SURFSIDE GIRLS

THE SECRET OF DANGER POINT

KIM DWINELL

Top Shelf Productions

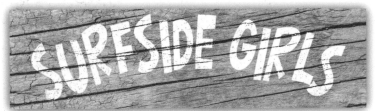

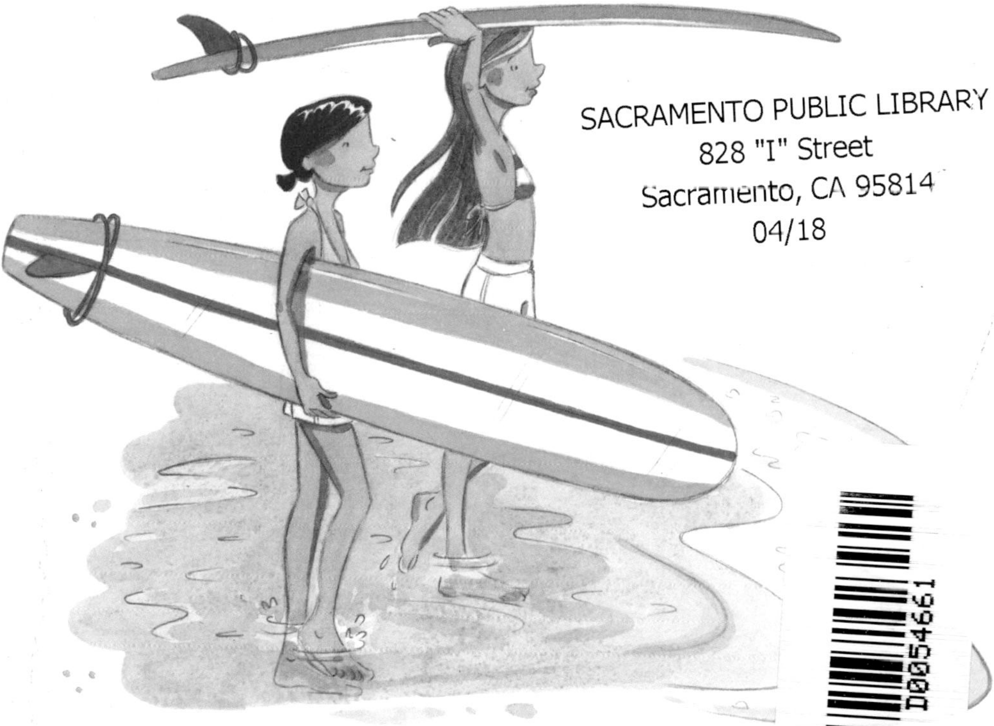

SURFSIDE GIRLS: THE SECRET OF DANGER POINT © 2017 Kim Dwinell.

ISBN: 978-1-60309-411-5   20 19 18 17   2 3 4 5

Published by Top Shelf Productions, PO Box 1282, Marietta, GA 30061-1282, USA. Top Shelf Productions is an imprint of IDW Publishing, a division of Idea and Design Works, LLC. Offices: 2765 Truxtun Road, San Diego, CA 92106. Top Shelf Productions®, the Top Shelf logo, Idea and Design Works®, and the IDW logo are registered trademarks of Idea and Design Works, LLC. All Rights Reserved. With the exception of small excerpts of artwork used for review purposes, none of the contents of this publication may be reprinted without the permission of IDW Publishing. IDW Publishing does not read or accept unsolicited submissions of ideas, stories, or artwork.

Editor-in-Chief: Chris Staros.
Edited by Chris Staros.
Designed by Gilberto Lazcano.
Visit our online catalog at www.topshelfcomix.com.

Printed in Korea.

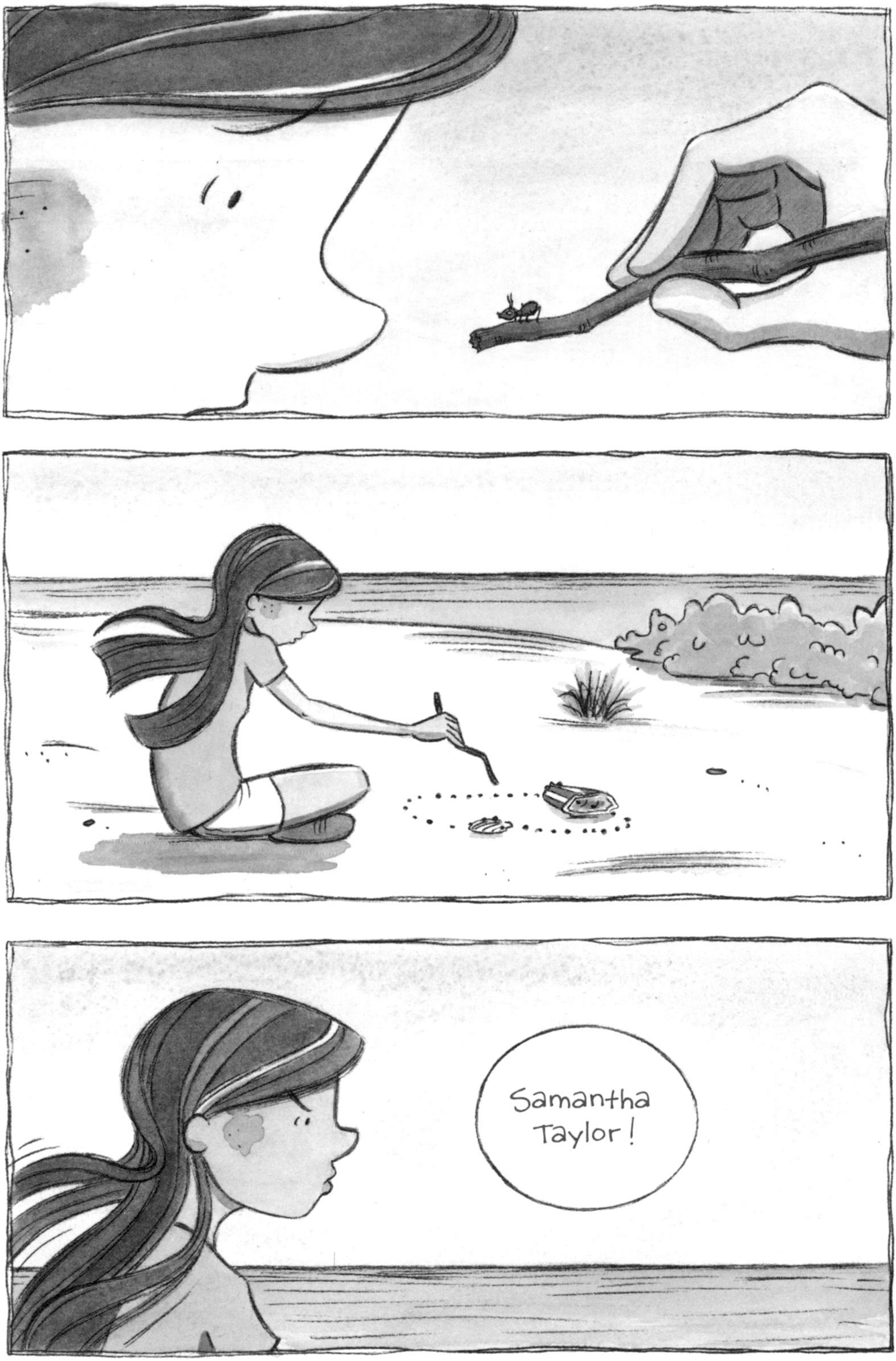
Samantha Taylor!

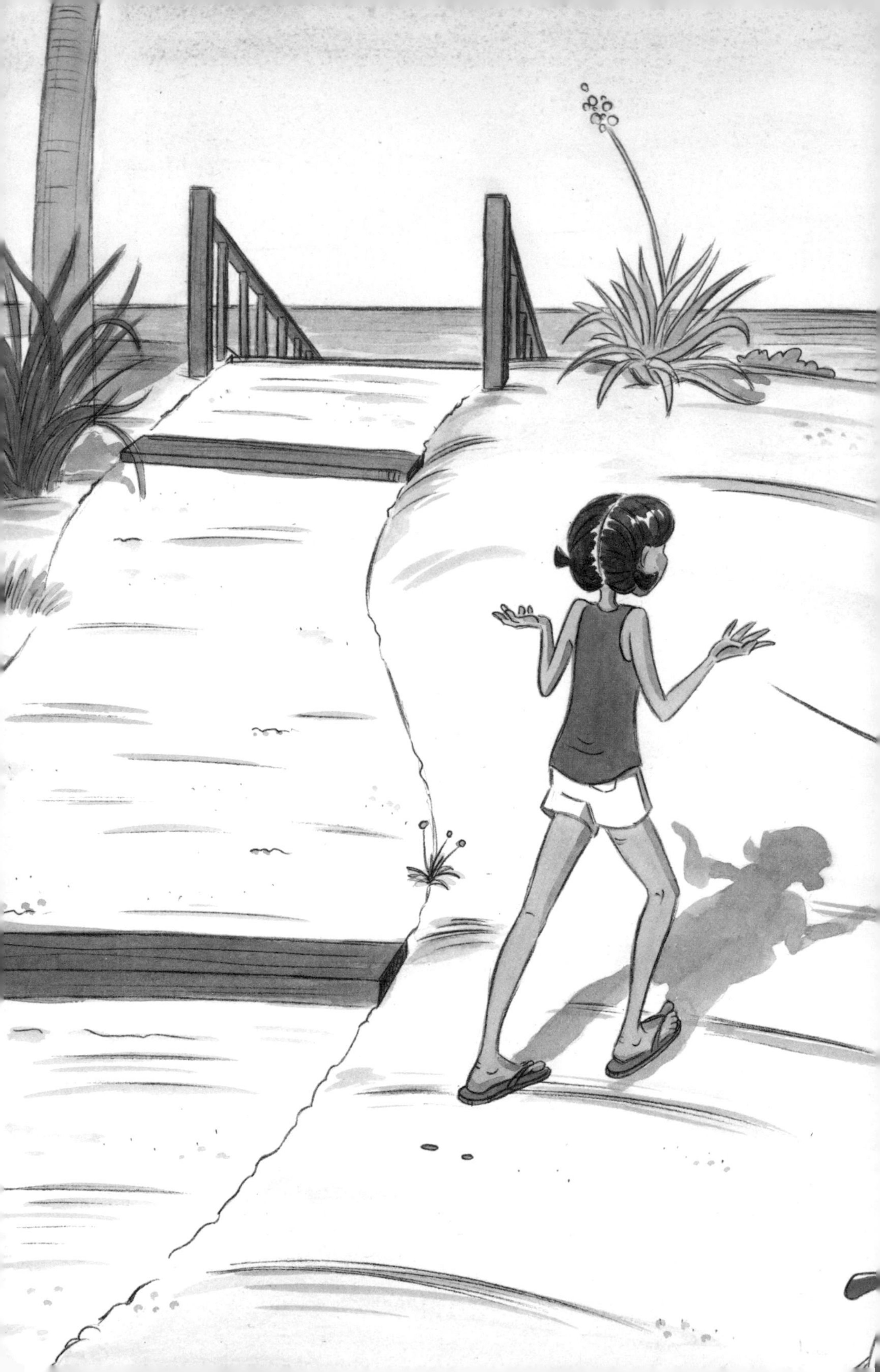

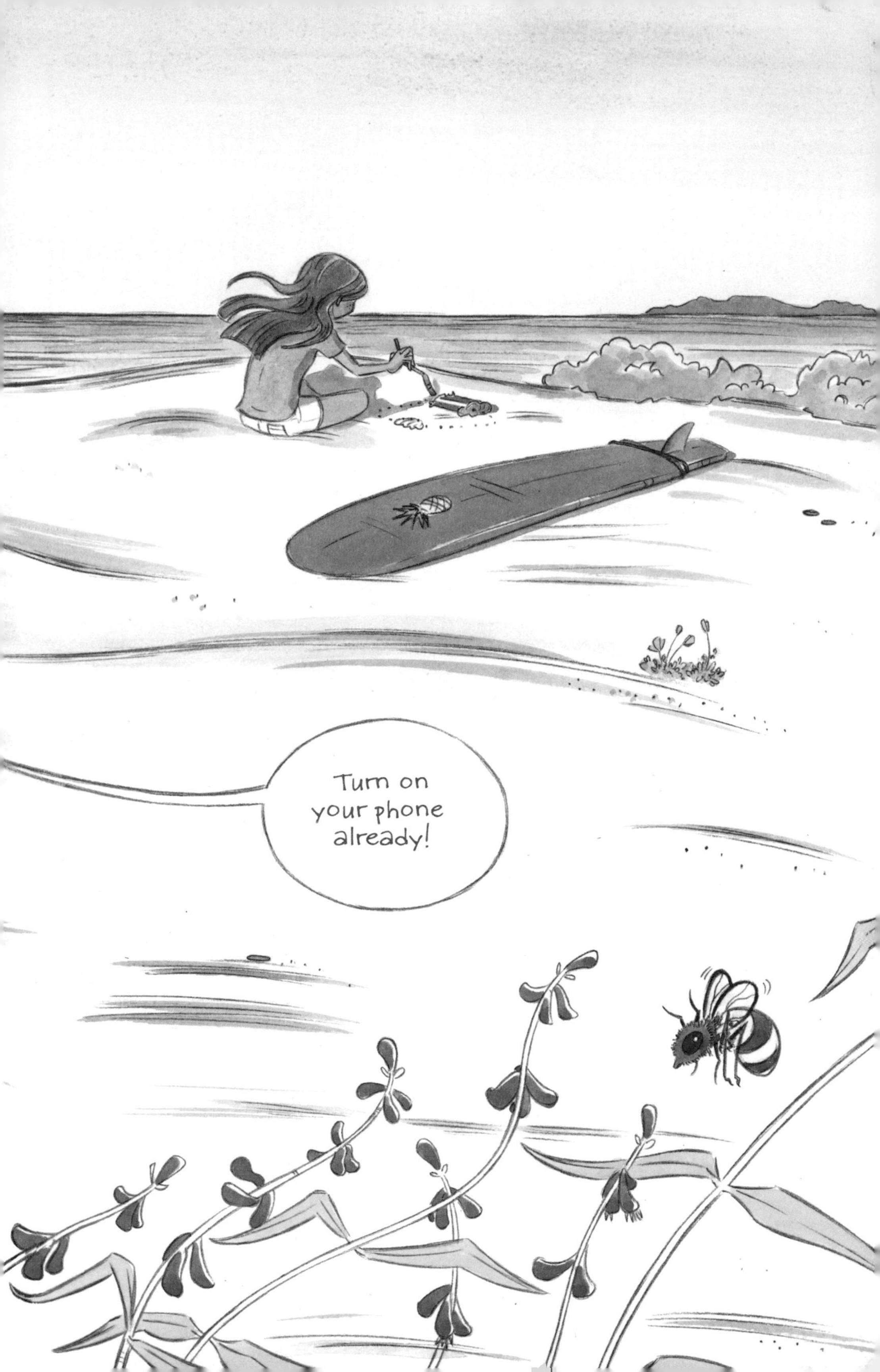
Turn on your phone already!

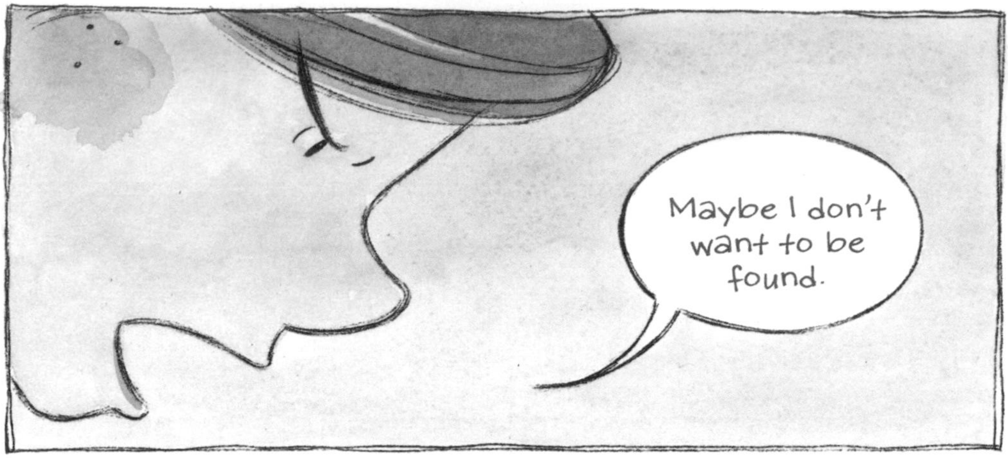
Maybe I don't want to be found.

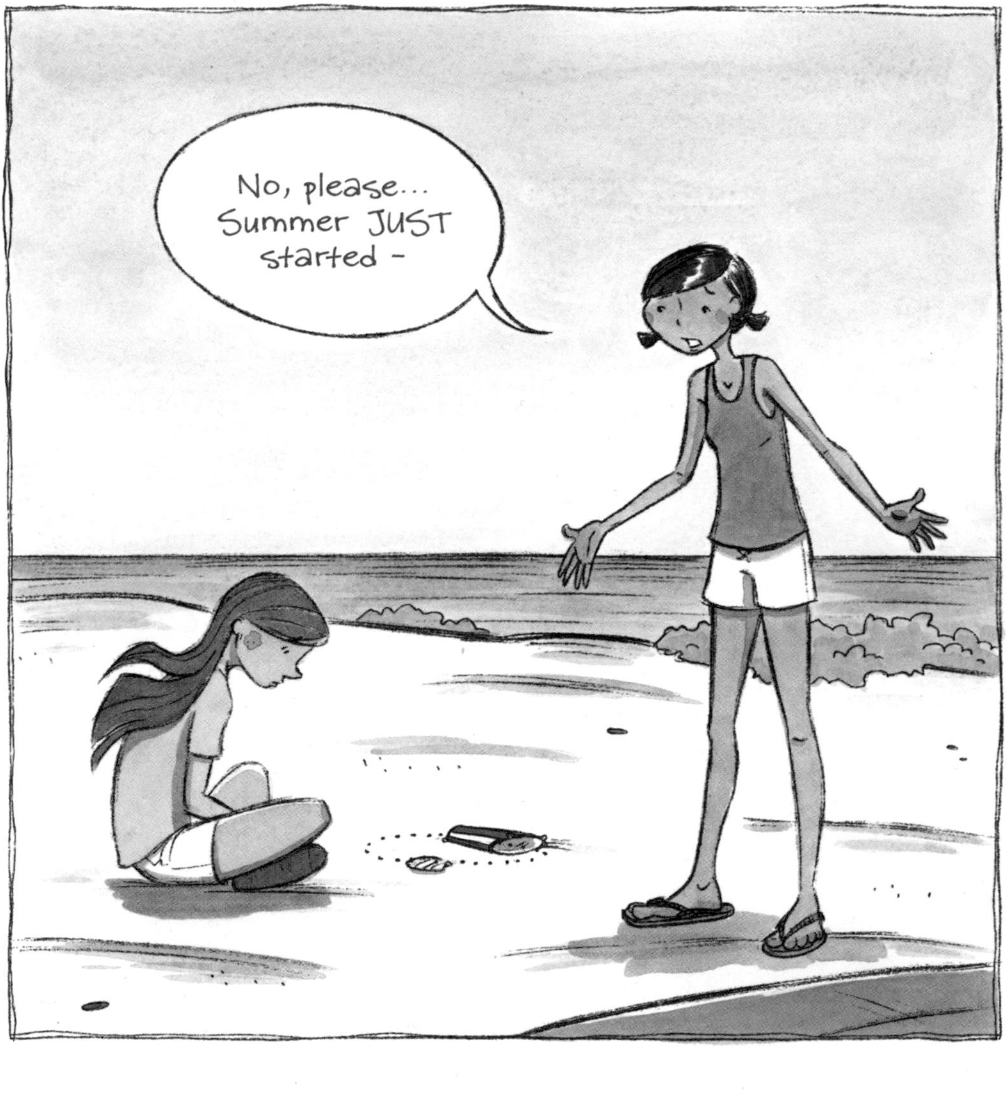
No, please... Summer JUST started -

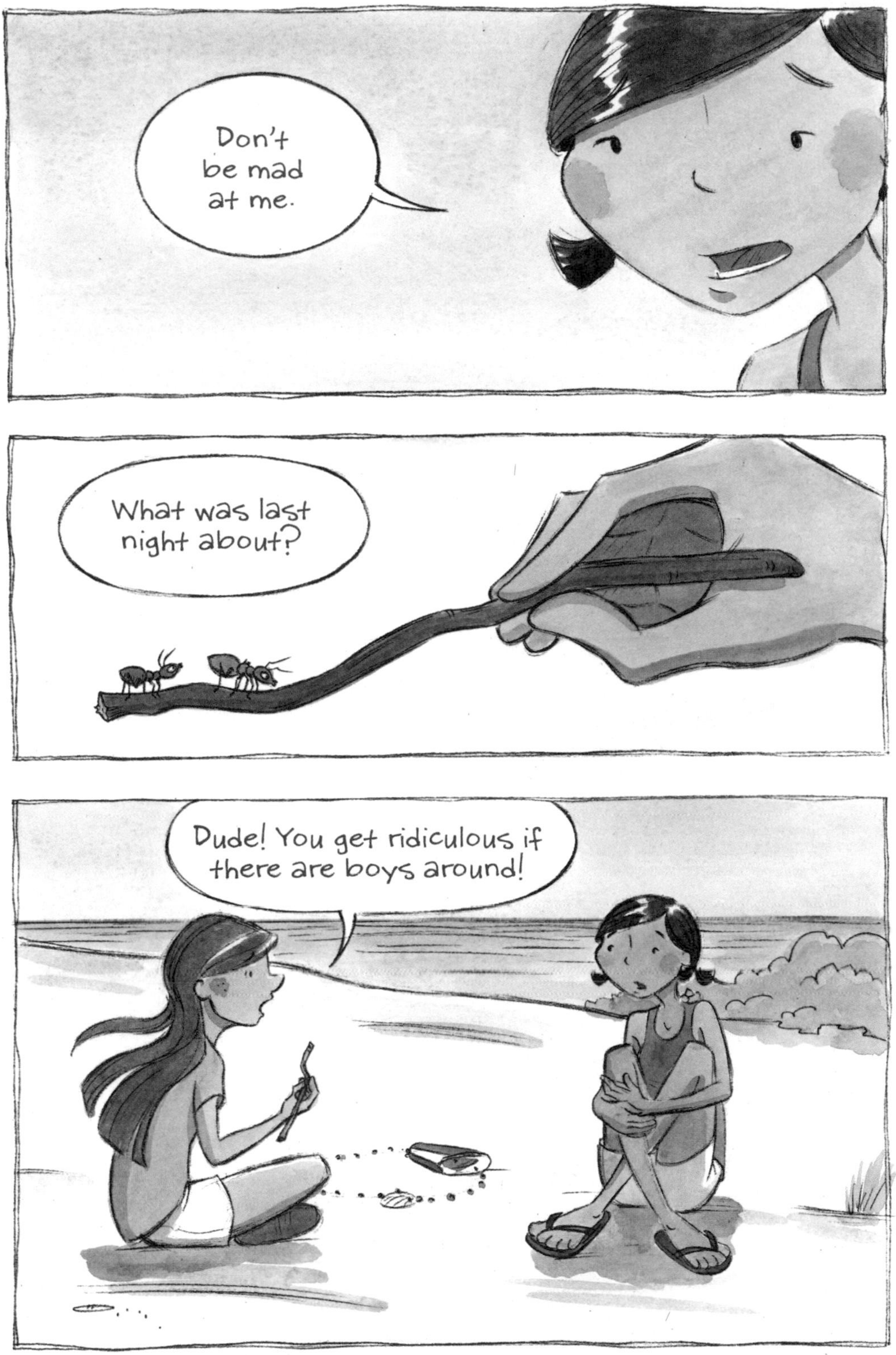
Don't be mad at me.
What was last night about?
Dude! You get ridiculous if there are boys around!

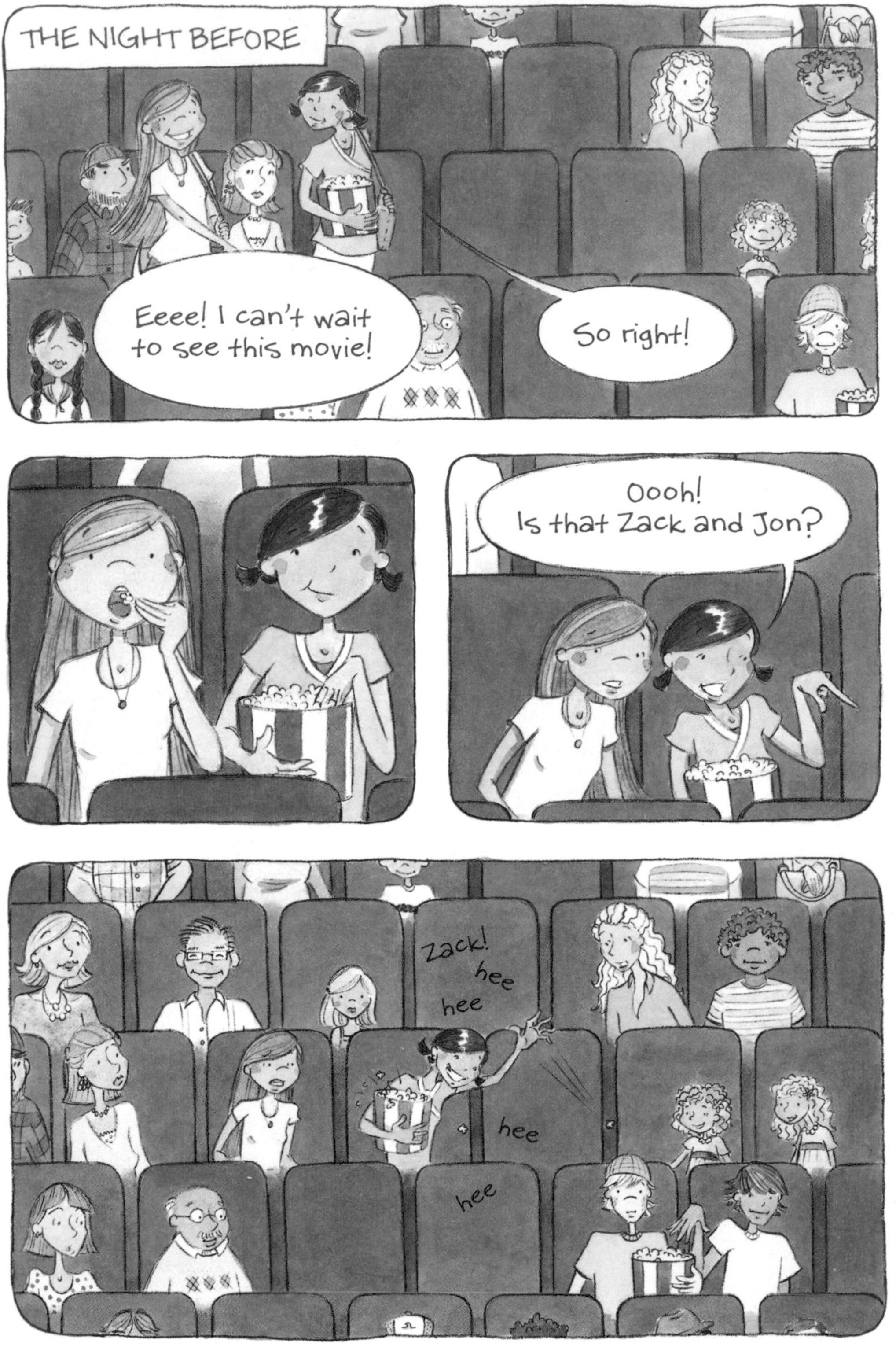
THE NIGHT BEFORE
Eeee! I can't wait to see this movie!
So right!
Oooh! Is that Zack and Jon?
Zack! hee hee
hee
hee

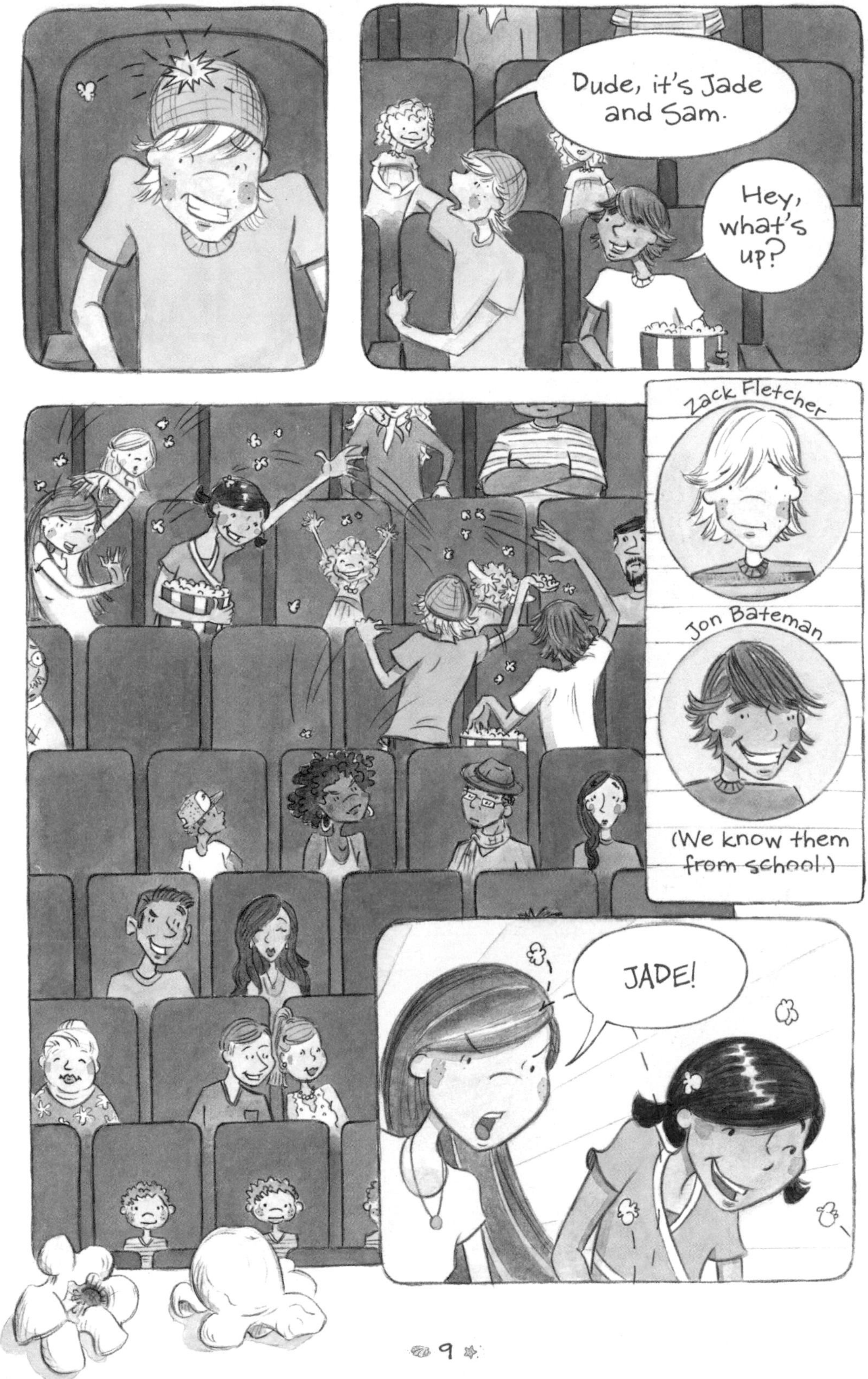

Dude, it's Jade and Sam.
Hey, what's up?
Zack Fletcher
Jon Bateman
(We know them from school.)
JADE!

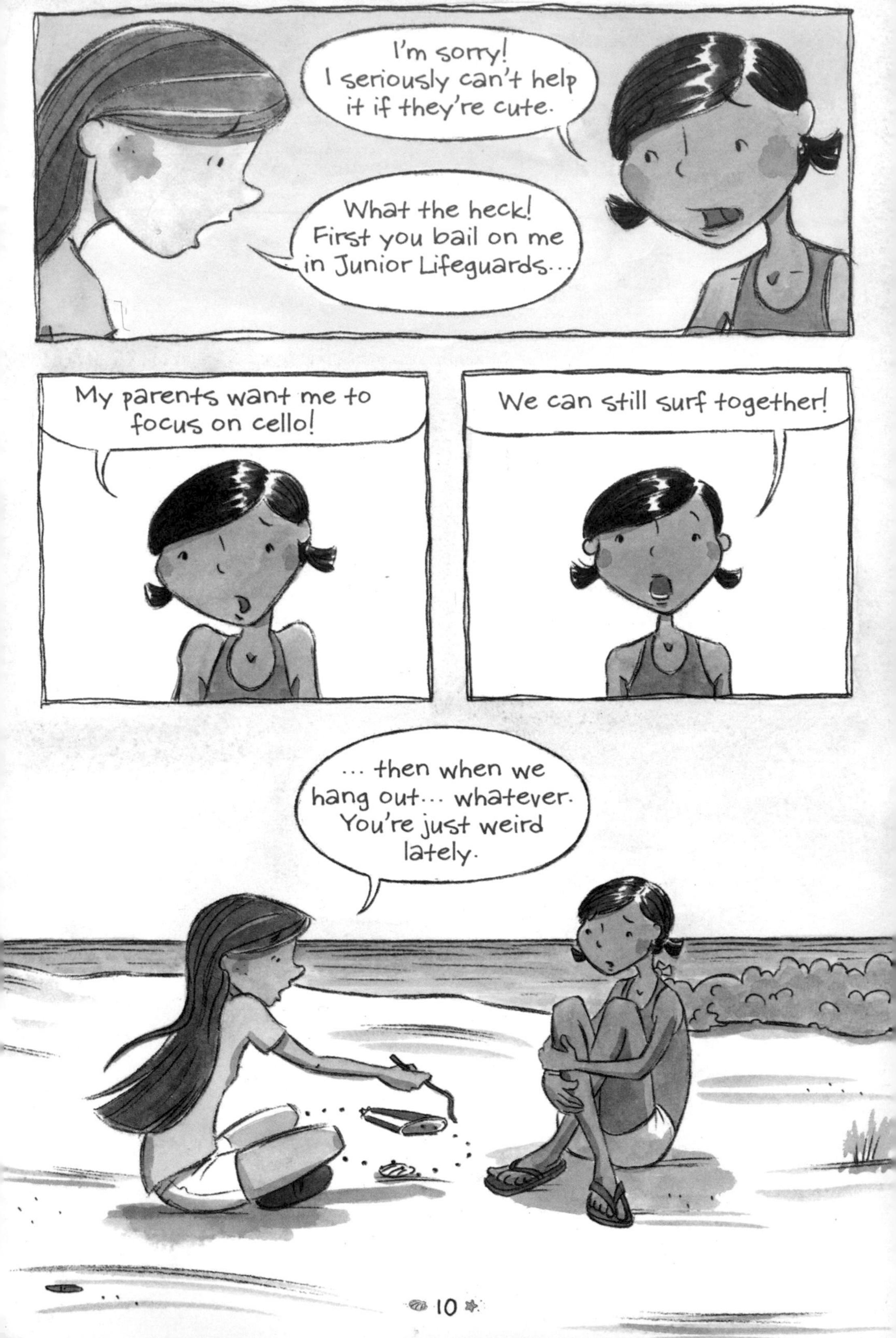
What the heck! First you bail on me in Junior Lifeguards...
I'm sorry! I seriously can't help it if they're cute.
My parents want me to focus on cello!
We can still surf together!
... then when we hang out... whatever. You're just weird lately.

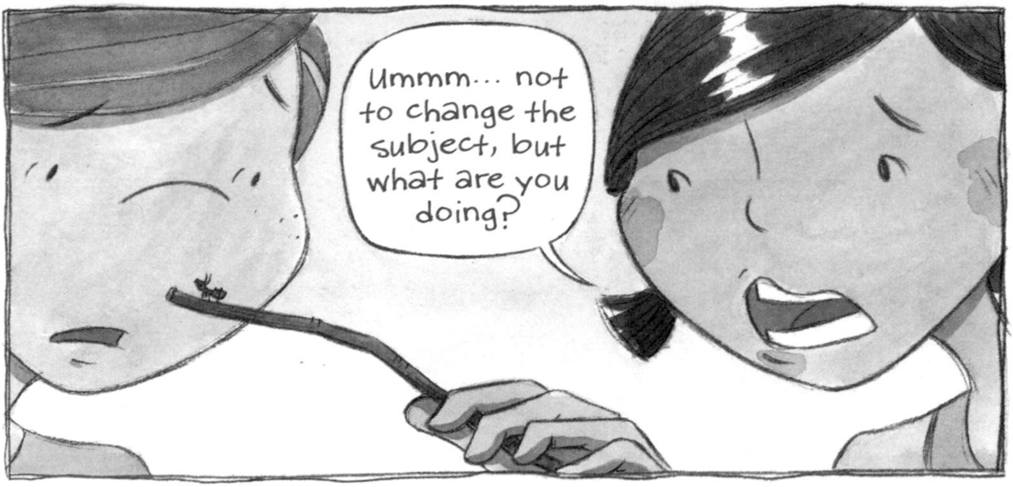
Ummm... not to change the subject, but what are you doing?

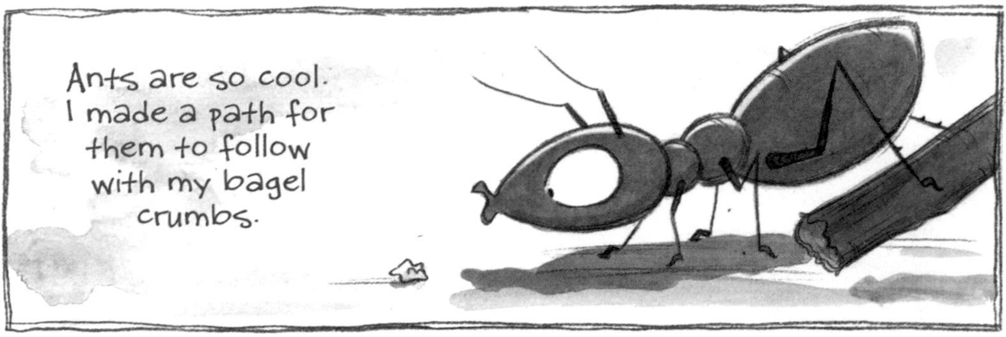
Ants are so cool. I made a path for them to follow with my bagel crumbs.

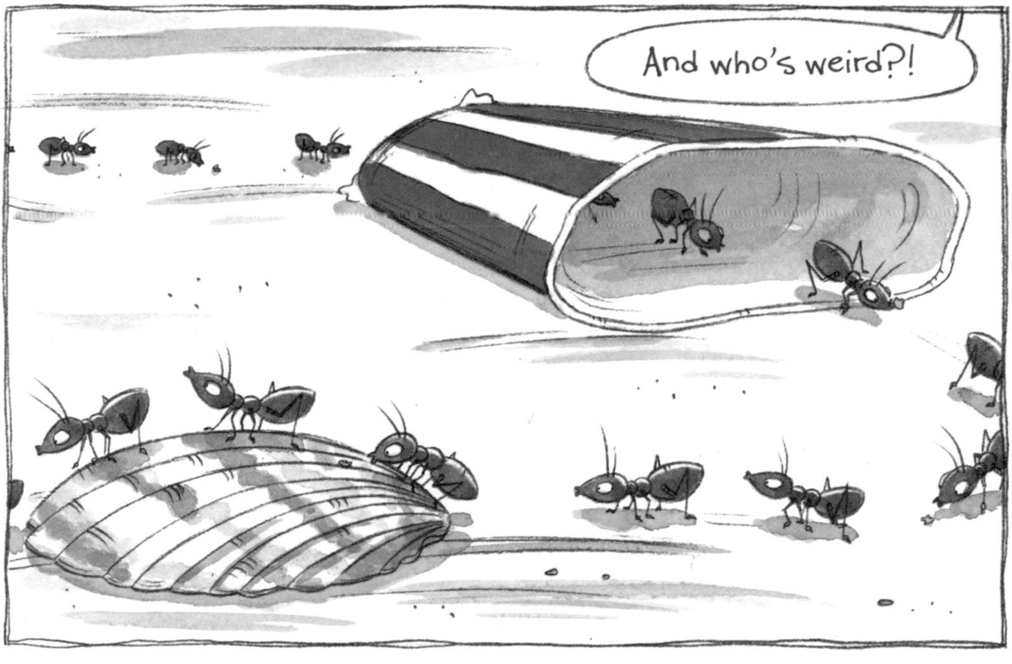
And who's weird?!

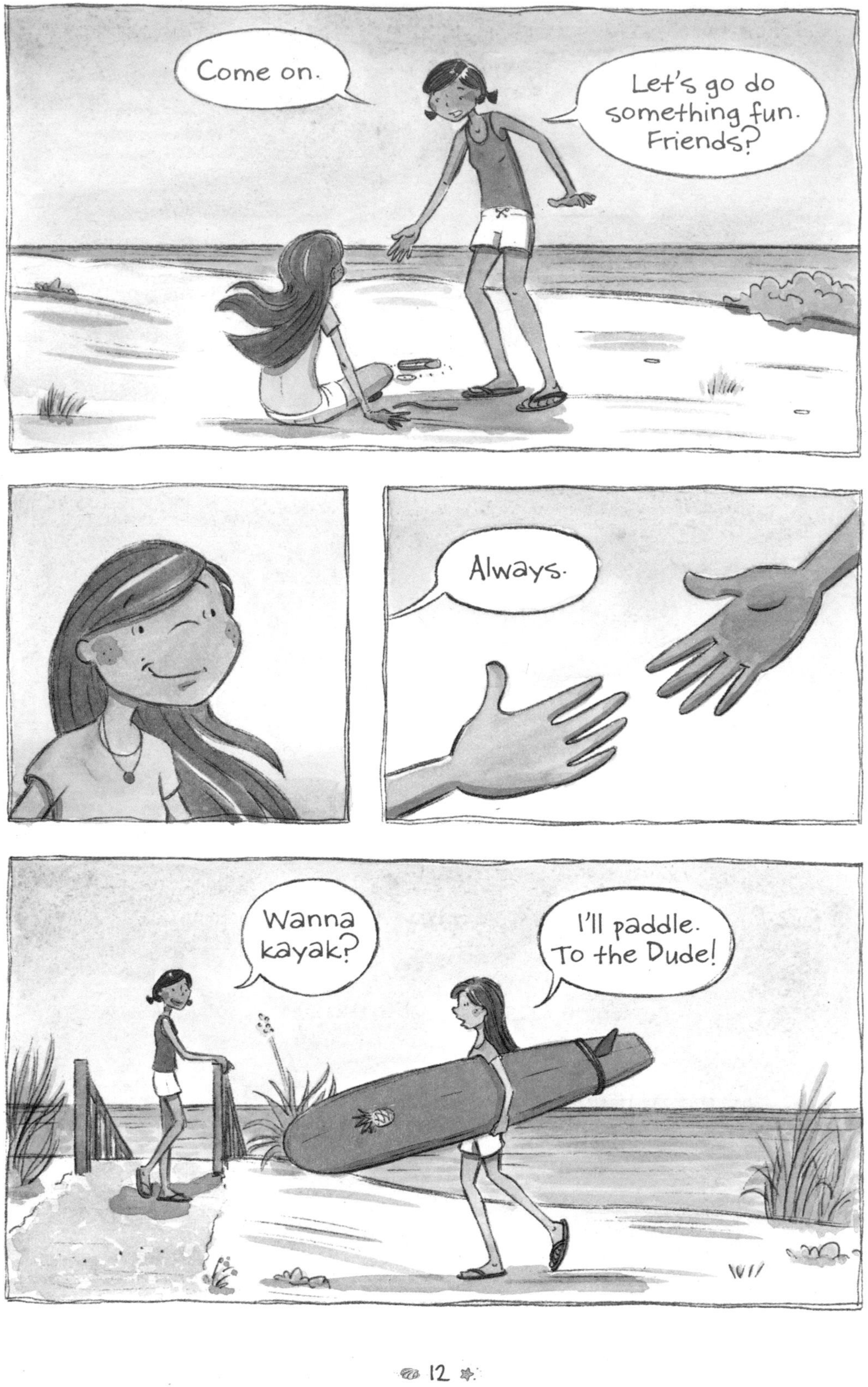
Come on.
Let's go do something fun. Friends?
Always.
Wanna kayak?
I'll paddle. To the Dude!

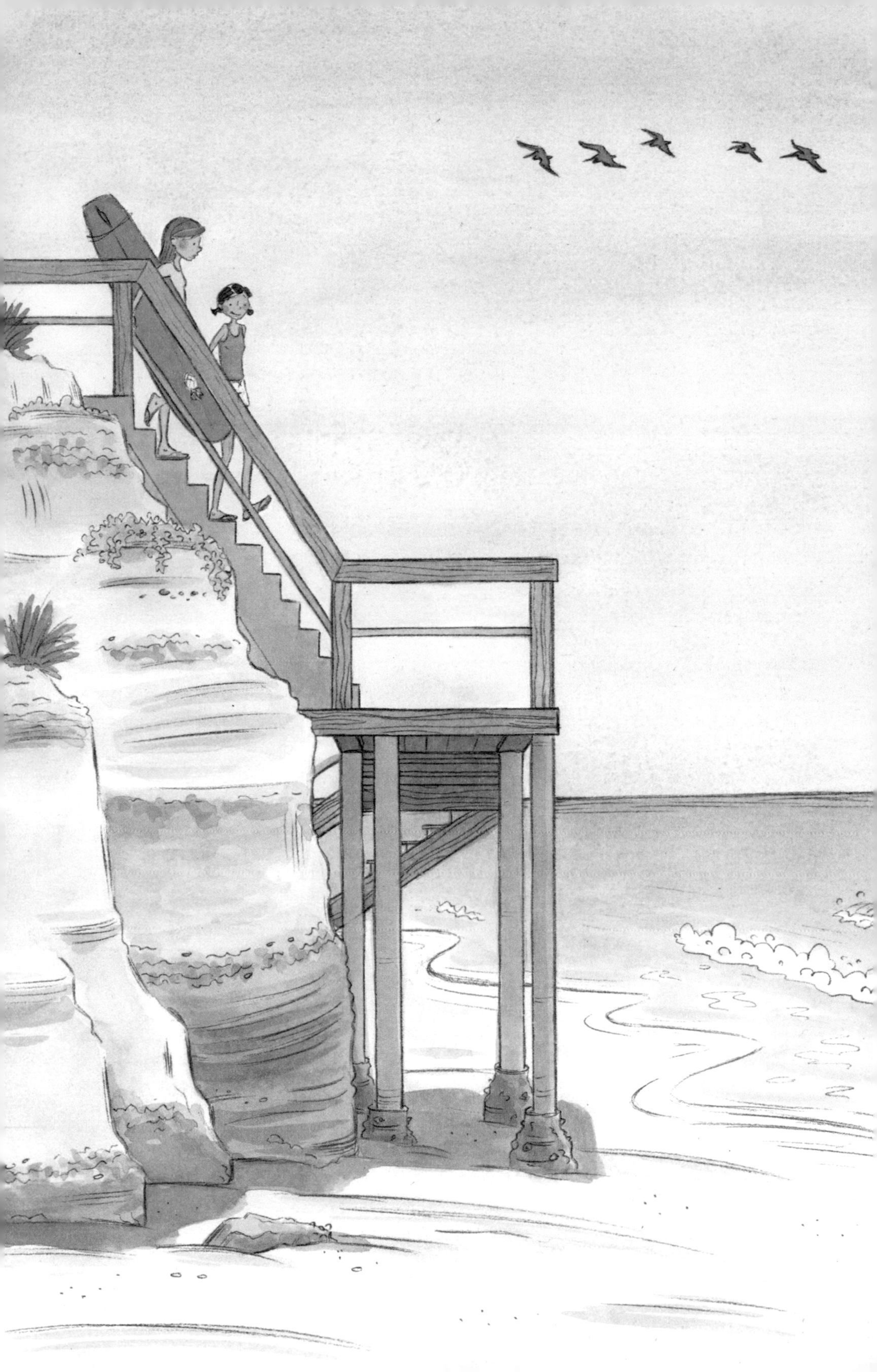

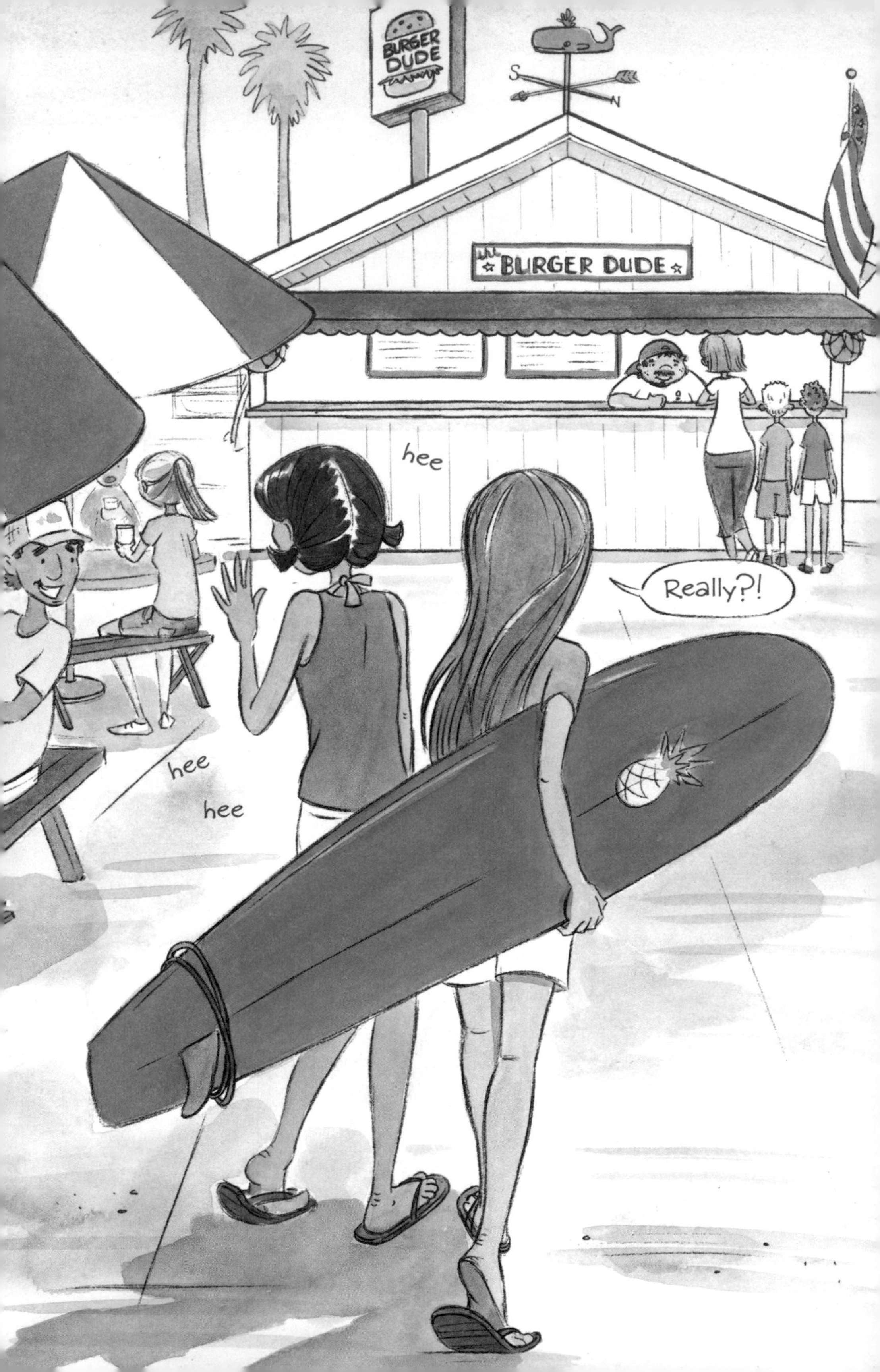
BURGER DUDE
S
N
BURGER DUDE
hee
Really?!
hee
hee

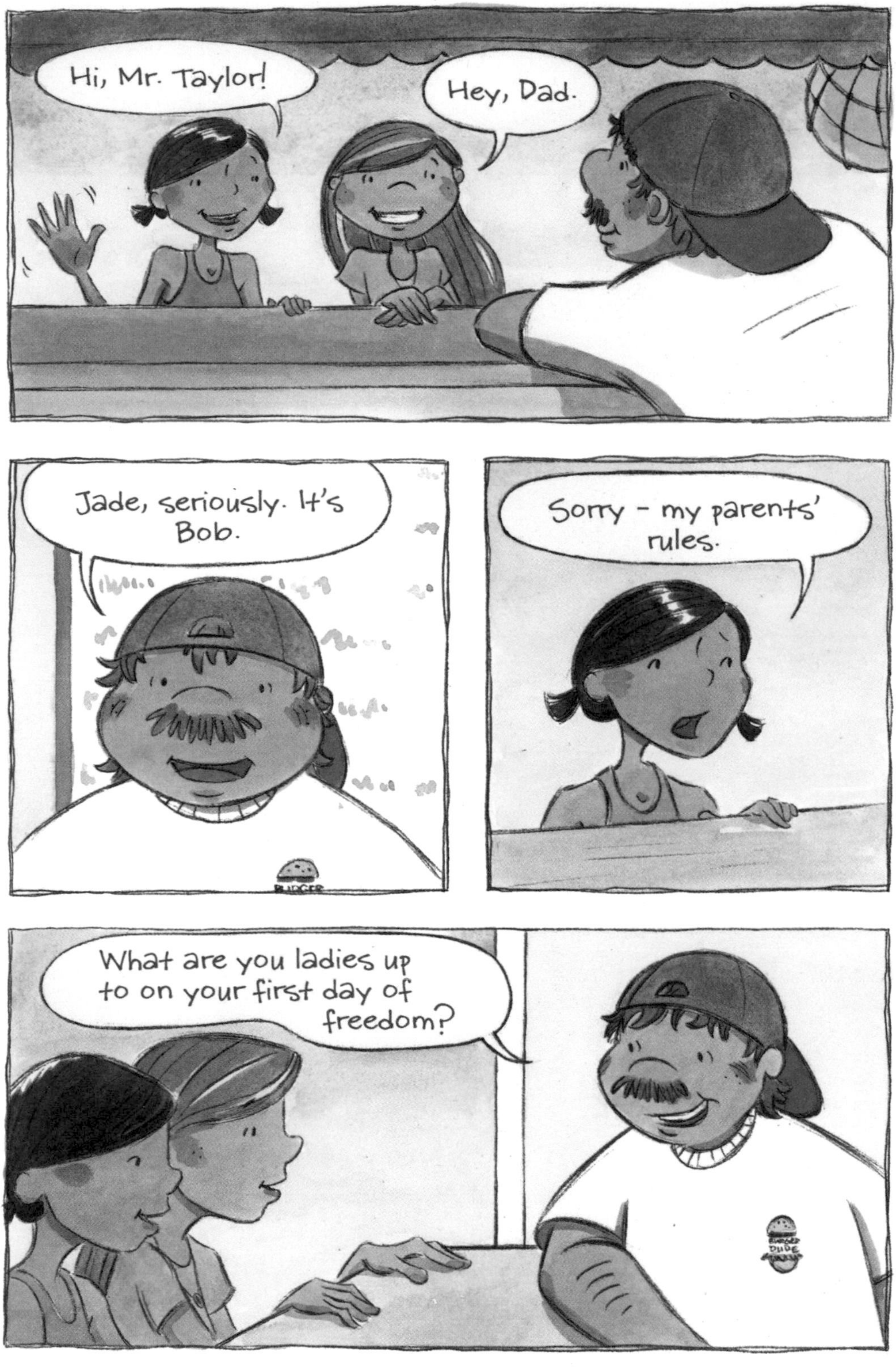

Hi, Mr. Taylor!
Hey, Dad.
Jade, seriously. It's Bob.
Sorry - my parents' rules.
What are you ladies up to on your first day of freedom?

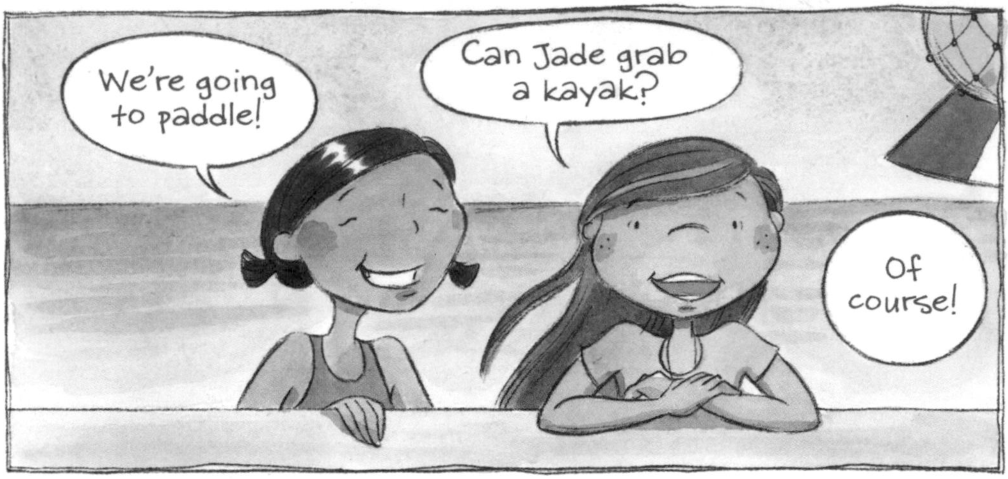
We're going to paddle!
Can Jade grab a kayak?
Of course!

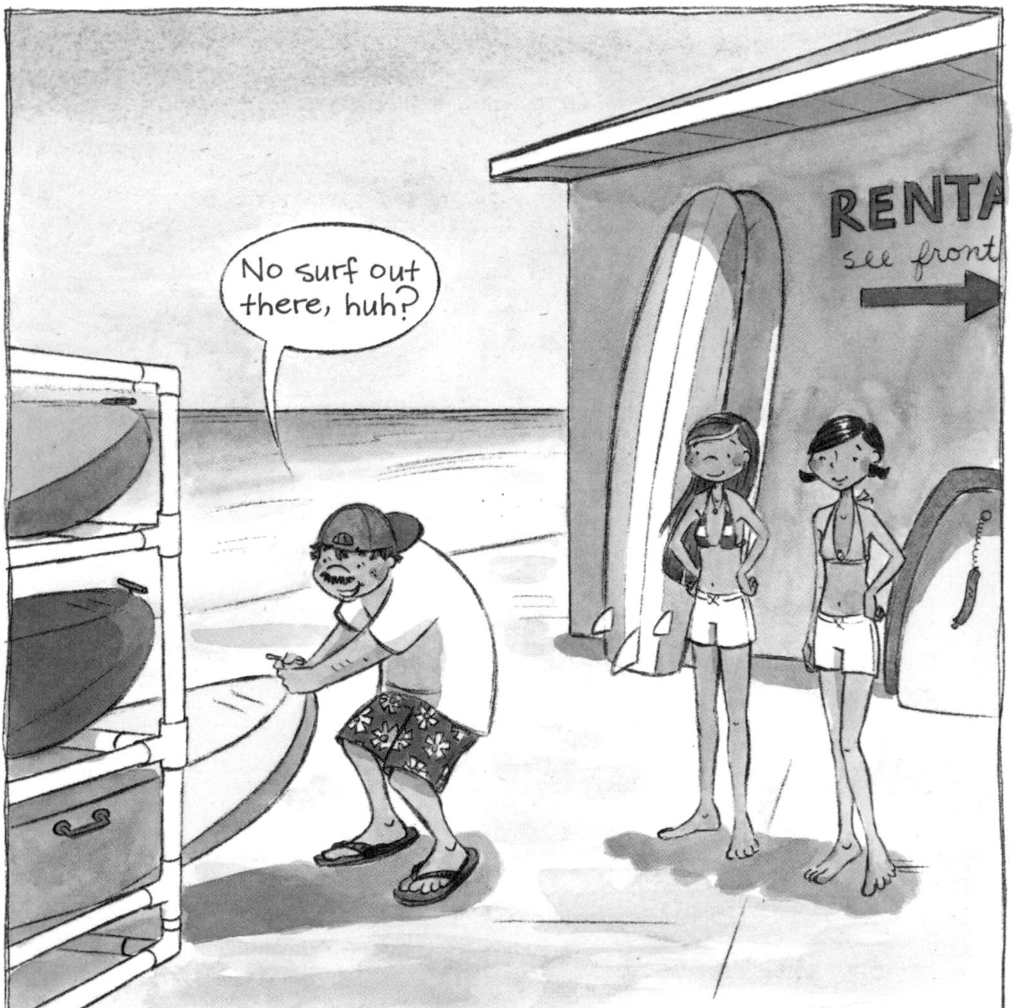
RENTA
see front
No surf out there, huh?

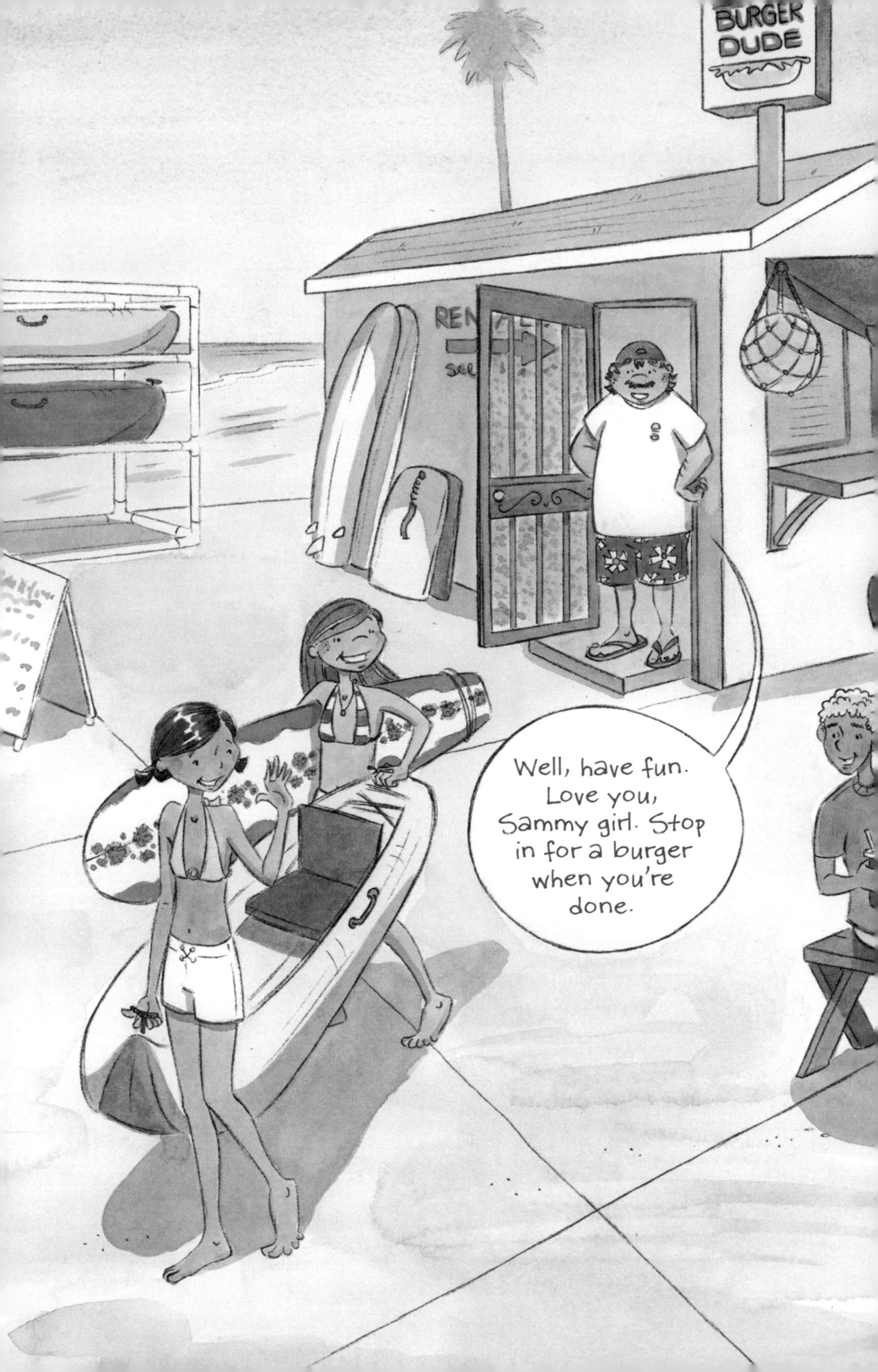
BURGER DUDE
Well, have fun. Love you, Sammy girl. Stop in for a burger when you're done.

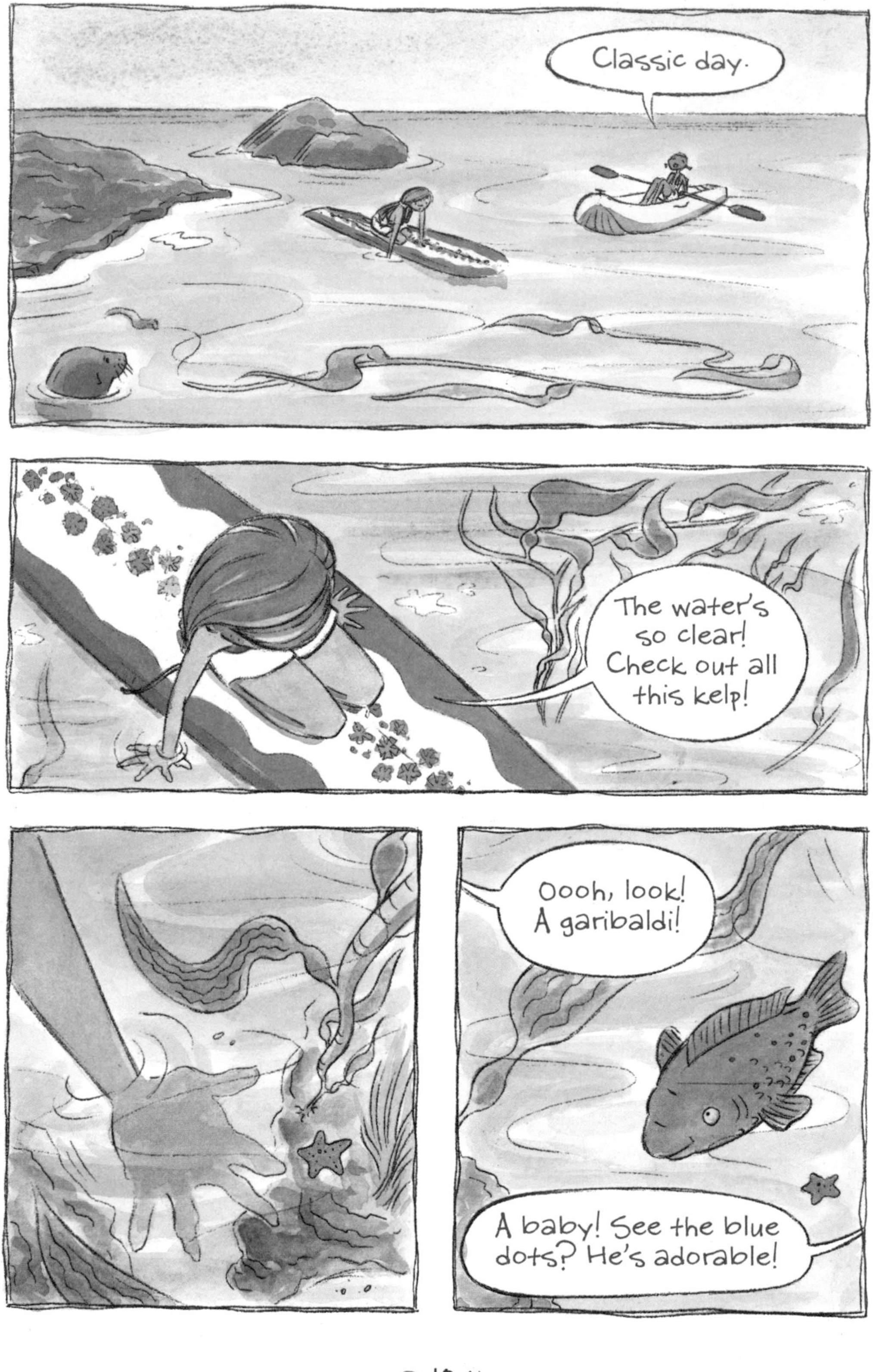
Classic day.
The water's so clear! Check out all this kelp!
Oooh, look! A garibaldi!
A baby! See the blue dots? He's adorable!

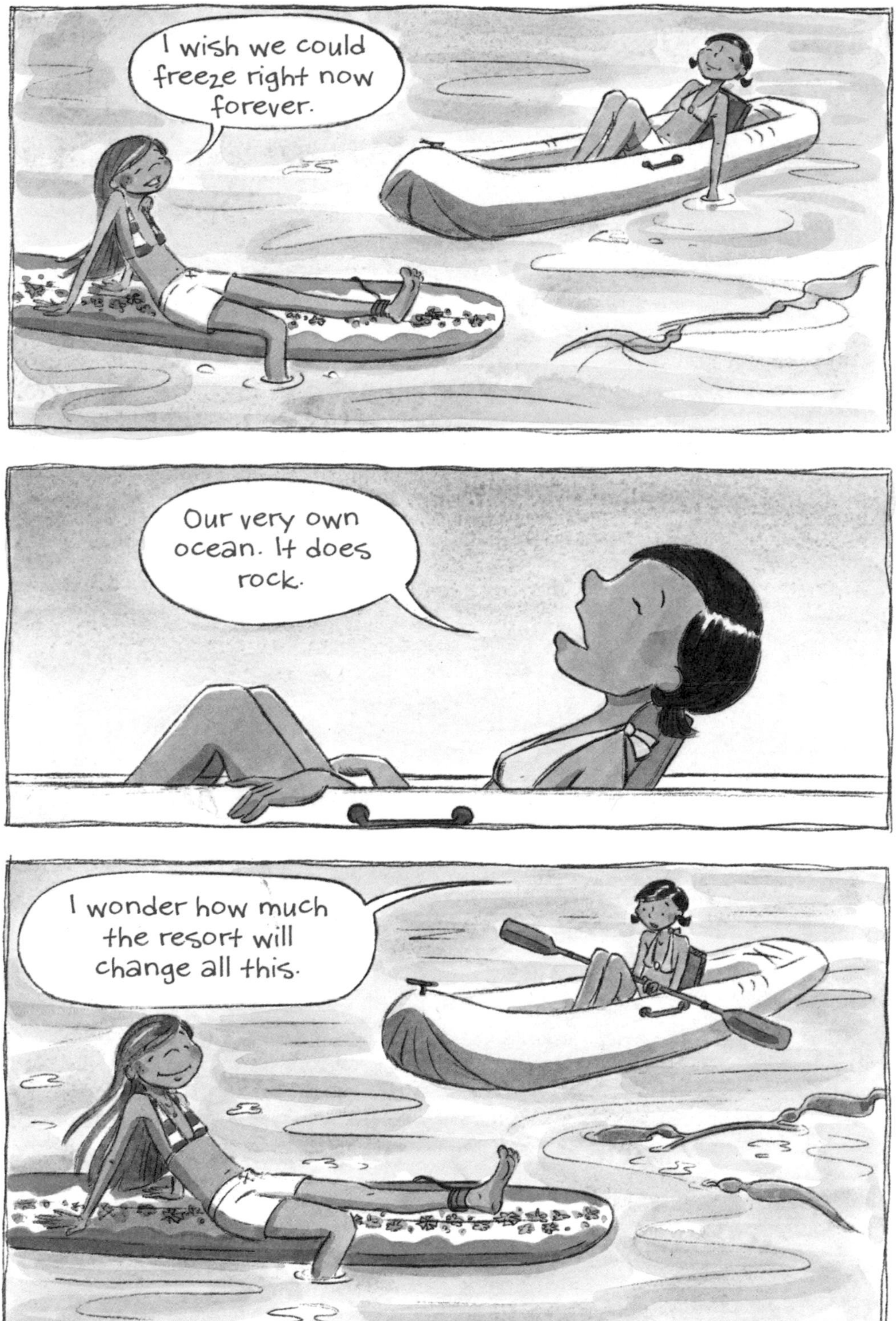
I wish we could freeze right now forever.
Our very own ocean. It does rock.
I wonder how much the resort will change all this.

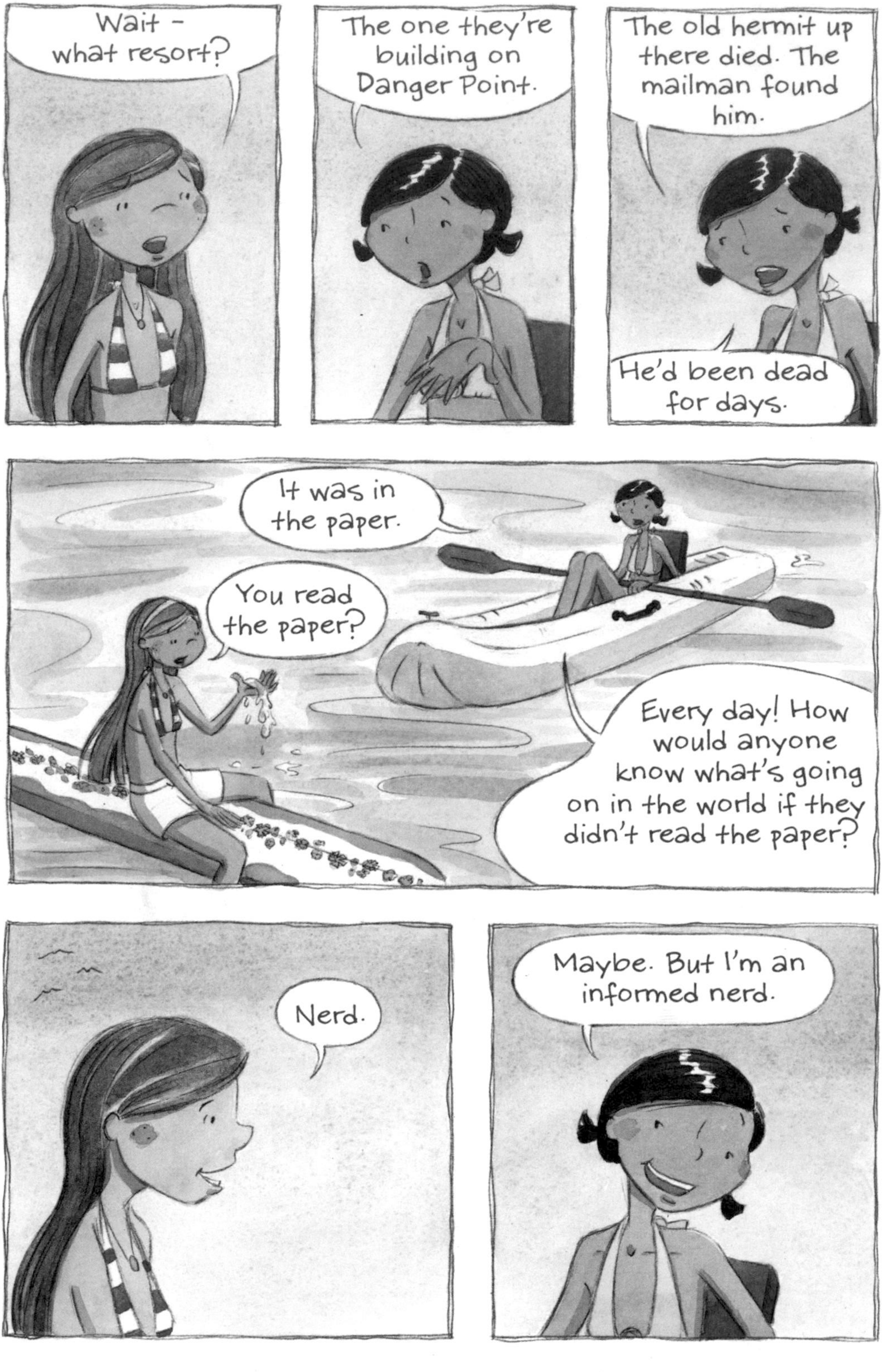
Wait - what resort?
The one they're building on Danger Point.
The old hermit up there died. The mailman found him.
He'd been dead for days.
It was in the paper.
You read the paper?
Every day! How would anyone know what's going on in the world if they didn't read the paper?
Nerd.
Maybe. But I'm an informed nerd.

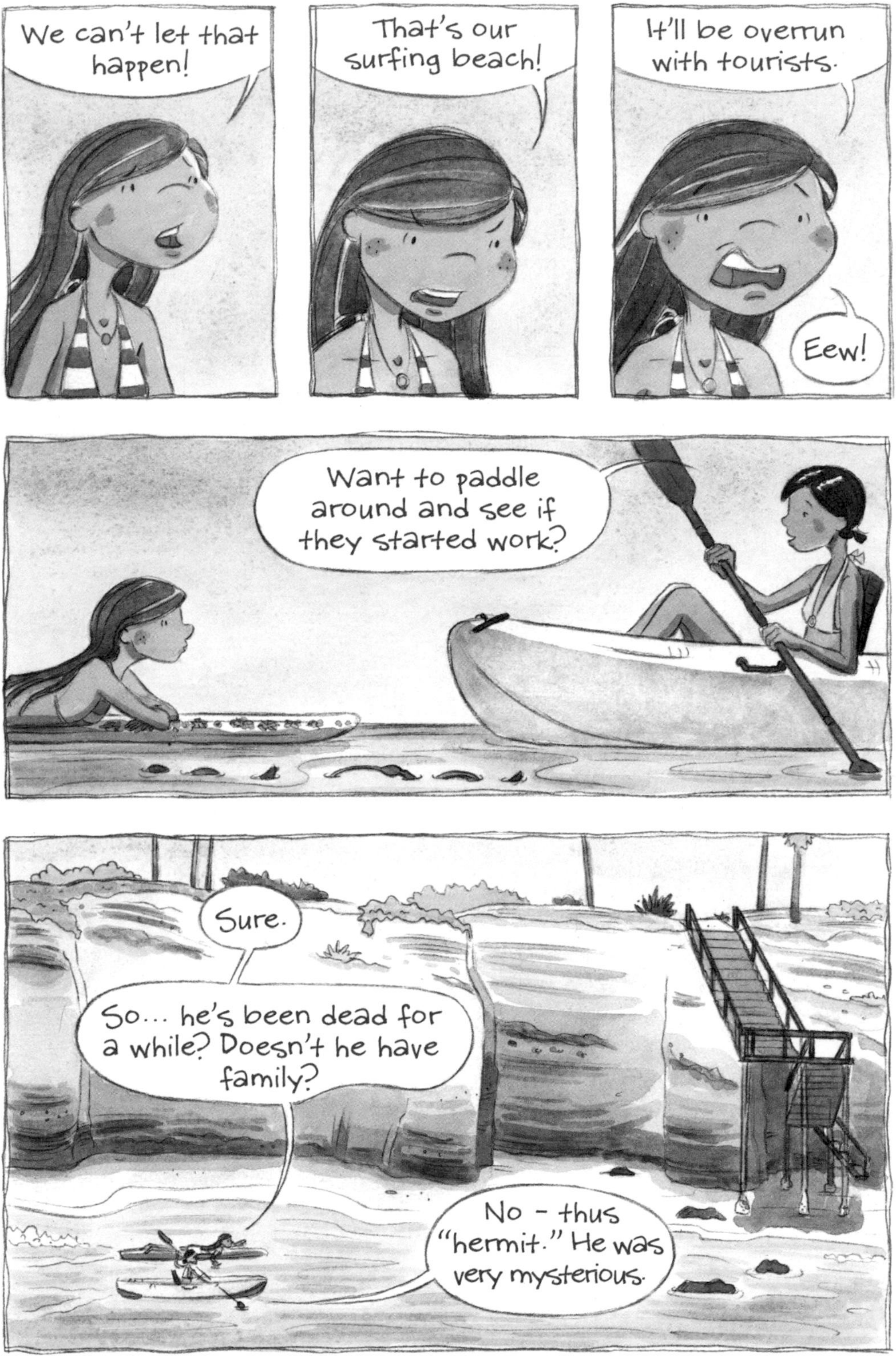
We can't let that happen!
That's our surfing beach!
It'll be overrun with tourists.
Eew!
Want to paddle around and see if they started work?
Sure.
So... he's been dead for a while? Doesn't he have family?
No - thus "hermit." He was very mysterious.

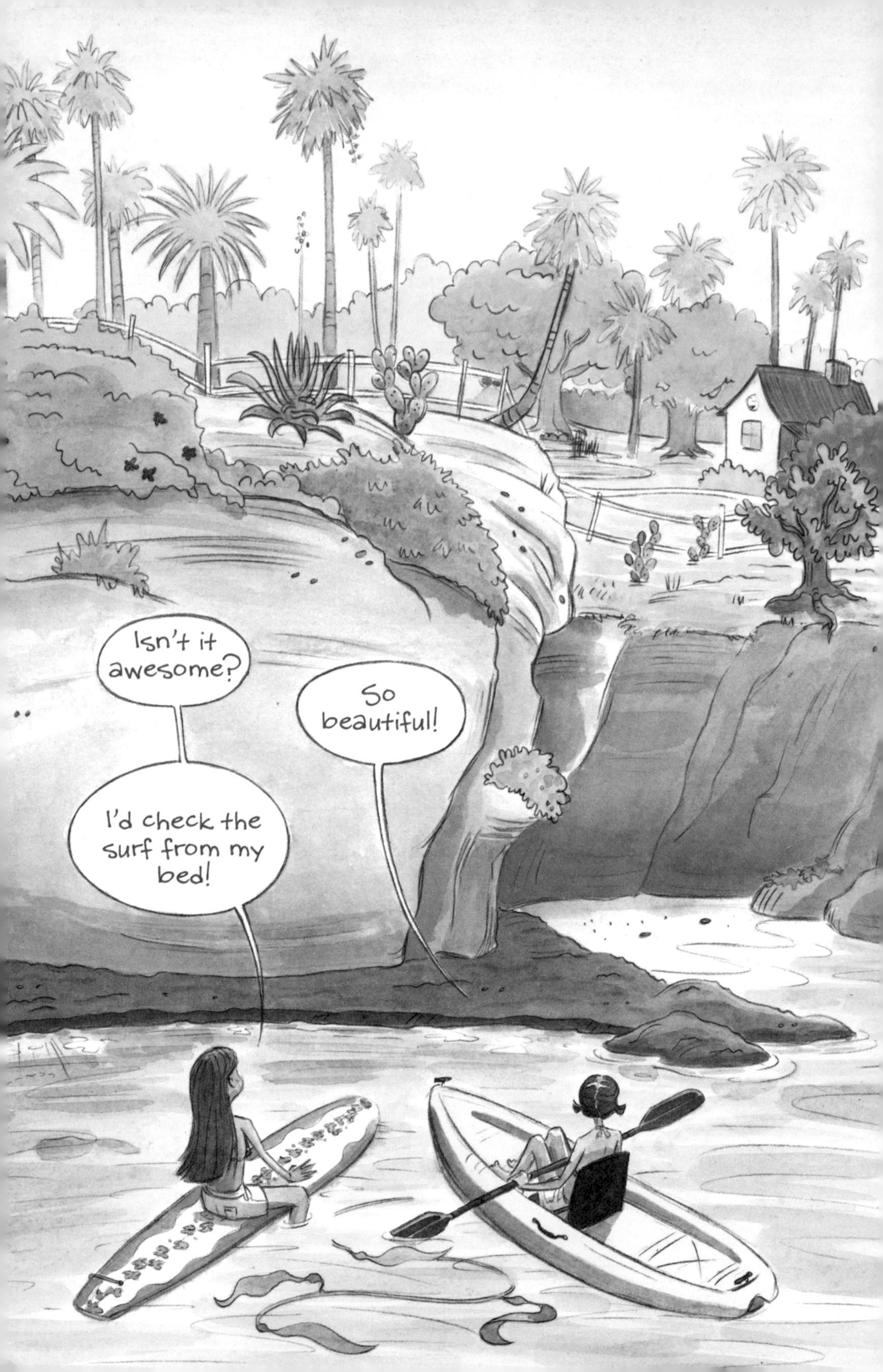
Isn't it awesome?
I'd check the surf from my bed!
So beautiful!

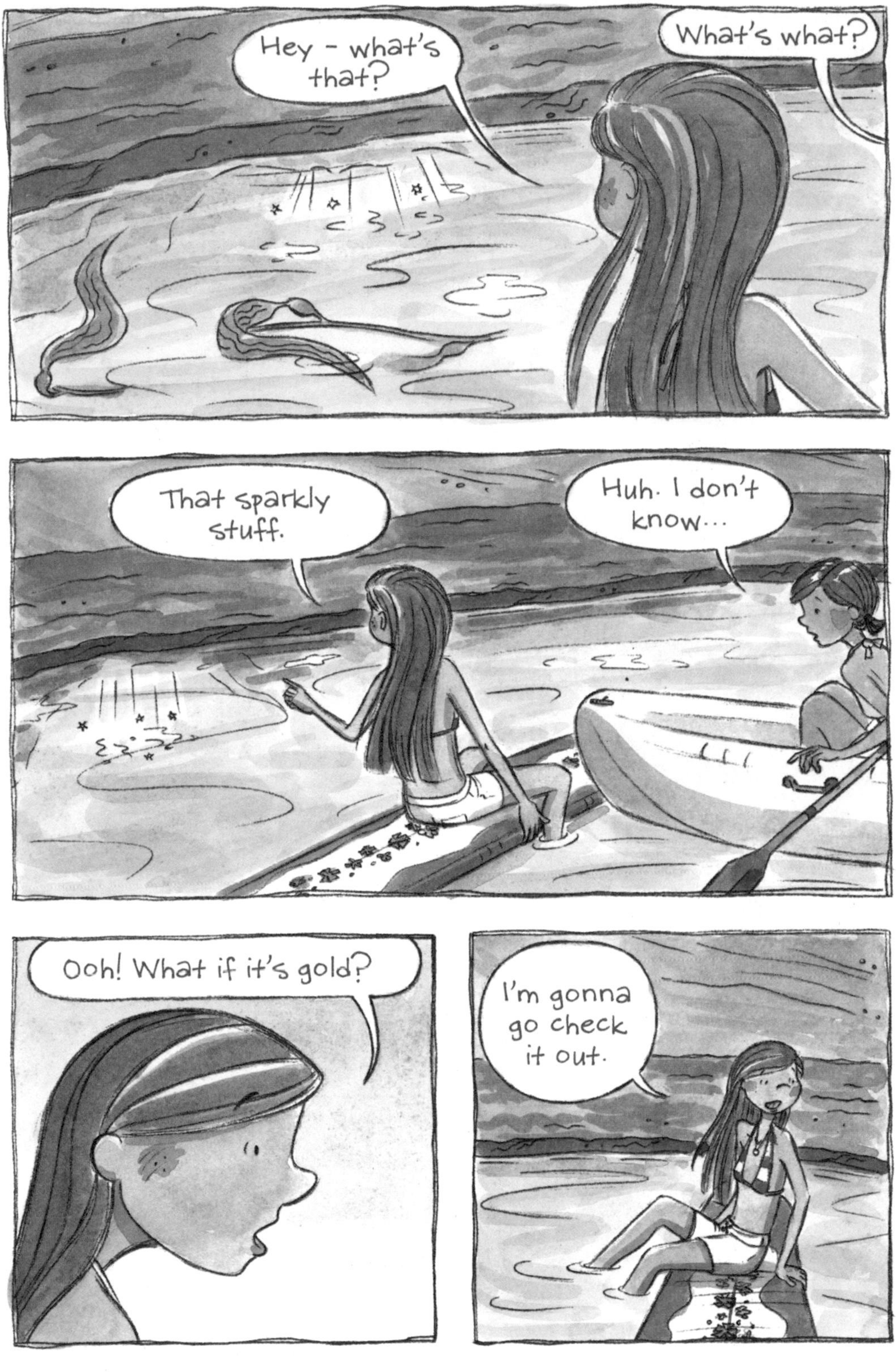
Hey - what's that?
What's what?
That sparkly stuff.
Huh. I don't know...
Ooh! What if it's gold?
I'm gonna go check it out.

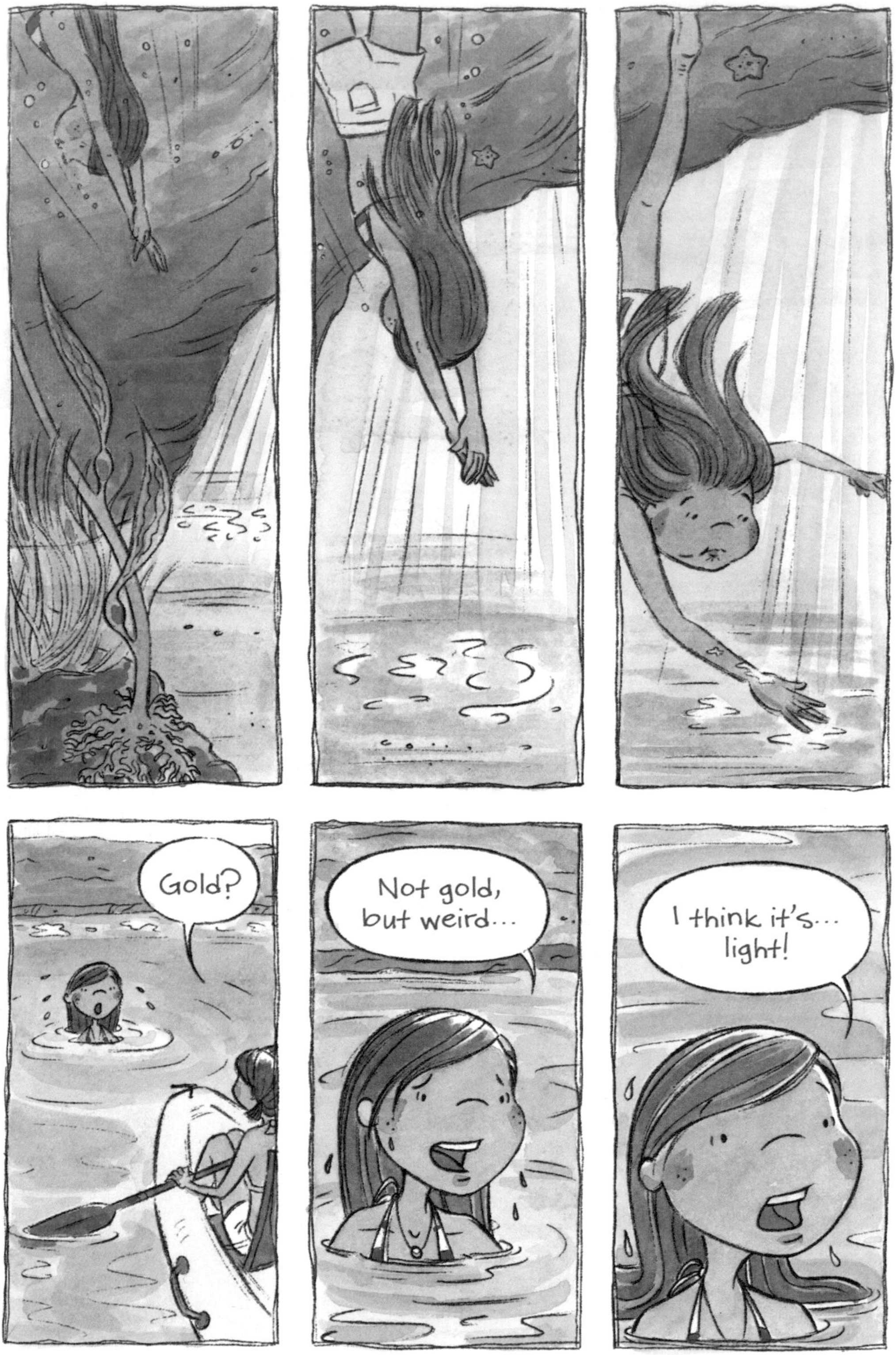
Gold?
Not gold, but weird...
I think it's... light!

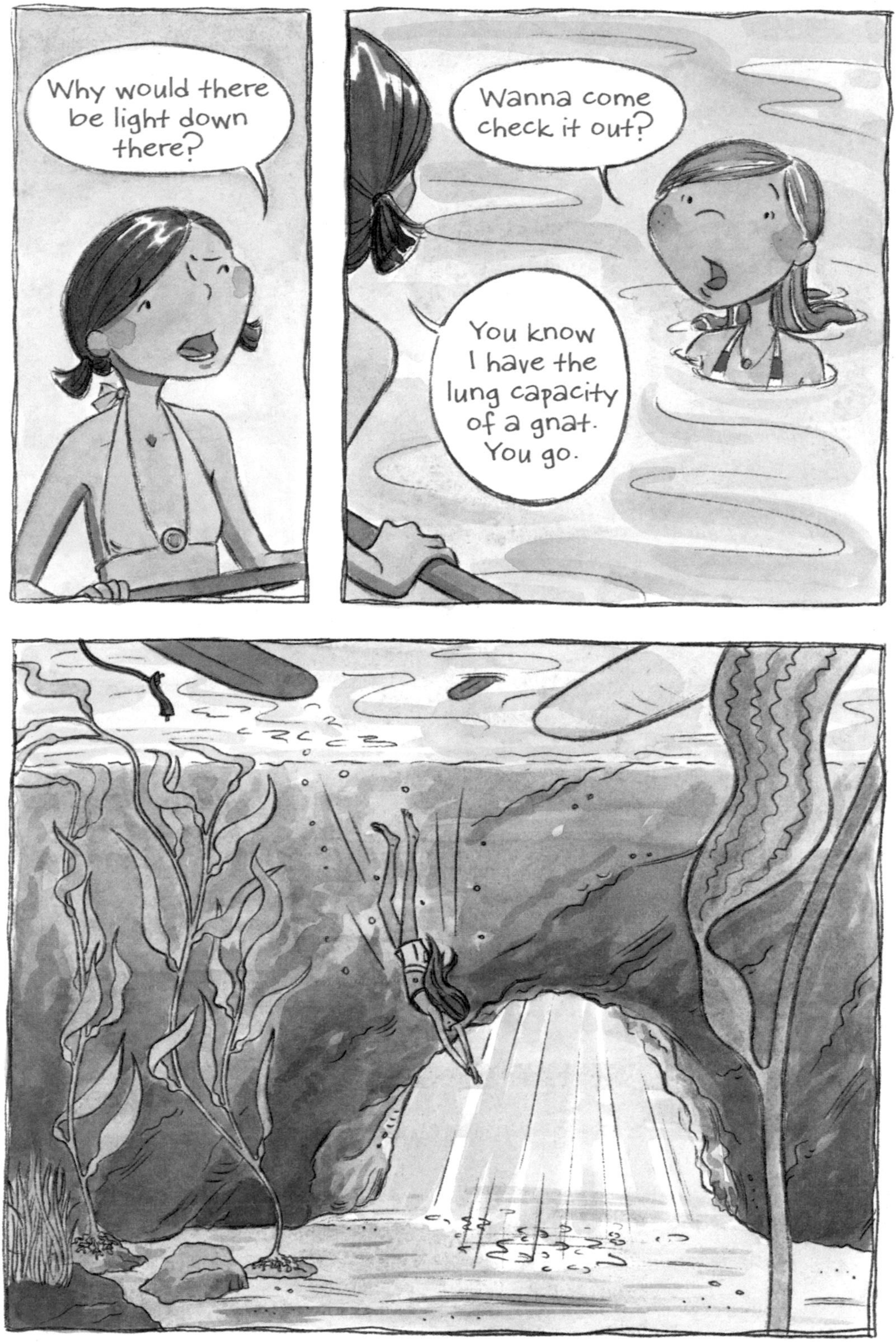
Why would there be light down there?
Wanna come check it out?
You know I have the lung capacity of a gnat. You go.

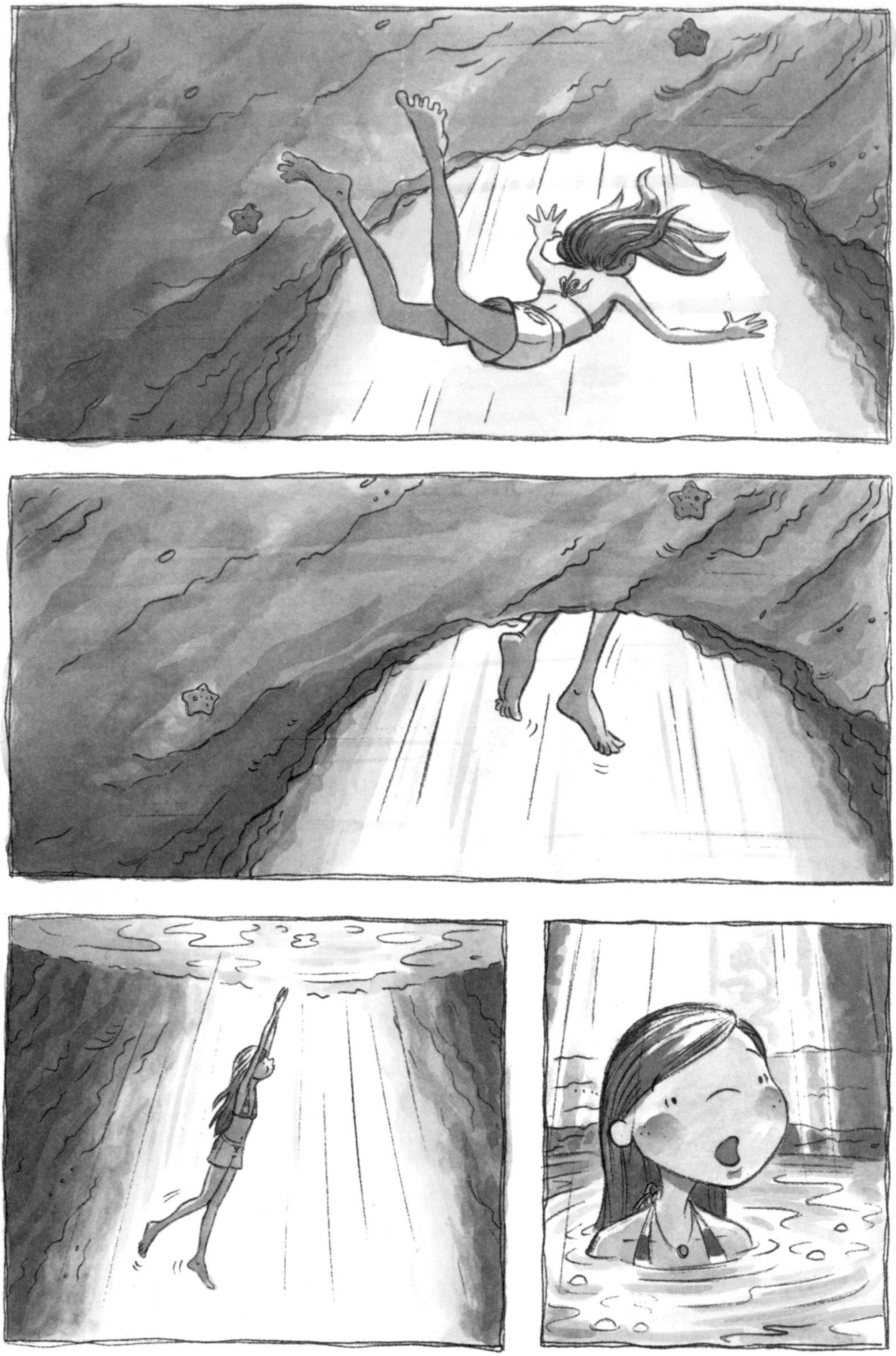

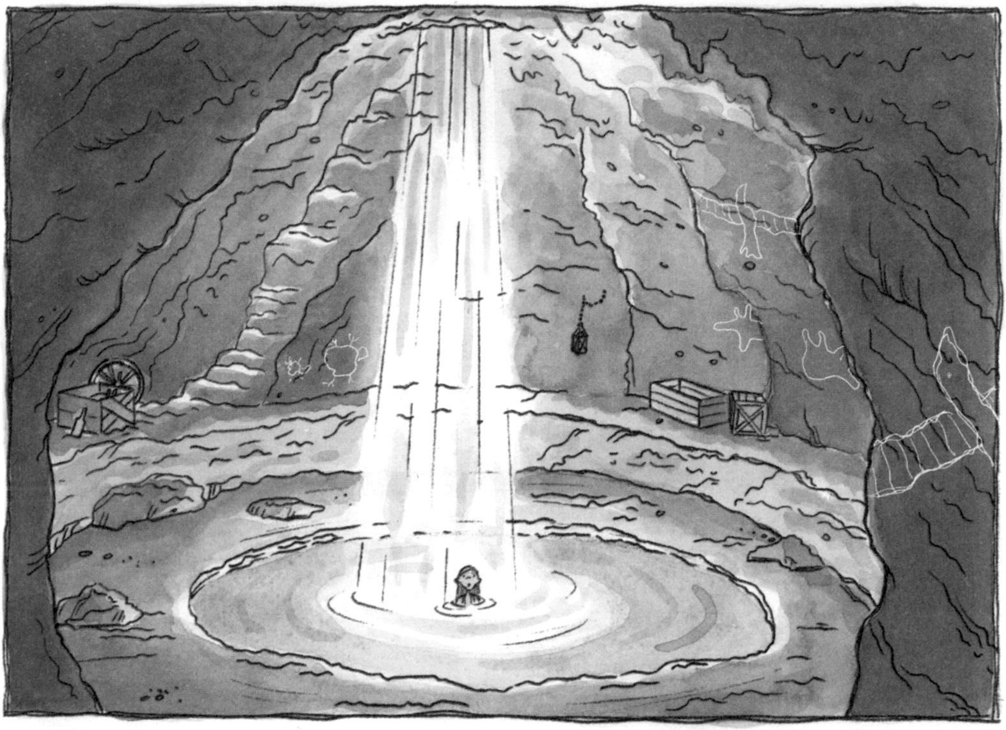

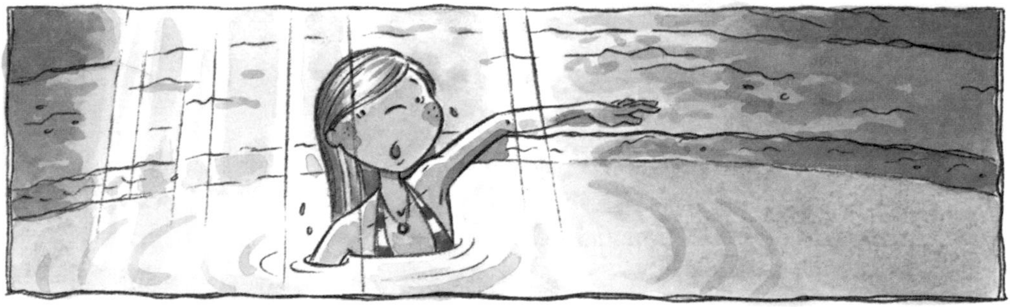

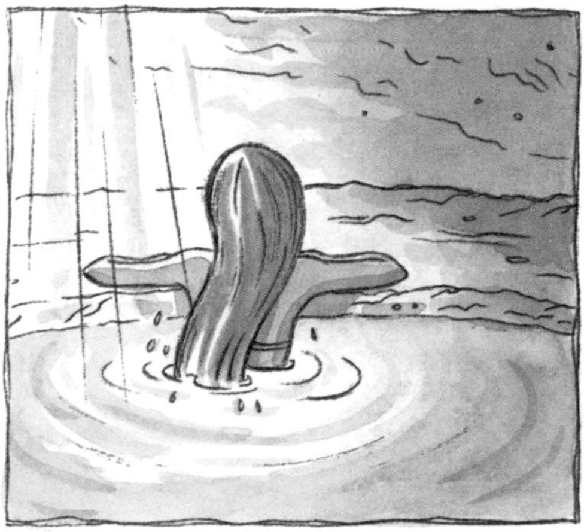

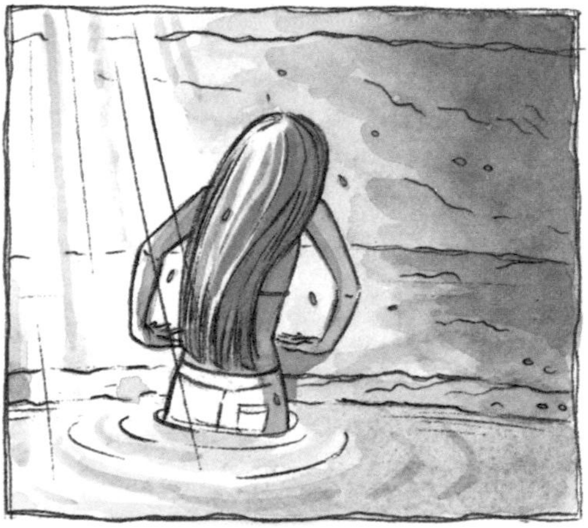

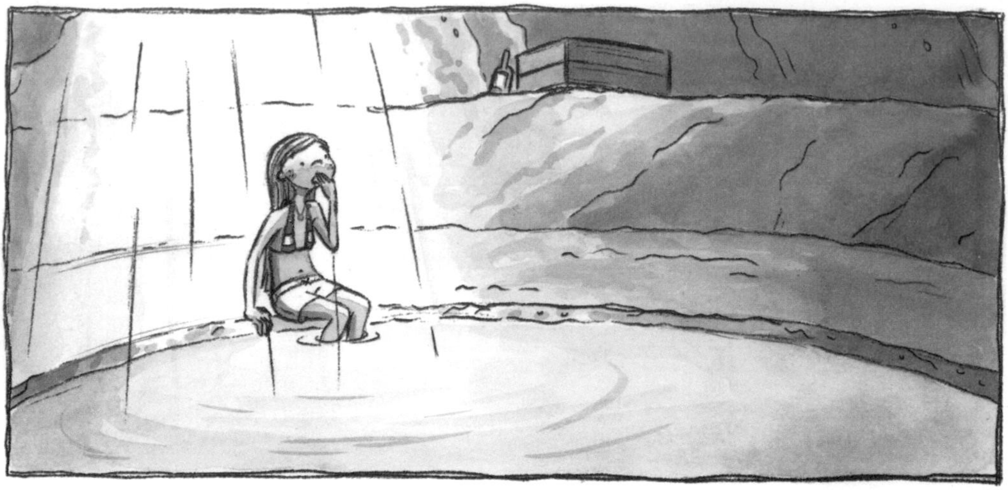

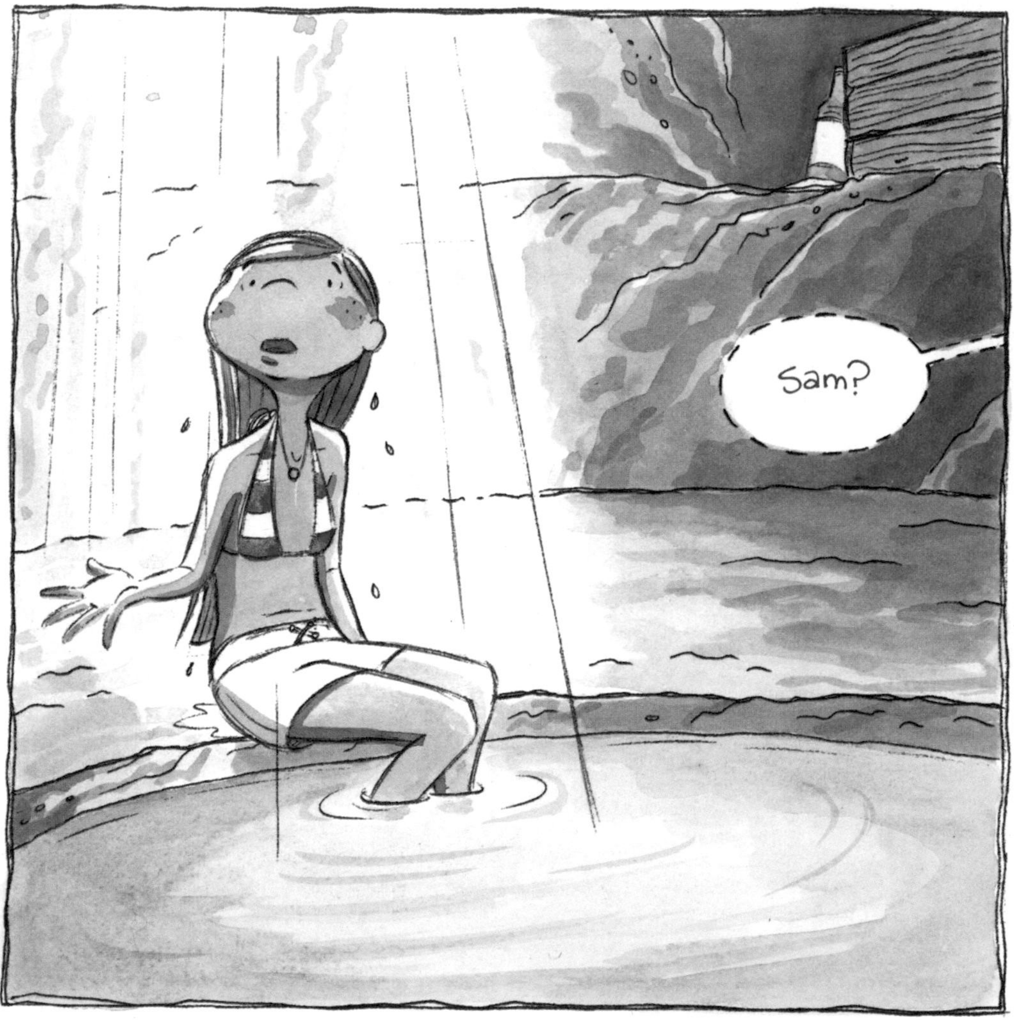
Sam?

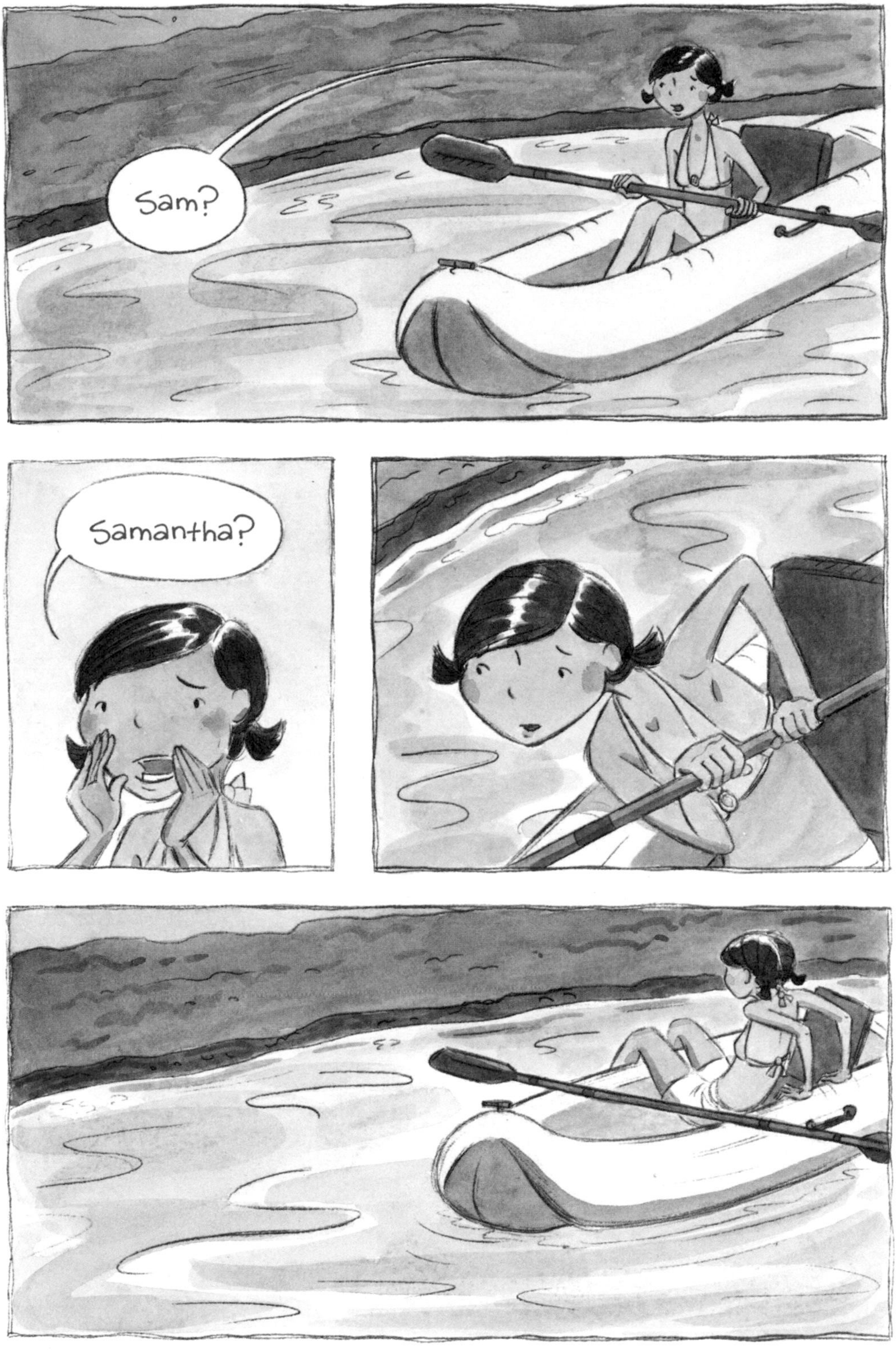
Sam?
Samantha?

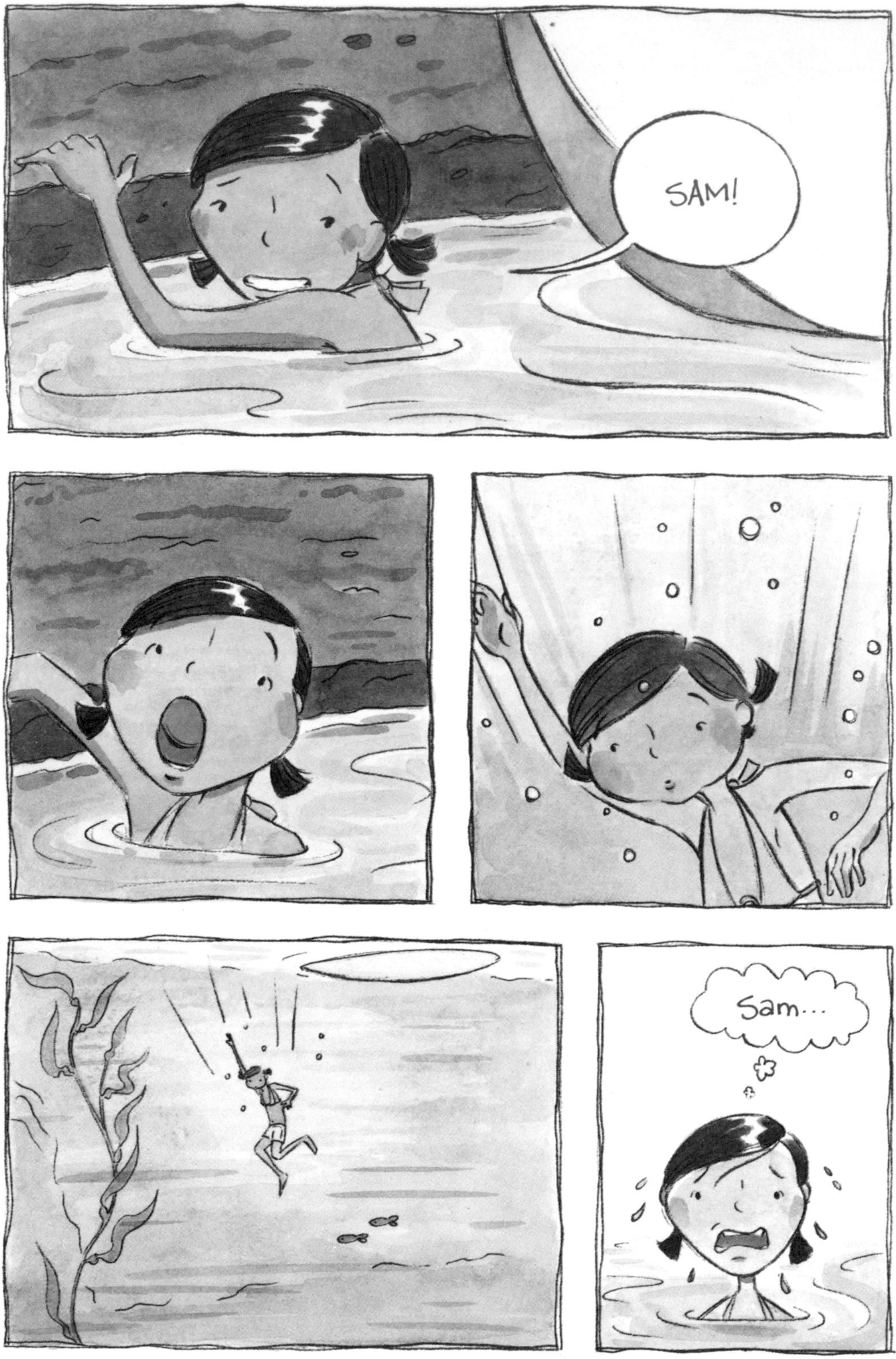
SAM!
Sam...

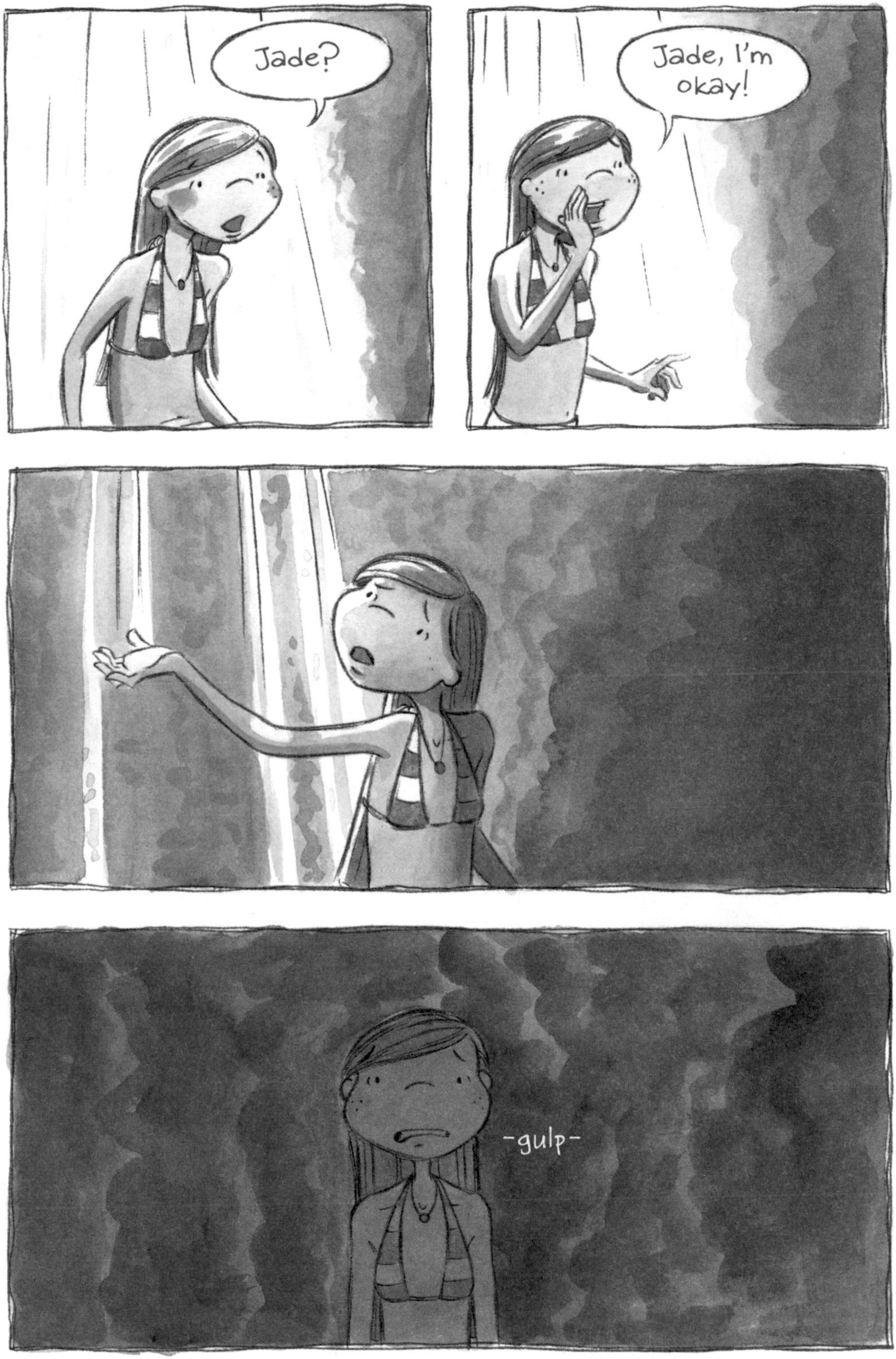
Jade?
Jade, I'm okay!
-gulp-

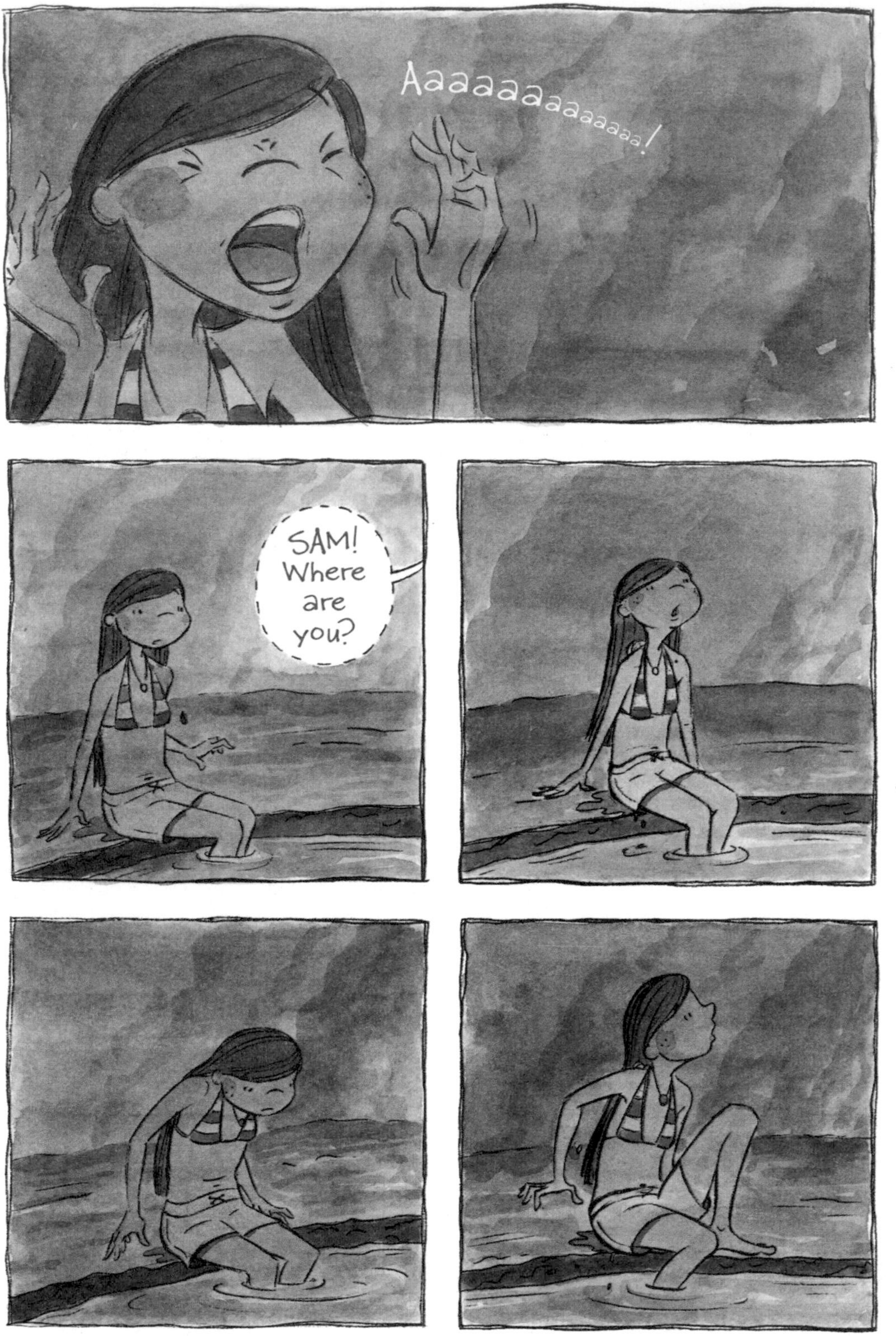
Aaaaaaaaaaaaaa!
SAM! Where are you?

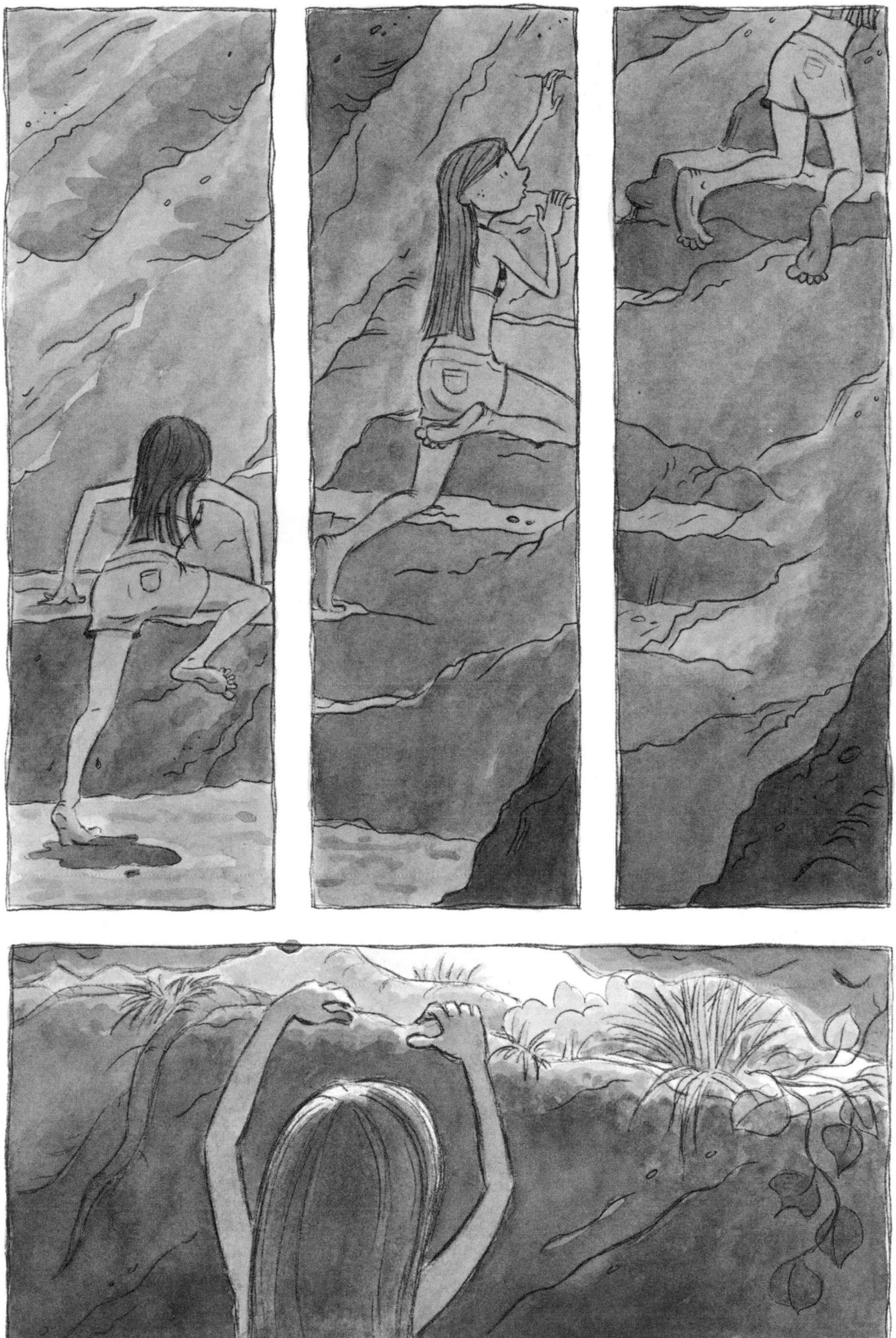

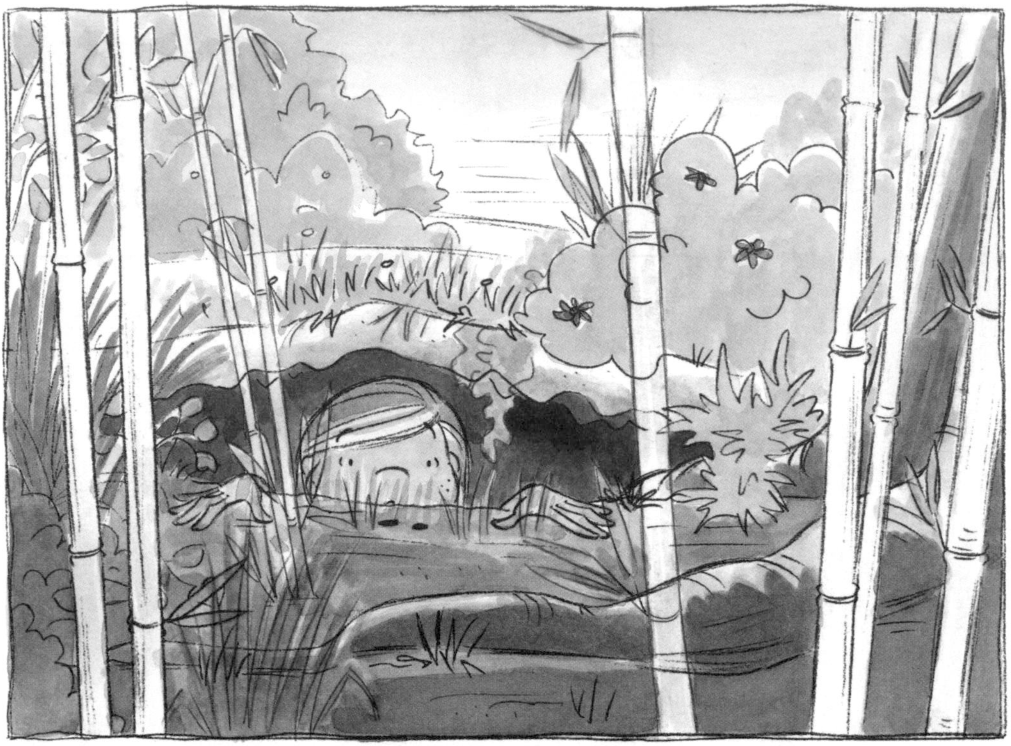

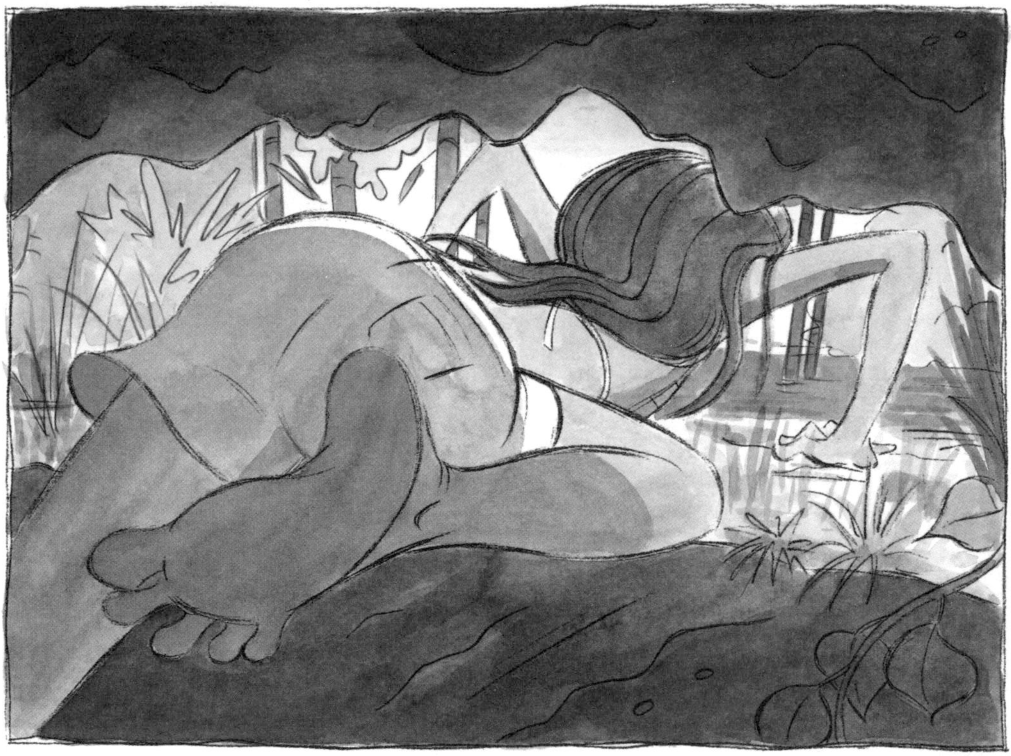

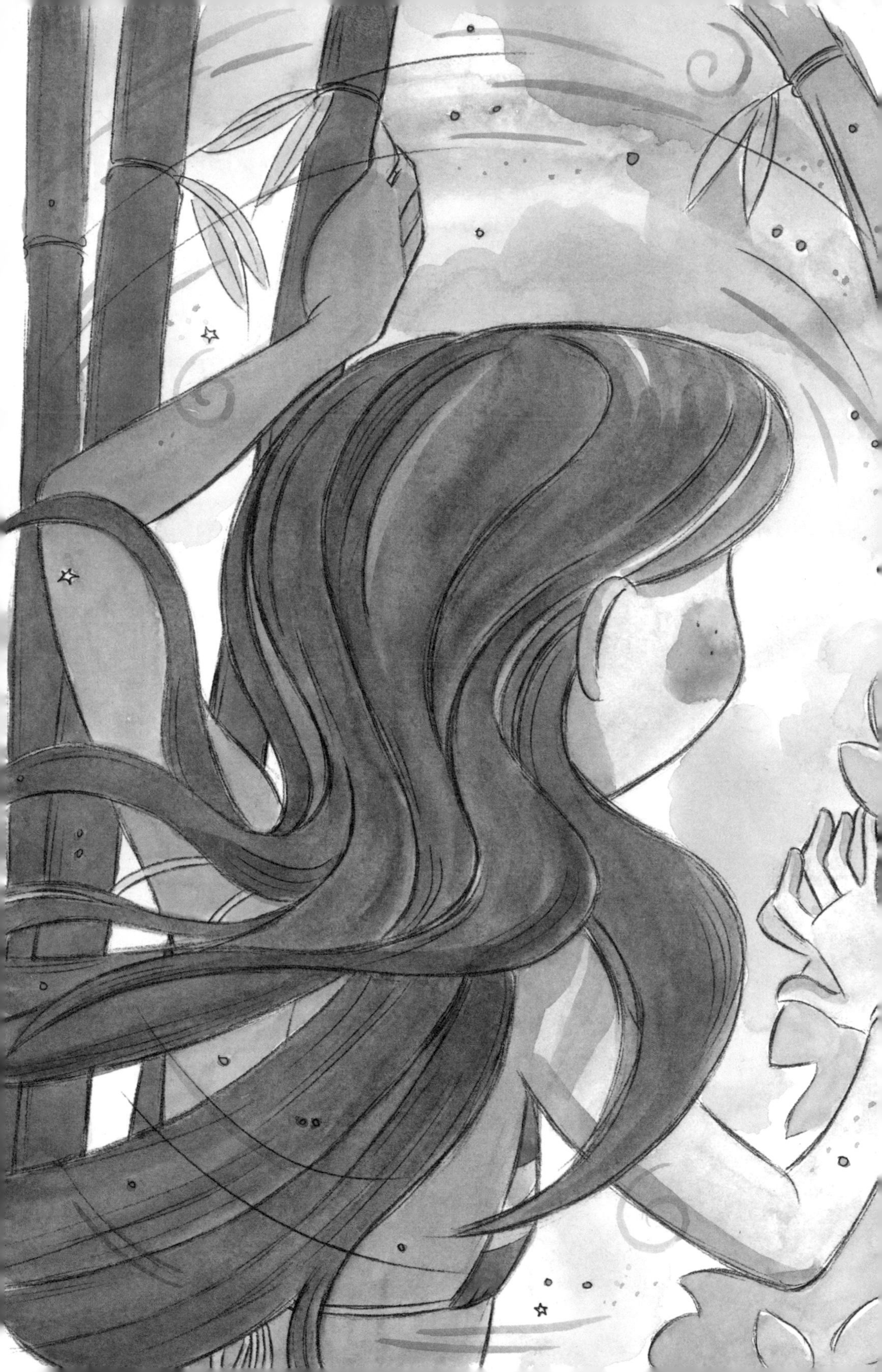

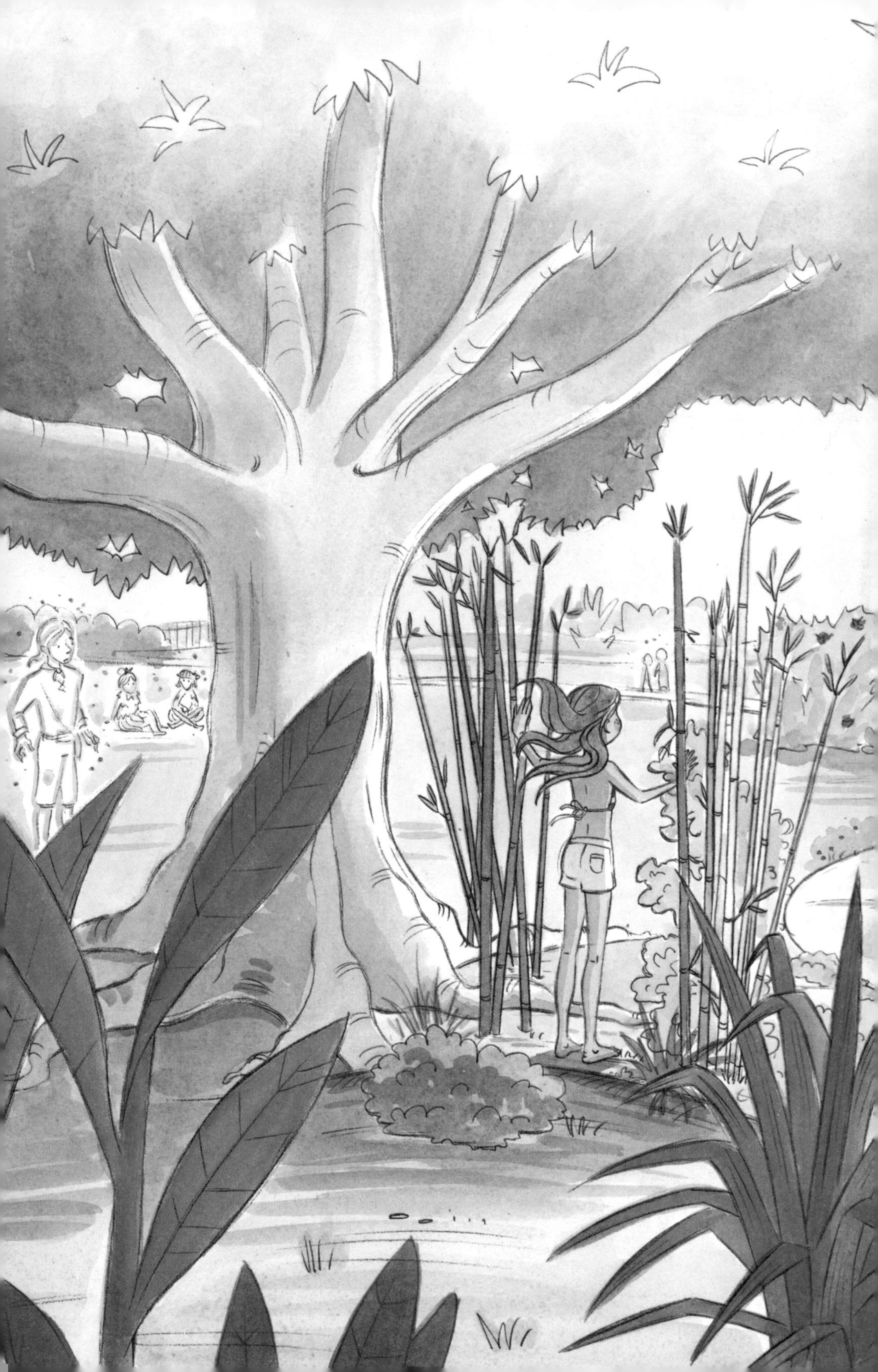

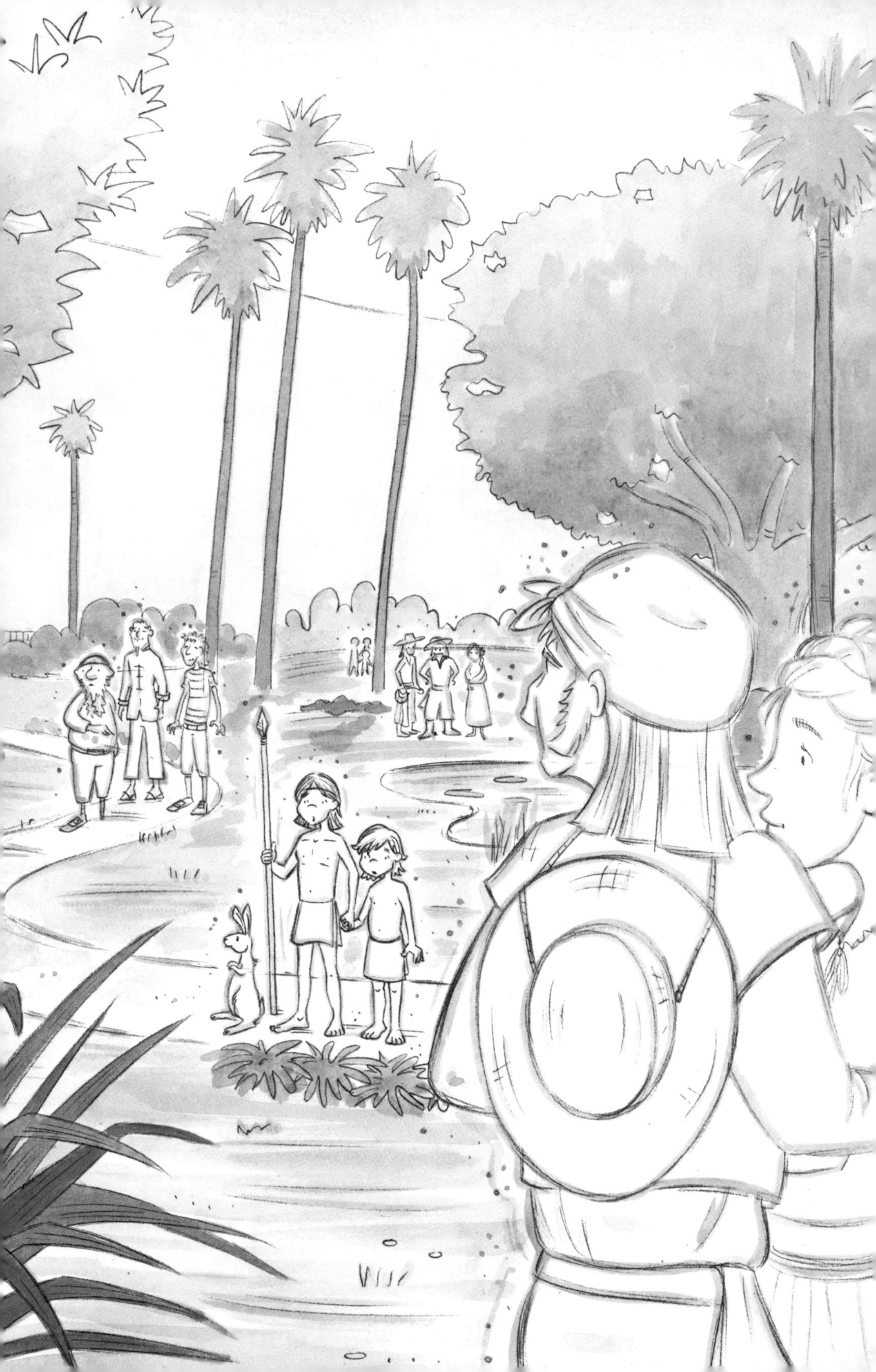

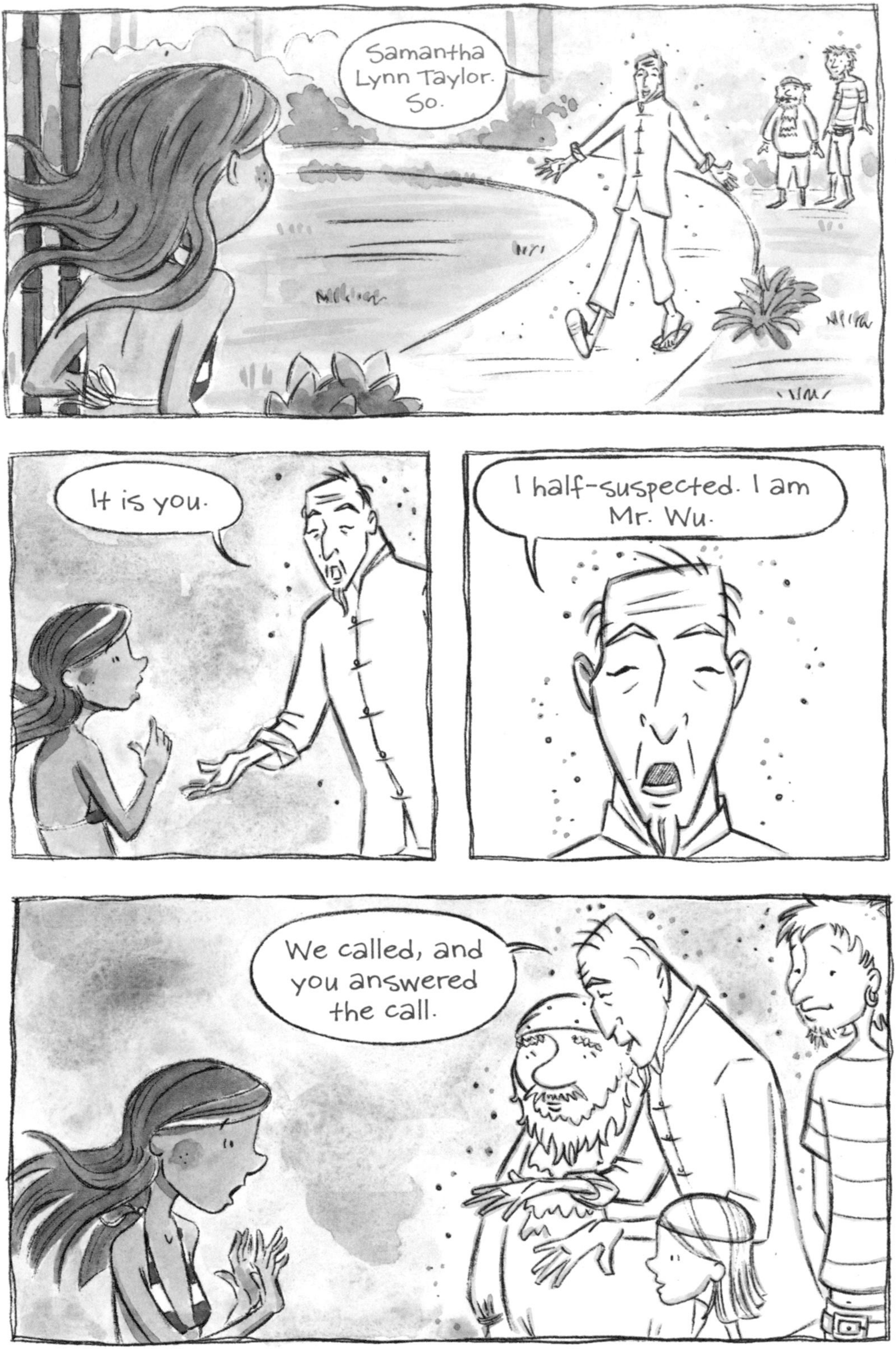
Samantha Lynn Taylor. So.
It is you.
I half-suspected. I am Mr. Wu.
We called, and you answered the call.

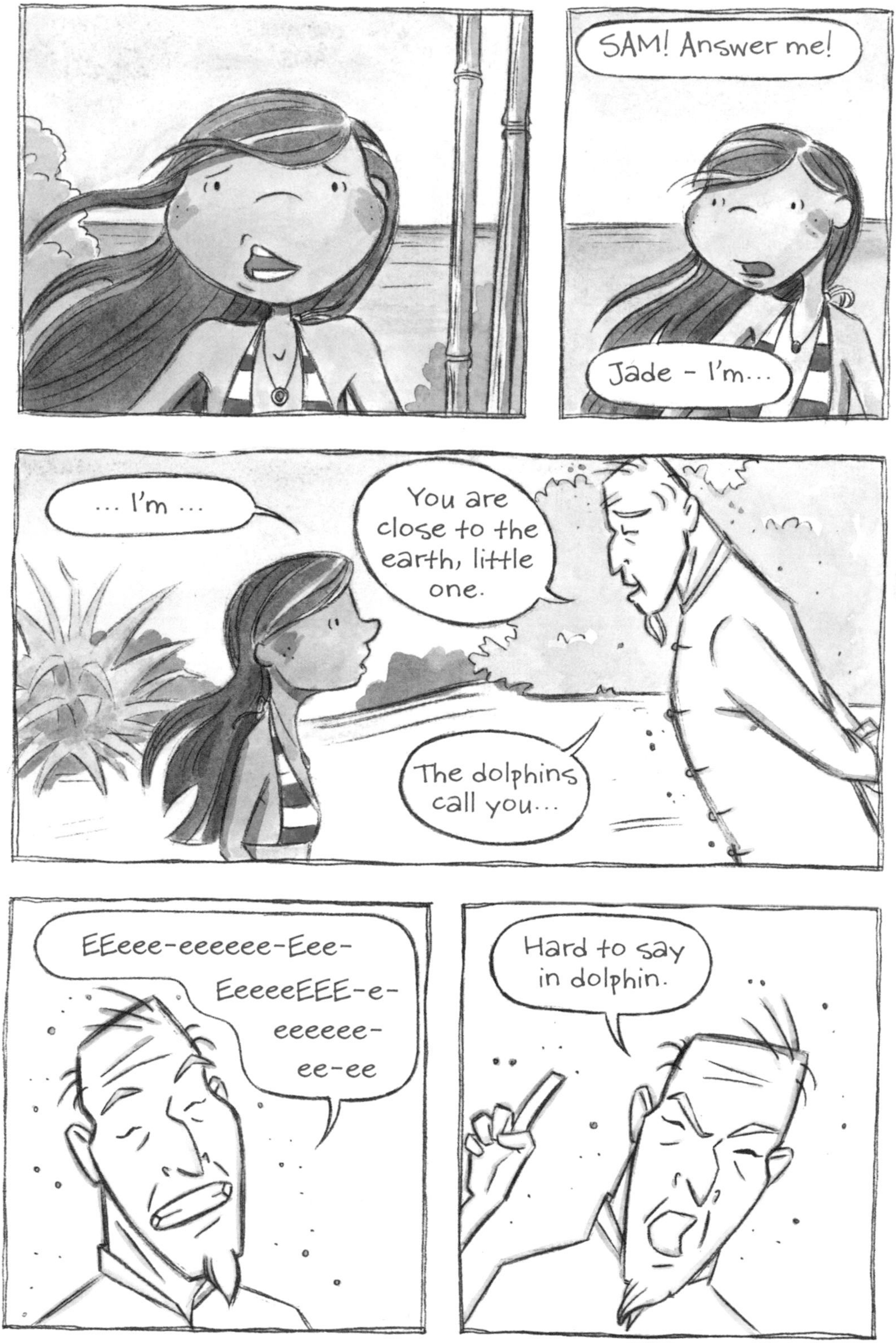
SAM! Answer me!
Jade - I'm...
... I'm ...
You are close to the earth, little one.
The dolphins call you...
EEeee-eeeeee-Eee-EeeeeEEE-e-eeeeee-ee-ee
Hard to say in dolphin.

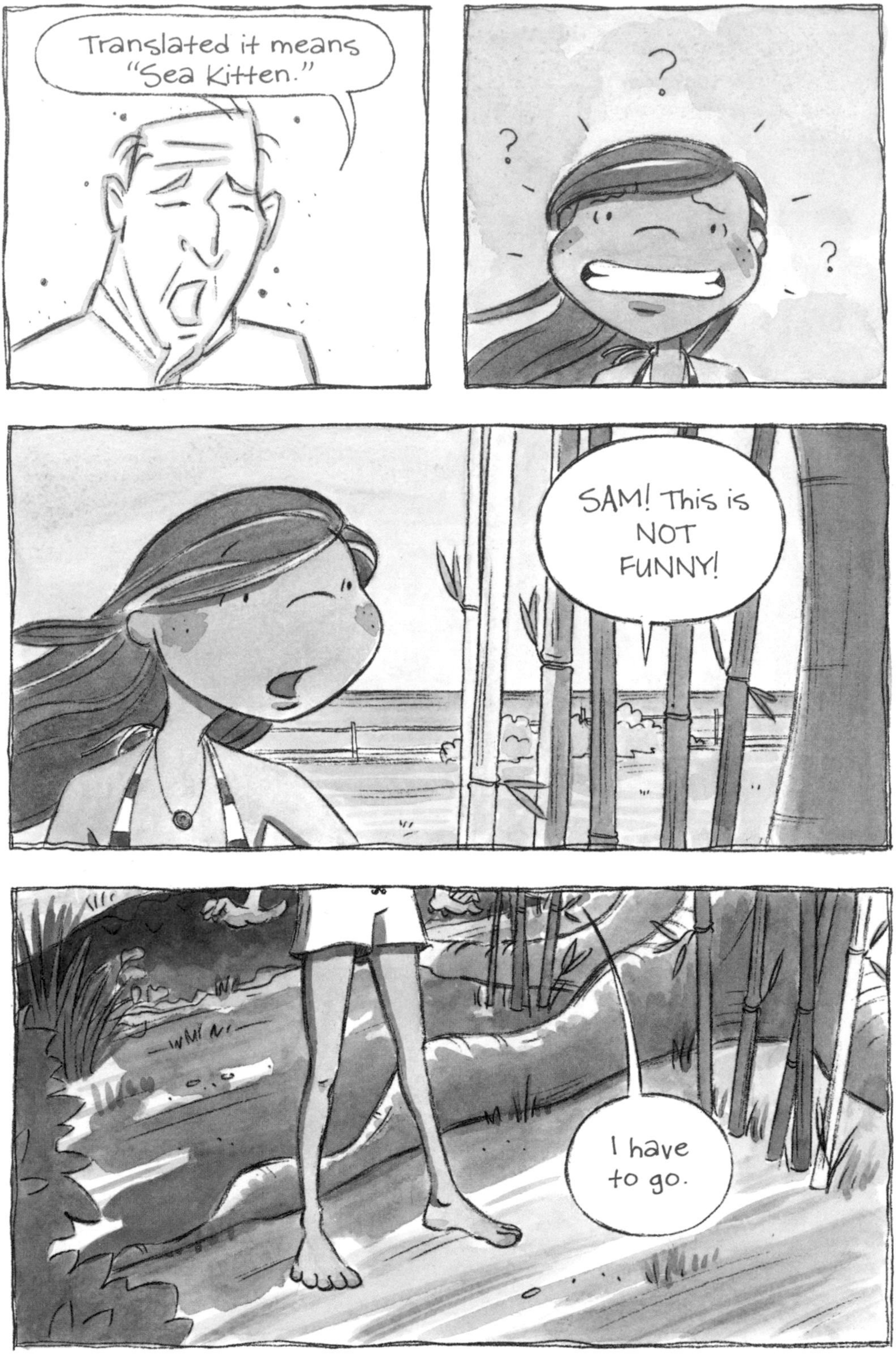
Translated it means "Sea Kitten."
?
?
?
SAM! This is NOT FUNNY!
I have to go.

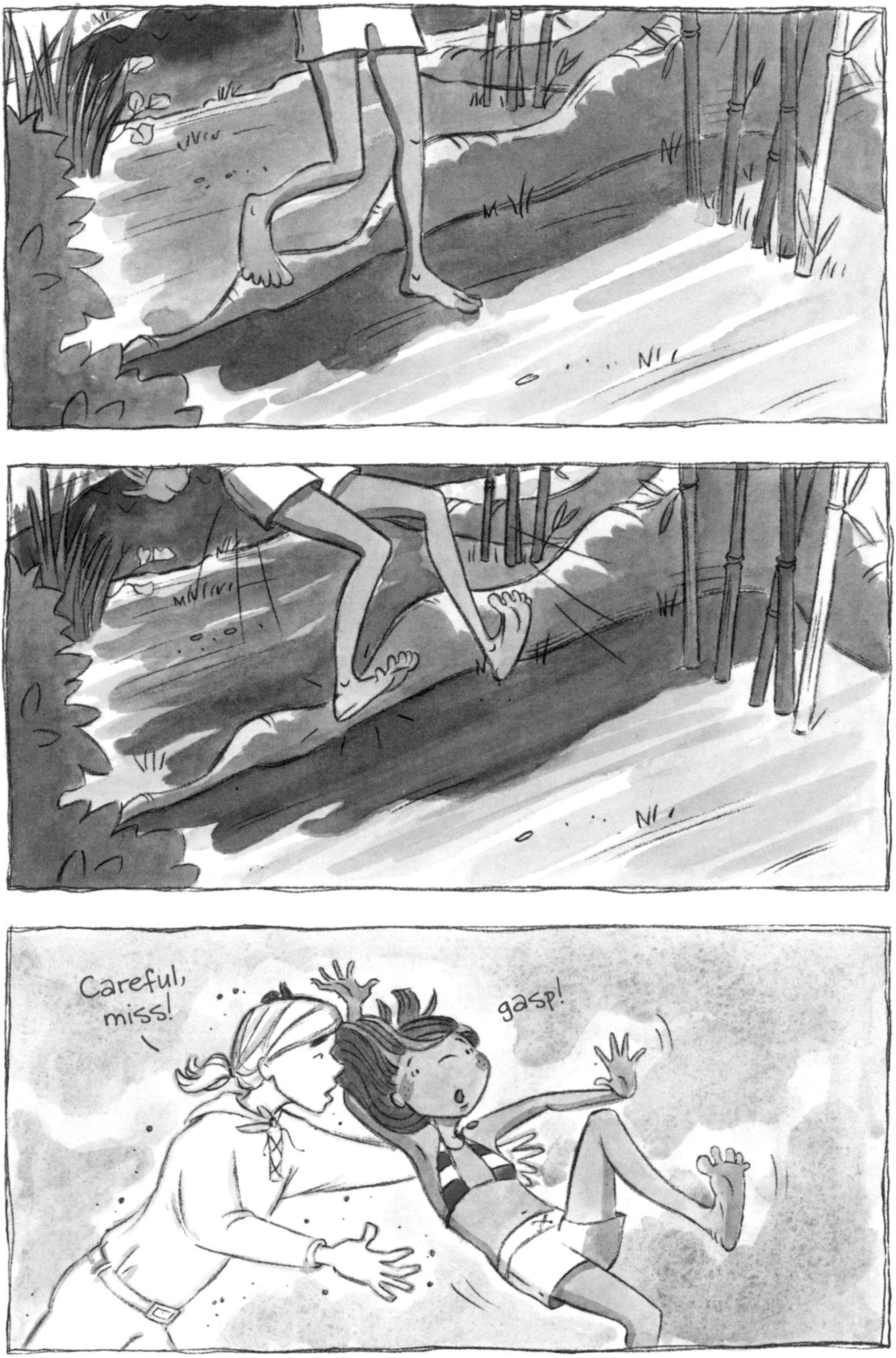
Careful, miss!
gasp!

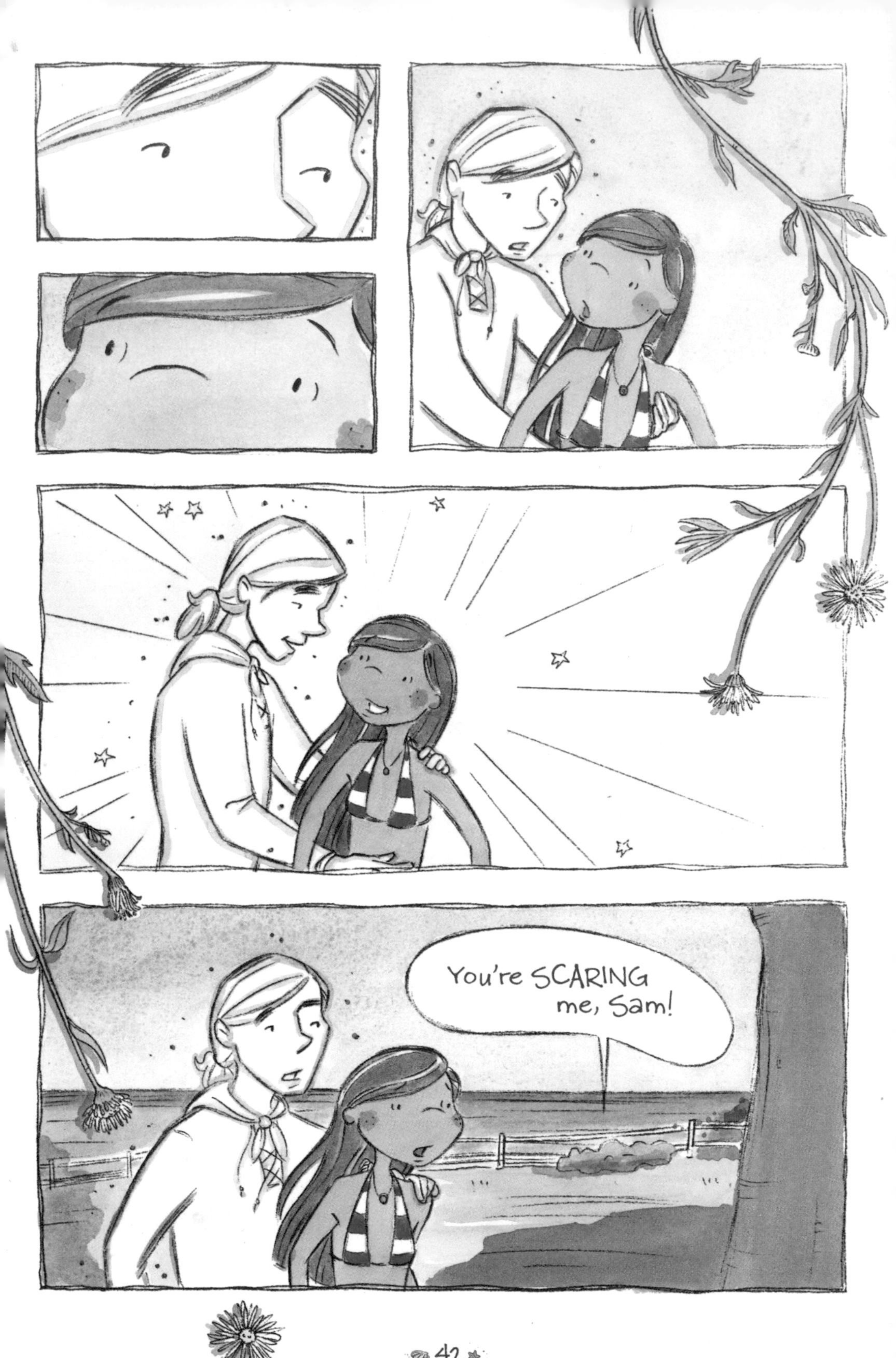
You're SCARING me, Sam!

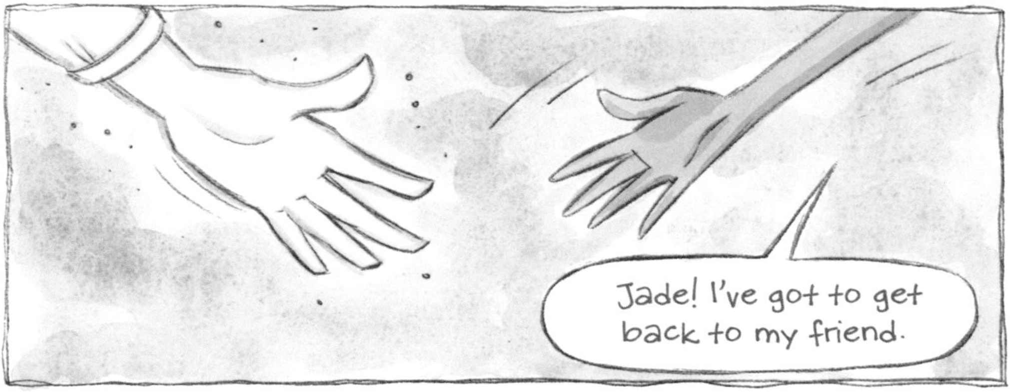
Jade! I've got to get back to my friend.

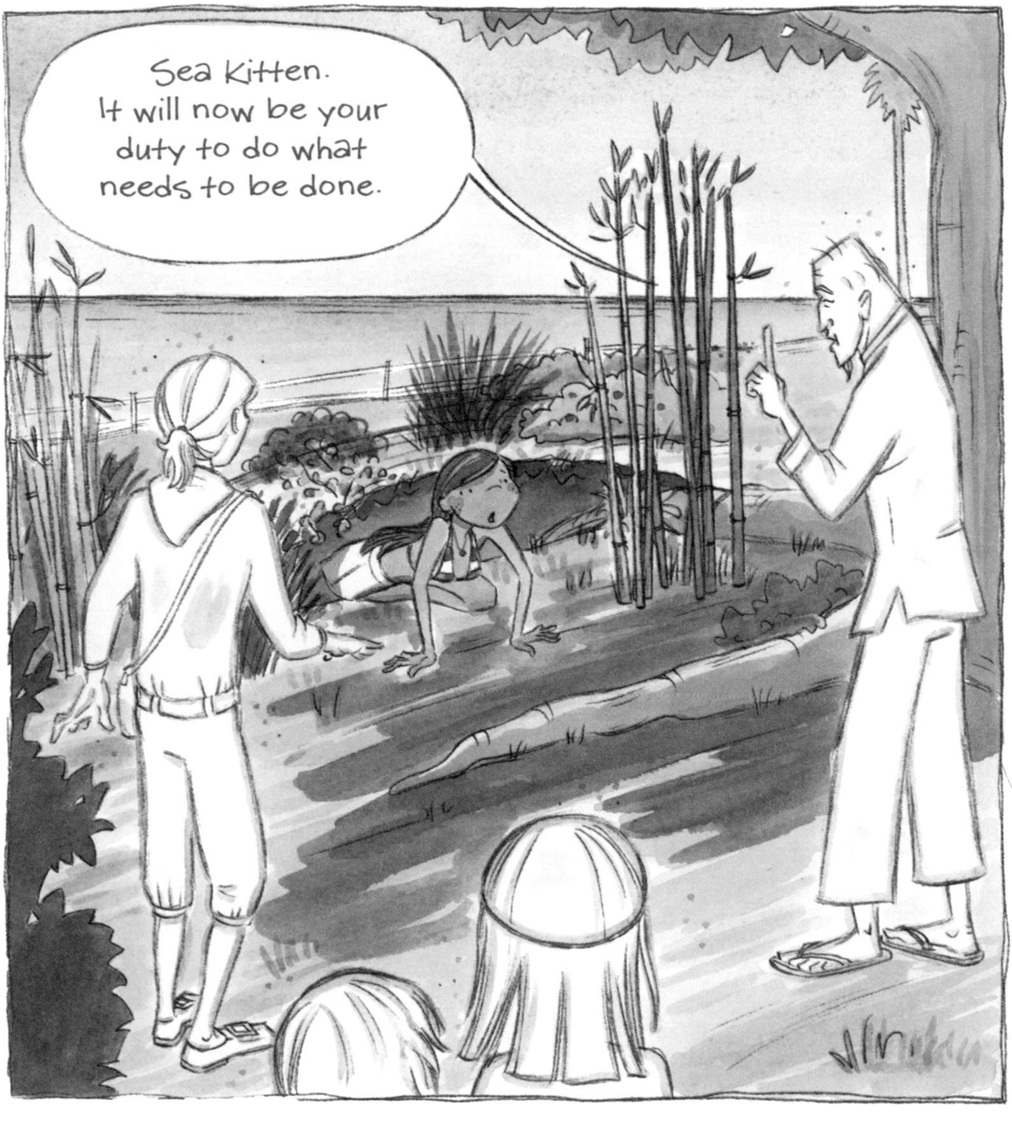
Sea Kitten. It will now be your duty to do what needs to be done.

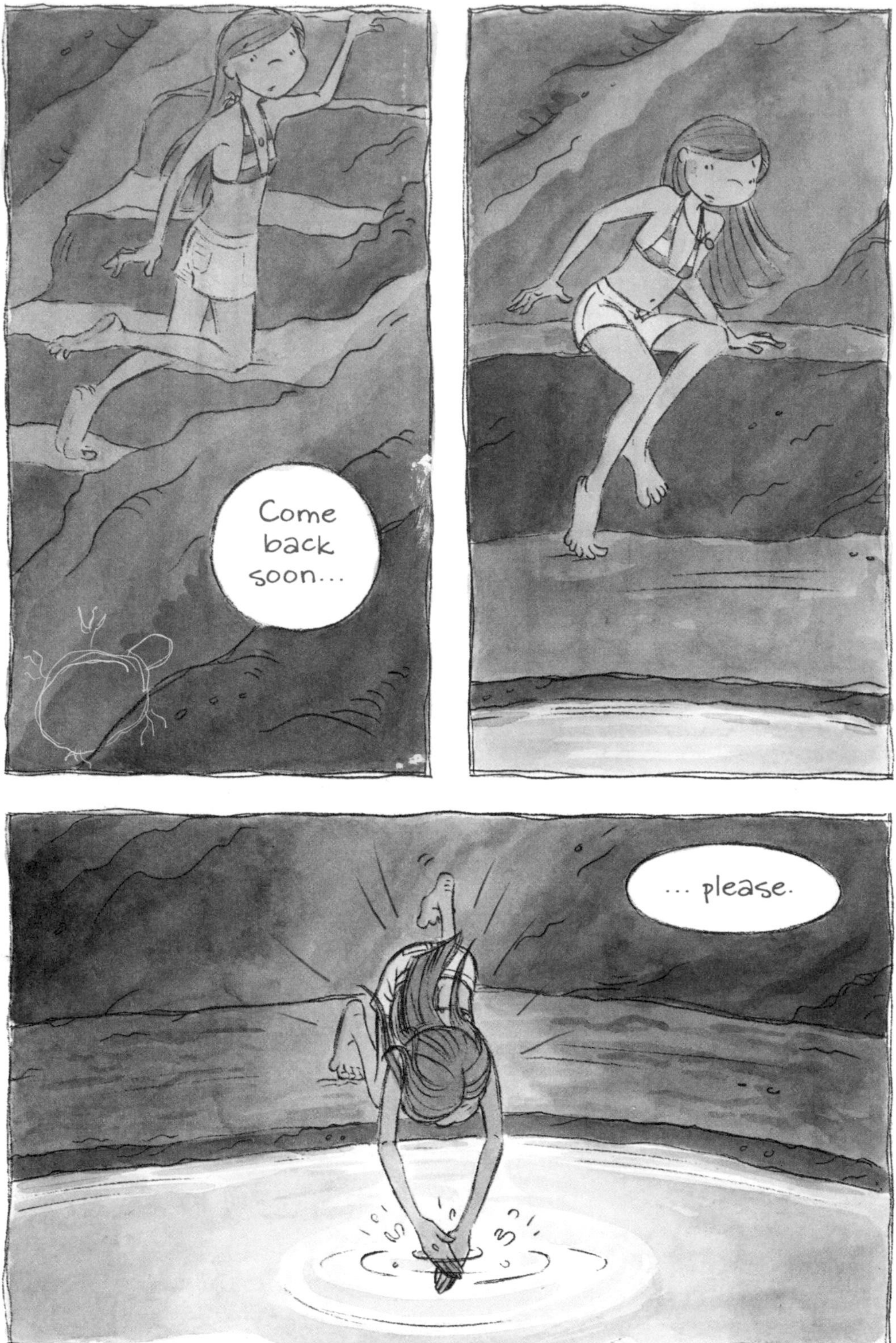
Come back soon...
... please.

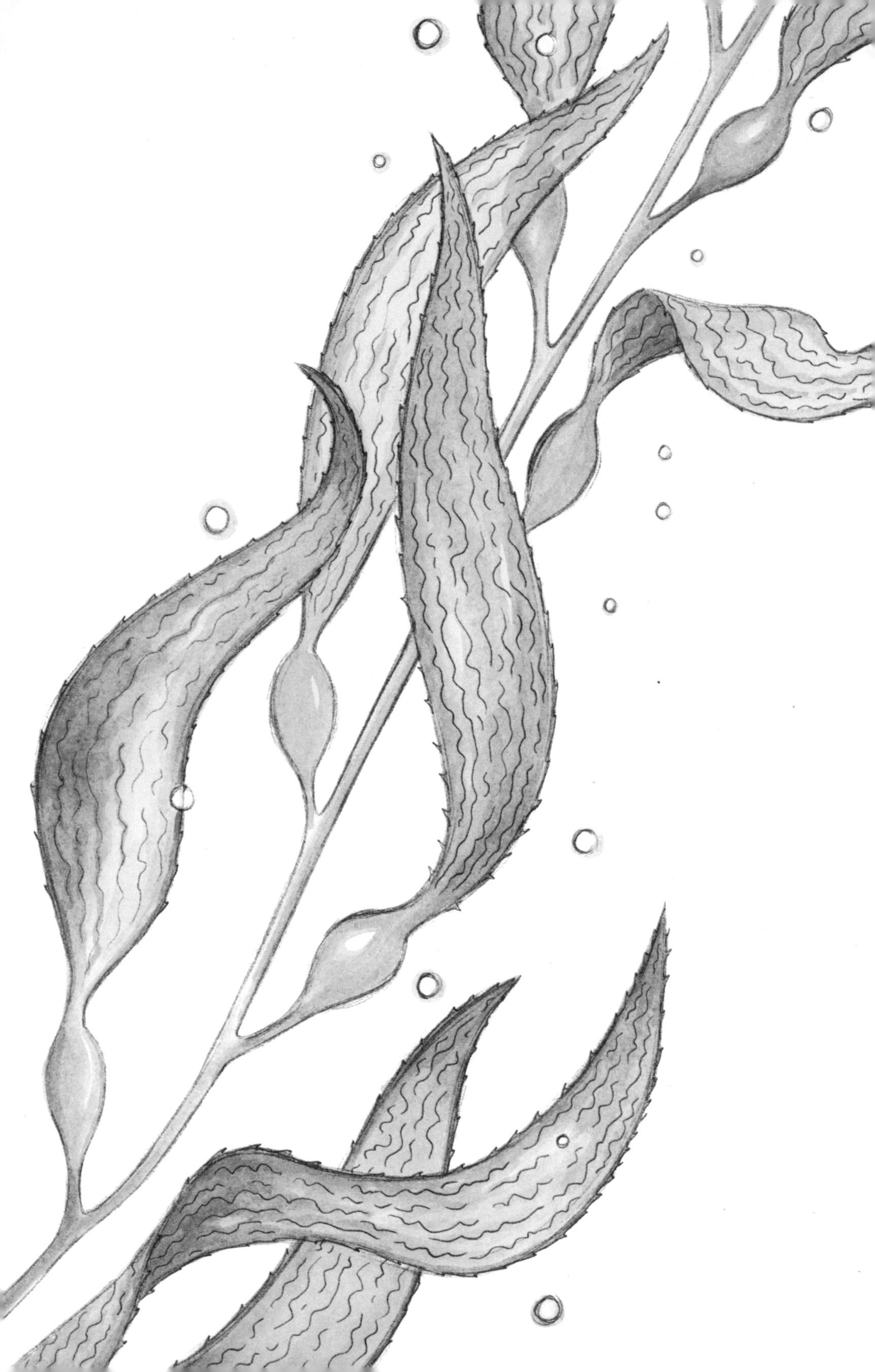

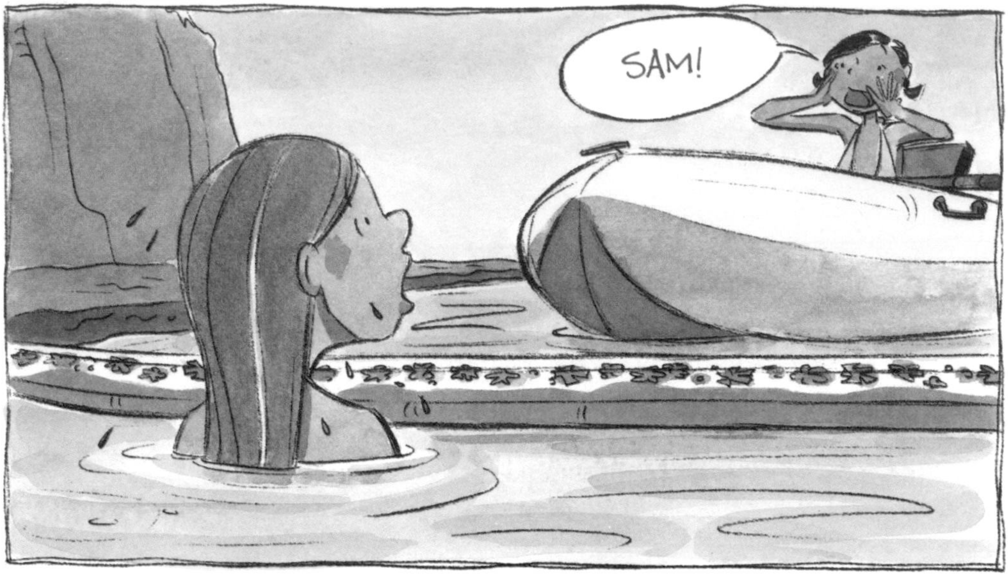
SAM!

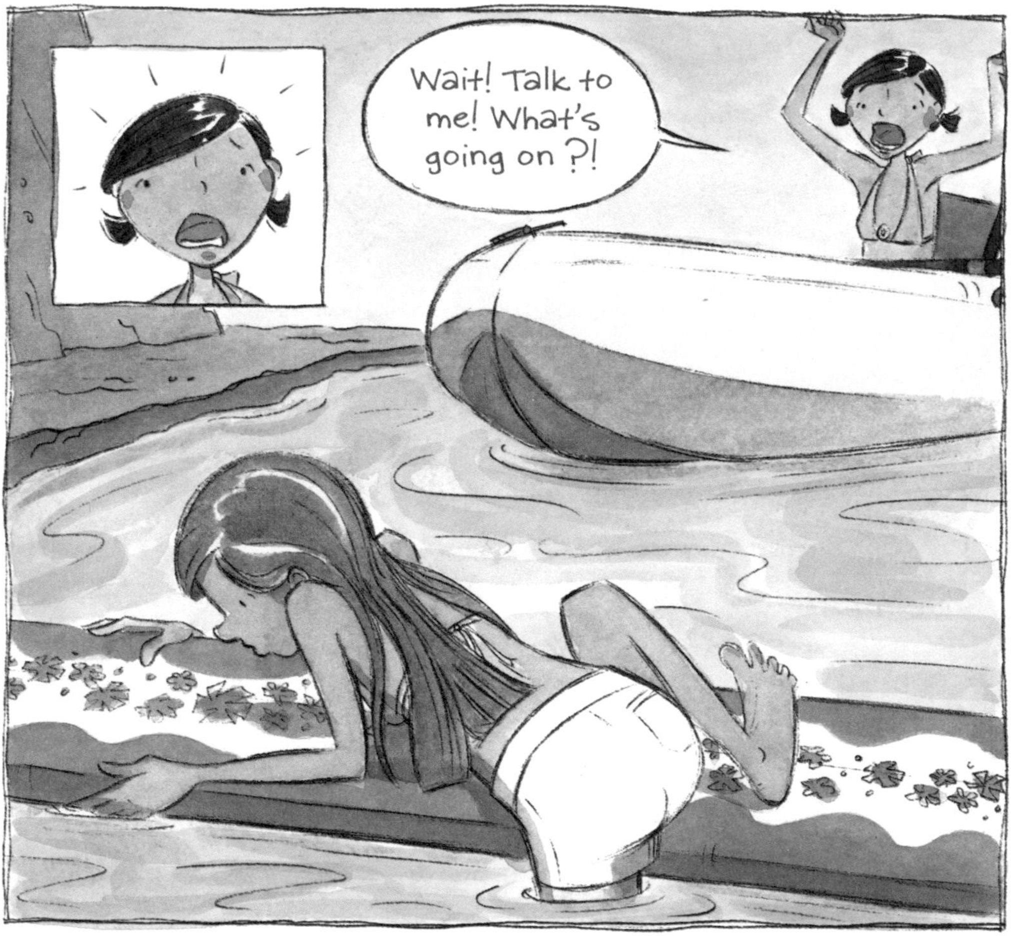
Wait! Talk to me! What's going on ?!

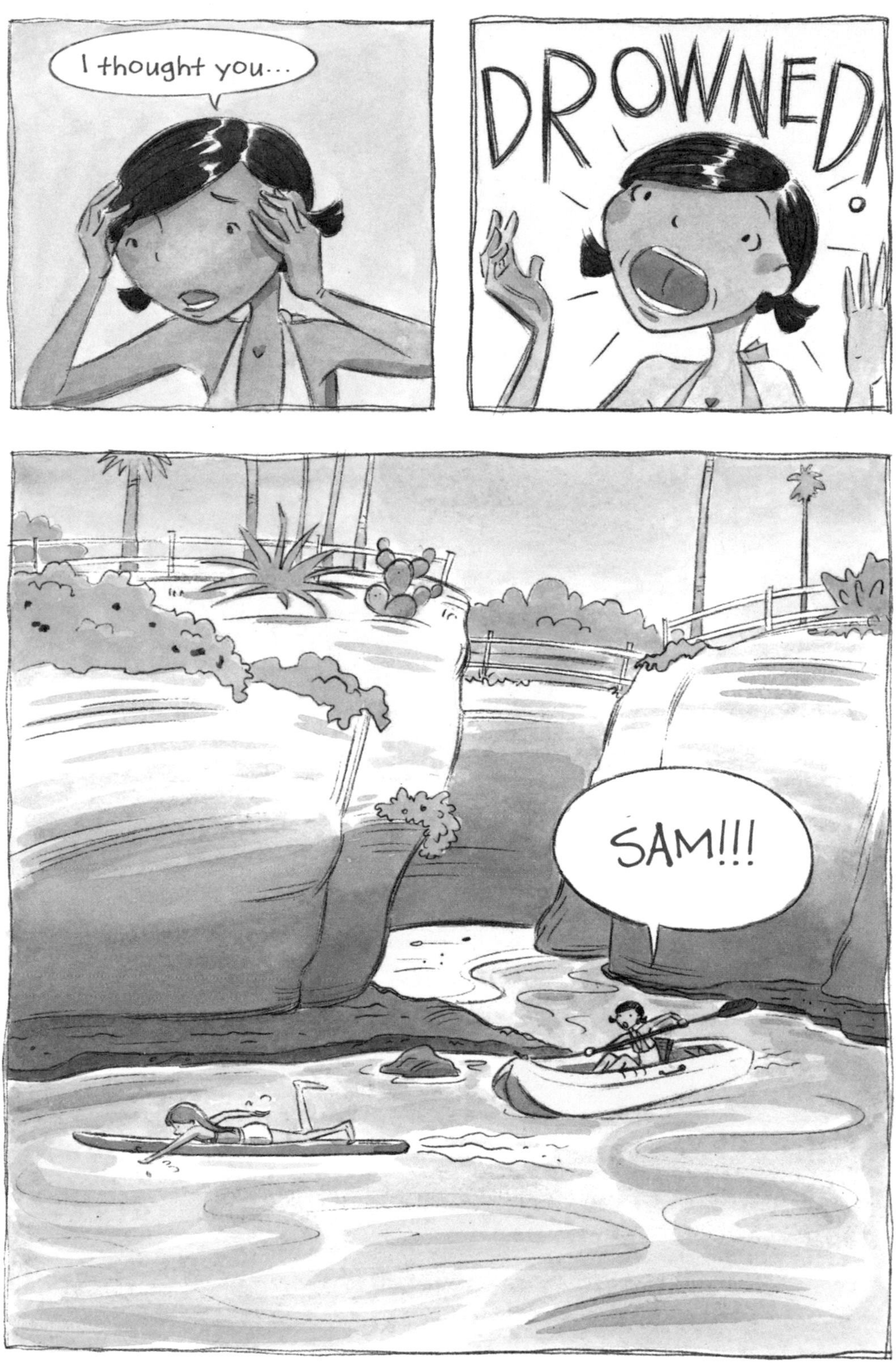
I thought you...
DROWNED!
SAM!!!

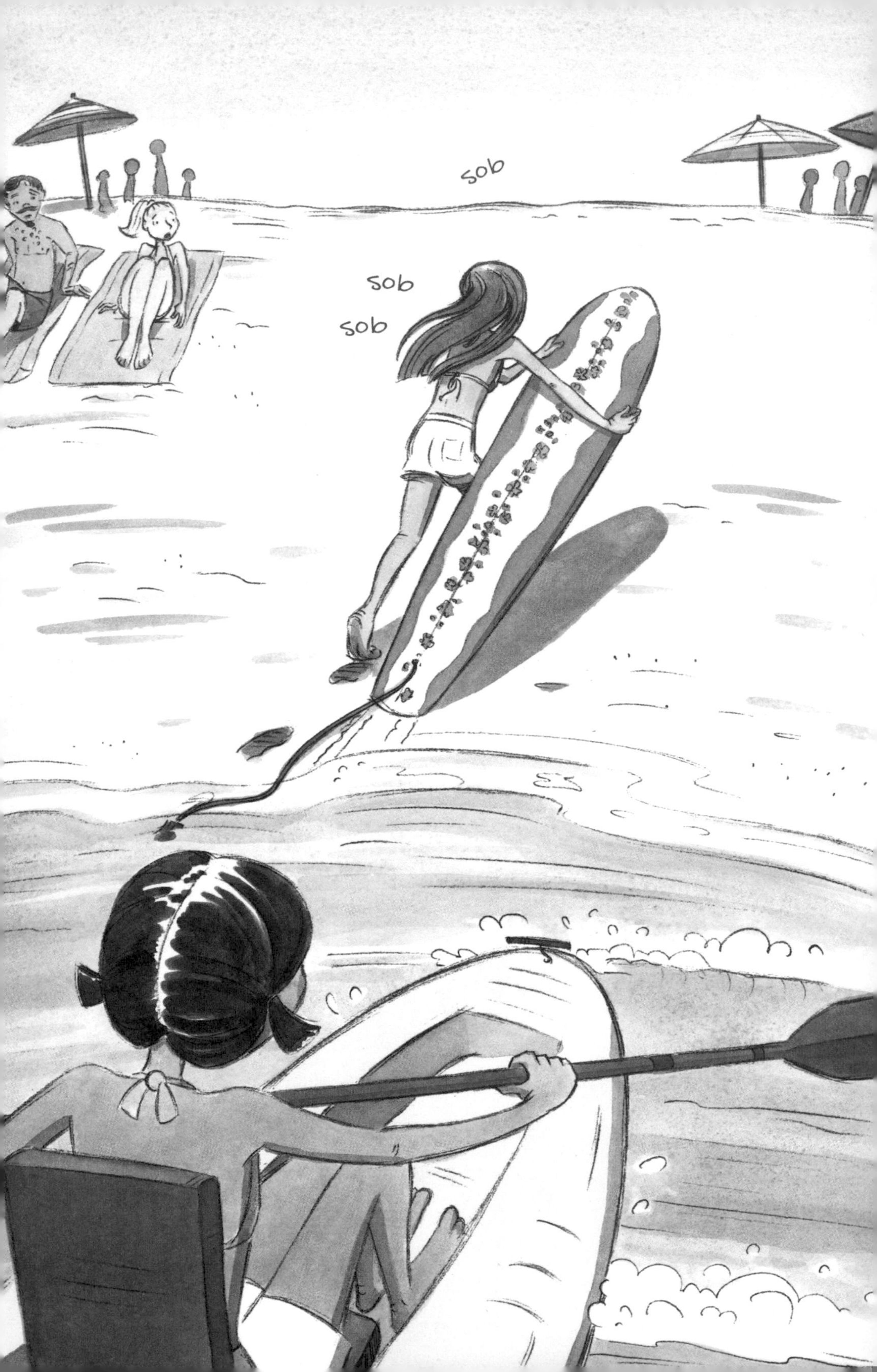
sob
sob
sob

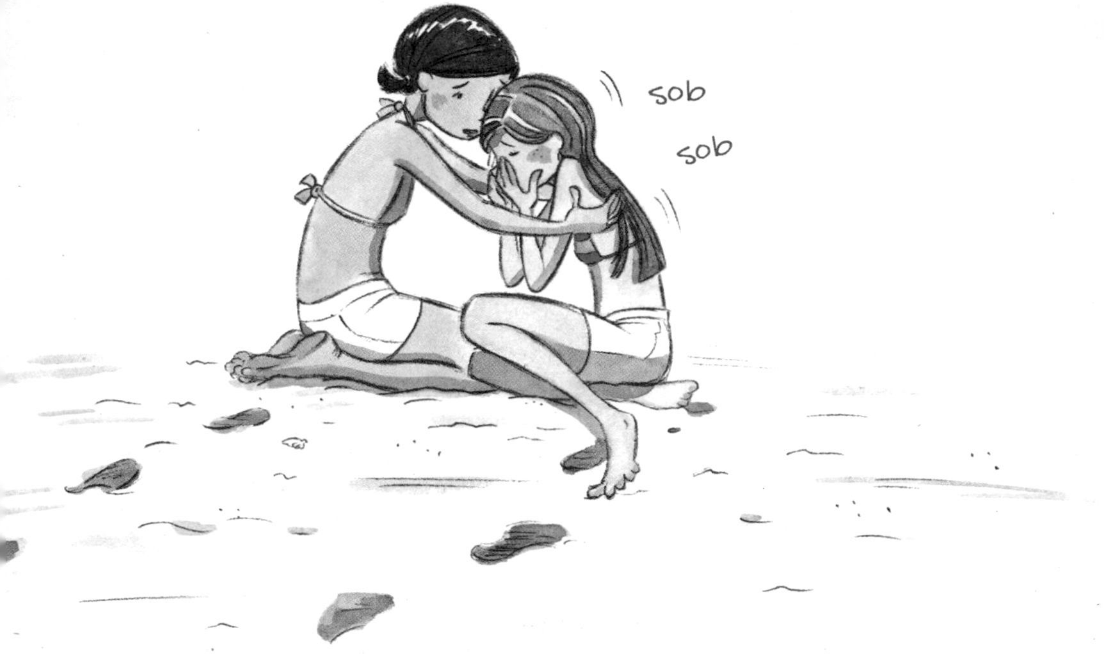
sob
sob

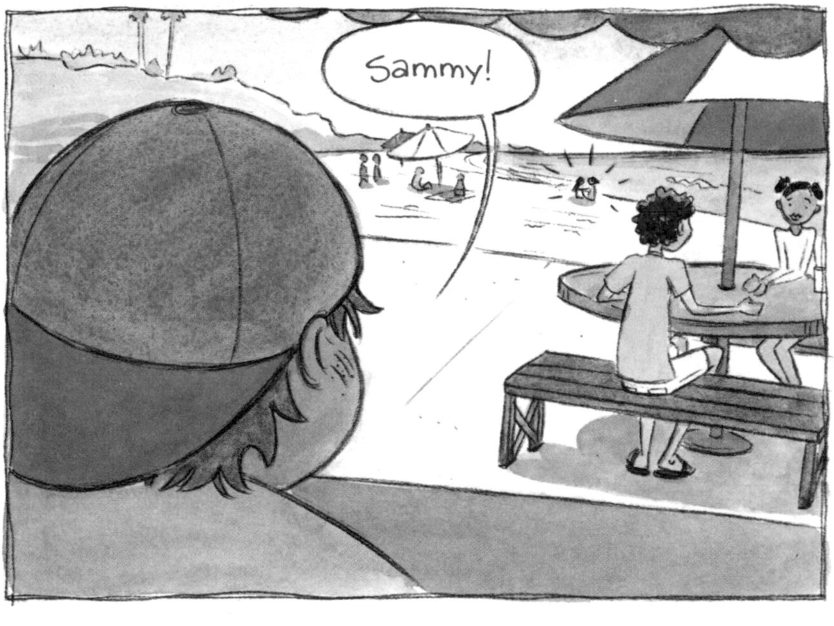
Sammy!

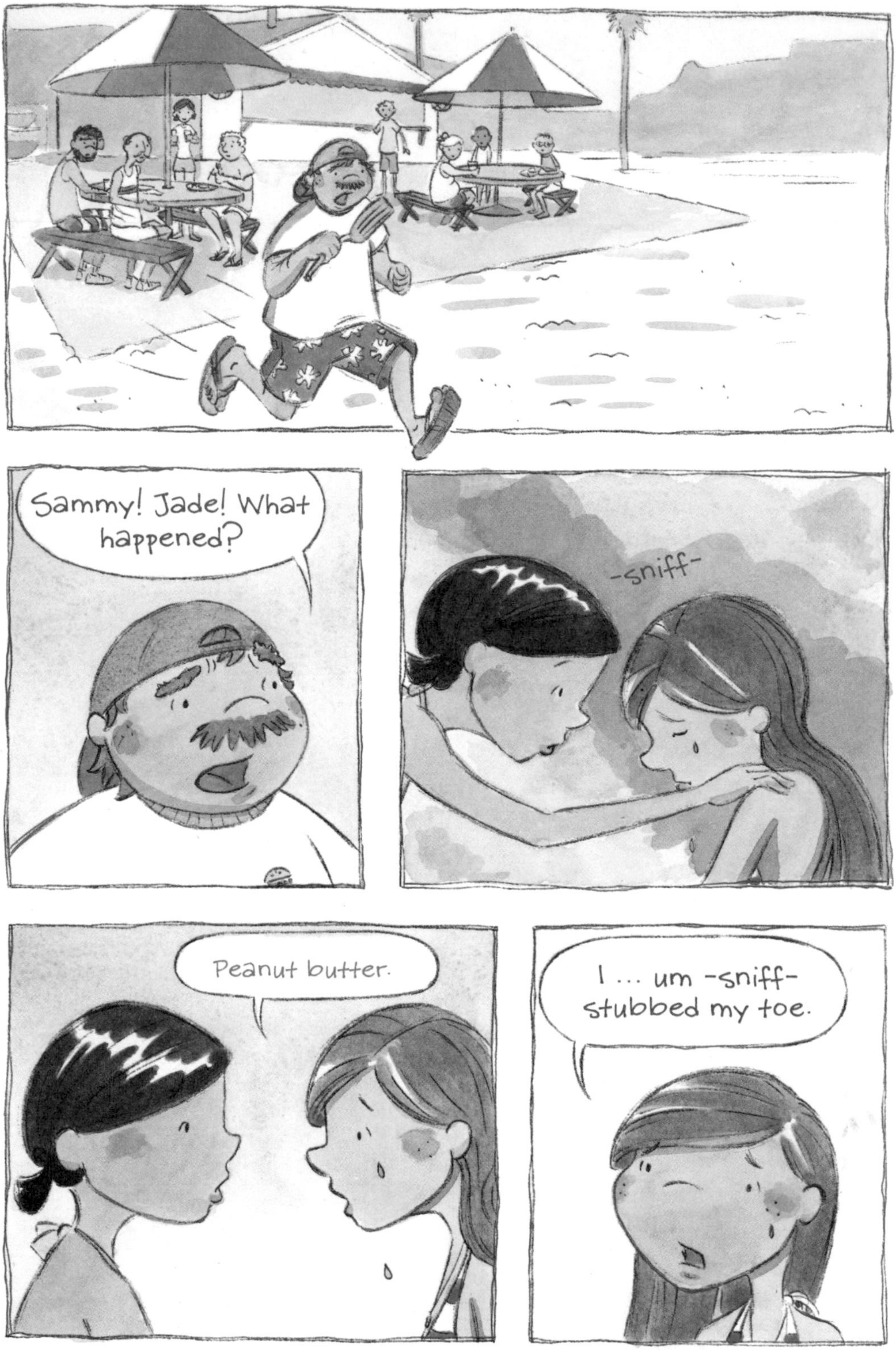
Sammy! Jade! What happened?
-sniff-
Peanut butter.
I ... um -sniff- stubbed my toe.

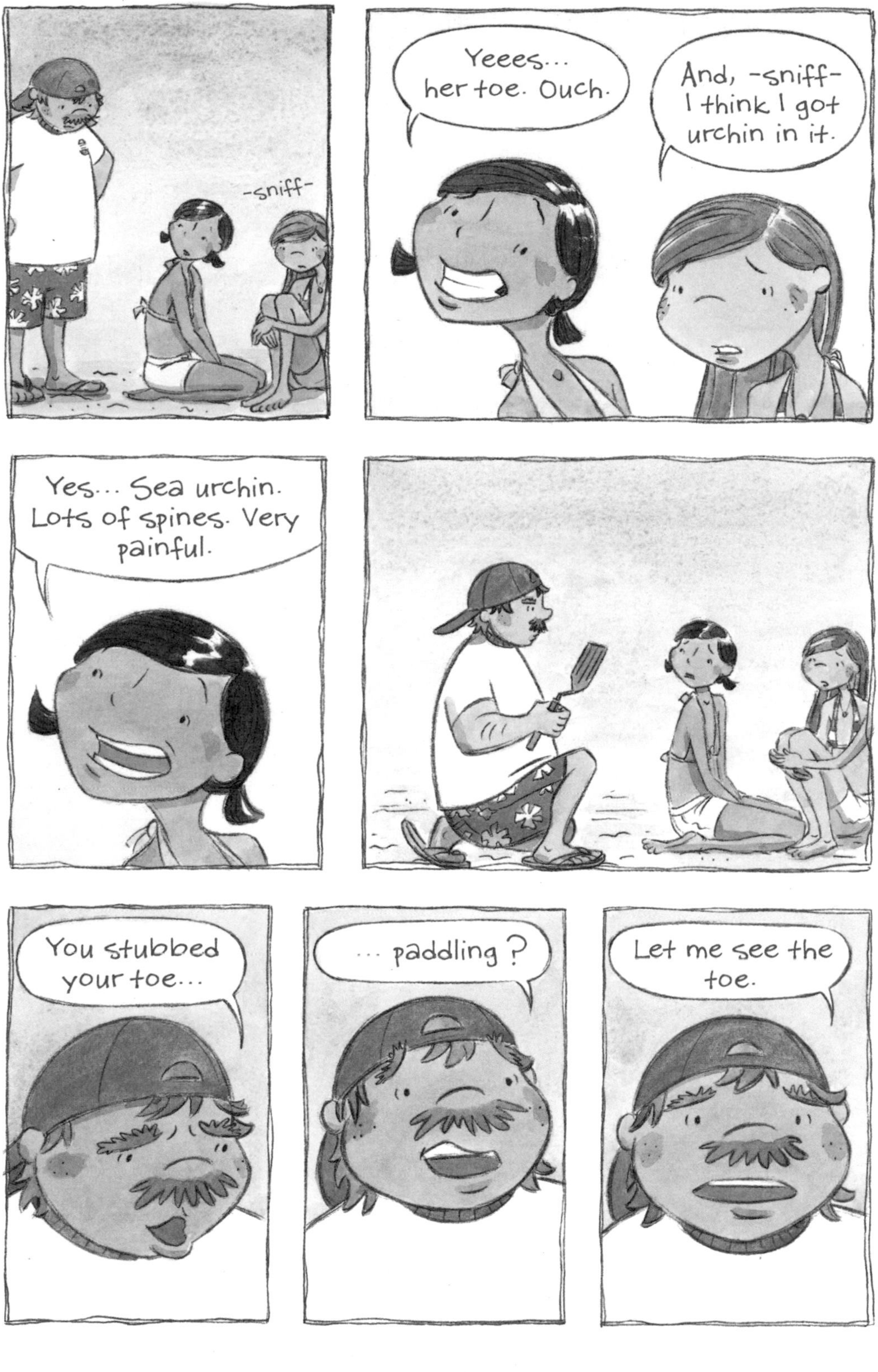
-sniff-
Yeees... her toe. Ouch.
And, -sniff- I think I got urchin in it.
Yes... Sea urchin. Lots of spines. Very painful.
You stubbed your toe...
... paddling?
Let me see the toe.

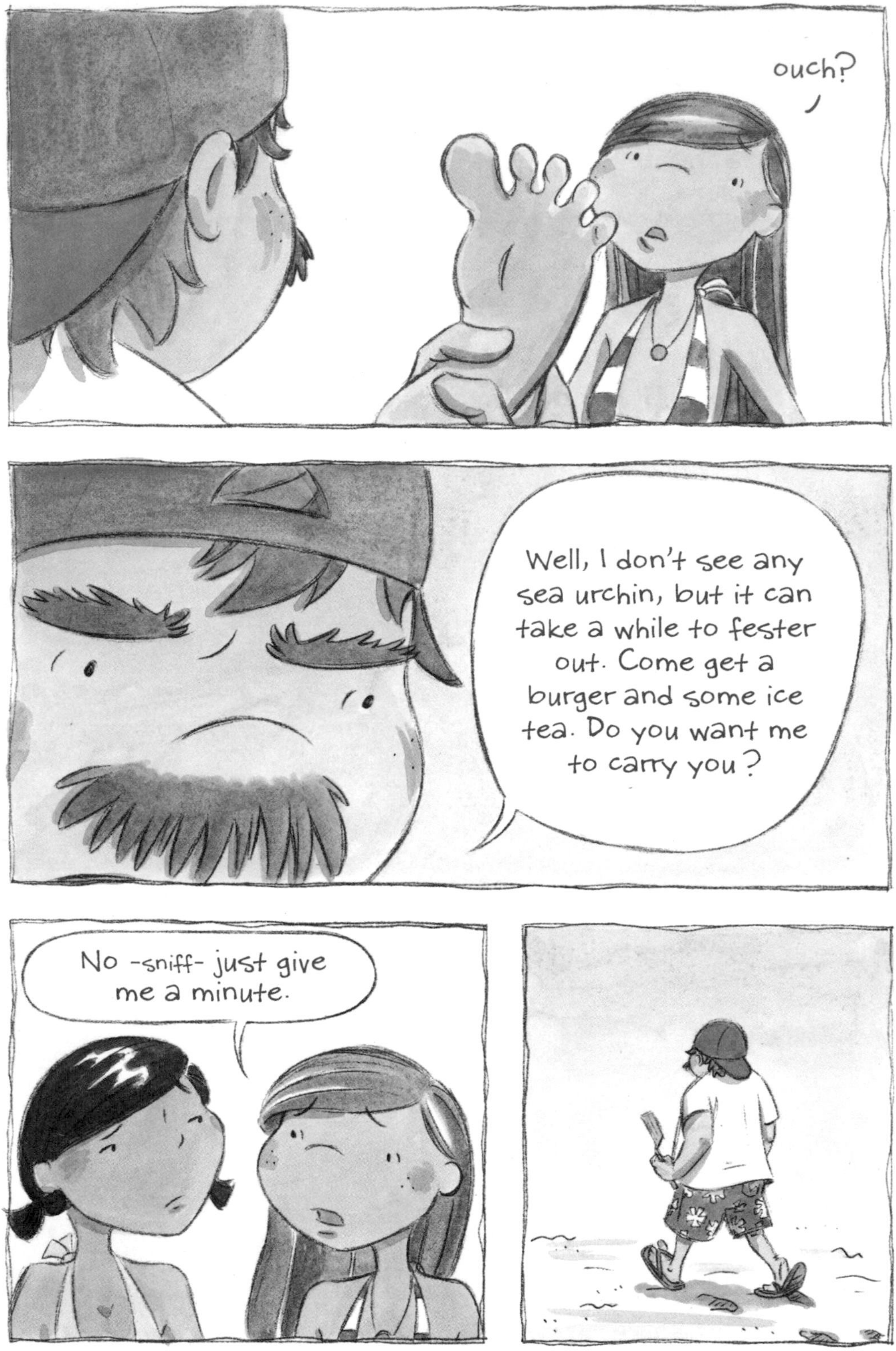
ouch?
Well, I don't see any sea urchin, but it can take a while to fester out. Come get a burger and some ice tea. Do you want me to carry you?
No -sniff- just give me a minute.

Tell me the peanut butter NOW.
Later...
Faker.
Shush.

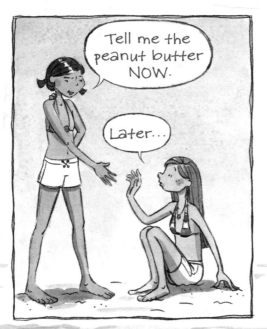

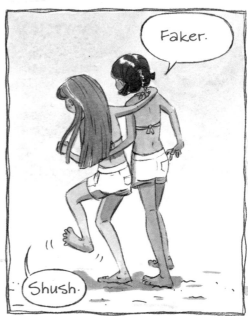

"Peanut butter" is a secret code word that me and Jade use when we can't talk about an important thing right that minute, but we totally have to remember it to talk about it later. Like, when a lady shouldn't be wearing a bikini that small, or a German tourist guy is jogging in speedos and shoes and a fanny pack.

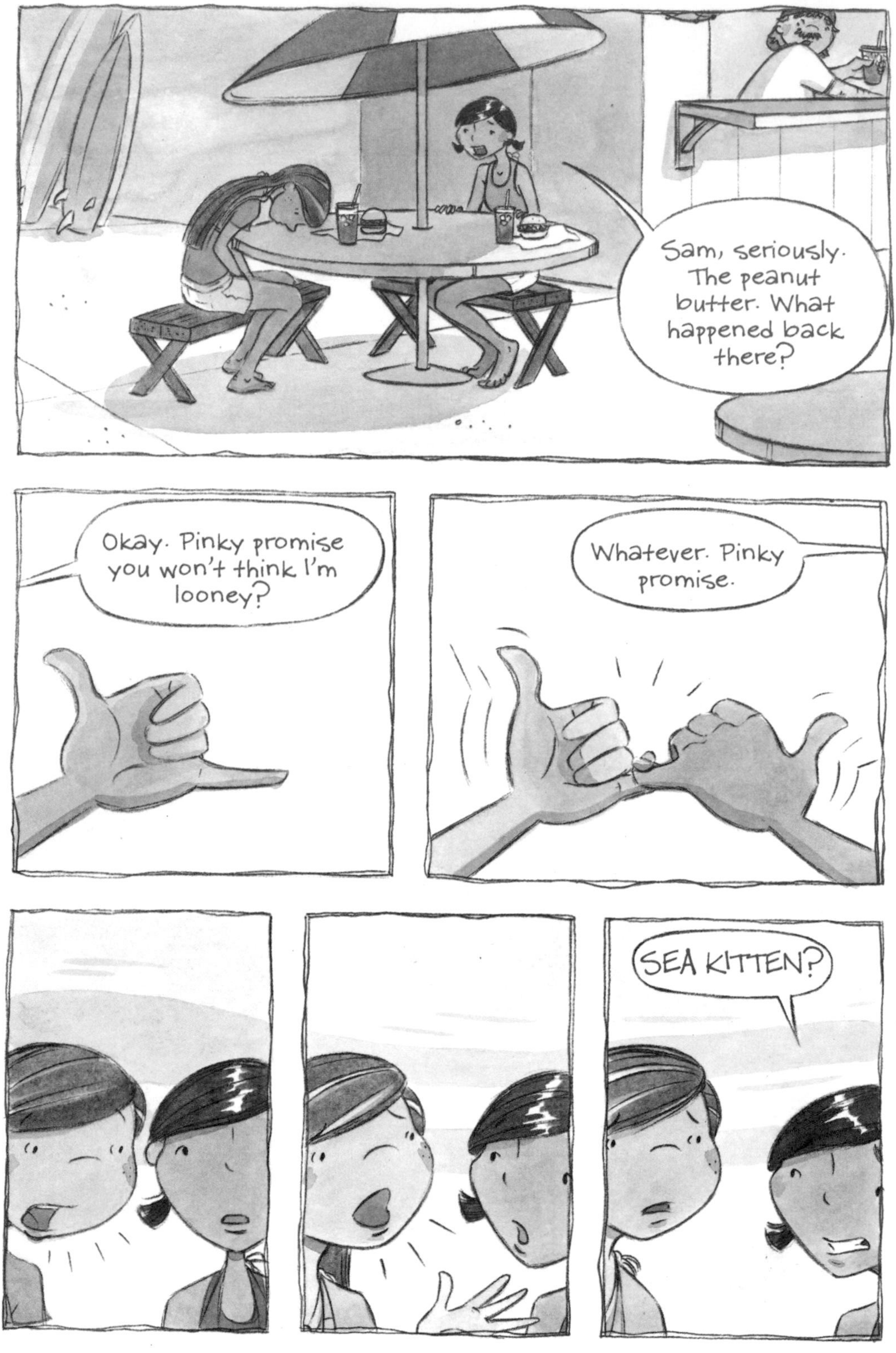
Sam, seriously. The peanut butter. What happened back there?
Okay. Pinky promise you won't think I'm looney?
Whatever. Pinky promise.
SEA KITTEN?

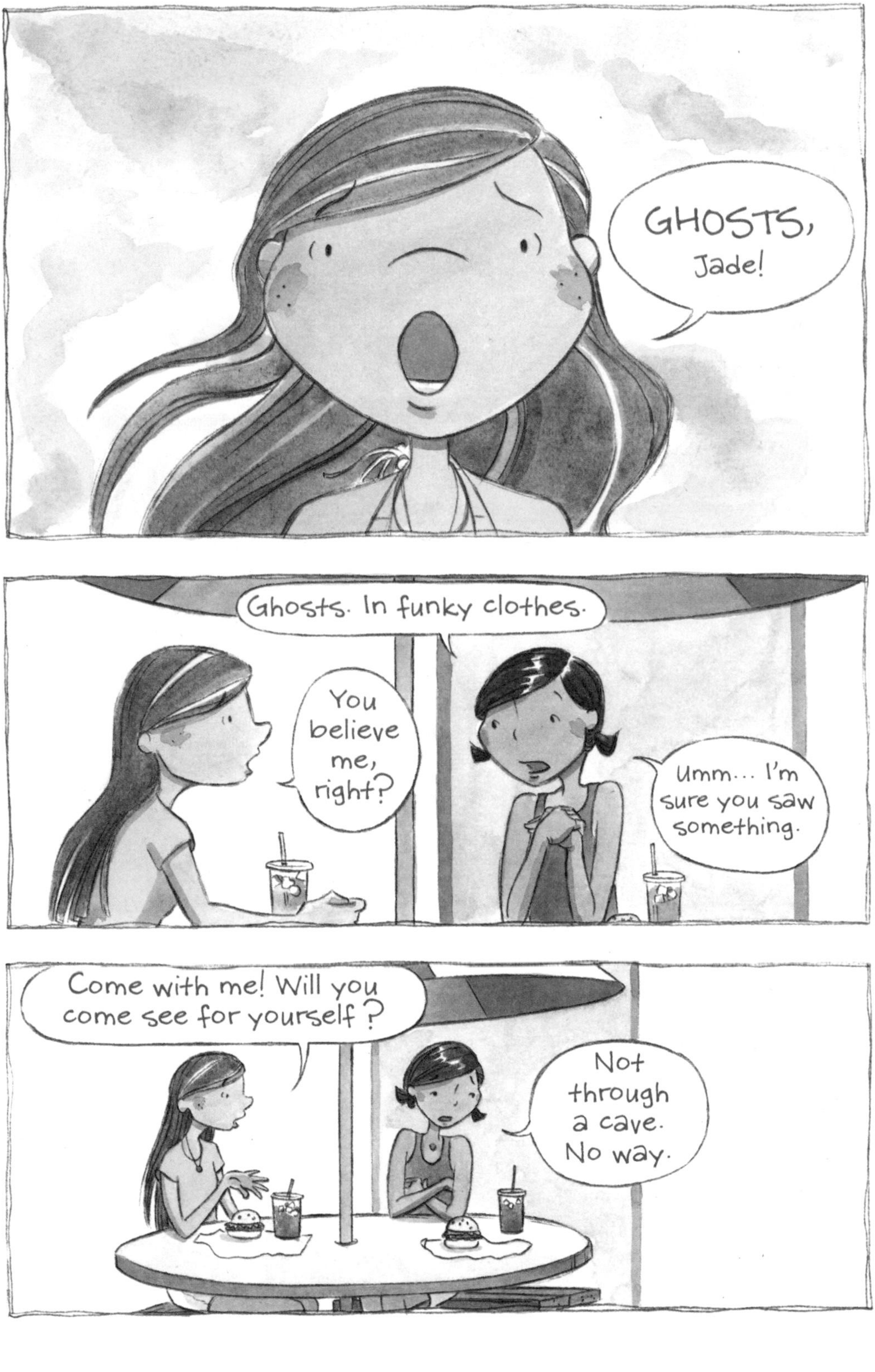
GHOSTS, Jade!
Ghosts. In funky clothes.
You believe me, right?
Umm... I'm sure you saw something.
Come with me! Will you come see for yourself?
Not through a cave. No way.

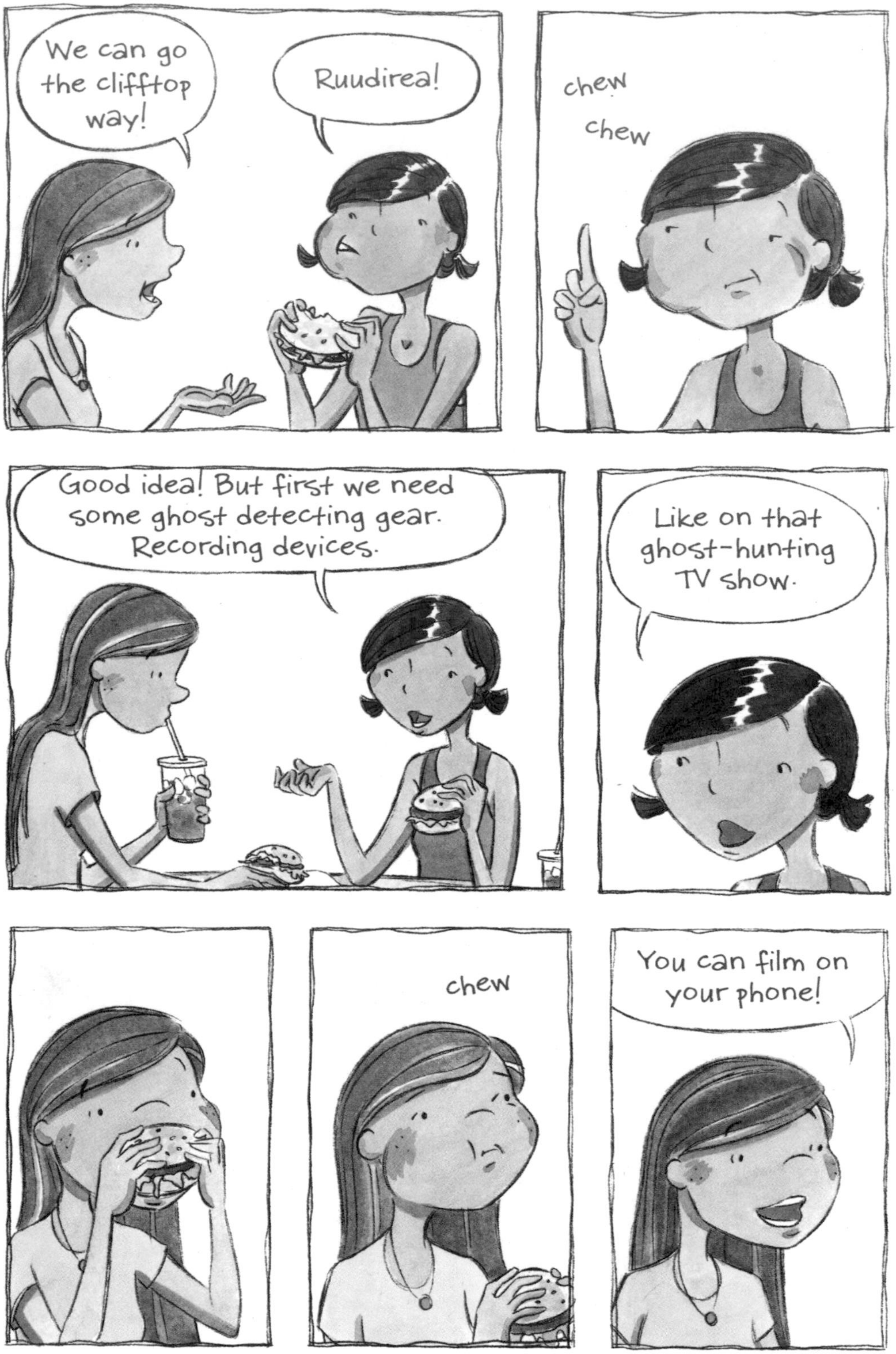
We can go the clifftop way!
Ruudirea!
chew
chew
Good idea! But first we need some ghost detecting gear. Recording devices.
Like on that ghost-hunting TV show.
chew
You can film on your phone!

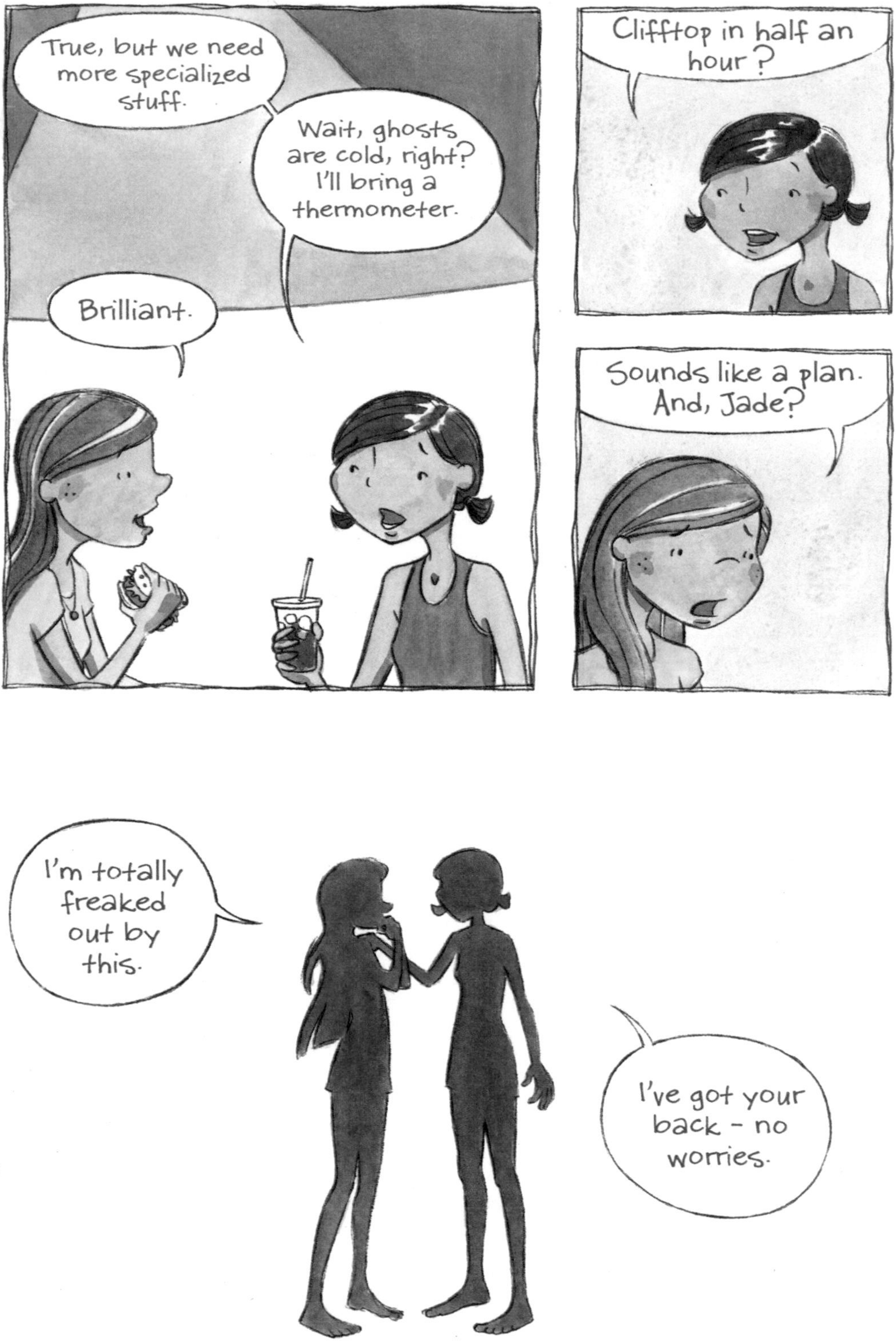
True, but we need more specialized stuff.
Wait, ghosts are cold, right? I'll bring a thermometer.
Brilliant.
Clifftop in half an hour?
Sounds like a plan. And, Jade?
I'm totally freaked out by this.
I've got your back - no worries.

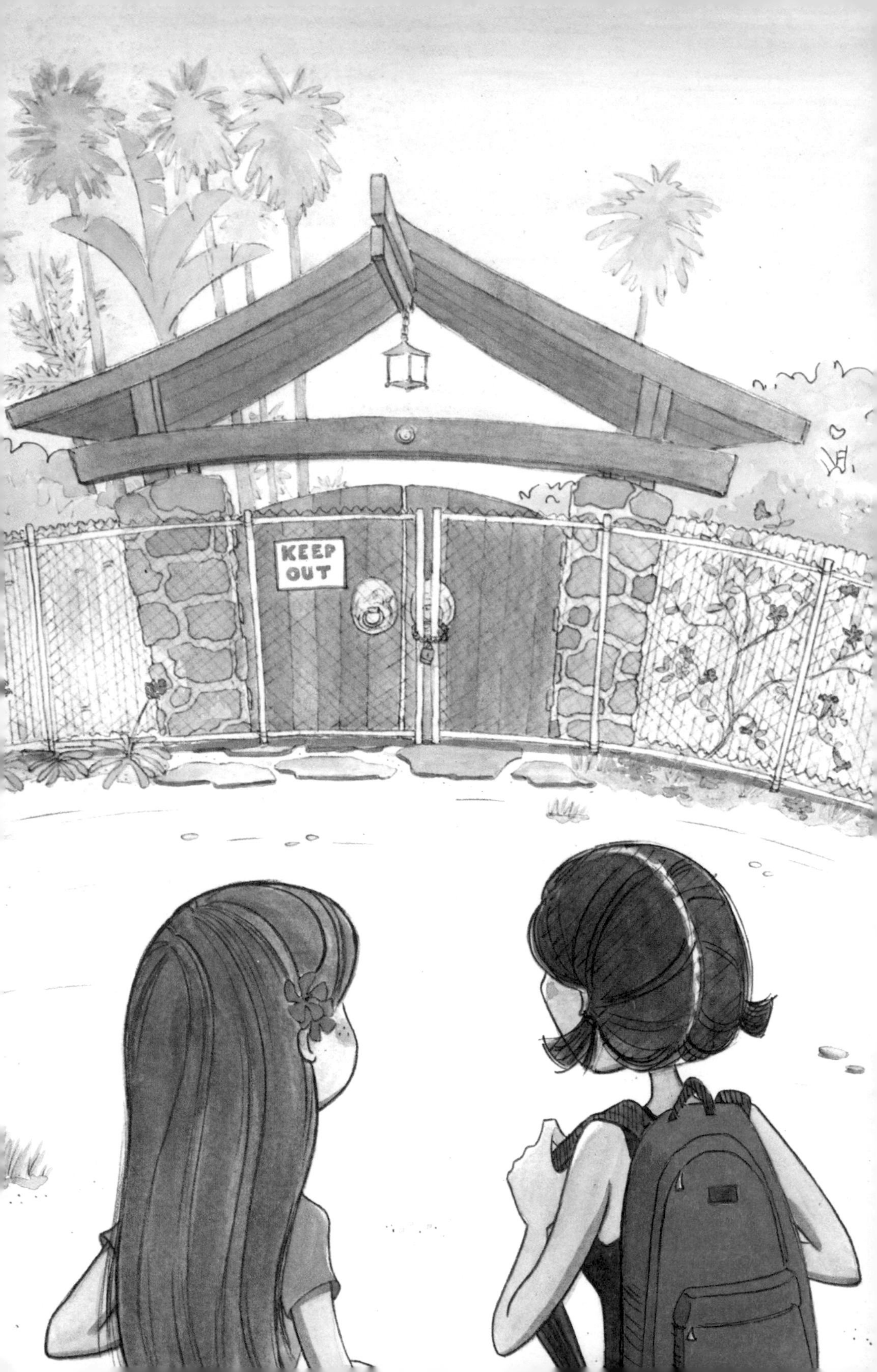
KEEP OUT

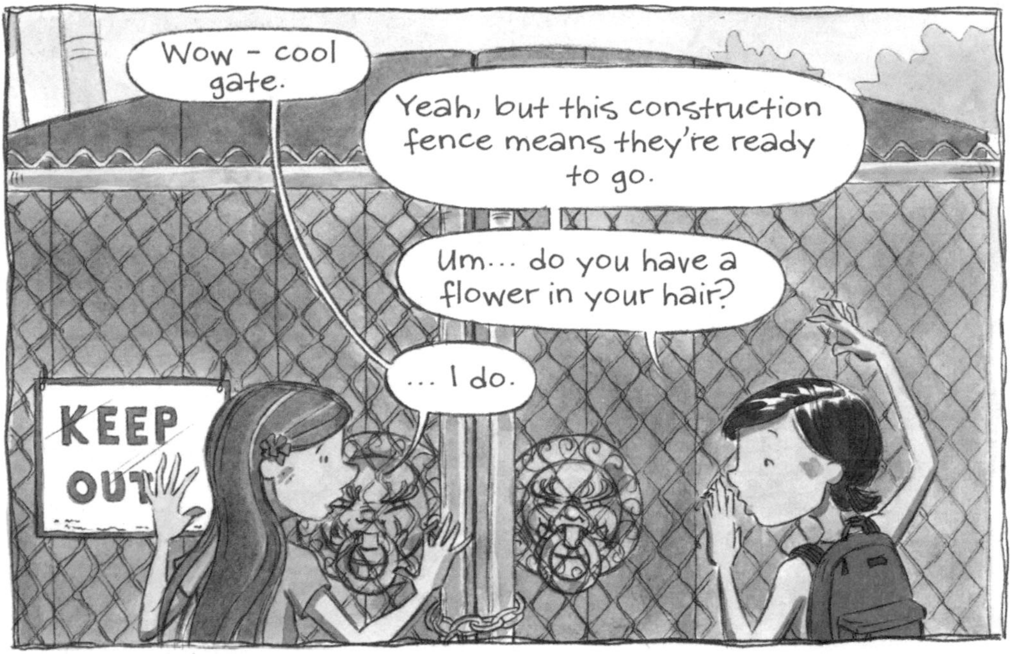
Wow - cool gate.
Yeah, but this construction fence means they're ready to go.
Um... do you have a flower in your hair?
... I do.
KEEP OUT

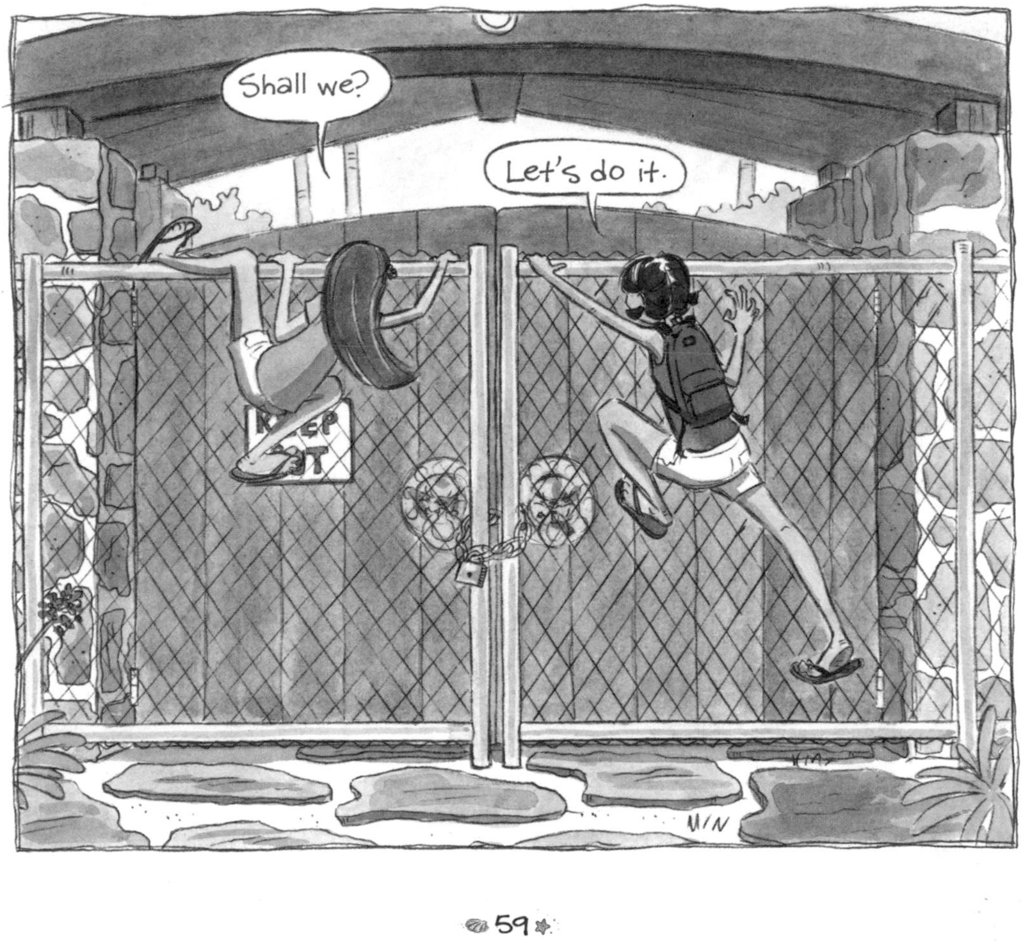
Shall we?
Let's do it.

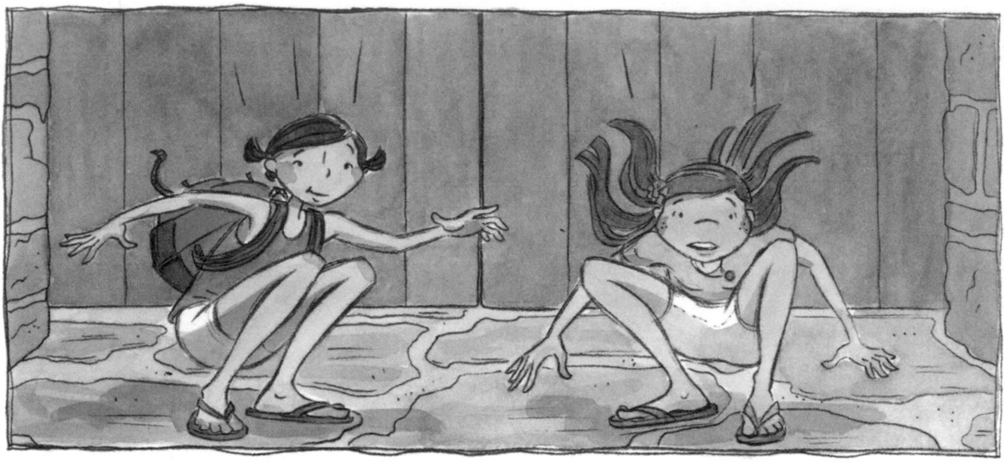

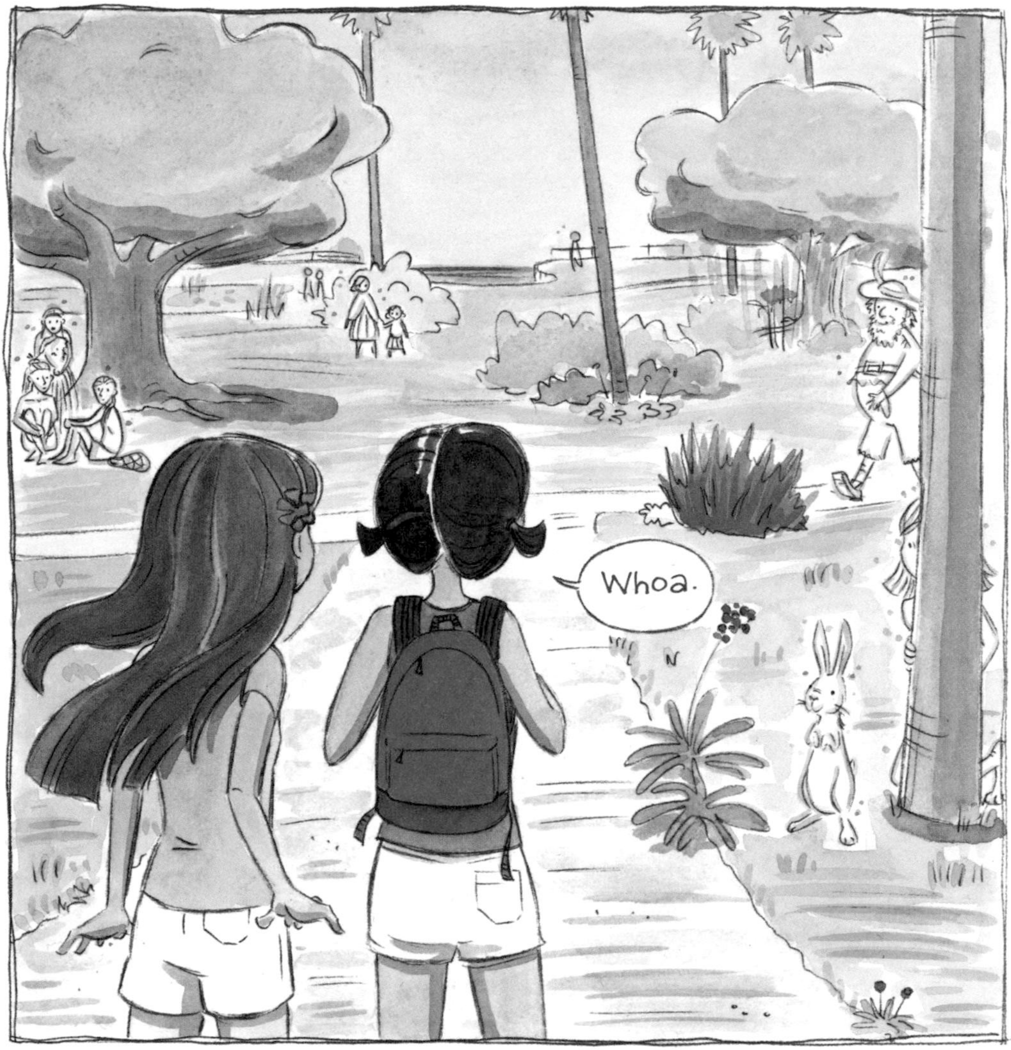
Whoa.

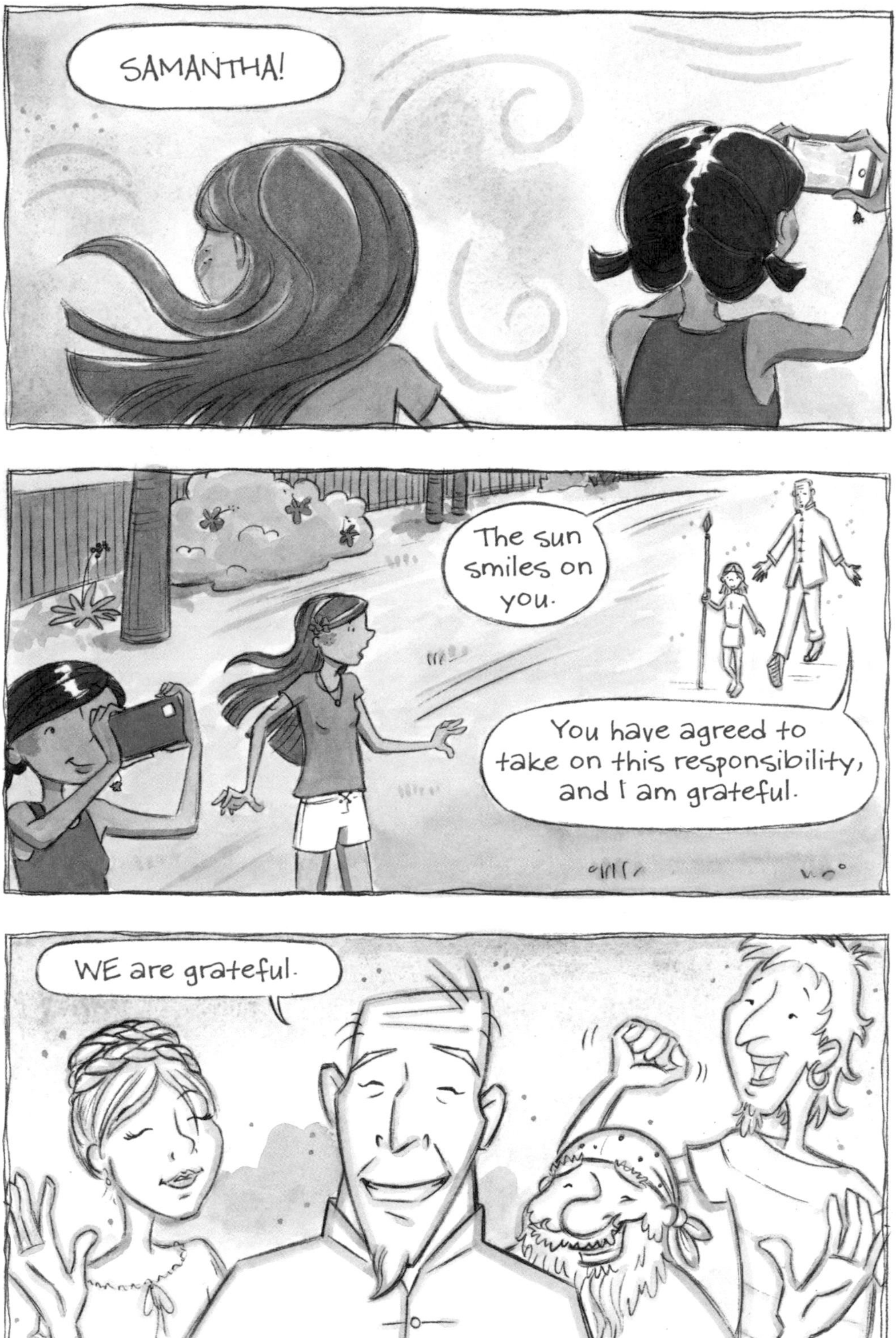
SAMANTHA!
The sun smiles on you.
You have agreed to take on this responsibility, and I am grateful.
WE are grateful.

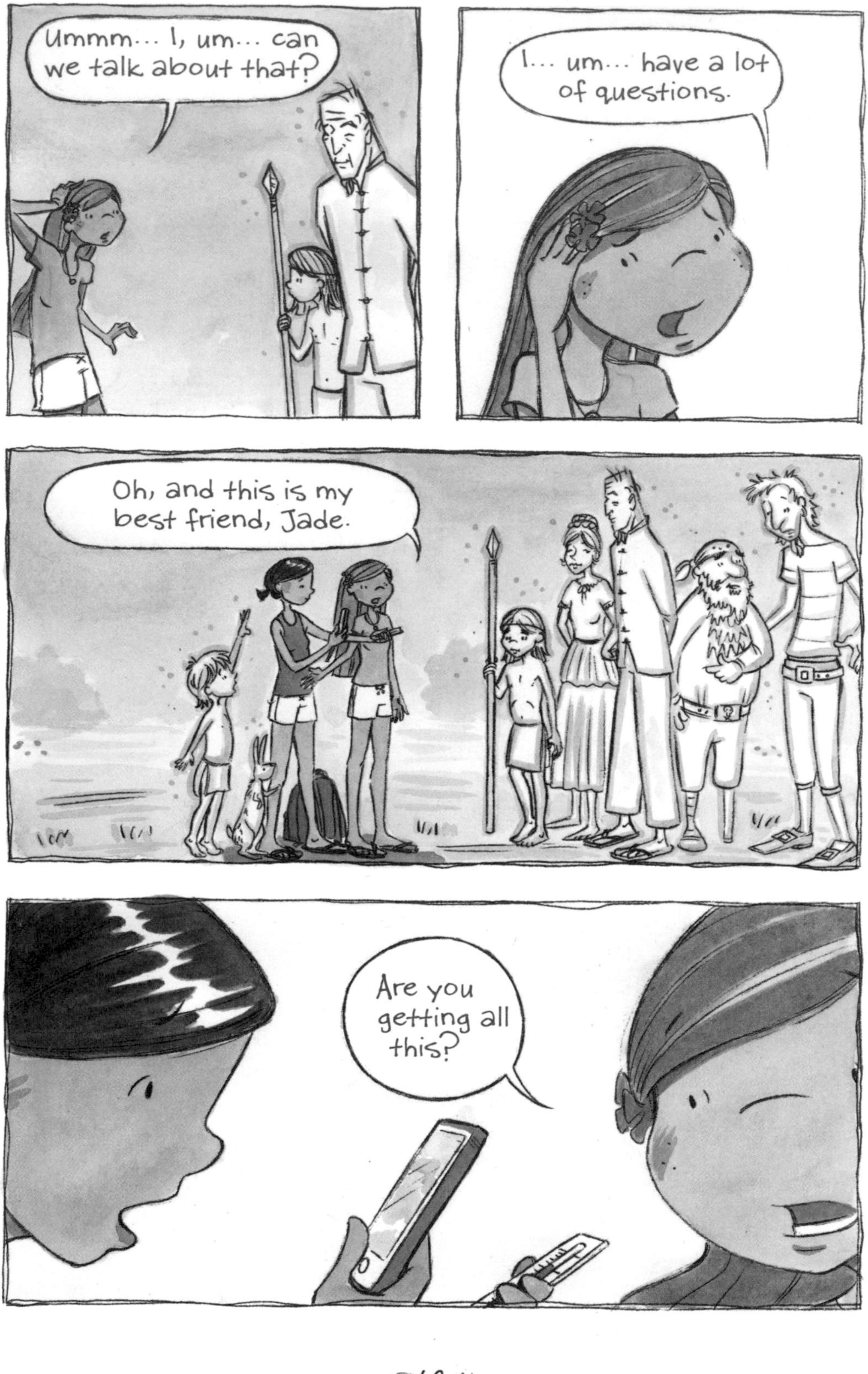
Ummm... I, um... can we talk about that?
I... um... have a lot of questions.
Oh, and this is my best friend, Jade.
Are you getting all this?

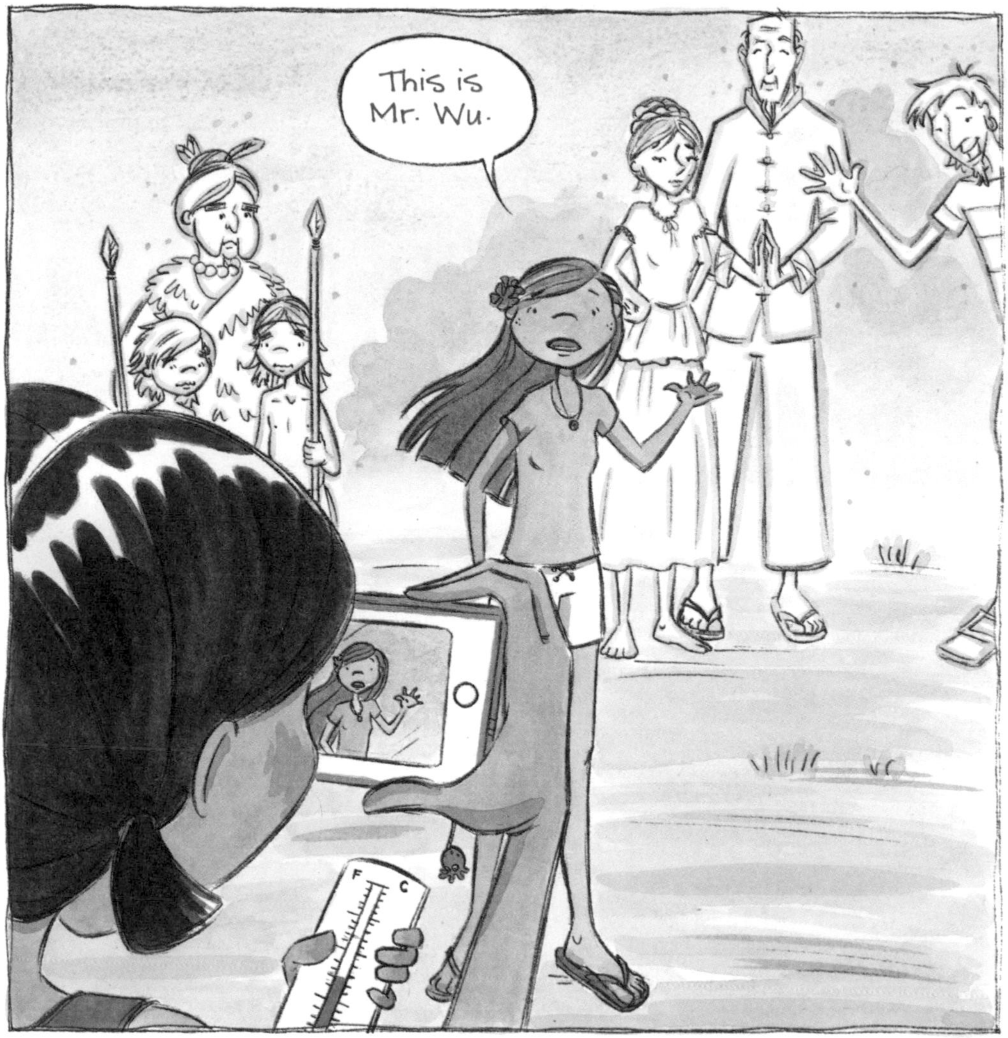
This is Mr. Wu.
F C

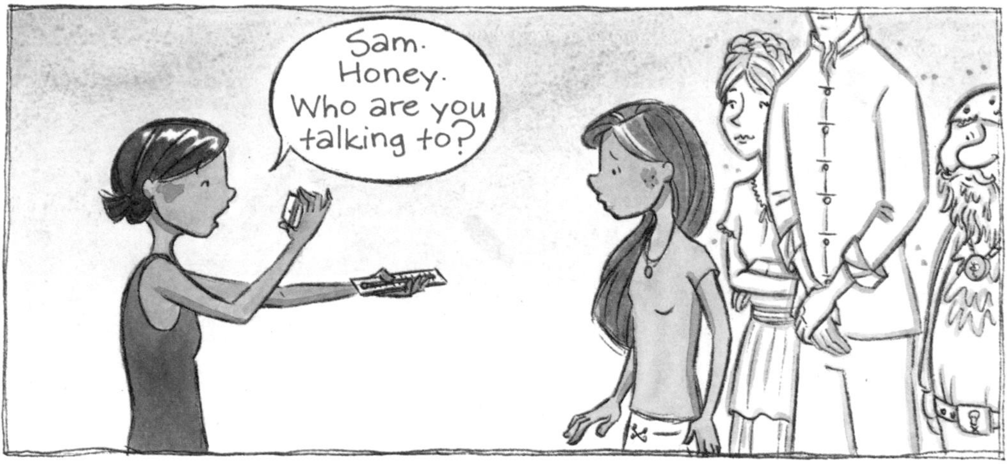
Sam. Honey. Who are you talking to?

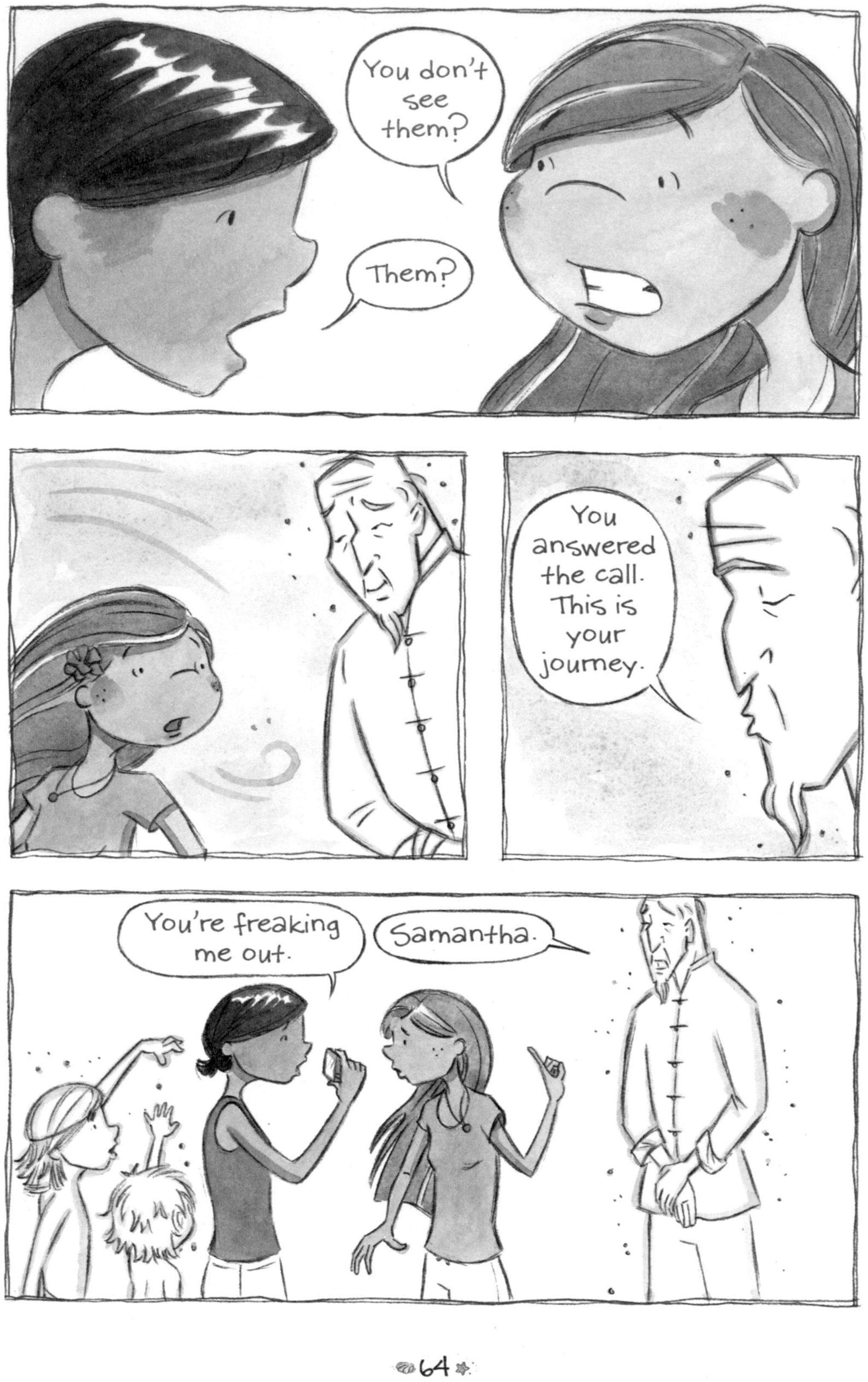
You don't see them?
Them?
You answered the call. This is your journey.
You're freaking me out.
Samantha.

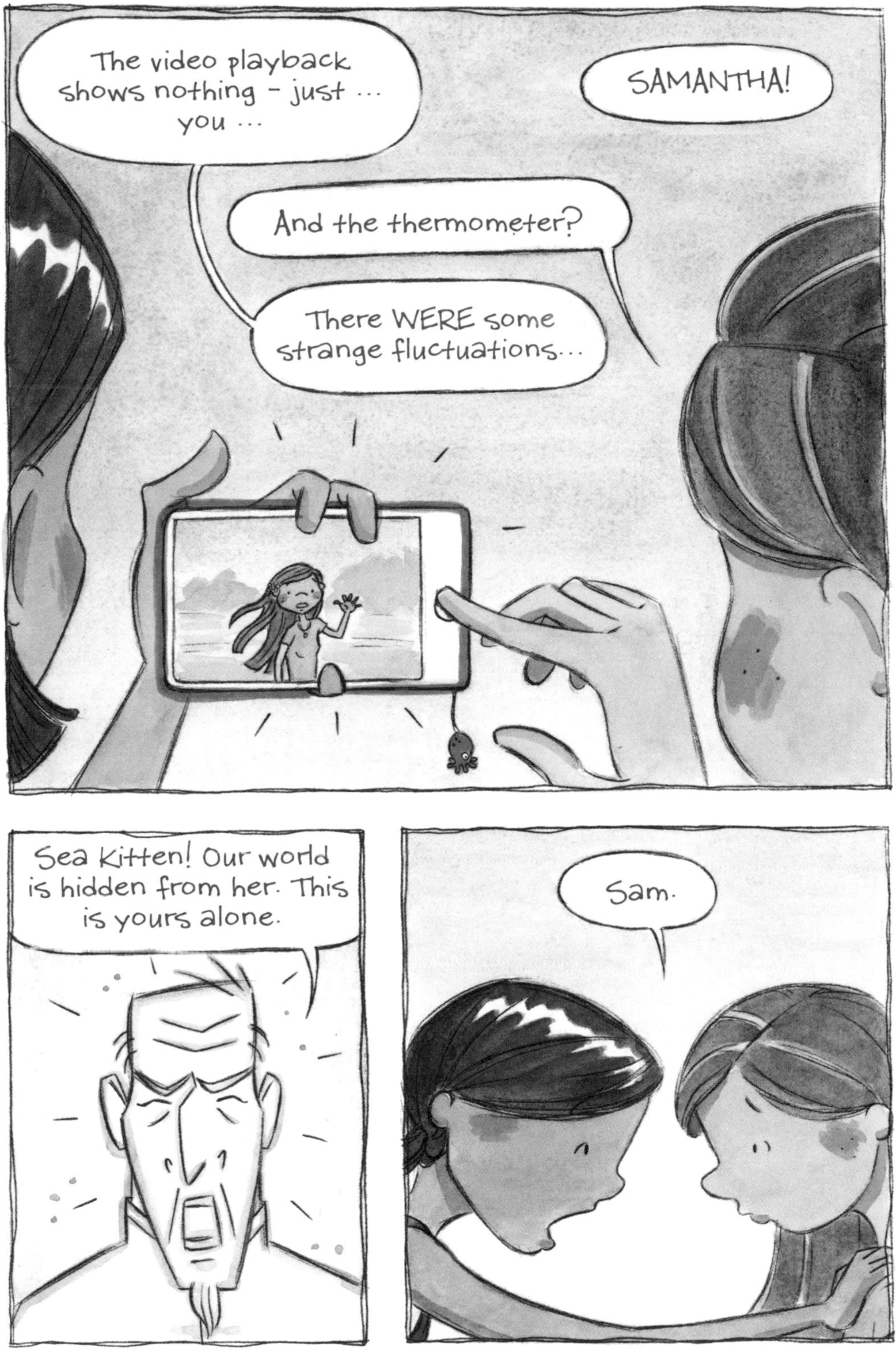
The video playback shows nothing - just ... you ...
SAMANTHA!
And the thermometer?
There WERE some strange fluctuations...
Sea Kitten! Our world is hidden from her. This is yours alone.
Sam.

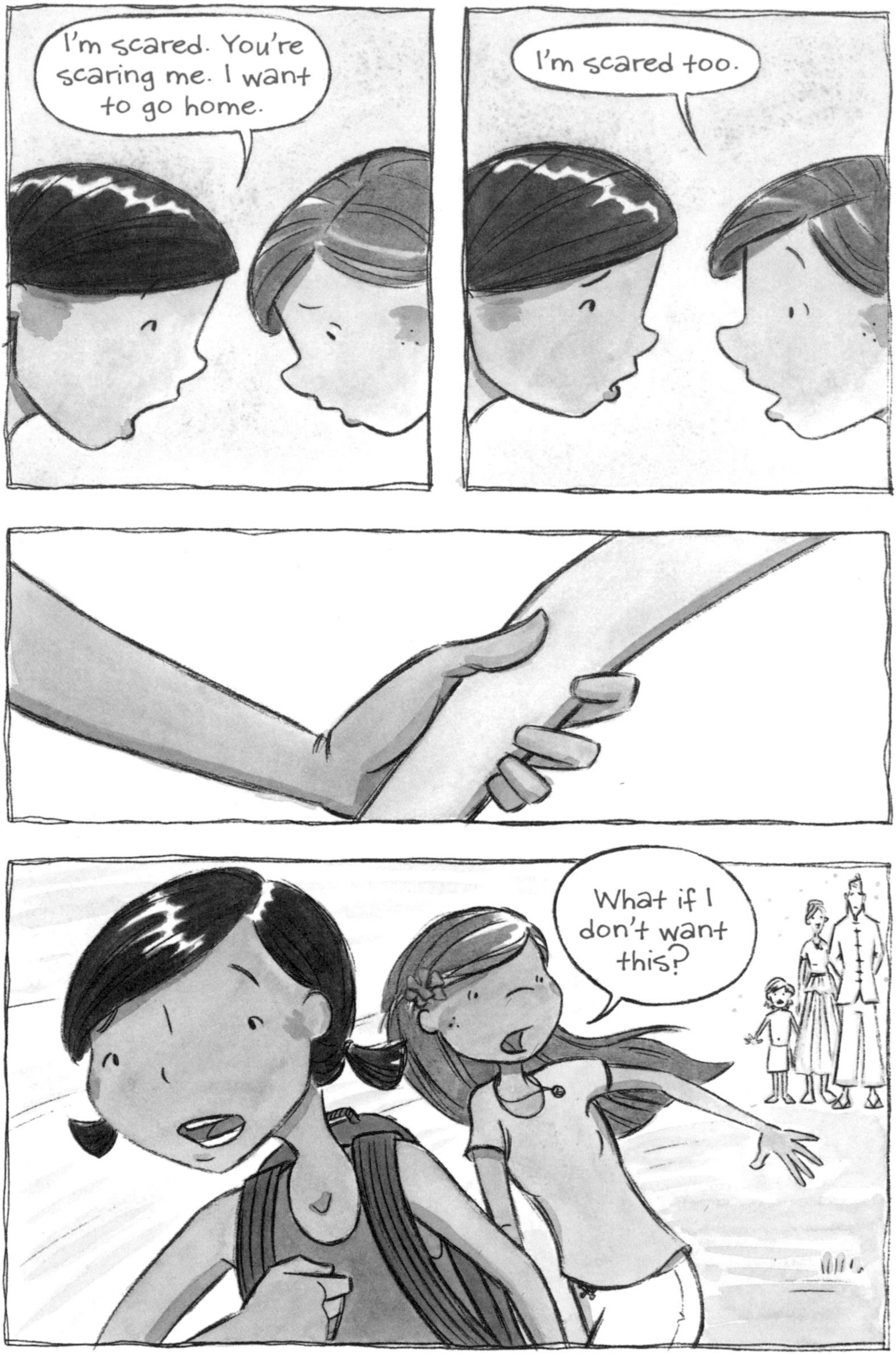
I'm scared. You're scaring me. I want to go home.
I'm scared too.
What if I don't want this?

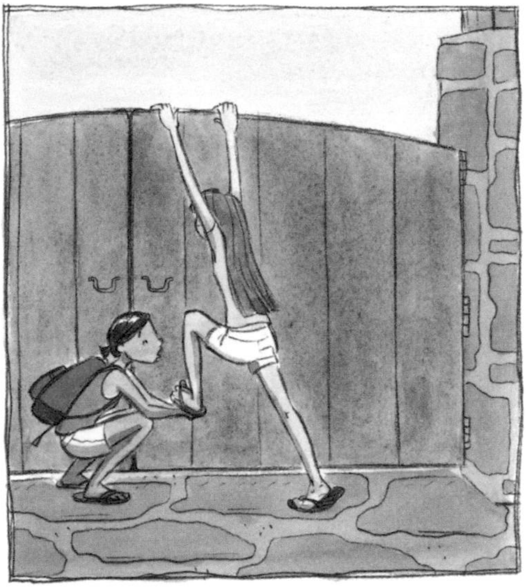

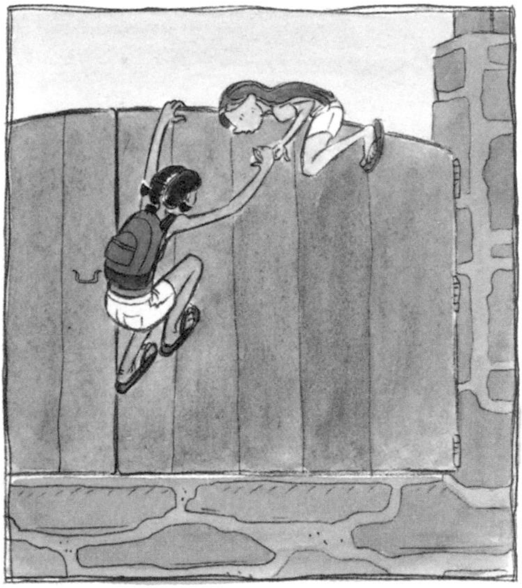

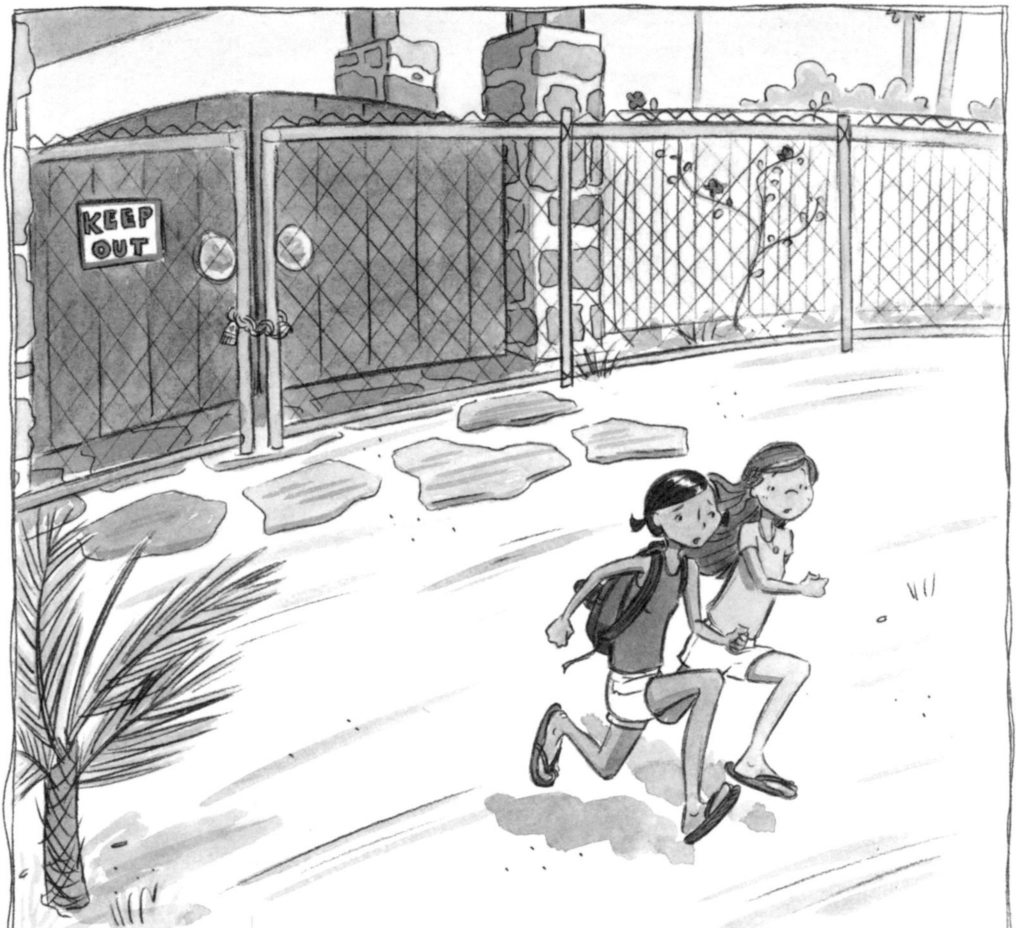
KEEP OUT

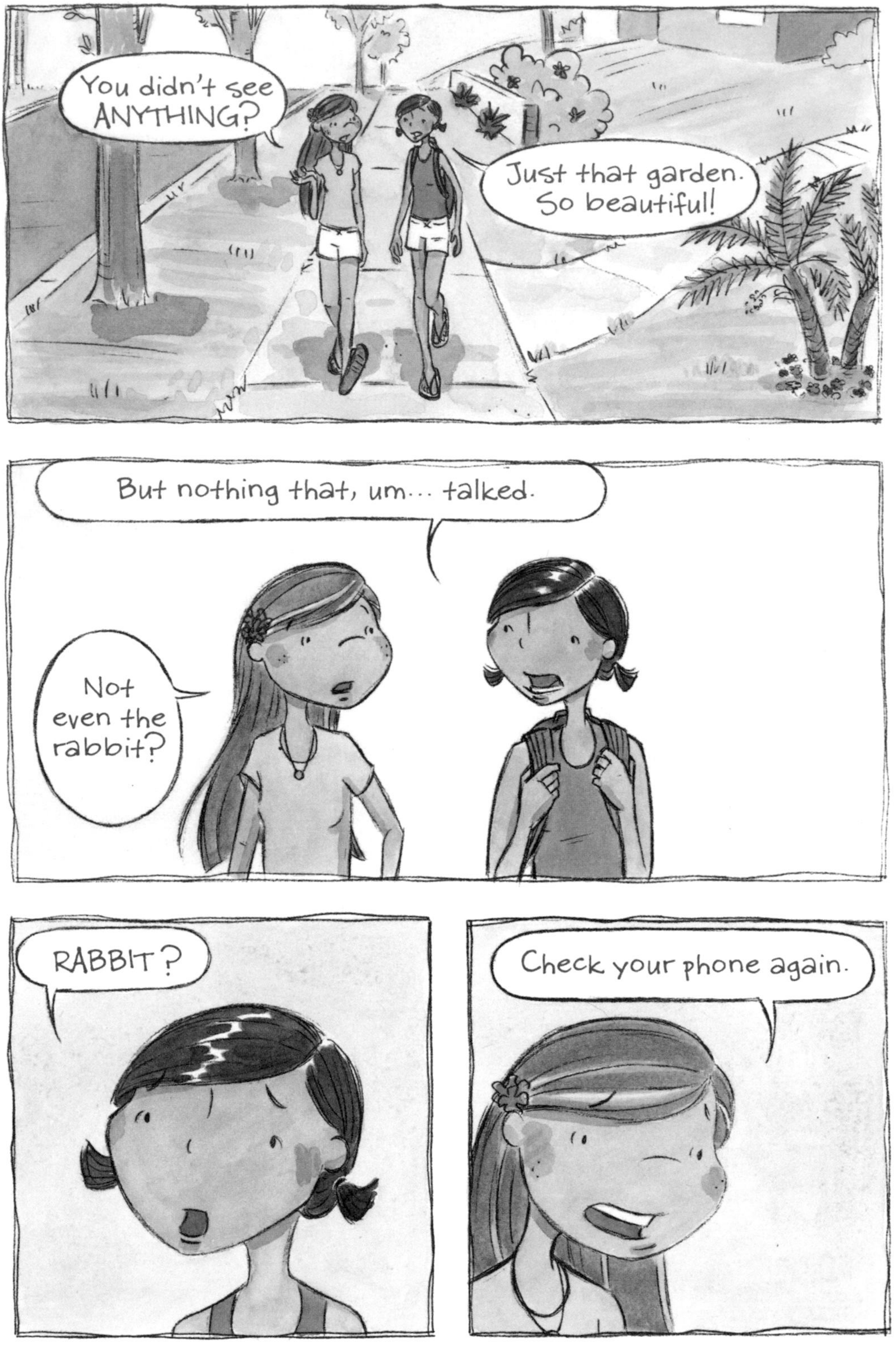
You didn't see ANYTHING?
Just that garden. So beautiful!
But nothing that, um... talked.
Not even the rabbit?
RABBIT?
Check your phone again.

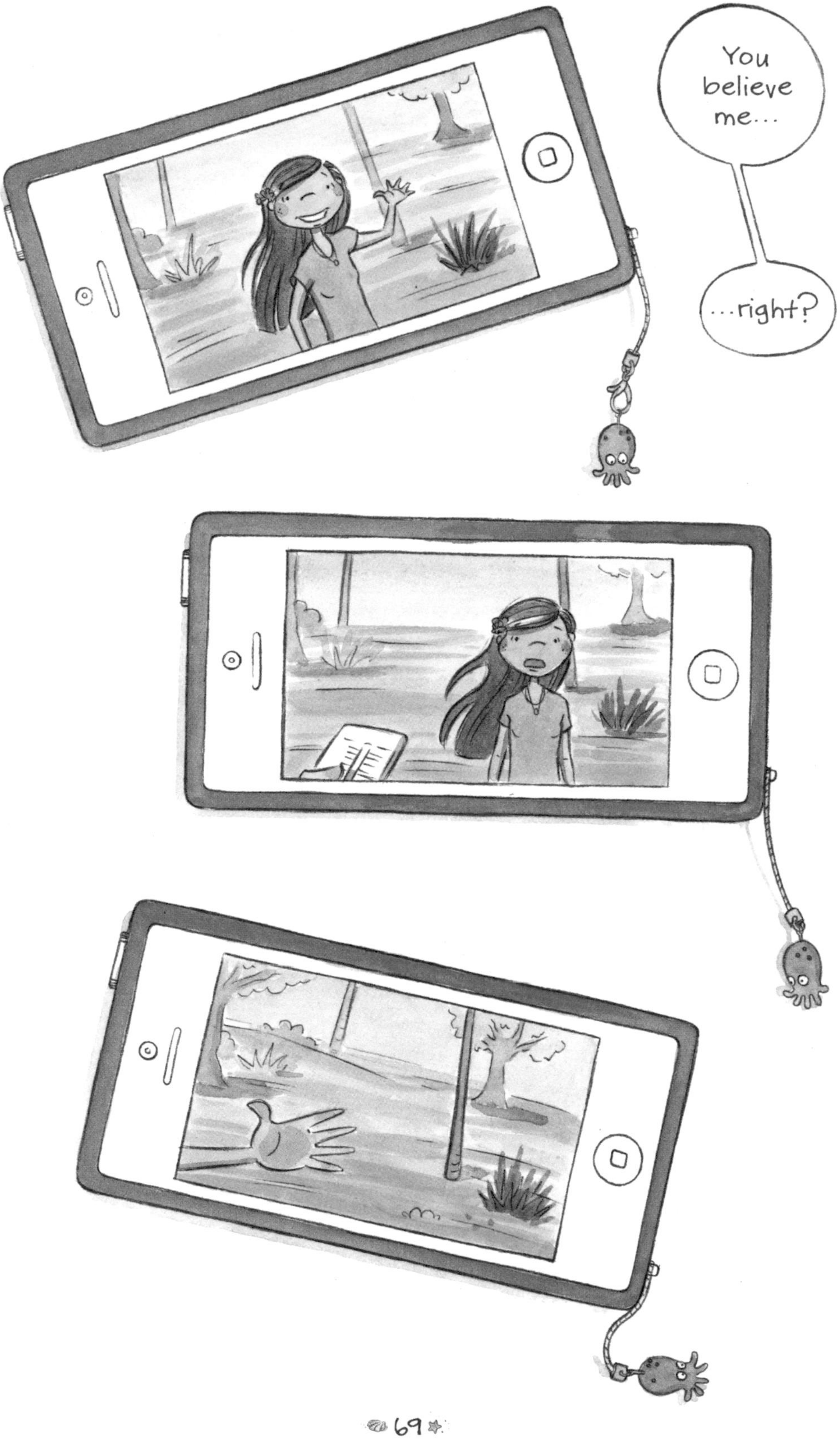
You believe me...
...right?

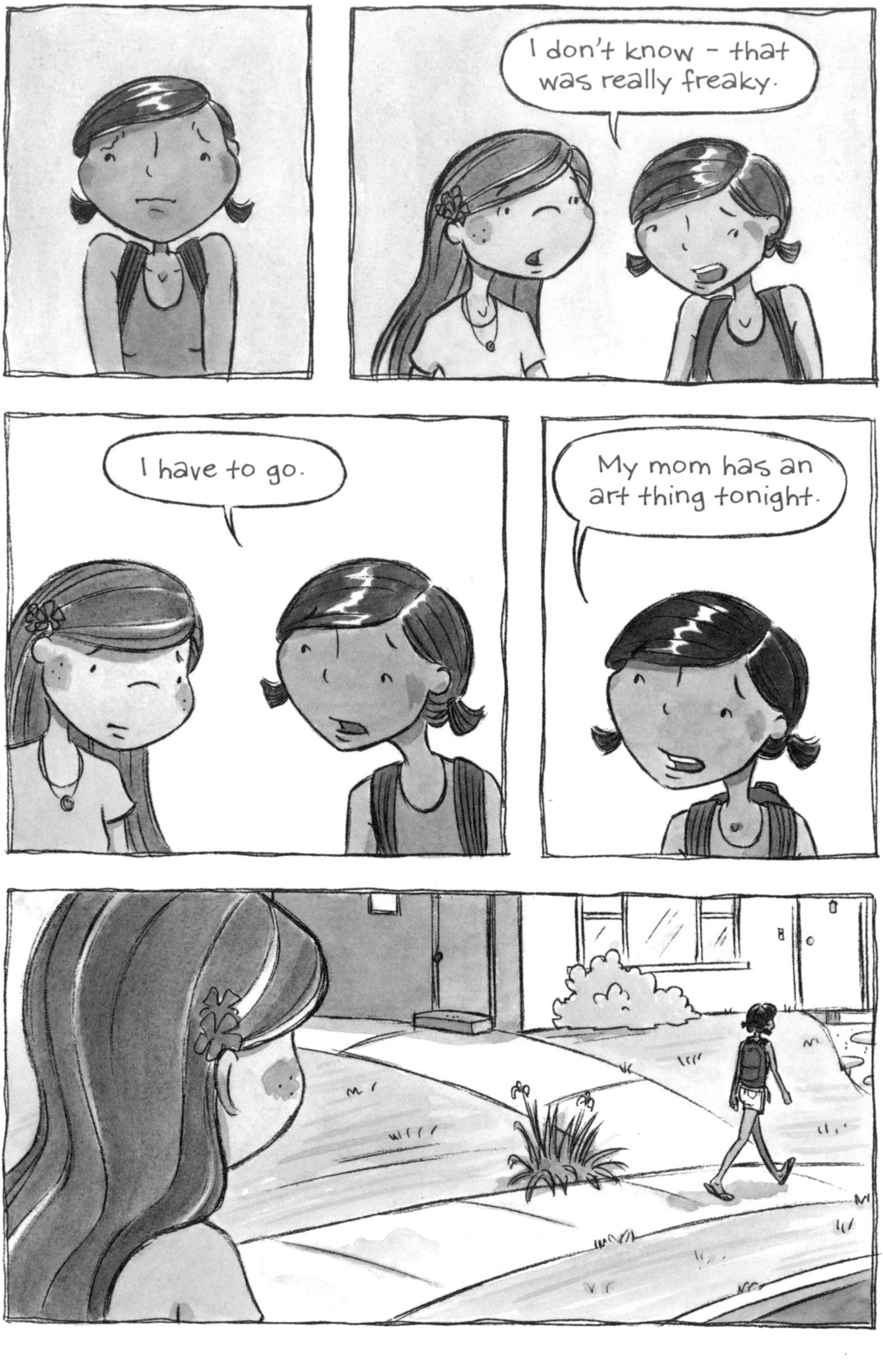

I don't know - that was really freaky.
I have to go.
My mom has an art thing tonight.

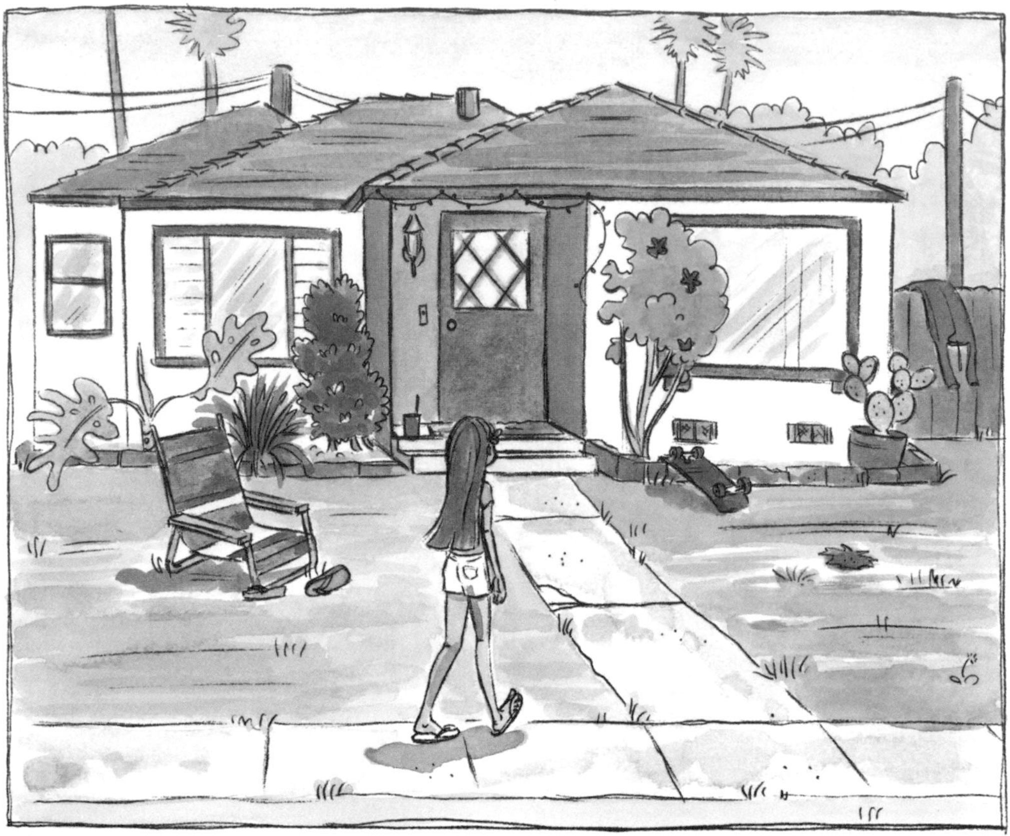

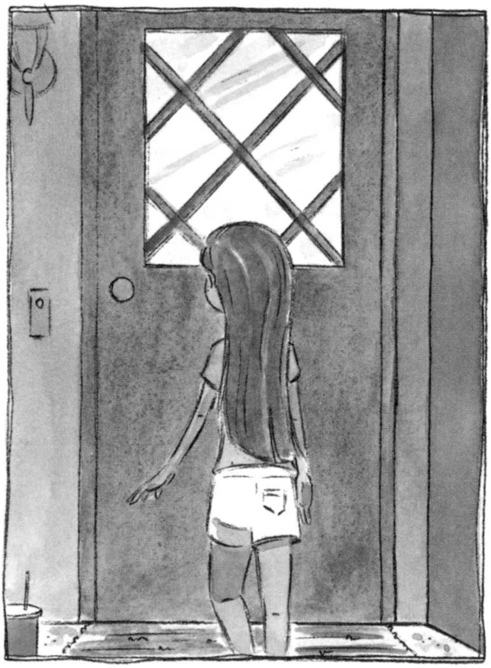

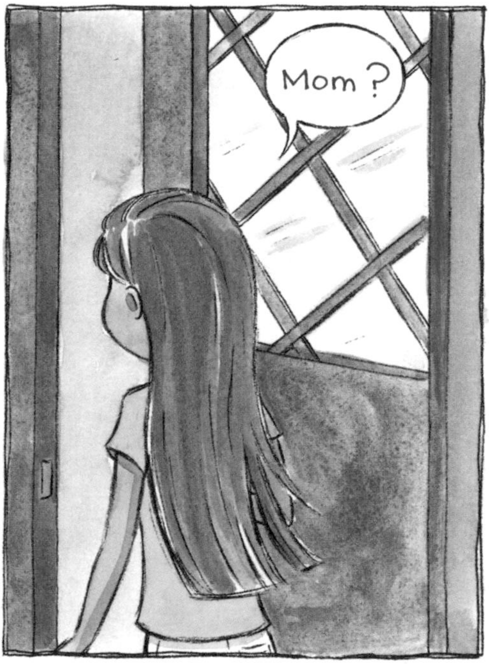
Mom?

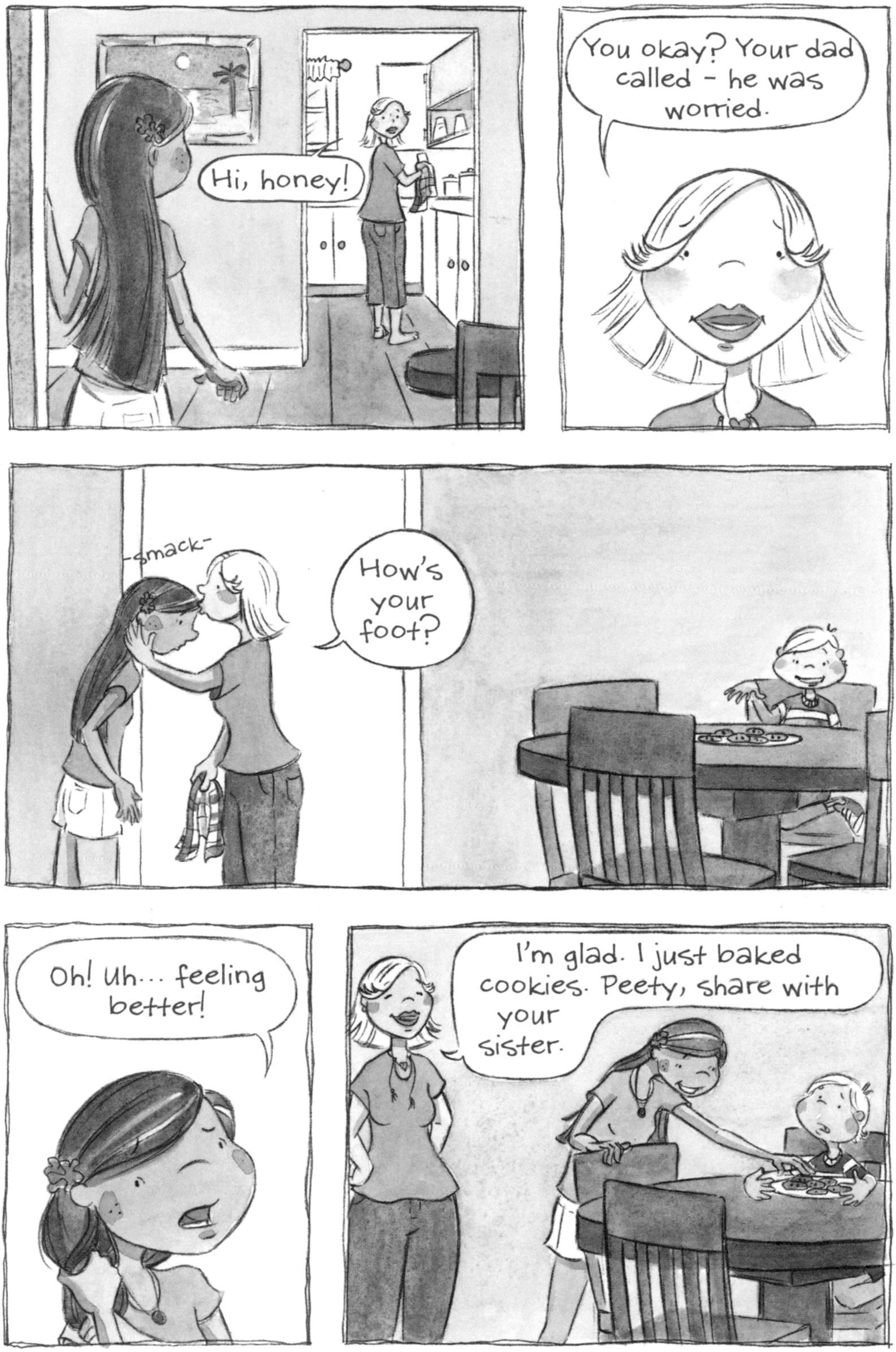
Hi, honey!
You okay? Your dad called - he was worried.
-smack-
How's your foot?
Oh! Uh... feeling better!
I'm glad. I just baked cookies. Peety, share with your sister.

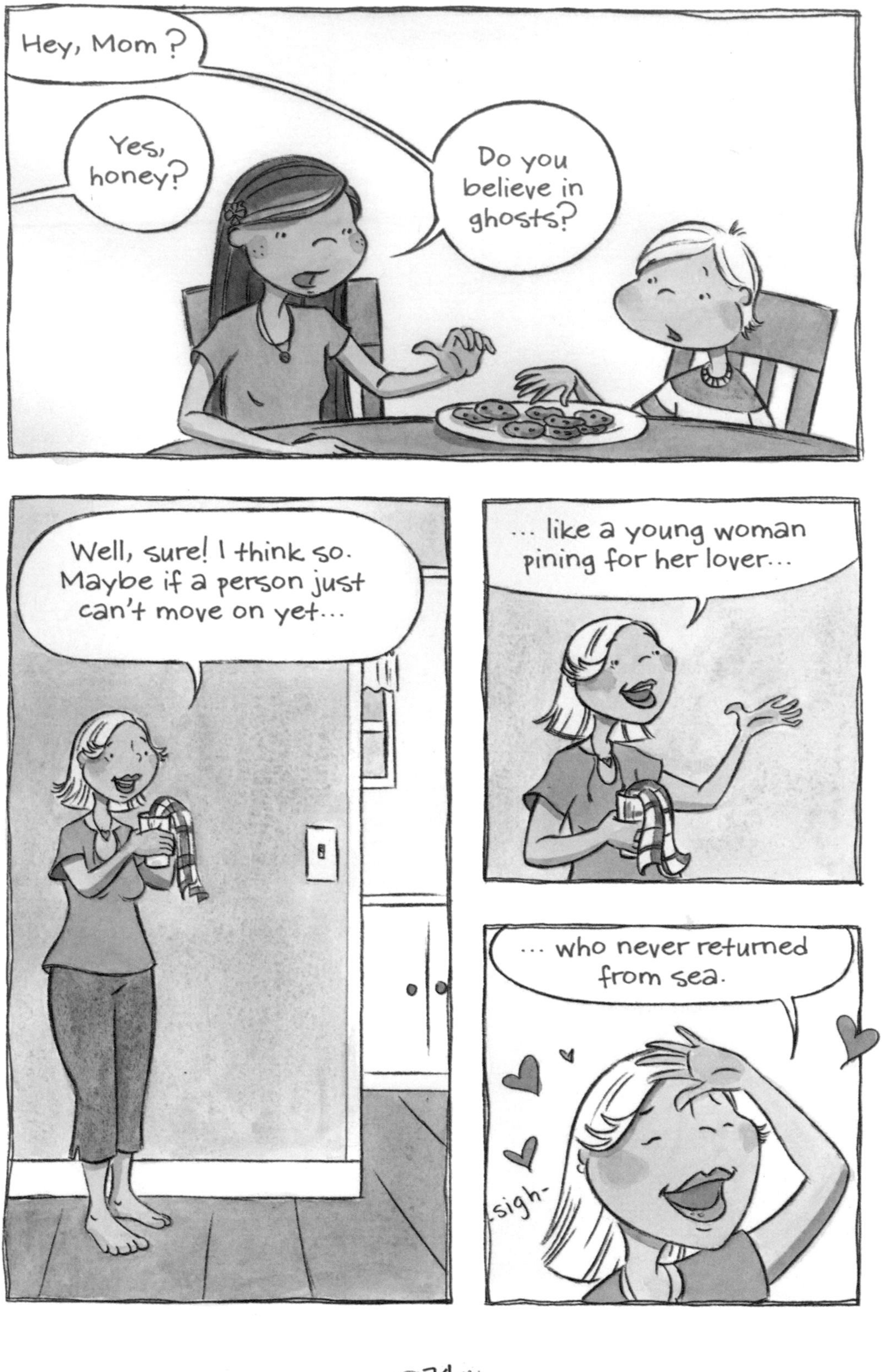
Hey, Mom?
Yes, honey?
Do you believe in ghosts?
Well, sure! I think so. Maybe if a person just can't move on yet...
... like a young woman pining for her lover...
... who never returned from sea.
-sigh-

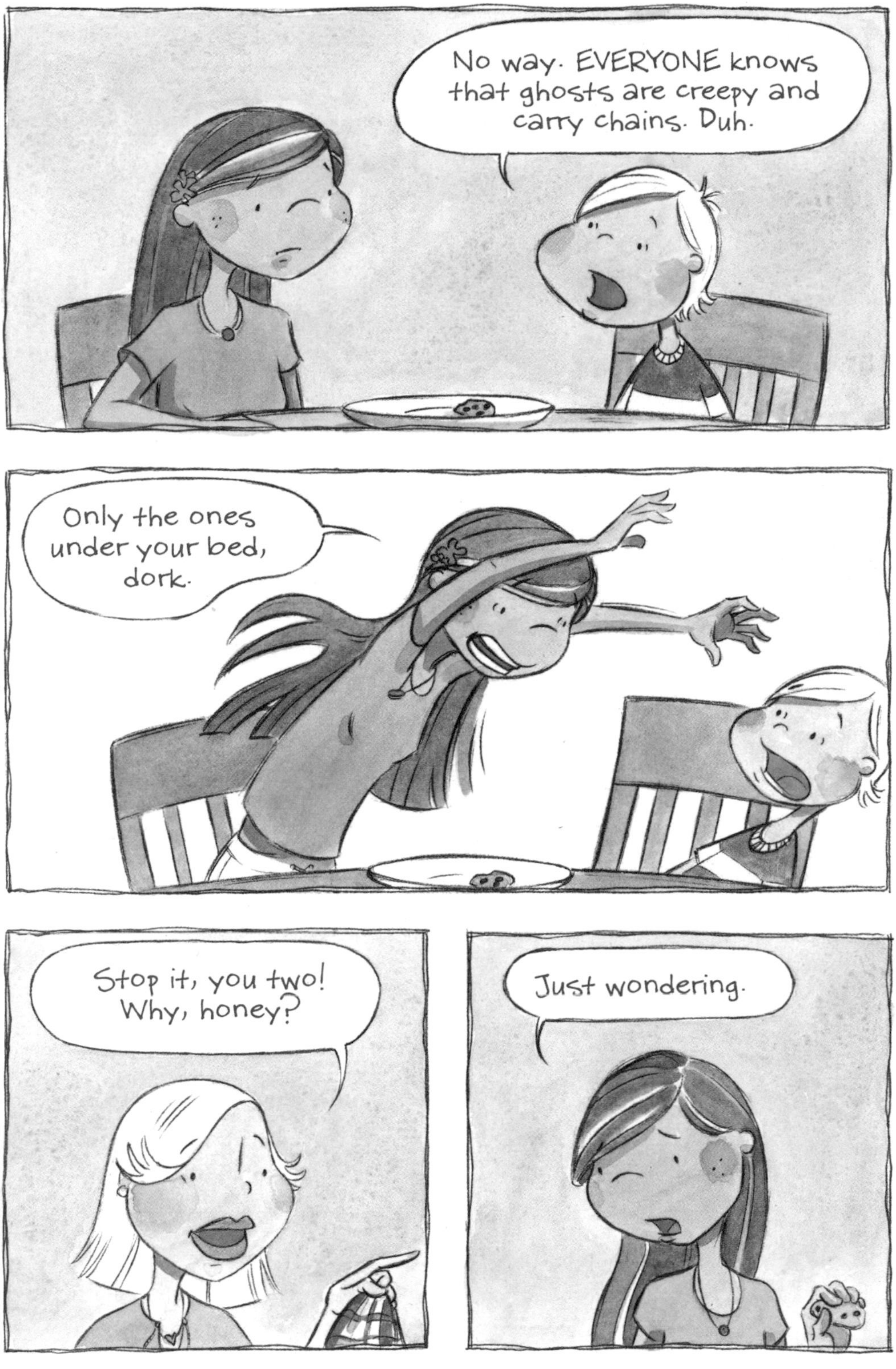
No way. EVERYONE knows that ghosts are creepy and carry chains. Duh.
Only the ones under your bed, dork.
Stop it, you two! Why, honey?
Just wondering.

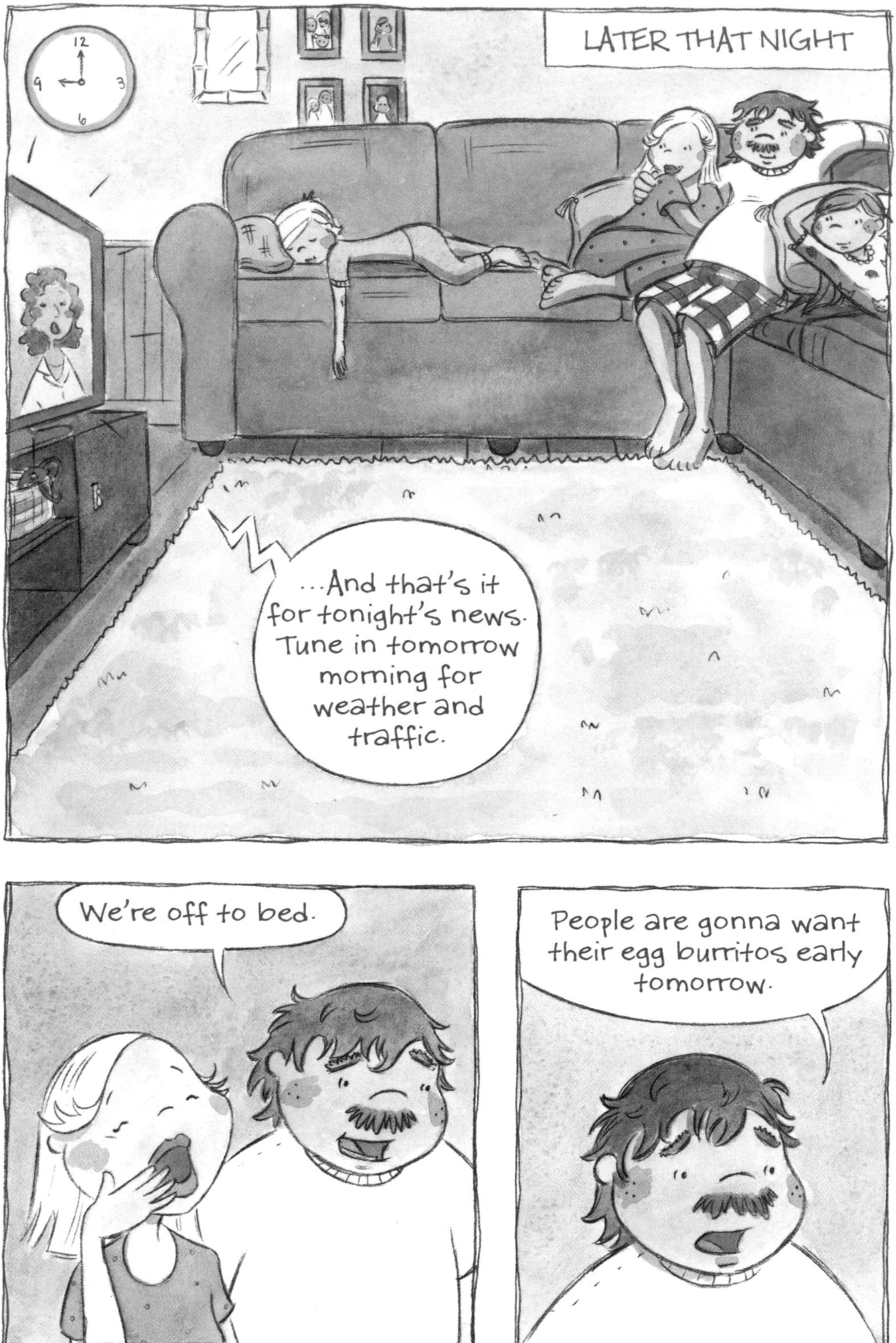
LATER THAT NIGHT
...And that's it for tonight's news. Tune in tomorrow morning for weather and traffic.
We're off to bed.
People are gonna want their egg burritos early tomorrow.

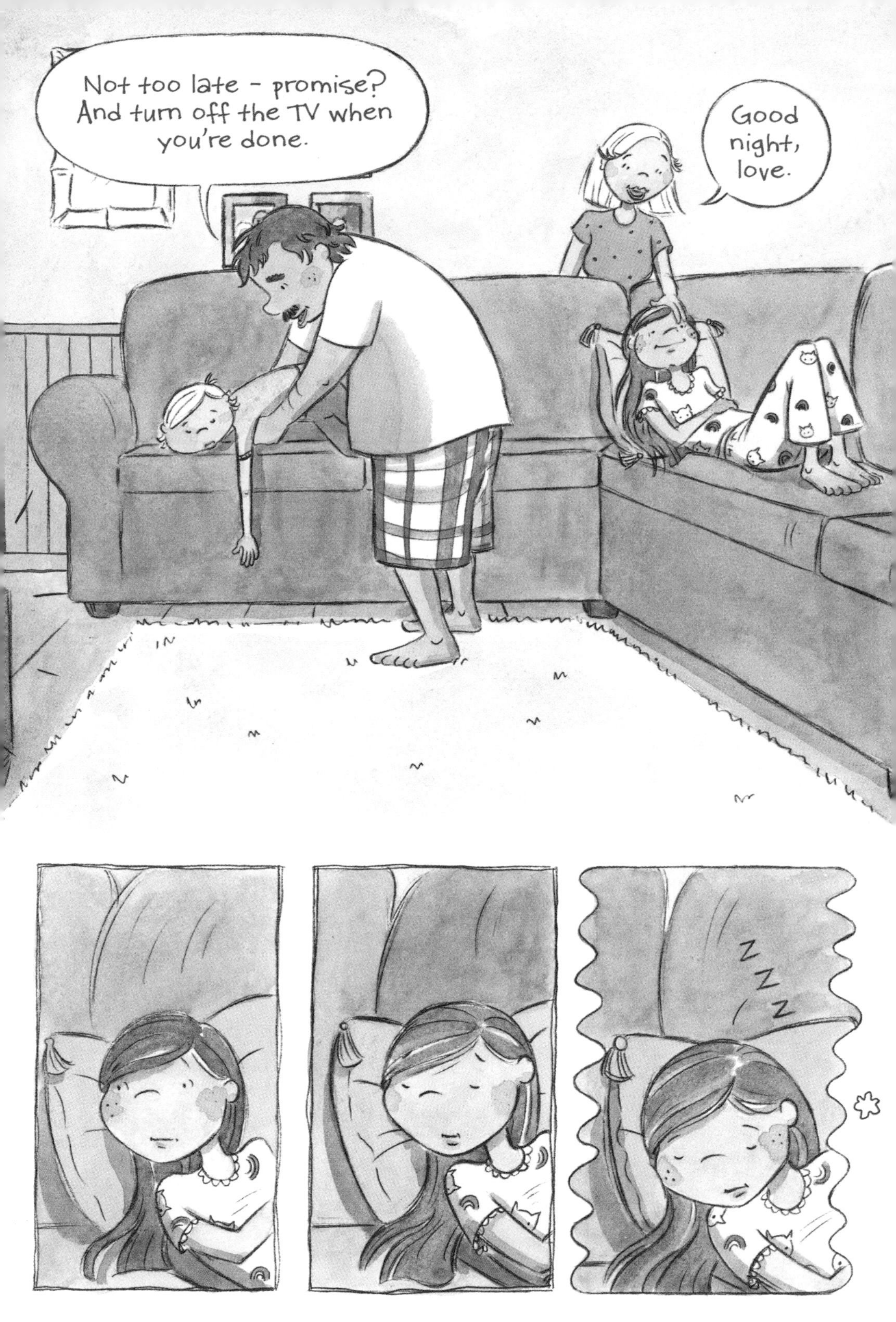
Not too late - promise? And turn off the TV when you're done.
Good night, love.
Z Z Z

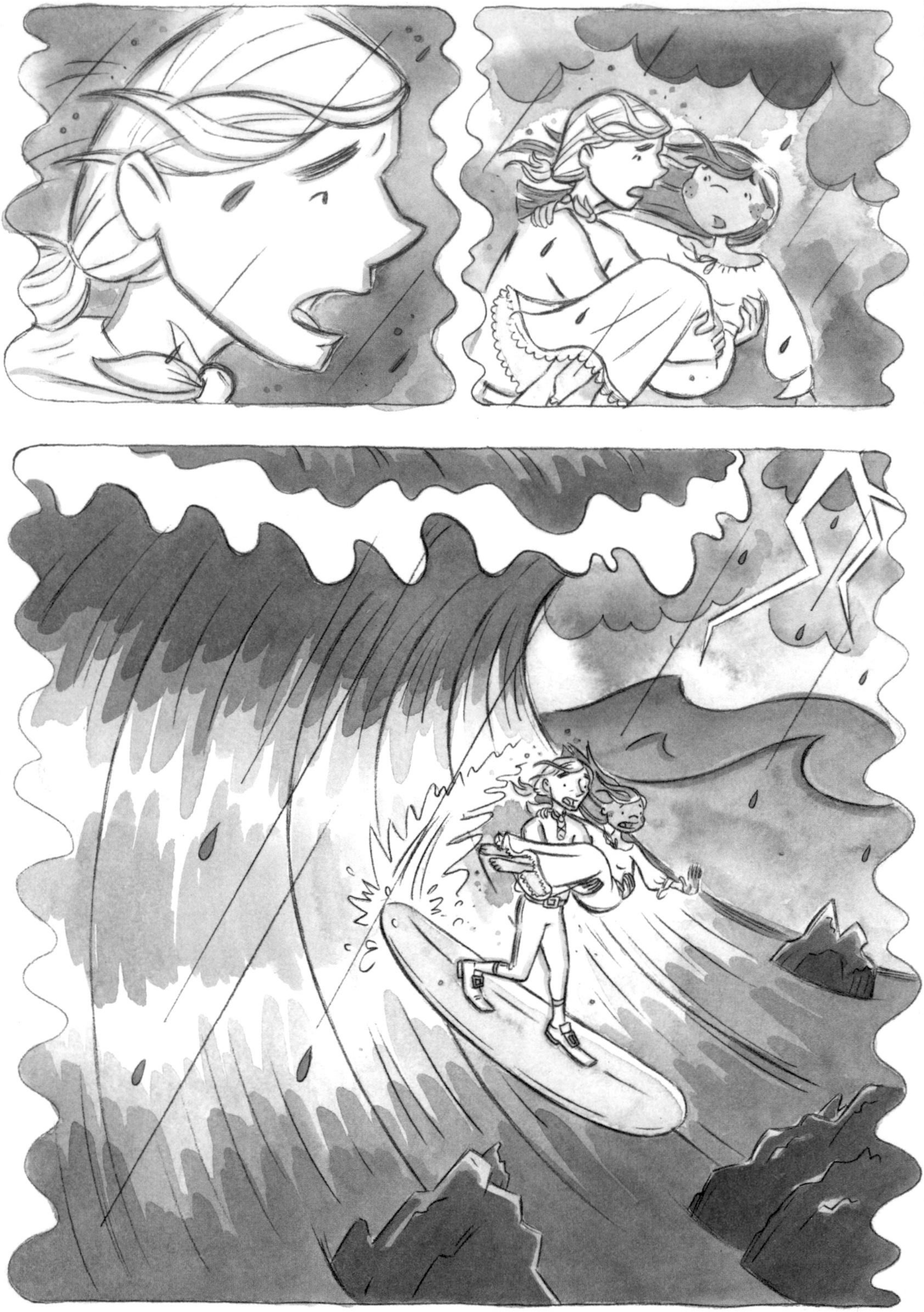

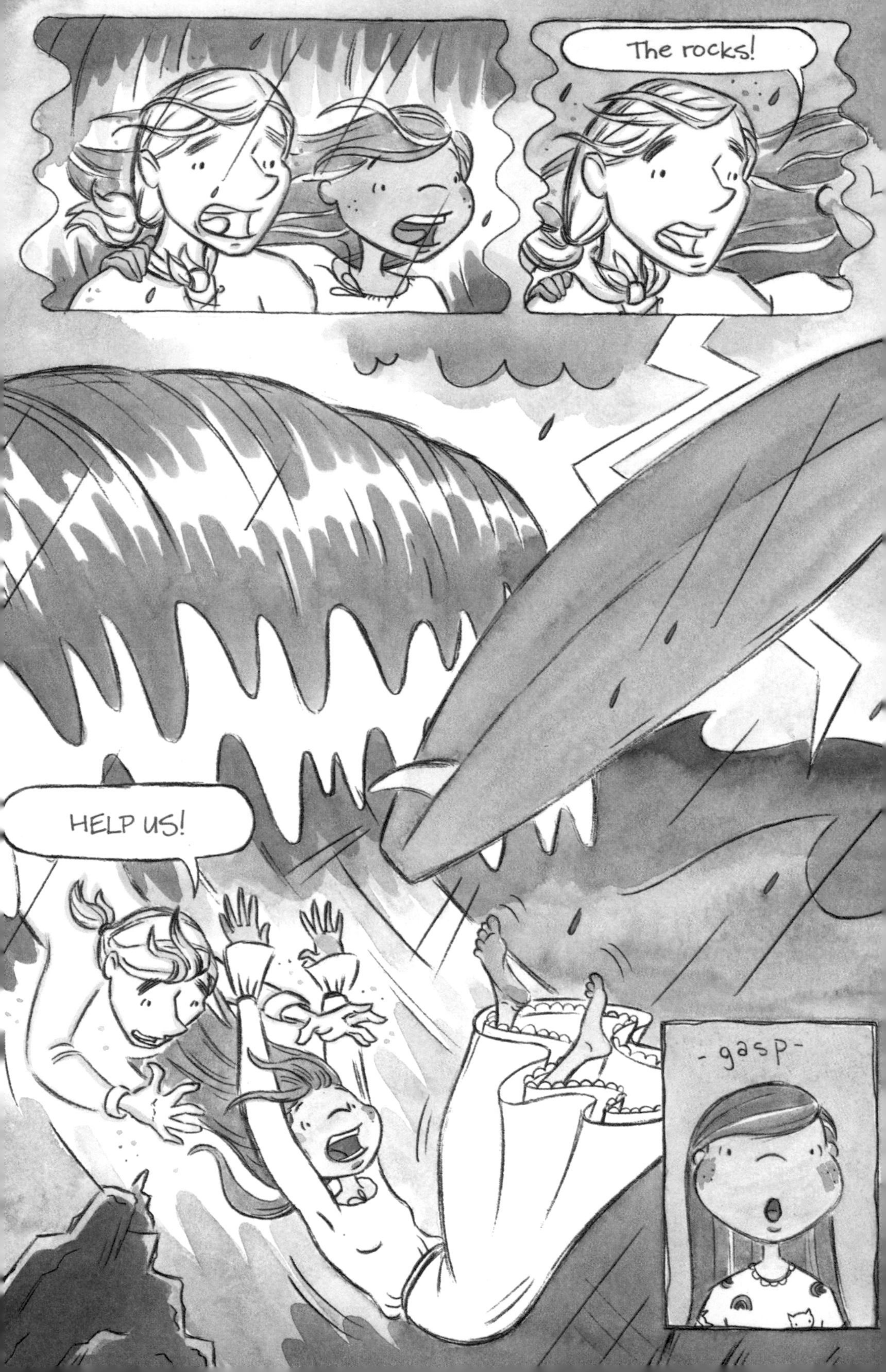
The rocks!
HELP US!
-gasp-

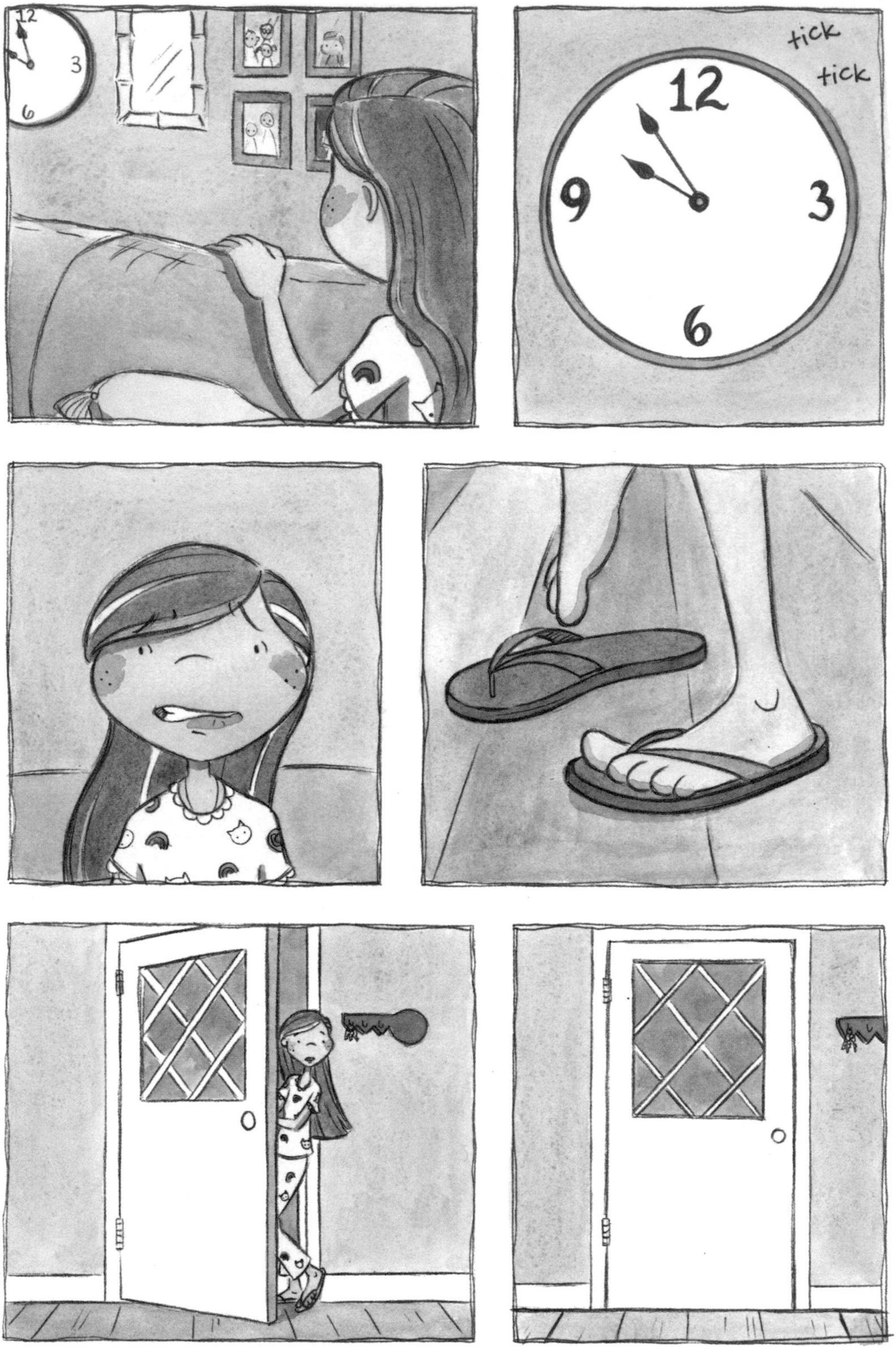
tick
tick

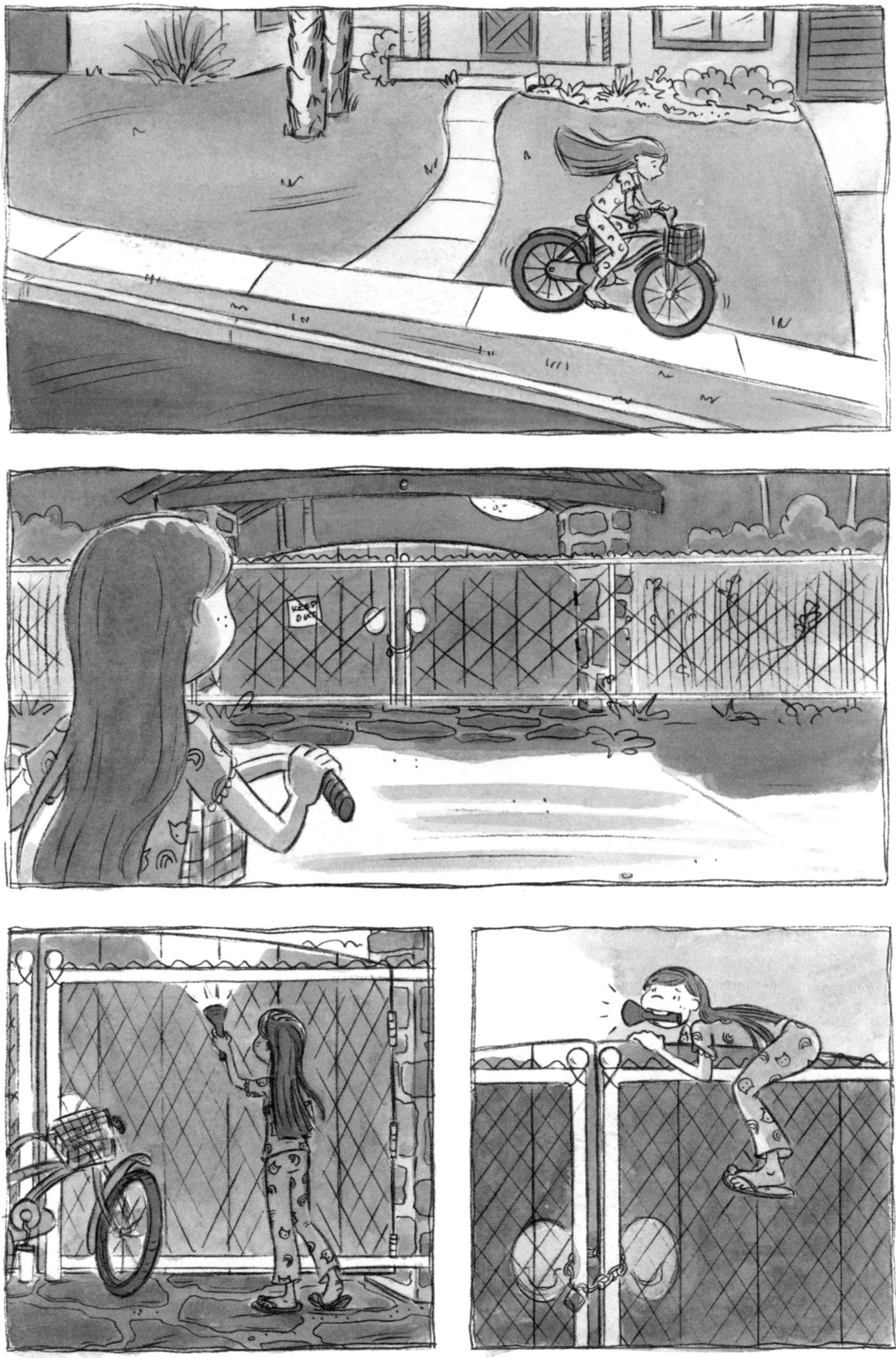
KEEP OUT

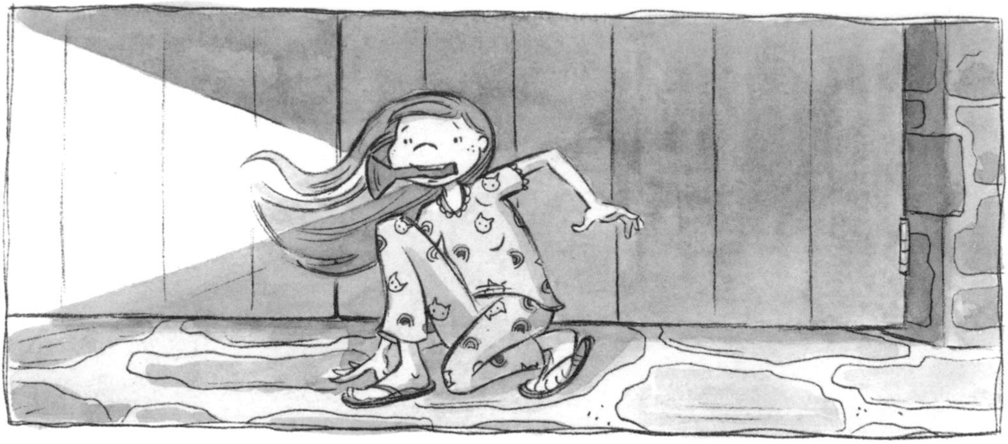

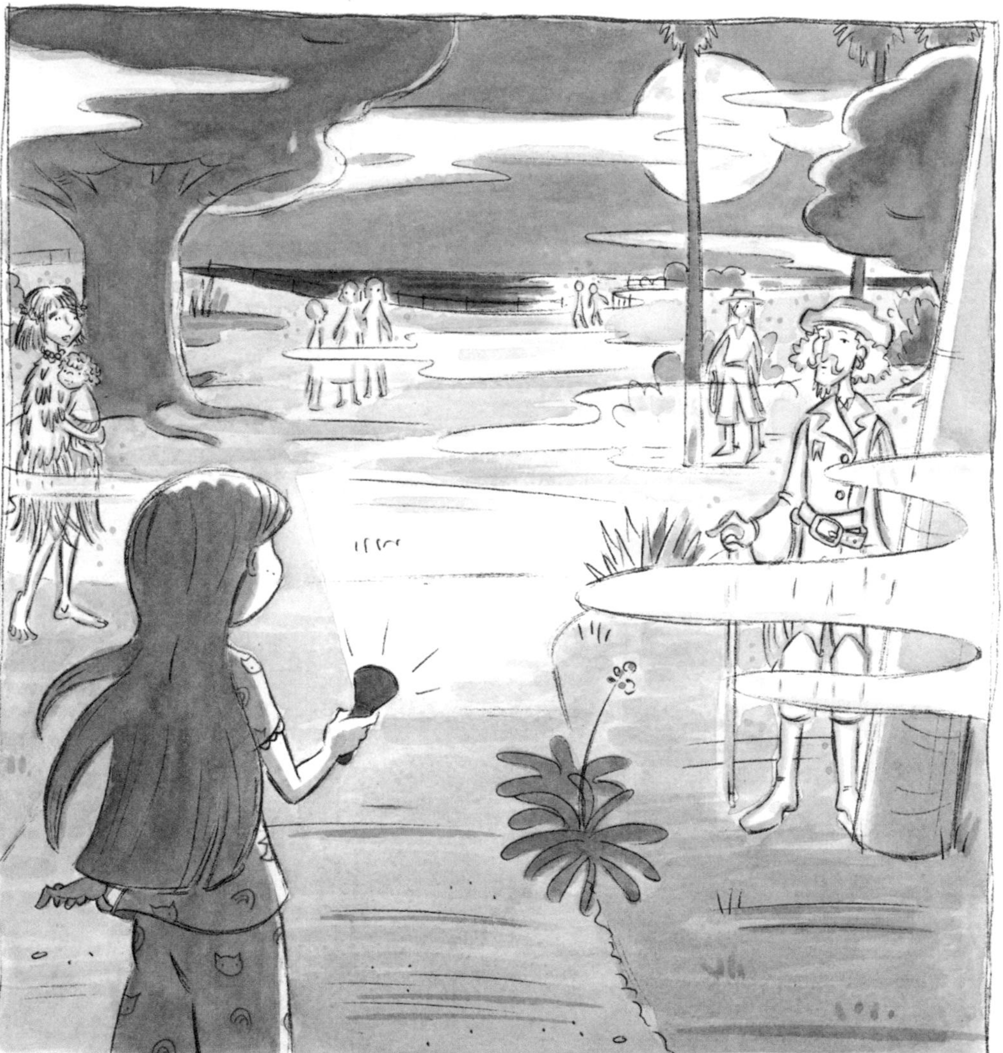

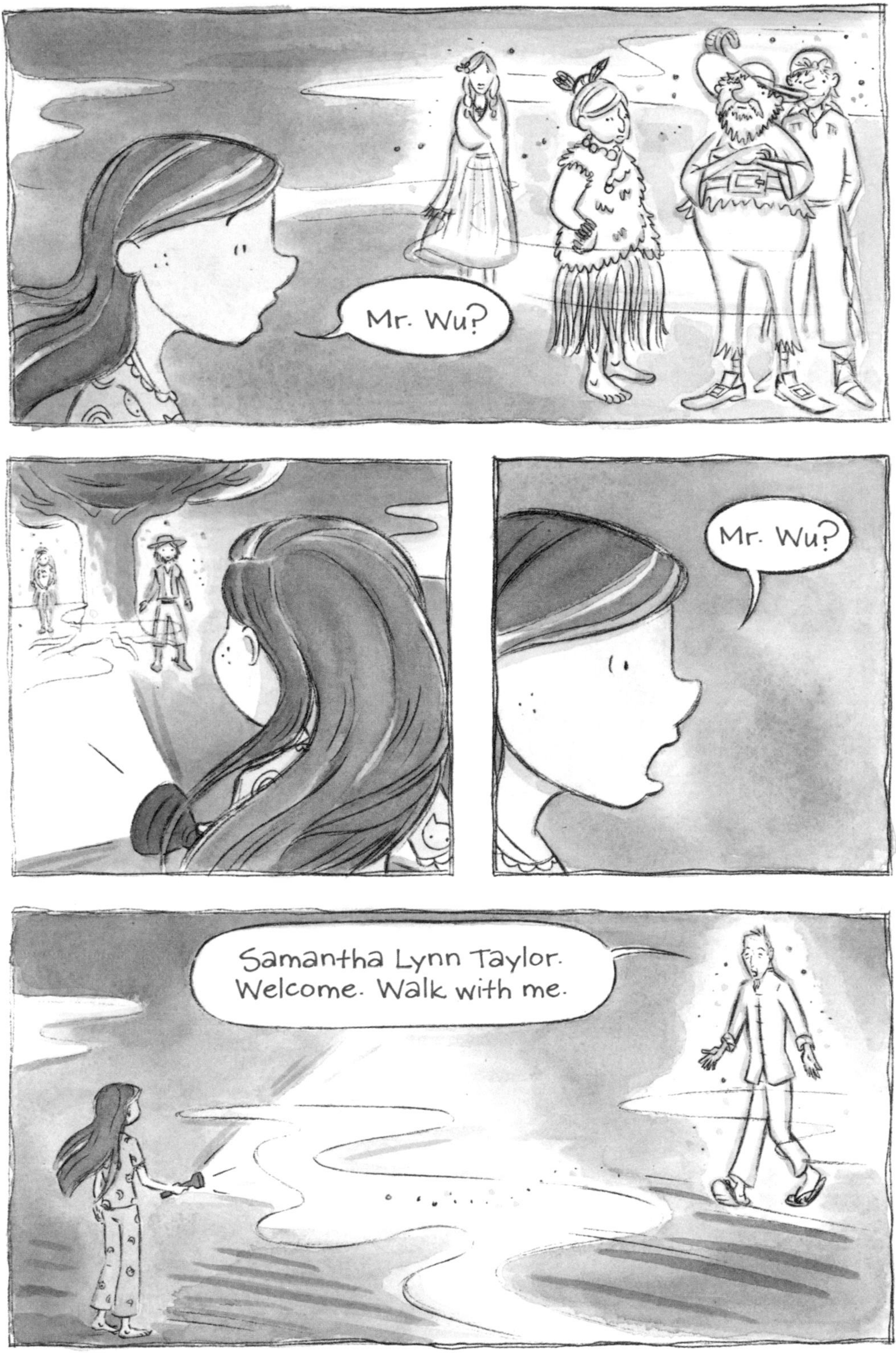
Mr. Wu?
Mr. Wu?
Samantha Lynn Taylor. Welcome. Walk with me.

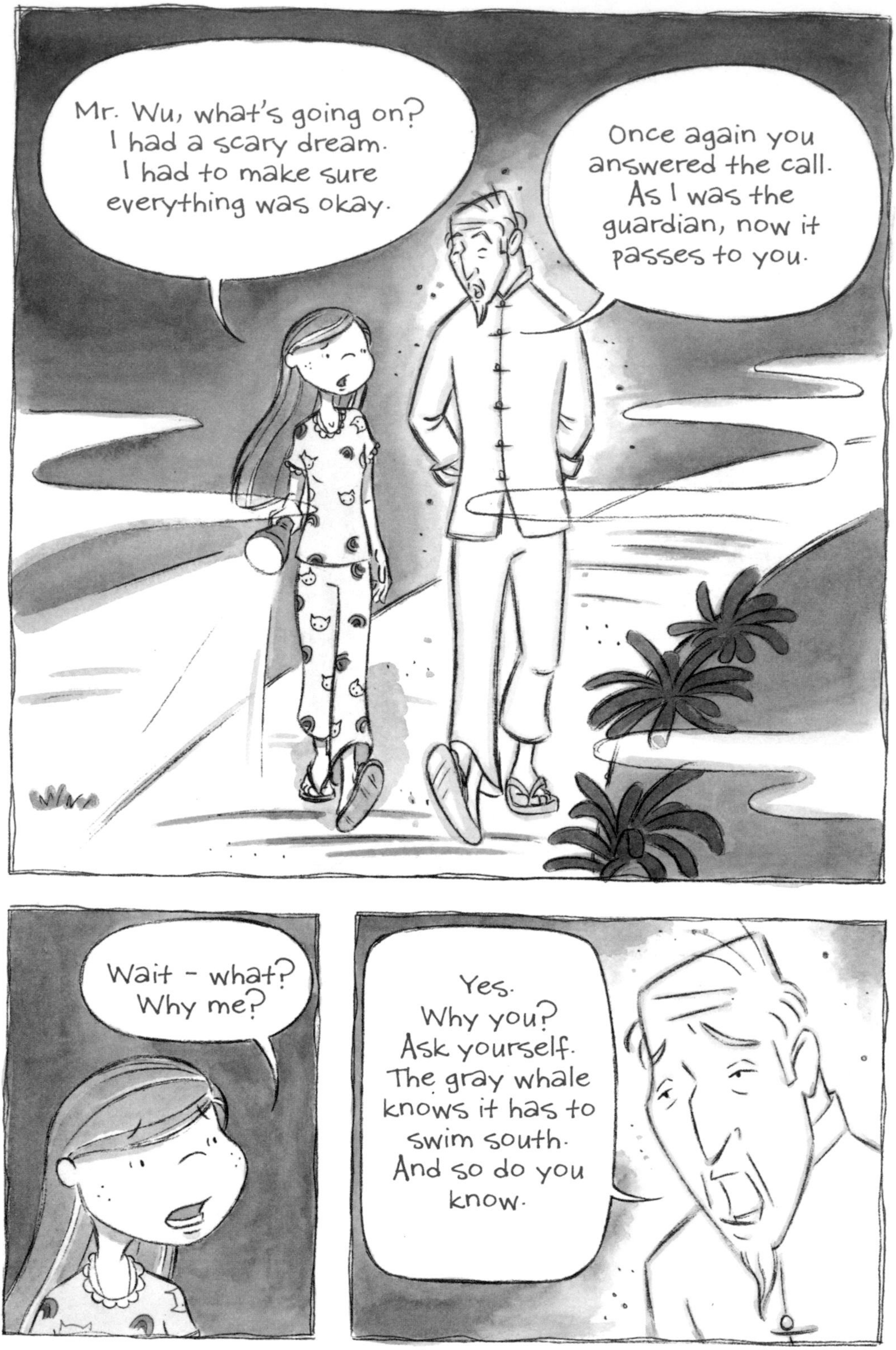
Mr. Wu, what's going on? I had a scary dream. I had to make sure everything was okay.
Once again you answered the call. As I was the guardian, now it passes to you.
Wait - what? Why me?
Yes. Why you? Ask yourself. The gray whale knows it has to swim south. And so do you know.

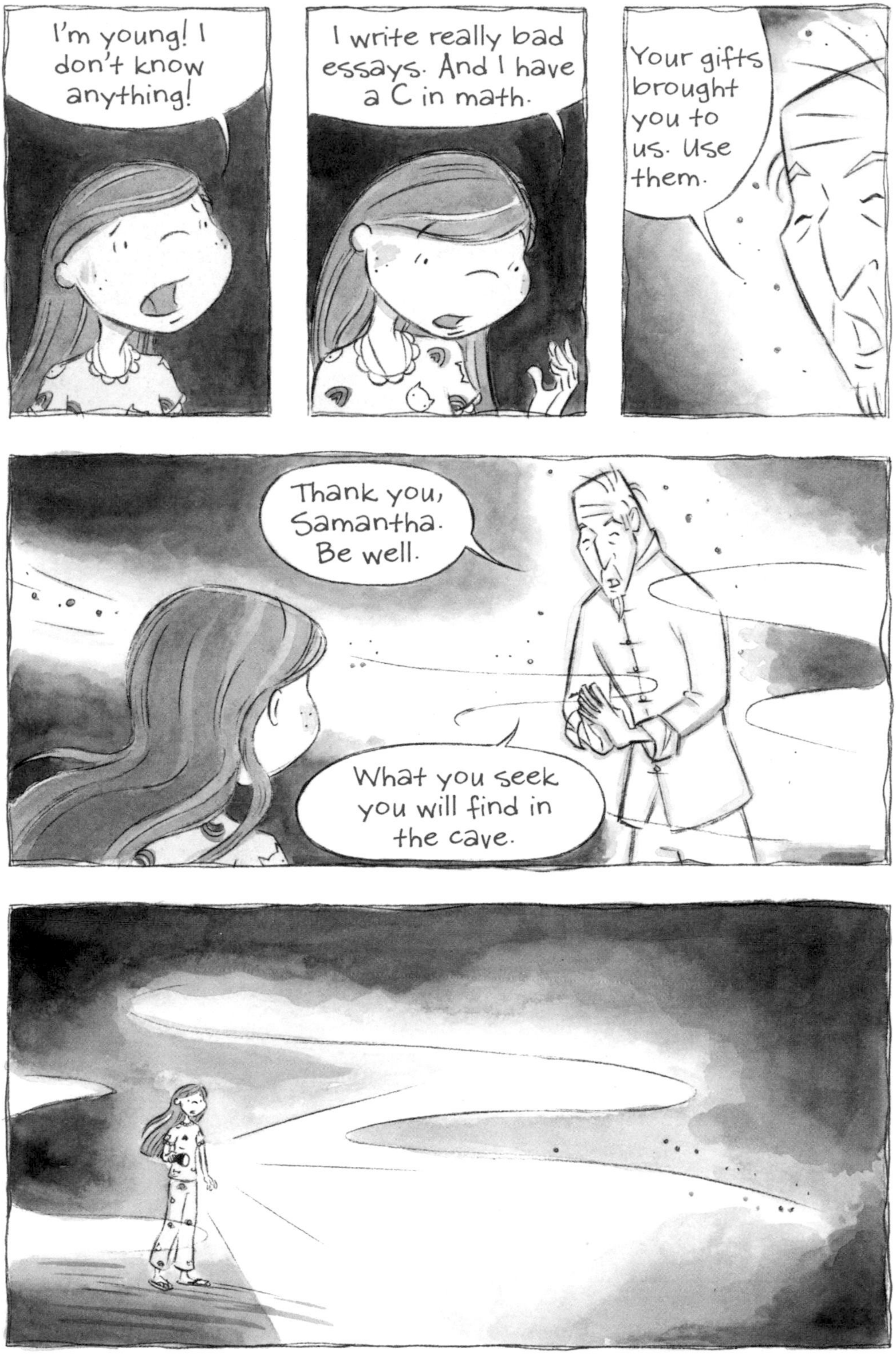
I'm young! I don't know anything!
I write really bad essays. And I have a C in math.
Your gifts brought you to us. Use them.
Thank you, Samantha. Be well.
What you seek you will find in the cave.

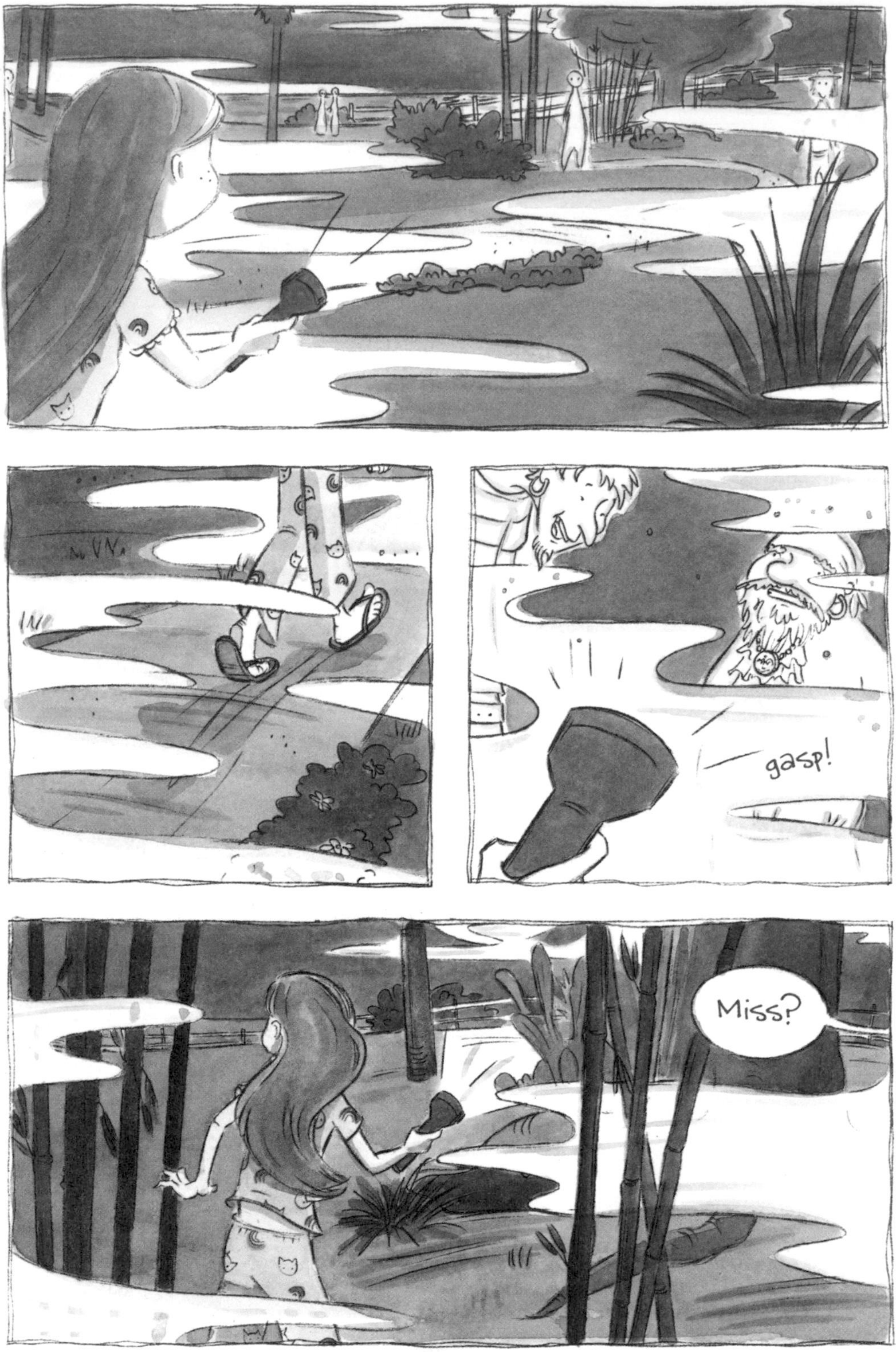
gasp!
Miss?

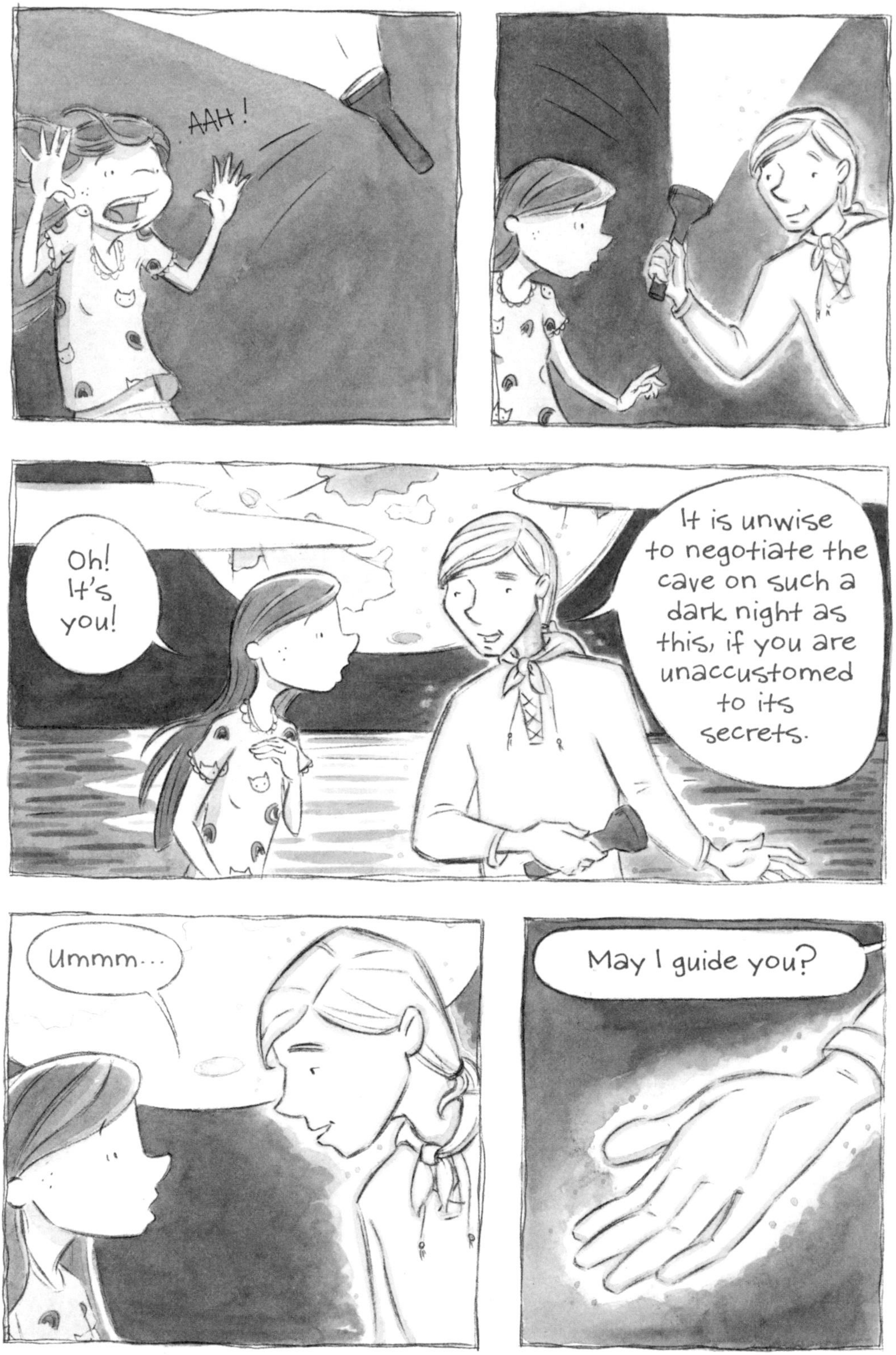
AAH!
Oh! It's you!
It is unwise to negotiate the cave on such a dark night as this, if you are unaccustomed to its secrets.
Ummm...
May I guide you?

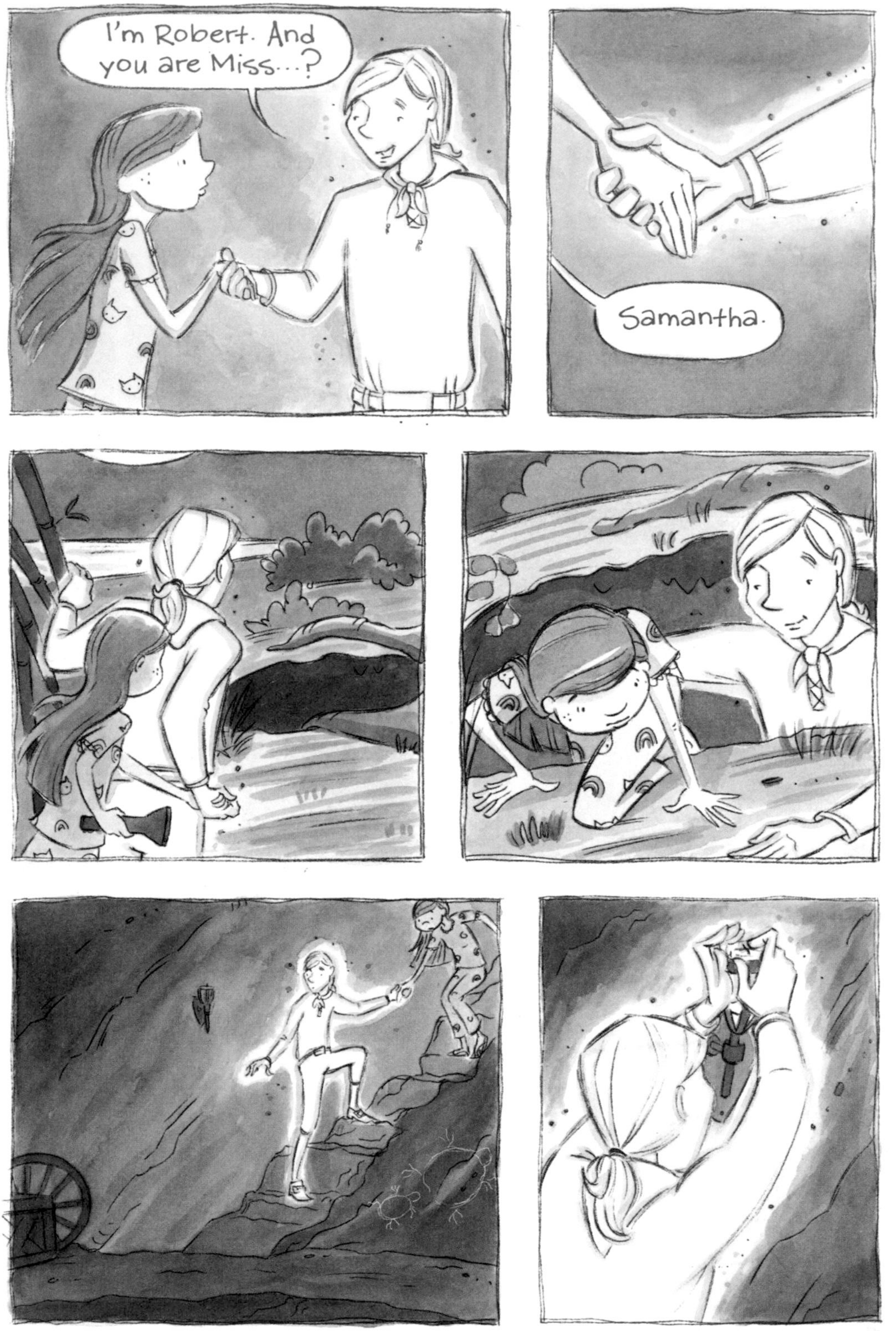
I'm Robert. And you are Miss...?
Samantha.

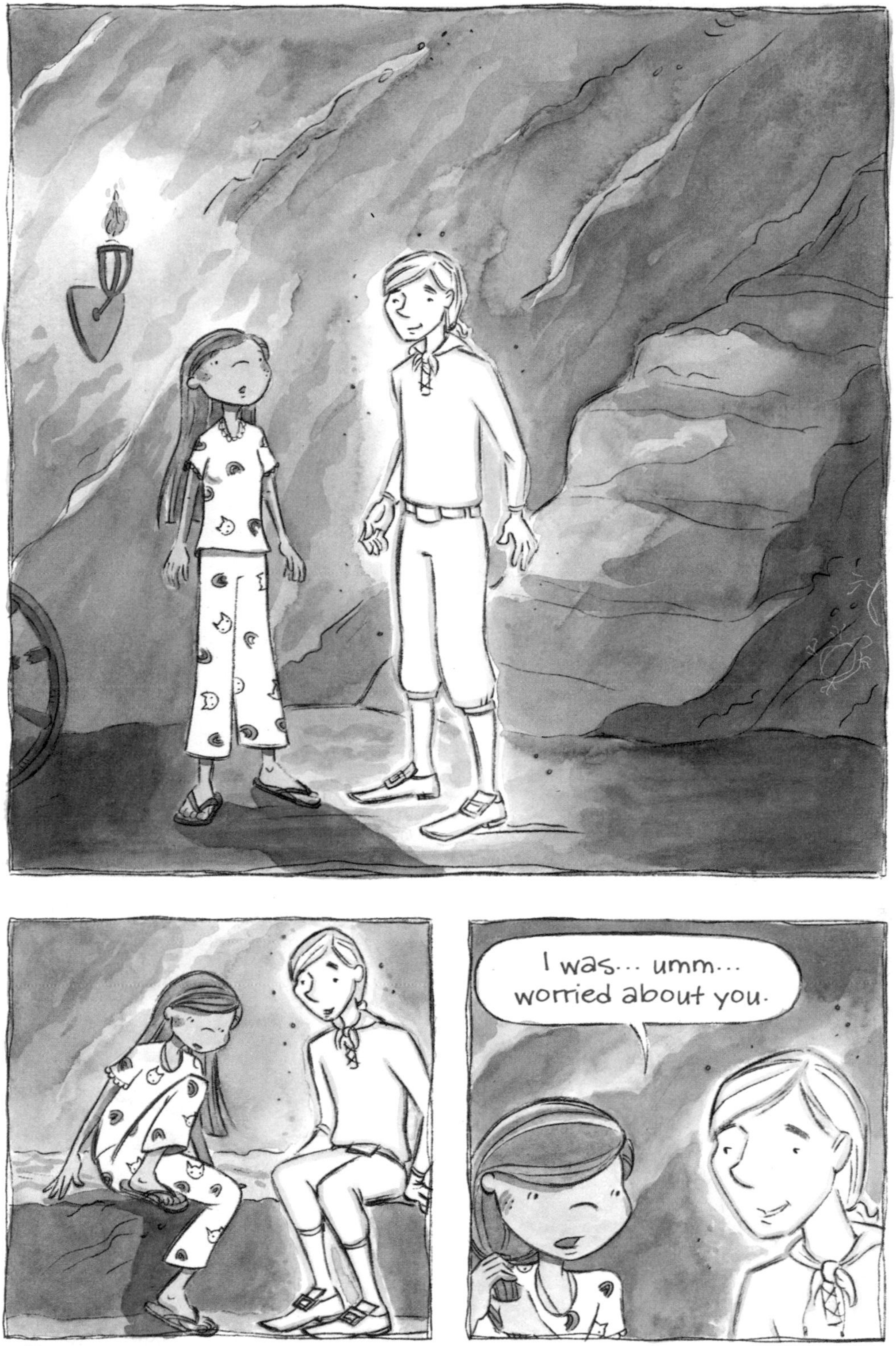
I was... umm...
worried about you.

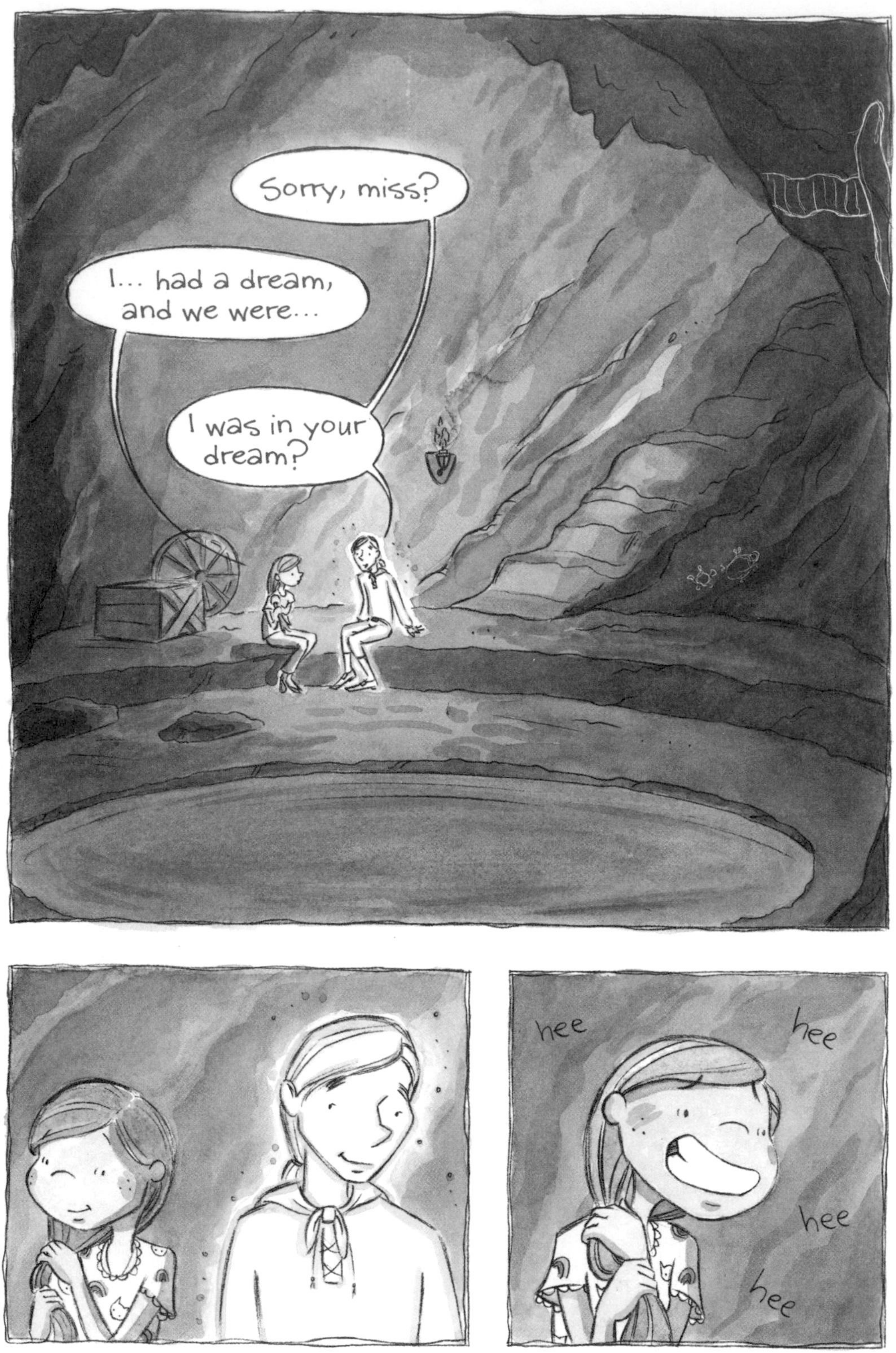
Sorry, miss?
I... had a dream, and we were...
I was in your dream?
hee
hee
hee
hee

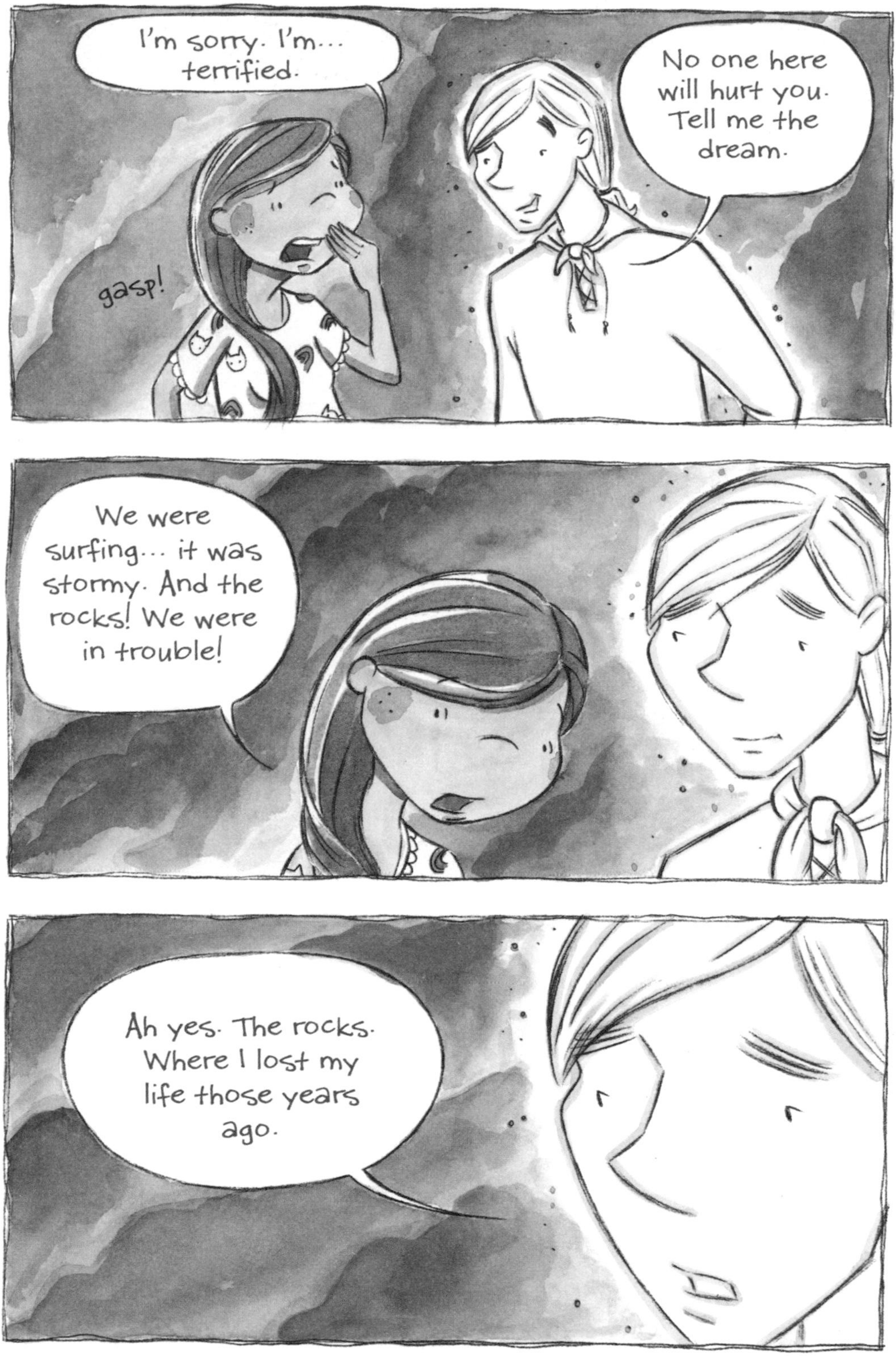
I'm sorry. I'm... terrified.
No one here will hurt you. Tell me the dream.
gasp!
We were surfing... it was stormy. And the rocks! We were in trouble!
Ah yes. The rocks. Where I lost my life those years ago.

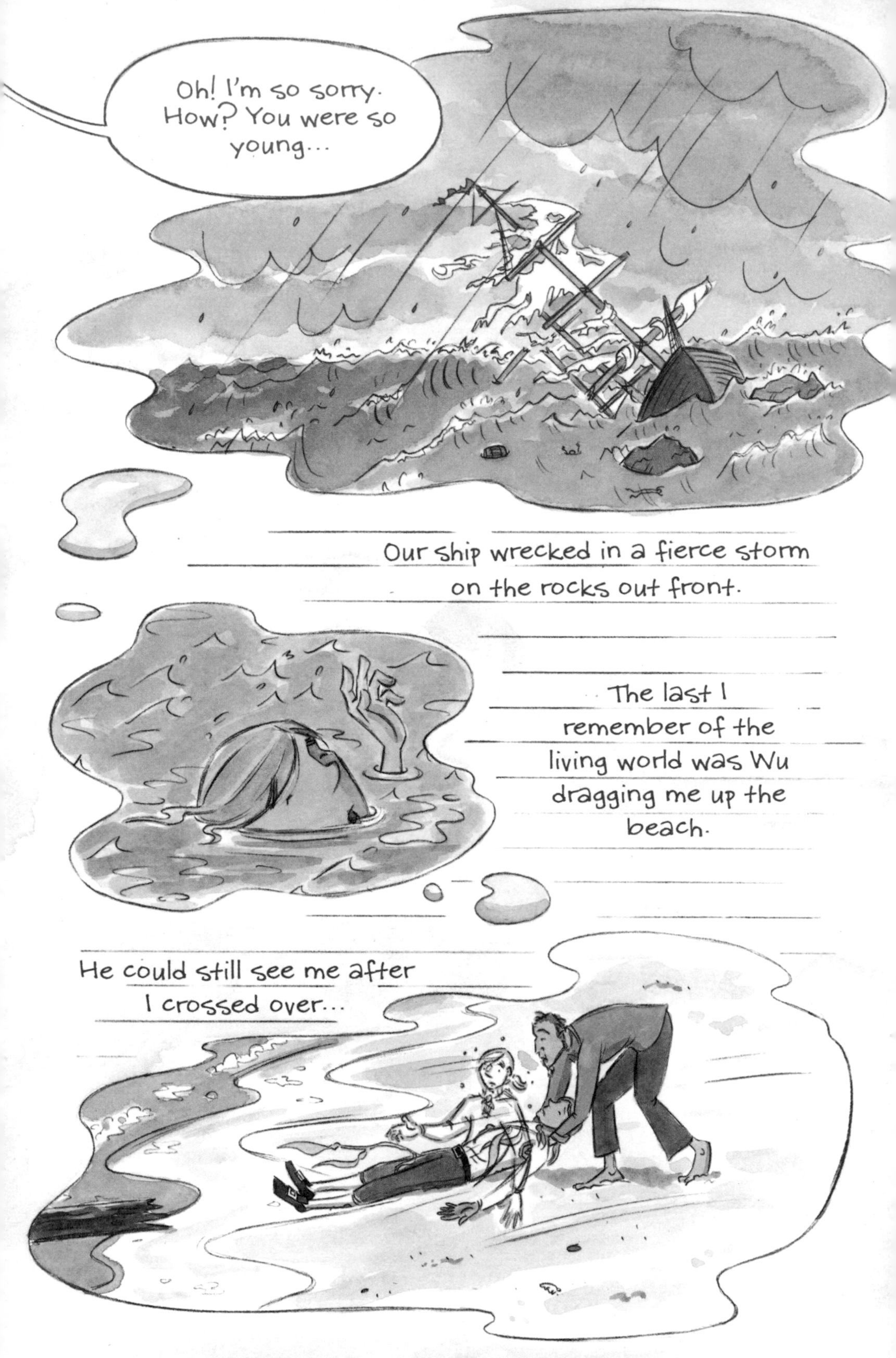
Oh! I'm so sorry. How? You were so young...
Our ship wrecked in a fierce storm on the rocks out front.
The last I remember of the living world was Wu dragging me up the beach.
He could still see me after I crossed over...

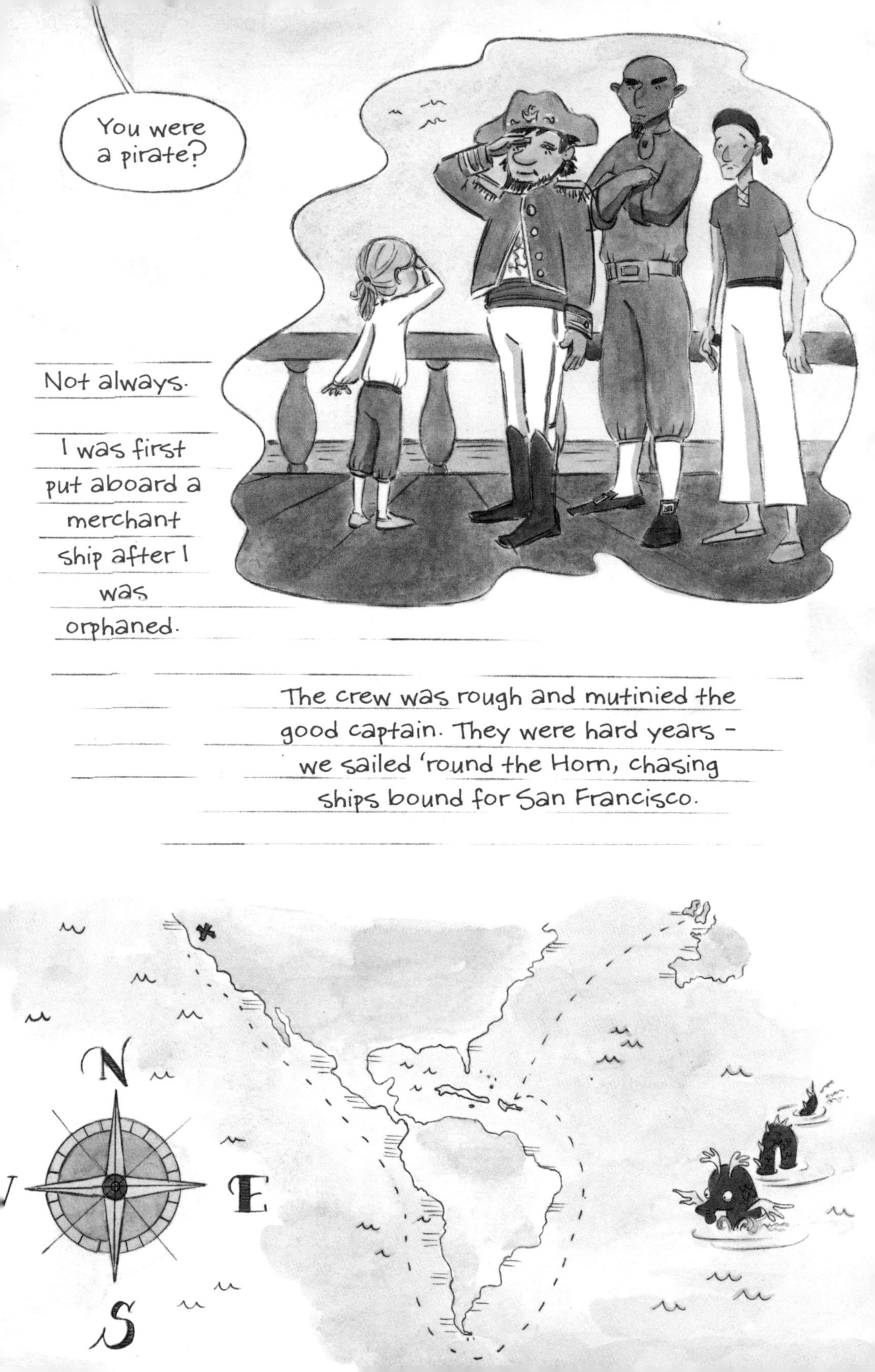
You were a pirate?
Not always.
I was first put aboard a merchant ship after I was orphaned.
The crew was rough and mutinied the good captain. They were hard years – we sailed 'round the Horn, chasing ships bound for San Francisco.
N
E
S

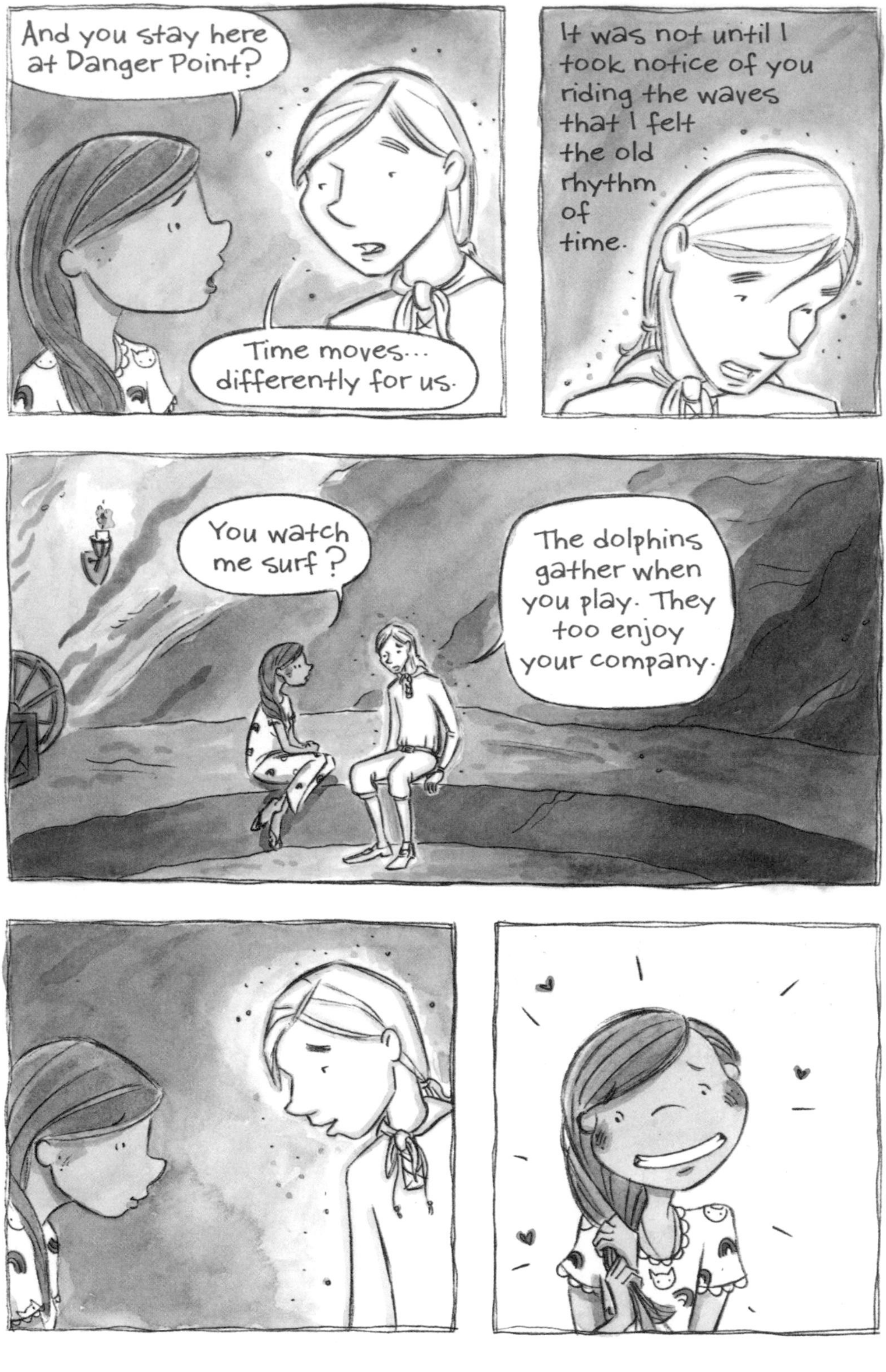

And you stay here at Danger Point?
Time moves... differently for us.
It was not until I took notice of you riding the waves that I felt the old rhythm of time.
You watch me surf?
The dolphins gather when you play. They too enjoy your company.

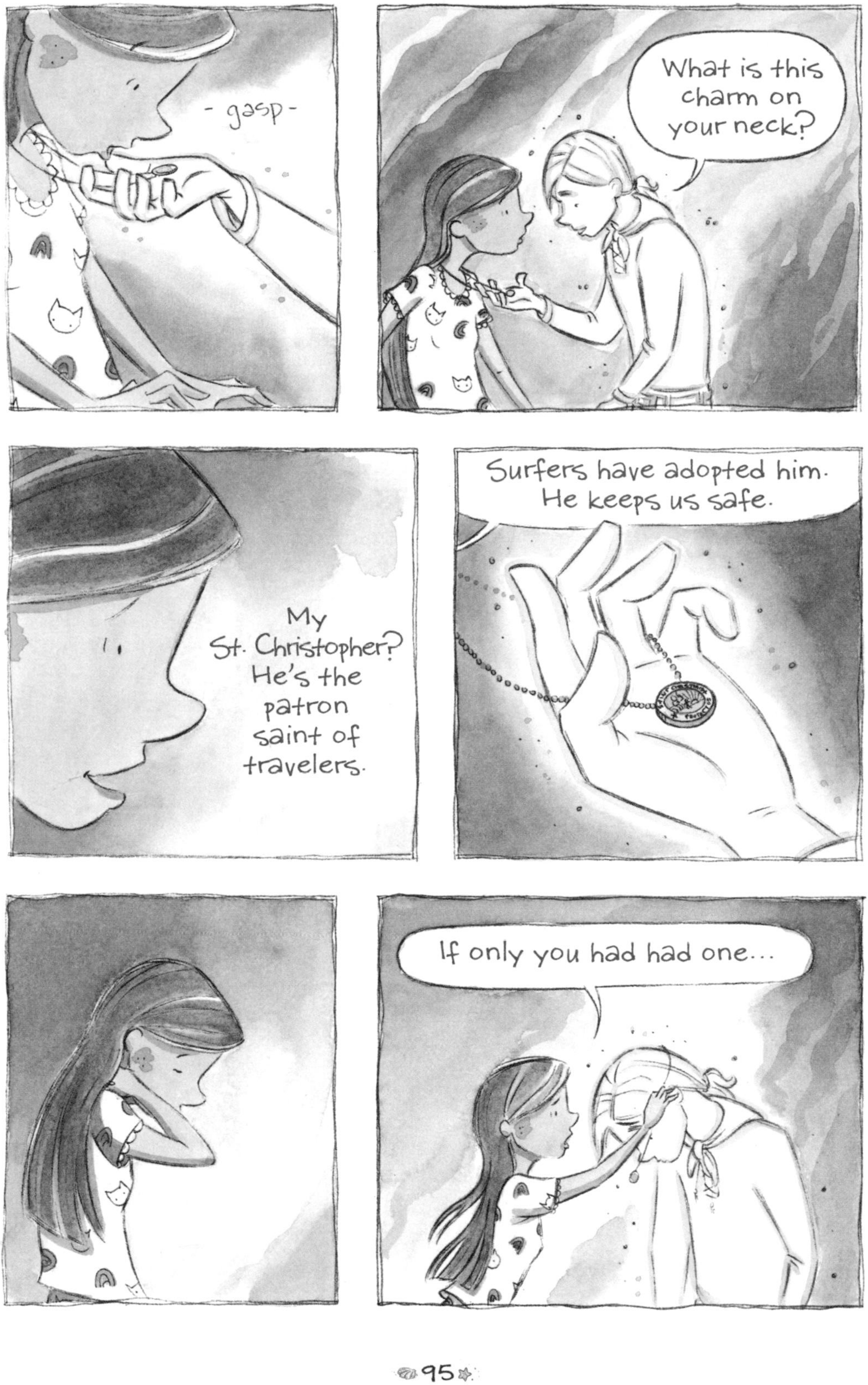
- gasp -
What is this charm on your neck?
My St. Christopher? He's the patron saint of travelers.
Surfers have adopted him. He keeps us safe.
If only you had had one...

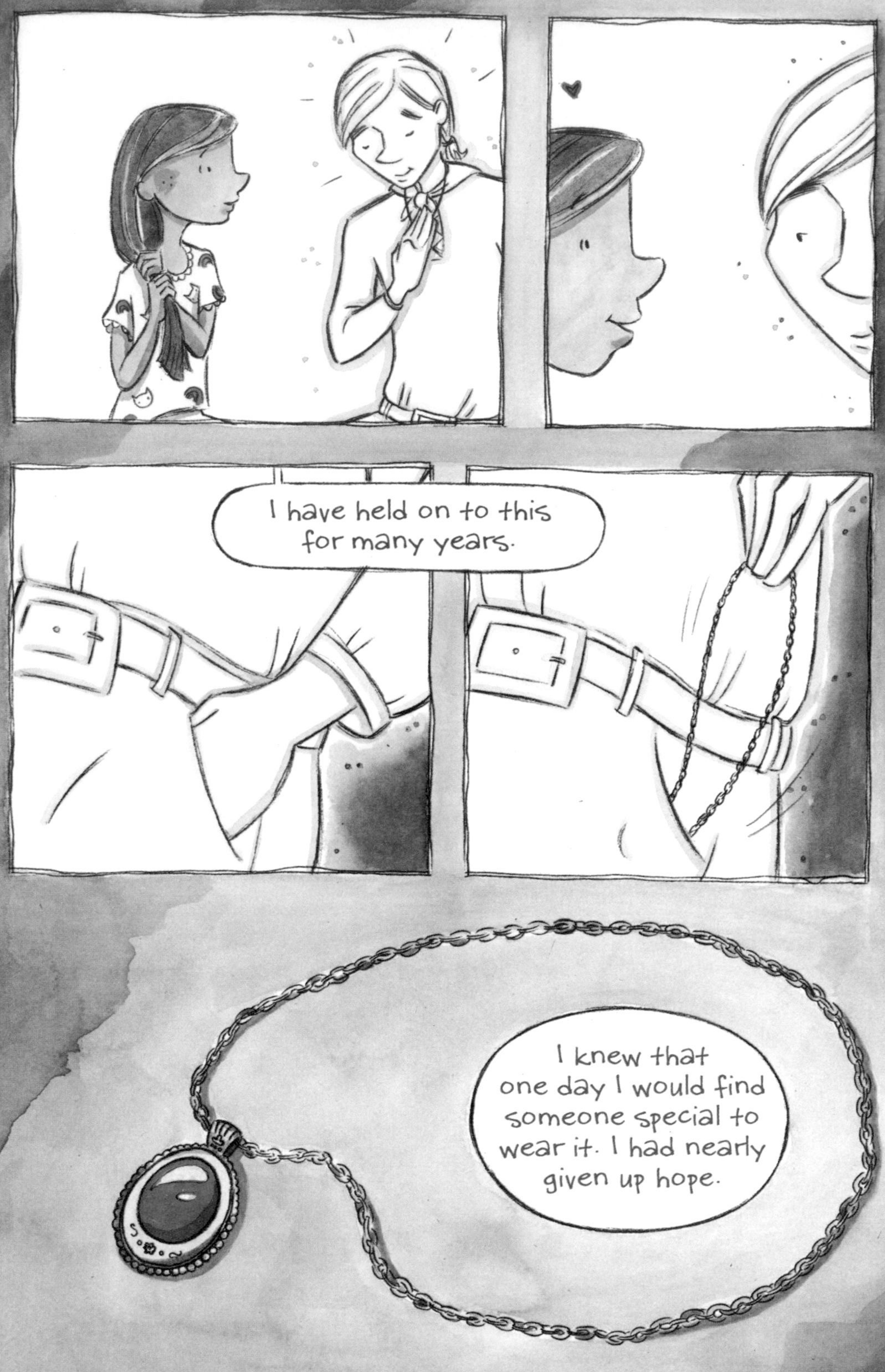
I have held on to this for many years.
I knew that one day I would find someone special to wear it. I had nearly given up hope.

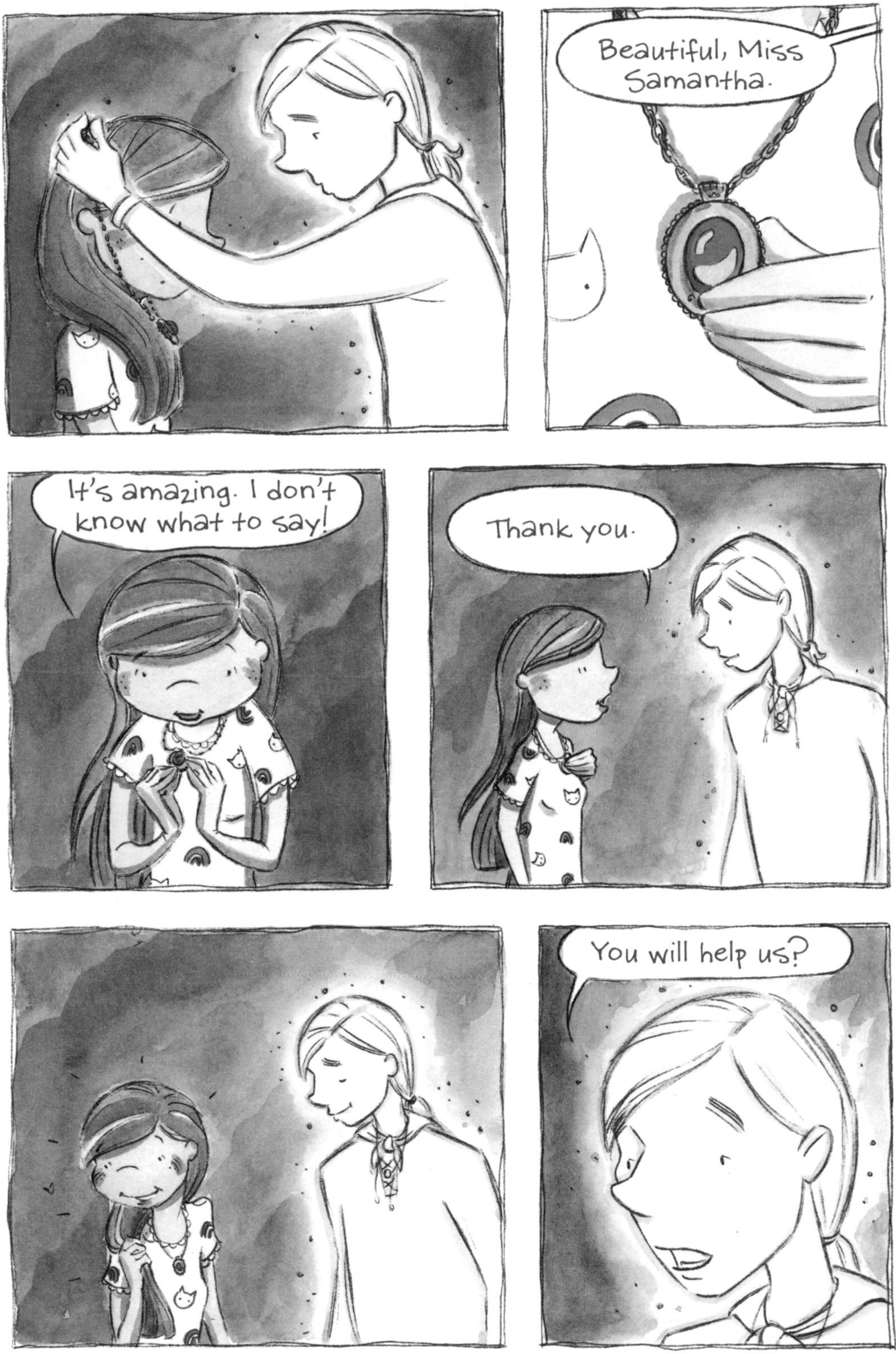
Beautiful, Miss Samantha.
It's amazing. I don't know what to say!
Thank you.
You will help us?

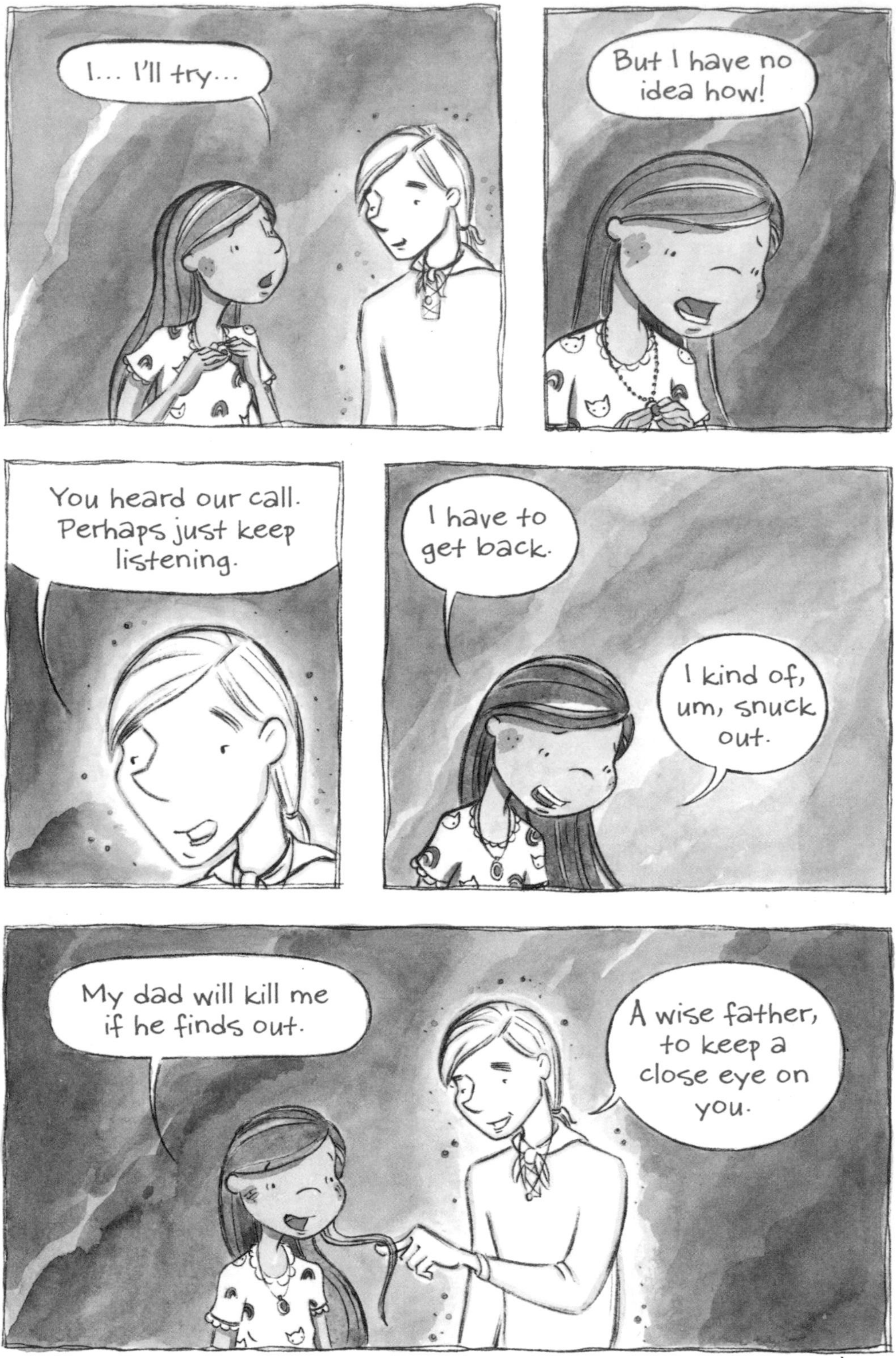
I... I'll try...
But I have no idea how!
You heard our call. Perhaps just keep listening.
I have to get back.
I kind of, um, snuck out.
My dad will kill me if he finds out.
A wise father, to keep a close eye on you.

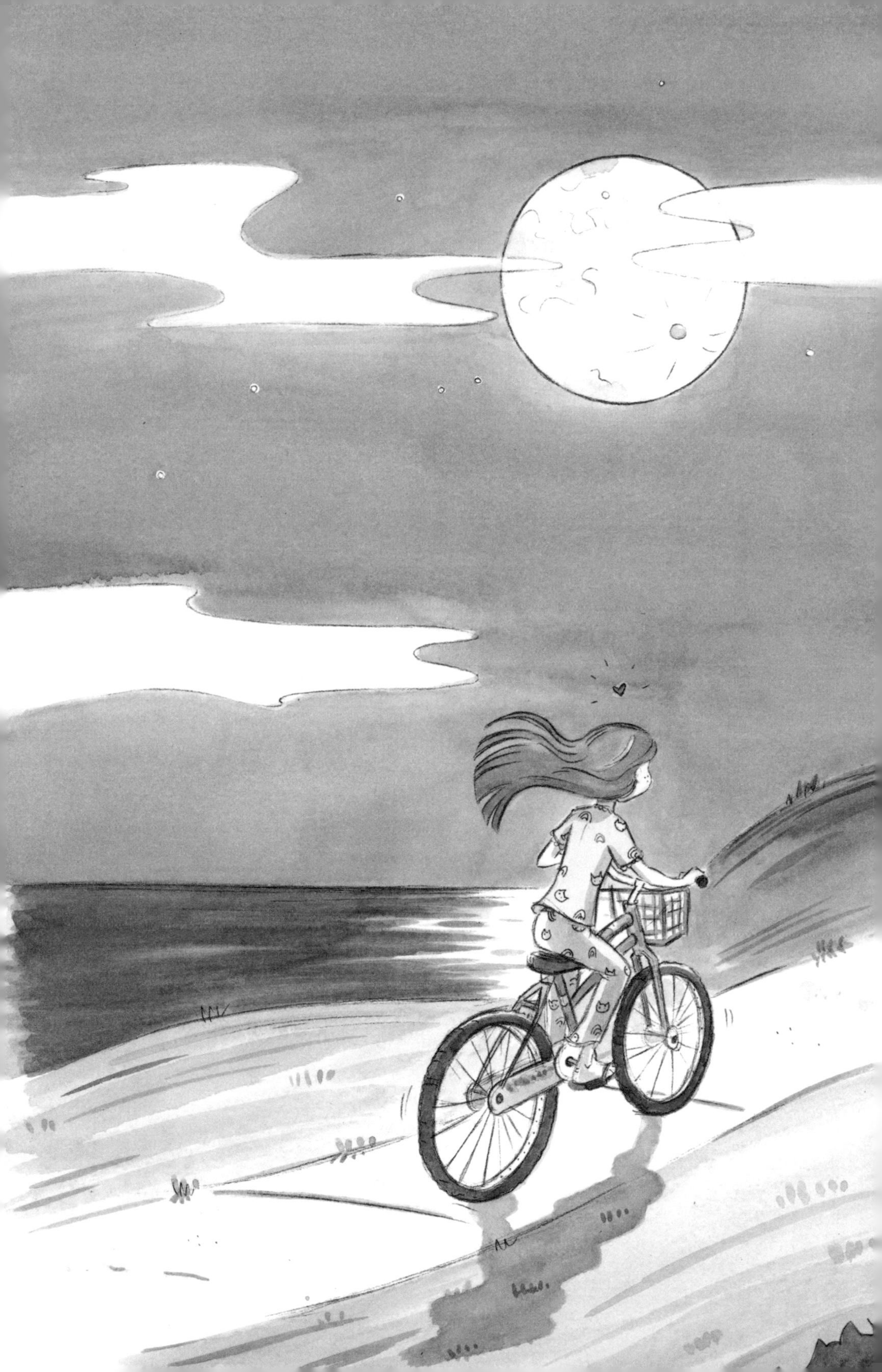

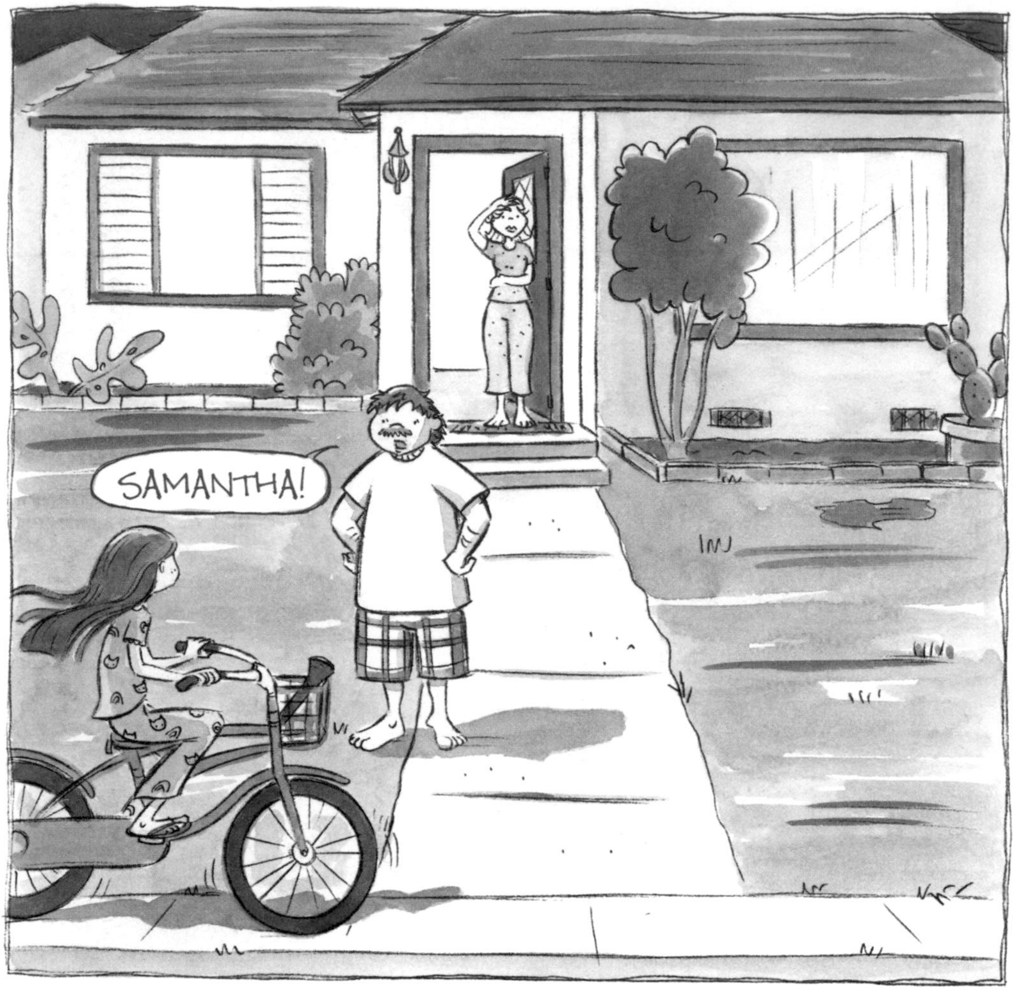
SAMANTHA!

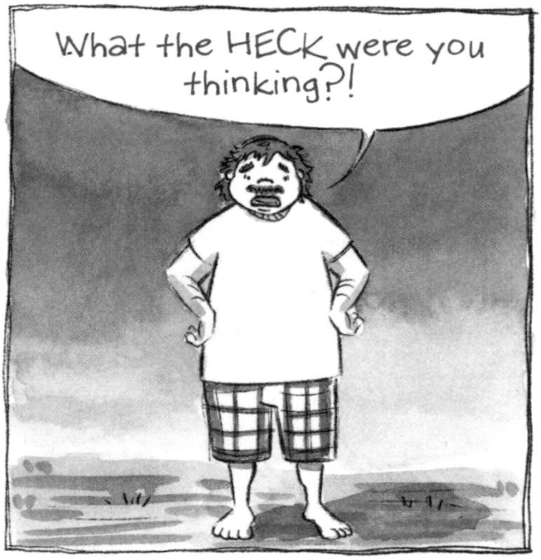
What the HECK were you thinking?!

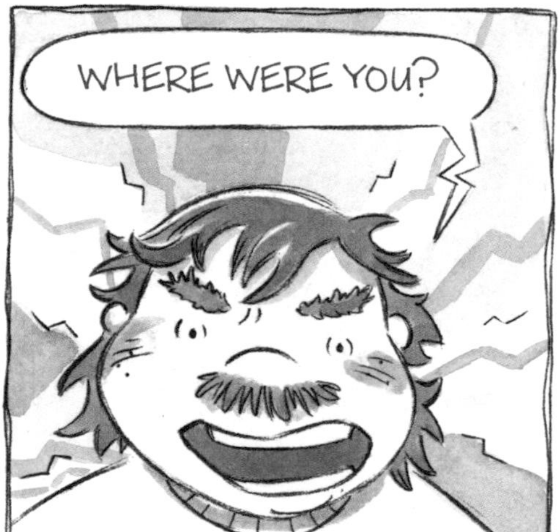
WHERE WERE YOU?

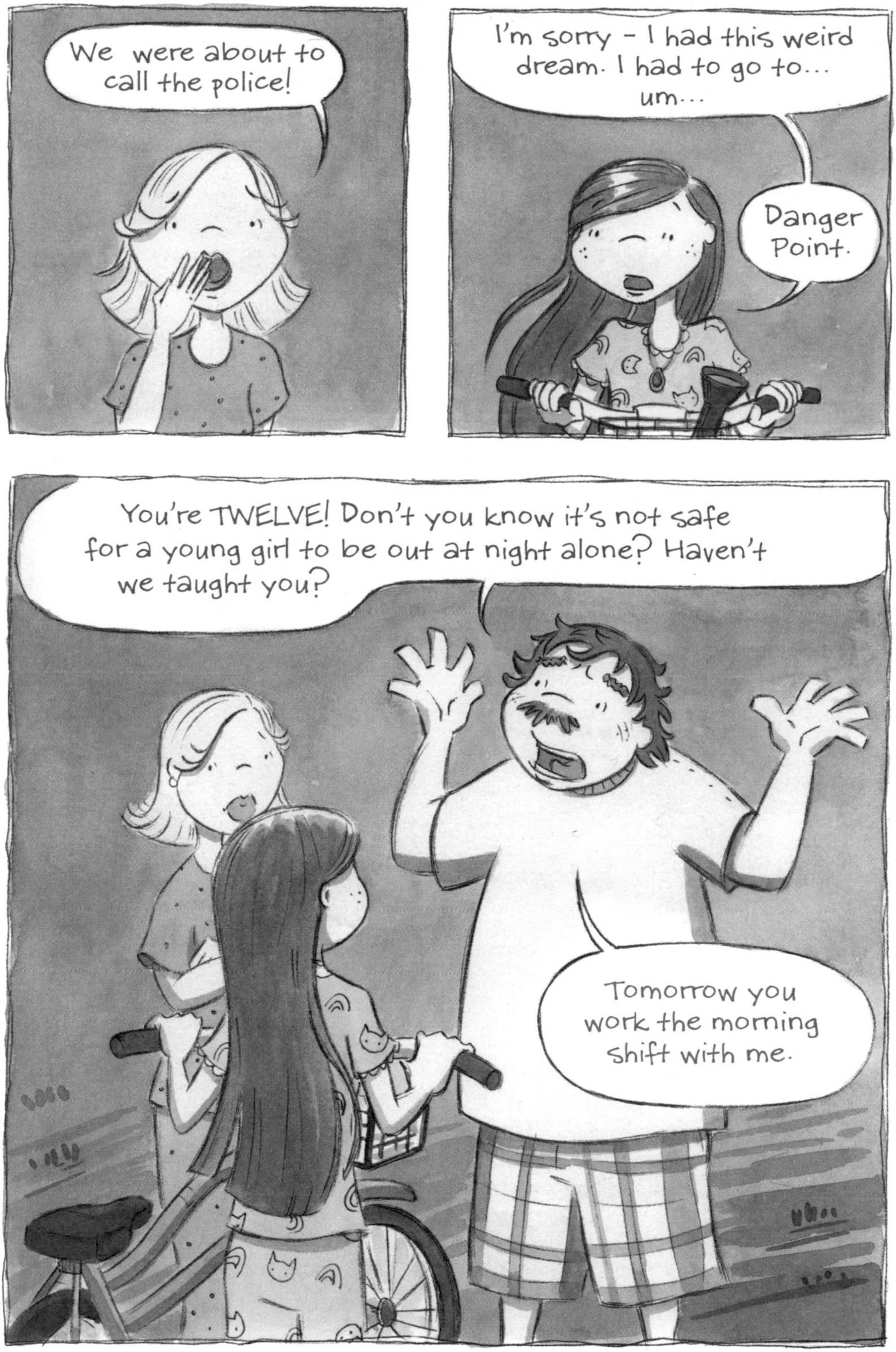
We were about to call the police!
I'm sorry - I had this weird dream. I had to go to... um...
Danger Point.
You're TWELVE! Don't you know it's not safe for a young girl to be out at night alone? Haven't we taught you?
Tomorrow you work the morning shift with me.

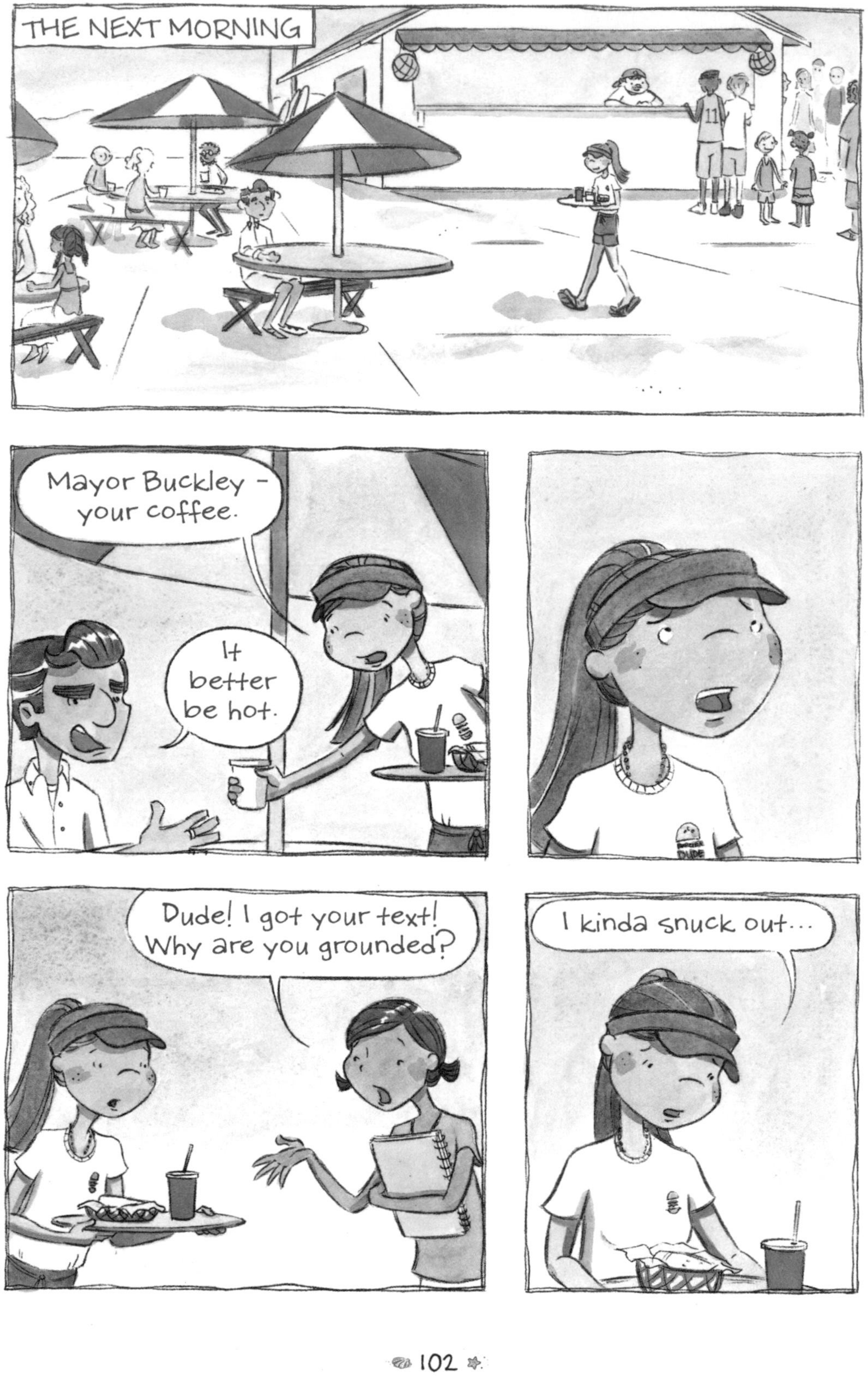
THE NEXT MORNING
Mayor Buckley - your coffee.
It better be hot.
Dude! I got your text! Why are you grounded?
I kinda snuck out...

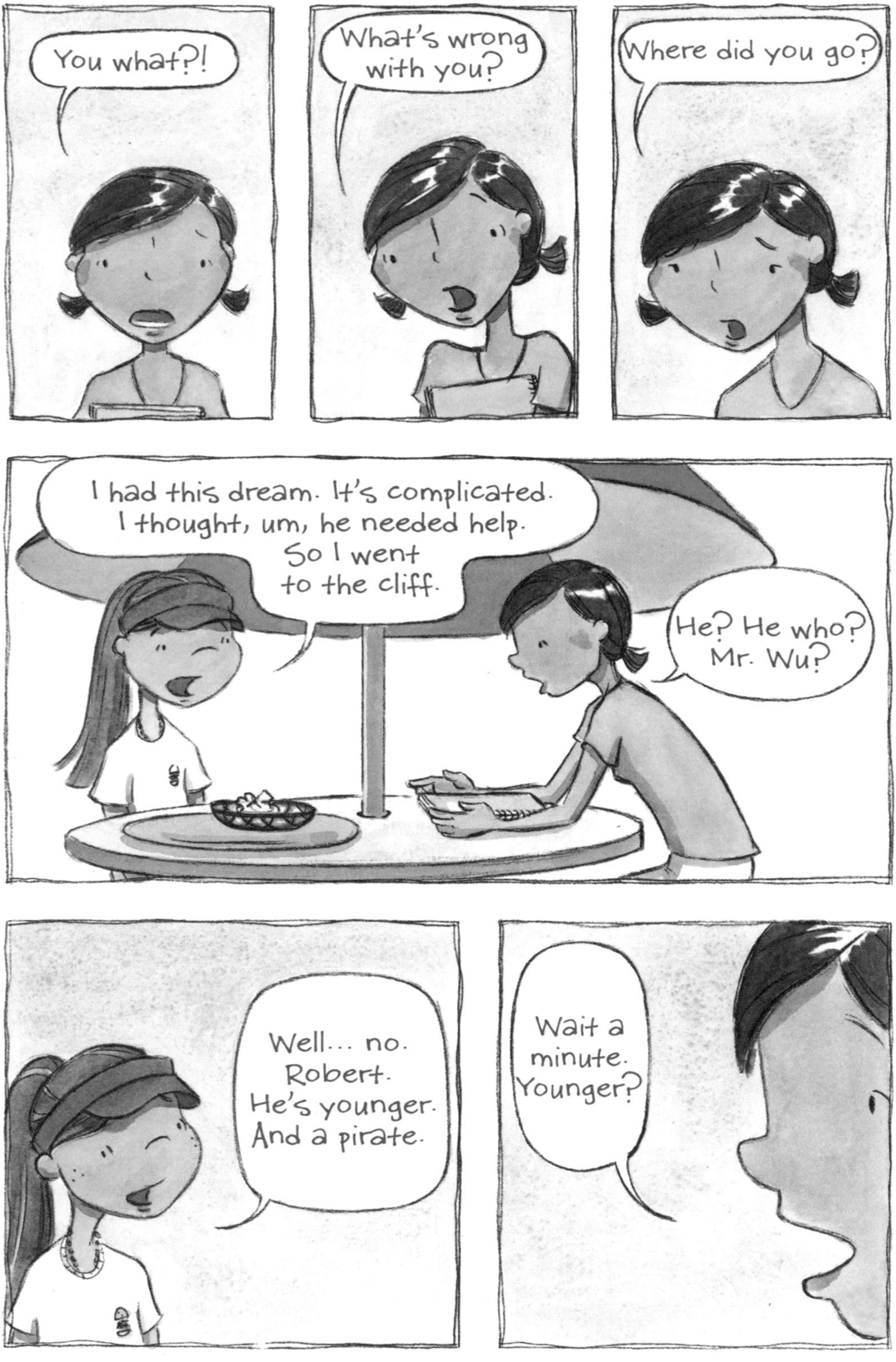
You what?!
What's wrong with you?
Where did you go?
I had this dream. It's complicated. I thought, um, he needed help. So I went to the cliff.
He? He who? Mr. Wu?
Well... no. Robert. He's younger. And a pirate.
Wait a minute. Younger?

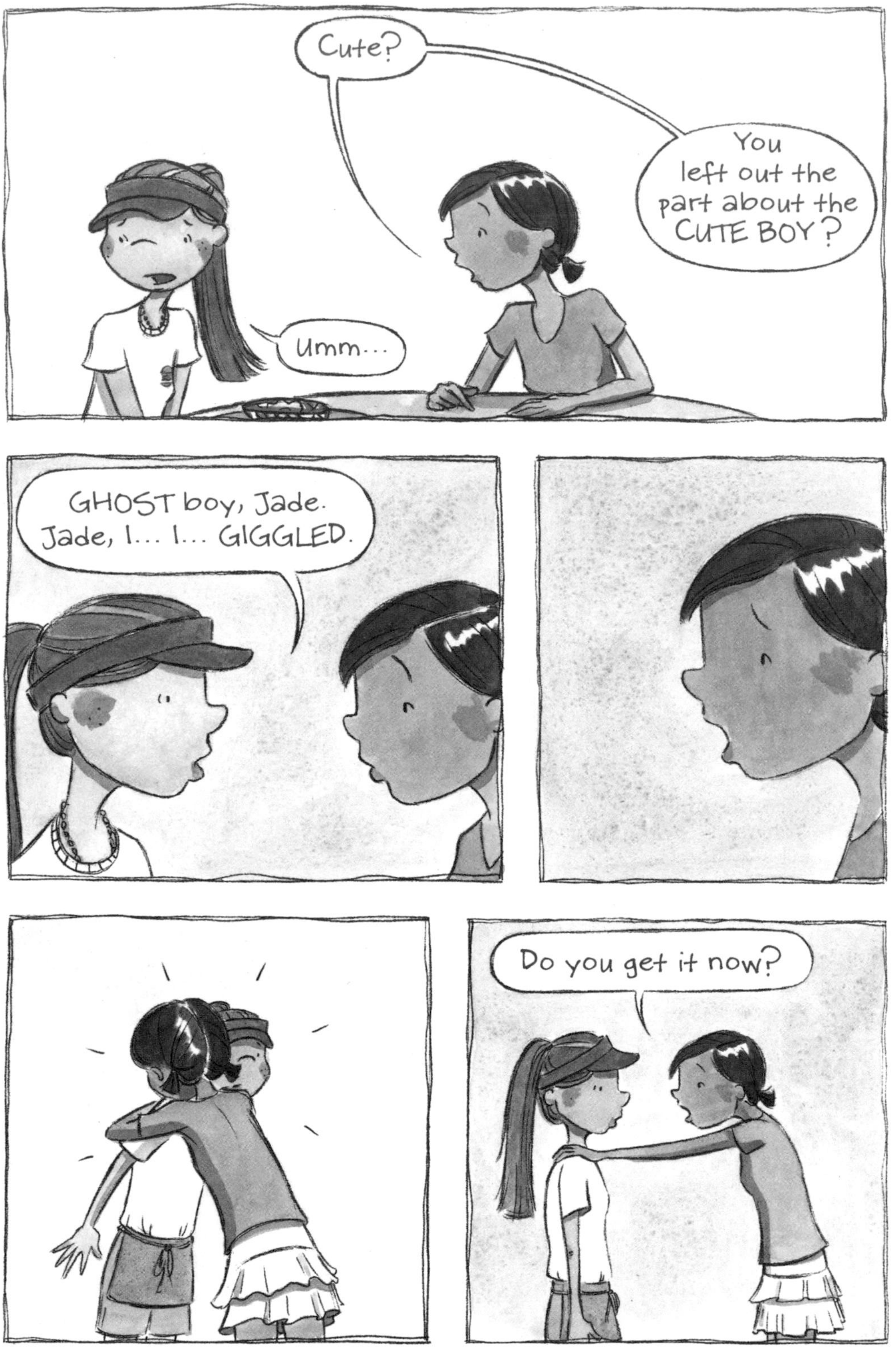
Cute?
You left out the part about the CUTE BOY?
Umm...
GHOST boy, Jade. Jade, I... I... GIGGLED.
Do you get it now?

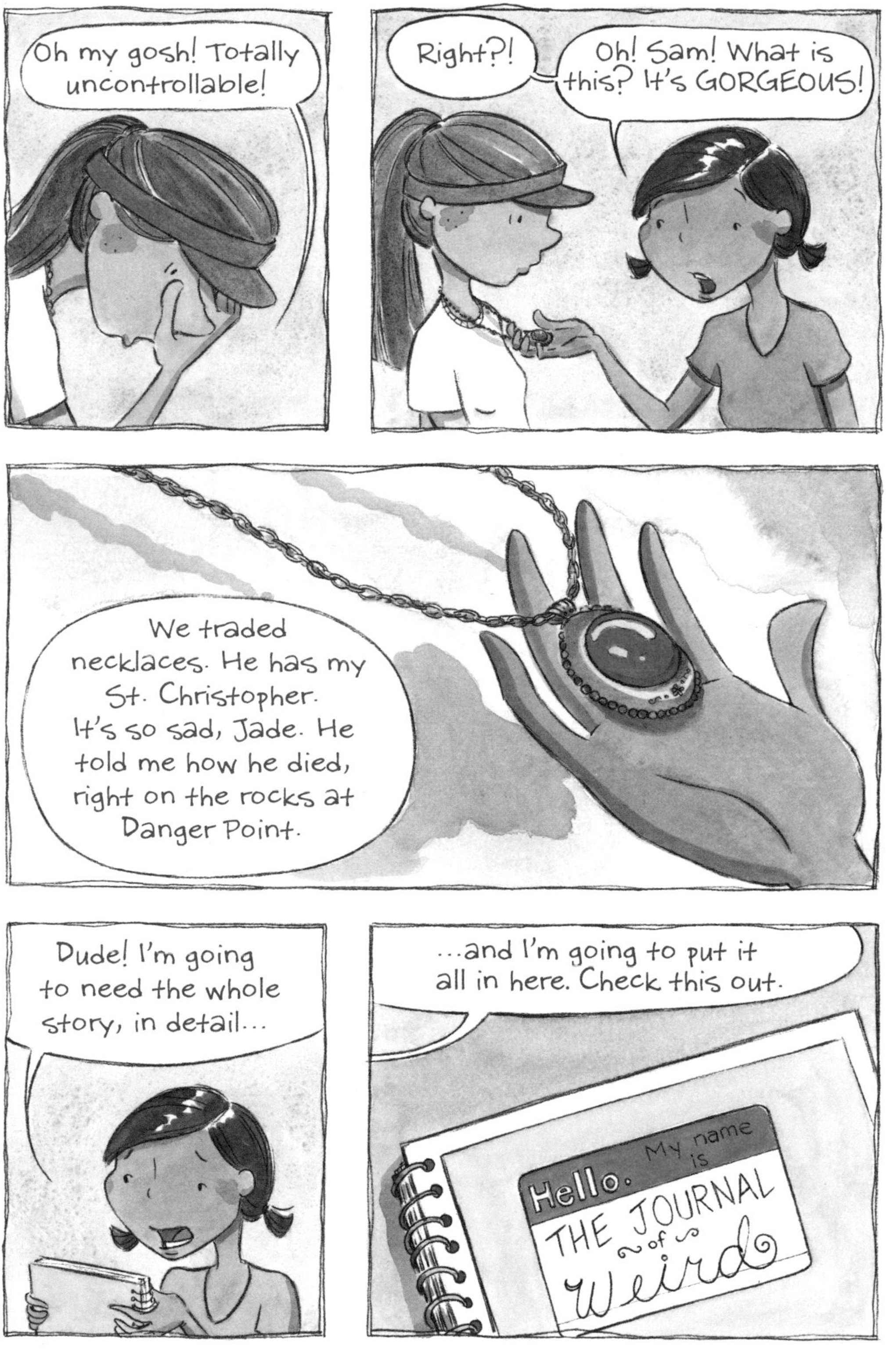

Oh my gosh! Totally uncontrollable!
Right?!
Oh! Sam! What is this? It's GORGEOUS!
We traded necklaces. He has my St. Christopher. It's so sad, Jade. He told me how he died, right on the rocks at Danger Point.
Dude! I'm going to need the whole story, in detail...
...and I'm going to put it all in here. Check this out.
Hello. My name is
THE JOURNAL of Weird

THE JOURNAL OF WEIRD

A documentation of strange occurrences and clues as recorded by JADE LEE

1) GHOSTS- DANGER POINT CLIFF: as seen and described by SAMANTHA TAYLOR:

a) Ghosts in pirate costumes
- large boots with buckles
- pirate hats

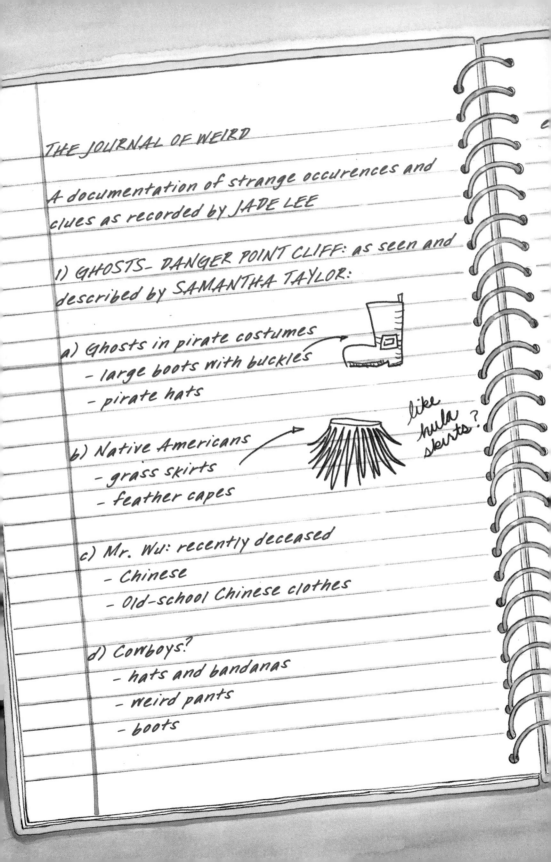

b) Native Americans
- grass skirts
- feather capes

like hula skirts?

c) Mr. Wu: recently deceased
- Chinese
- Old-school Chinese clothes

d) Cowboys?
- hats and bandanas
- weird pants
- boots

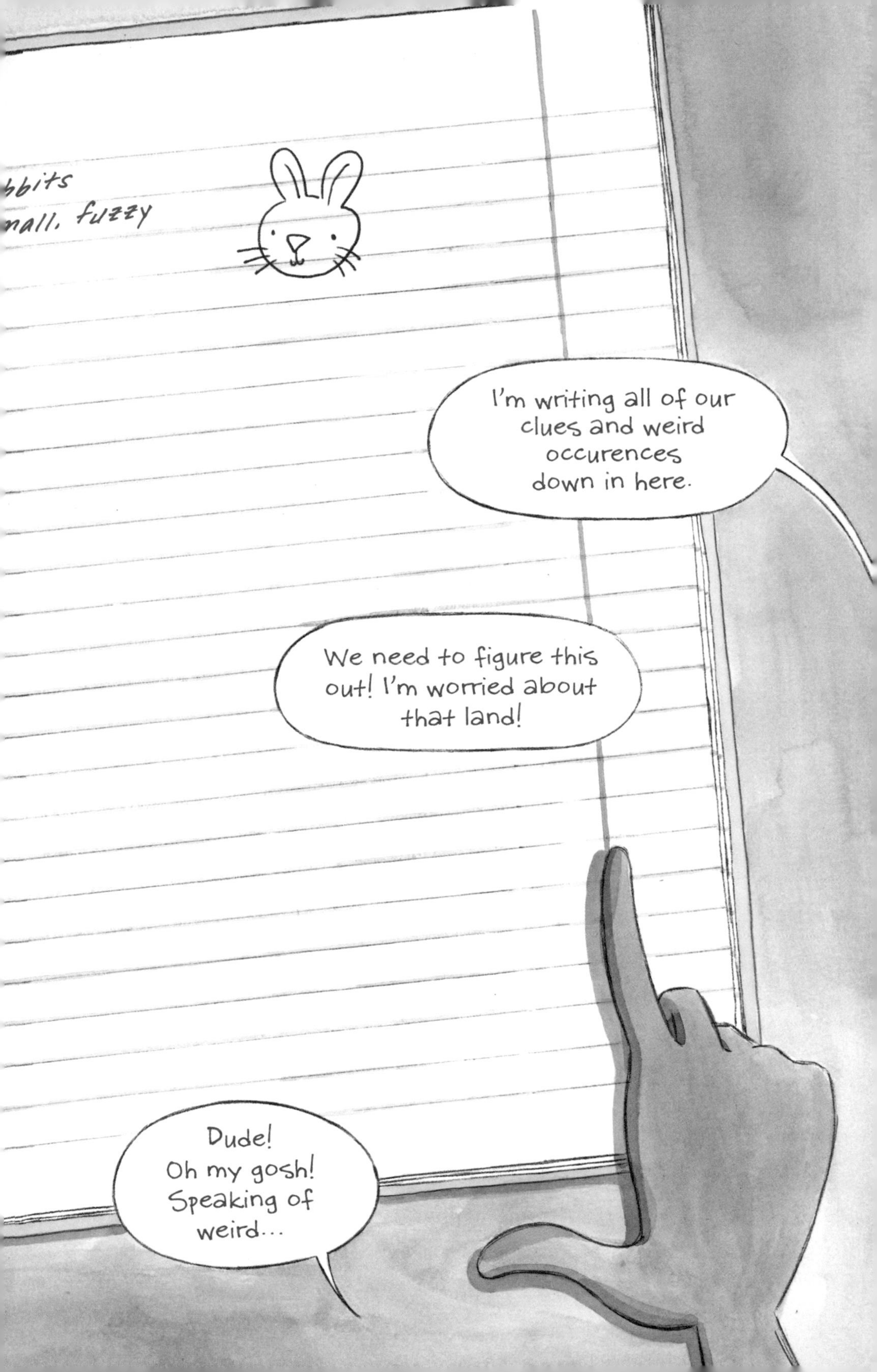
bbits
nall, fuzzy
I'm writing all of our clues and weird occurences down in here.
We need to figure this out! I'm worried about that land!
Dude! Oh my gosh! Speaking of weird...

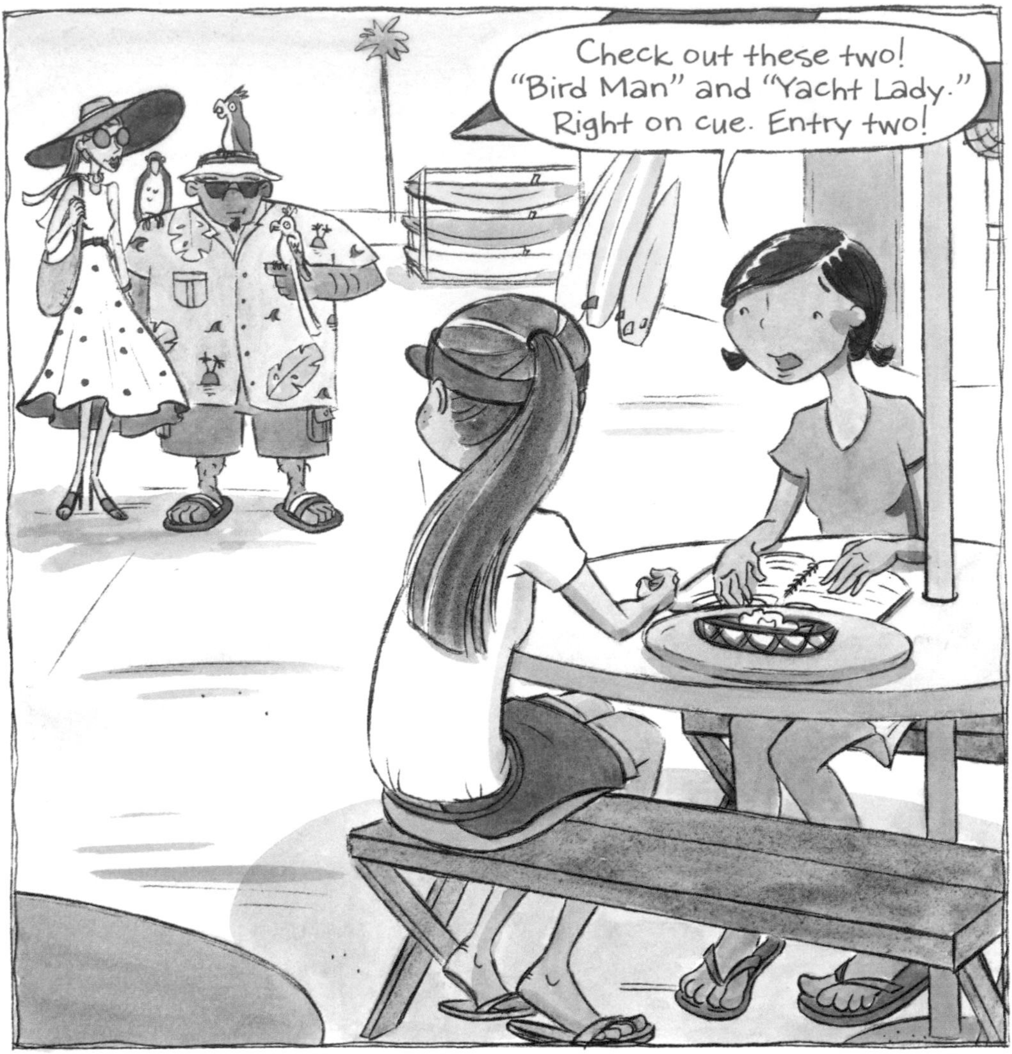
Check out these two!
"Bird Man" and "Yacht Lady."
Right on cue. Entry two!

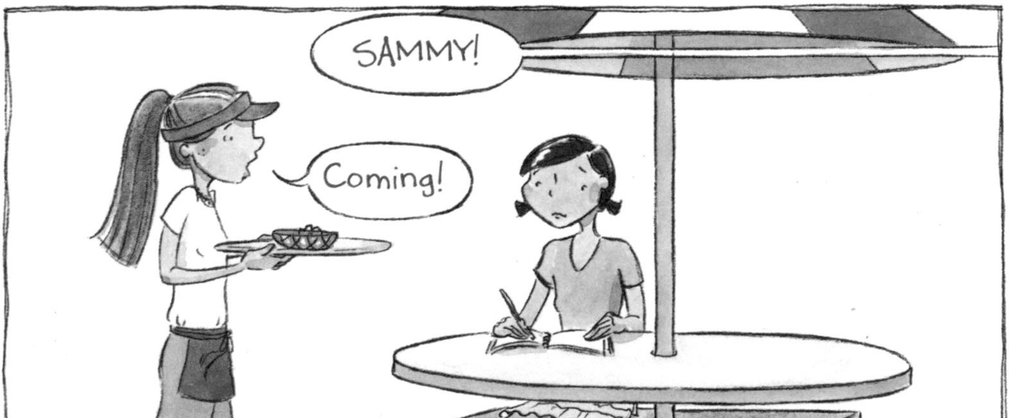
SAMMY!
Coming!

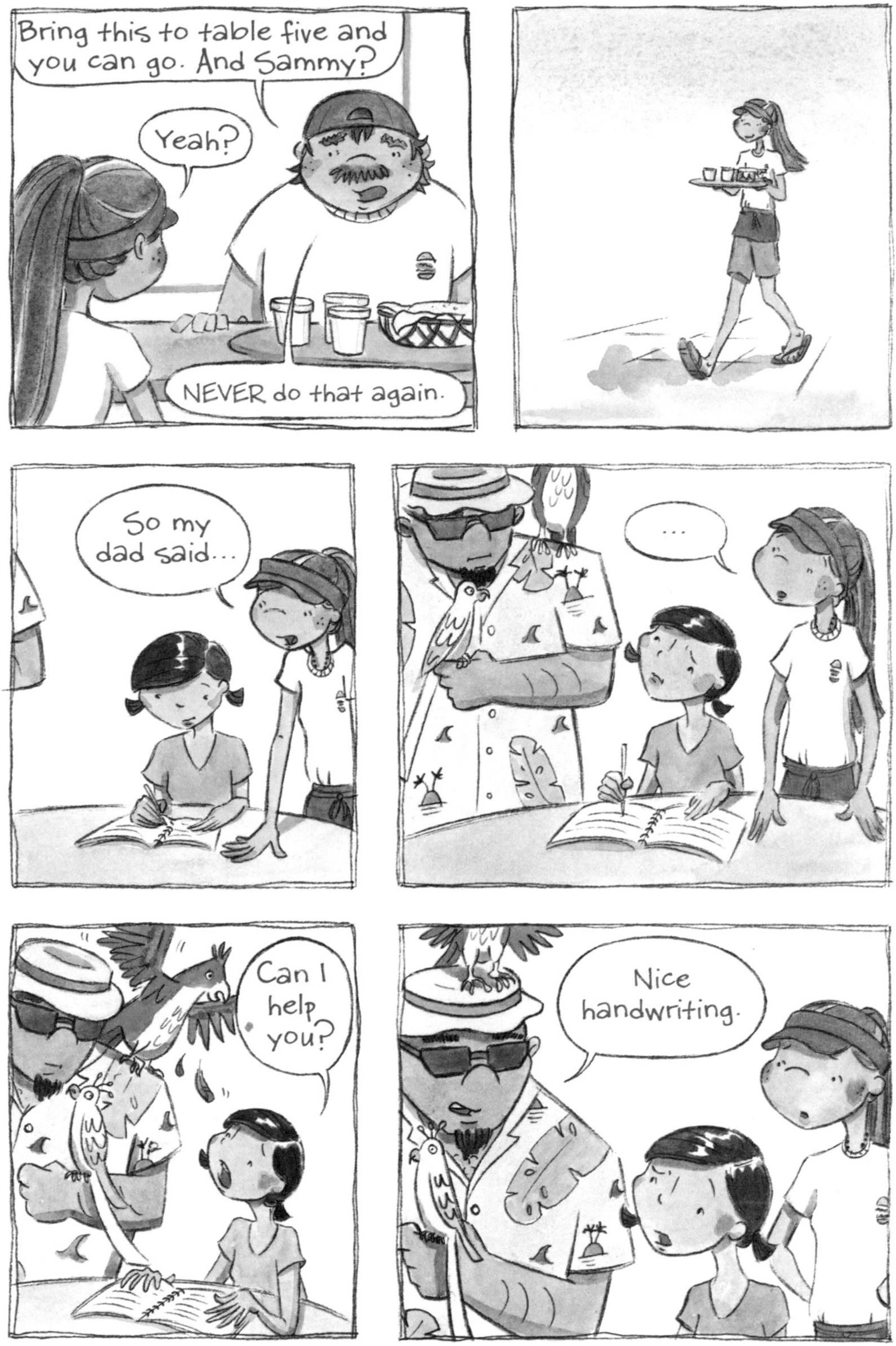
Bring this to table five and you can go. And Sammy?
Yeah?
NEVER do that again.
So my dad said...
...
Can I help you?
Nice handwriting.

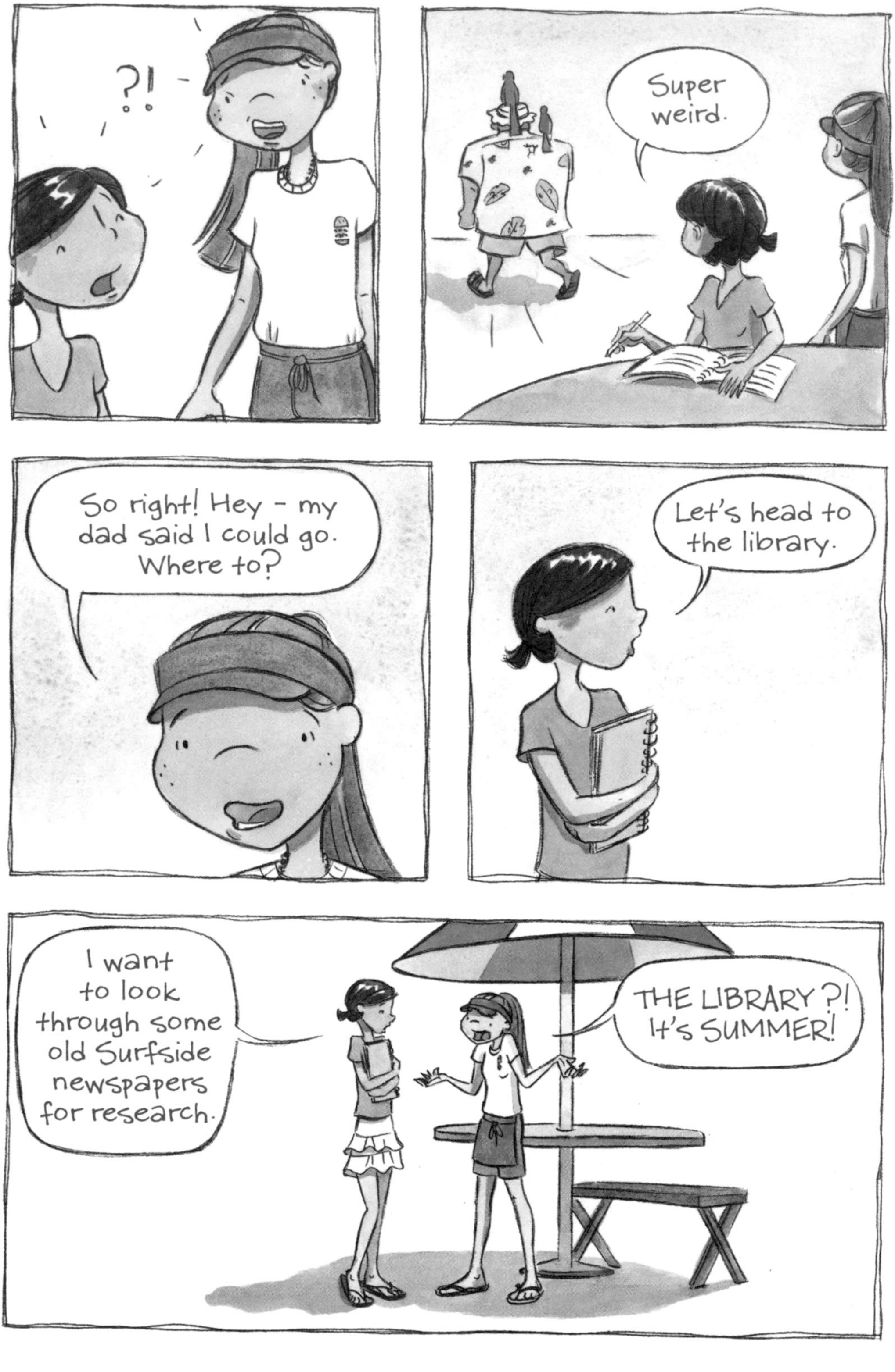
?!
Super weird.
So right! Hey - my dad said I could go. Where to?
Let's head to the library.
I want to look through some old Surfside newspapers for research.
THE LIBRARY?! It's SUMMER!

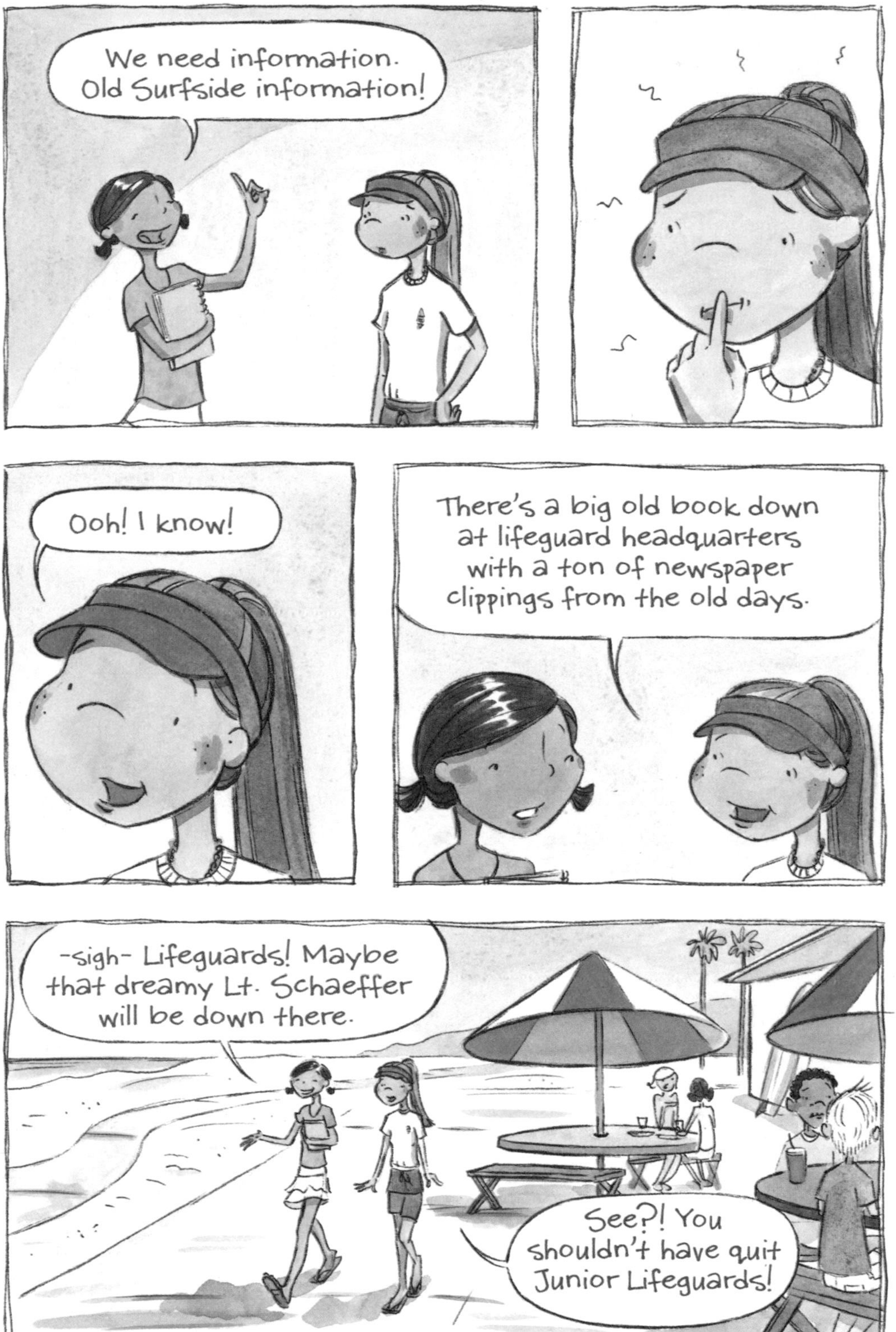
We need information. Old Surfside information!
Ooh! I know!
There's a big old book down at lifeguard headquarters with a ton of newspaper clippings from the old days.
-sigh- Lifeguards! Maybe that dreamy Lt. Schaeffer will be down there.
See?! You shouldn't have quit Junior Lifeguards!

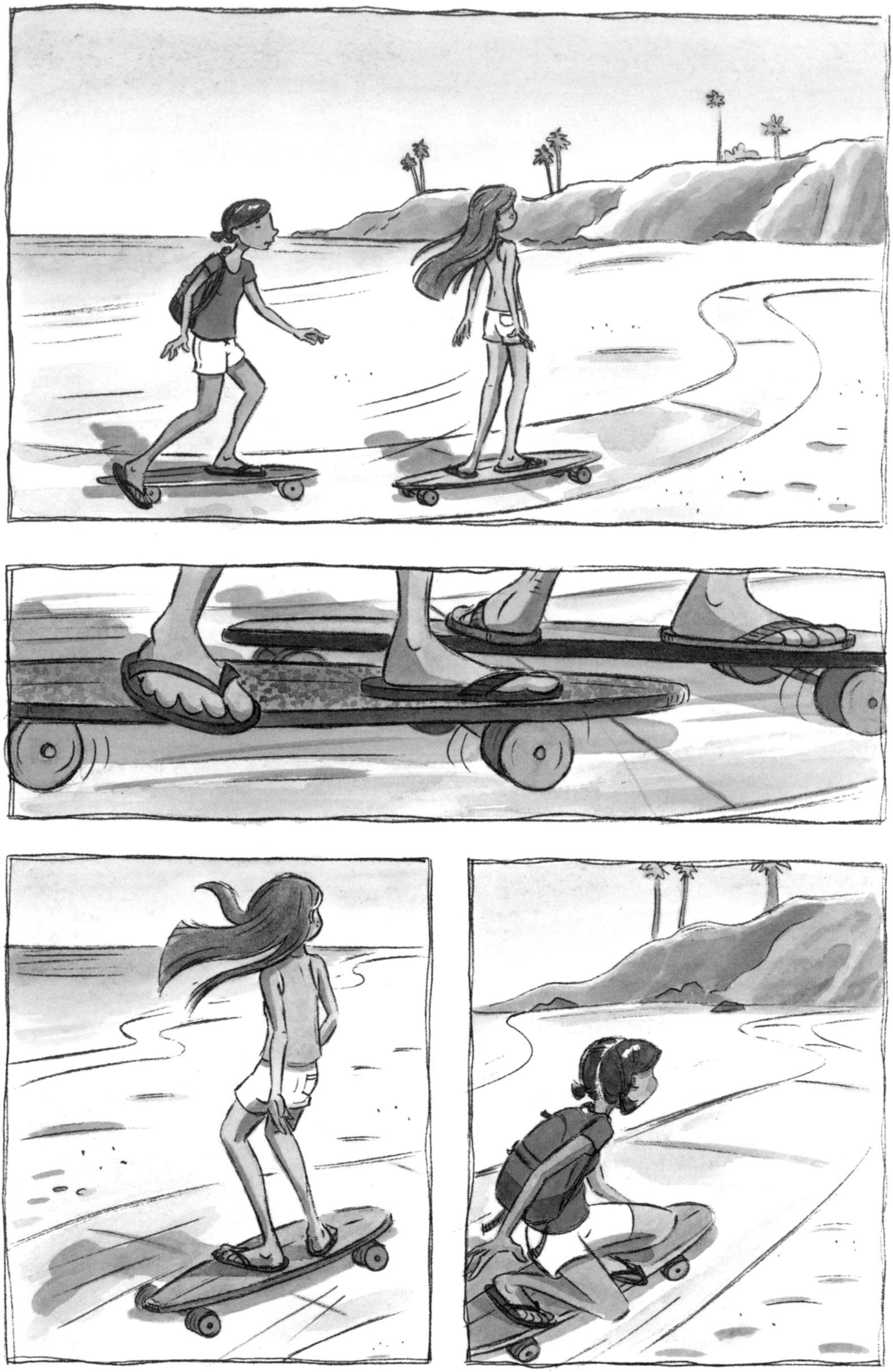

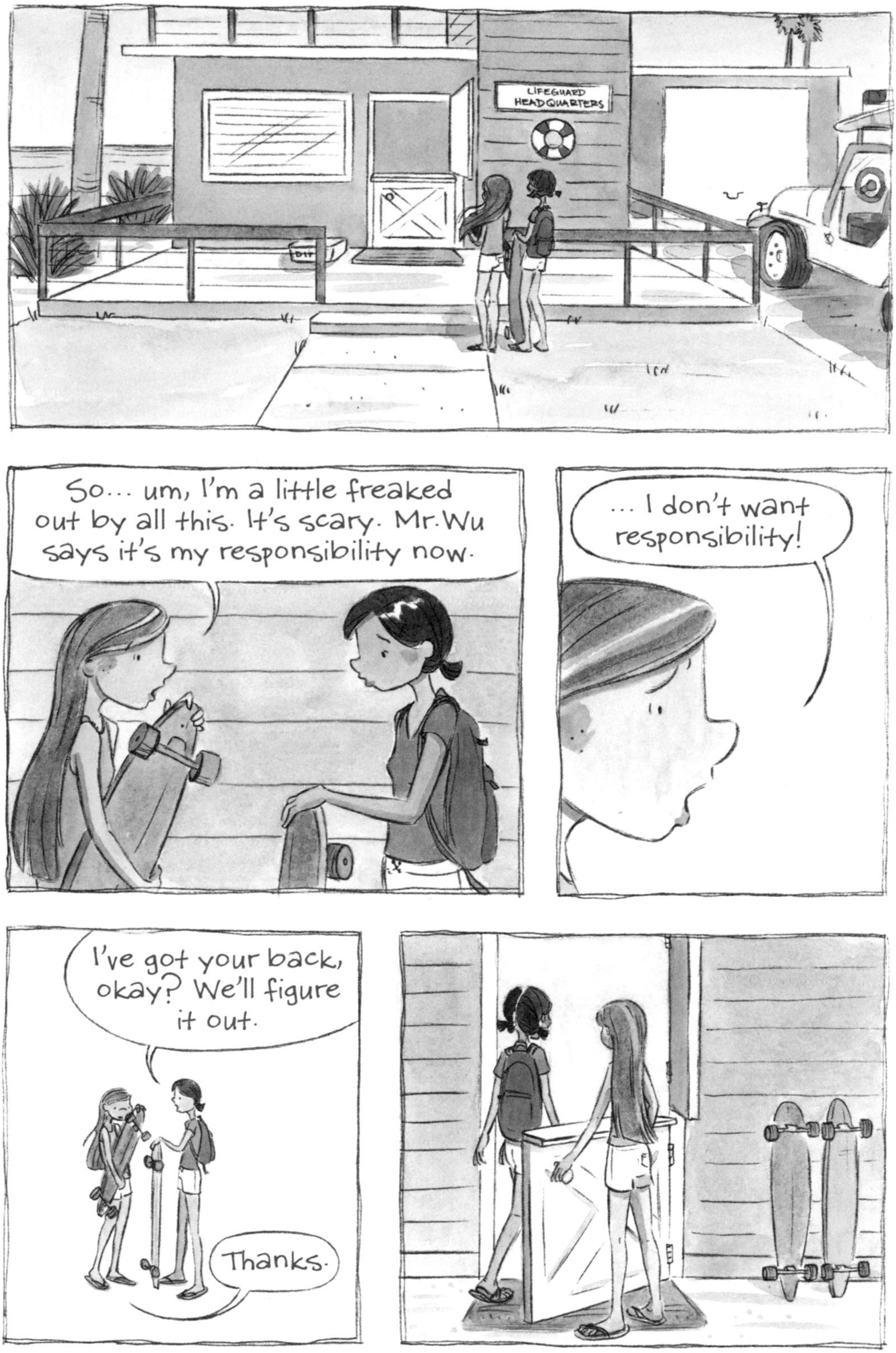
LIFEGUARD HEADQUARTERS
So... um, I'm a little freaked out by all this. It's scary. Mr. Wu says it's my responsibility now.
... I don't want responsibility!
I've got your back, okay? We'll figure it out.
Thanks.

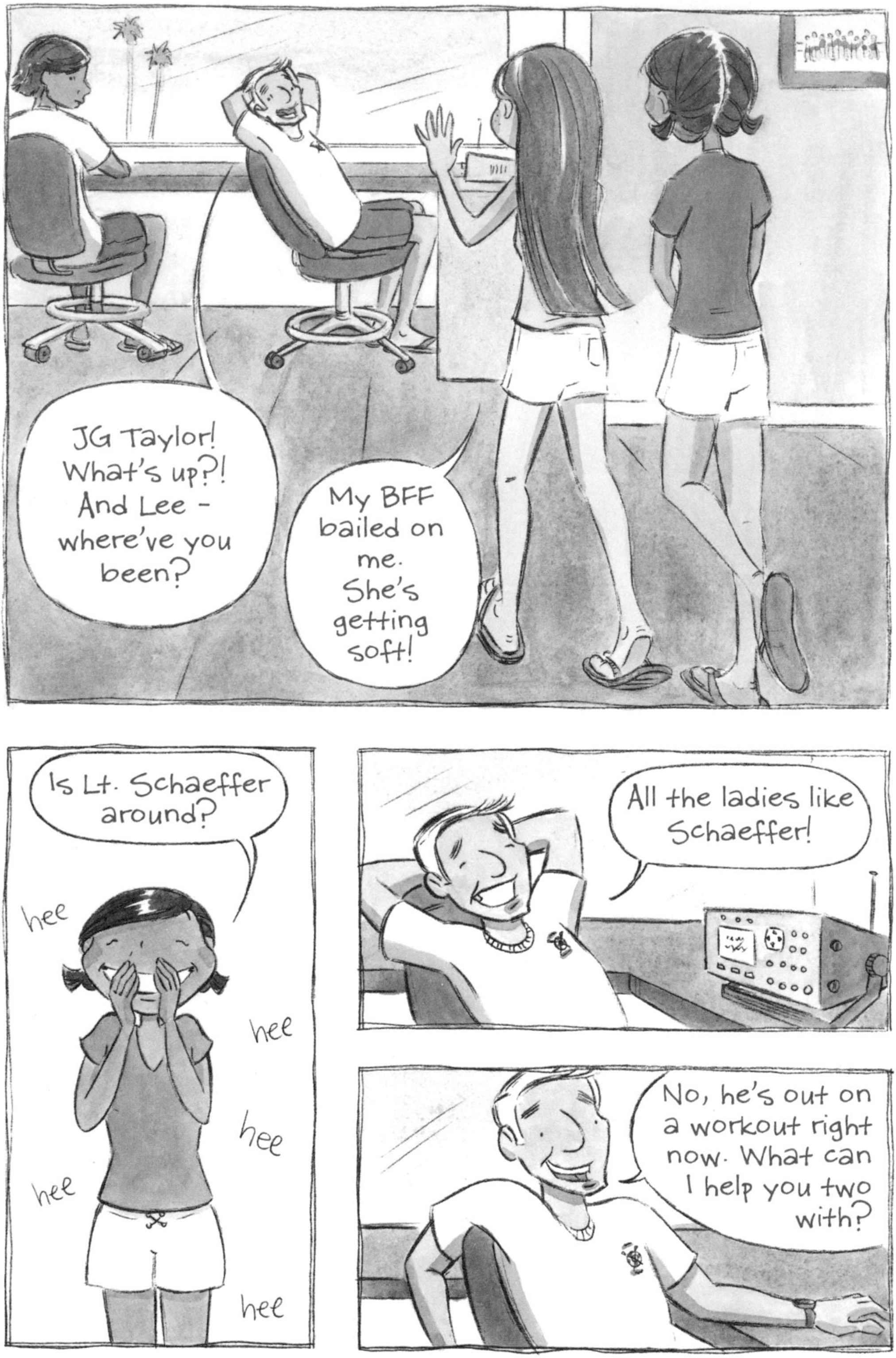
JG Taylor! What's up?! And Lee - where've you been?
My BFF bailed on me. She's getting soft!
Is Lt. Schaeffer around?
hee
hee
hee
hee
hee
All the ladies like Schaeffer!
No, he's out on a workout right now. What can I help you two with?

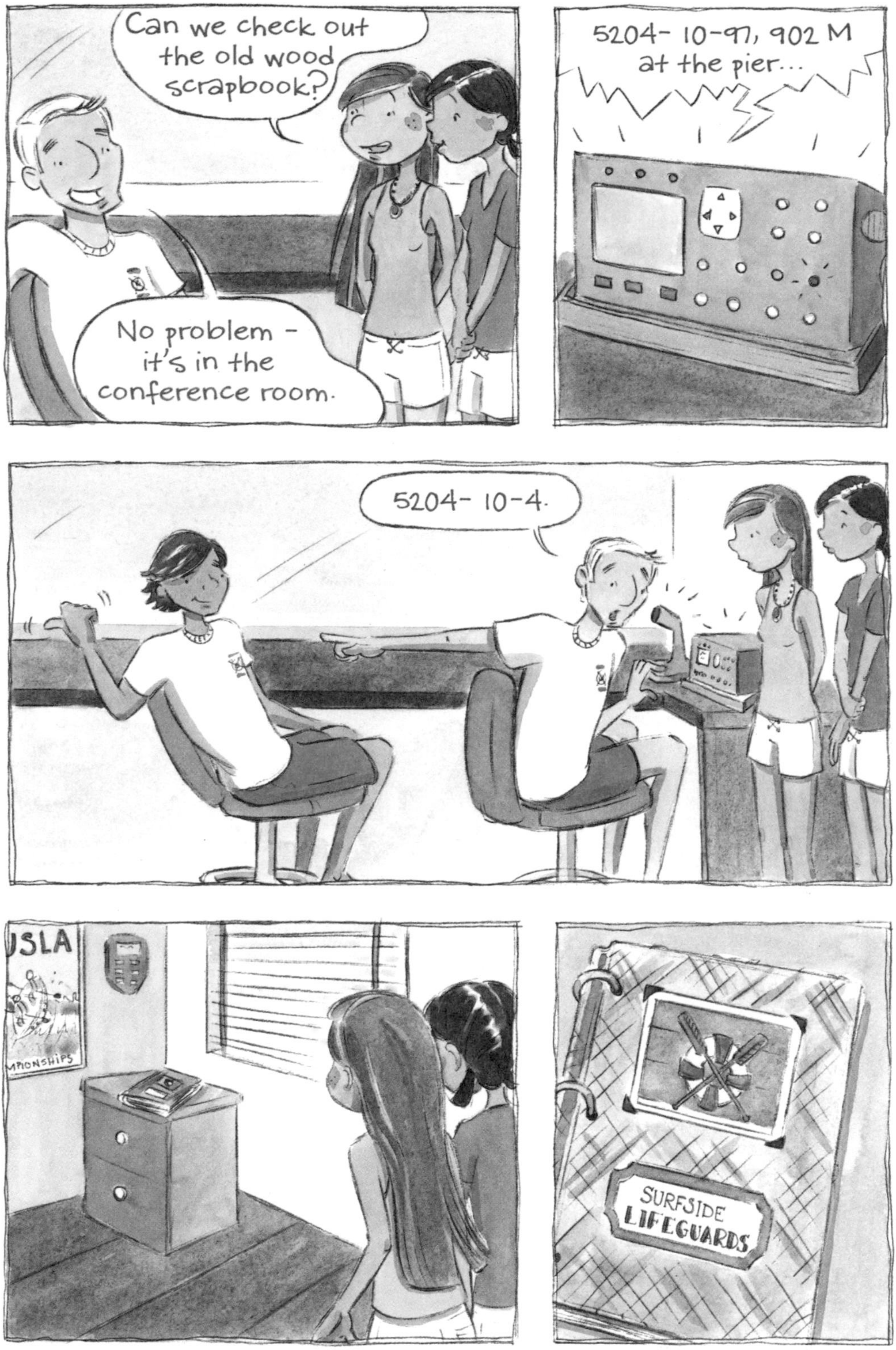
Can we check out the old wood scrapbook?
No problem - it's in the conference room.
5204- 10-97, 902 M at the pier...
5204- 10-4.
USLA
MPIONSHIPS
SURFSIDE LIFEGUARDS

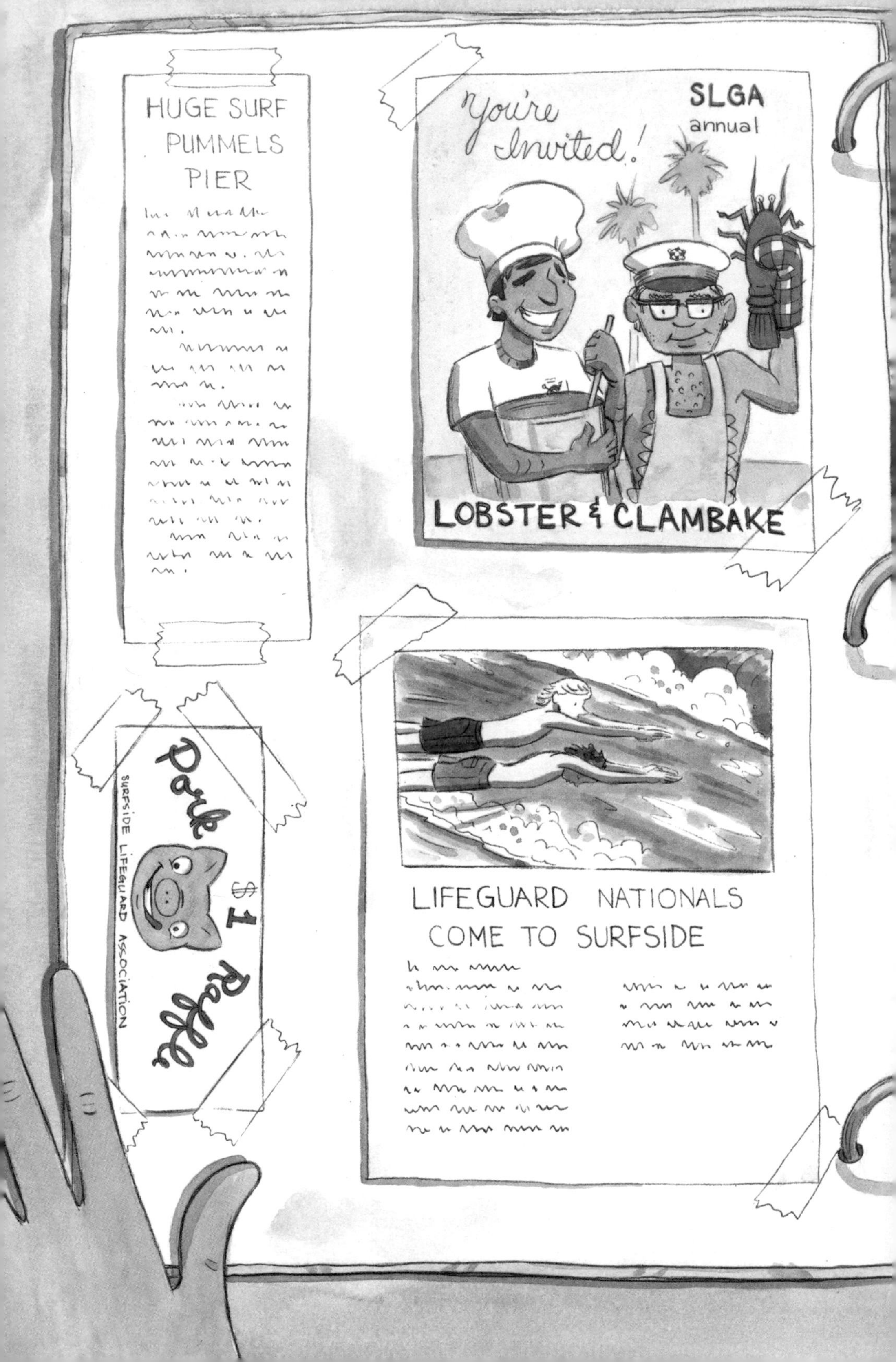
HUGE SURF PUMMELS PIER
You're Invited!
SLGA annual
LOBSTER & CLAMBAKE
Pork Raffle
$1
SURFSIDE LIFEGUARD ASSOCIATION
LIFEGUARD NATIONALS COME TO SURFSIDE

1ST PLACE

MEN'S DORY

USLA · 1951

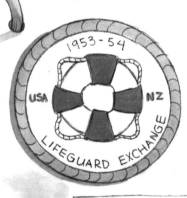

1953-54

USA · NZ

LIFEGUARD EXCHANGE

1972 SUMMER INTRODUCES FIRST FEMALE LIFEGUARD

Lifeguard Chief Retires

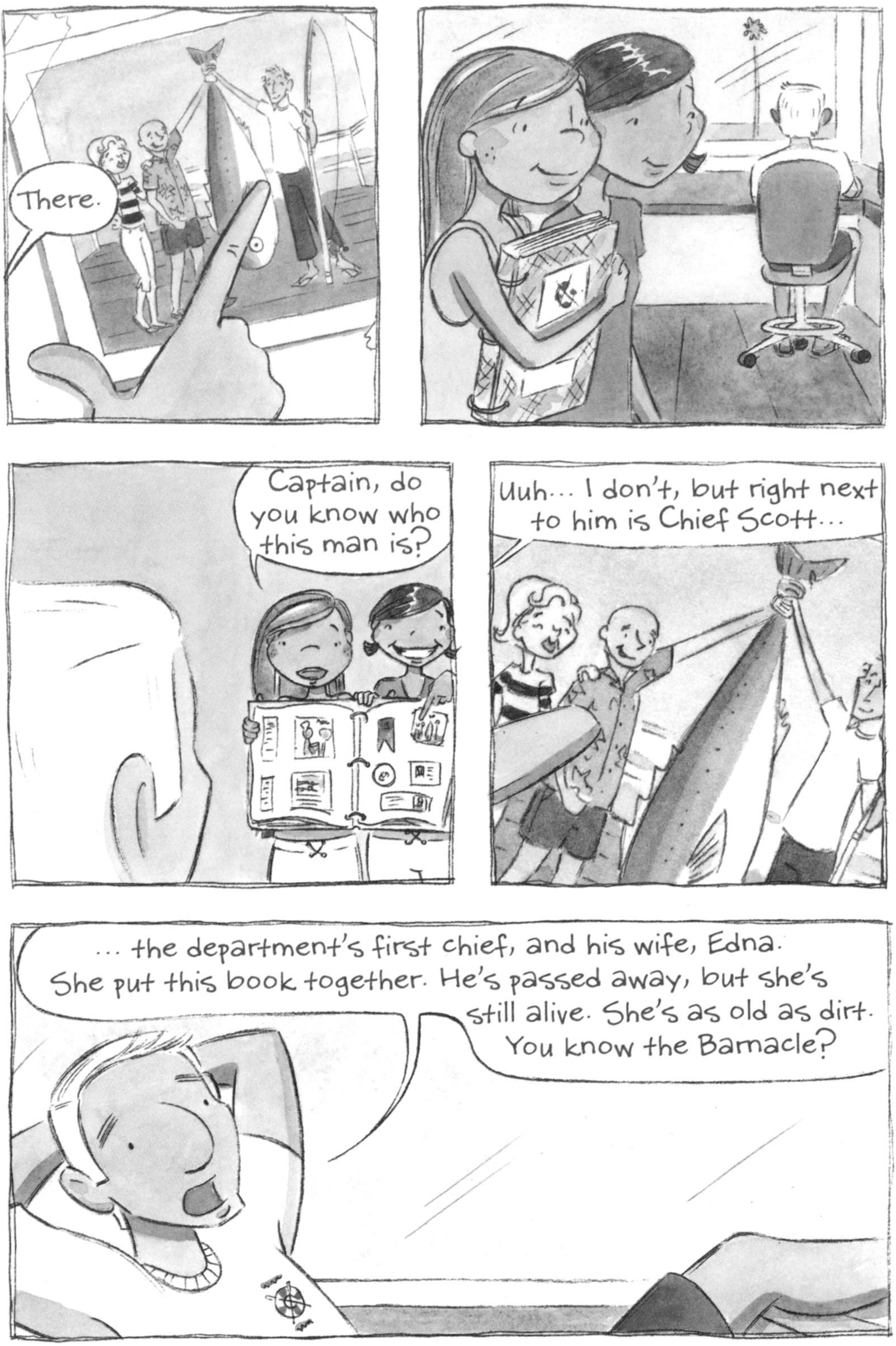
There.
Captain, do you know who this man is?
Uuh... I don't, but right next to him is Chief Scott...
... the department's first chief, and his wife, Edna. She put this book together. He's passed away, but she's still alive. She's as old as dirt. You know the Barnacle?

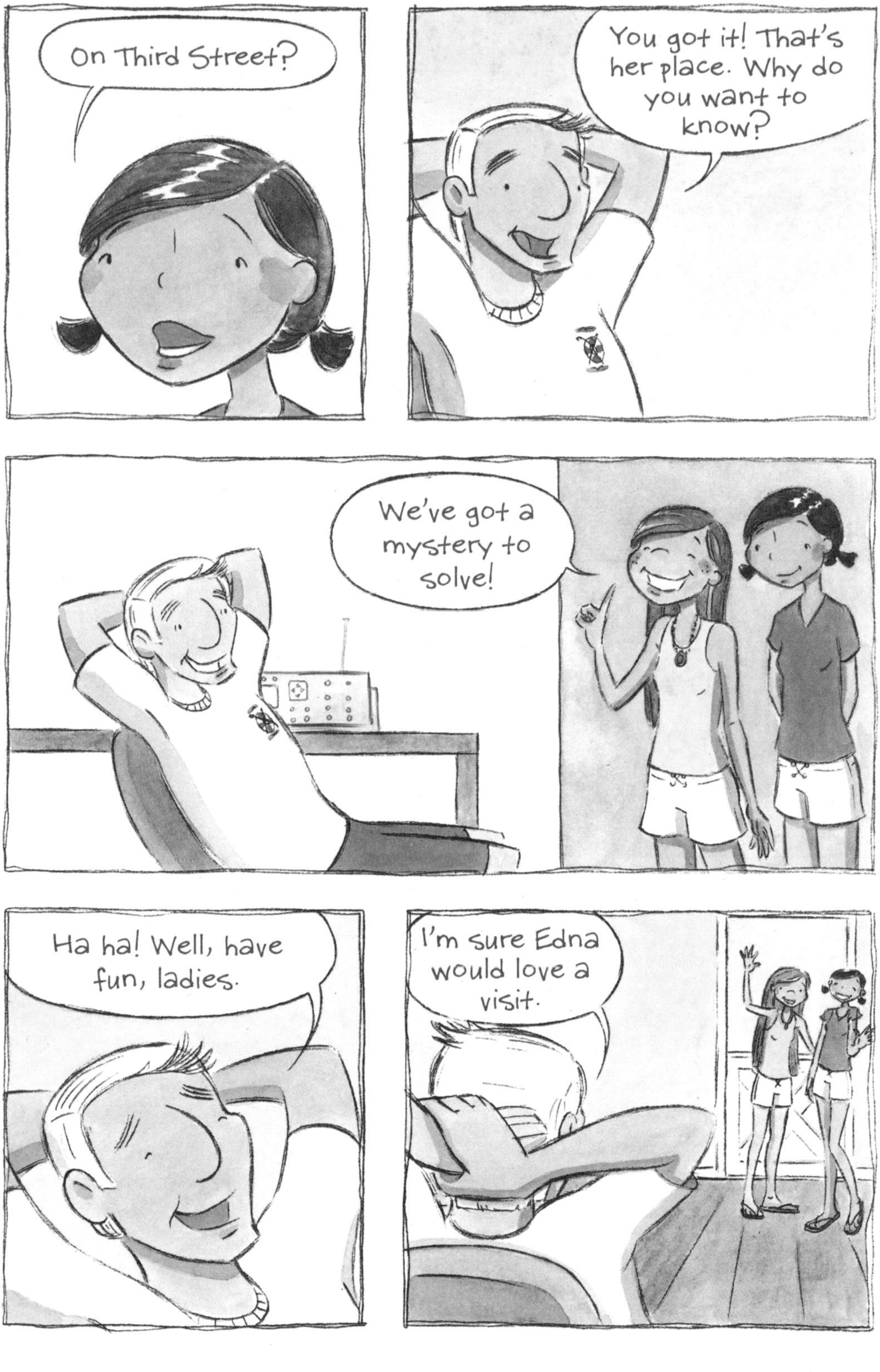
On Third Street?
You got it! That's her place. Why do you want to know?
We've got a mystery to solve!
Ha ha! Well, have fun, ladies.
I'm sure Edna would love a visit.

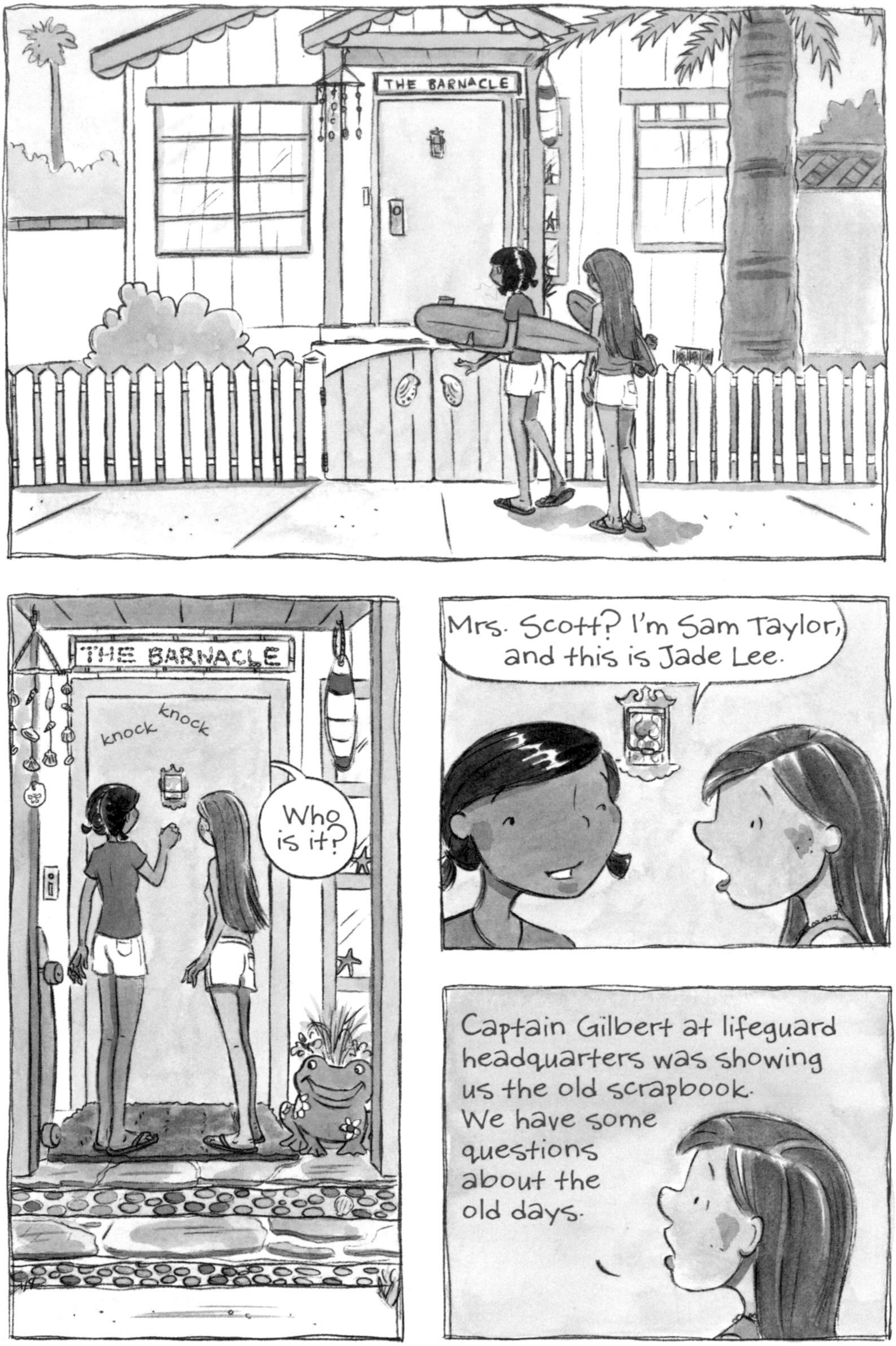
THE BARNACLE
THE BARNACLE
knock knock
Who is it?
Mrs. Scott? I'm Sam Taylor, and this is Jade Lee.
Captain Gilbert at lifeguard headquarters was showing us the old scrapbook. We have some questions about the old days.

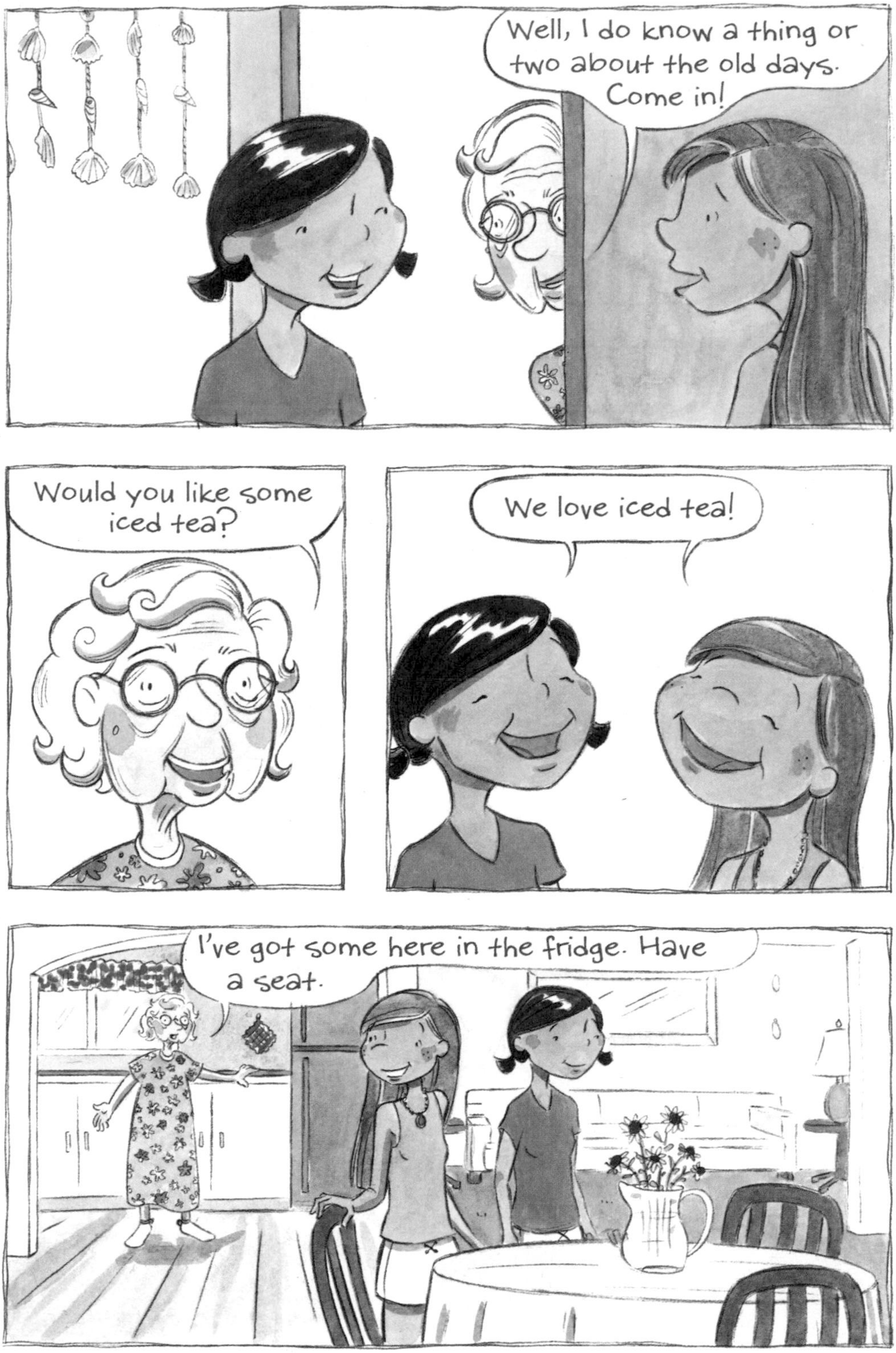
Well, I do know a thing or two about the old days. Come in!
Would you like some iced tea?
We love iced tea!
I've got some here in the fridge. Have a seat.

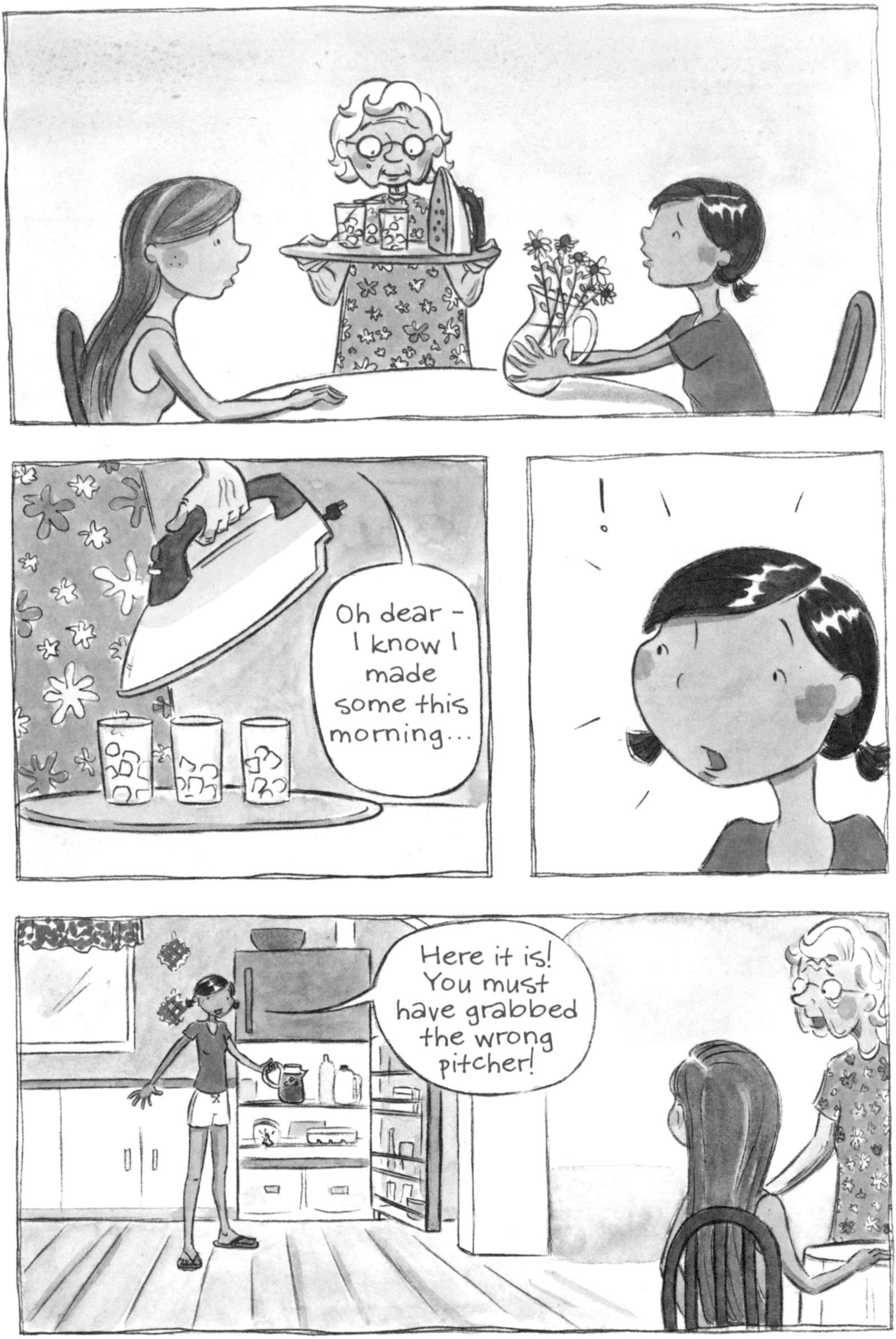
Oh dear - I know I made some this morning...
!
Here it is! You must have grabbed the wrong pitcher!

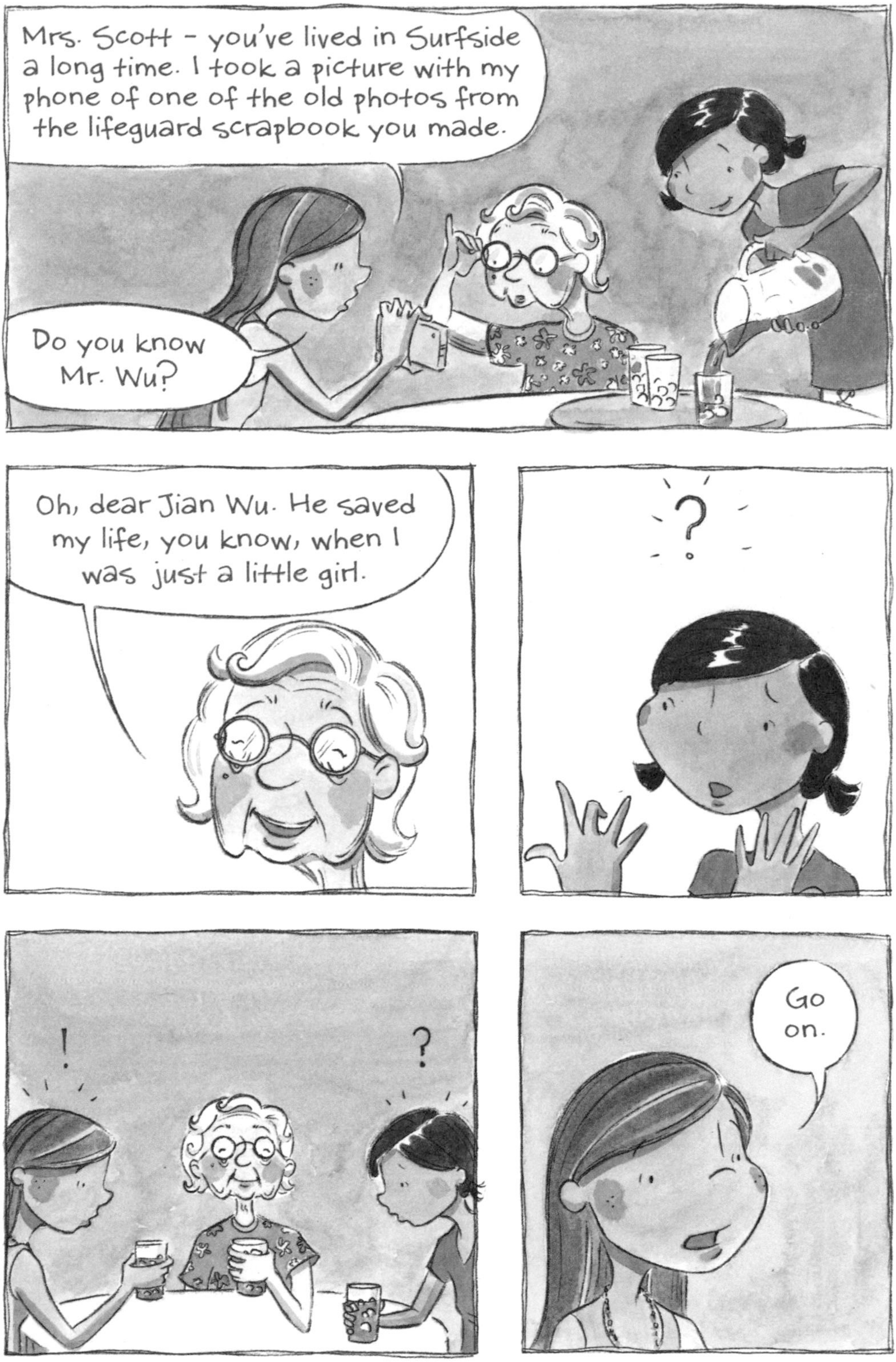
Mrs. Scott - you've lived in Surfside a long time. I took a picture with my phone of one of the old photos from the lifeguard scrapbook you made.
Do you know Mr. Wu?
Oh, dear Jian Wu. He saved my life, you know, when I was just a little girl.
?
!
?
Go on.

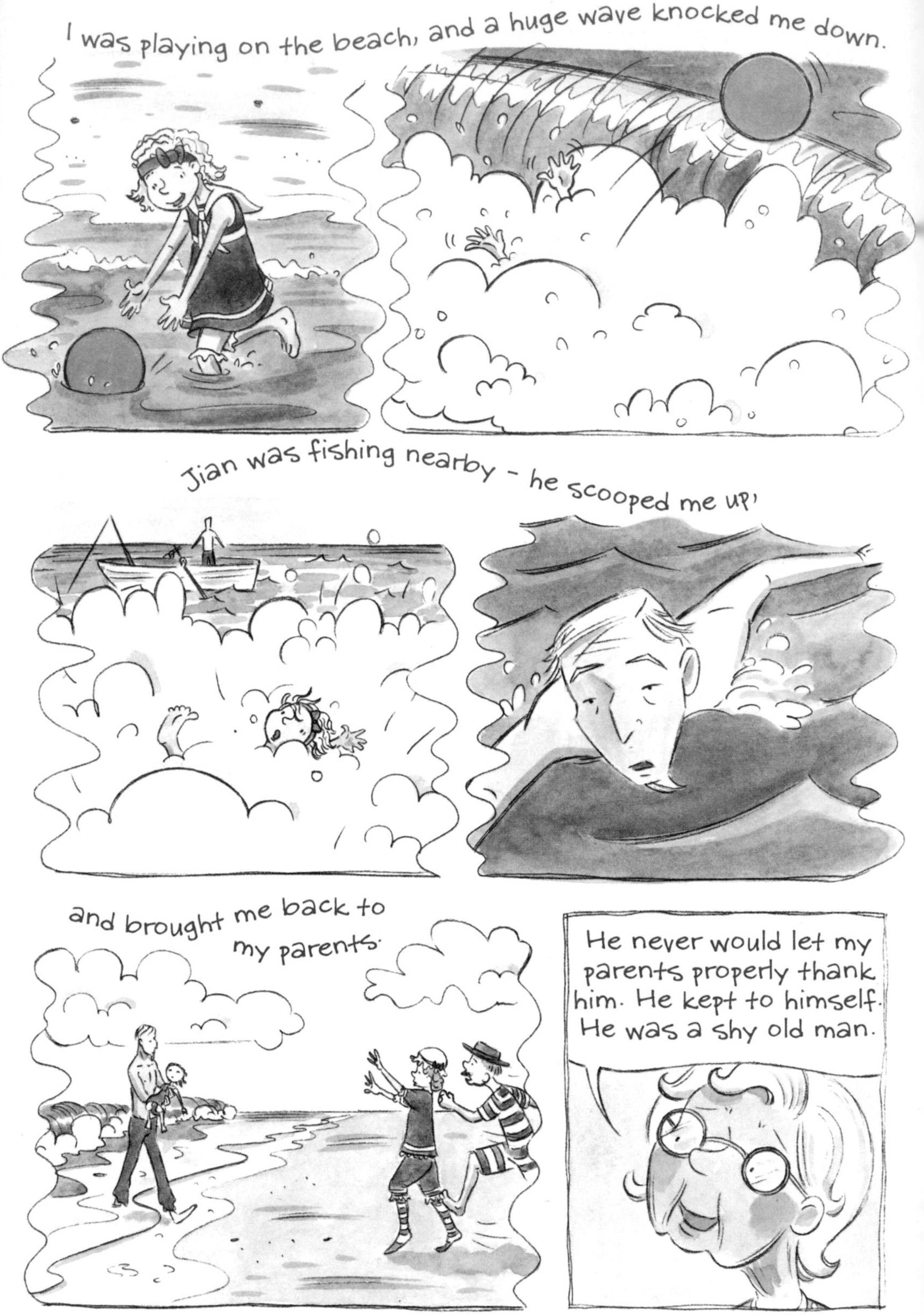
I was playing on the beach, and a huge wave knocked me down.
Jian was fishing nearby - he scooped me up,
and brought me back to my parents.
He never would let my parents properly thank him. He kept to himself. He was a shy old man.

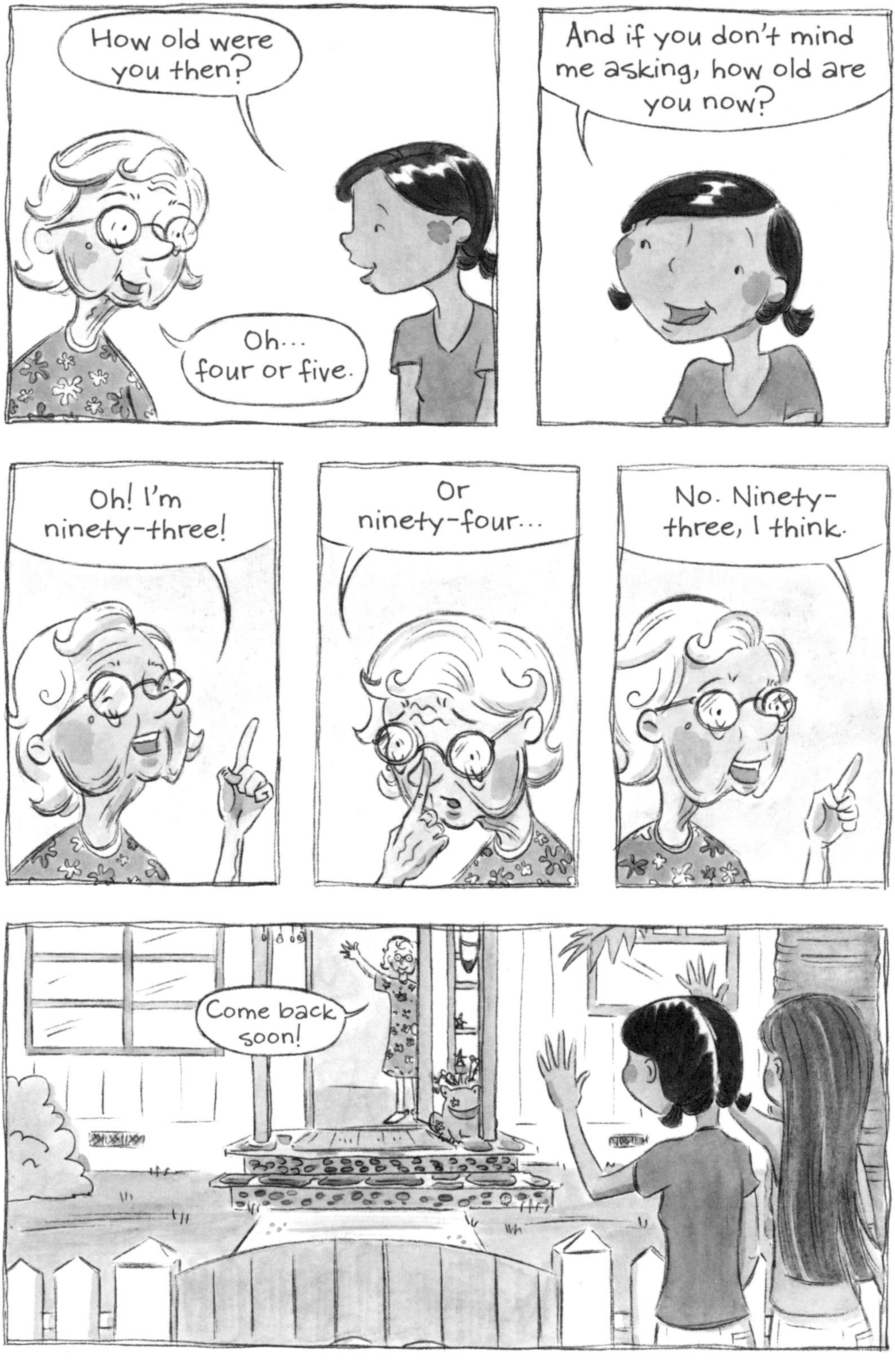
How old were you then?
Oh... four or five.
And if you don't mind me asking, how old are you now?
Oh! I'm ninety-three!
Or ninety-four...
No. Ninety-three, I think.
Come back soon!

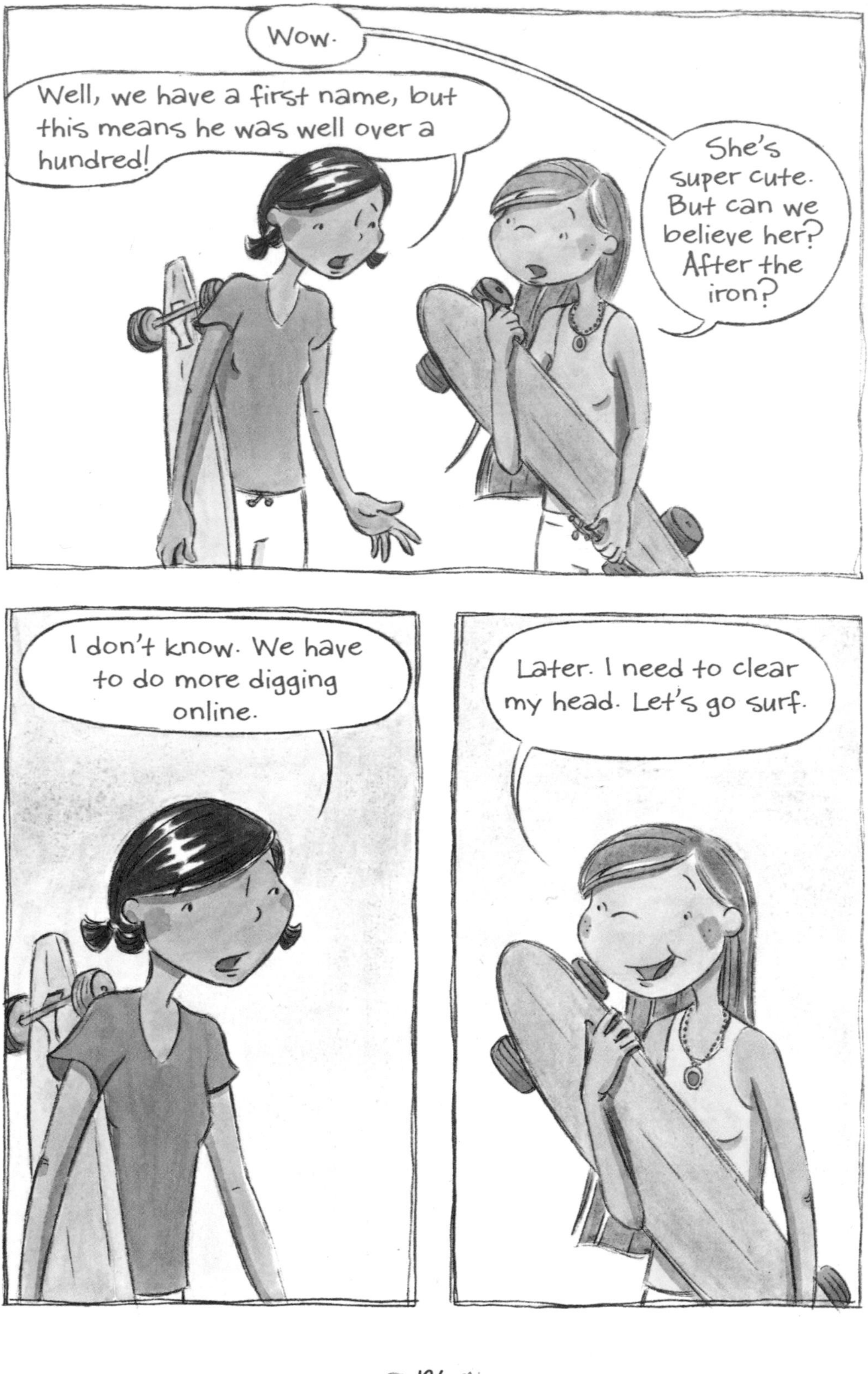
Wow.
Well, we have a first name, but this means he was well over a hundred!
She's super cute. But can we believe her? After the iron?
I don't know. We have to do more digging online.
Later. I need to clear my head. Let's go surf.

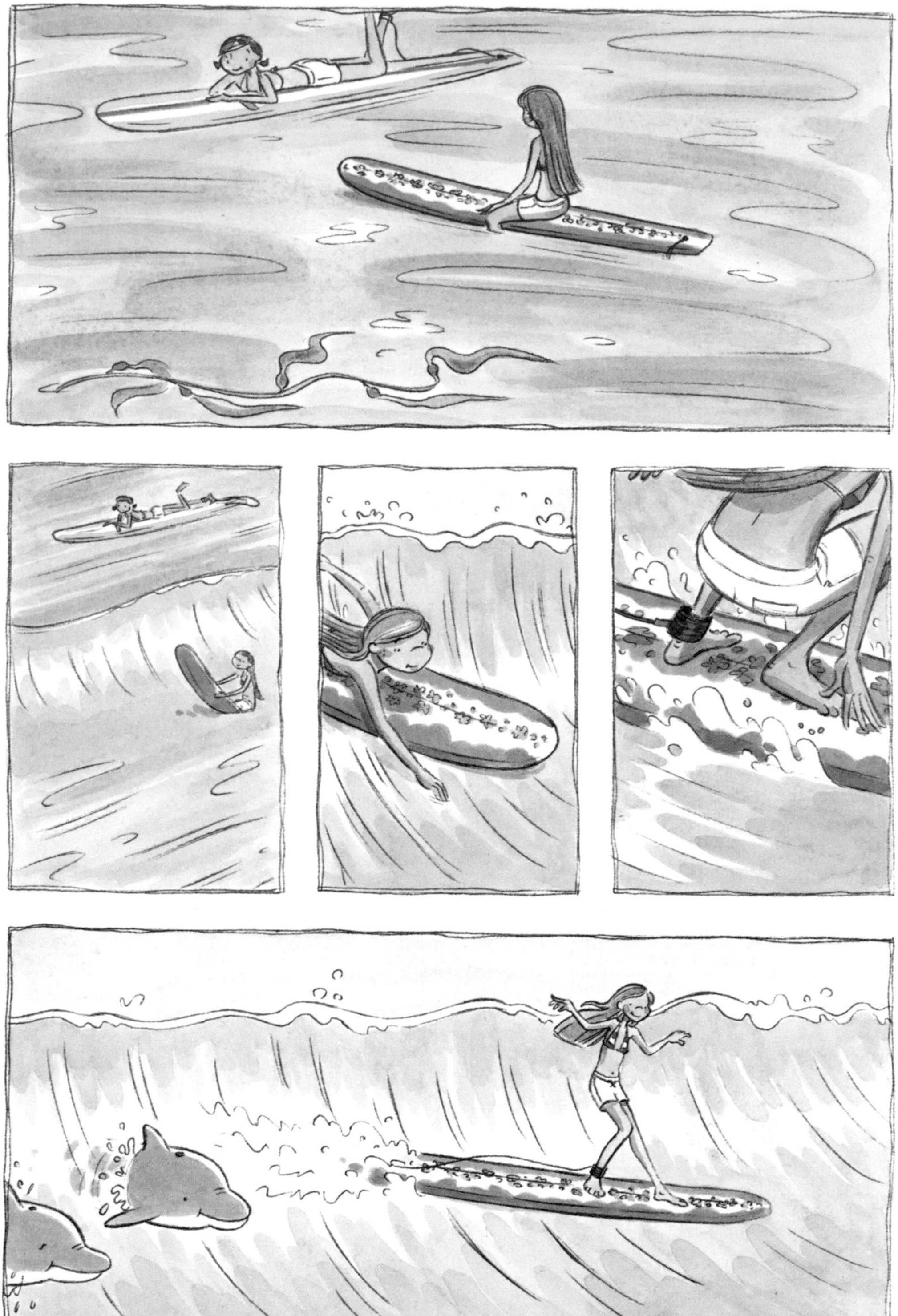

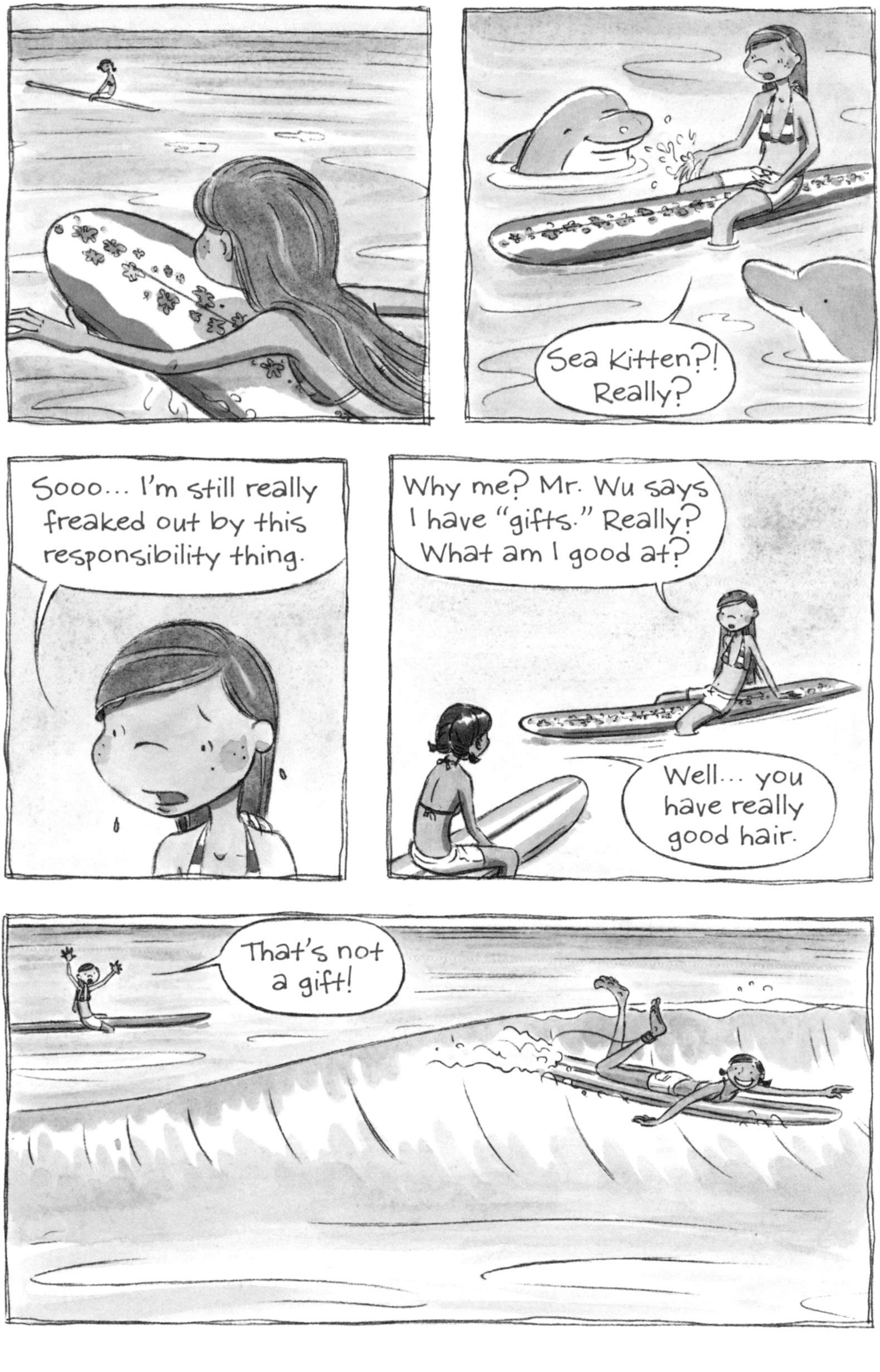

Sea Kitten?! Really?
Sooo... I'm still really freaked out by this responsibility thing.
Why me? Mr. Wu says I have "gifts." Really? What am I good at?
Well... you have really good hair.
That's not a gift!

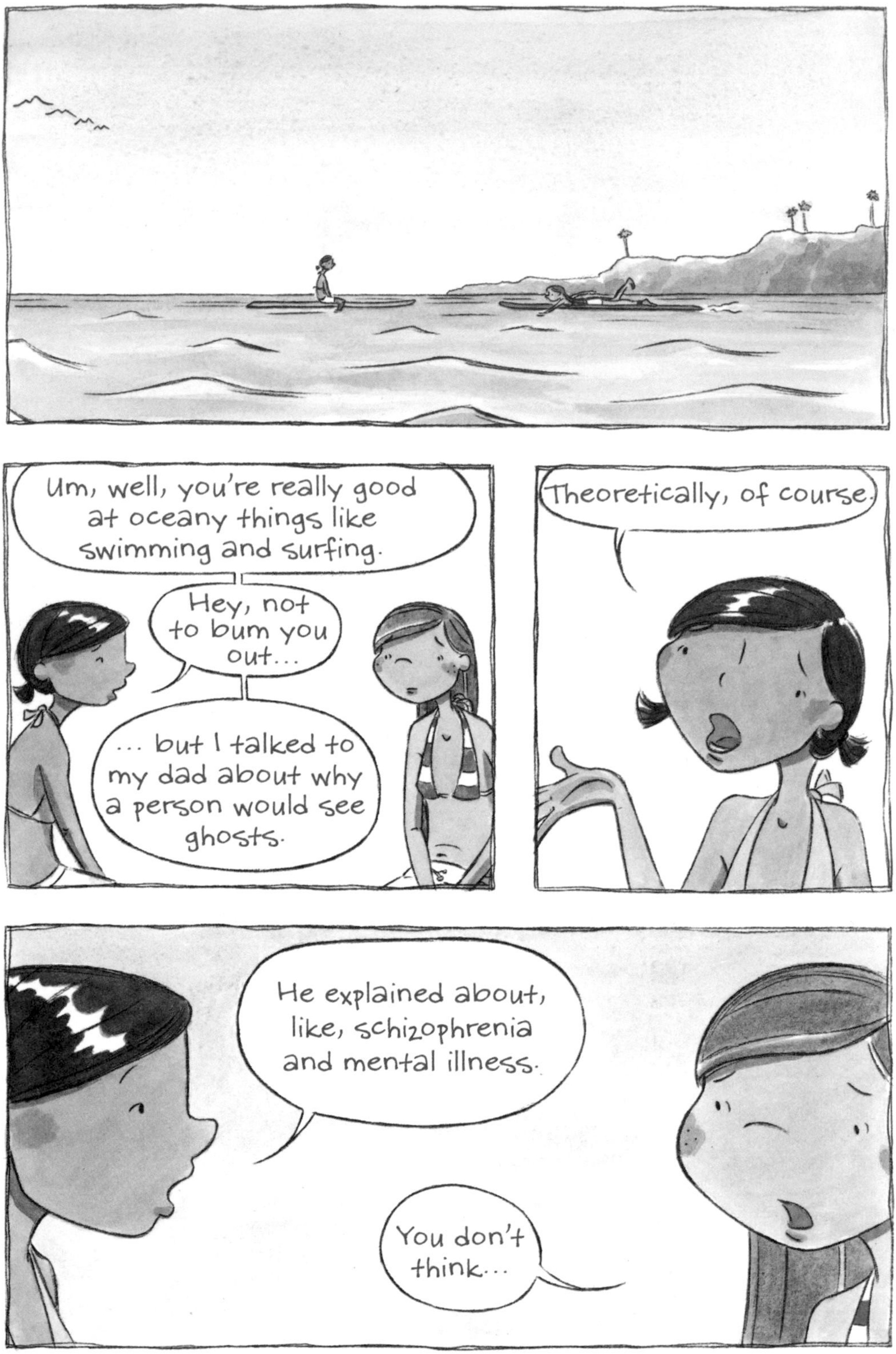

Um, well, you're really good at oceany things like swimming and surfing.
Hey, not to bum you out...
... but I talked to my dad about why a person would see ghosts.
Theoretically, of course.
He explained about, like, schizophrenia and mental illness.
You don't think...

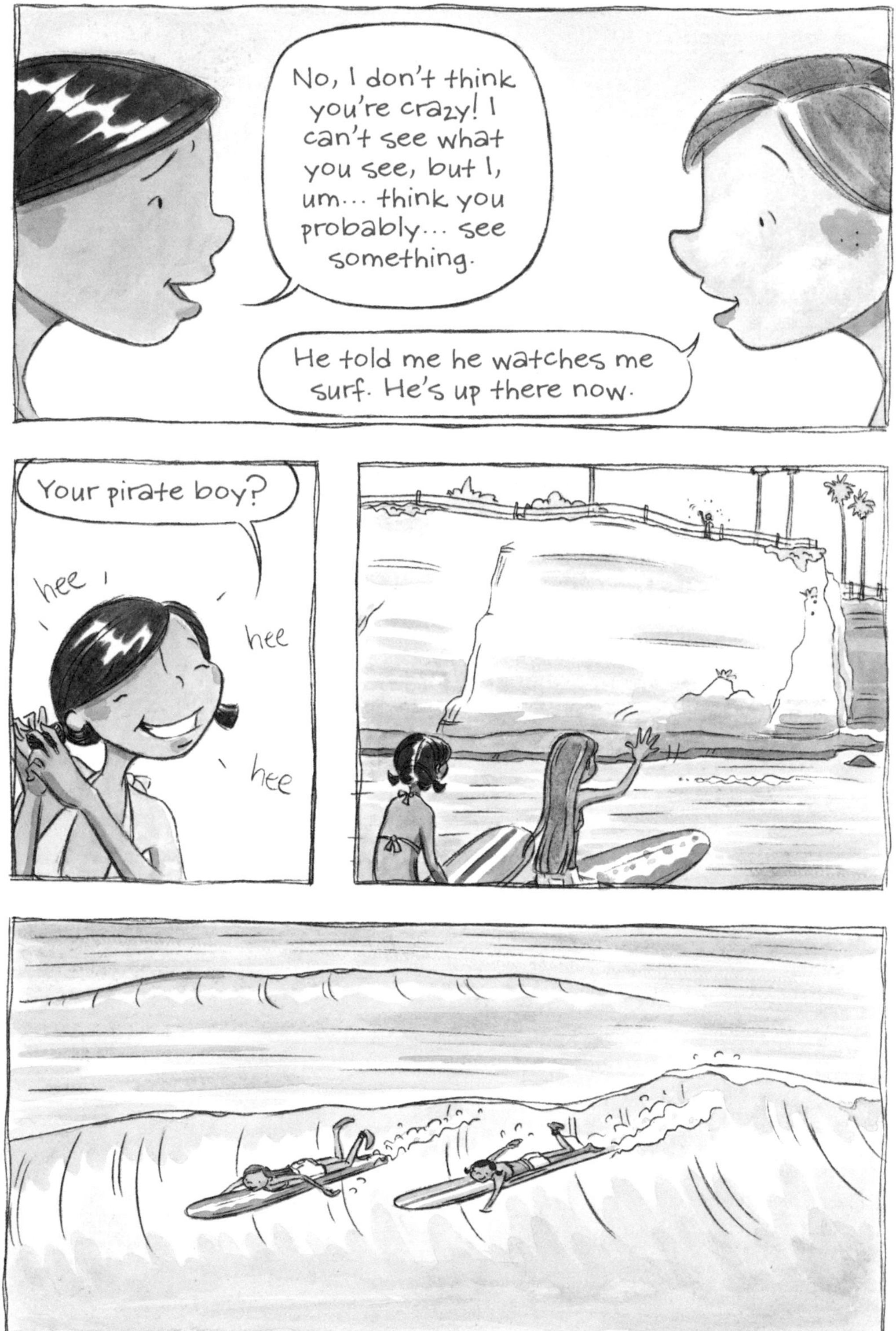
No, I don't think you're crazy! I can't see what you see, but I, um... think you probably... see something.
He told me he watches me surf. He's up there now.
Your pirate boy?
hee
hee
hee

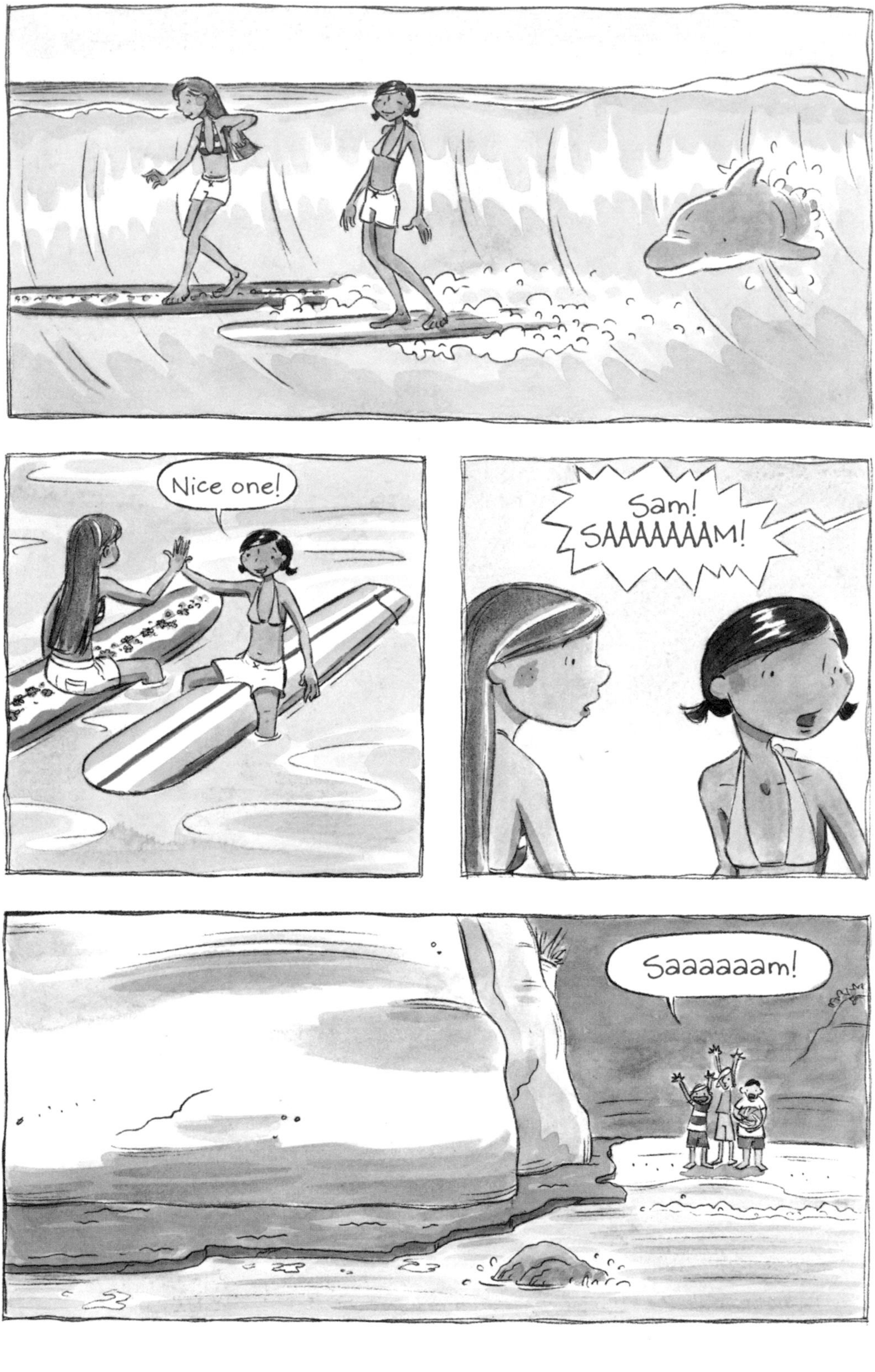
Nice one!
Sam! SAAAAAAAM!
Saaaaaam!

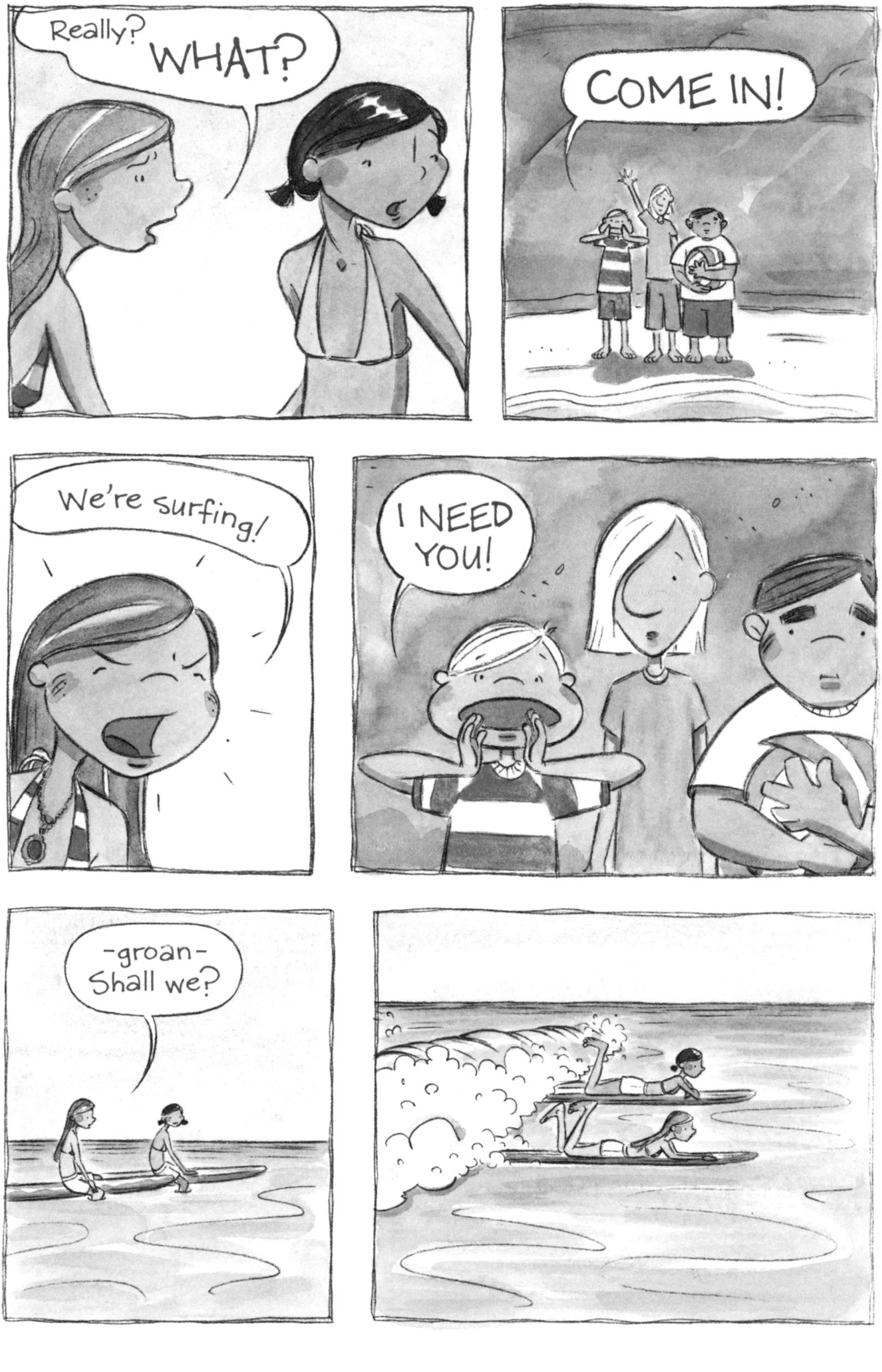
Really? WHAT?
COME IN!
We're surfing!
I NEED YOU!
-groan-
Shall we?

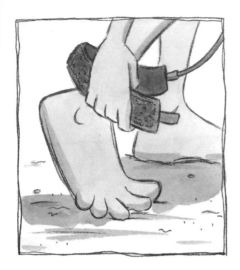

Peety! You're not supposed to leave Main Beach without Mom or Dad!

But look!

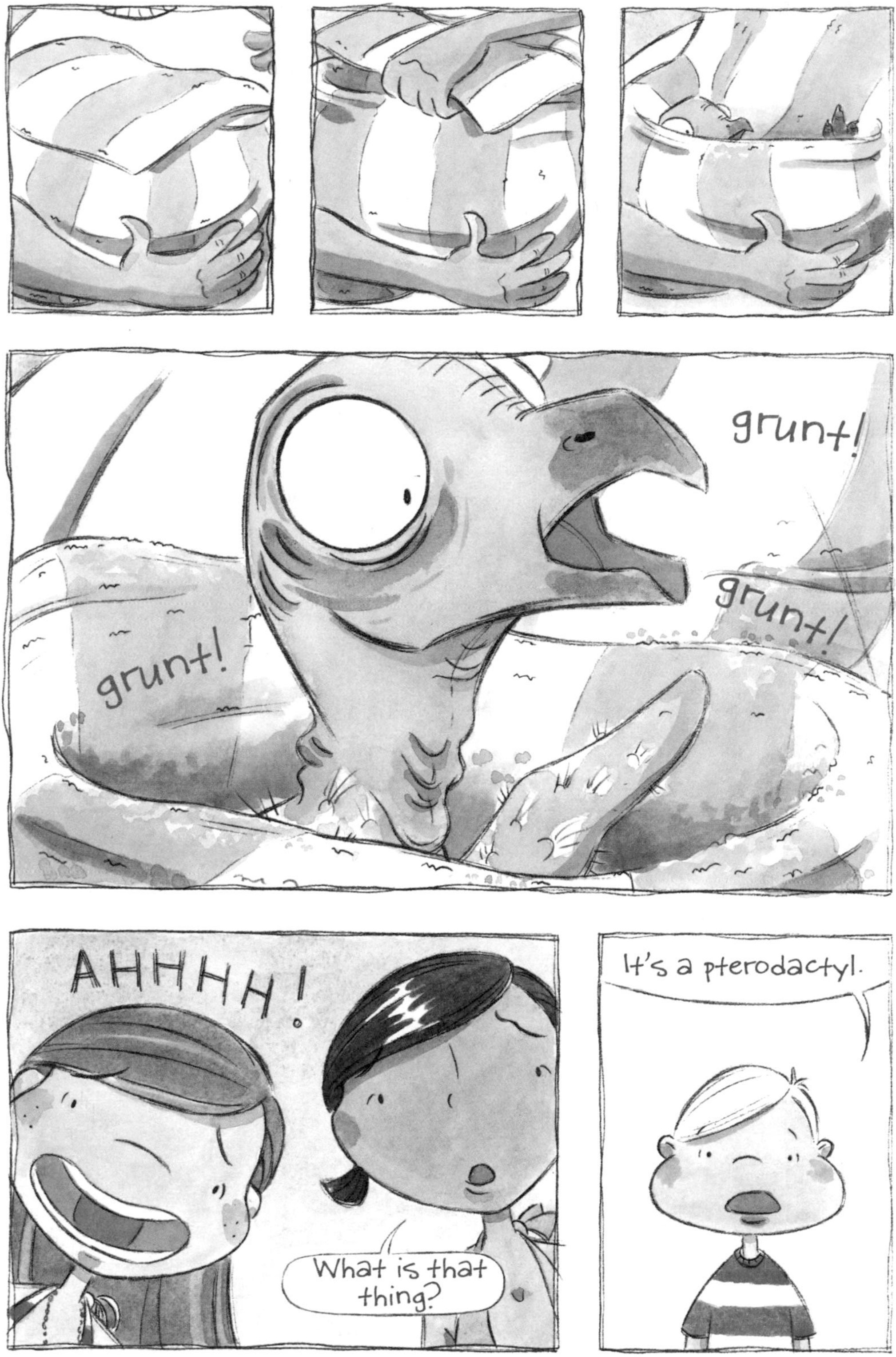

grunt!
grunt!
grunt!
AHHHH!
What is that thing?
It's a pterodactyl.

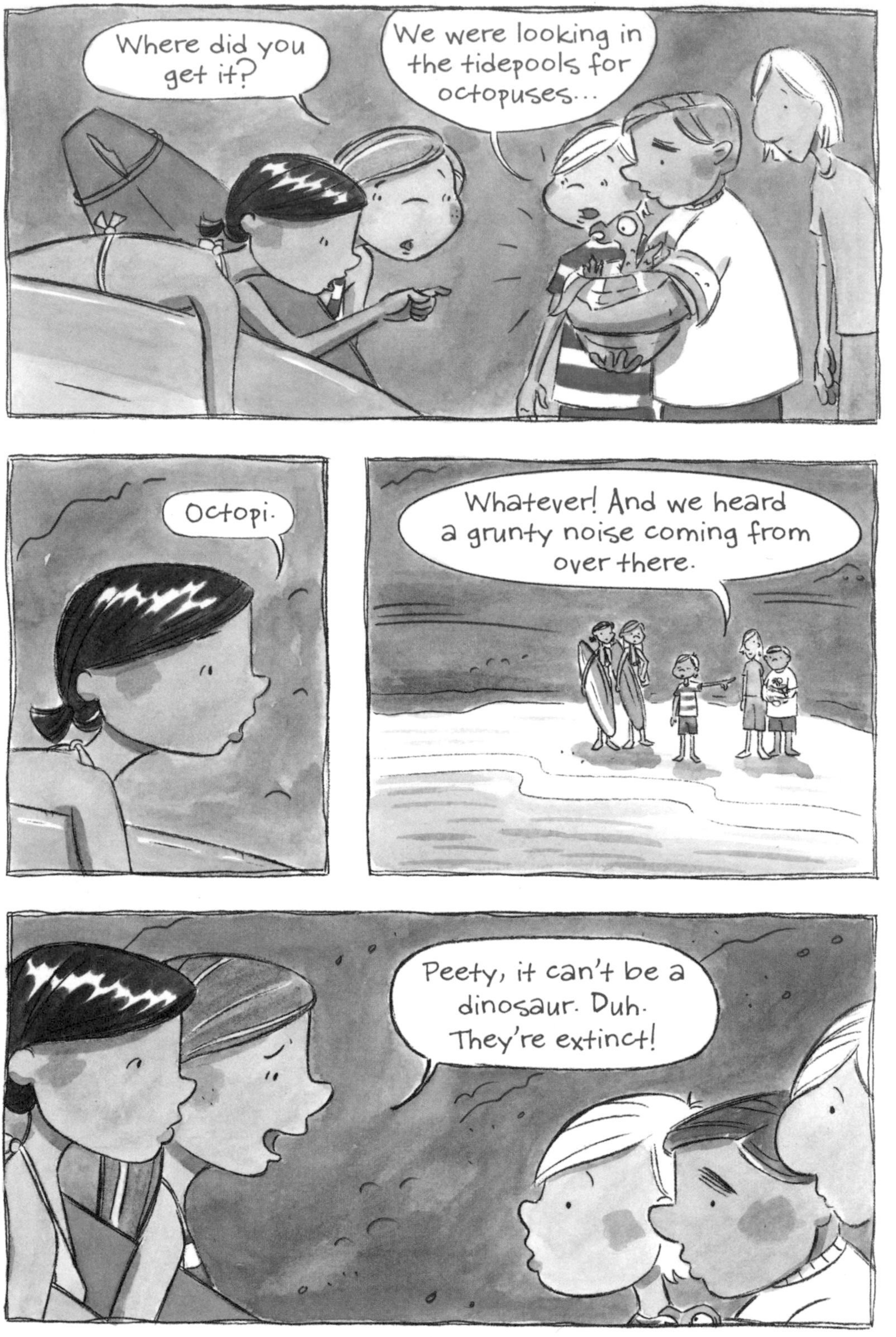
Where did you get it?
We were looking in the tidepools for octopuses...
Octopi.
Whatever! And we heard a grunty noise coming from over there.
Peety, it can't be a dinosaur. Duh. They're extinct!

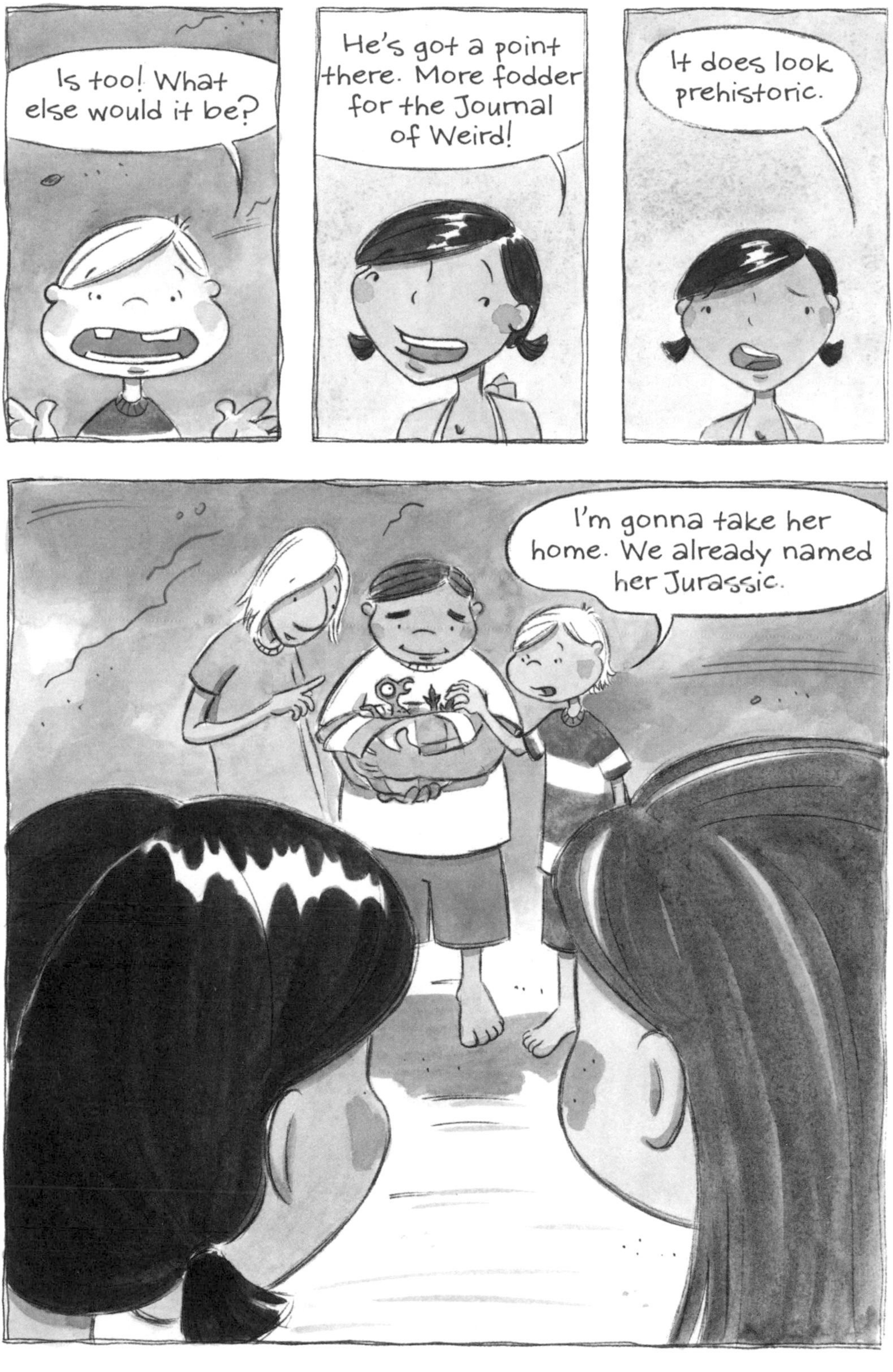
Is too! What else would it be?
He's got a point there. More fodder for the Journal of Weird!
It does look prehistoric.
I'm gonna take her home. We already named her Jurassic.

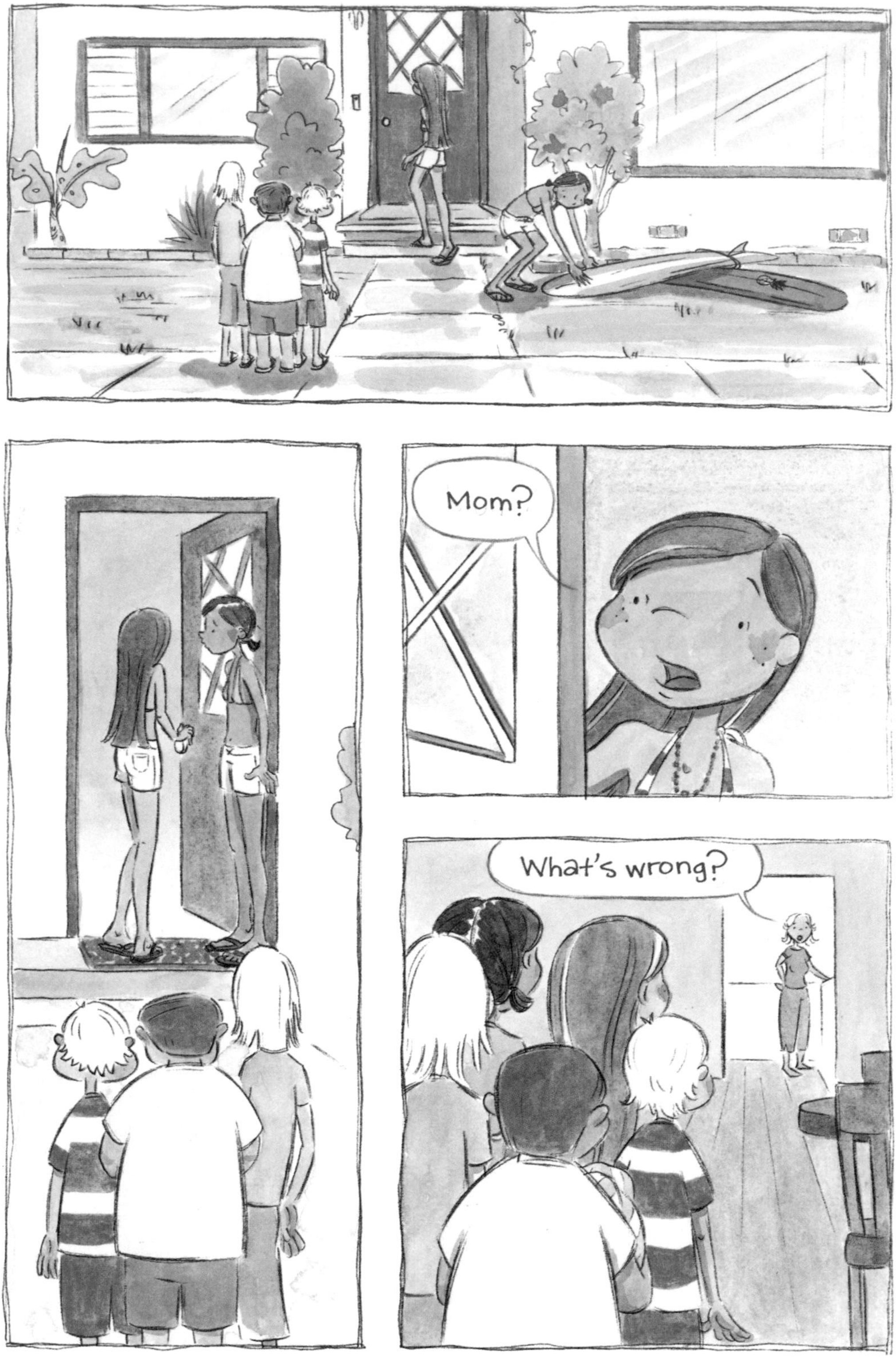
Mom?
What's wrong?

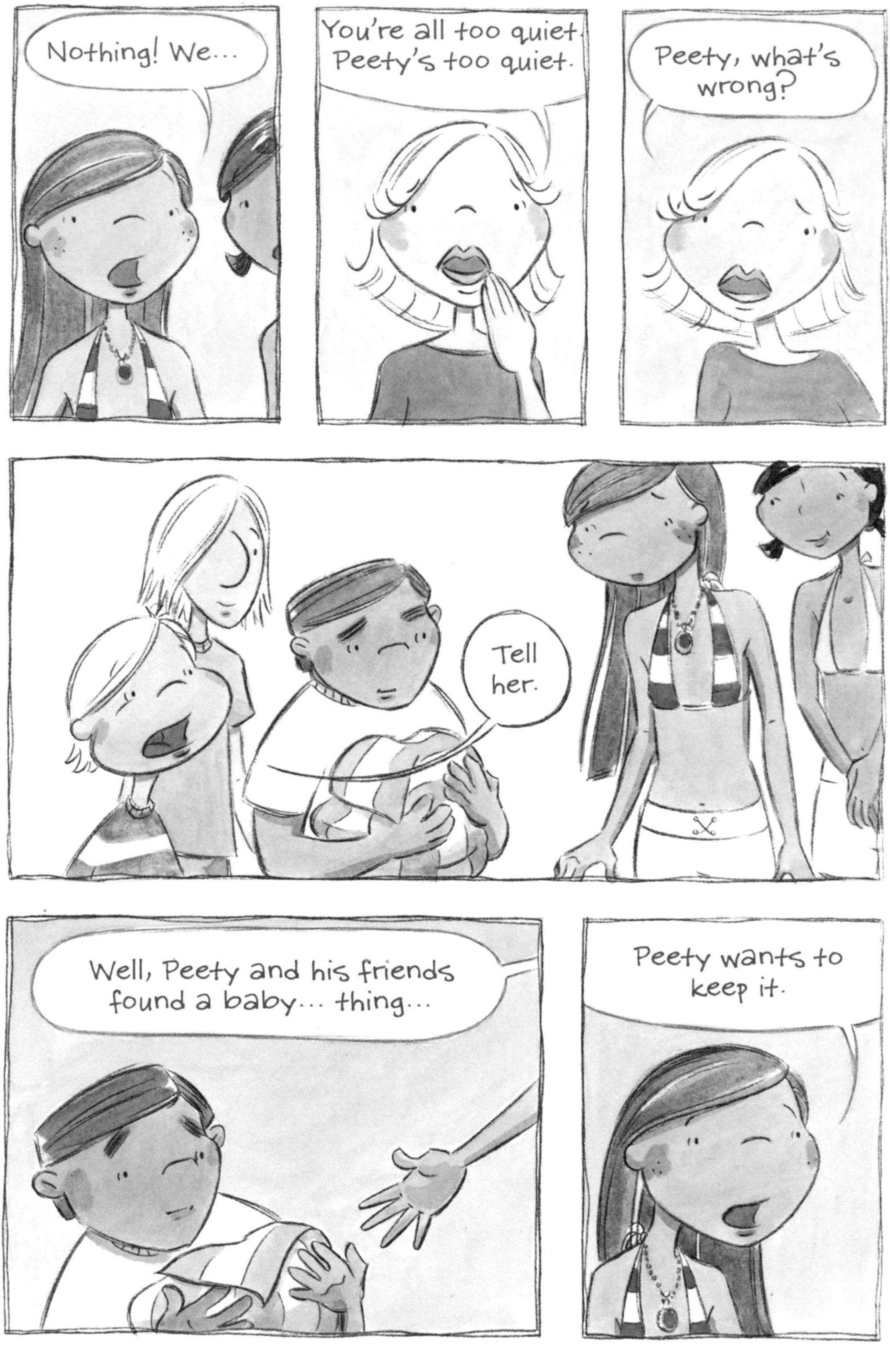
Nothing! We...
You're all too quiet. Peety's too quiet.
Peety, what's wrong?
Tell her.
Well, Peety and his friends found a baby... thing...
Peety wants to keep it.

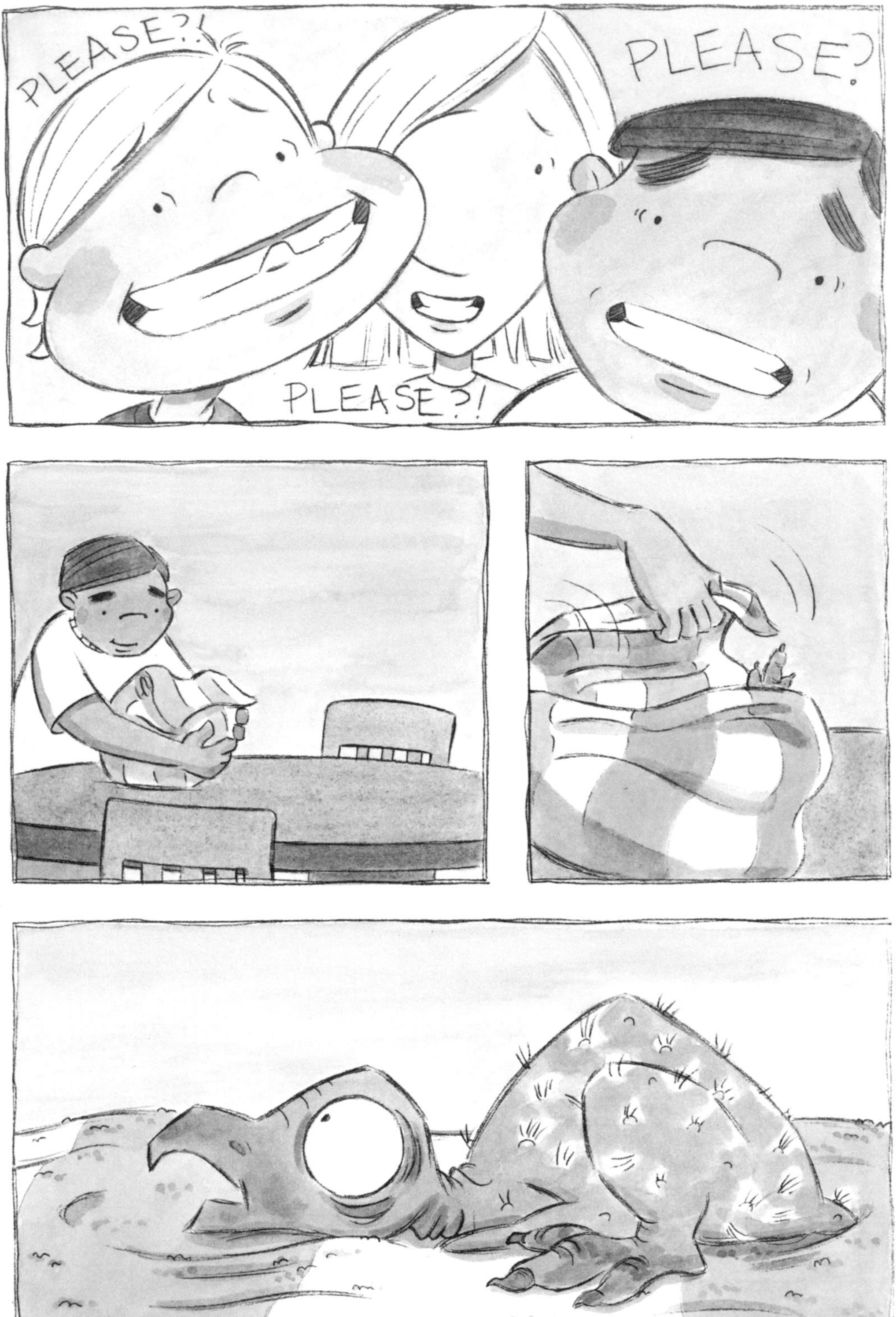
PLEASE?!
PLEASE?!
PLEASE?

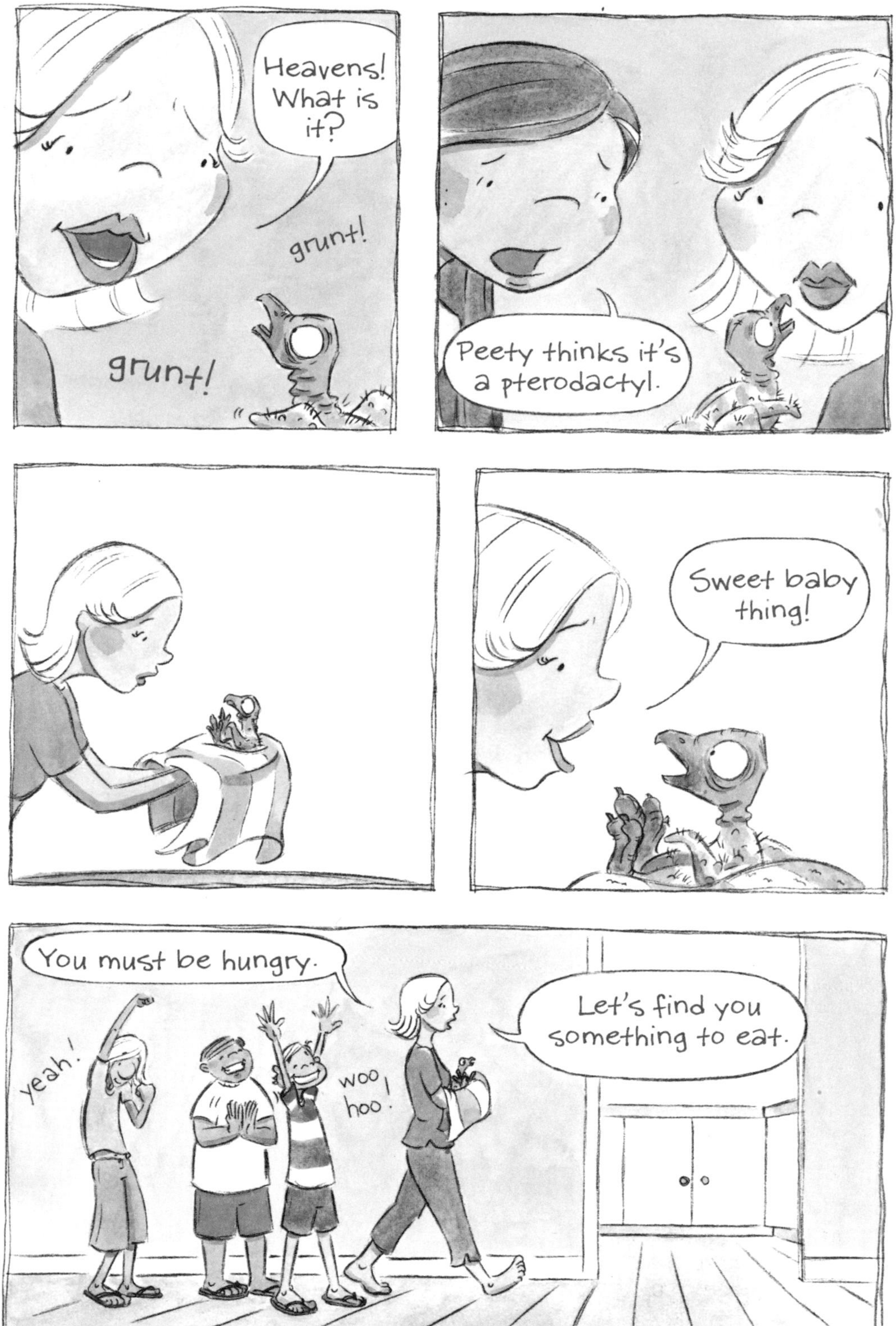
Heavens! What is it?
grunt!
grunt!
Peety thinks it's a pterodactyl.
Sweet baby thing!
You must be hungry.
yeah!
woo hoo!
Let's find you something to eat.

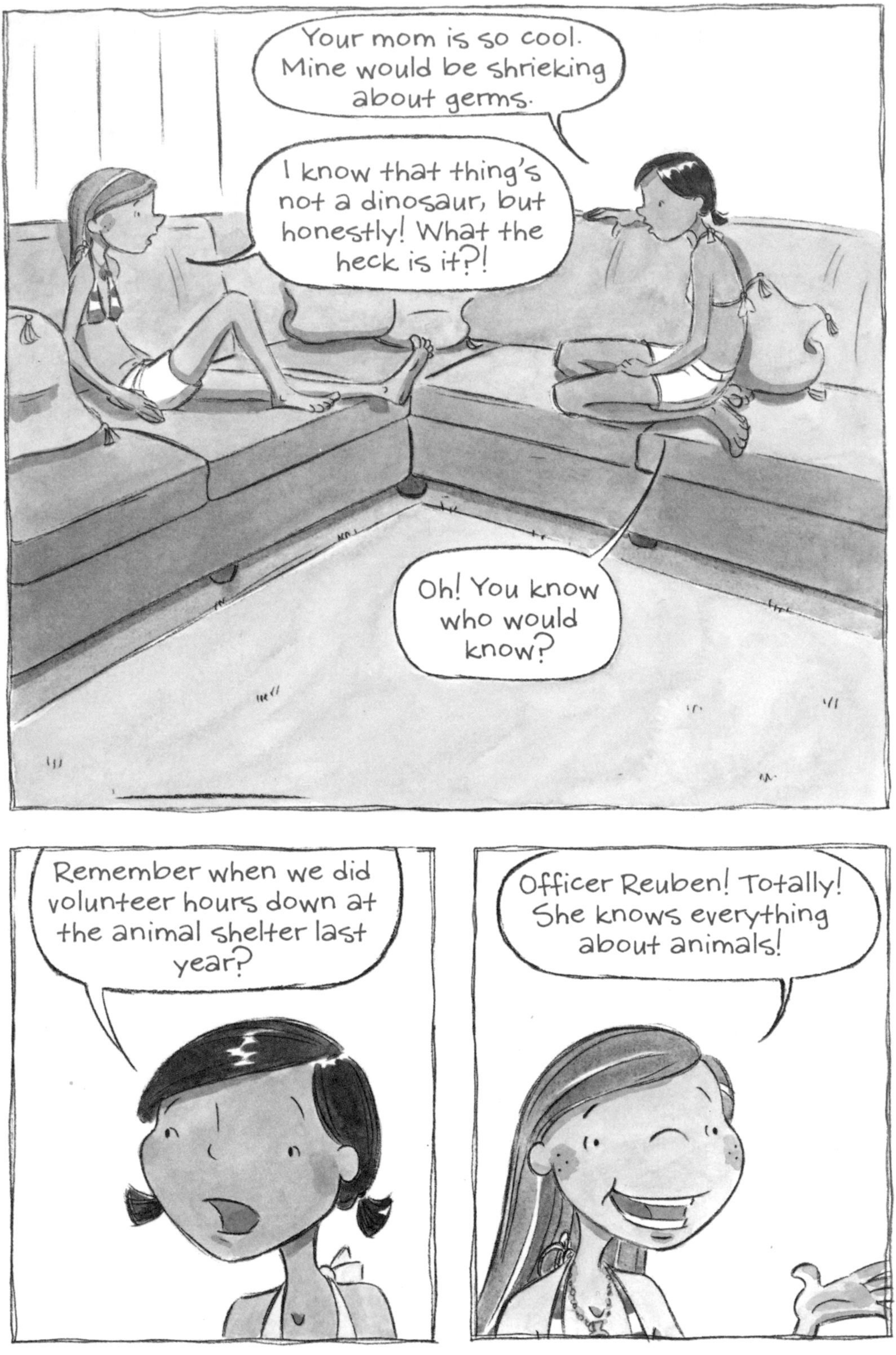
Your mom is so cool. Mine would be shrieking about germs.
I know that thing's not a dinosaur, but honestly! What the heck is it?!
Oh! You know who would know?
Remember when we did volunteer hours down at the animal shelter last year?
Officer Reuben! Totally! She knows everything about animals!

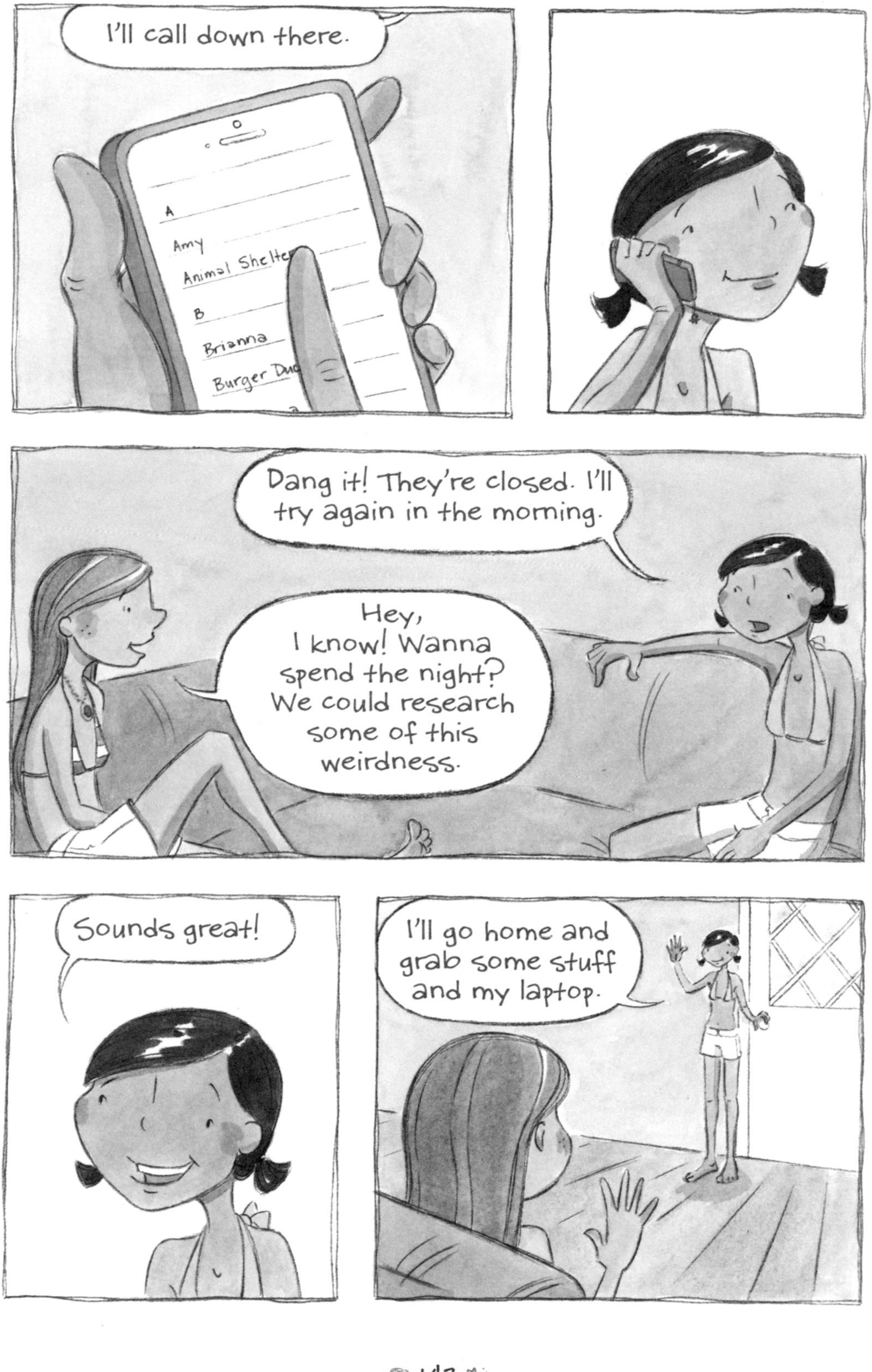
I'll call down there.
A
Amy
Animal Shelte
B
Brianna
Burger Du
Dang it! They're closed. I'll try again in the morning.
Hey, I know! Wanna spend the night? We could research some of this weirdness.
Sounds great!
I'll go home and grab some stuff and my laptop.

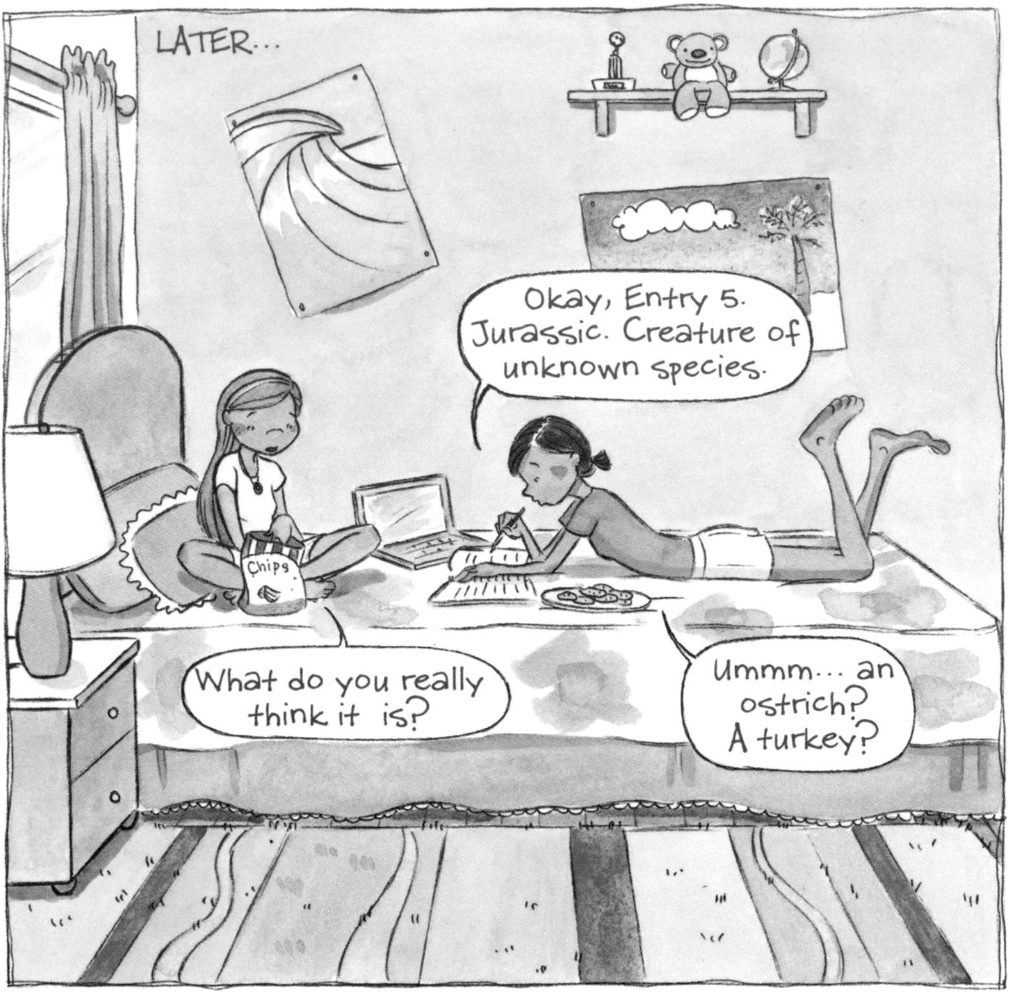
LATER...
Okay, Entry 5. Jurassic. Creature of unknown species.
Chips
What do you really think it is?
Ummm... an ostrich? A turkey?

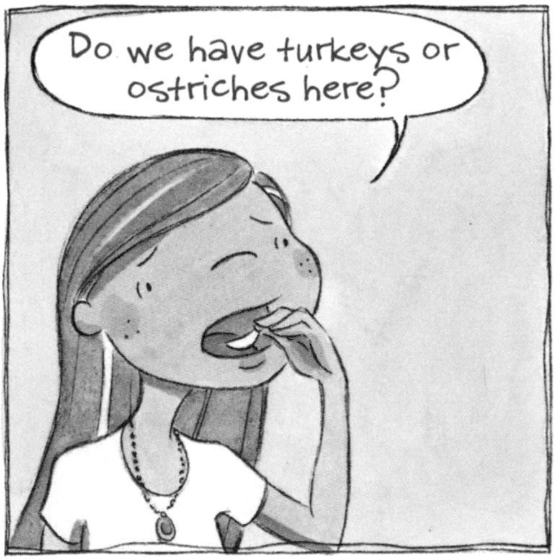
Do we have turkeys or ostriches here?

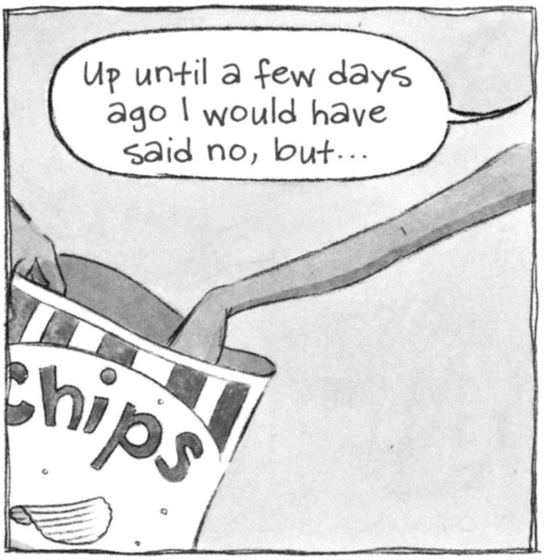
Up until a few days ago I would have said no, but...
Chips

Right!? So what have you logged in the Journal?

2. Edna Scott's account of Mr. Wu:

- first name Jian (John?)
- rescued Mrs. Scott
- was old a long time ago (over 100 years old?!!!!)

3. Mrs. Taylor's view of ghosts:

- romantic, like yearning for a lost lover

4. Dr. Lee (Dad)'s view of ghosts:

- effect of drug use, or
- mental illness (hallucination)

Here's the latest.

5. FOUND! Creature of Unknown Species:

-Peet thinks it's a pterodactyl
-found near Danger Point
-put a call in to Officer Reuben @ Animal Shelter

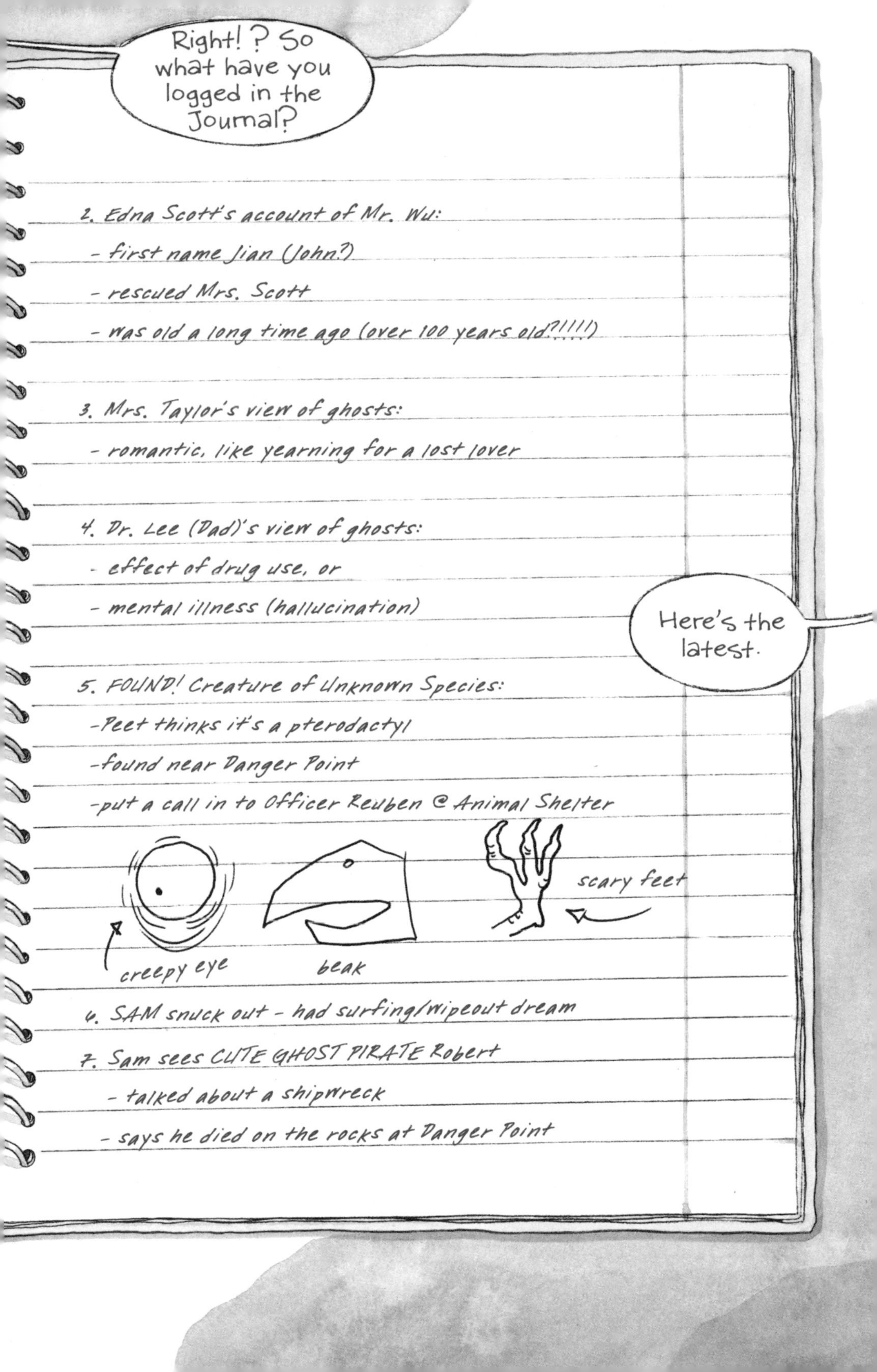

scary feet
creepy eye
beak

6. SAM snuck out - had surfing/wipeout dream

7. Sam sees CUTE GHOST PIRATE Robert

- talked about a shipwreck
- says he died on the rocks at Danger Point

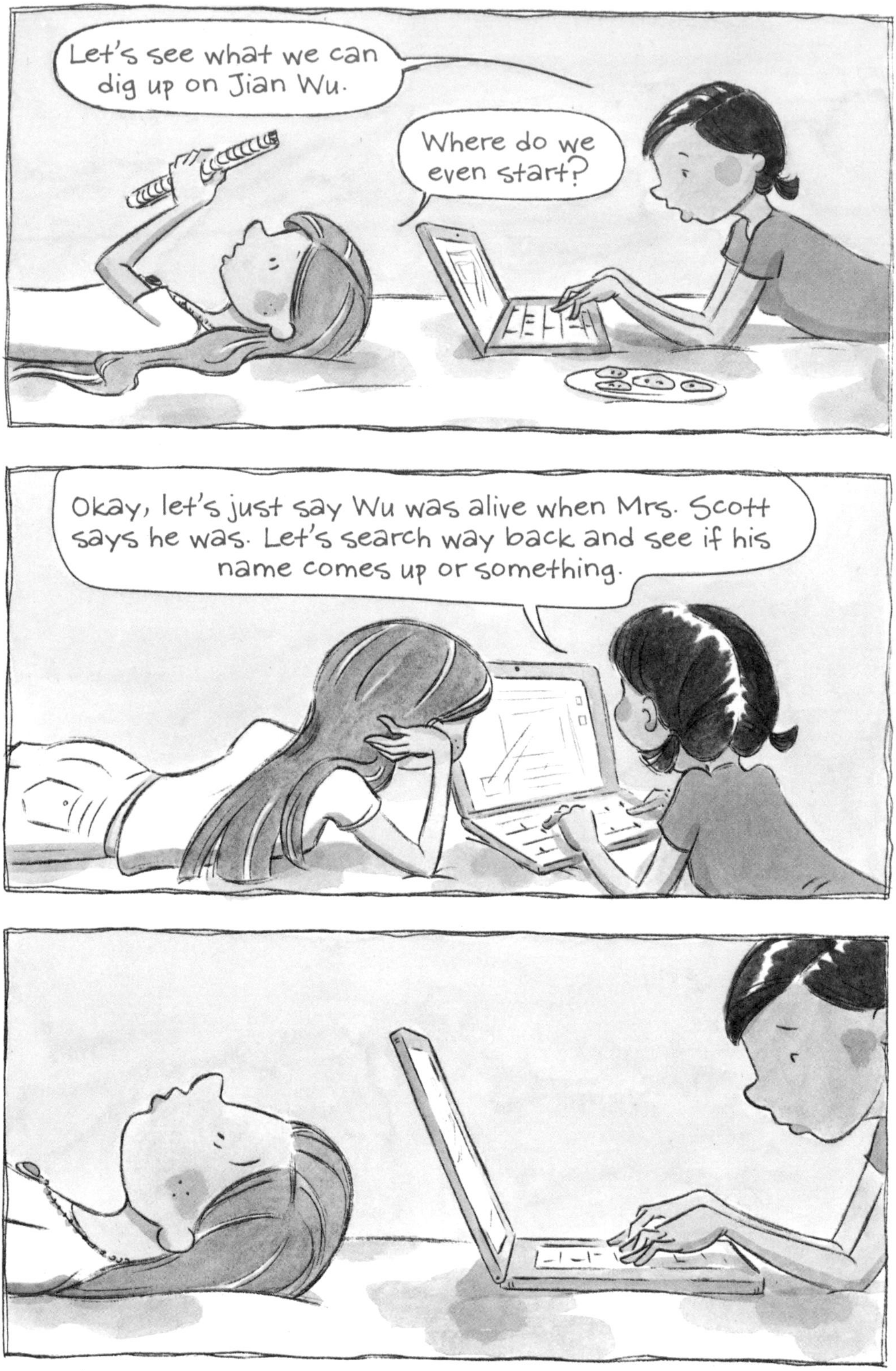
Let's see what we can dig up on Jian Wu.
Where do we even start?
Okay, let's just say Wu was alive when Mrs. Scott says he was. Let's search way back and see if his name comes up or something.

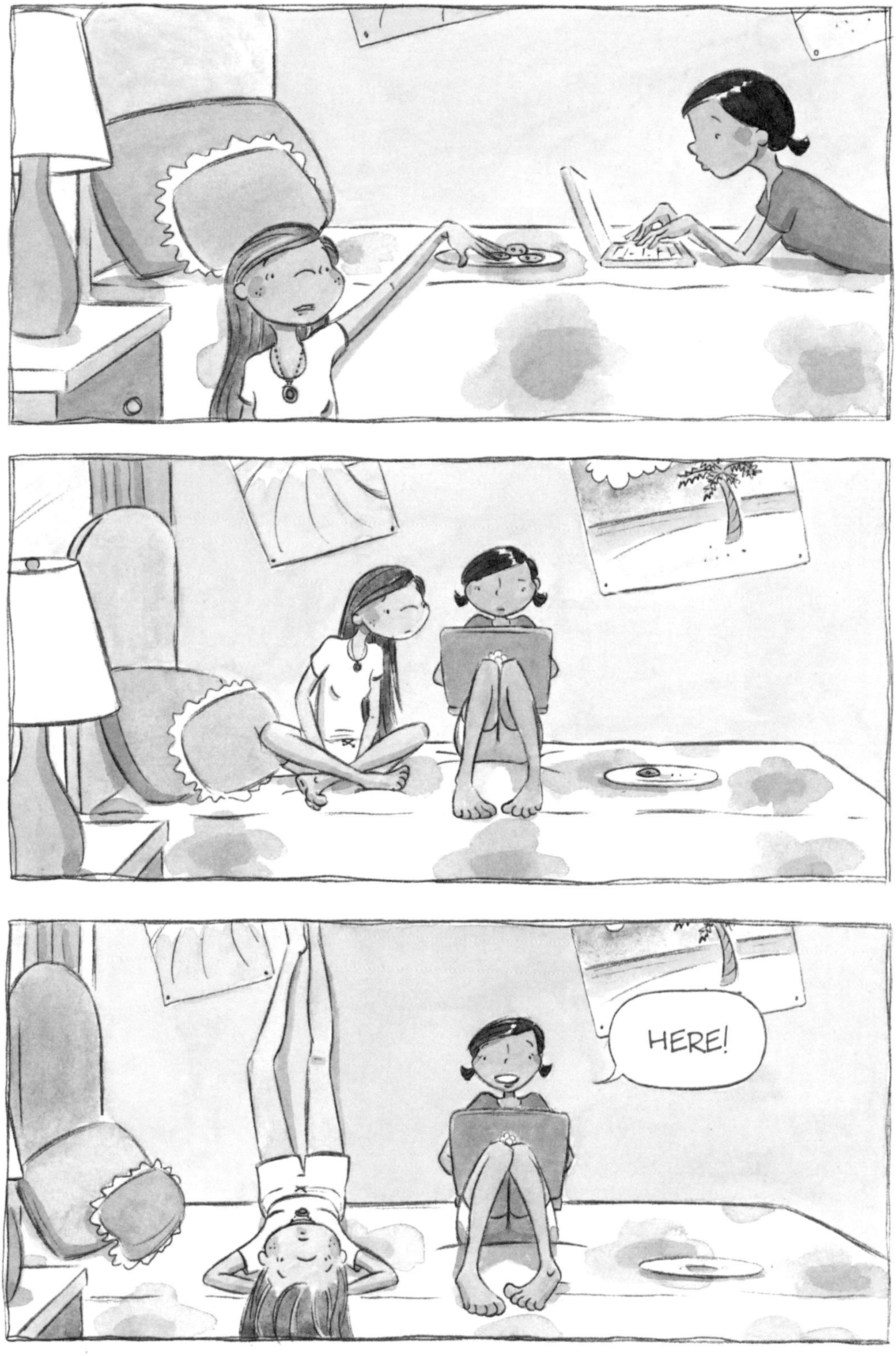
HERE!

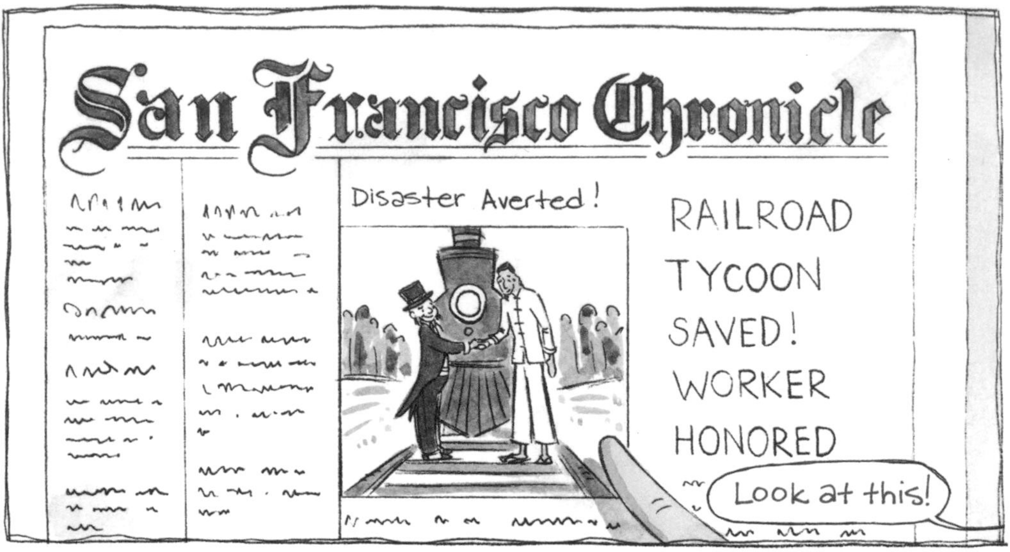
San Francisco Chronicle
Disaster Averted!
RAILROAD TYCOON SAVED! WORKER HONORED
Look at this!

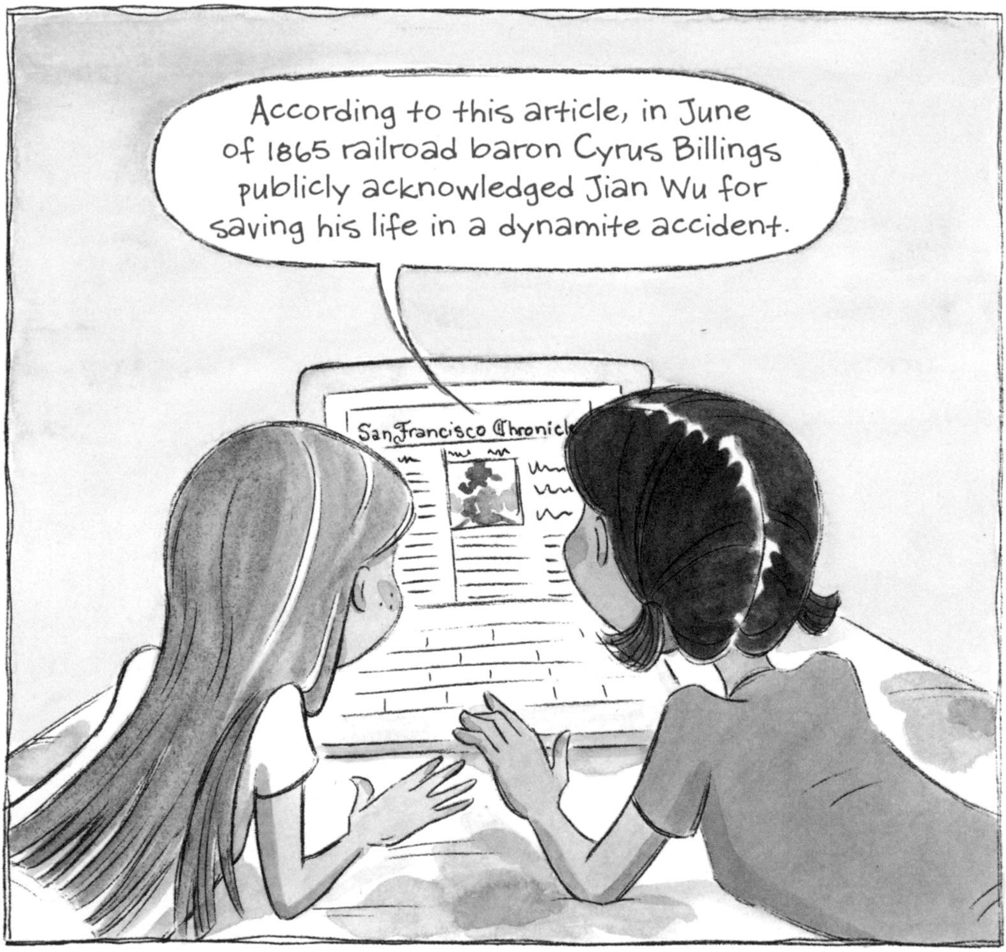
According to this article, in June of 1865 railroad baron Cyrus Billings publicly acknowledged Jian Wu for saving his life in a dynamite accident.
San Francisco Chronicle

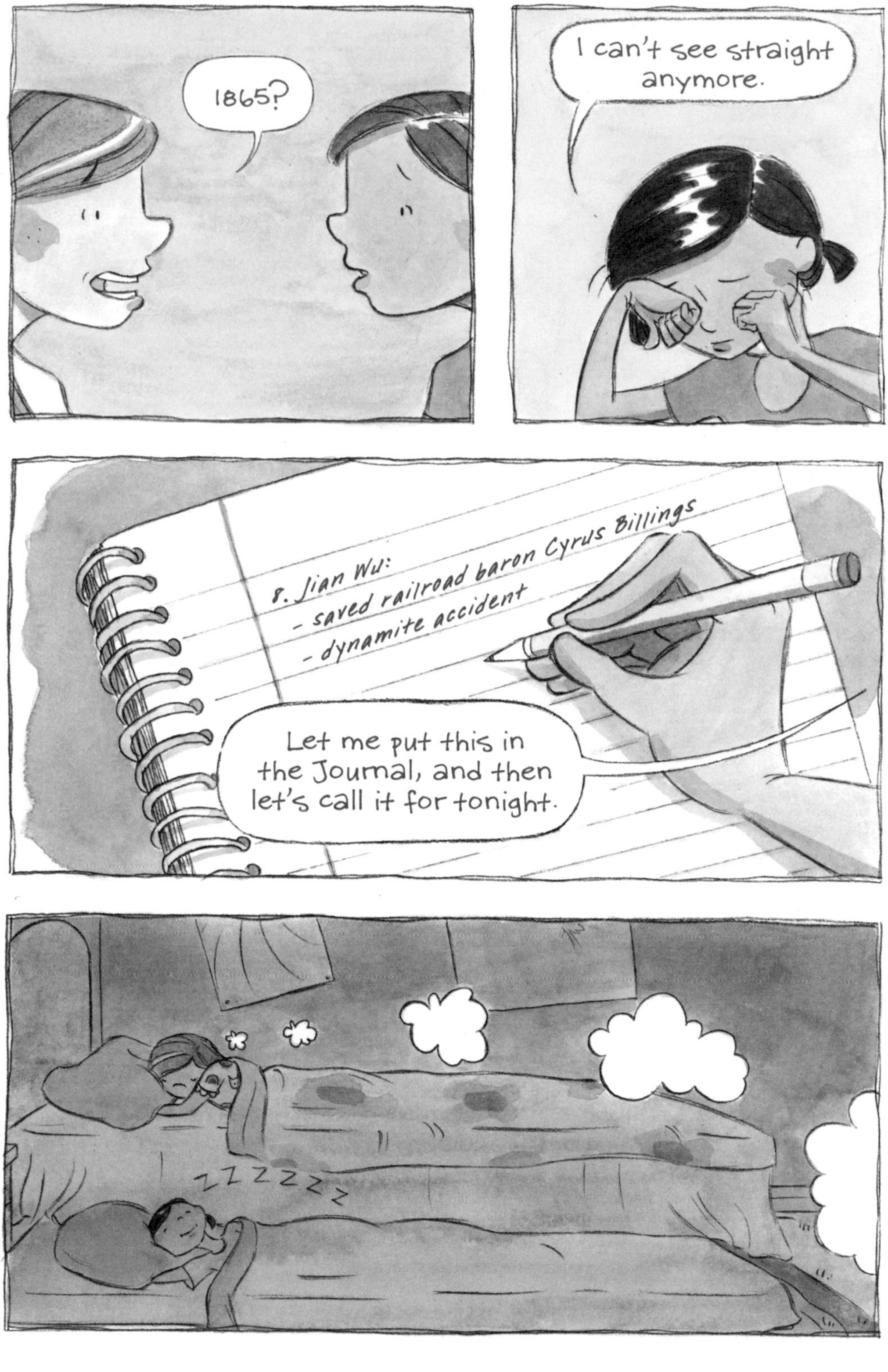
1865?
I can't see straight anymore.
8. Jian Wu:
- saved railroad baron Cyrus Billings
- dynamite accident
Let me put this in the Journal, and then let's call it for tonight.
ZZZZZZ

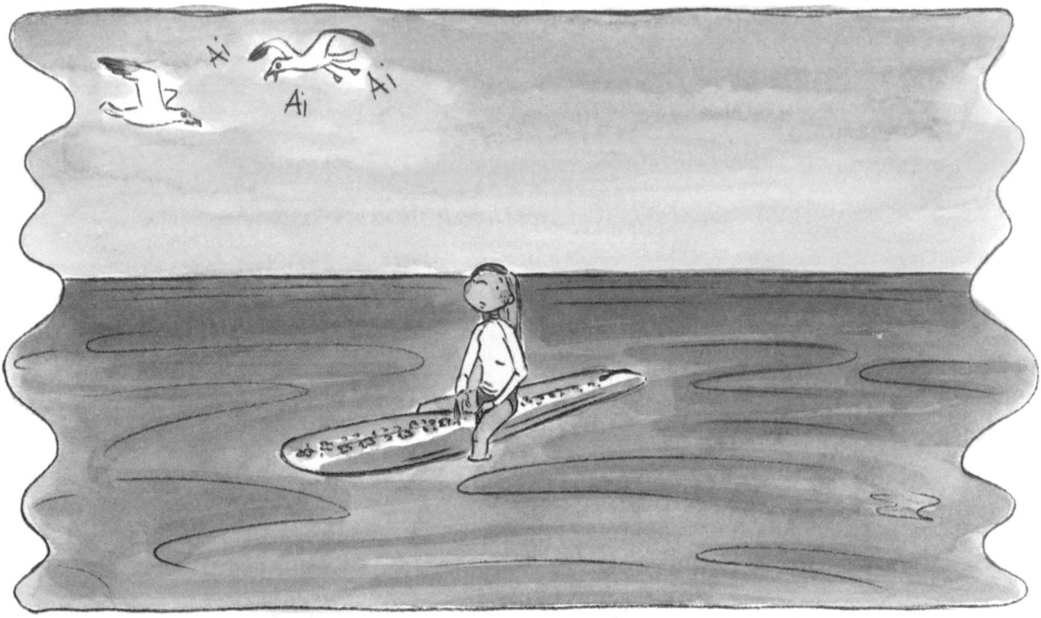
Ai
Ai
Ai

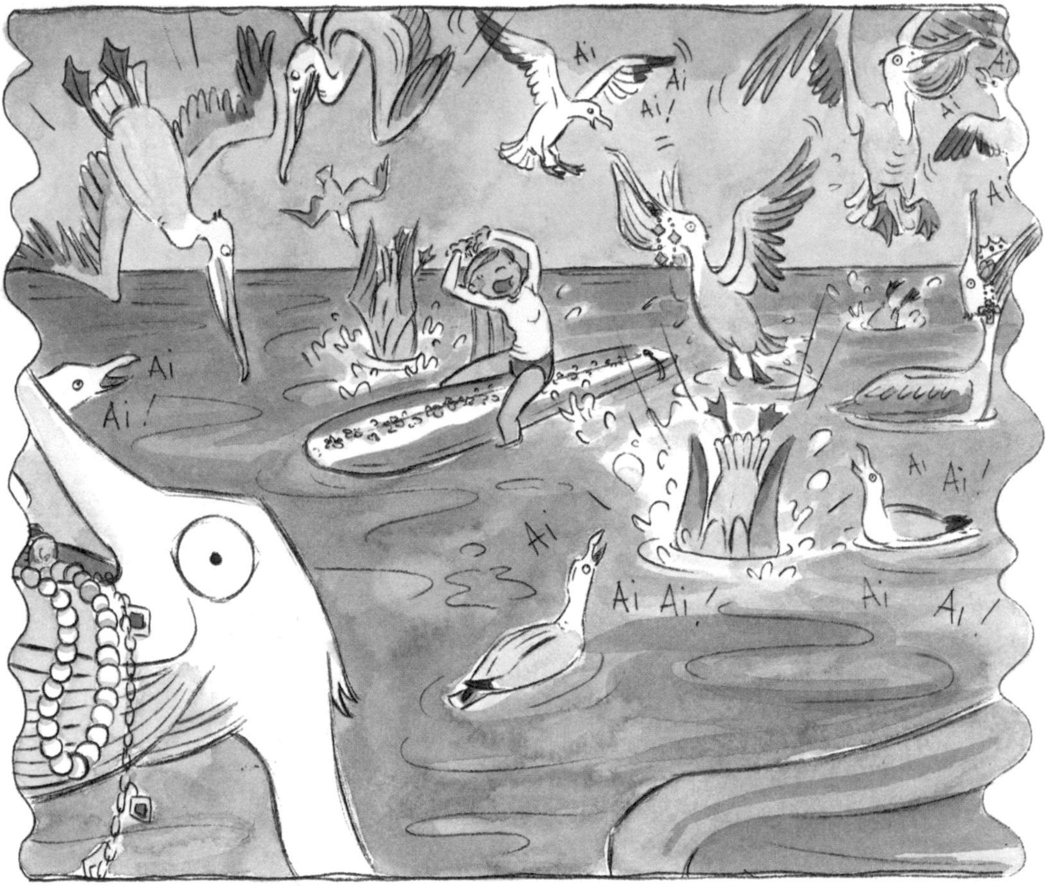
Ai
Ai
Ai!
Ai
Ai
Ai
Ai
Ai!
Ai
Ai!
Ai
Ai Ai!
Ai
Ai!

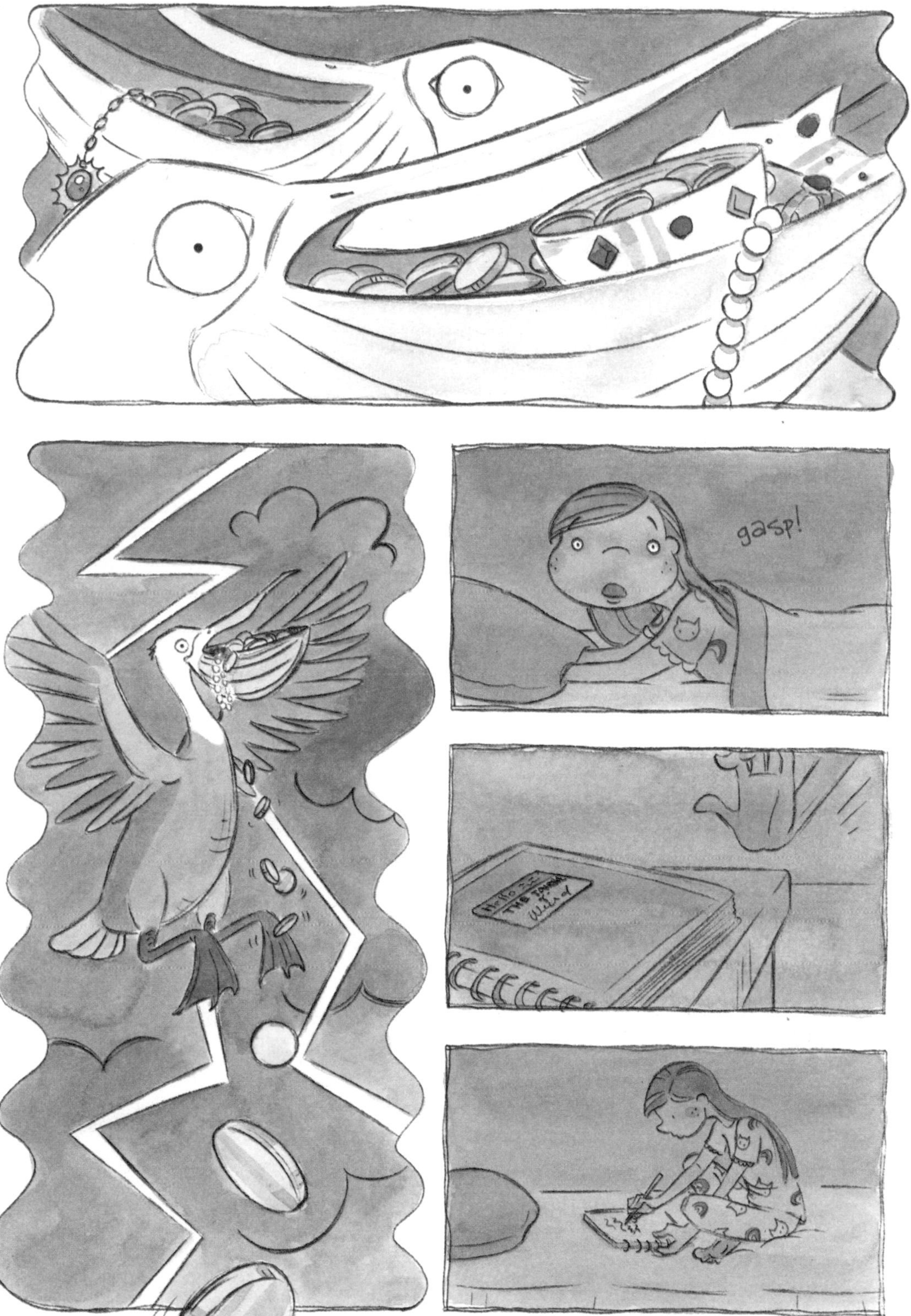
gasp!

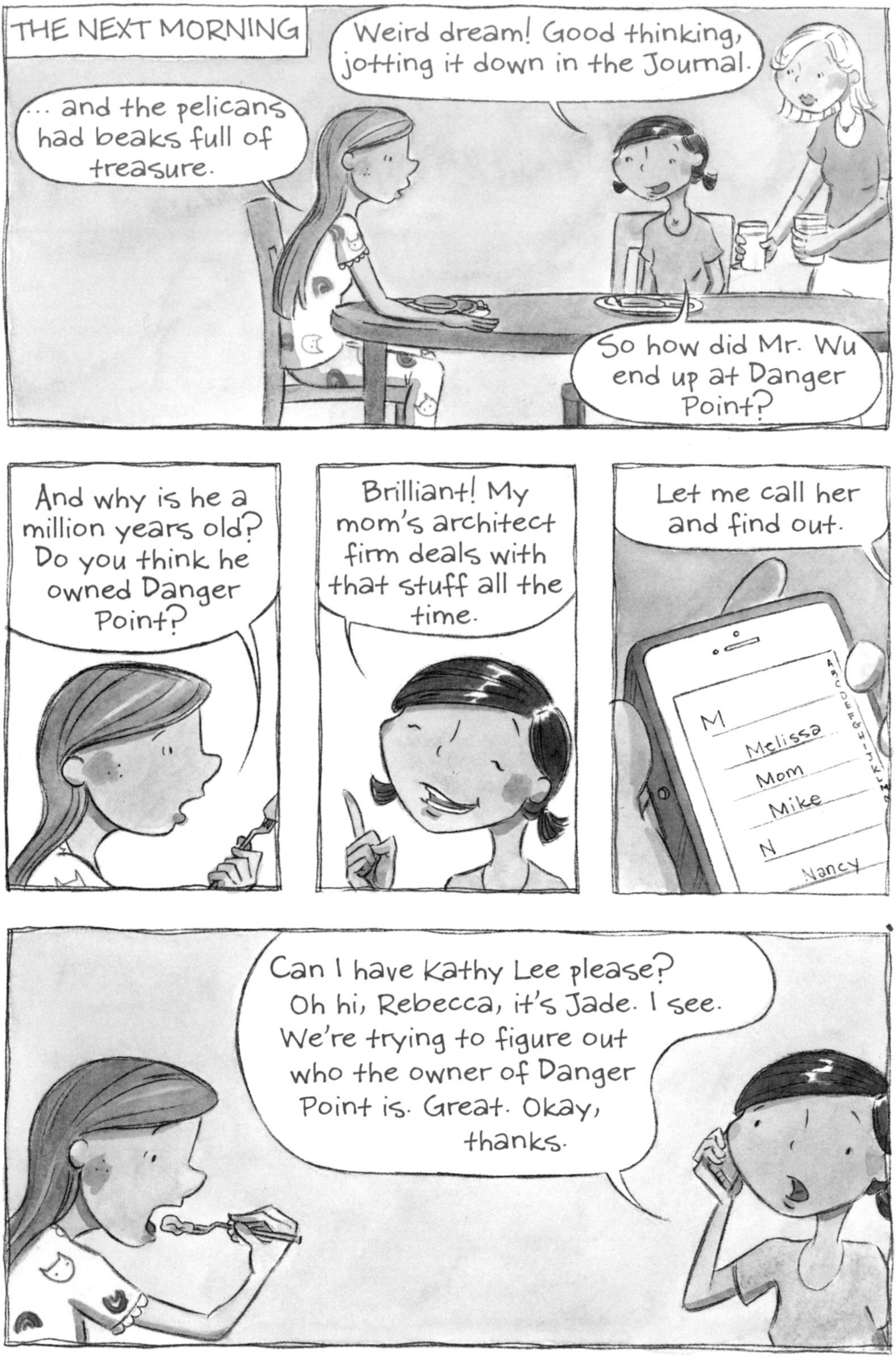
THE NEXT MORNING
... and the pelicans had beaks full of treasure.
Weird dream! Good thinking, jotting it down in the Journal.
So how did Mr. Wu end up at Danger Point?
And why is he a million years old? Do you think he owned Danger Point?
Brilliant! My mom's architect firm deals with that stuff all the time.
Let me call her and find out.
M
Melissa
Mom
Mike
N
Nancy
Can I have Kathy Lee please? Oh hi, Rebecca, it's Jade. I see. We're trying to figure out who the owner of Danger Point is. Great. Okay, thanks.

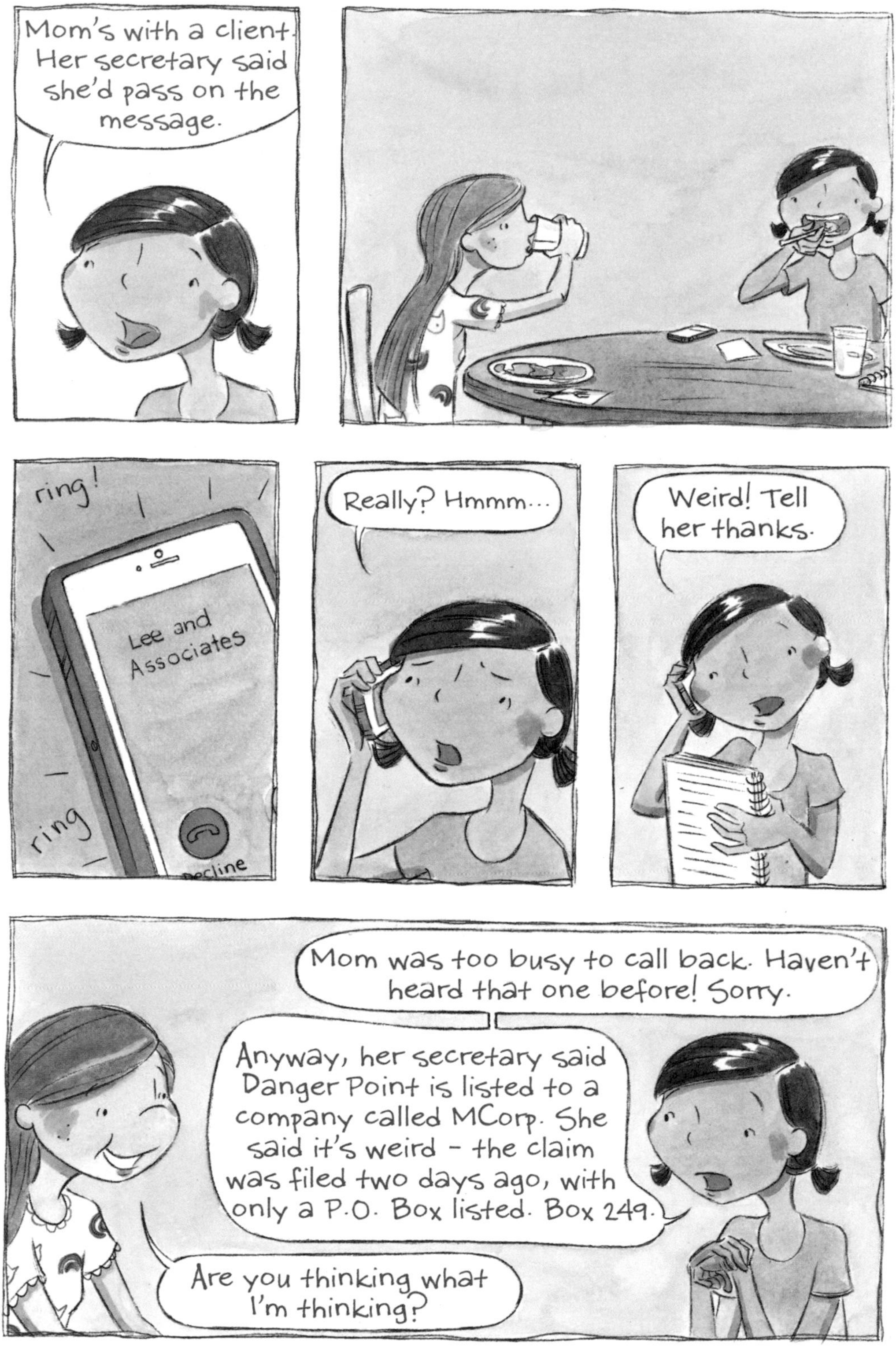
Mom's with a client. Her secretary said she'd pass on the message.
ring!
Lee and Associates
ring
Decline
Really? Hmmm...
Weird! Tell her thanks.
Mom was too busy to call back. Haven't heard that one before! Sorry.
Anyway, her secretary said Danger Point is listed to a company called MCorp. She said it's weird - the claim was filed two days ago, with only a P.O. Box listed. Box 249.
Are you thinking what I'm thinking?

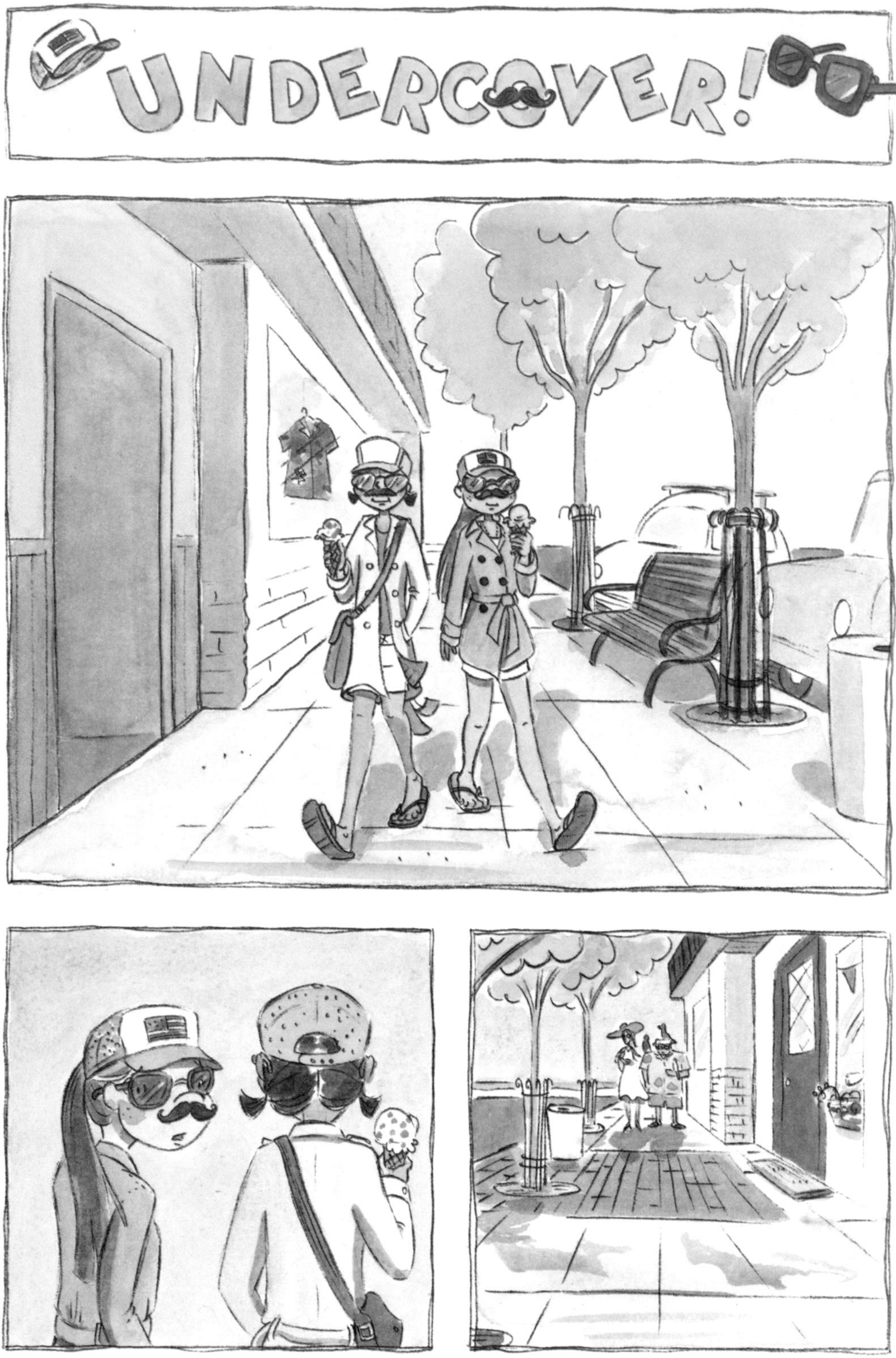
UNDERCOVER!

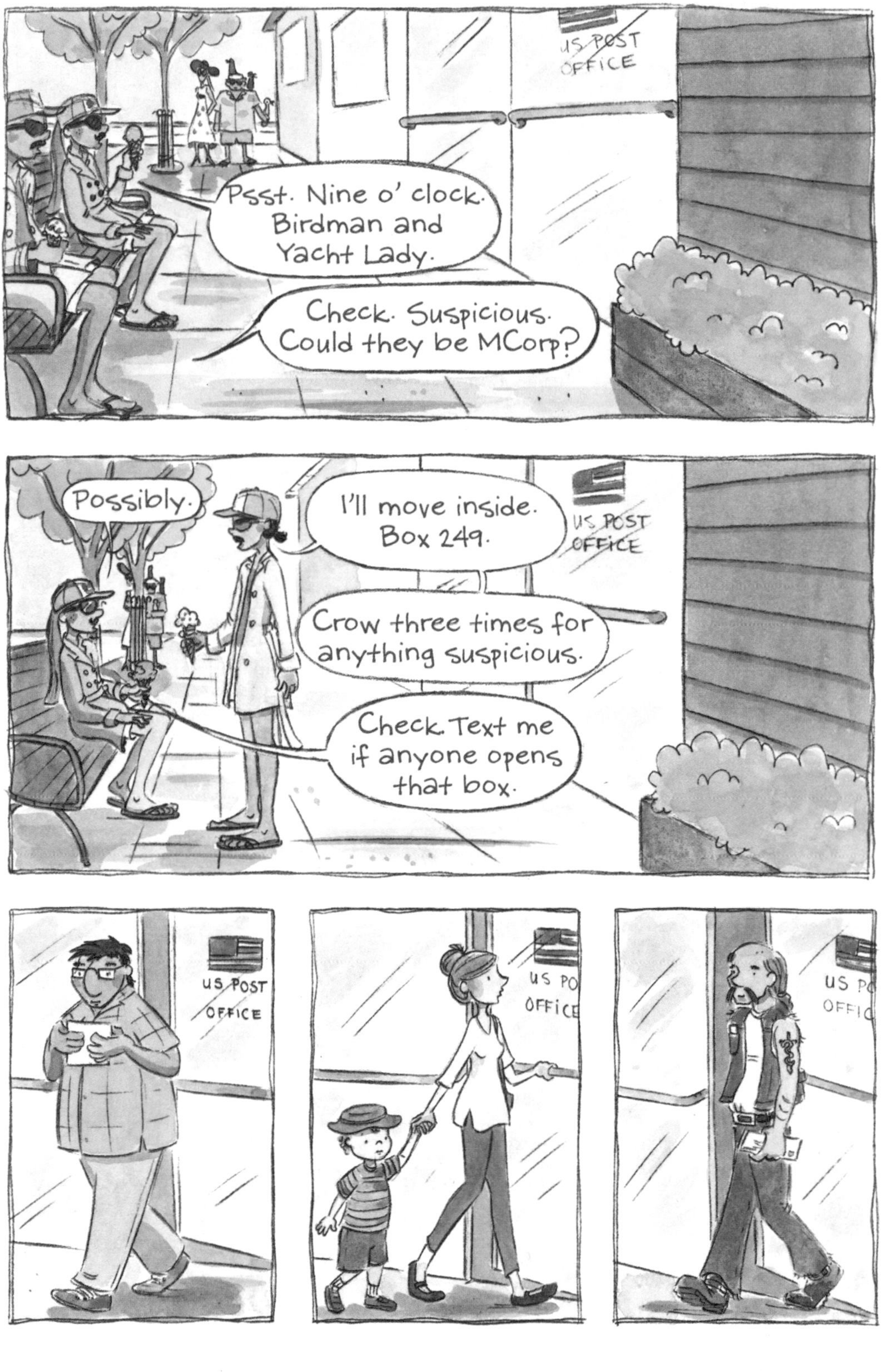
US POST OFFICE
Psst. Nine o' clock. Birdman and Yacht Lady.
Check. Suspicious. Could they be MCorp?
Possibly.
I'll move inside. Box 249.
Crow three times for anything suspicious.
Check. Text me if anyone opens that box.
US POST OFFICE
US POST OFFICE

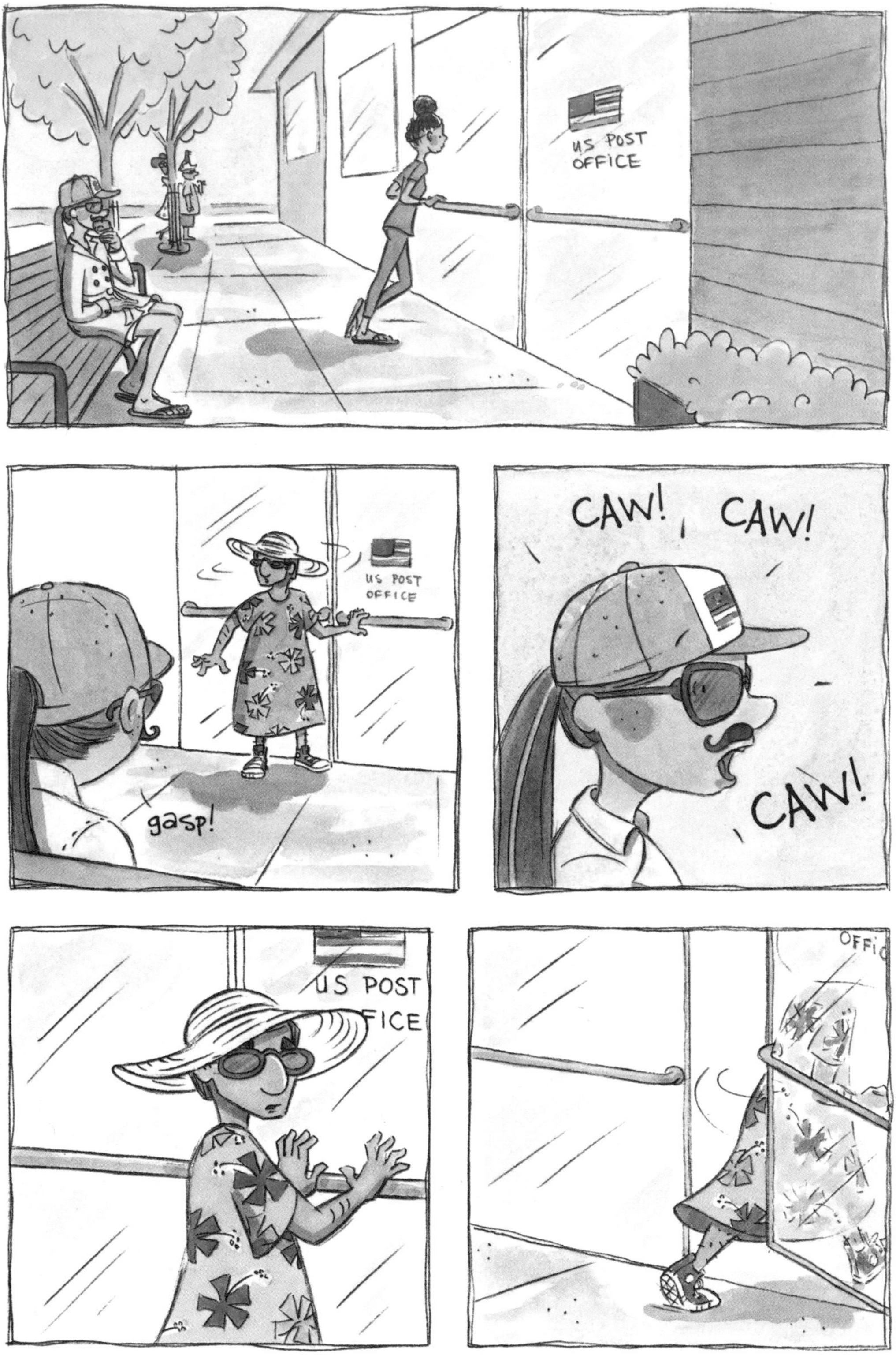
US POST OFFICE
US POST OFFICE
gasp!
CAW! CAW!
CAW!
US POST
FICE
OFFIC

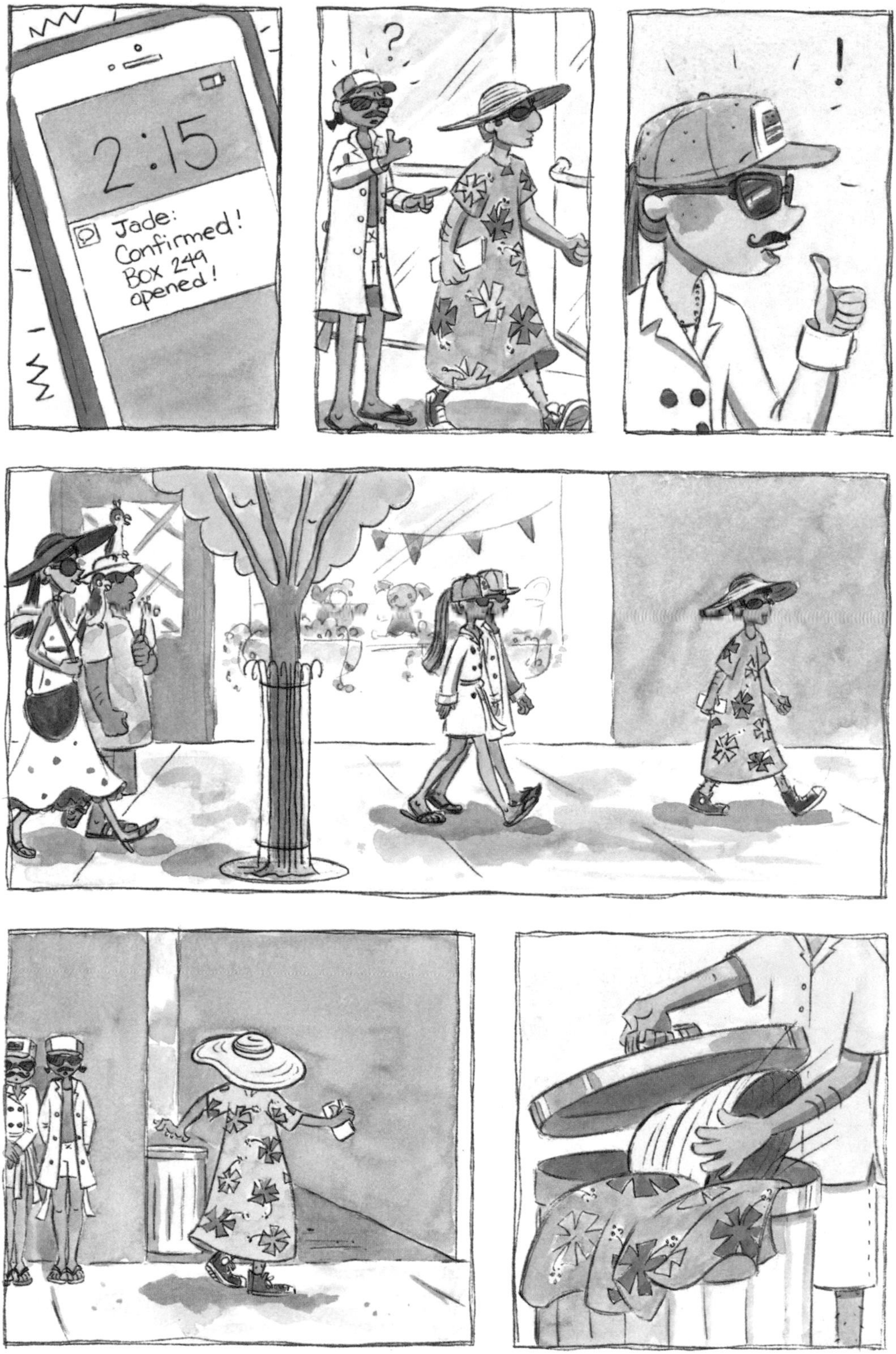
2:15
Jade:
Confirmed!
Box 249
opened!
?
!

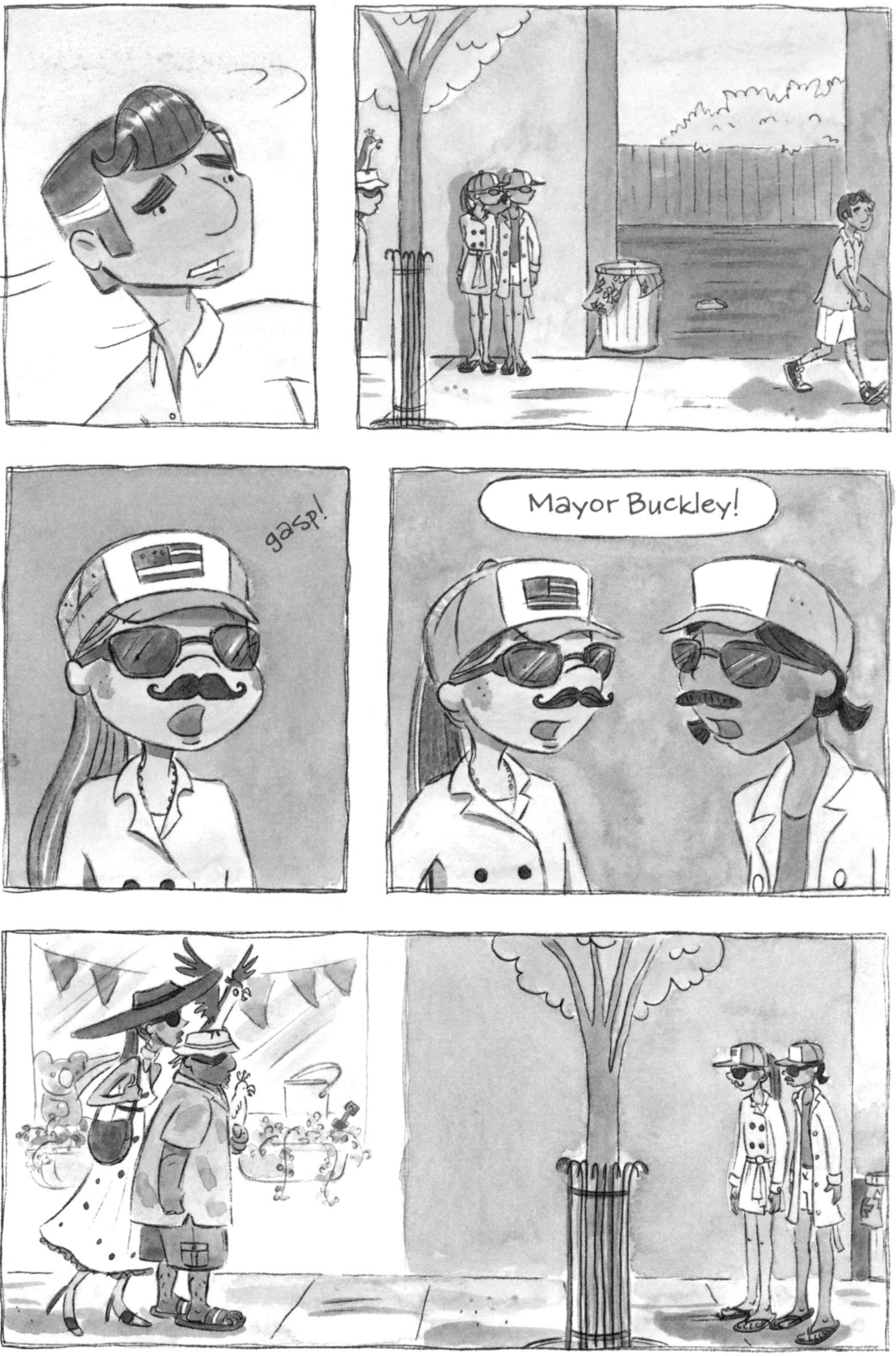
gasp!
Mayor Buckley!

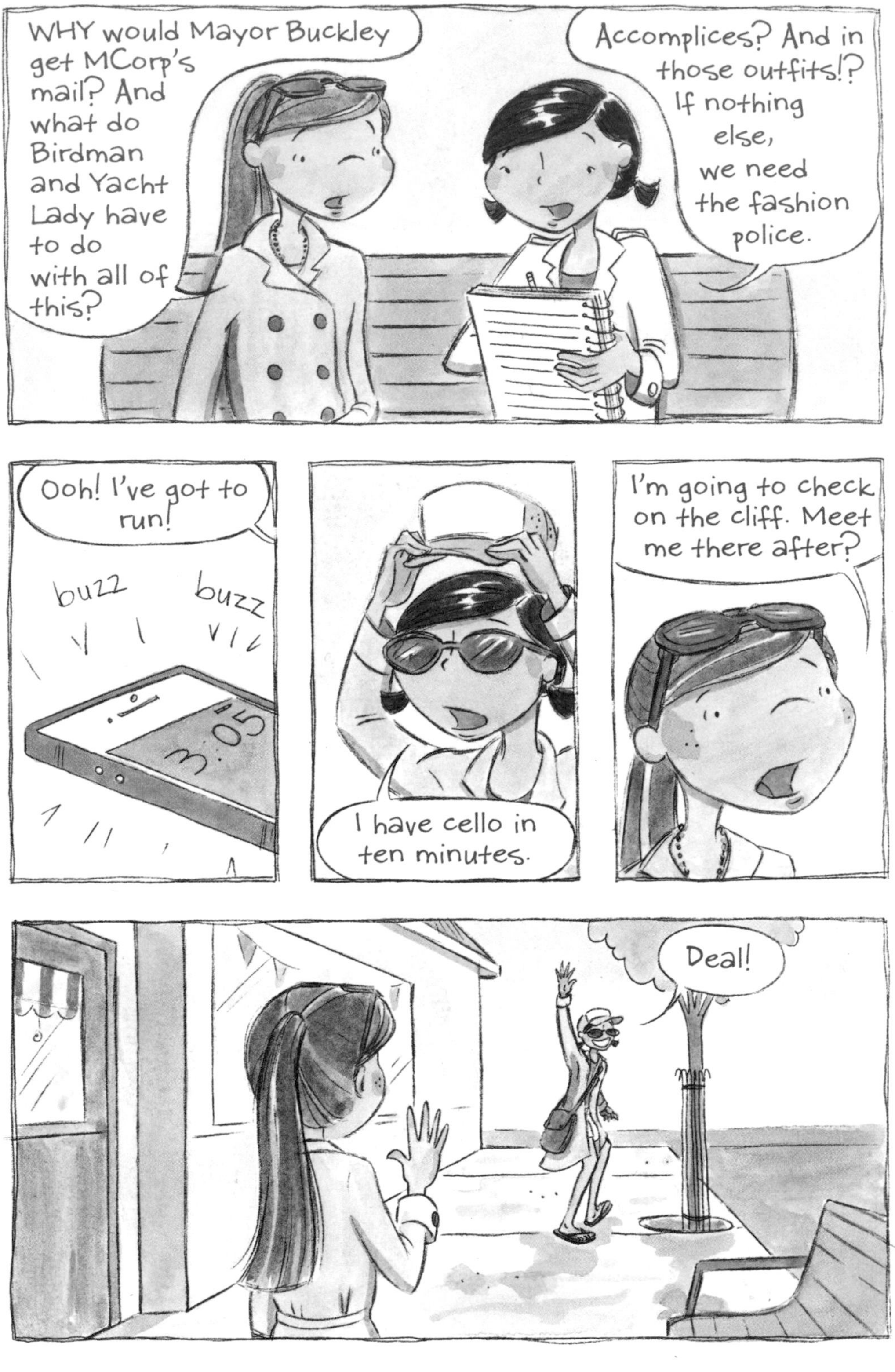
WHY would Mayor Buckley get MCorp's mail? And what do Birdman and Yacht Lady have to do with all of this?
Accomplices? And in those outfits!? If nothing else, we need the fashion police.
Ooh! I've got to run!
buzz
buzz
3:05
I have cello in ten minutes.
I'm going to check on the cliff. Meet me there after?
Deal!

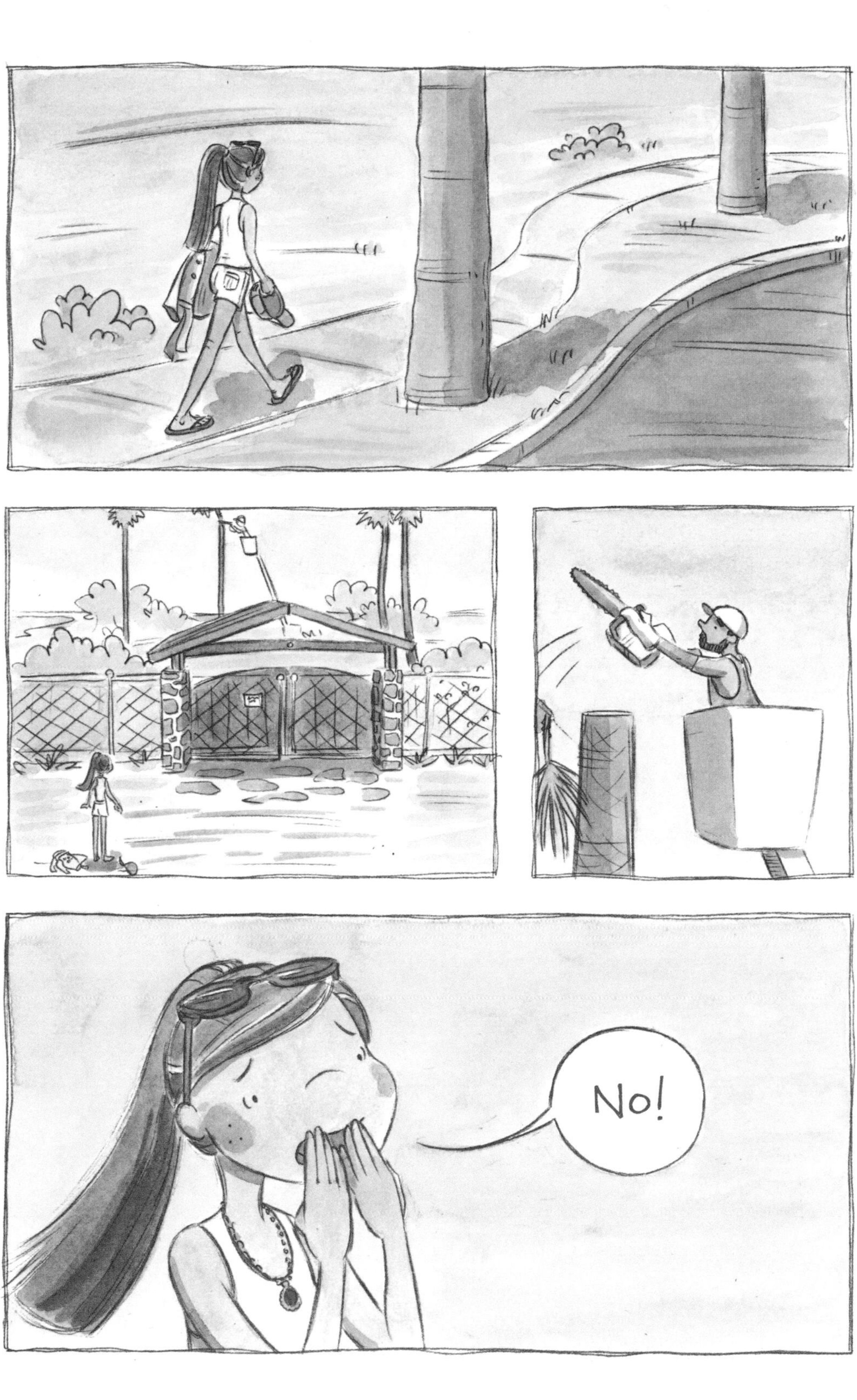
No!

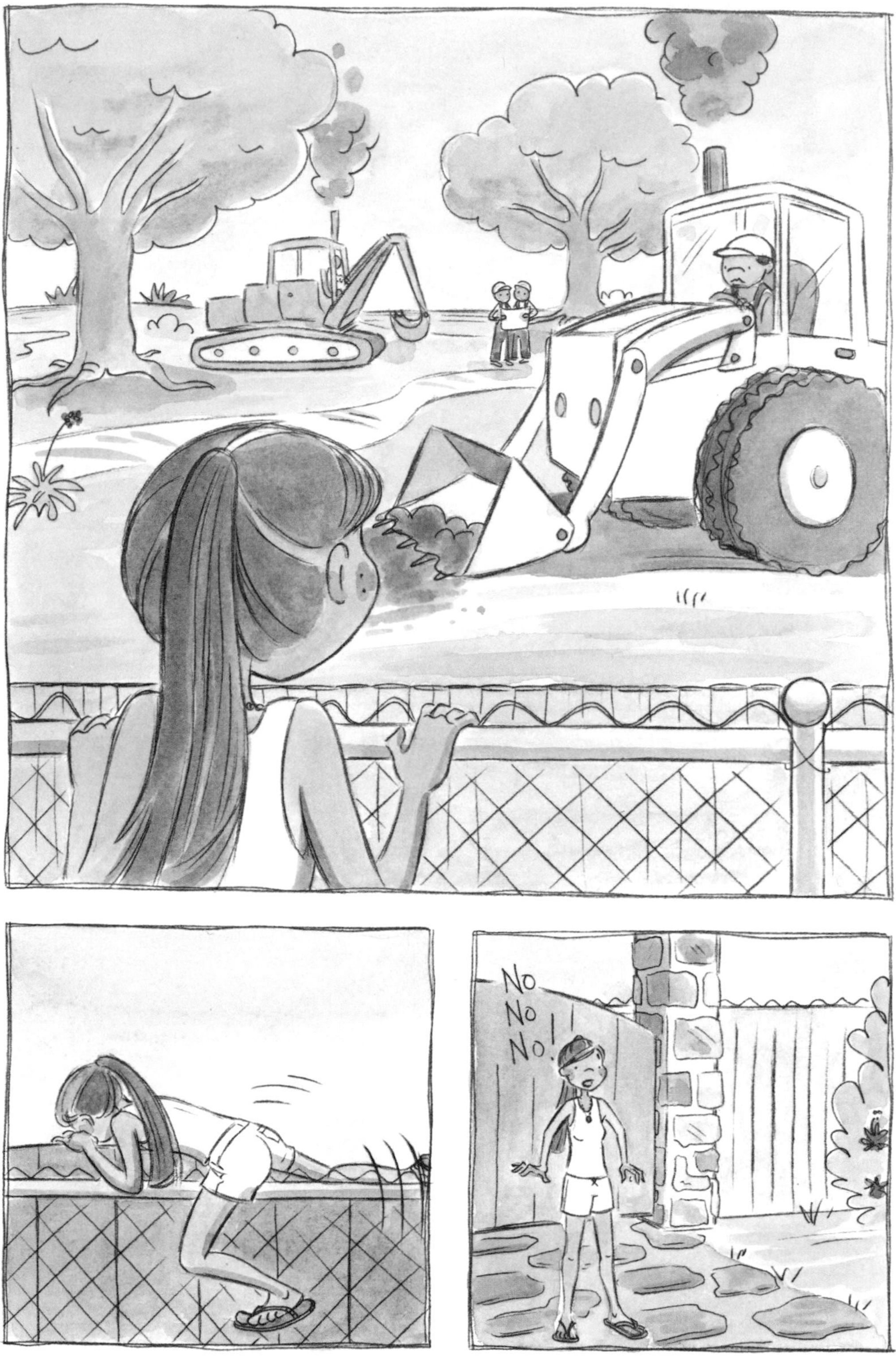
No
No
No!

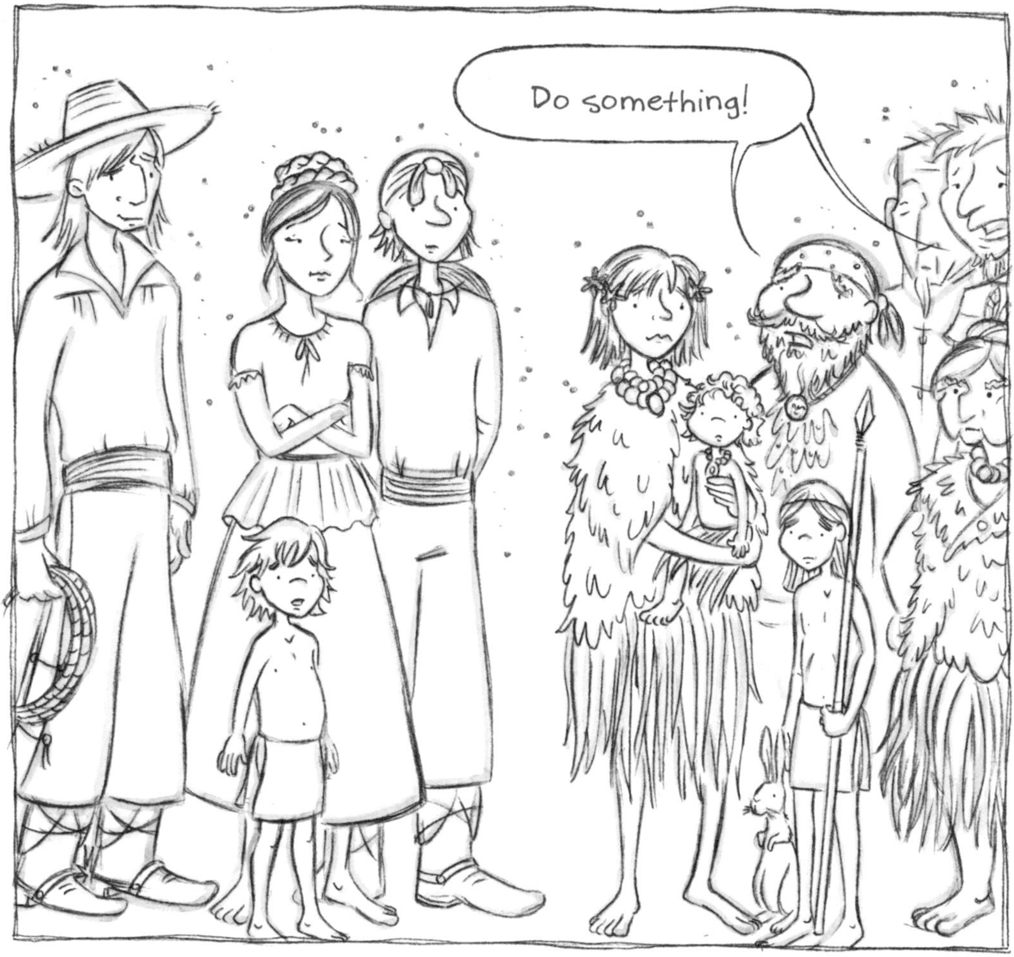
Do something!

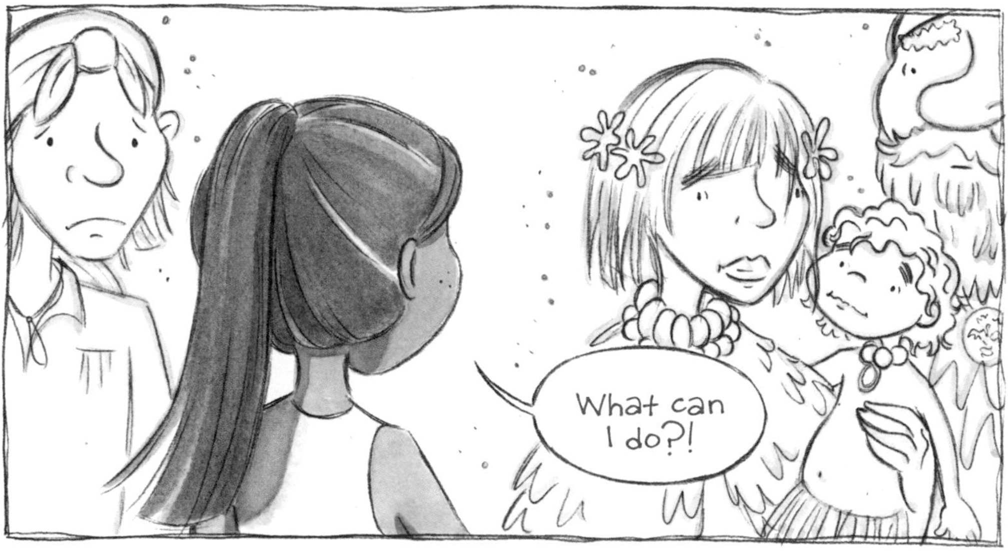
What can
I do?!

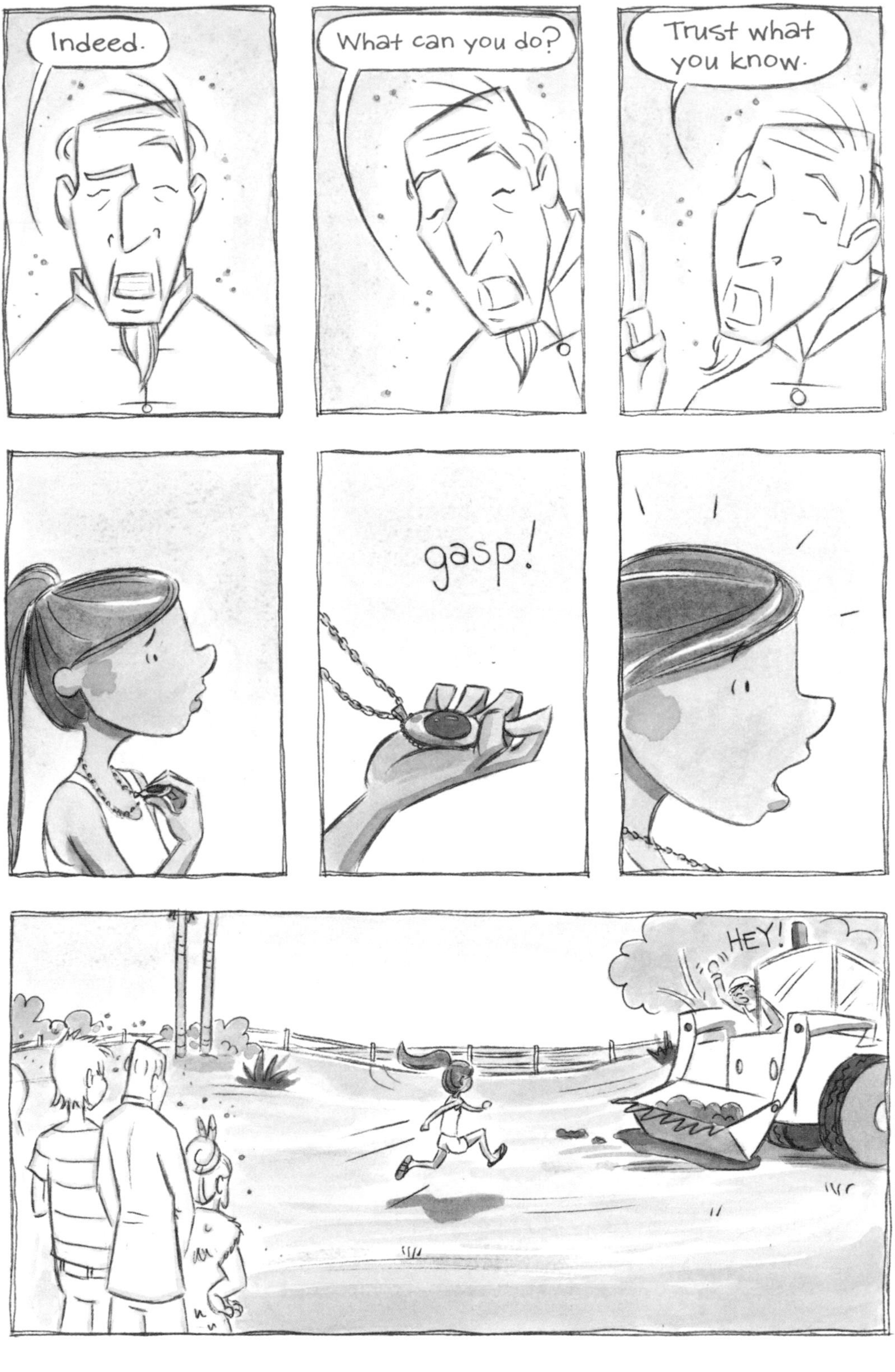
Indeed.
What can you do?
Trust what you know.
gasp!
HEY!

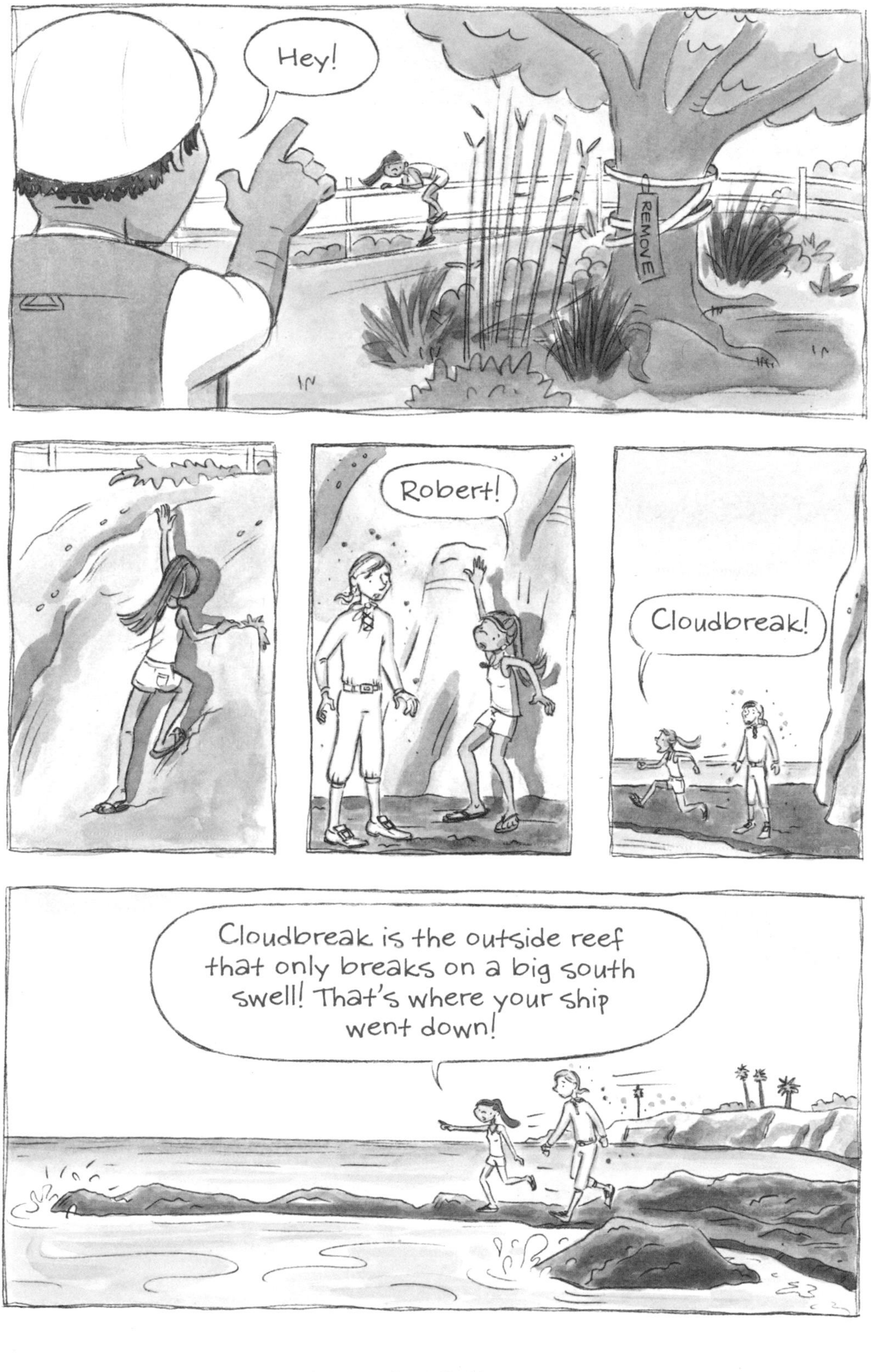
Hey!
REMOVE
Robert!
Cloudbreak!
Cloudbreak is the outside reef that only breaks on a big south swell! That's where your ship went down!

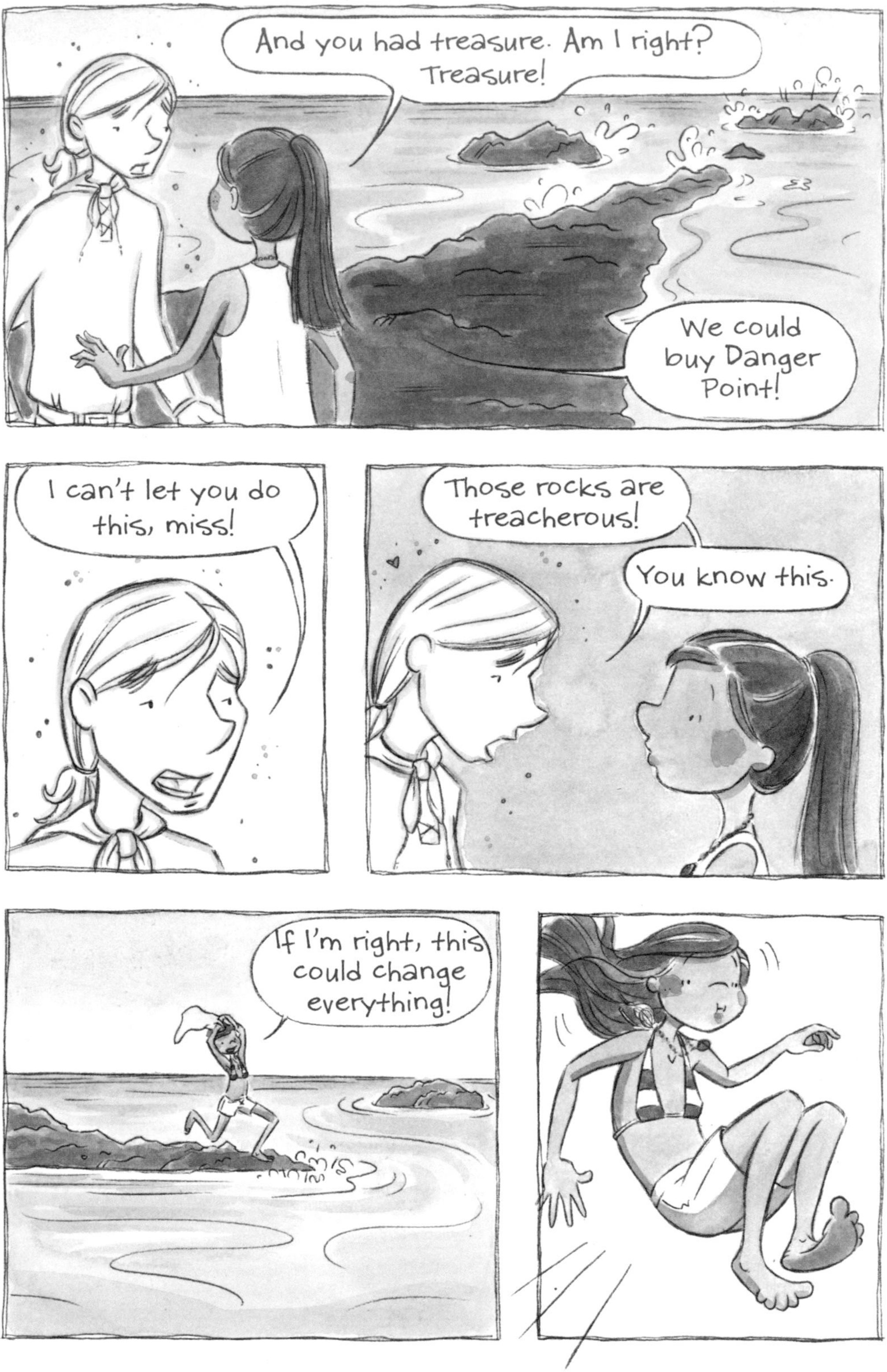
And you had treasure. Am I right? Treasure!
We could buy Danger Point!
I can't let you do this, miss!
Those rocks are treacherous!
You know this.
If I'm right, this could change everything!

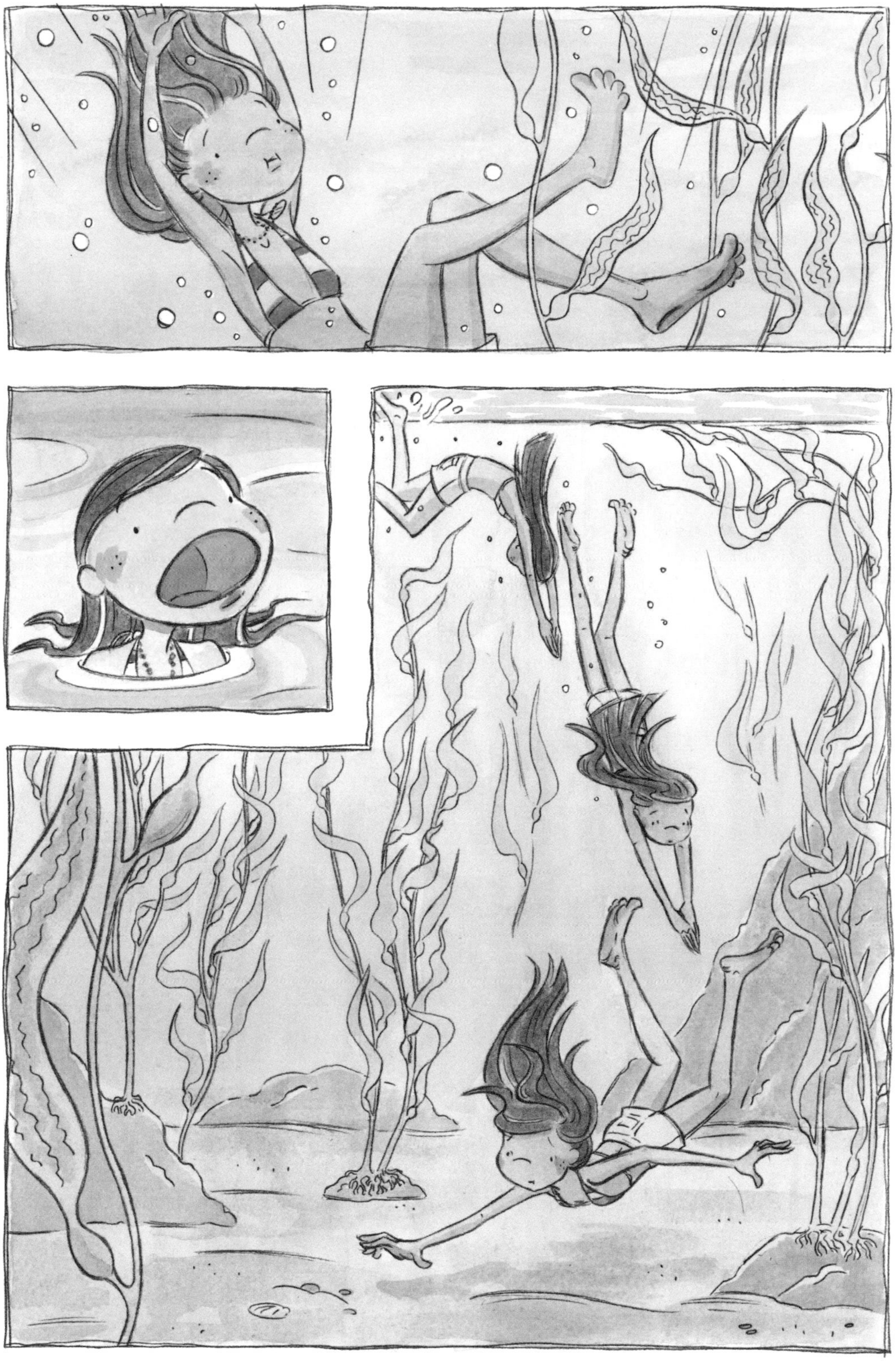

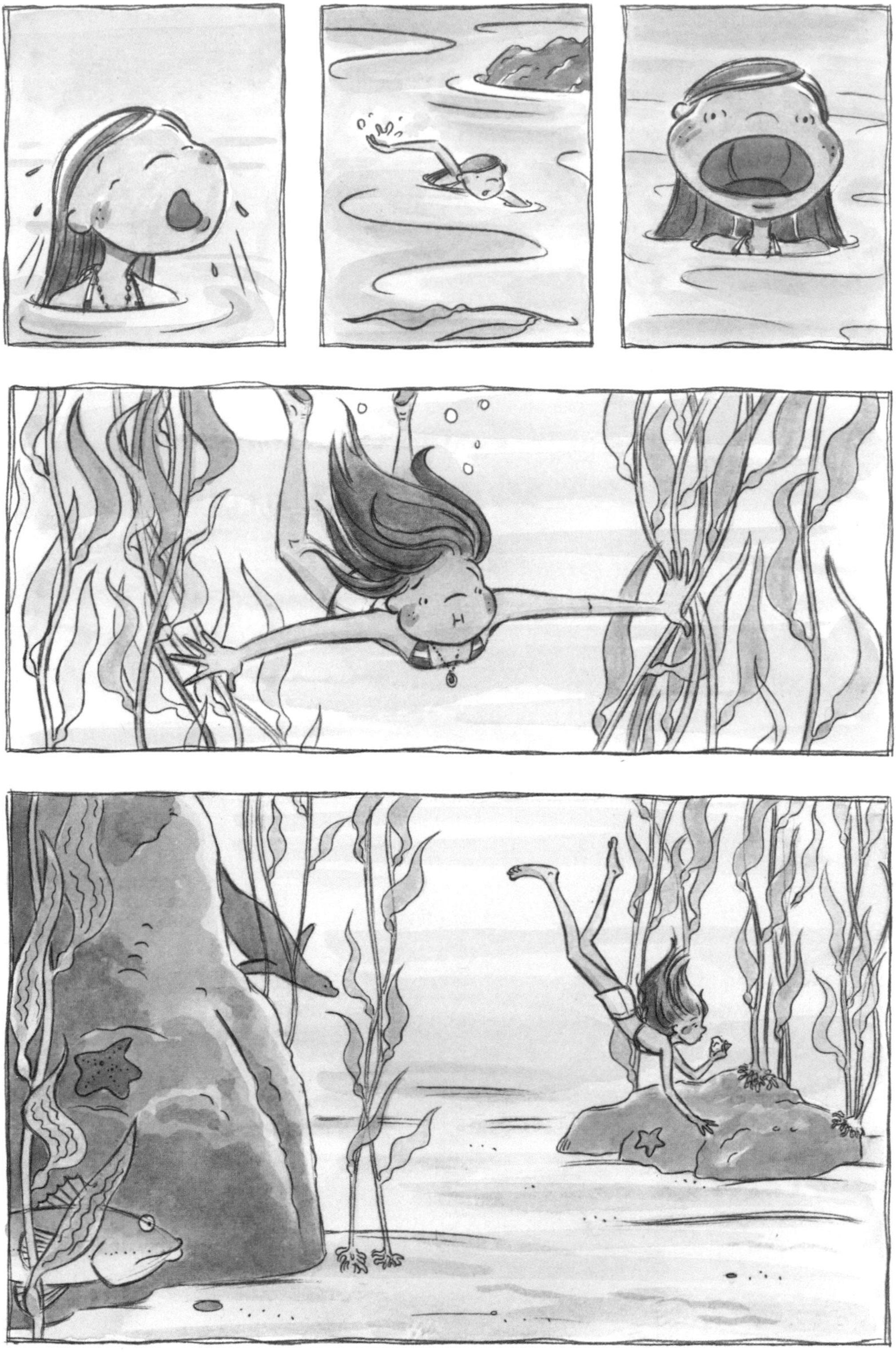

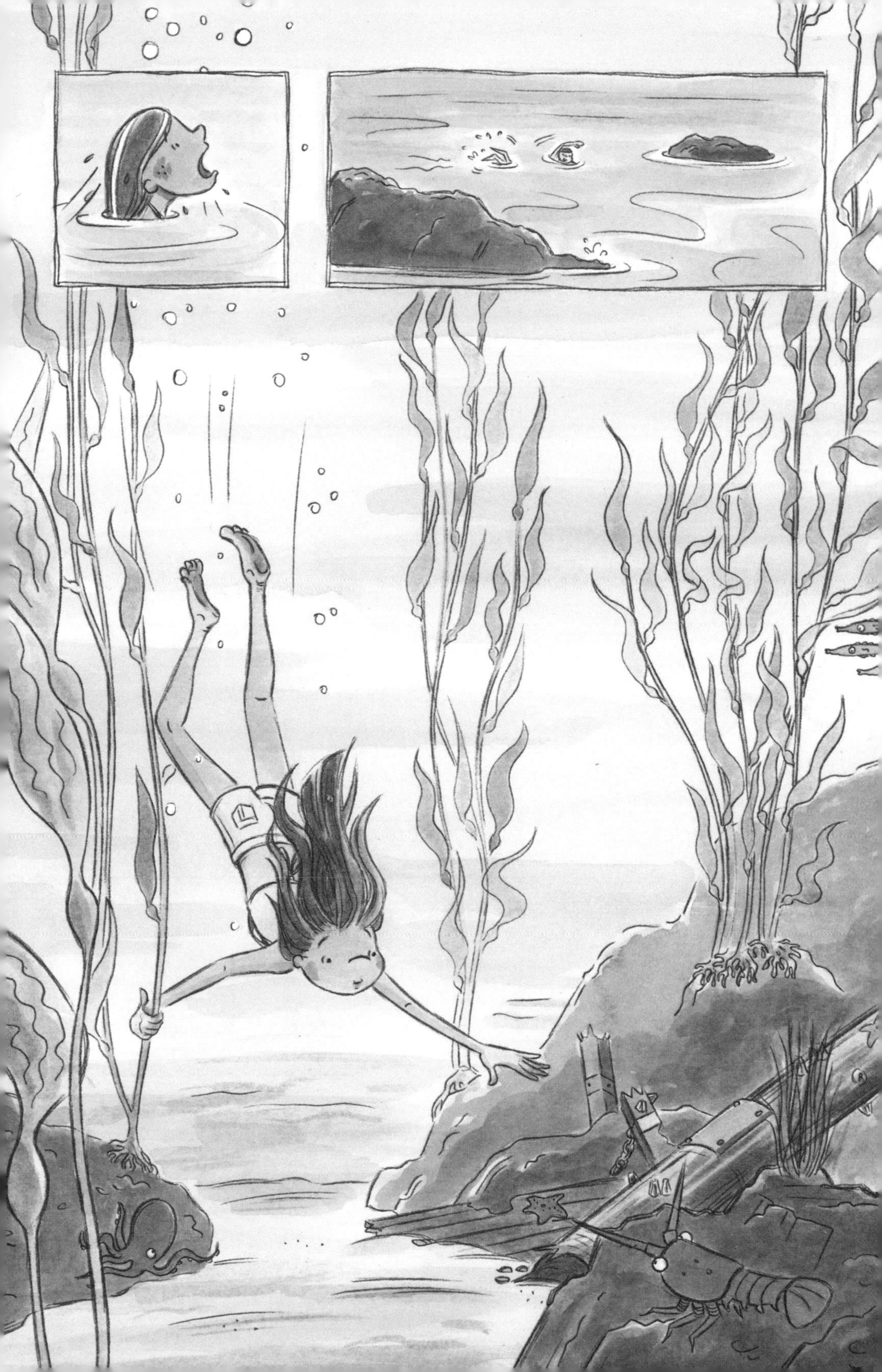

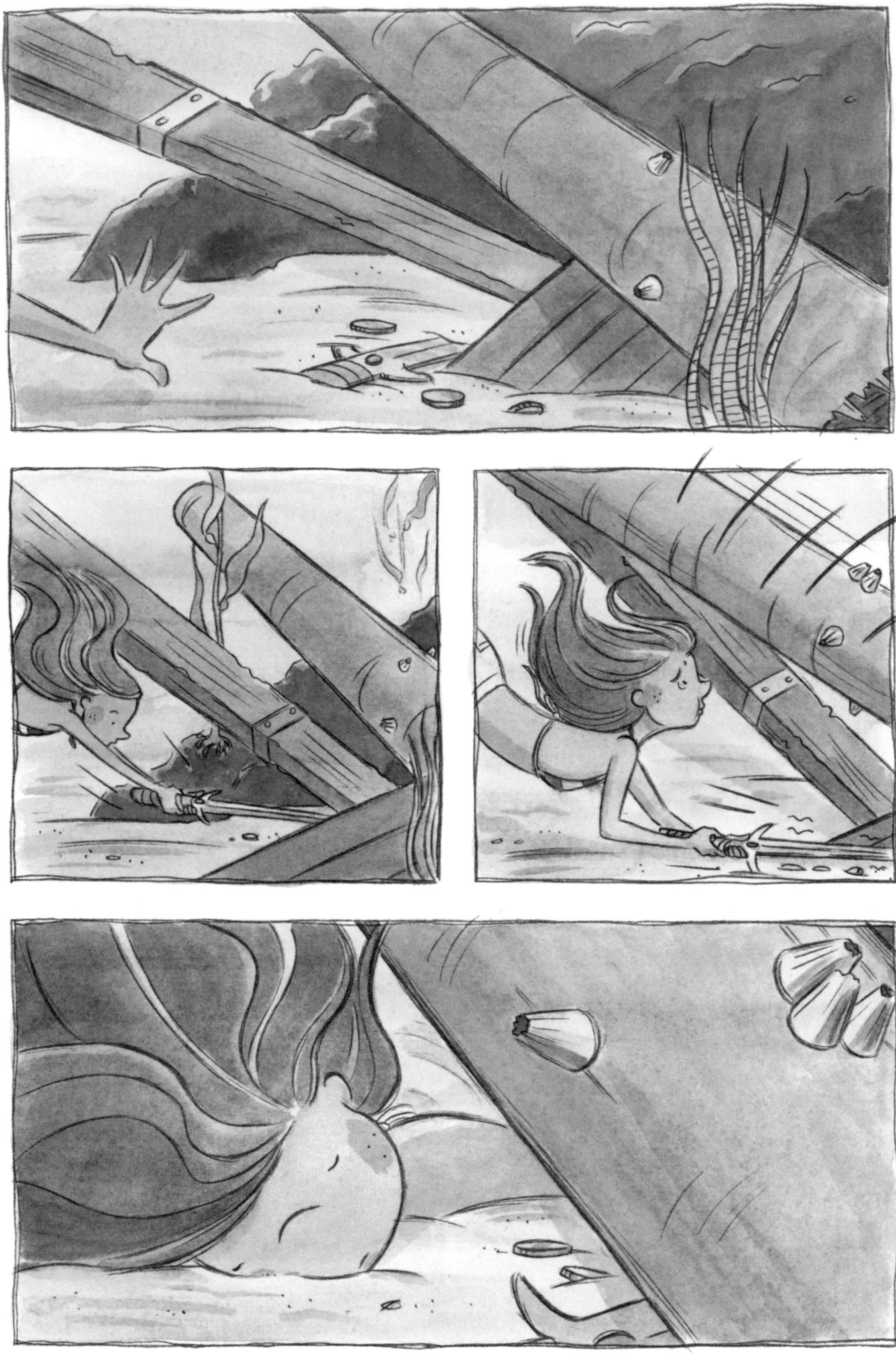

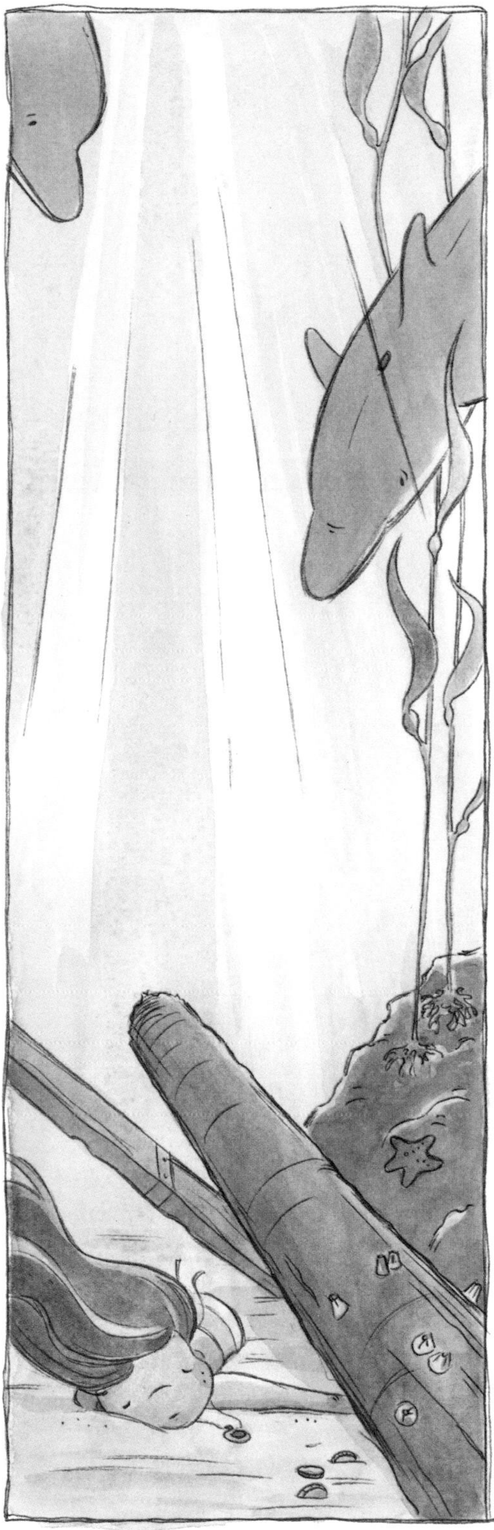

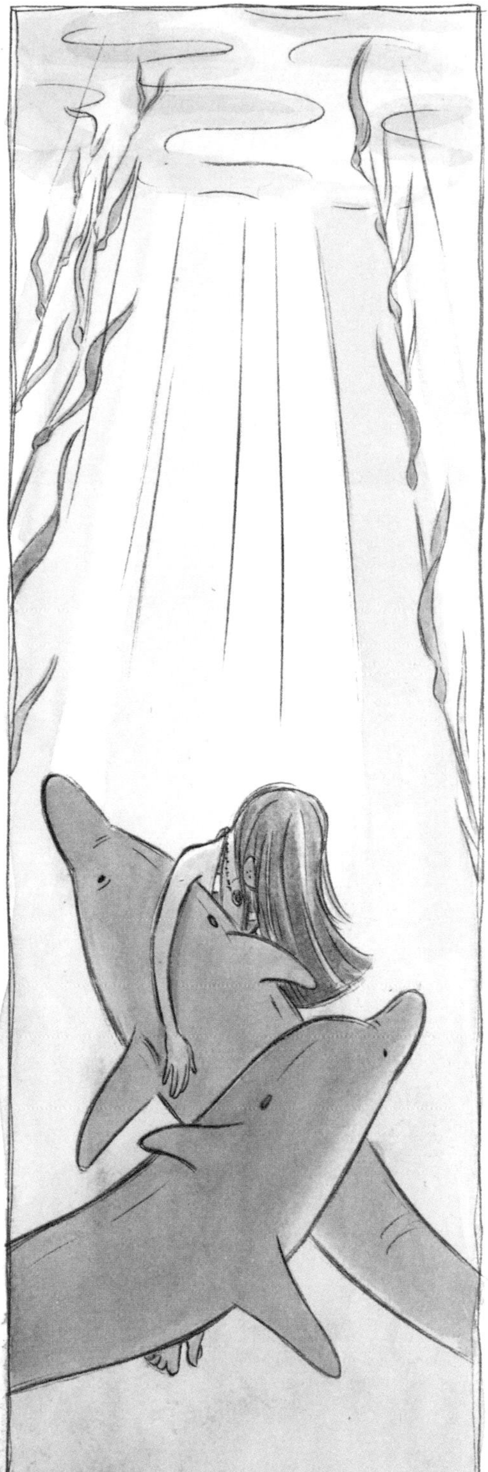

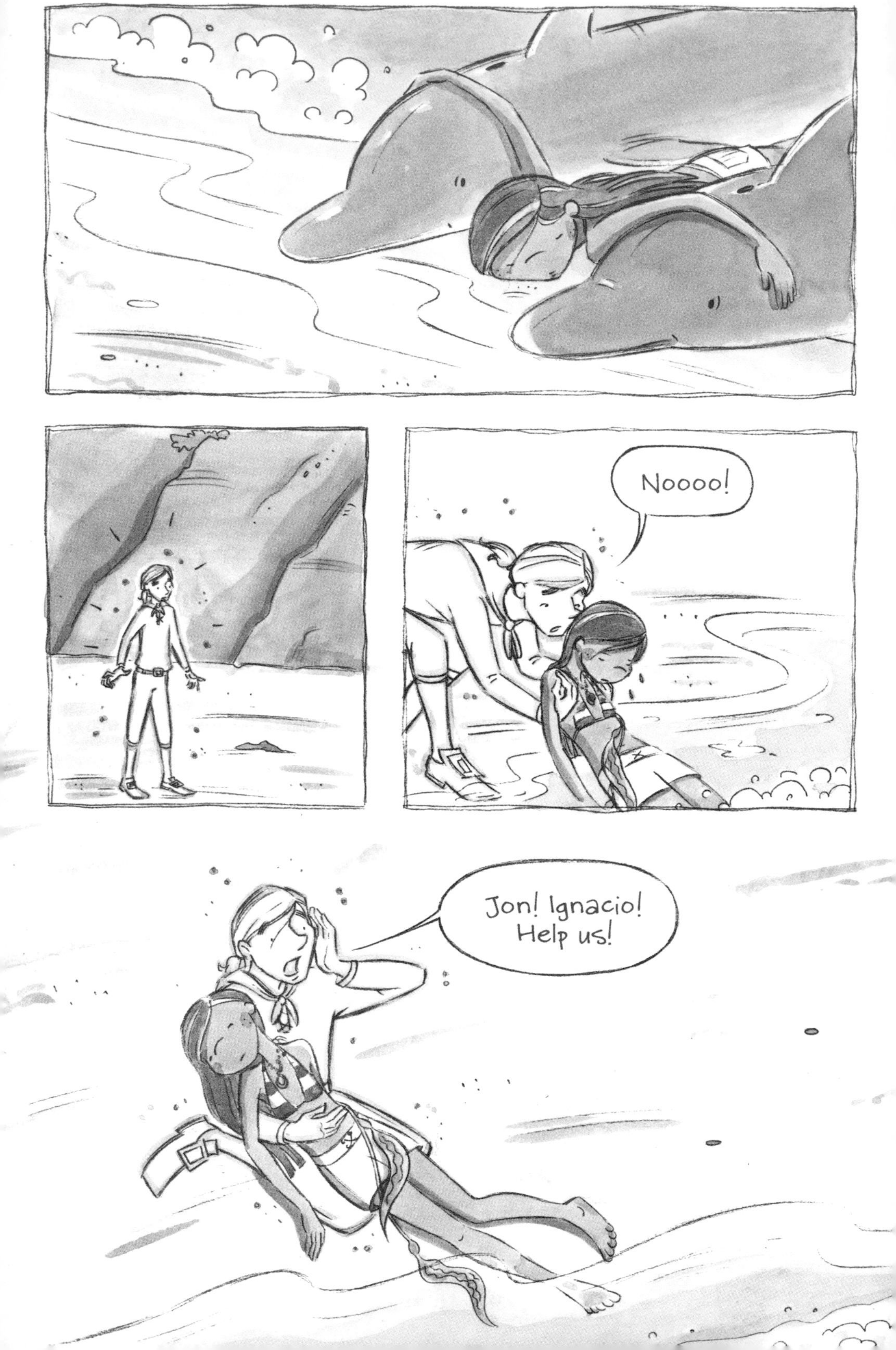
Noooo!
Jon! Ignacio! Help us!

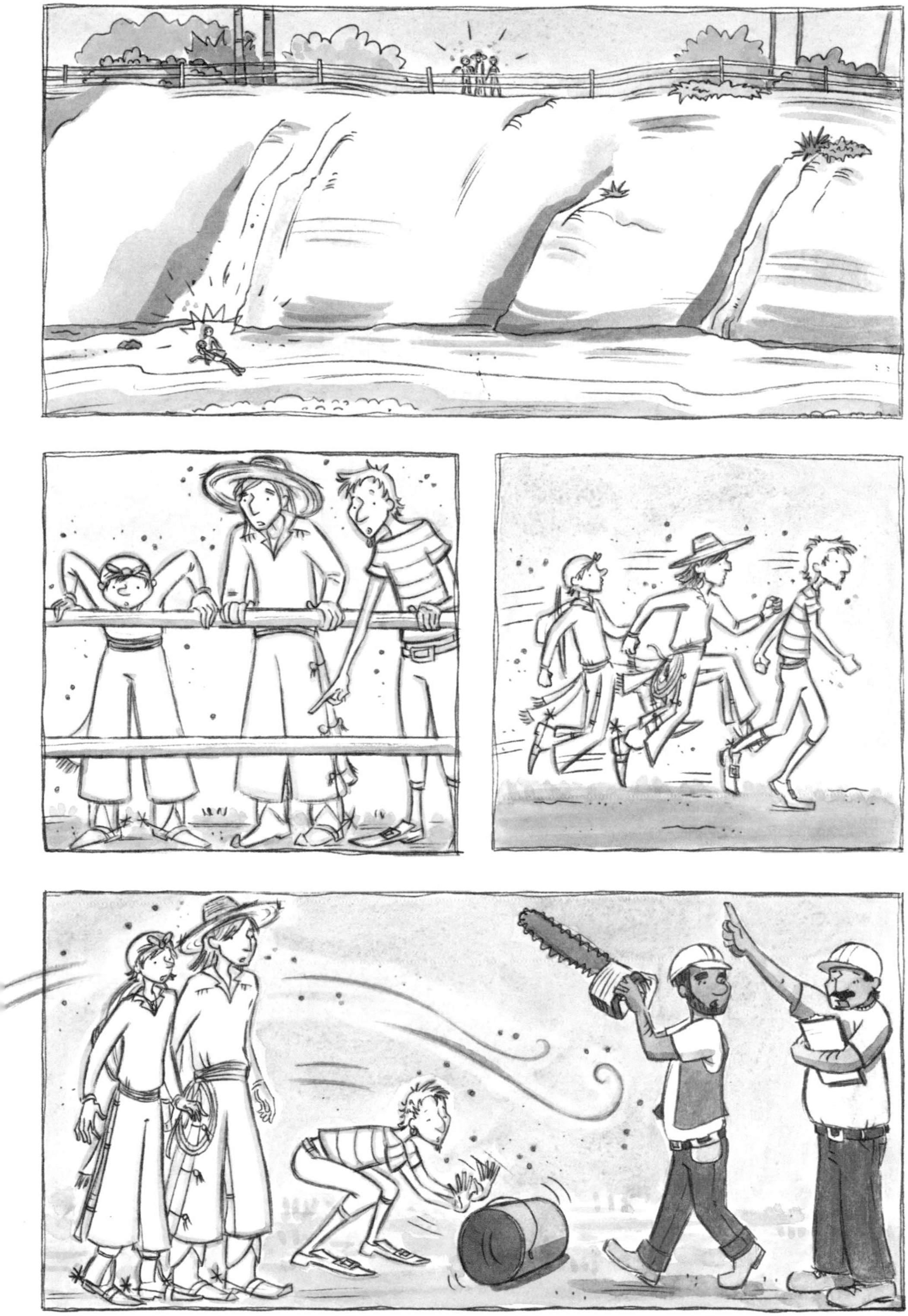

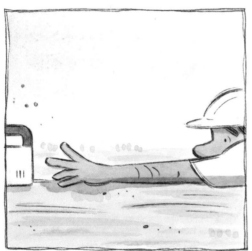

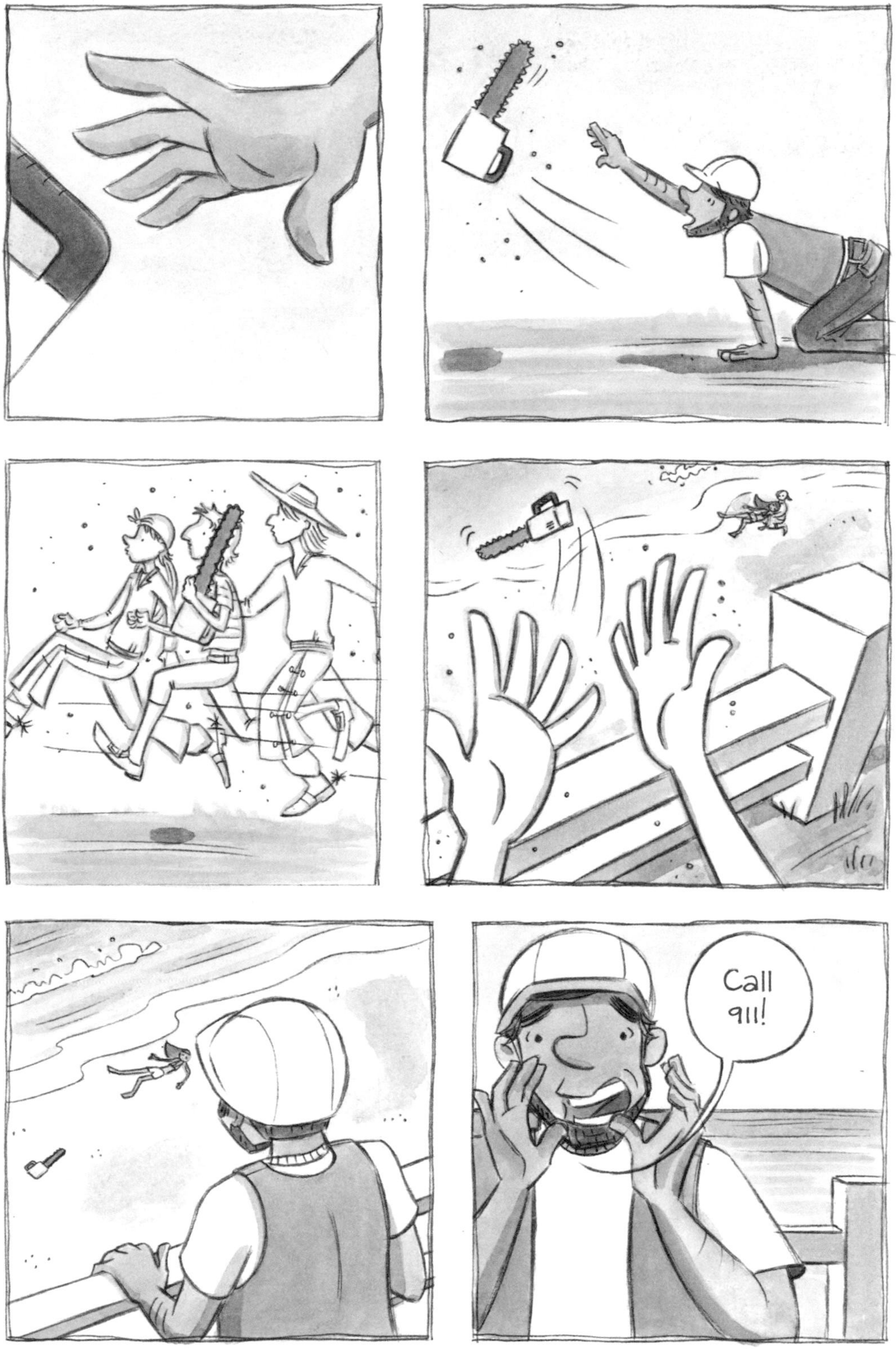
Call 911!

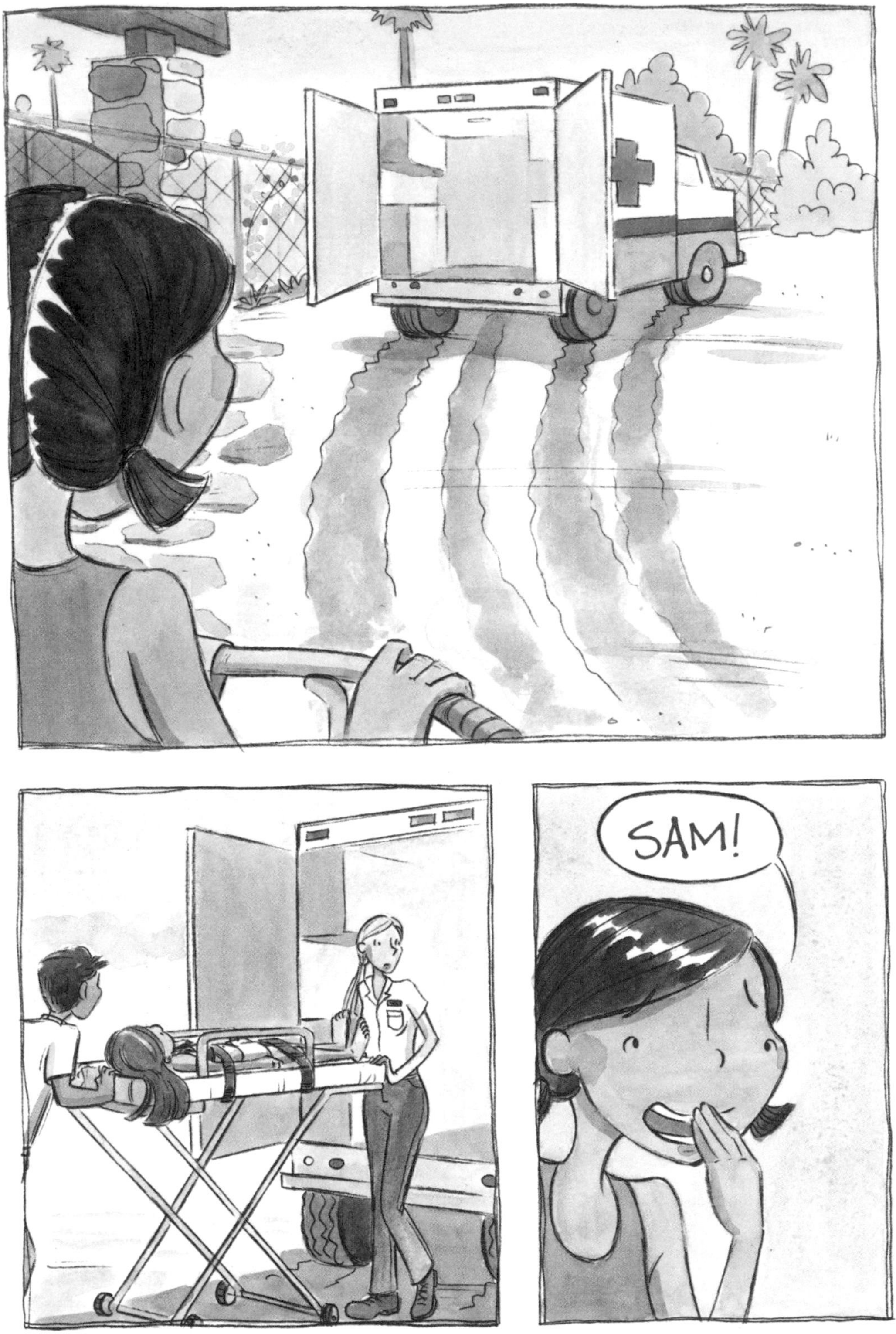
SAM!

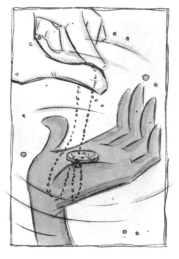

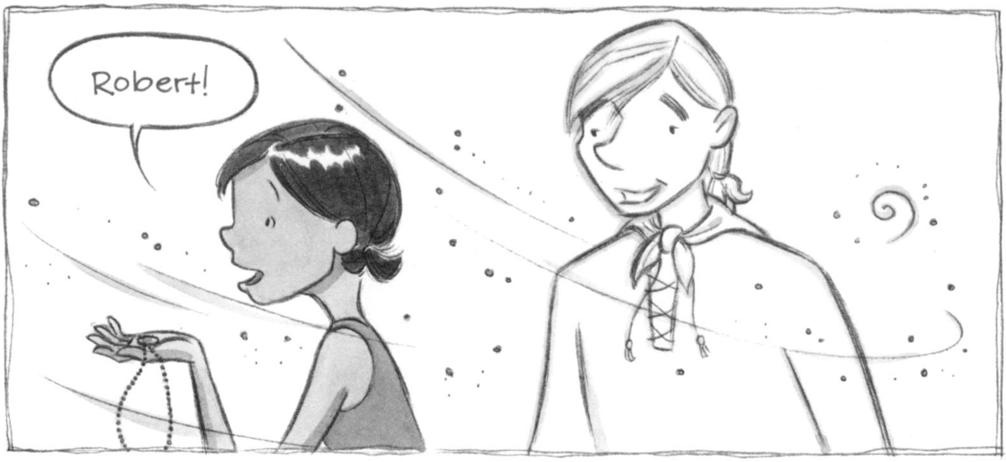
Robert!

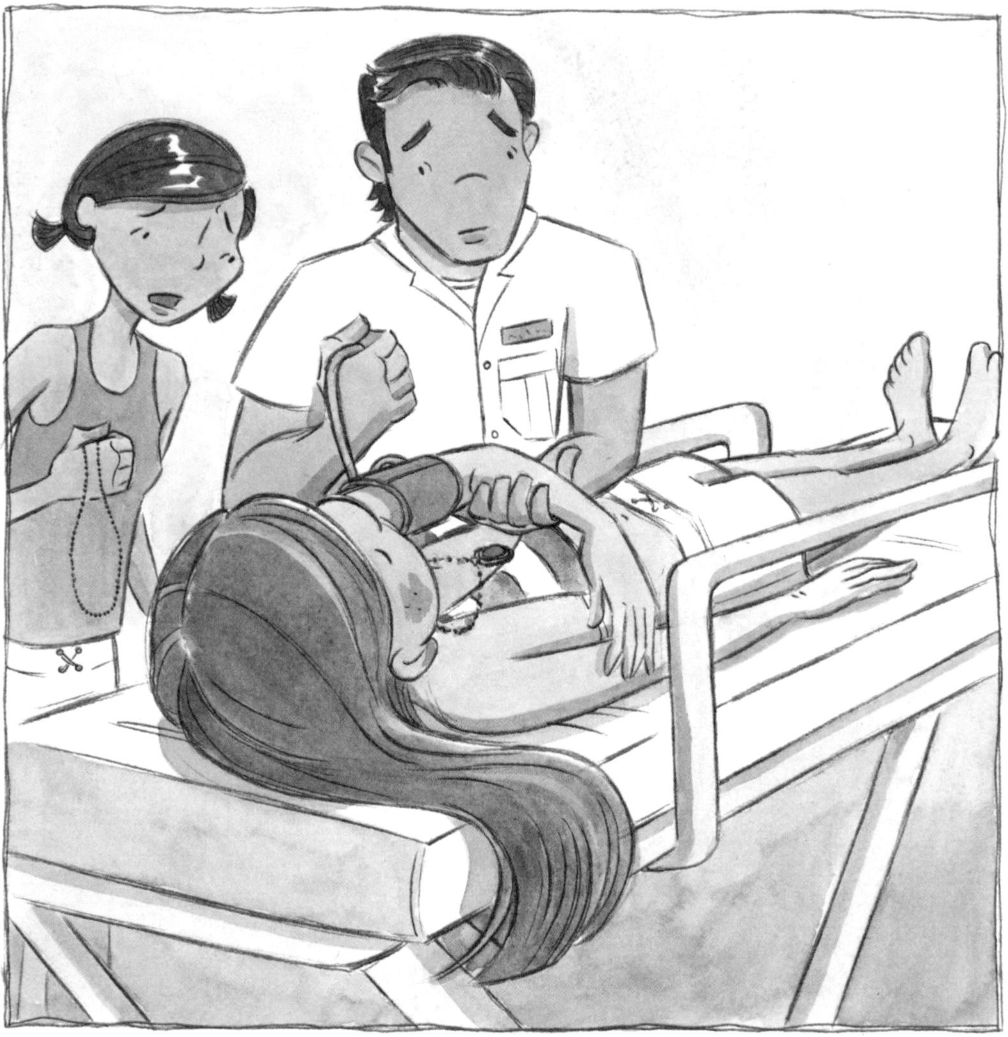

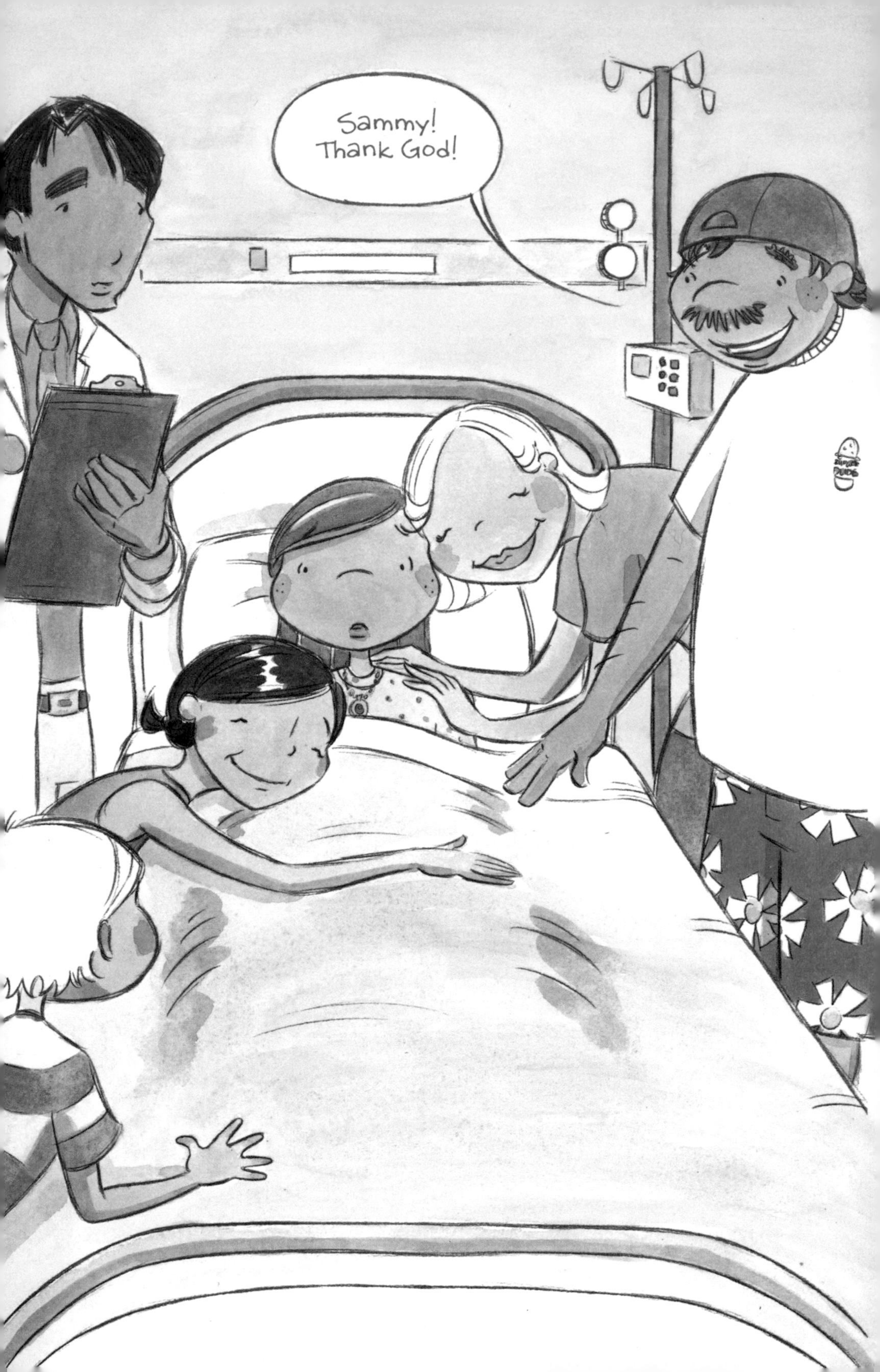
Sammy! Thank God!

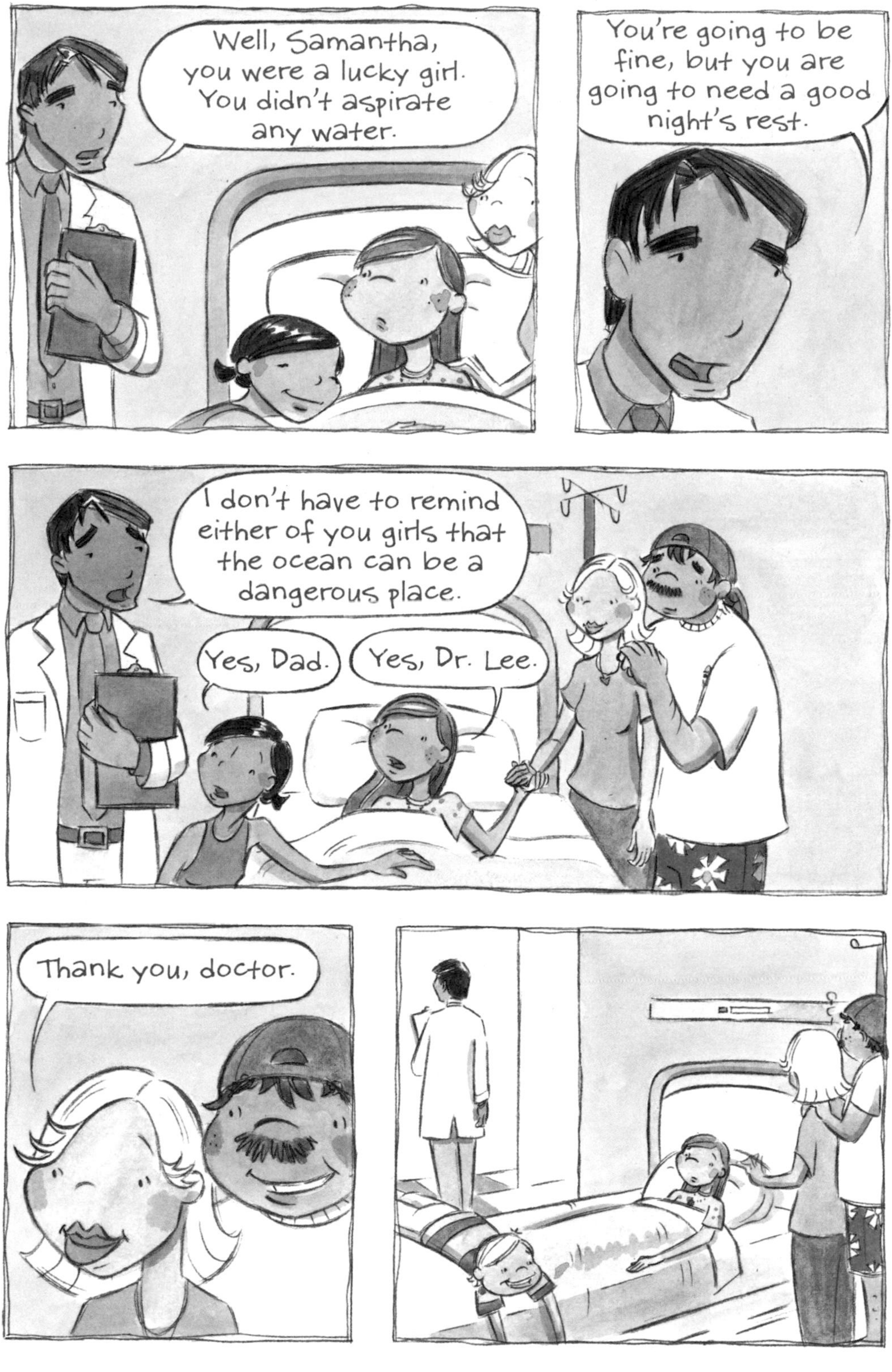
Well, Samantha, you were a lucky girl. You didn't aspirate any water.
You're going to be fine, but you are going to need a good night's rest.
I don't have to remind either of you girls that the ocean can be a dangerous place.
Yes, Dad.
Yes, Dr. Lee.
Thank you, doctor.

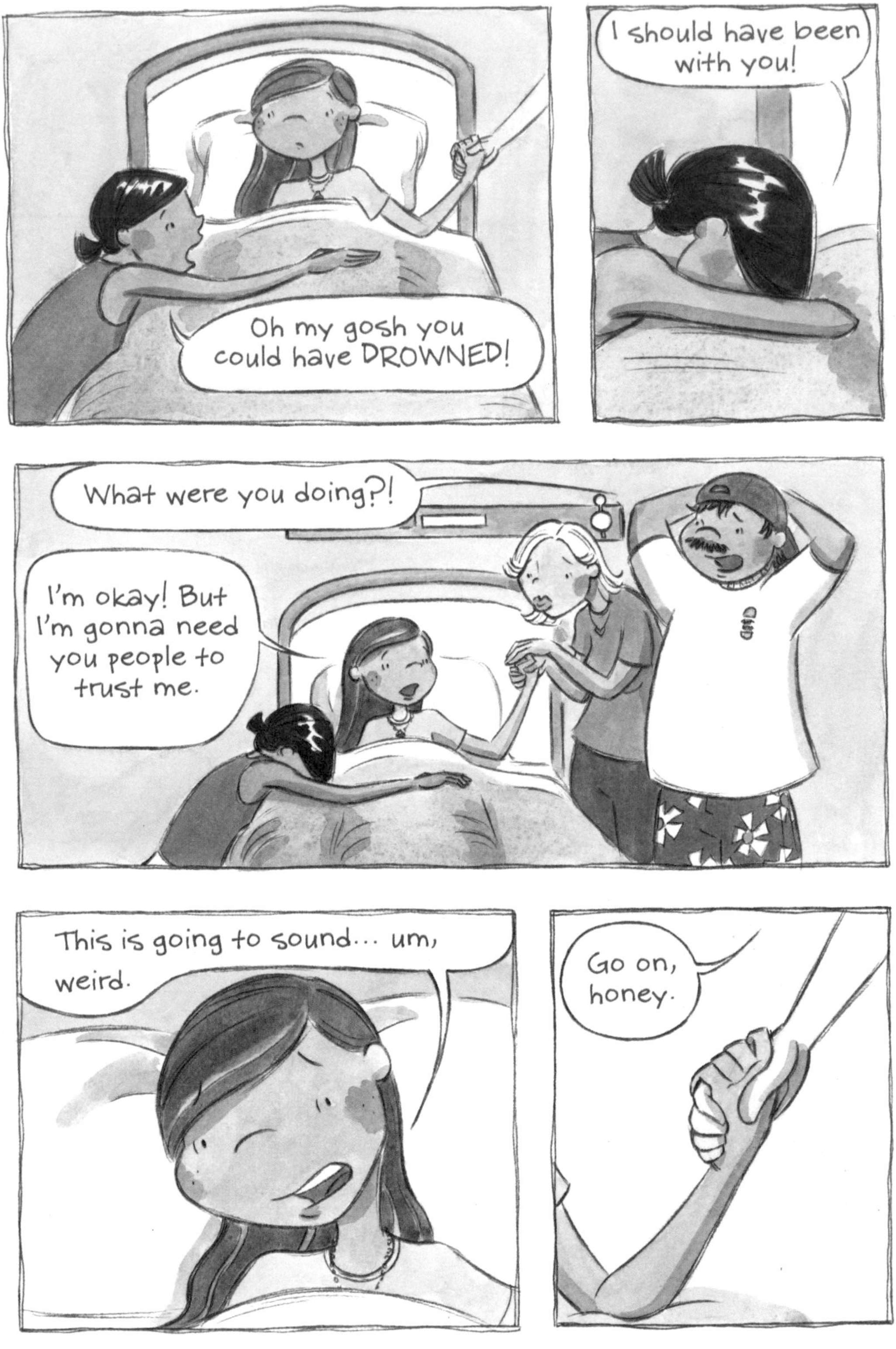
Oh my gosh you could have DROWNED!
I should have been with you!
What were you doing?!
I'm okay! But I'm gonna need you people to trust me.
This is going to sound... um, weird.
Go on, honey.

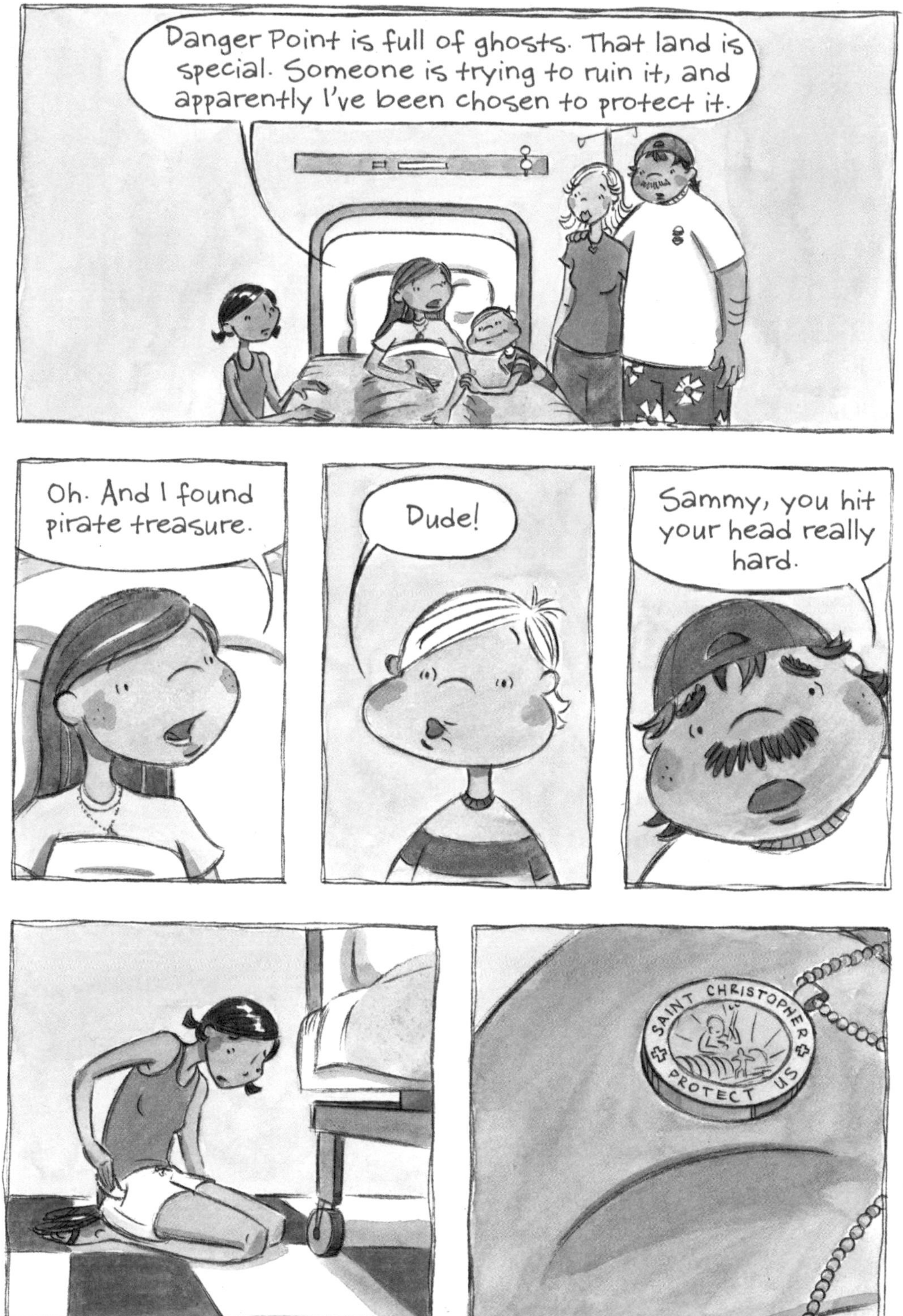
Danger Point is full of ghosts. That land is special. Someone is trying to ruin it, and apparently I've been chosen to protect it.
Oh. And I found pirate treasure.
Dude!
Sammy, you hit your head really hard.
SAINT CHRISTOPHER PROTECT US

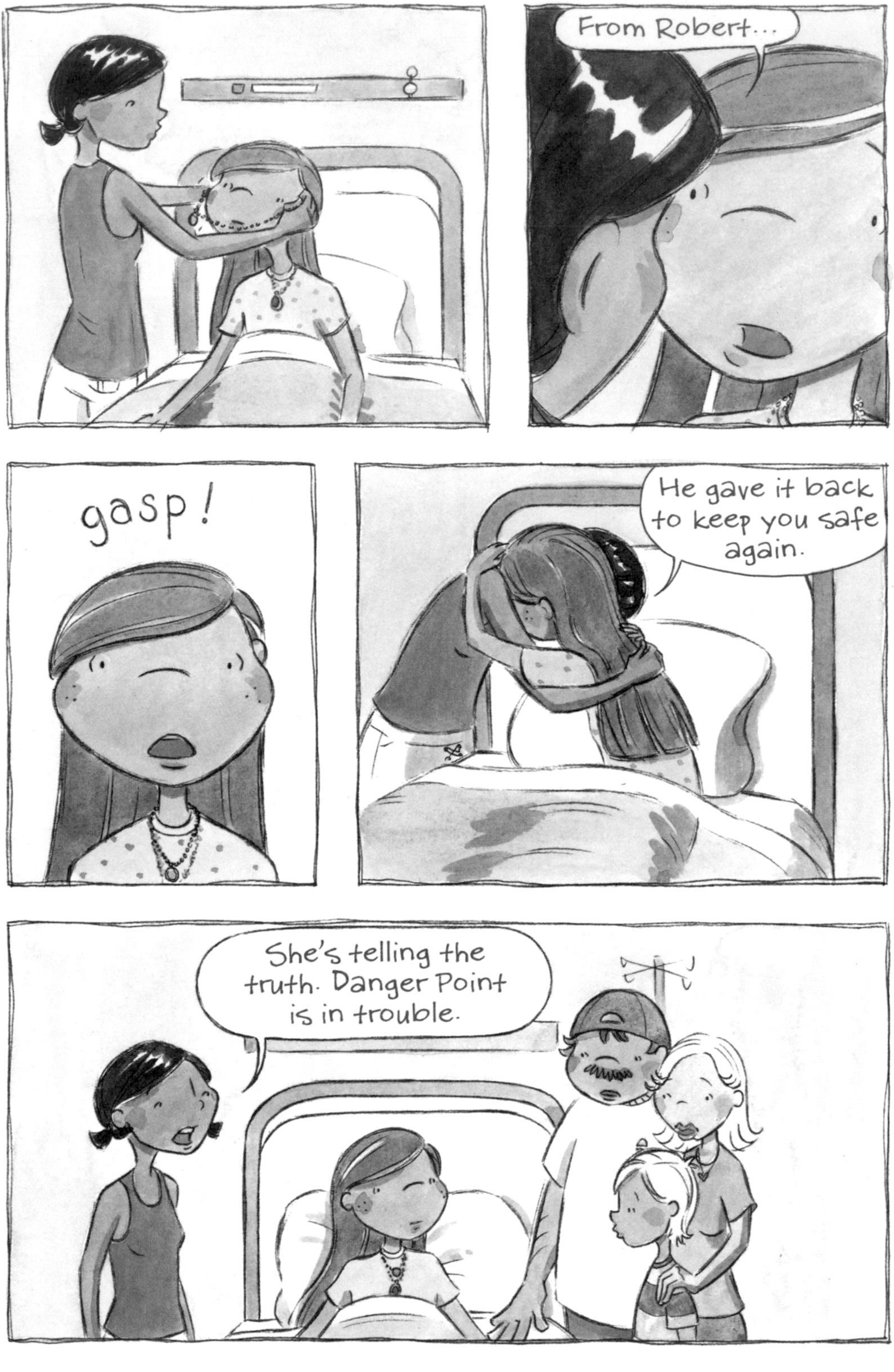
From Robert...
gasp!
He gave it back to keep you safe again.
She's telling the truth. Danger Point is in trouble.

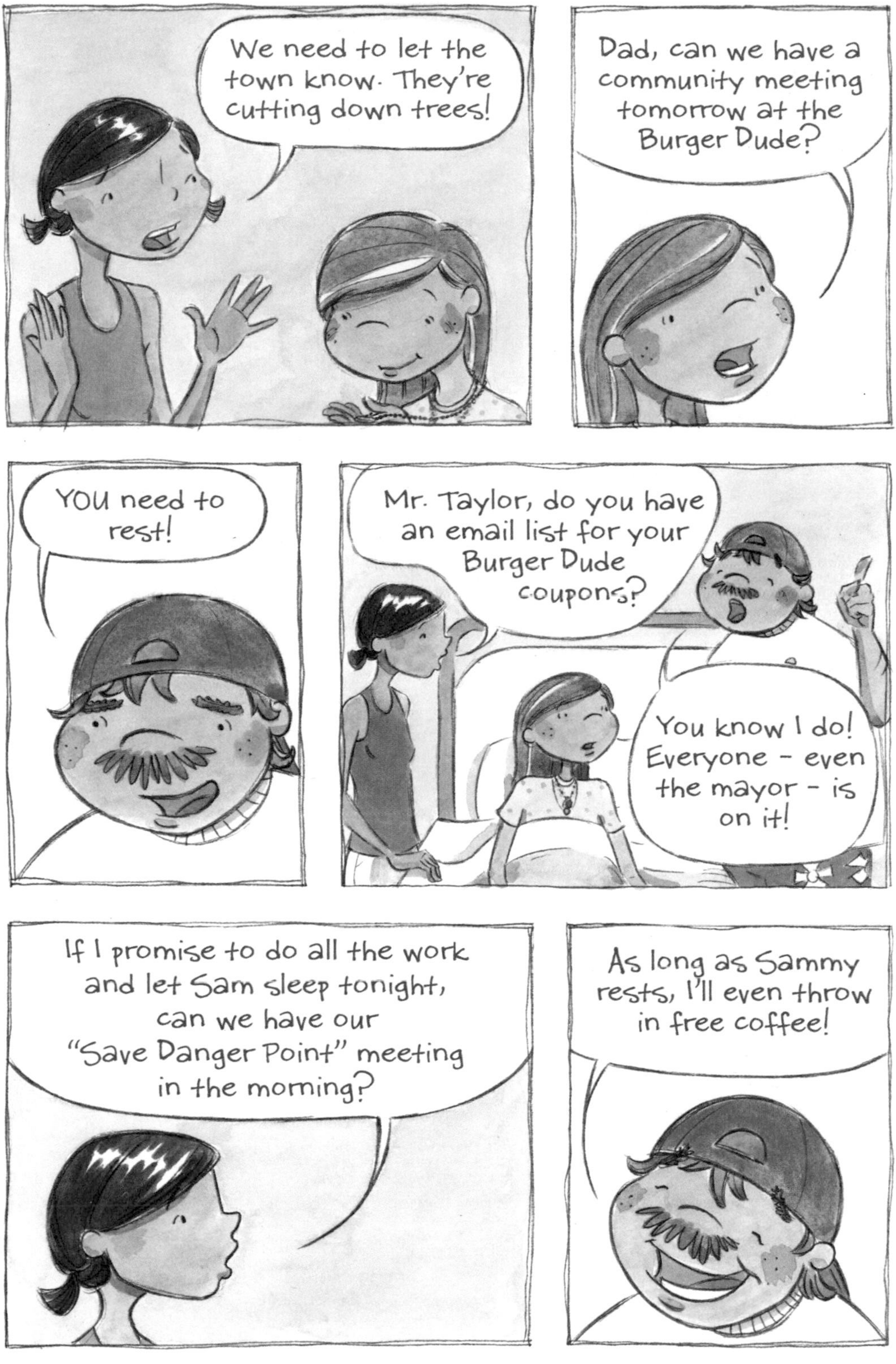
We need to let the town know. They're cutting down trees!
Dad, can we have a community meeting tomorrow at the Burger Dude?
YOU need to rest!
Mr. Taylor, do you have an email list for your Burger Dude coupons?
You know I do! Everyone - even the mayor - is on it!
If I promise to do all the work and let Sam sleep tonight, can we have our "Save Danger Point" meeting in the morning?
As long as Sammy rests, I'll even throw in free coffee!

LATER THAT EVENING

Ring!

Ring! Ring!

Hey, it's me. How're you feeling?

Better, thanks.

So I did some digging around online.

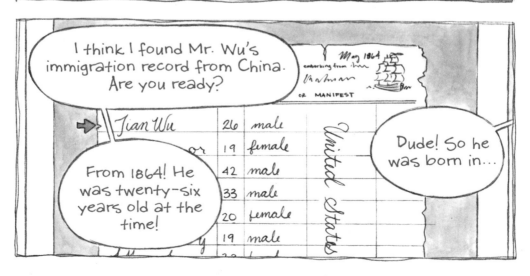

I think I found Mr. Wu's immigration record from China. Are you ready?

From 1864! He was twenty-six years old at the time!

Dude! So he was born in...

May 1864

embarking from

OR MANIFEST

Jian Wu	26	male
	19	female
	42	male
	33	male
	20	female
	19	male

United States

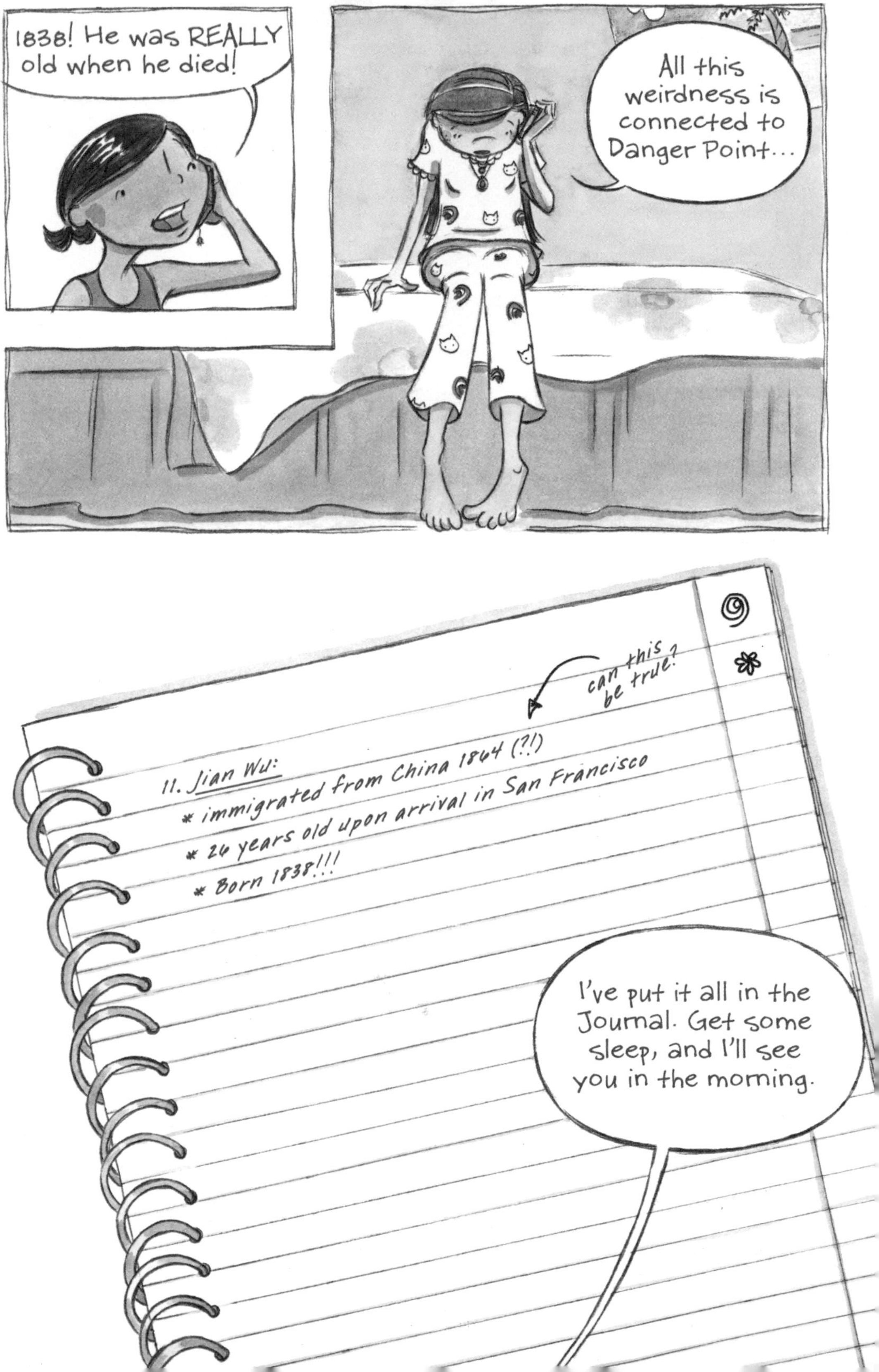
1838! He was REALLY old when he died!
All this weirdness is connected to Danger Point...
can this be true?
11. Jian Wu:
* immigrated from China 1864 (?!)
* 26 years old upon arrival in San Francisco
* Born 1838!!!
I've put it all in the Journal. Get some sleep, and I'll see you in the morning.

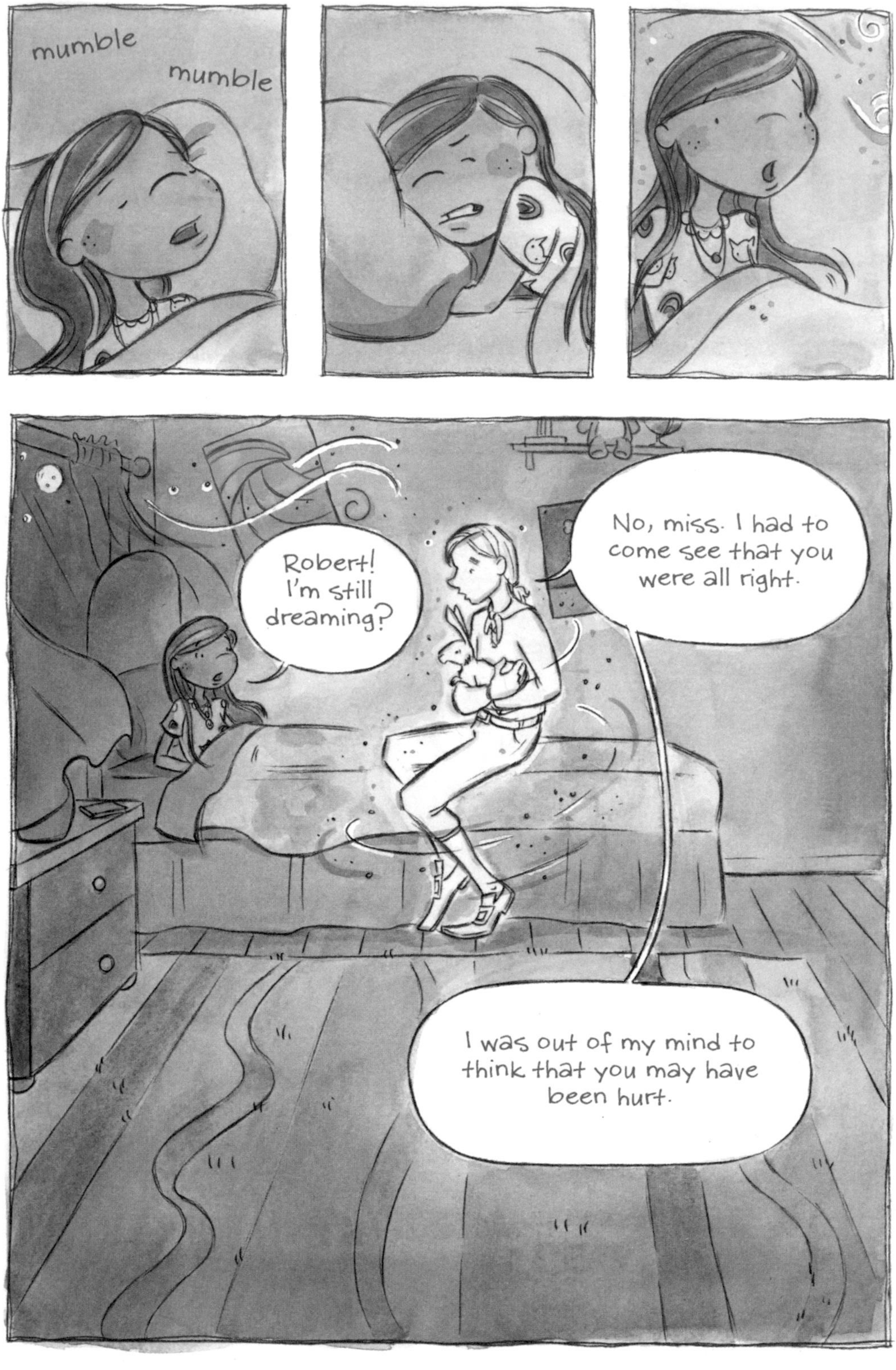
mumble
mumble
Robert! I'm still dreaming?
No, miss. I had to come see that you were all right.
I was out of my mind to think that you may have been hurt.

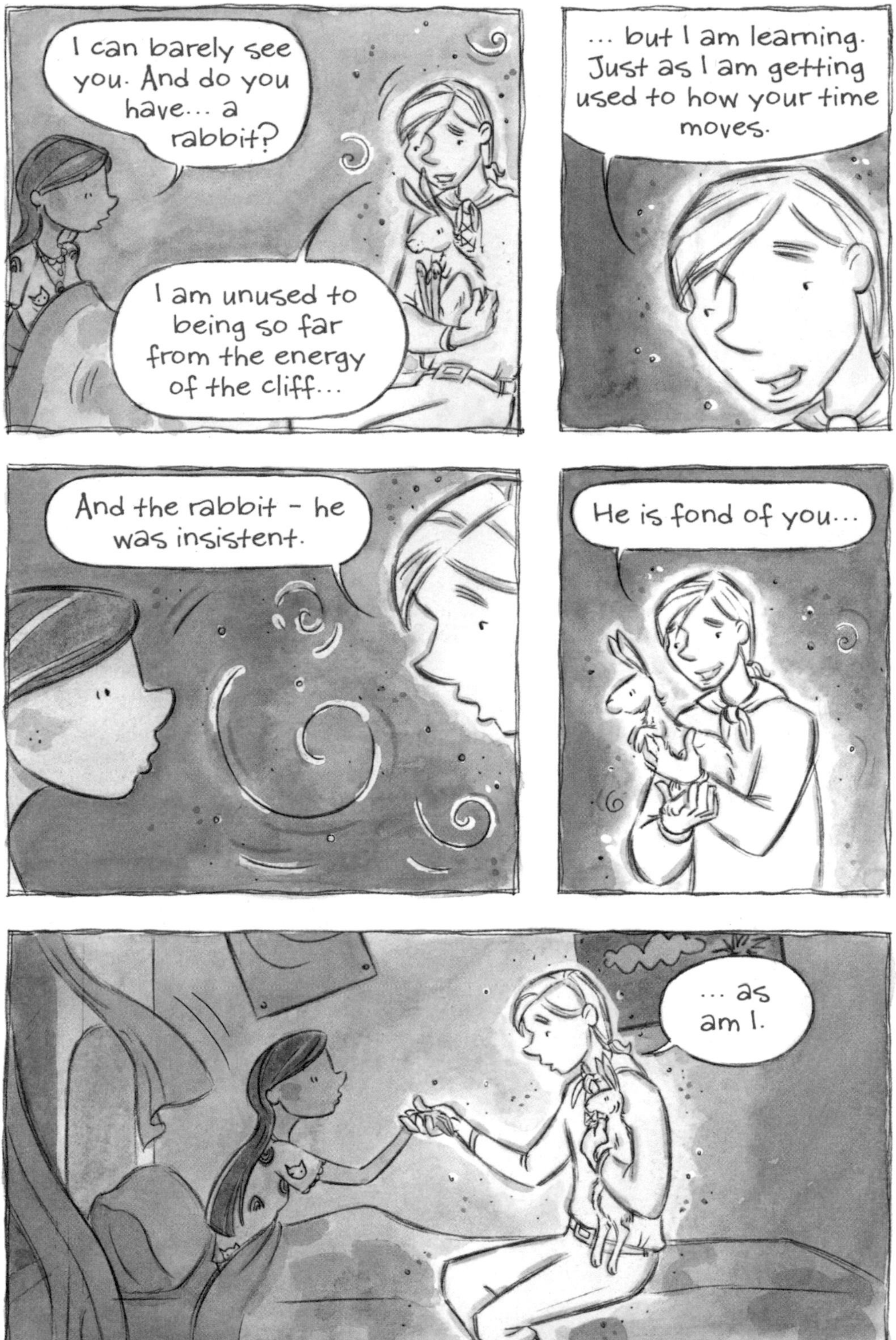
I can barely see you. And do you have... a rabbit?
I am unused to being so far from the energy of the cliff...
... but I am learning. Just as I am getting used to how your time moves.
And the rabbit - he was insistent.
He is fond of you...
... as am I.

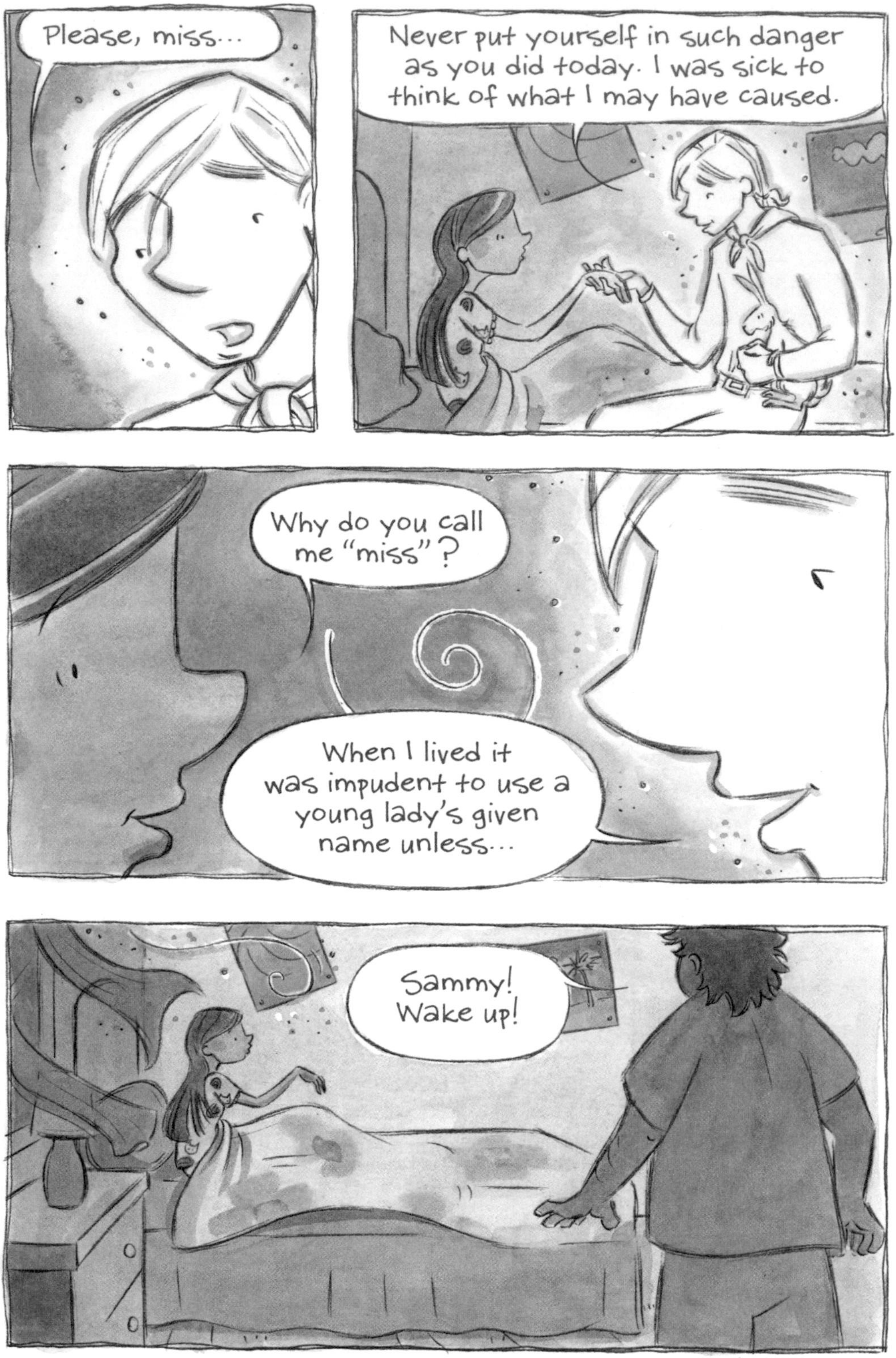
Please, miss...
Never put yourself in such danger as you did today. I was sick to think of what I may have caused.
Why do you call me "miss"?
When I lived it was impudent to use a young lady's given name unless...
Sammy! Wake up!

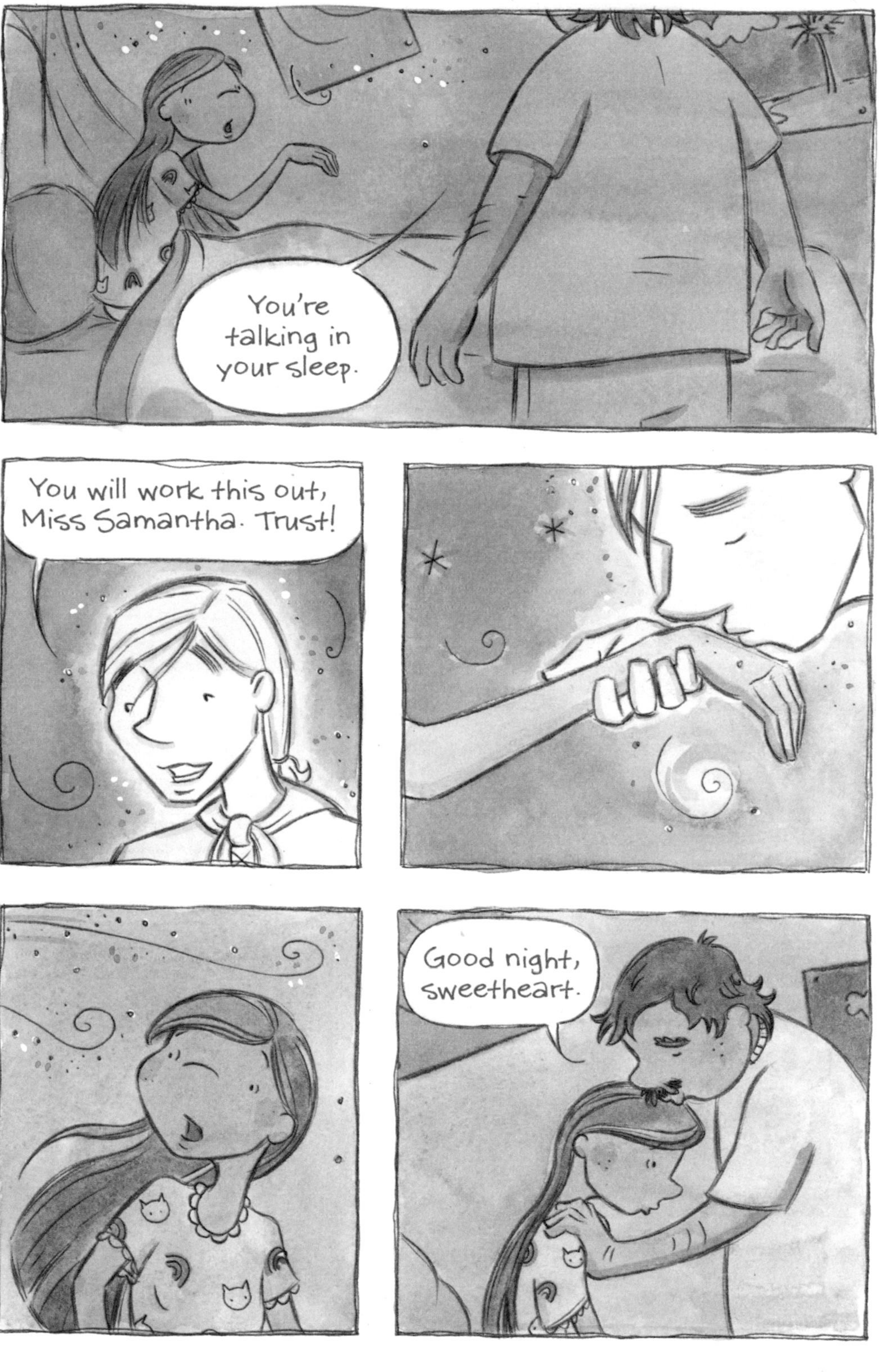
You're talking in your sleep.
You will work this out, Miss Samantha. Trust!
Good night, sweetheart.

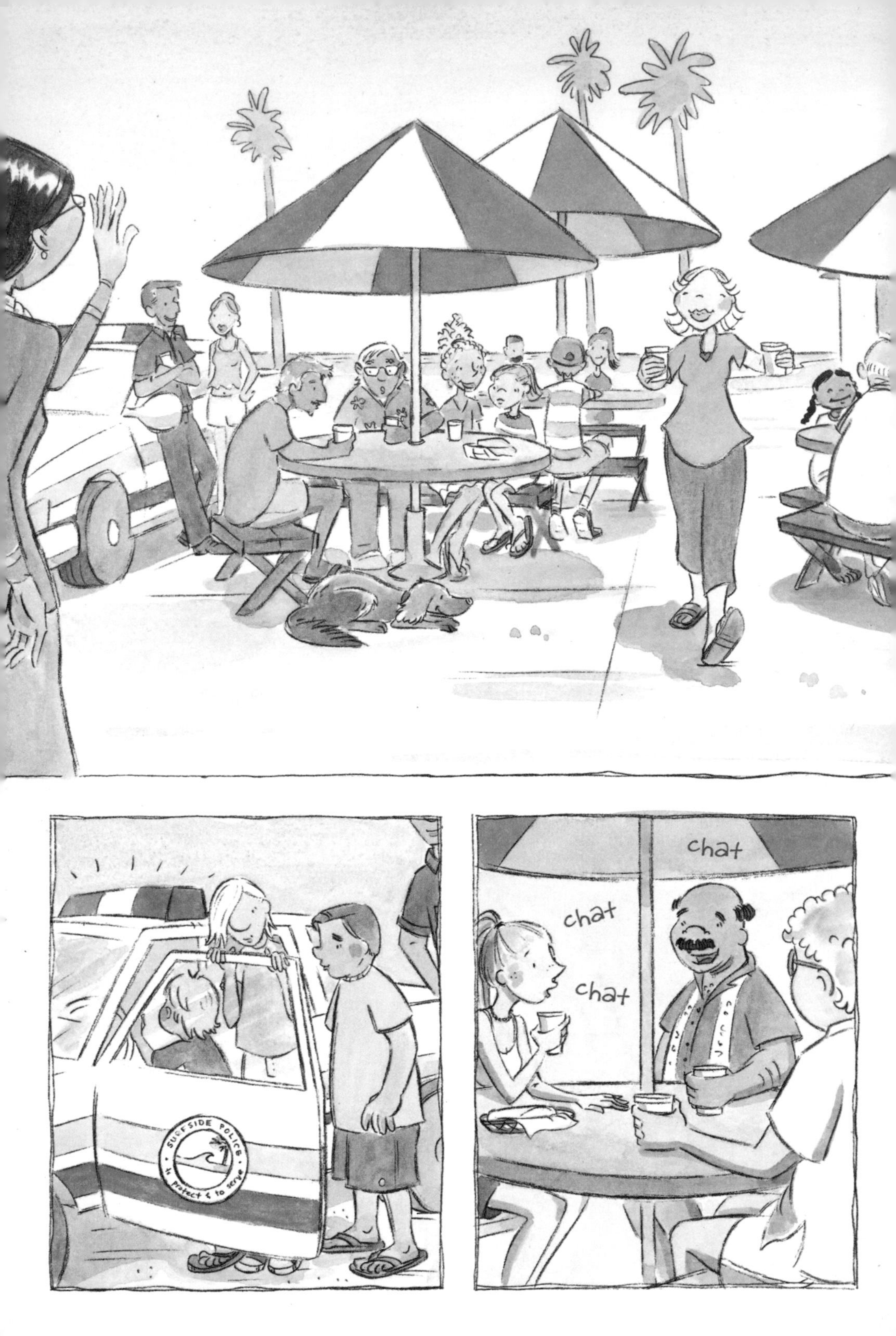
SURFSIDE POLICE
to protect & to serve
chat
chat
chat

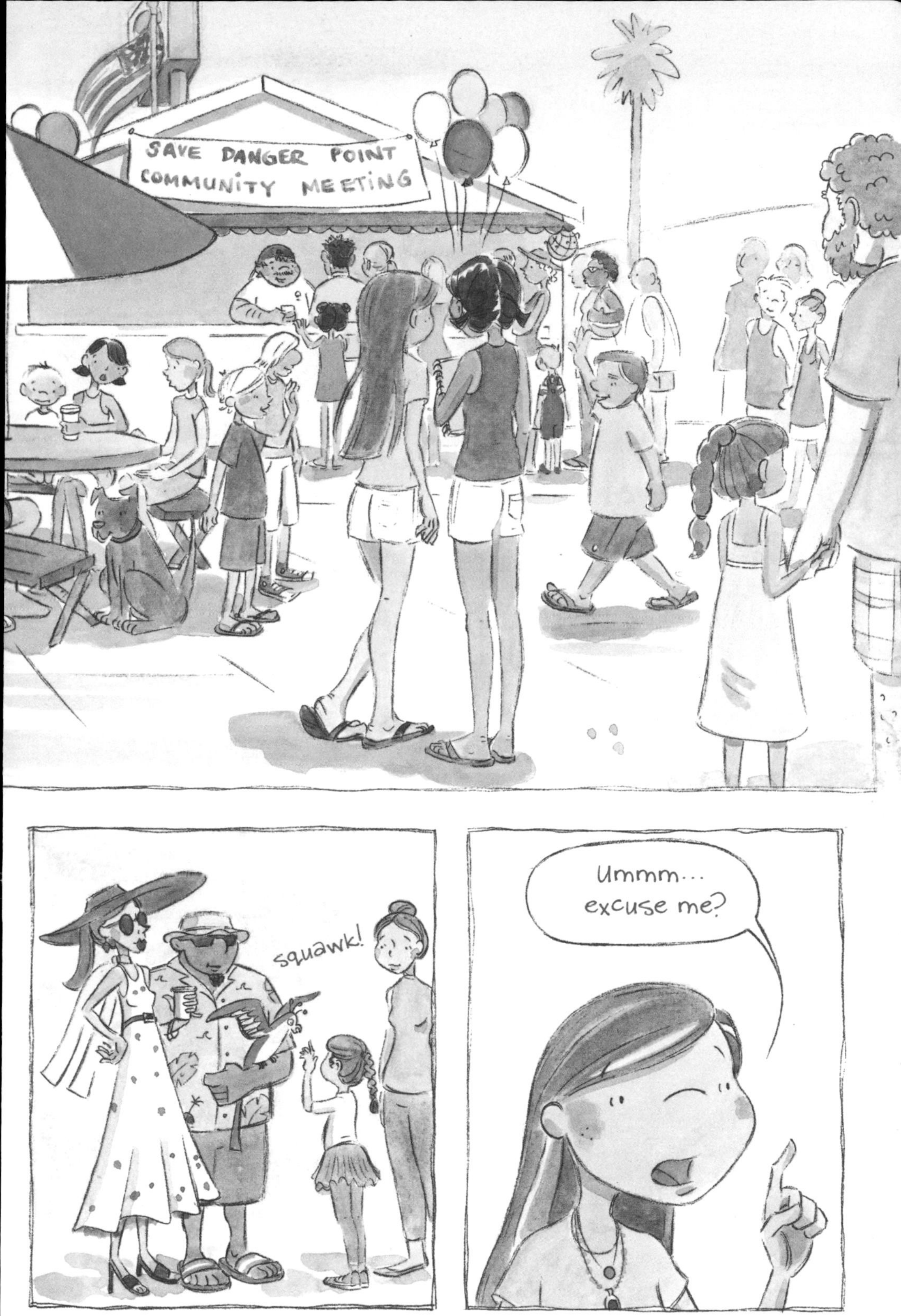
SAVE DANGER POINT
COMMUNITY MEETING
squawk!
Ummm...
excuse me?

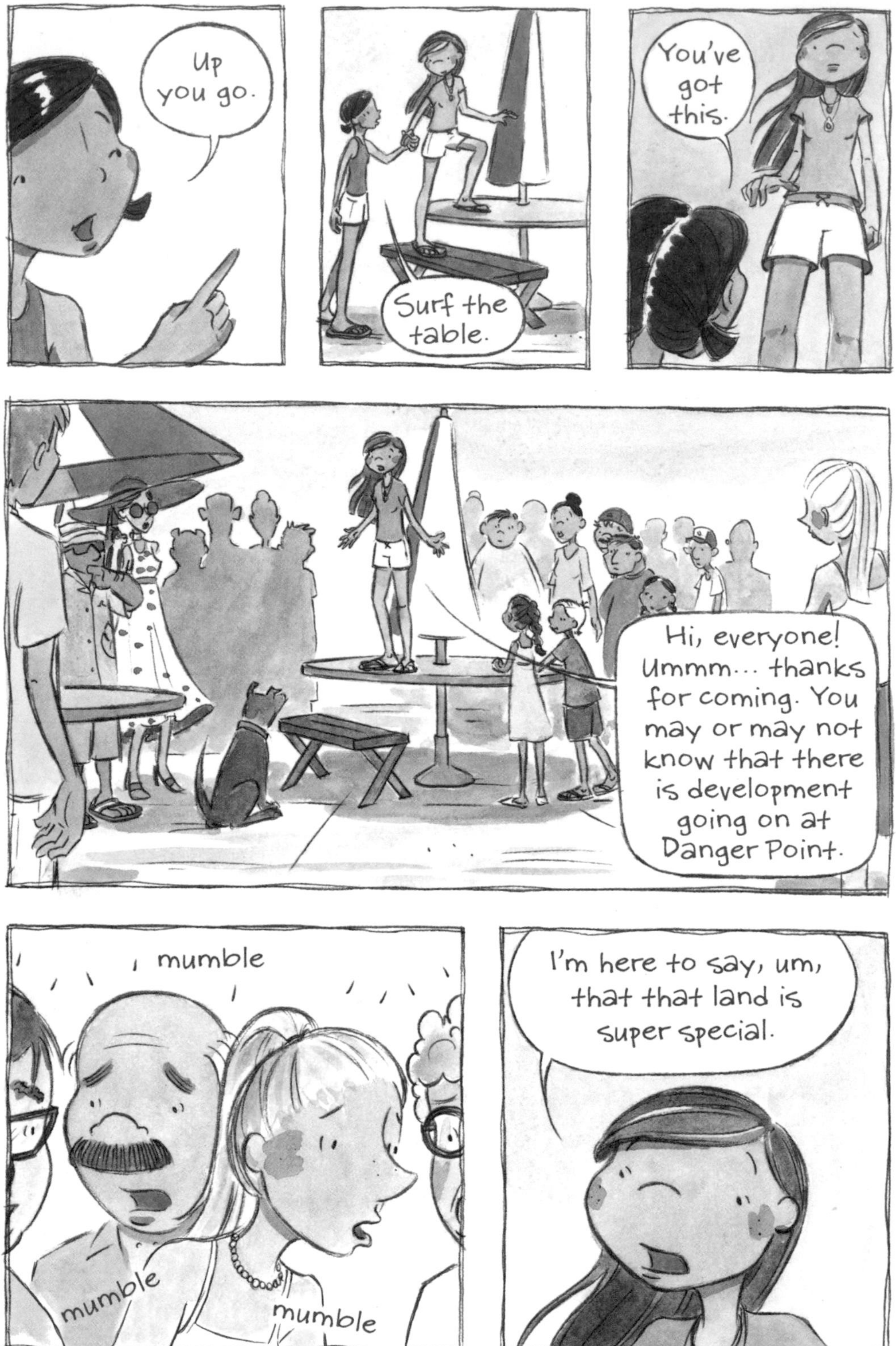
Up you go.
Surf the table.
You've got this.
Hi, everyone! Ummm... thanks for coming. You may or may not know that there is development going on at Danger Point.
mumble
mumble
mumble
I'm here to say, um, that that land is super special.

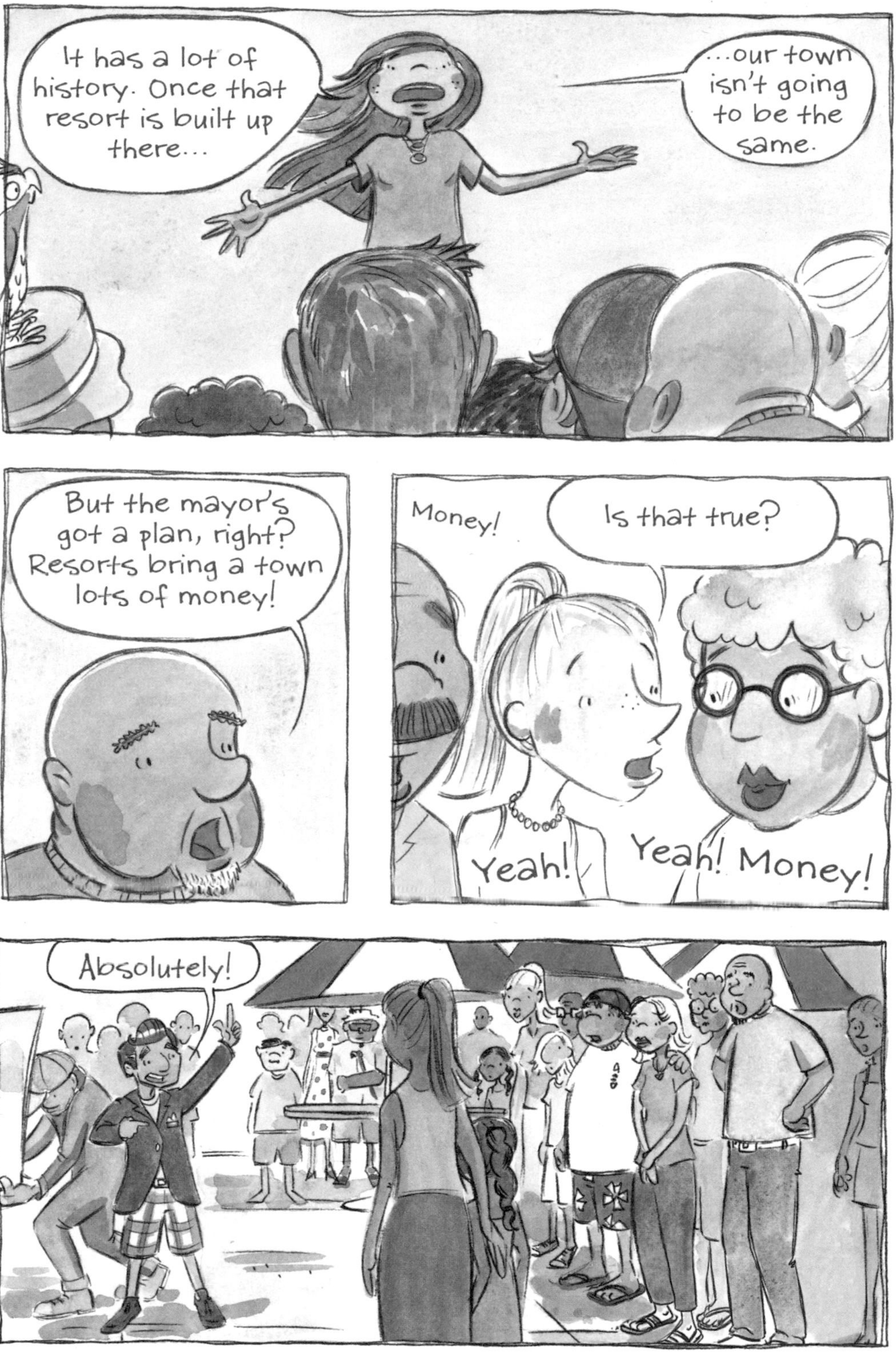
It has a lot of history. Once that resort is built up there...
...our town isn't going to be the same.
But the mayor's got a plan, right? Resorts bring a town lots of money!
Money!
Is that true?
Yeah!
Yeah! Money!
Absolutely!

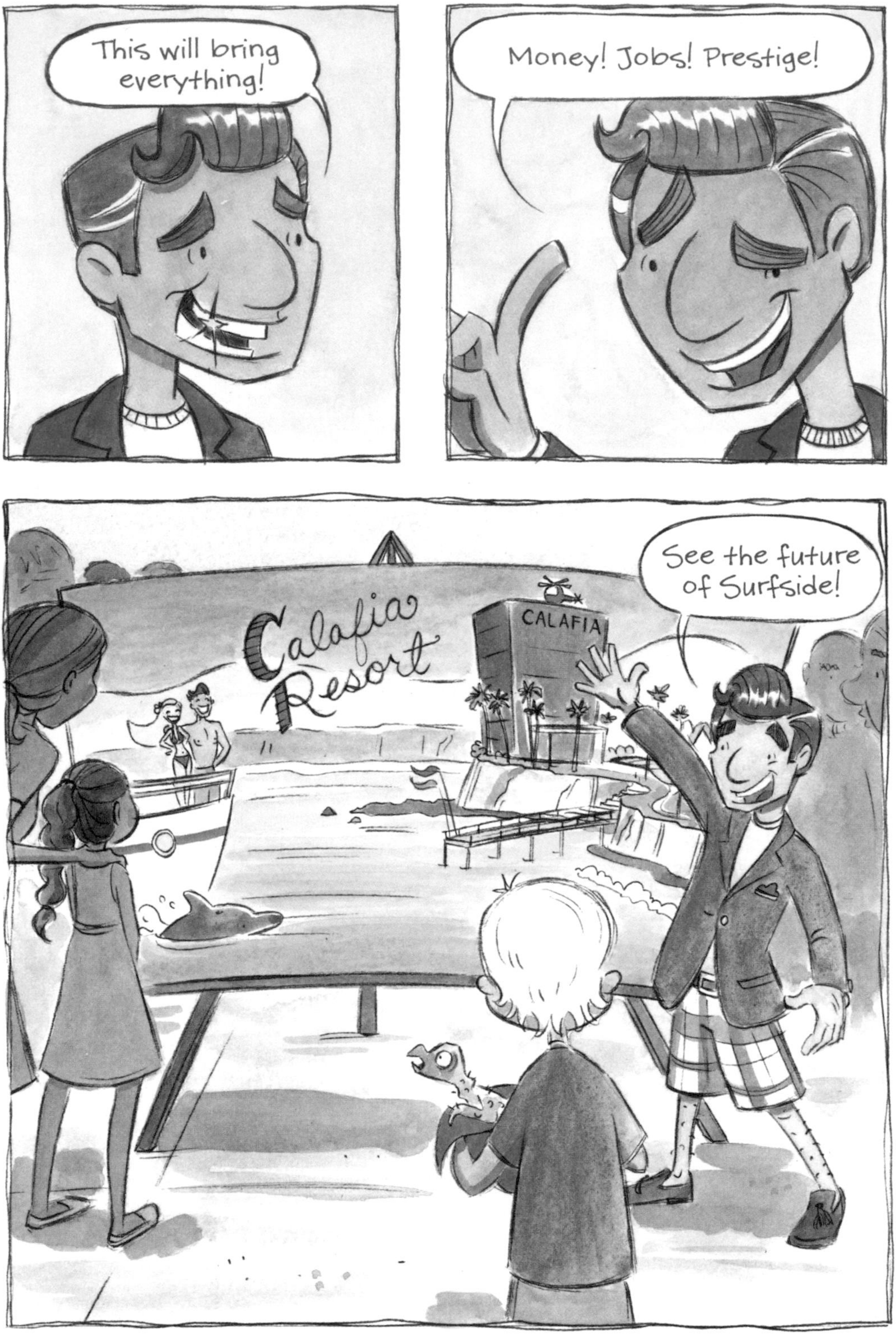
This will bring everything!
Money! Jobs! Prestige!
Calafia Resort
CALAFIA
See the future of Surfside!

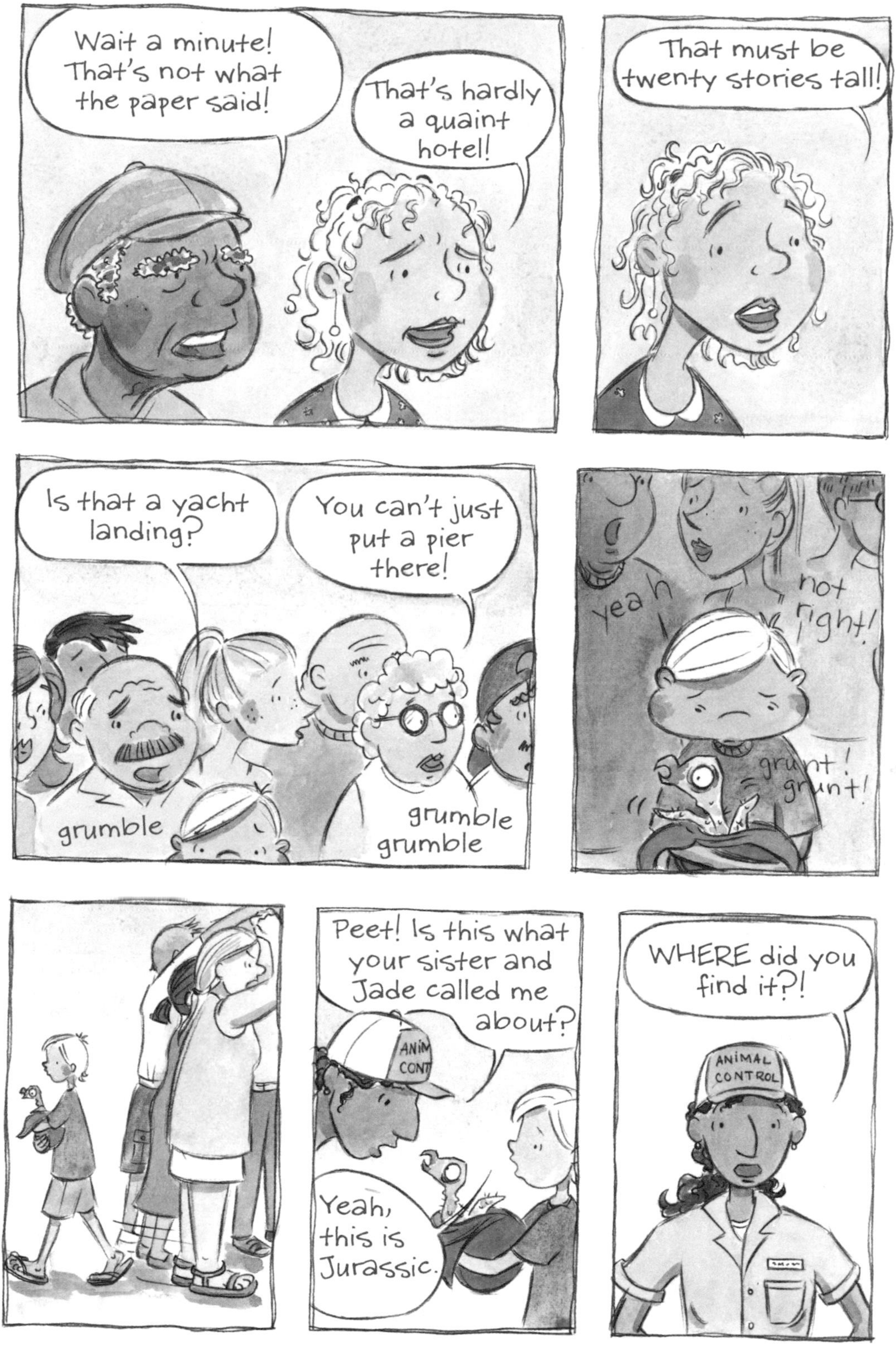
Wait a minute! That's not what the paper said!
That's hardly a quaint hotel!
That must be twenty stories tall!
Is that a yacht landing?
You can't just put a pier there!
grumble
grumble grumble
yeah
not right!
grunt! grunt!
Peet! Is this what your sister and Jade called me about?
ANIM CONT
Yeah, this is Jurassic.
WHERE did you find it?!
ANIMAL CONTROL

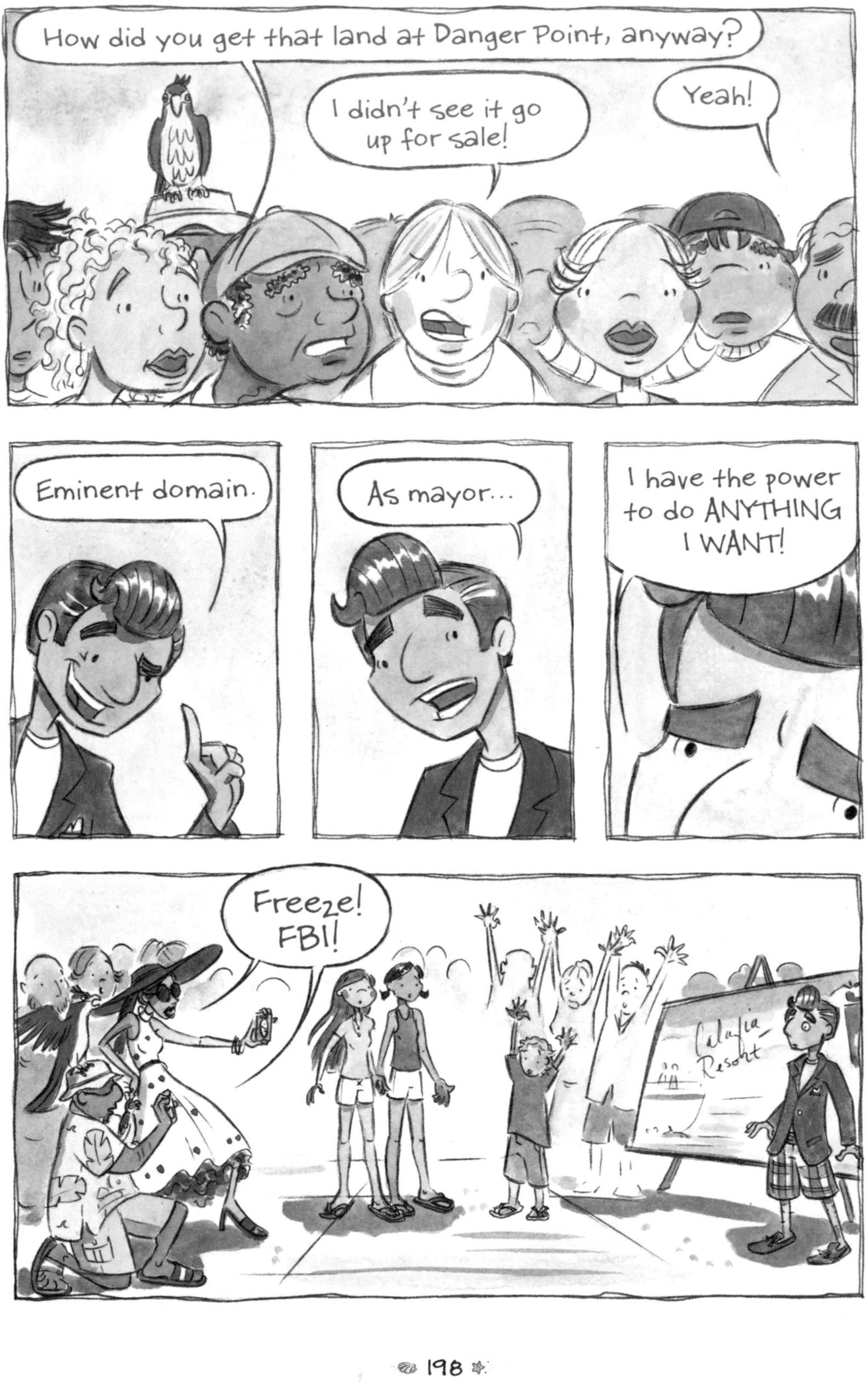
How did you get that land at Danger Point, anyway?
I didn't see it go up for sale!
Yeah!
Eminent domain.
As mayor...
I have the power to do ANYTHING I WANT!
Freeze! FBI!
Calafia Resort

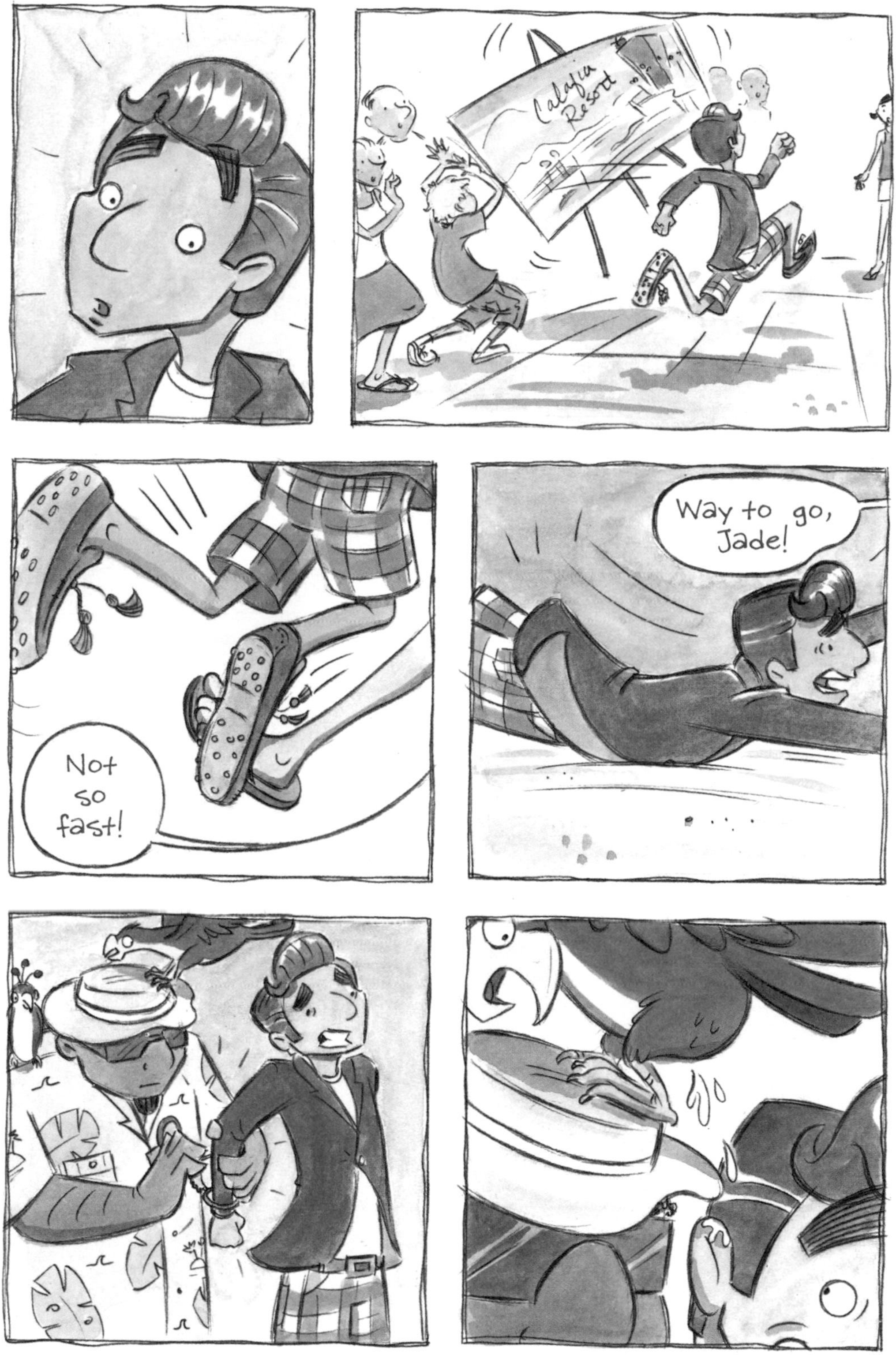
Calafia Resort
Not so fast!
Way to go, Jade!

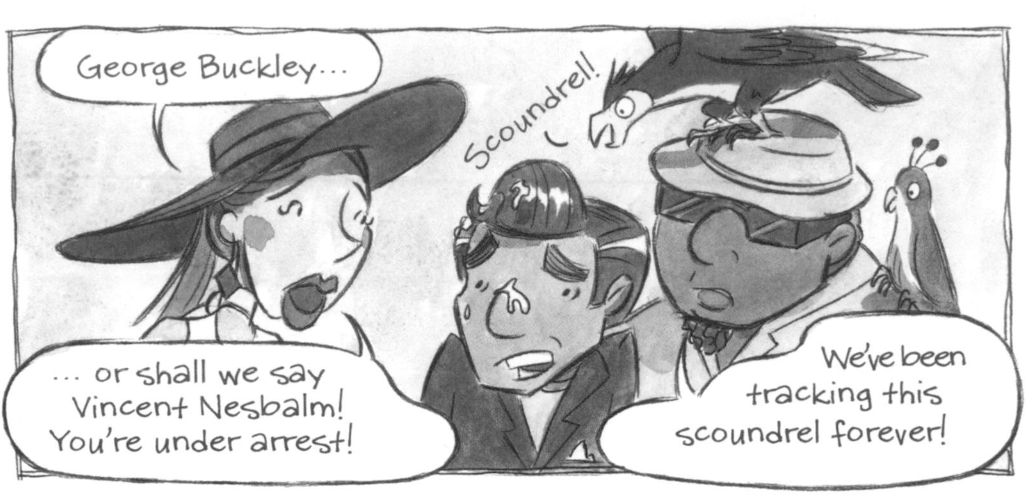
George Buckley...
Scoundrel!
... or shall we say Vincent Nesbalm! You're under arrest!
We've been tracking this scoundrel forever!

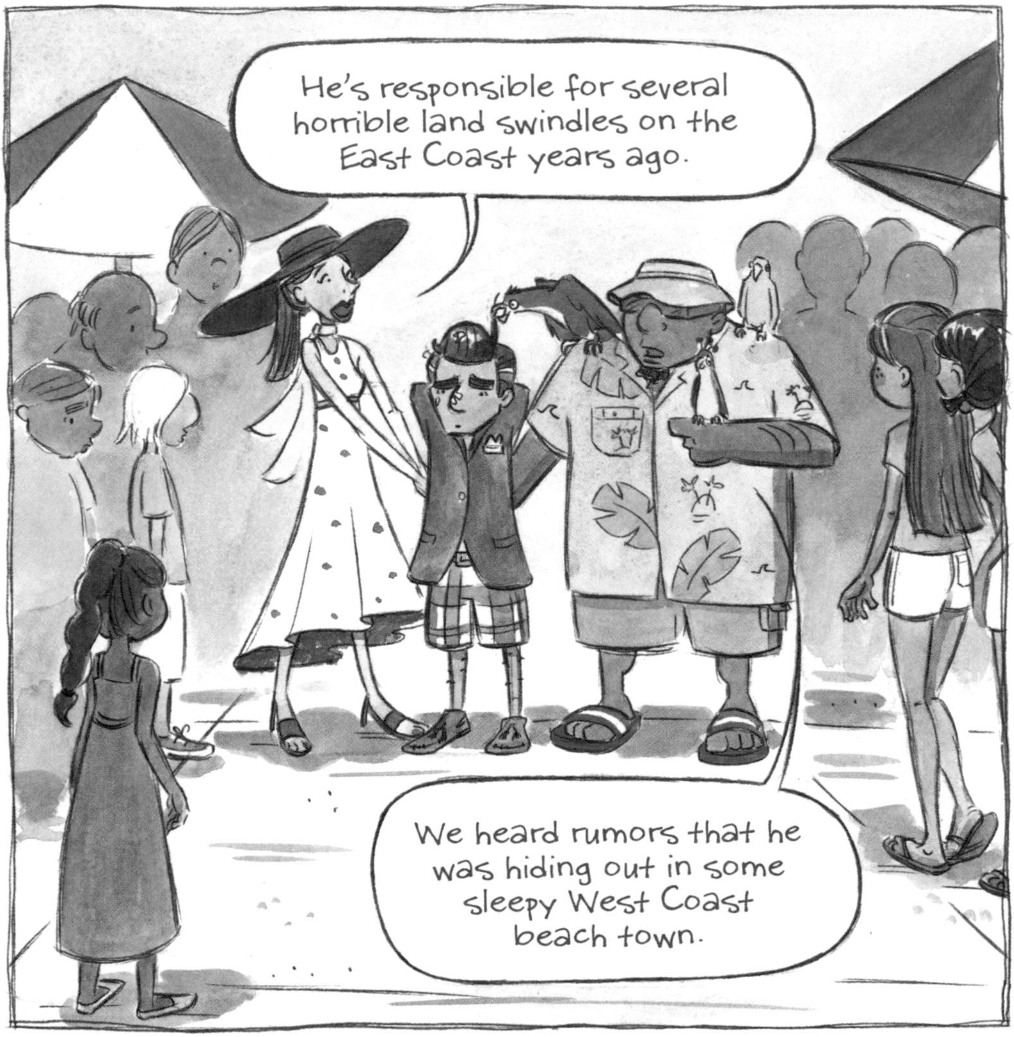
He's responsible for several horrible land swindles on the East Coast years ago.
We heard rumors that he was hiding out in some sleepy West Coast beach town.

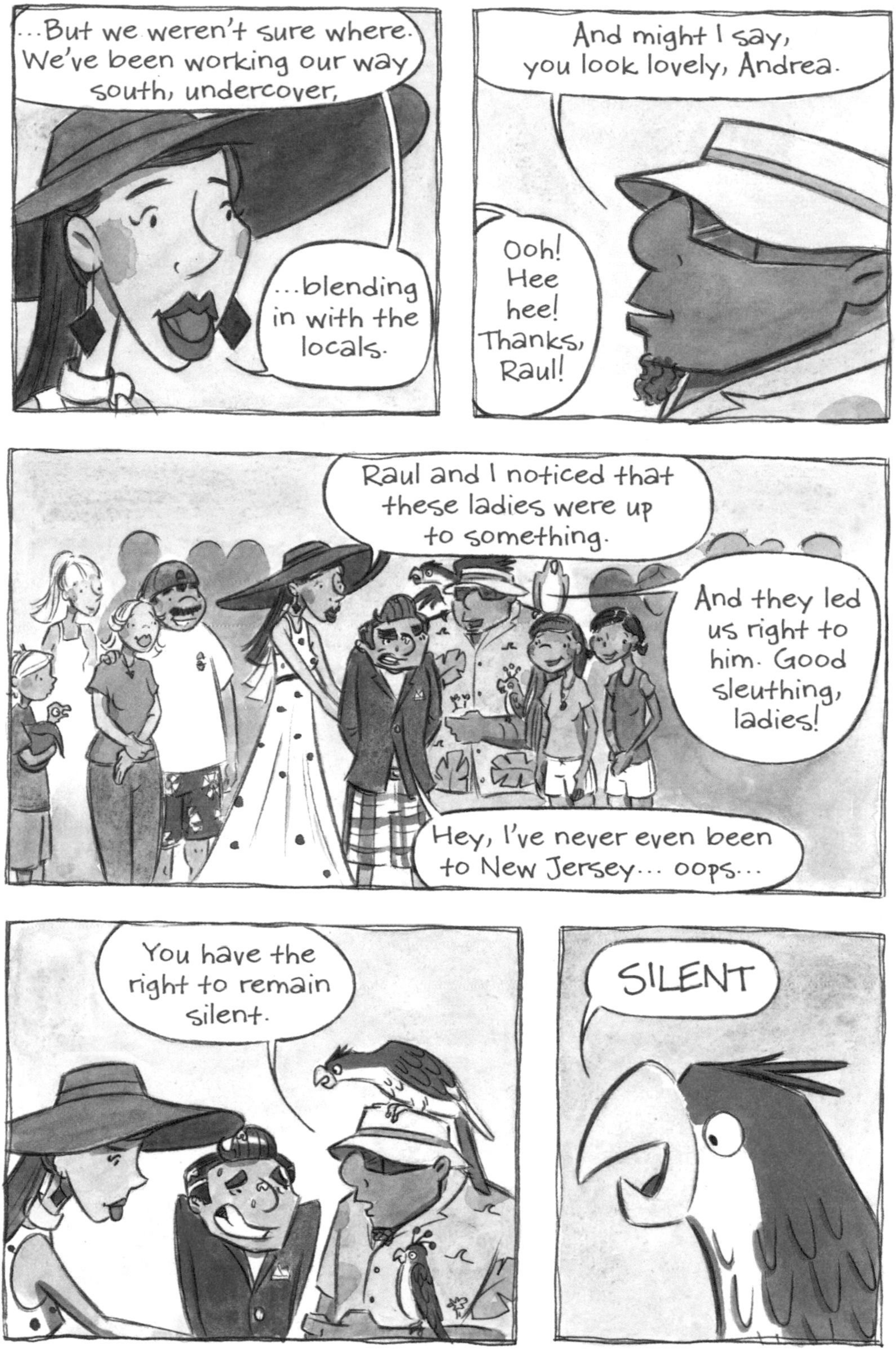
...But we weren't sure where. We've been working our way south, undercover,
...blending in with the locals.
And might I say, you look lovely, Andrea.
Ooh! Hee hee! Thanks, Raul!
Raul and I noticed that these ladies were up to something.
And they led us right to him. Good sleuthing, ladies!
Hey, I've never even been to New Jersey... oops...
You have the right to remain silent.
SILENT

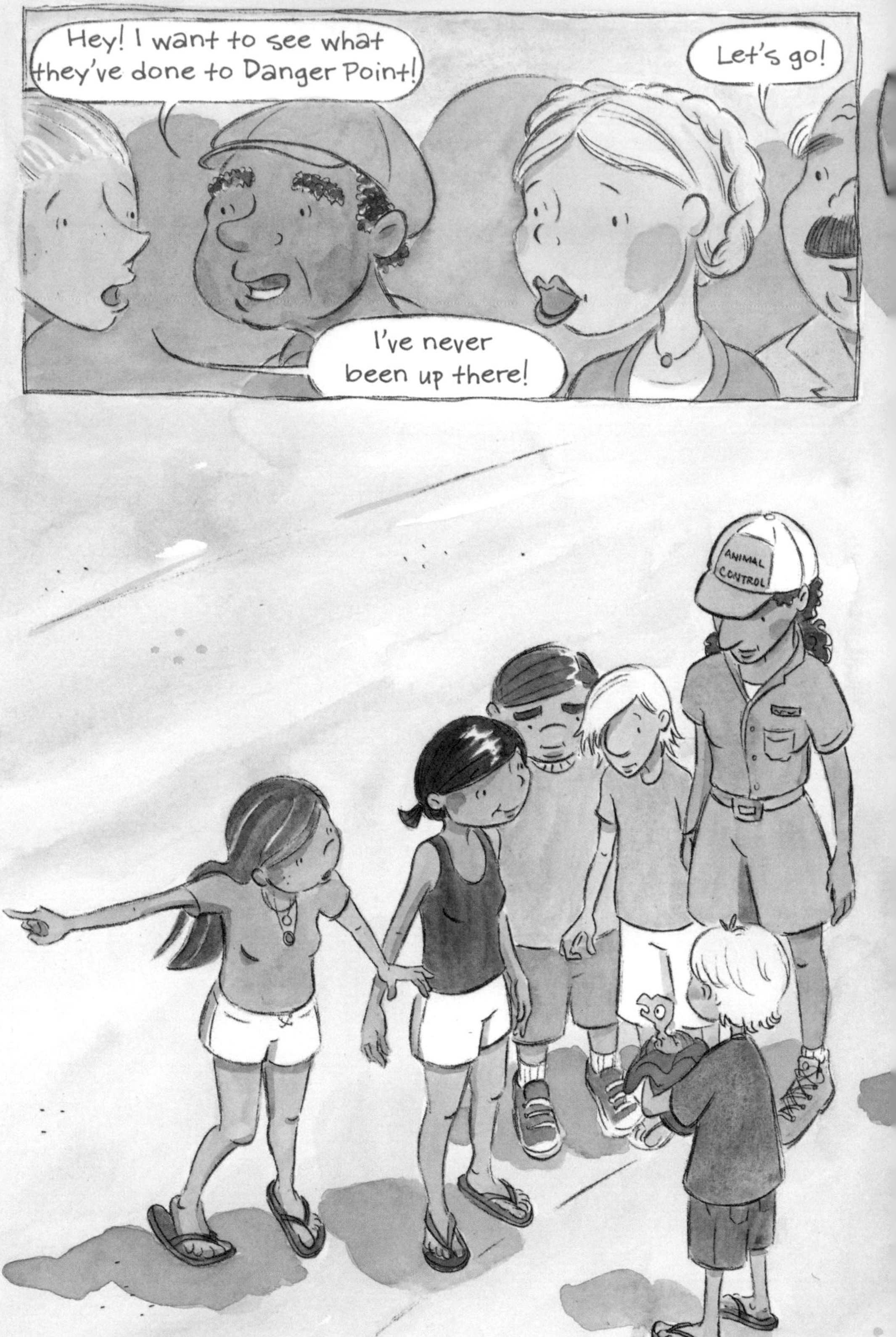
Hey! I want to see what they've done to Danger Point!
Let's go!
I've never been up there!
ANIMAL CONTROL

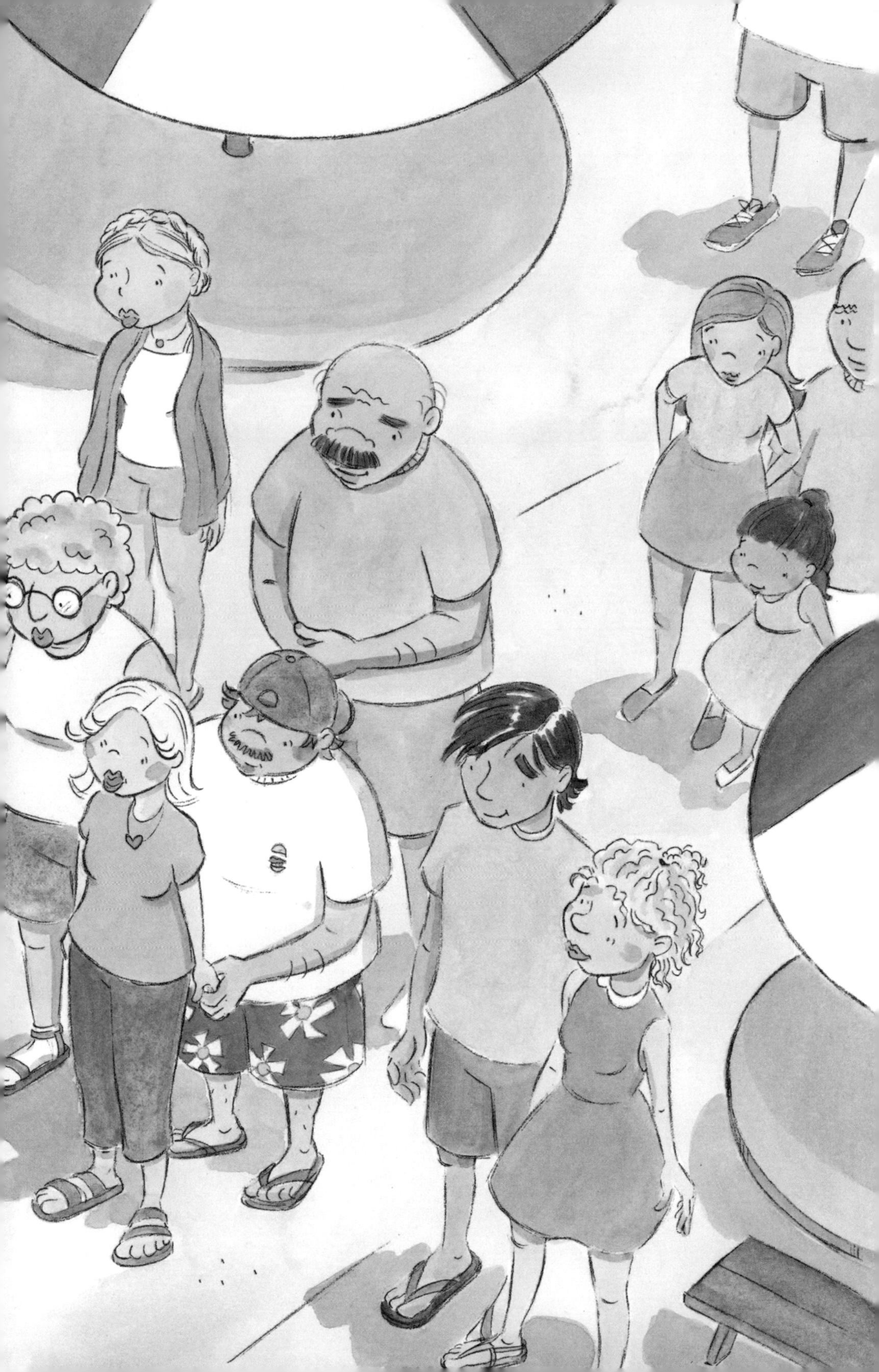

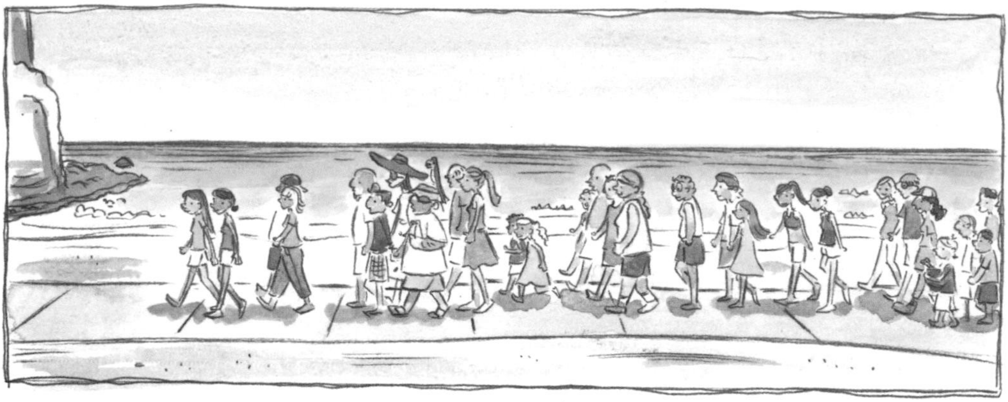

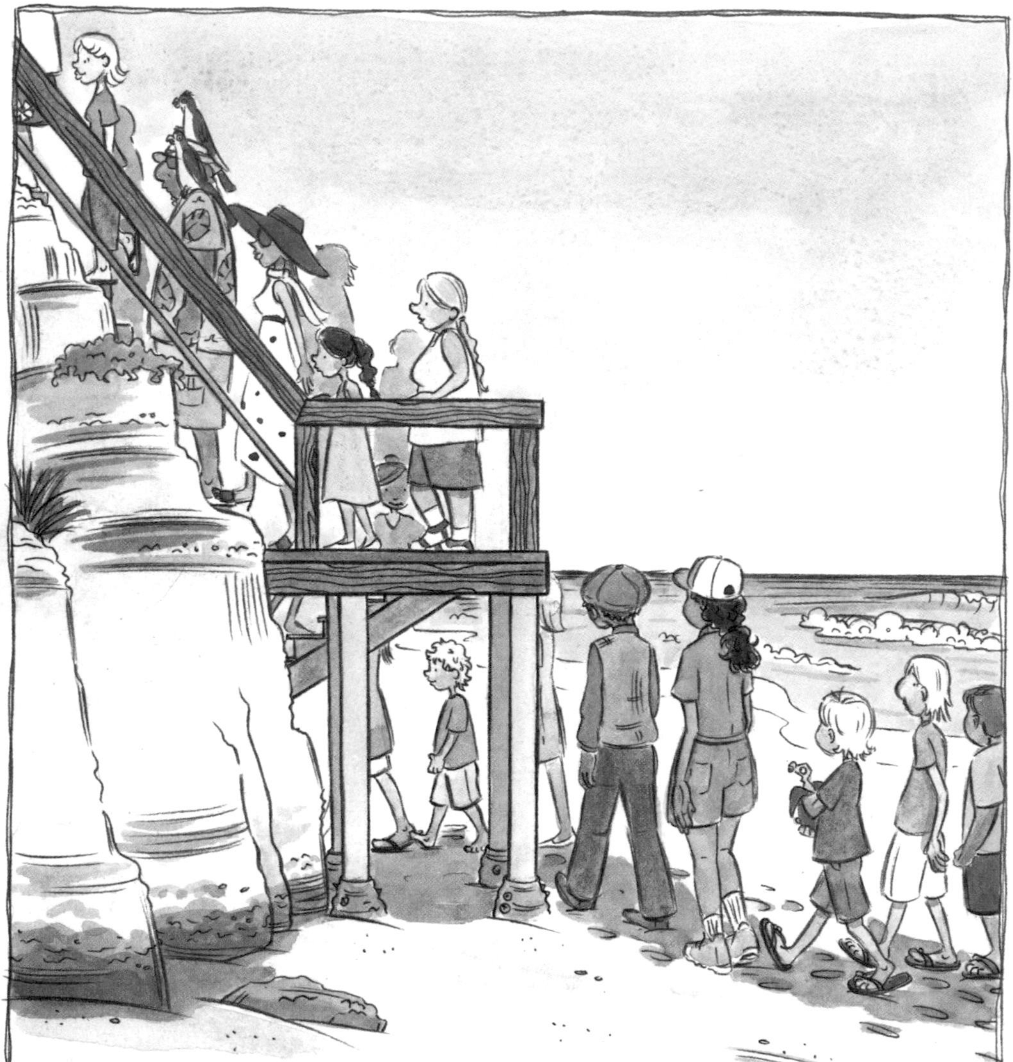

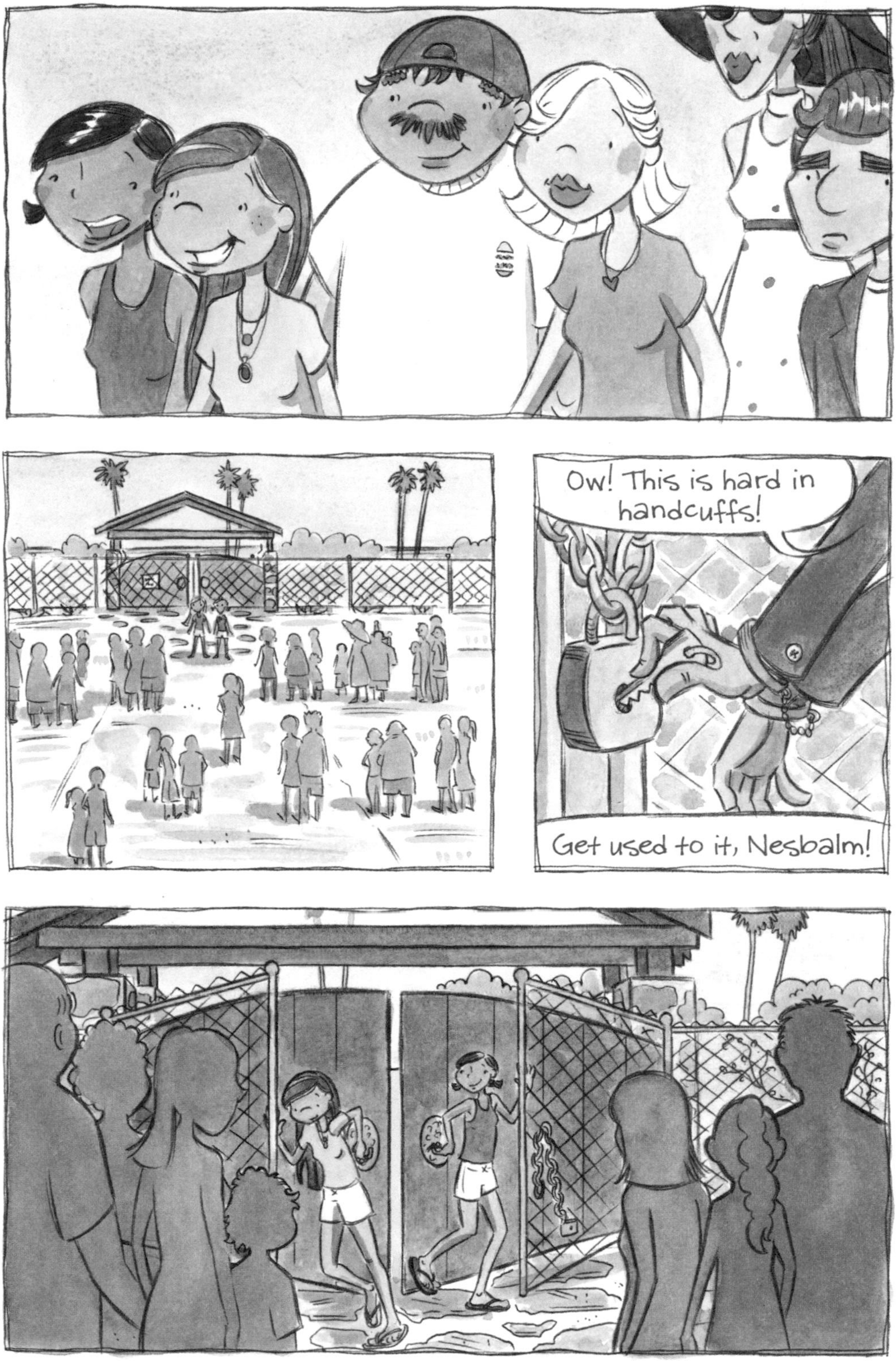
Ow! This is hard in handcuffs!
Get used to it, Nesbalm!

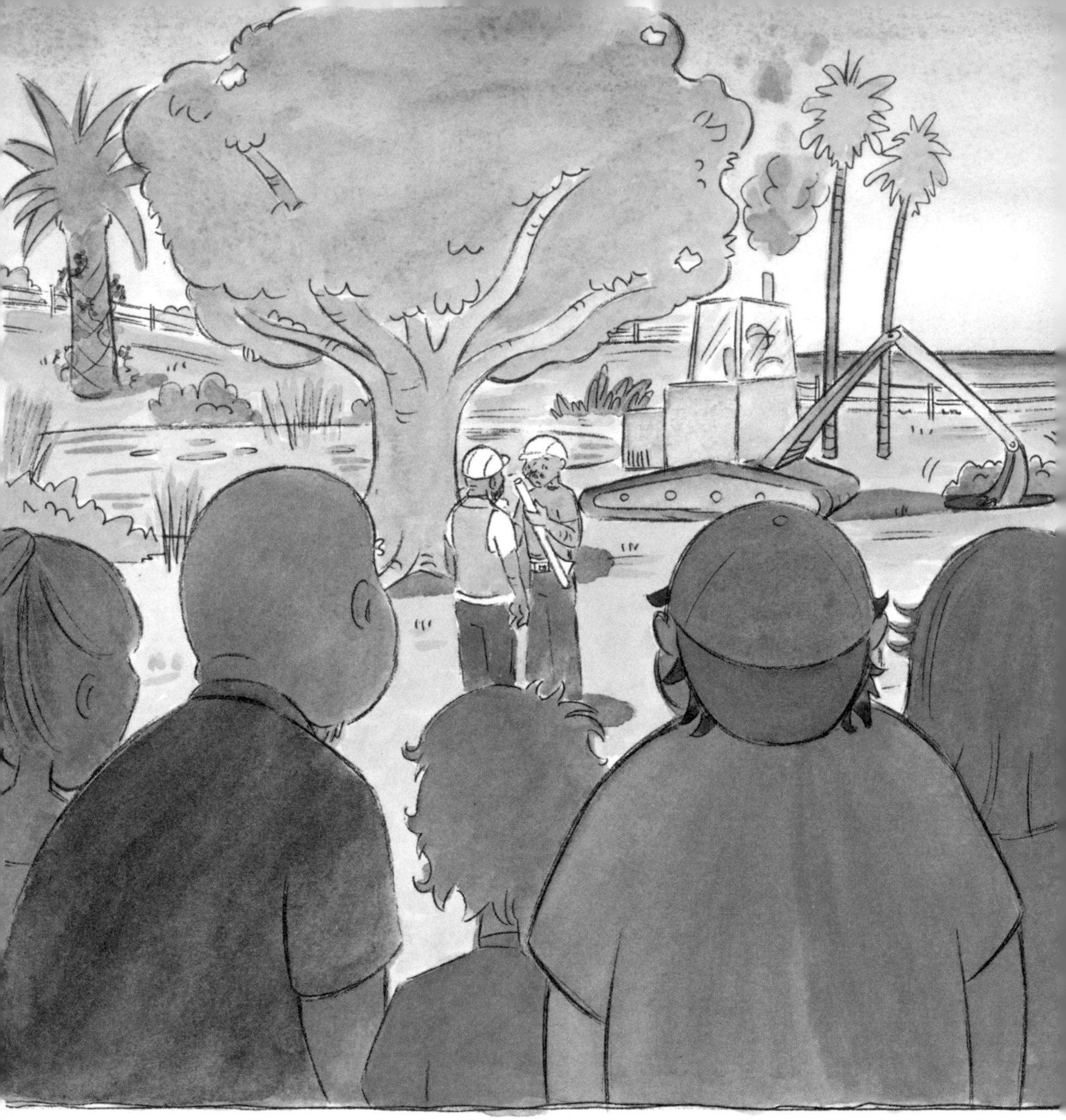

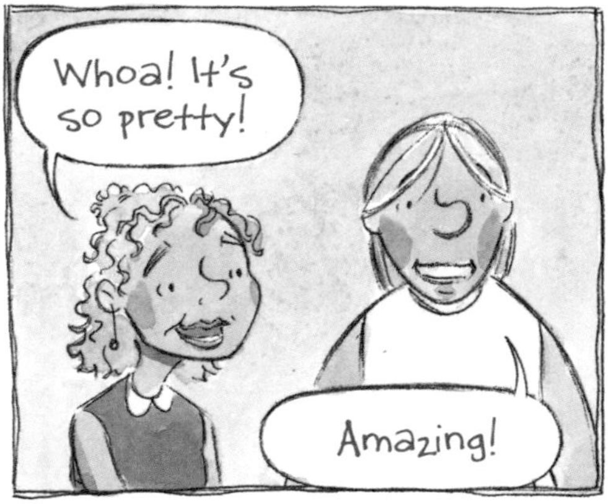
Whoa! It's so pretty!
Amazing!

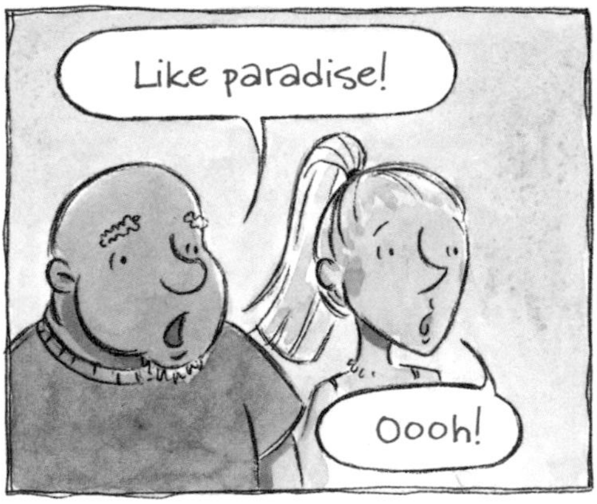
Like paradise!
Oooh!

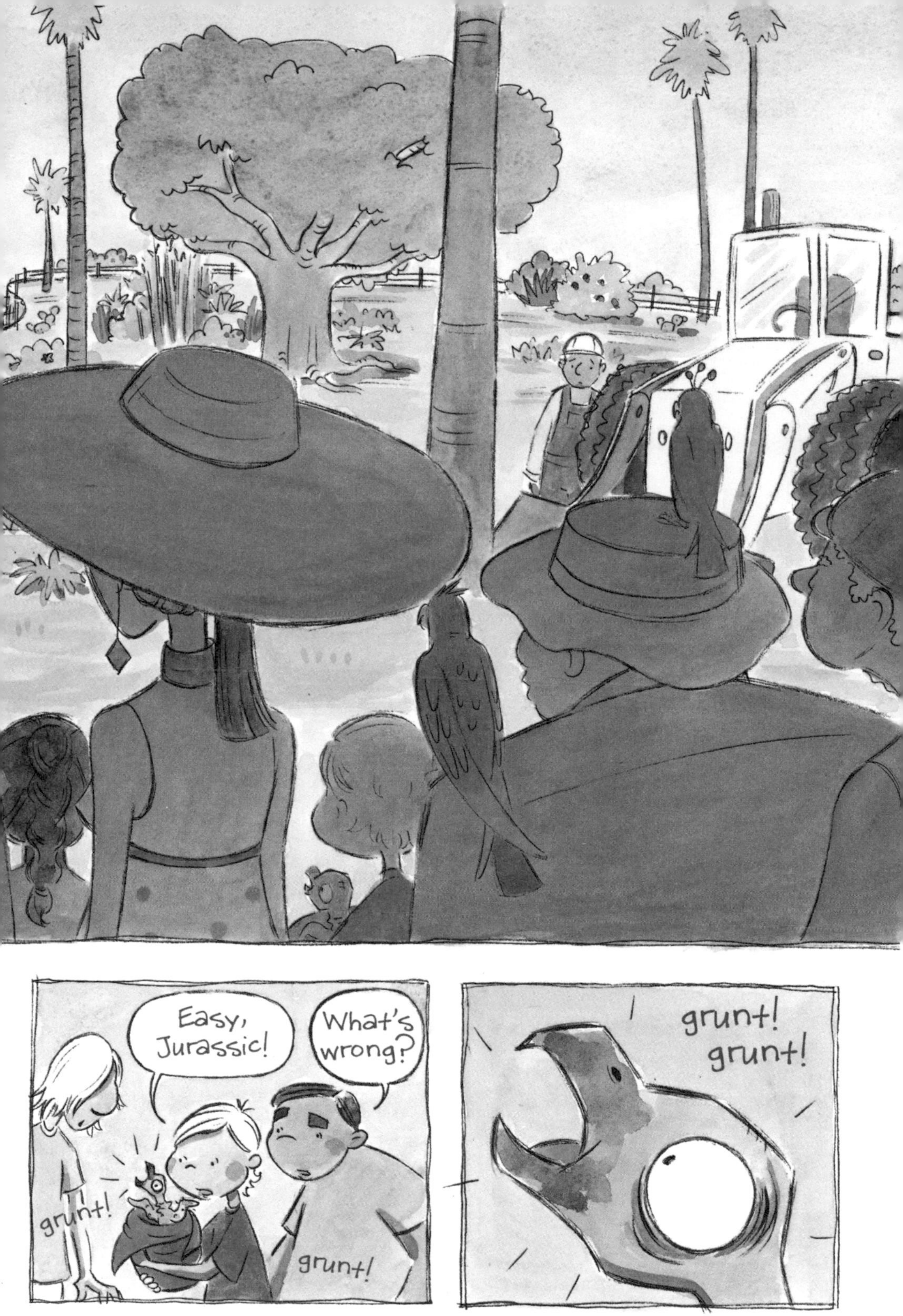
Easy, Jurassic!
What's wrong?
grunt!
grunt!
grunt! grunt!

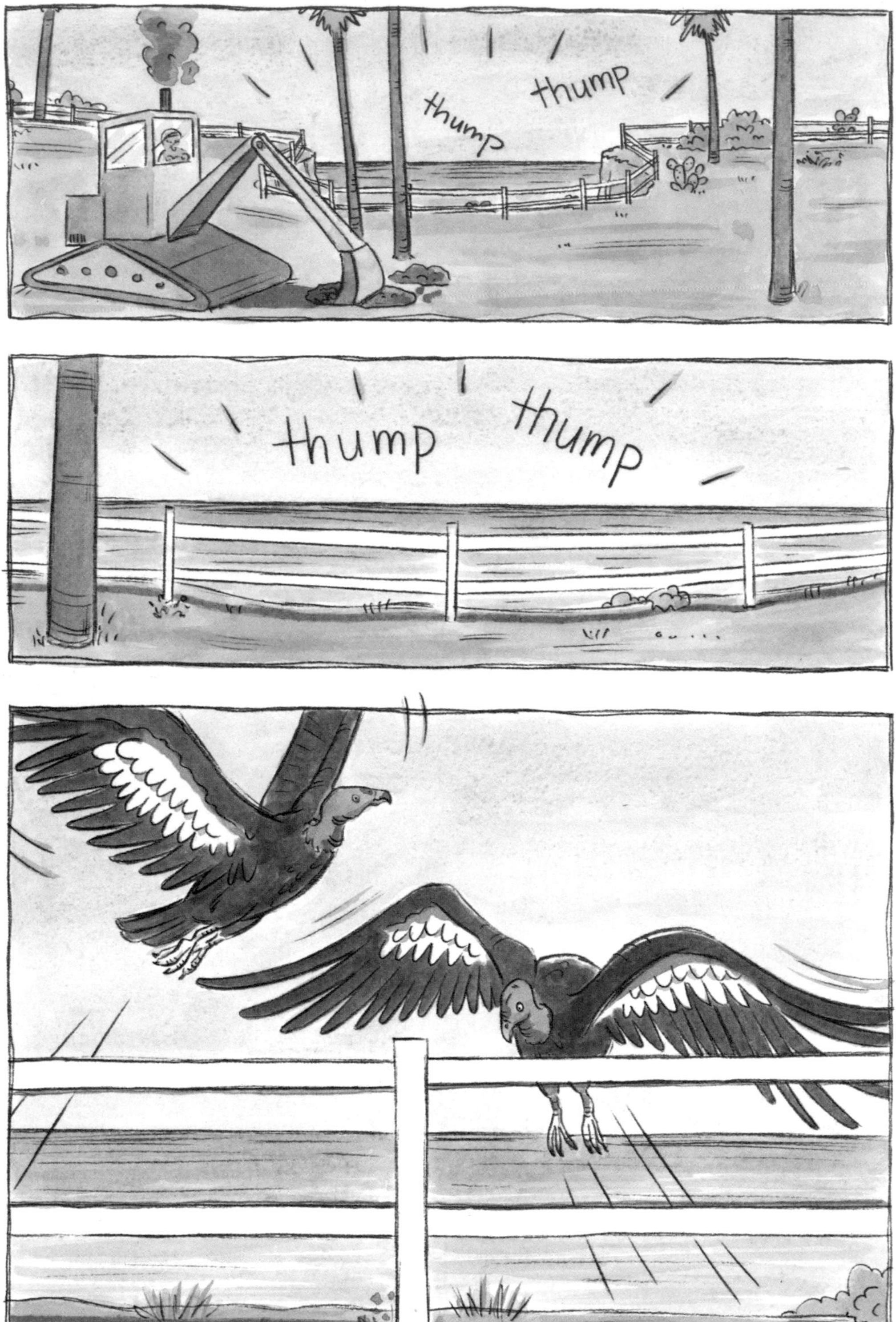
thump
thump
thump
thump

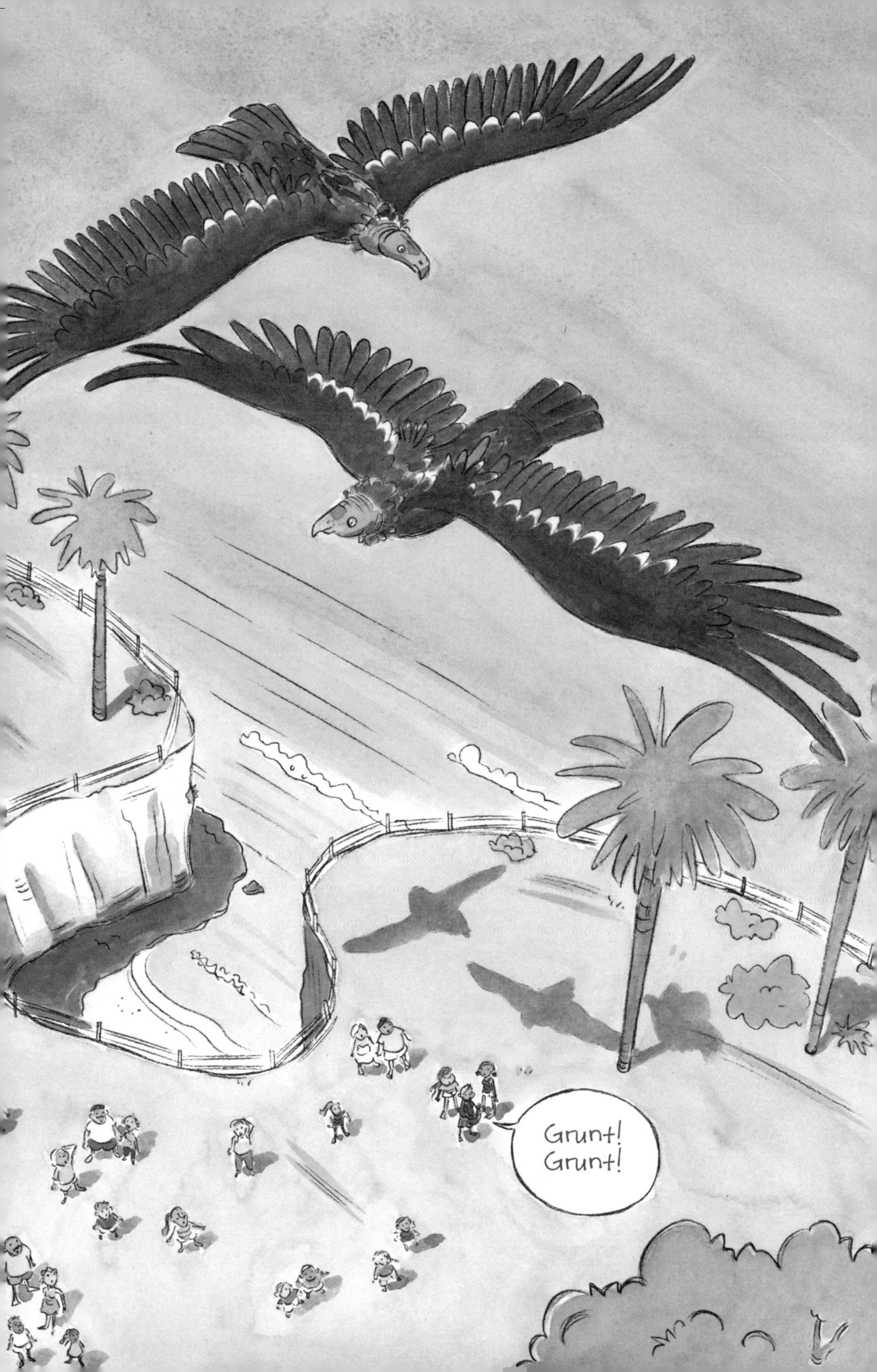
Grunt! Grunt!

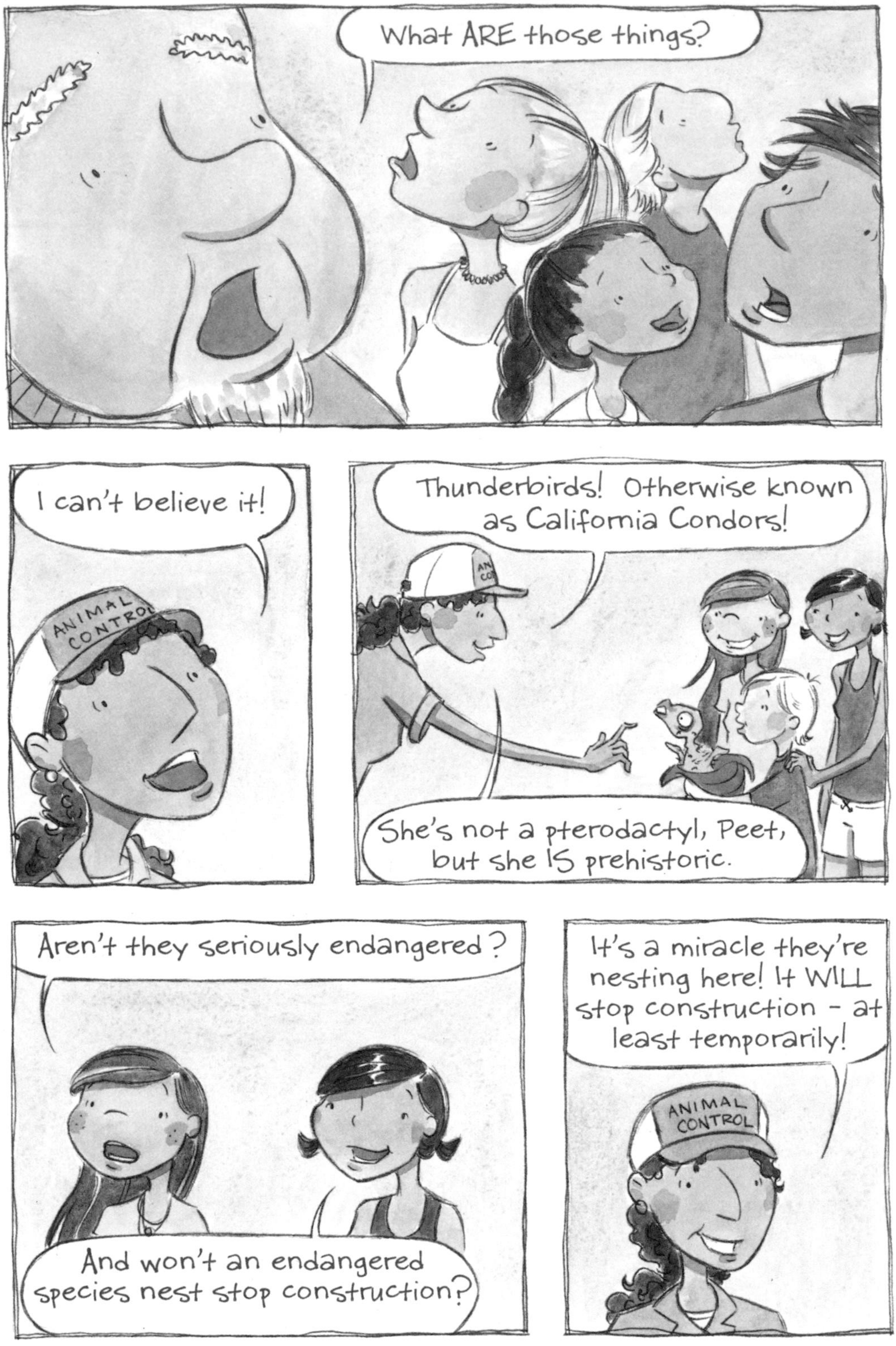
What ARE those things?
I can't believe it!
Thunderbirds! Otherwise known as California Condors!
She's not a pterodactyl, Peet, but she IS prehistoric.
Aren't they seriously endangered?
And won't an endangered species nest stop construction?
It's a miracle they're nesting here! It WILL stop construction - at least temporarily!
ANIMAL CONTROL

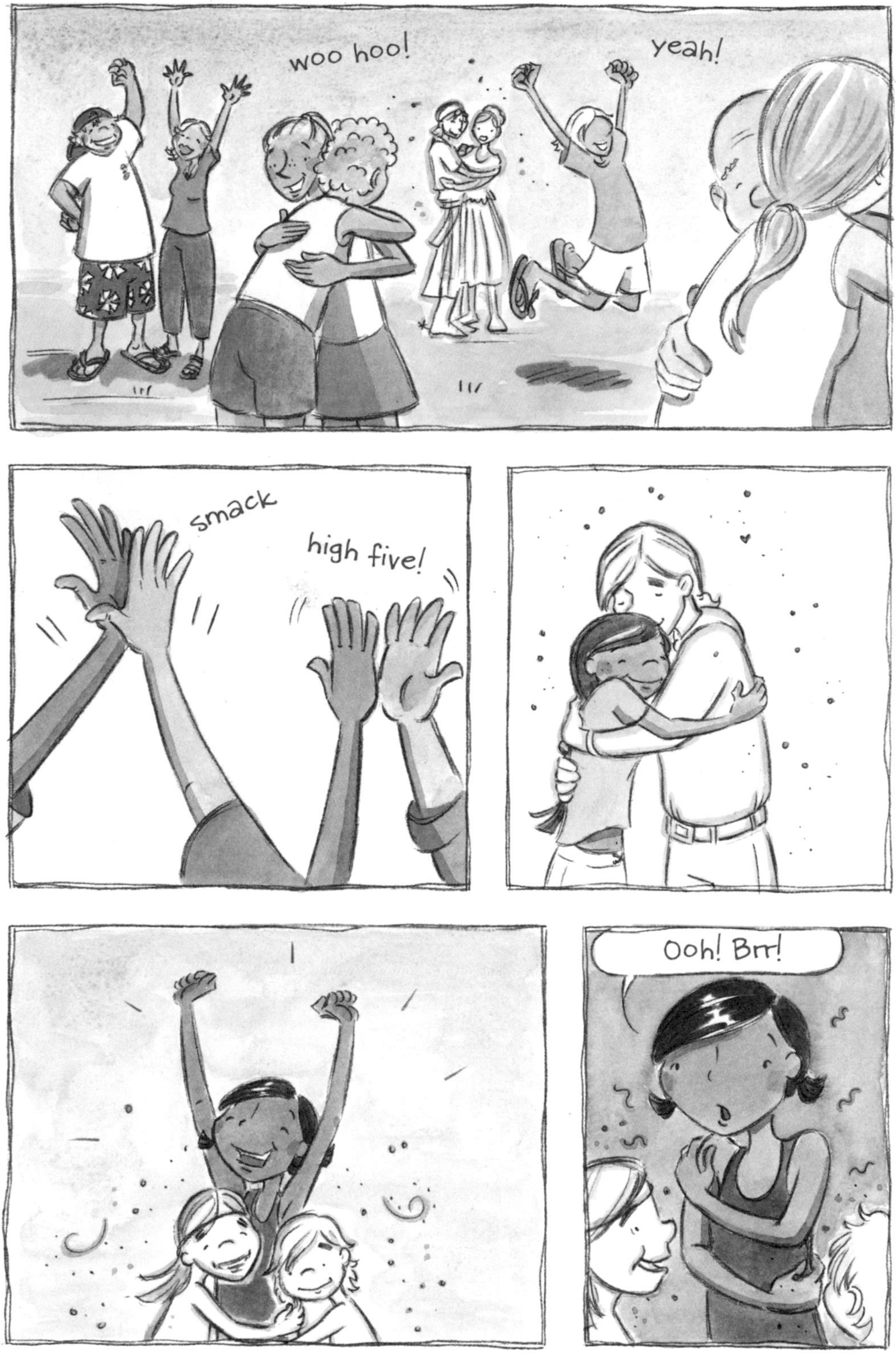
woo hoo!
yeah!
smack
high five!
Ooh! Brr!

THE SURFS
SUNDAY
SPECIAL
DANGER POINT
INCREDIBLE DISCOVERY
Endangered Condors nesting at Danger Point.
by
had been released
in Central California,
" It's a miracle!"
Peet Taylor and his friends
BOYS "THOUGHT IT WAS A DINOSAUR.
5'0"
MAYOR ARRESTED!
Awaiting trial on charges of land fraud.
by

IDE TIMES ⭐

EDITION $1.00

SCANDAL EXPOSED

FBI, LOCAL GIRLS THWART SECRET PLAN

Twelve-year-old heroes "used wits and disguises."

Samantha Taylor and Jade Lee expose Mayor's plot.

by ᷟᴗᴗᴗ ᴗᴗ ᴗᴗᴗᴗ

ᴗᴗᴗ ᴗᴗ ᴗᴗᴗ ᴗ ᴗᴗᴗᴗ ᴗᴗ ᴗᴗ ᴗᴗᴗᴗ ᴗ ᴗᴗ ᴗᴗᴗ ᴗᴗᴗᴗᴗ ᴗ ᴗᴗᴗᴗ ᴗ ᴗᴗ ᴗ ᴗᴗᴗ ᴗᴗᴗᴗ ᴗᴗᴗ ᴗᴗ.

ᴗᴗᴗᴗ ᴗᴗ ᴗᴗ ᴗᴗ ᴗᴗᴗ ᴗᴗ ᴗᴗ ᴗᴗᴗ ᴗᴗᴗ ᴗᴗᴗ ᴗᴗᴗ ᴗᴗ ᴗᴗ ᴗᴗ ᴗᴗ ᴗᴗᴗ ᴗᴗᴗ ᴗᴗᴗᴗᴗ. ᴗ ᴗ ᴗ ᴗᴗ ᴗᴗᴗᴗᴗ. ᴗ ᴗᴗ ᴗᴗᴗ ᴗᴗ ᴗᴗ ᴗᴗ ᴗᴗ ᴗᴗᴗ ᴗᴗᴗ ᴗᴗ ᴗᴗ.

ᴗᴗᴗ ᴗᴗᴗ ᴗᴗᴗ ᴗ ᴗᴗᴗ ᴗᴗᴗᴗ. ᴗ ᴗᴗᴗ ᴗᴗᴗ ᴗᴗ ᴗᴗ **Samantha and Jade** ᴗᴗ ᴗᴗ ᴗᴗ ᴗᴗᴗ ᴗᴗ ᴗᴗᴗ ᴗᴗ ᴗᴗ **the Burger Dude** ᴗᴗ ᴗᴗ ᴗᴗᴗ ᴗᴗ ᴗ ᴗᴗᴗᴗ.

ᴗᴗᴗ ᴗᴗ ᴗᴗᴗ ᴗᴗᴗ ᴗᴗ ᴗᴗ ᴗᴗ ᴗ ᴗᴗᴗ ᴗᴗ

ᴗᴗ ᴗᴗ ᴗᴗ, ᴗᴗᴗ ᴗᴗᴗ ᴗᴗᴗ ᴗ.

ᴗᴗ ᴗᴗᴗ ᴗᴗ ᴗᴗᴗ ᴗᴗᴗ ᴗᴗᴗ ᴗ, ᴗᴗᴗ ᴗᴗ ᴗᴗᴗ ᴗᴗ ᴗᴗᴗ ᴗ ᴗ.

ᴗᴗᴗ ᴗᴗᴗ ᴗᴗᴗ ᴗᴗᴗ ᴗ ᴗᴗ ᴗᴗ ᴗᴗ ᴗᴗ ᴗᴗ ᴗᴗᴗᴗ ᴗᴗᴗ ᴗᴗᴗᴗ ᴗᴗ ᴗᴗᴗ ᴗᴗᴗ ᴗᴗ ᴗᴗᴗ ᴗᴗᴗ ᴗᴗᴗ ᴗᴗ ᴗᴗᴗ ᴗᴗᴗ ᴗ ᴗᴗ ᴗᴗᴗ.

ᴗᴗᴗ ᴗᴗᴗ ᴗᴗᴗ ᴗᴗᴗ ᴗᴗᴗ ᴗᴗ ᴗ ᴗᴗ ᴗᴗᴗ ᴗ ᴗᴗᴗ ᴗᴗᴗ ᴗᴗᴗ ᴗ ᴗ ᴗᴗ. ᴗᴗ ᴗᴗ ᴗ ᴗᴗ ᴗᴗ ᴗᴗ ᴗᴗ ᴗᴗᴗ ᴗᴗᴗ ᴗ ᴗᴗ ᴗᴗᴗ ᴗᴗᴗ ᴗᴗᴗ ᴗᴗᴗ ᴗᴗ ᴗᴗᴗ ᴗᴗ, ᴗᴗᴗ ᴗ ᴗᴗ ᴗ.

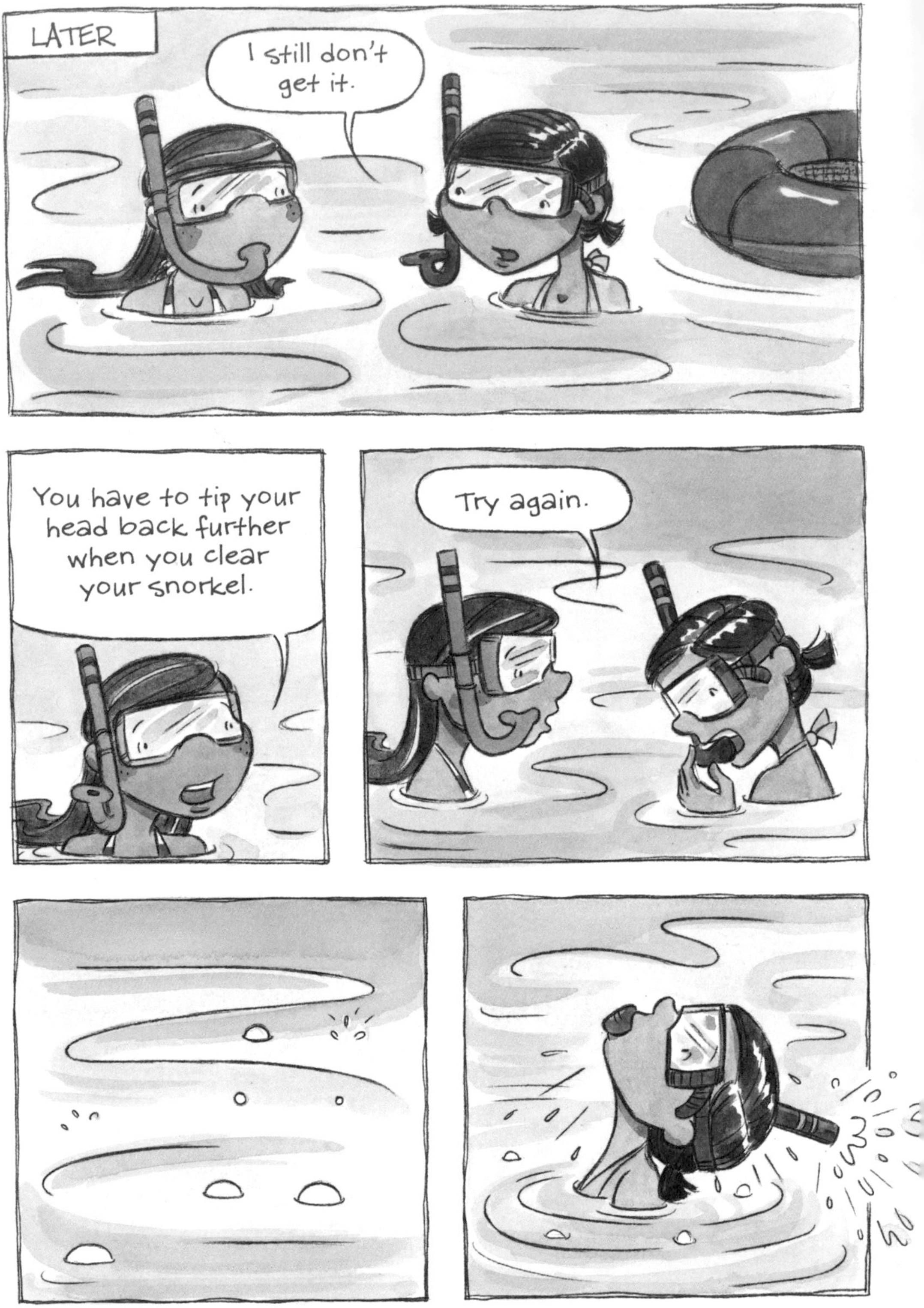
LATER
I still don't get it.
You have to tip your head back further when you clear your snorkel.
Try again.

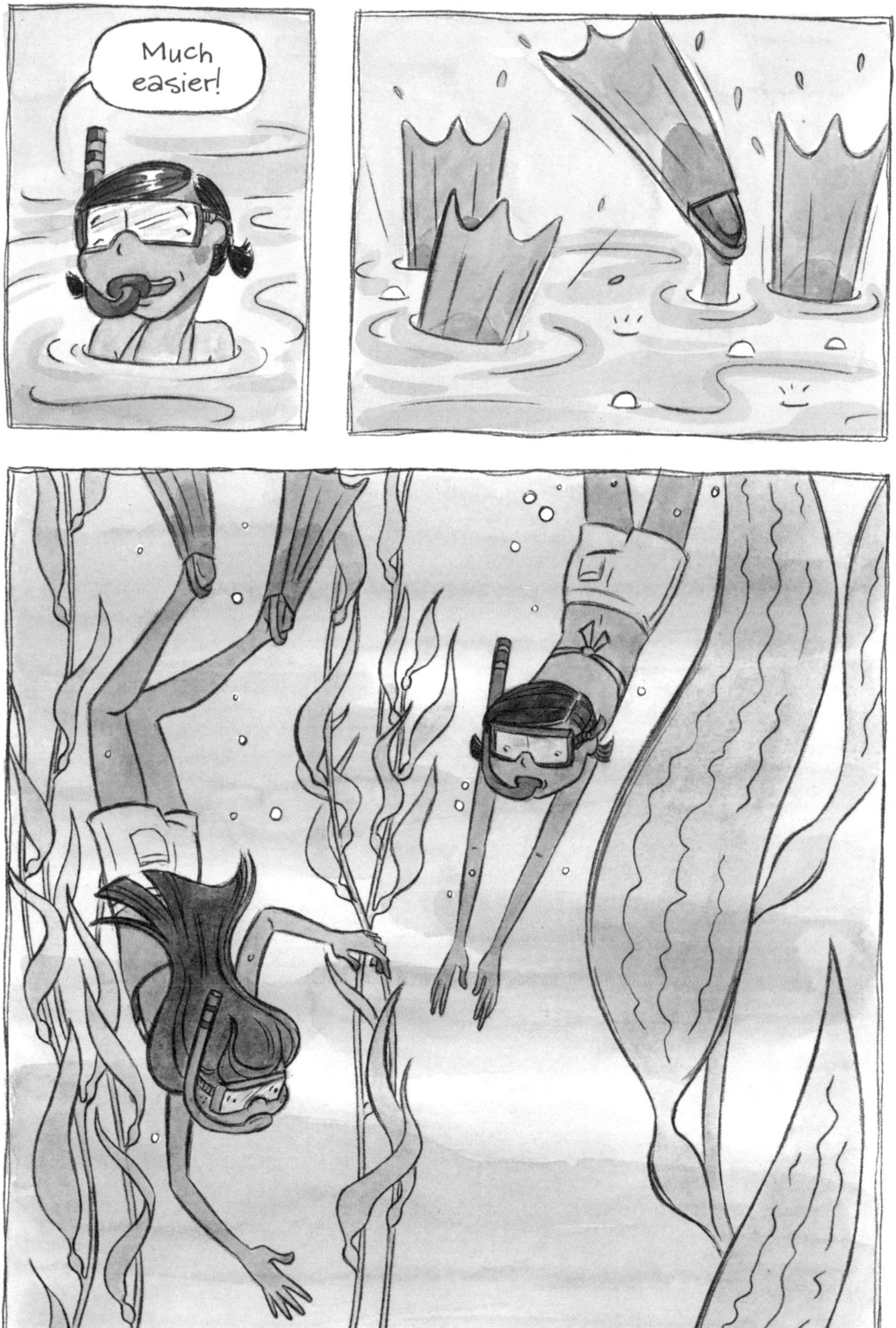
Much easier!

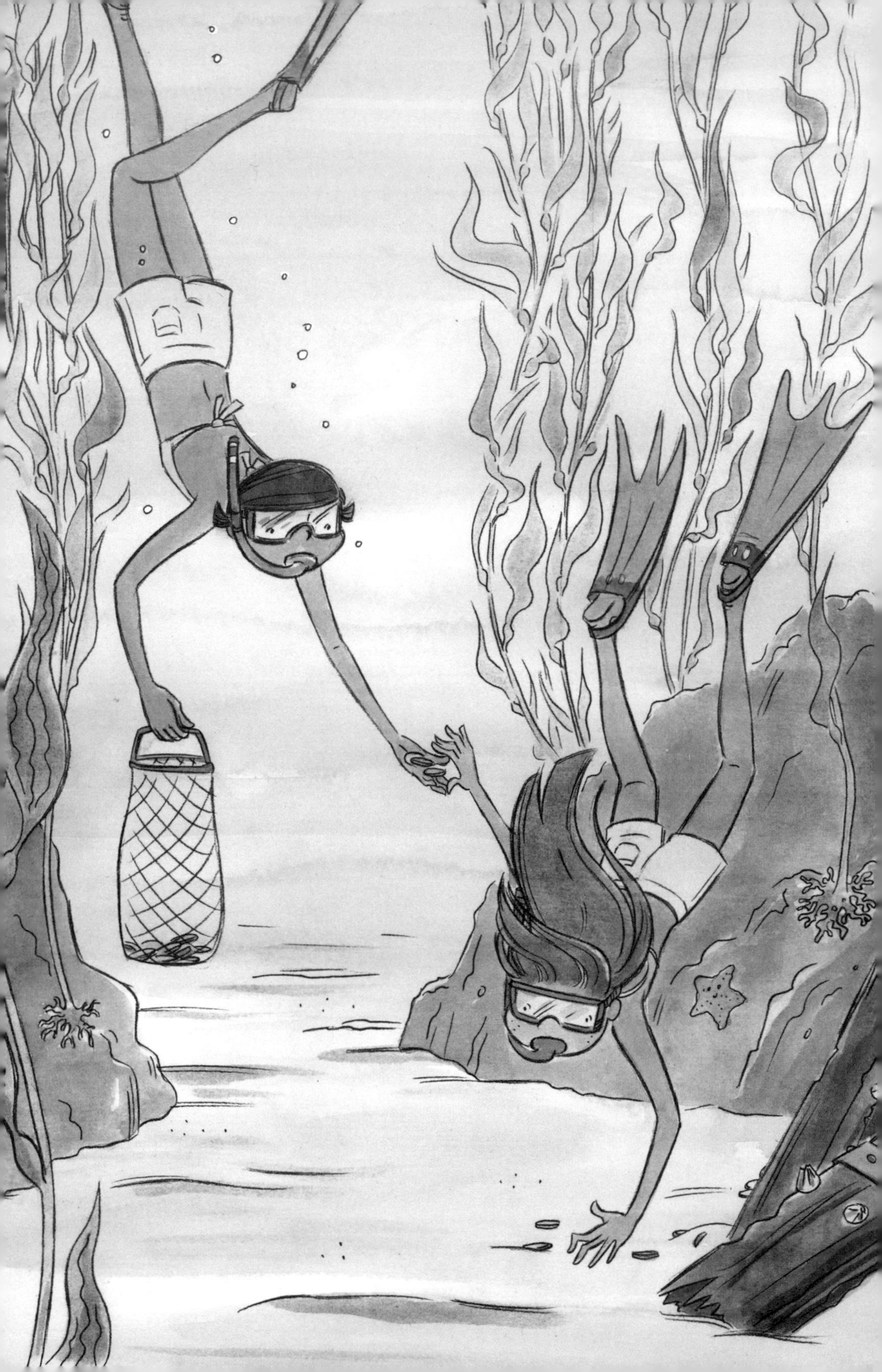

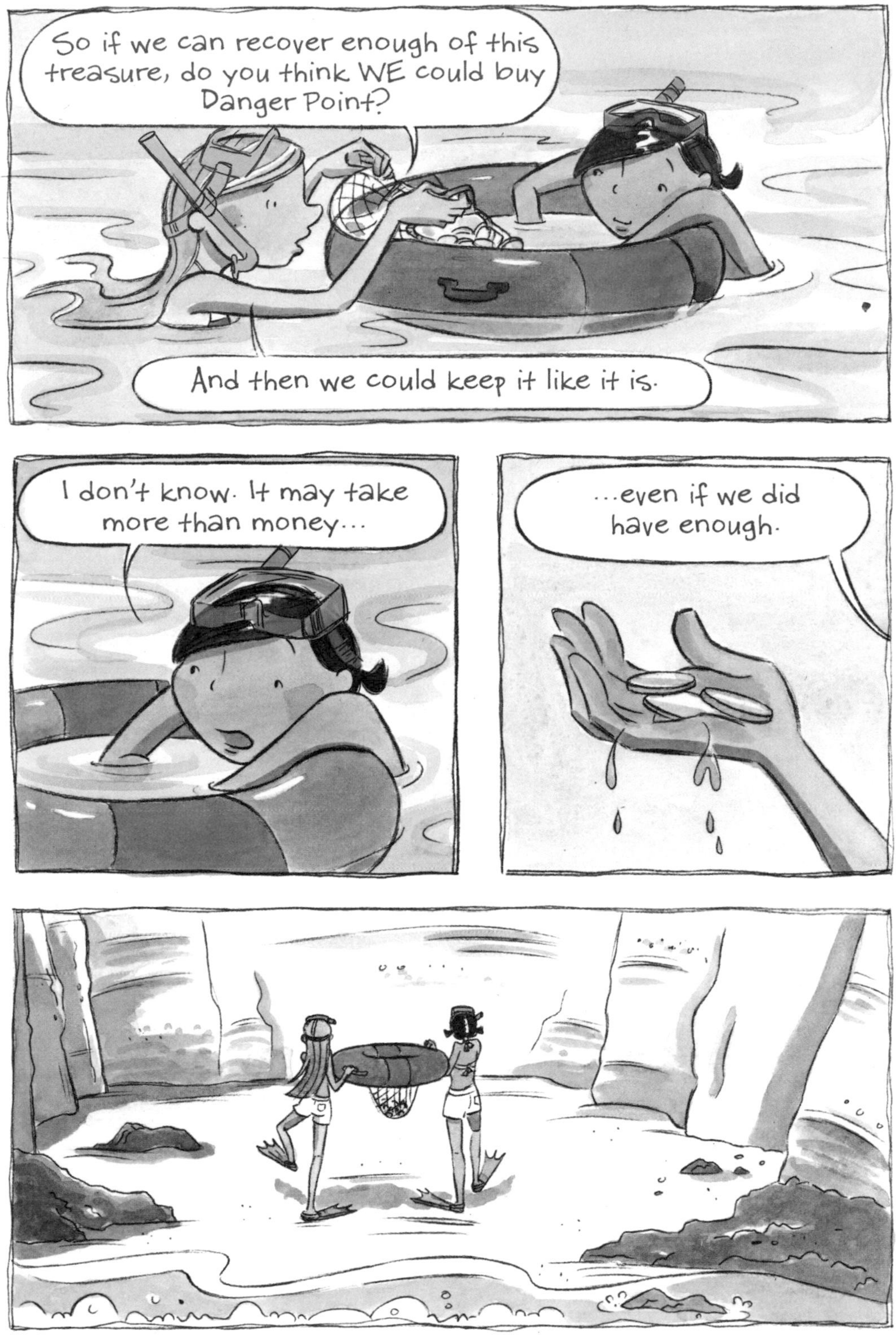
So if we can recover enough of this treasure, do you think WE could buy Danger Point?
And then we could keep it like it is.
I don't know. It may take more than money...
...even if we did have enough.

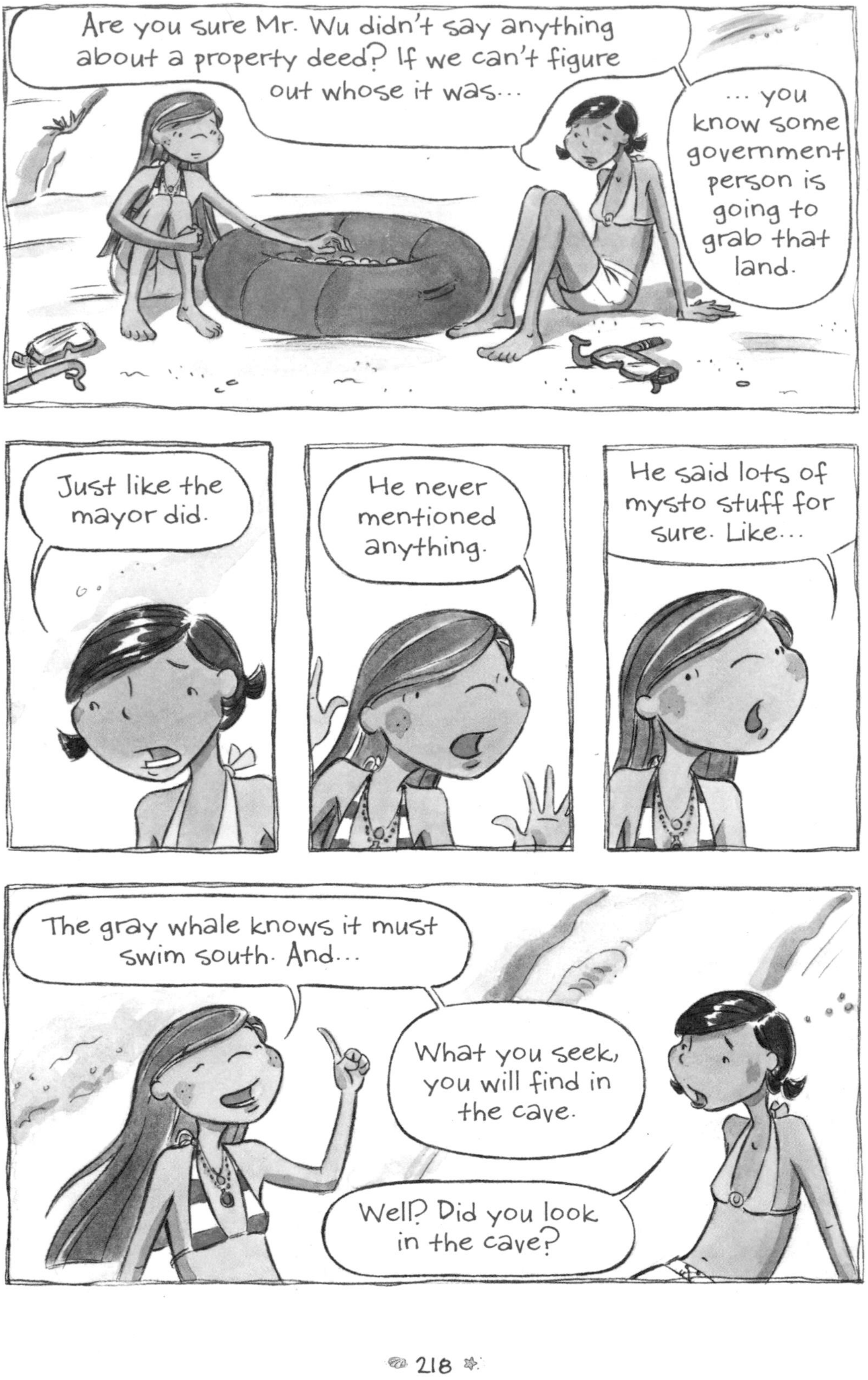
Are you sure Mr. Wu didn't say anything about a property deed? If we can't figure out whose it was...
... you know some government person is going to grab that land.
Just like the mayor did.
He never mentioned anything.
He said lots of mysto stuff for sure. Like...
The gray whale knows it must swim south. And...
What you seek, you will find in the cave.
Well? Did you look in the cave?

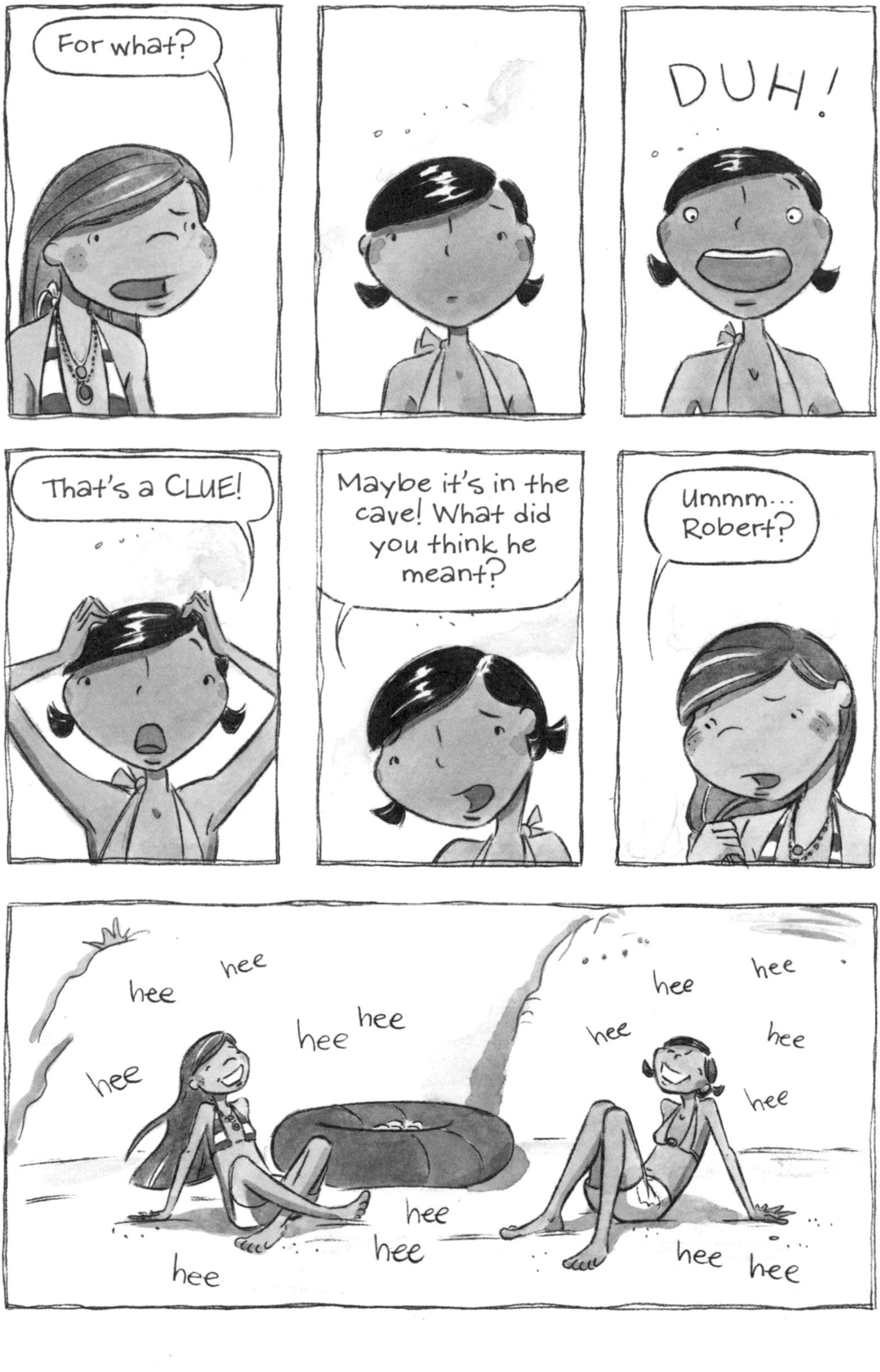
For what?
DUH!
That's a CLUE!
Maybe it's in the cave! What did you think he meant?
Ummm... Robert?
hee
hee
hee
hee
hee
hee
hee
hee
hee
hee
hee
hee
hee
hee
hee
hee

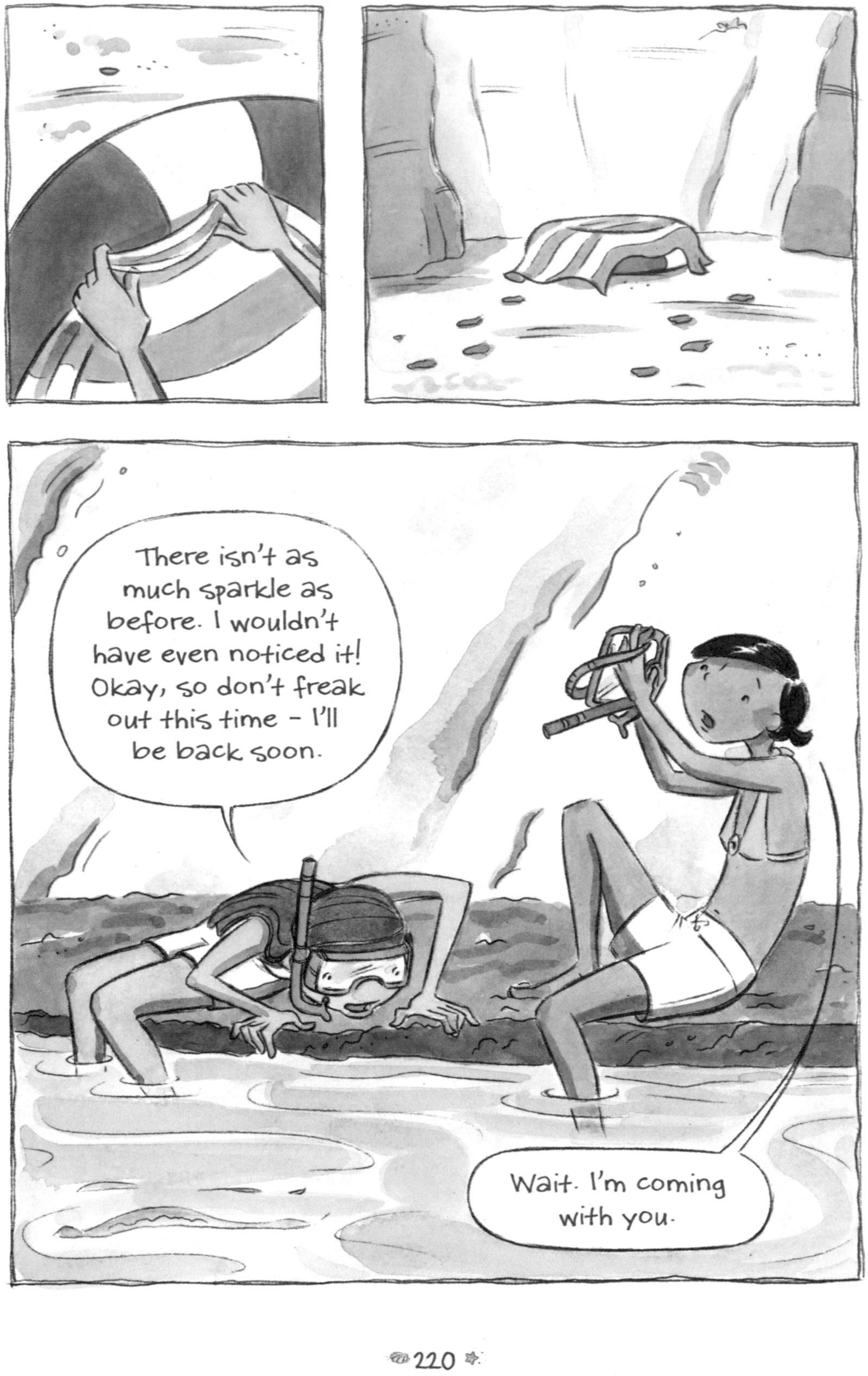
There isn't as much sparkle as before. I wouldn't have even noticed it! Okay, so don't freak out this time – I'll be back soon.
Wait. I'm coming with you.

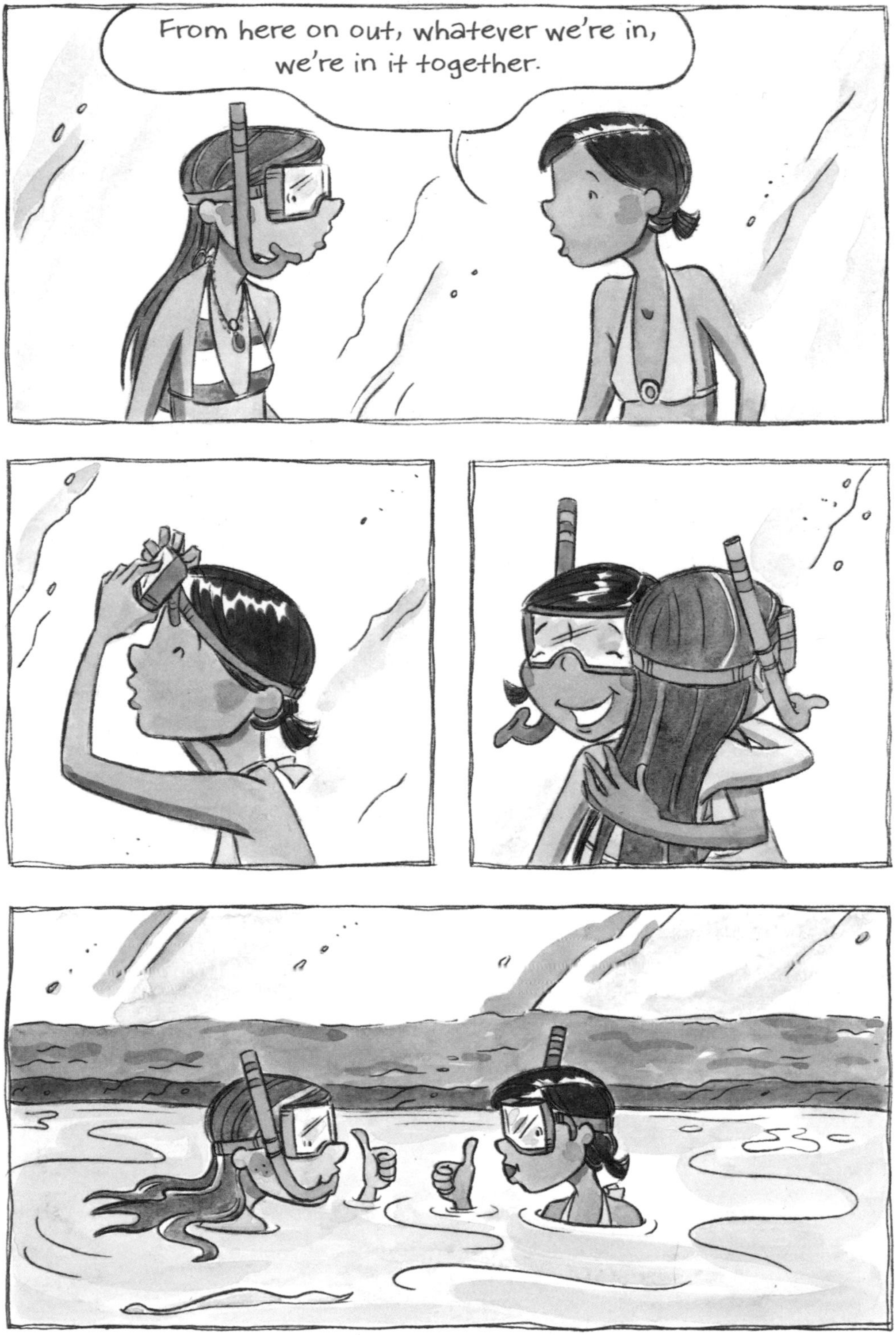
From here on out, whatever we're in, we're in it together.

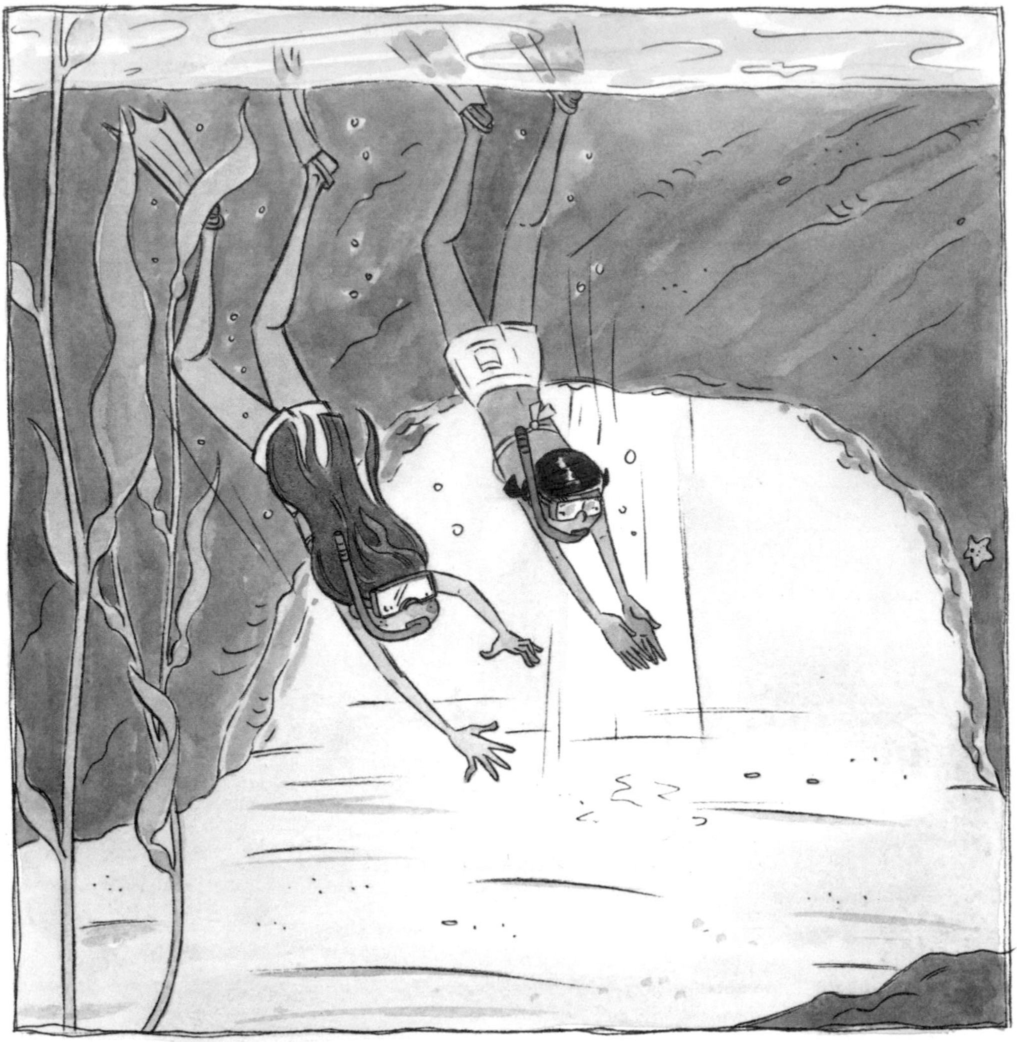

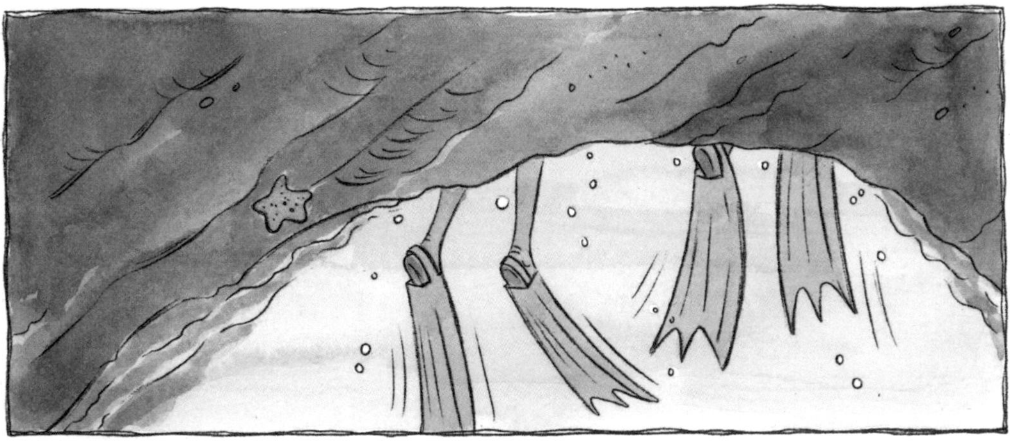

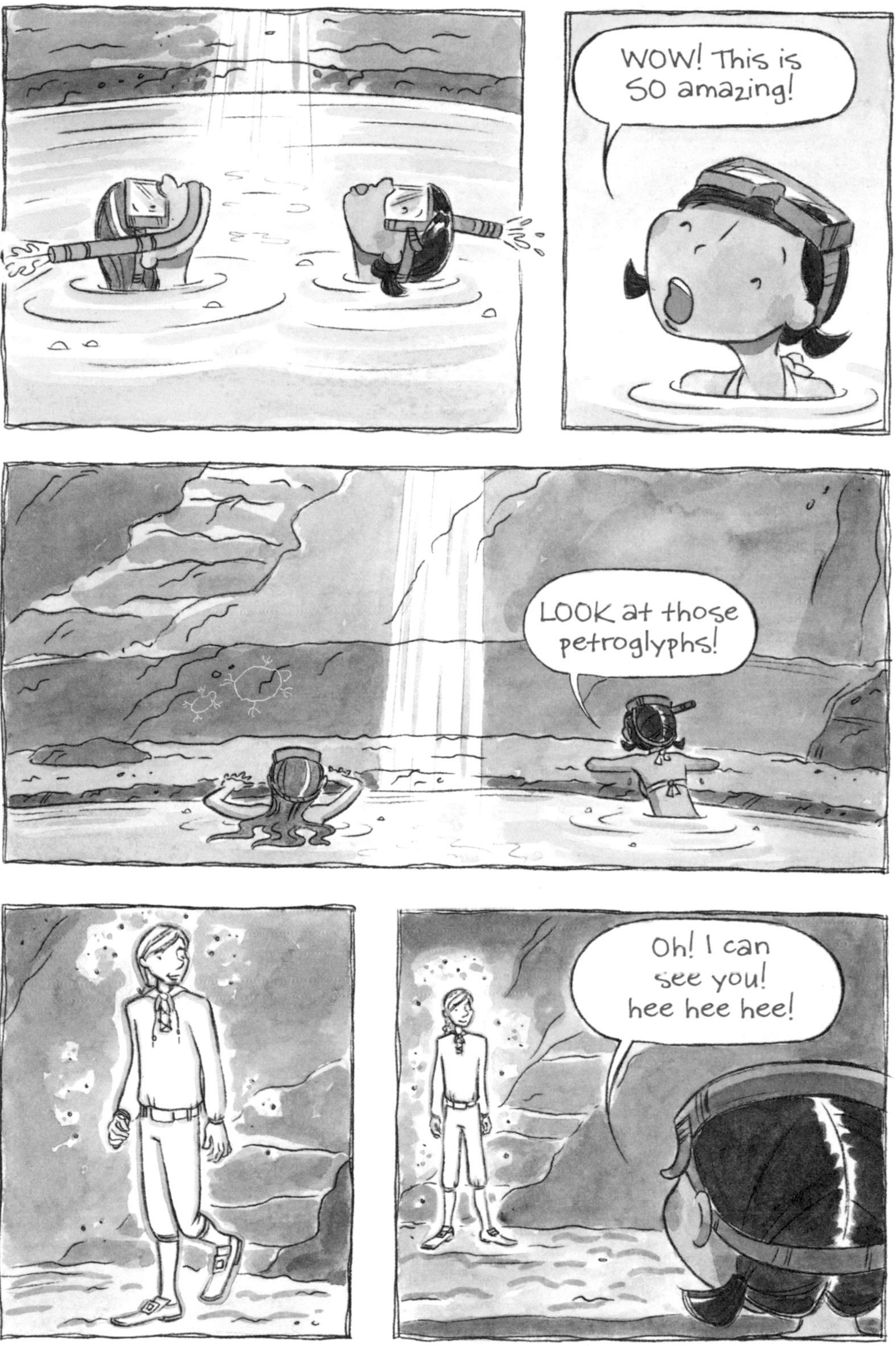
WOW! This is SO amazing!
LOOK at those petroglyphs!
Oh! I can see you! hee hee hee!

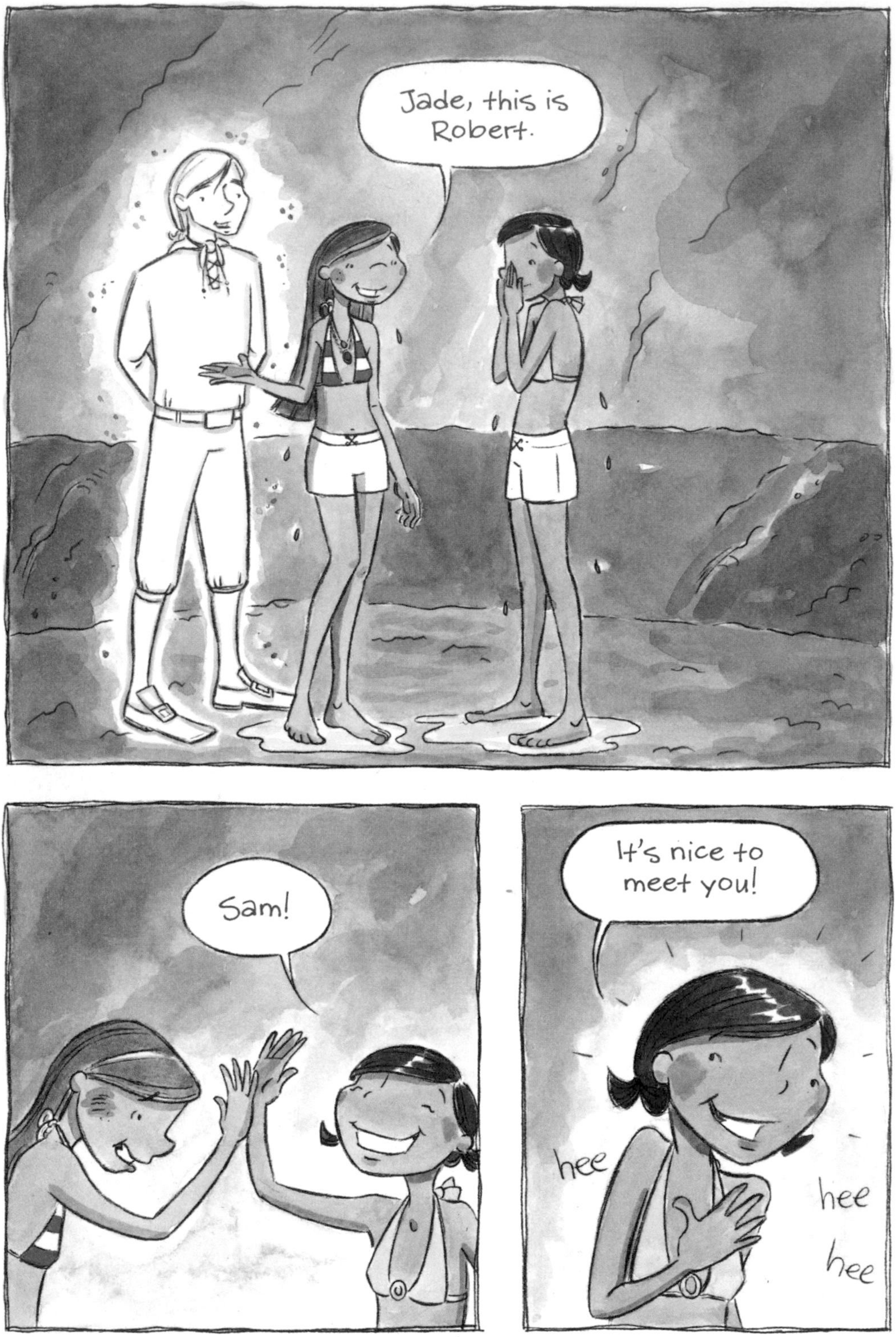
Jade, this is Robert.
Sam!
It's nice to meet you!
hee
hee
hee

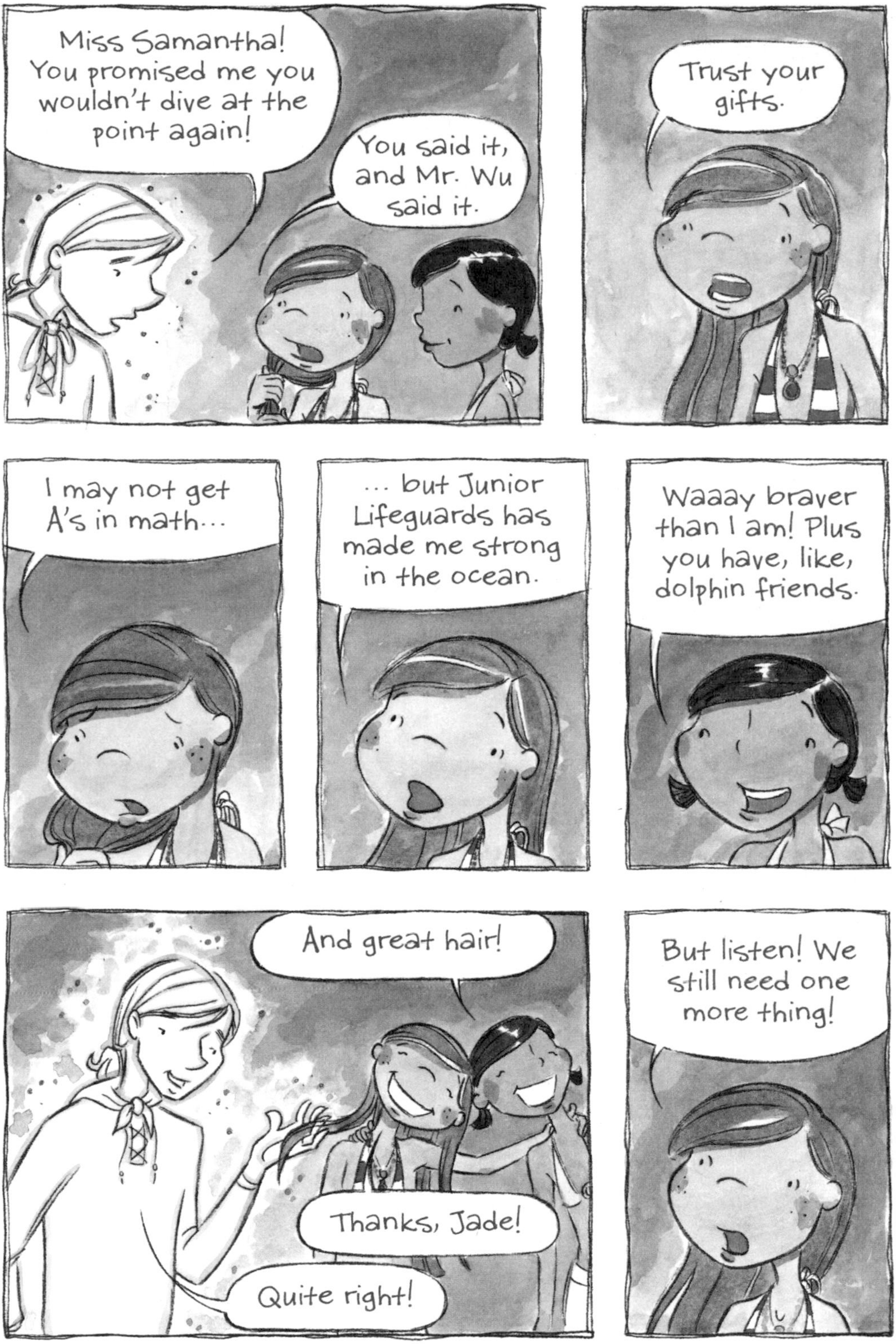
Miss Samantha! You promised me you wouldn't dive at the point again!
You said it, and Mr. Wu said it.
Trust your gifts.
I may not get A's in math...
... but Junior Lifeguards has made me strong in the ocean.
Waaay braver than I am! Plus you have, like, dolphin friends.
And great hair!
Thanks, Jade!
Quite right!
But listen! We still need one more thing!

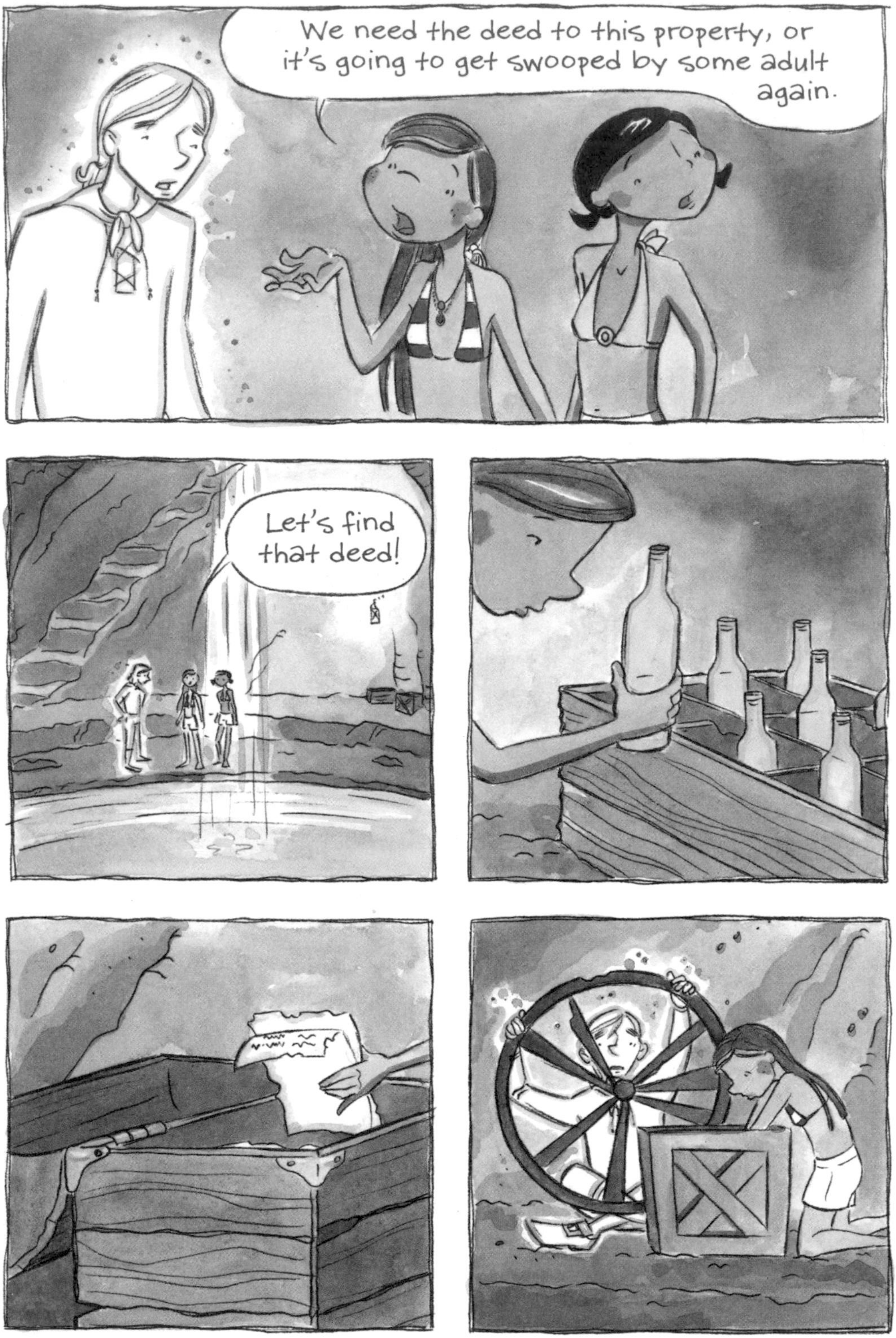
We need the deed to this property, or it's going to get swooped by some adult again.
Let's find that deed!

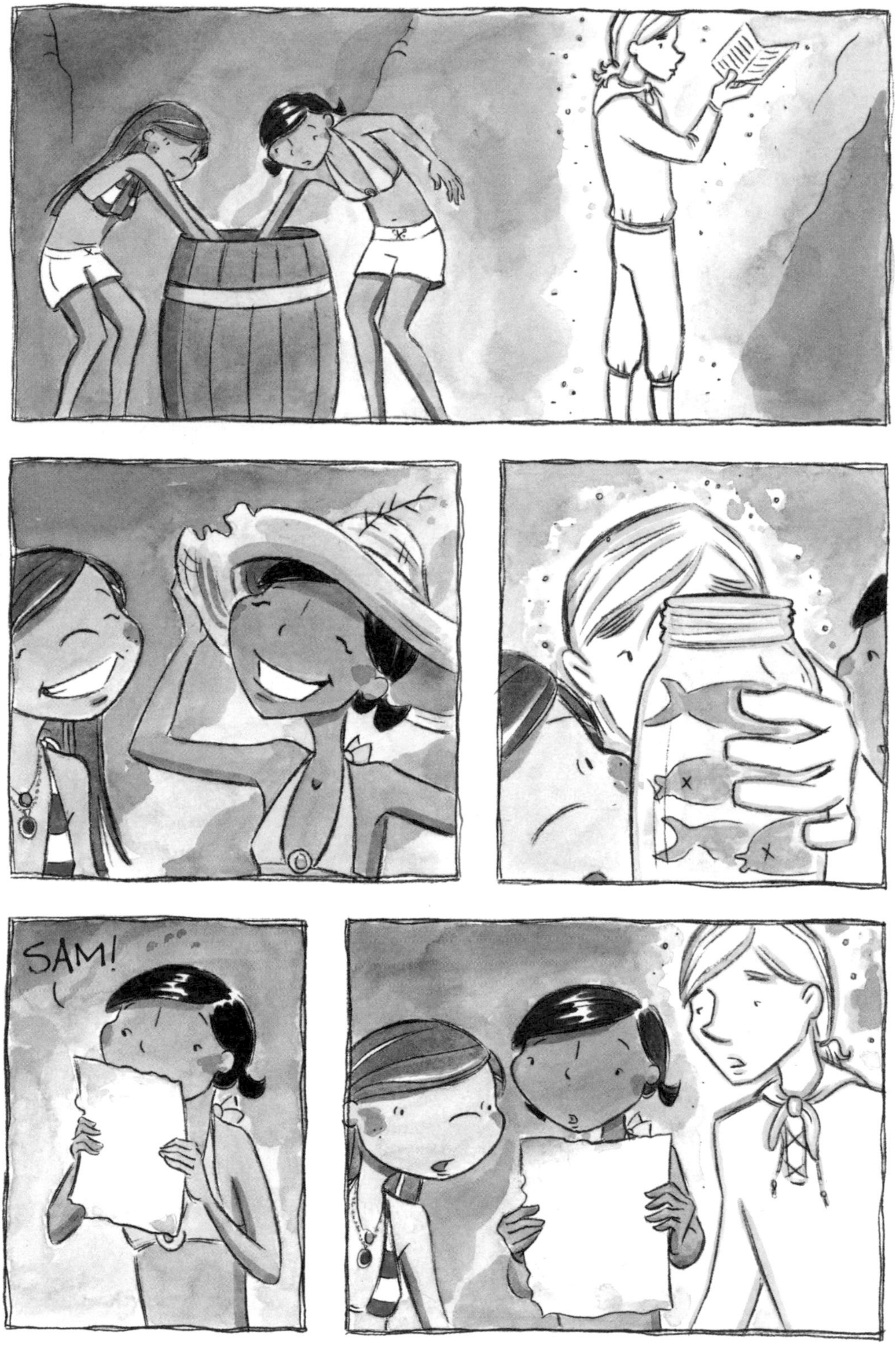
SAM!

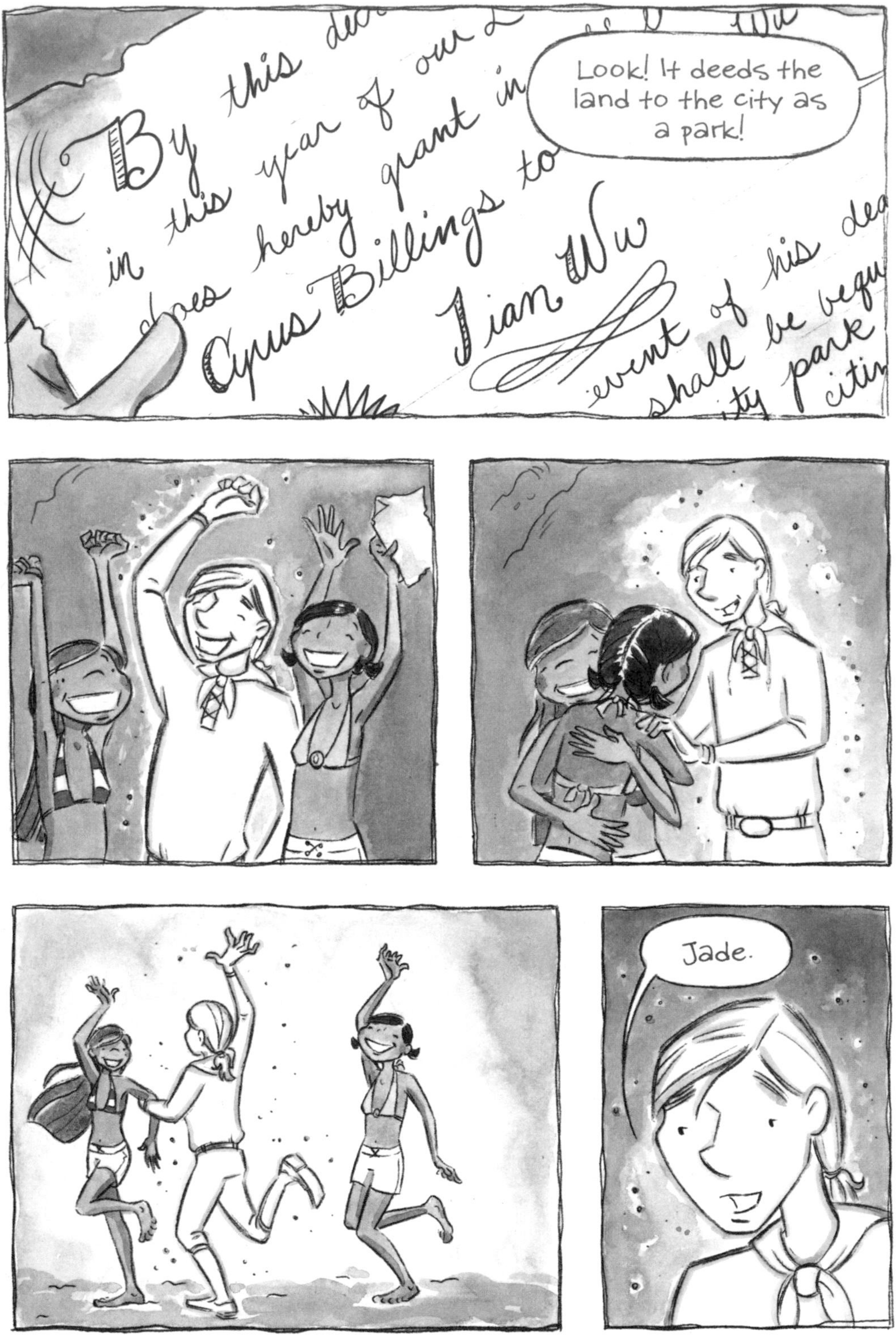
By this
in this year of our
does hereby grant in
Cyrus Billings to
Jian Wu
event of his
shall be
park
Look! It deeds the land to the city as a park!
Jade.

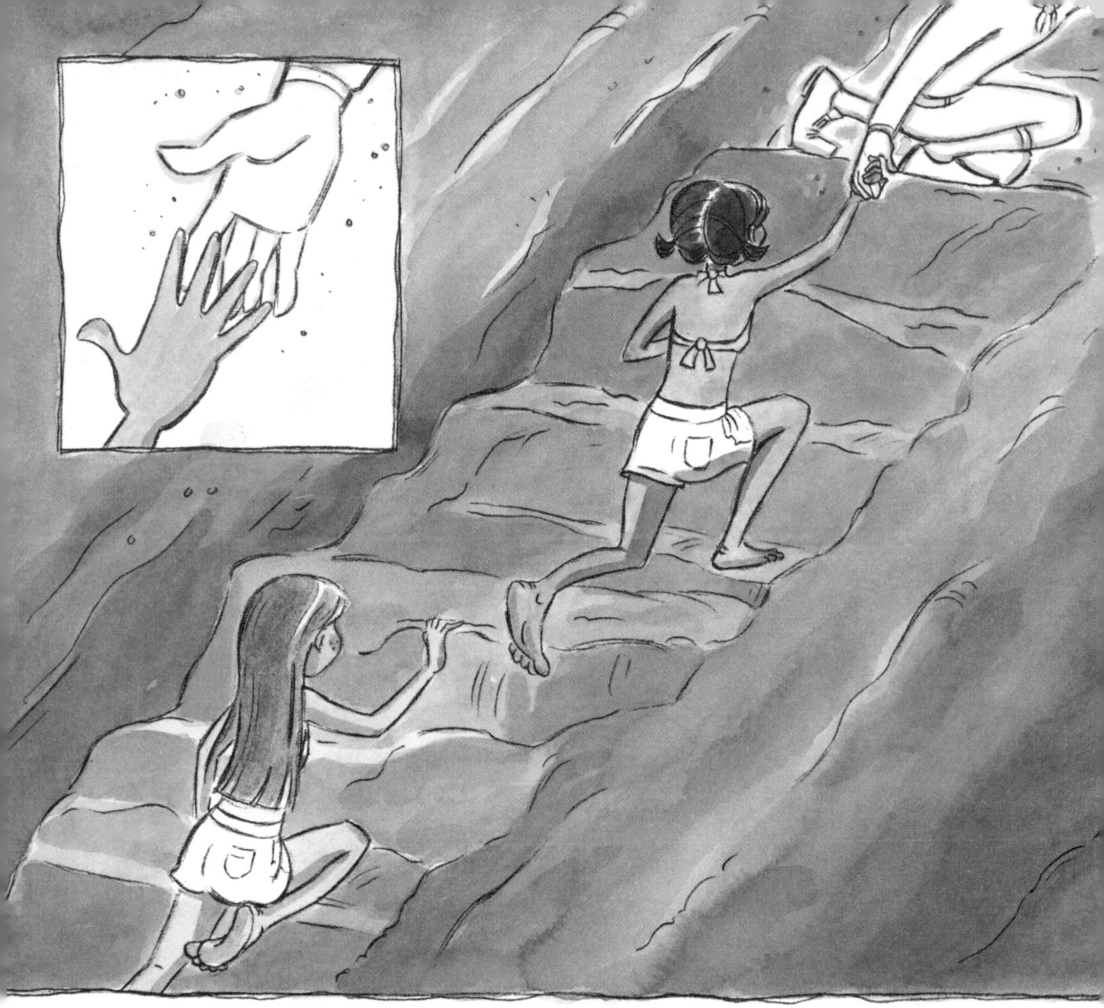

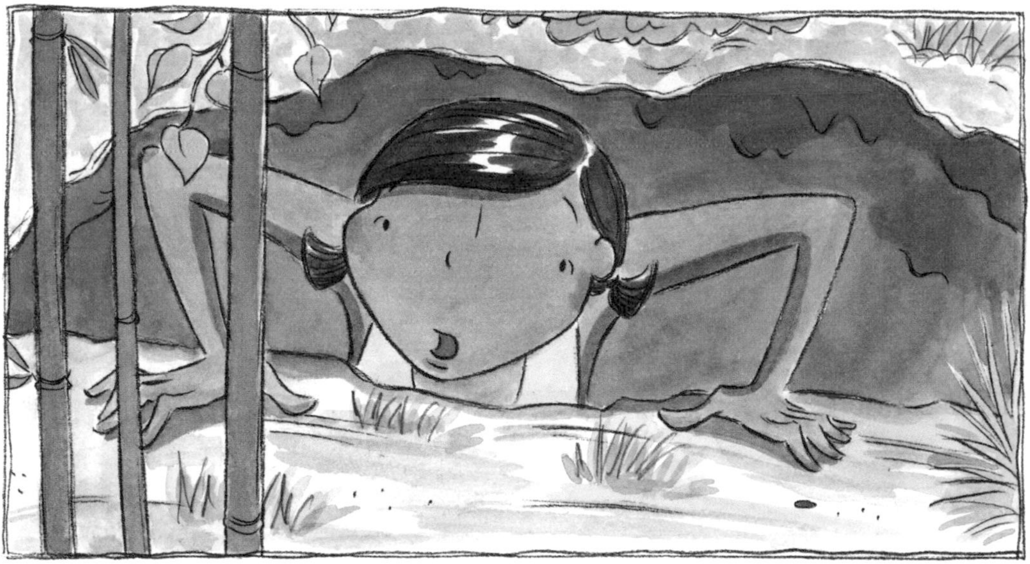

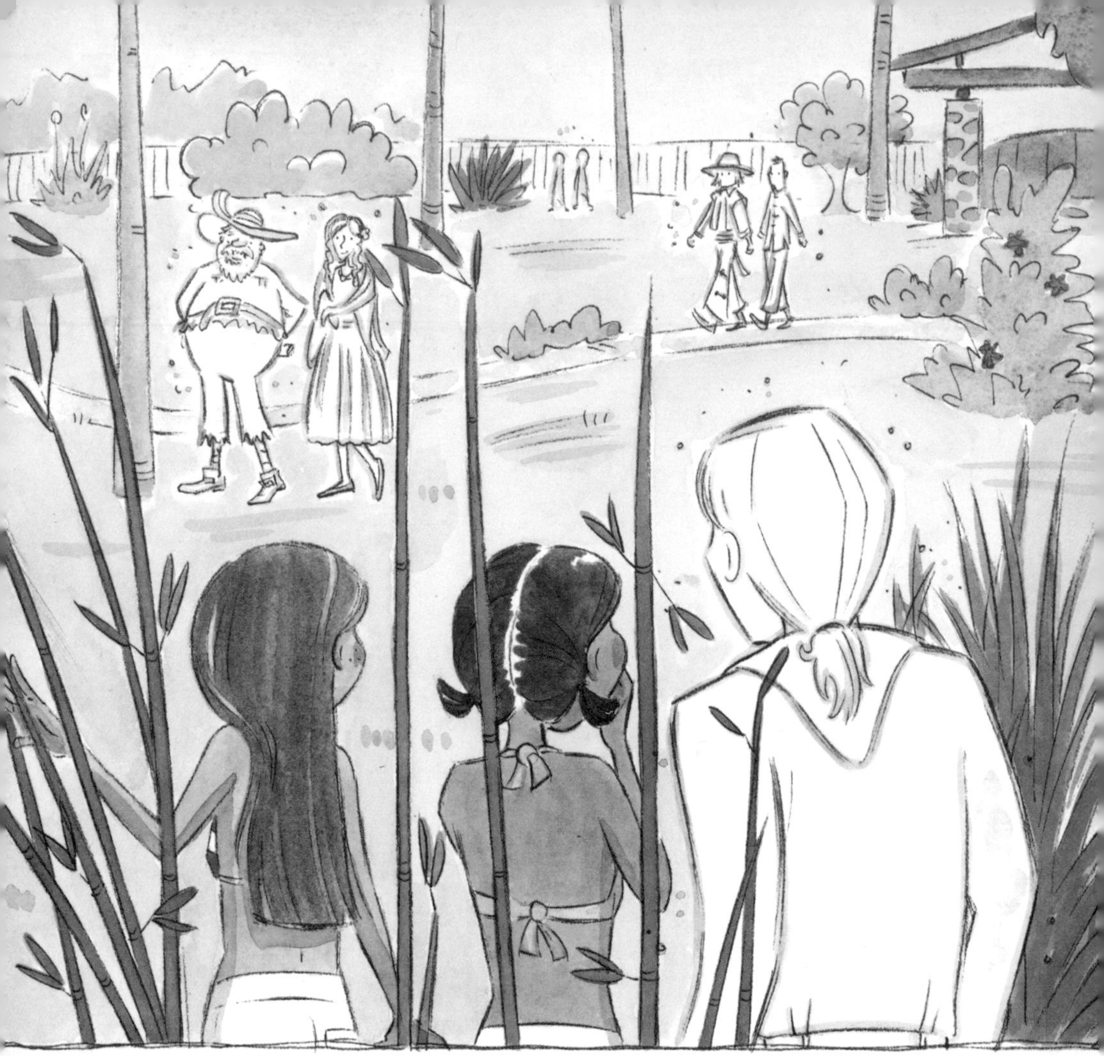

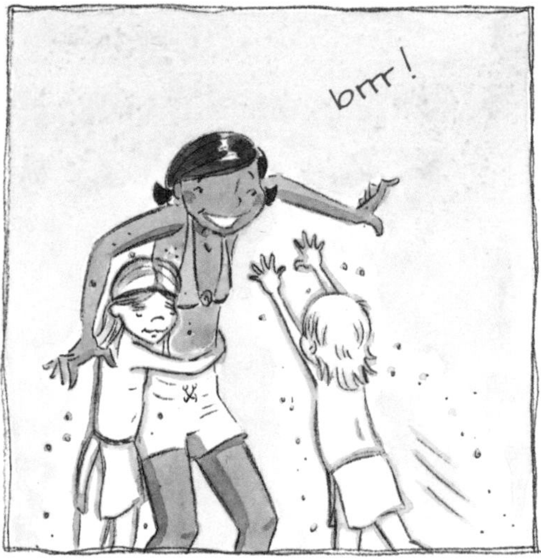
brrr!

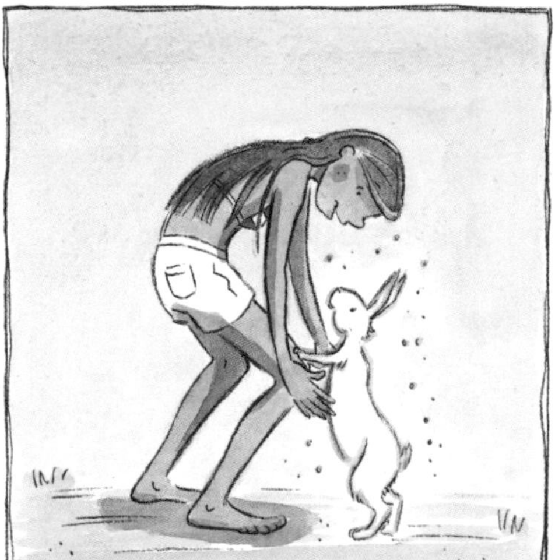

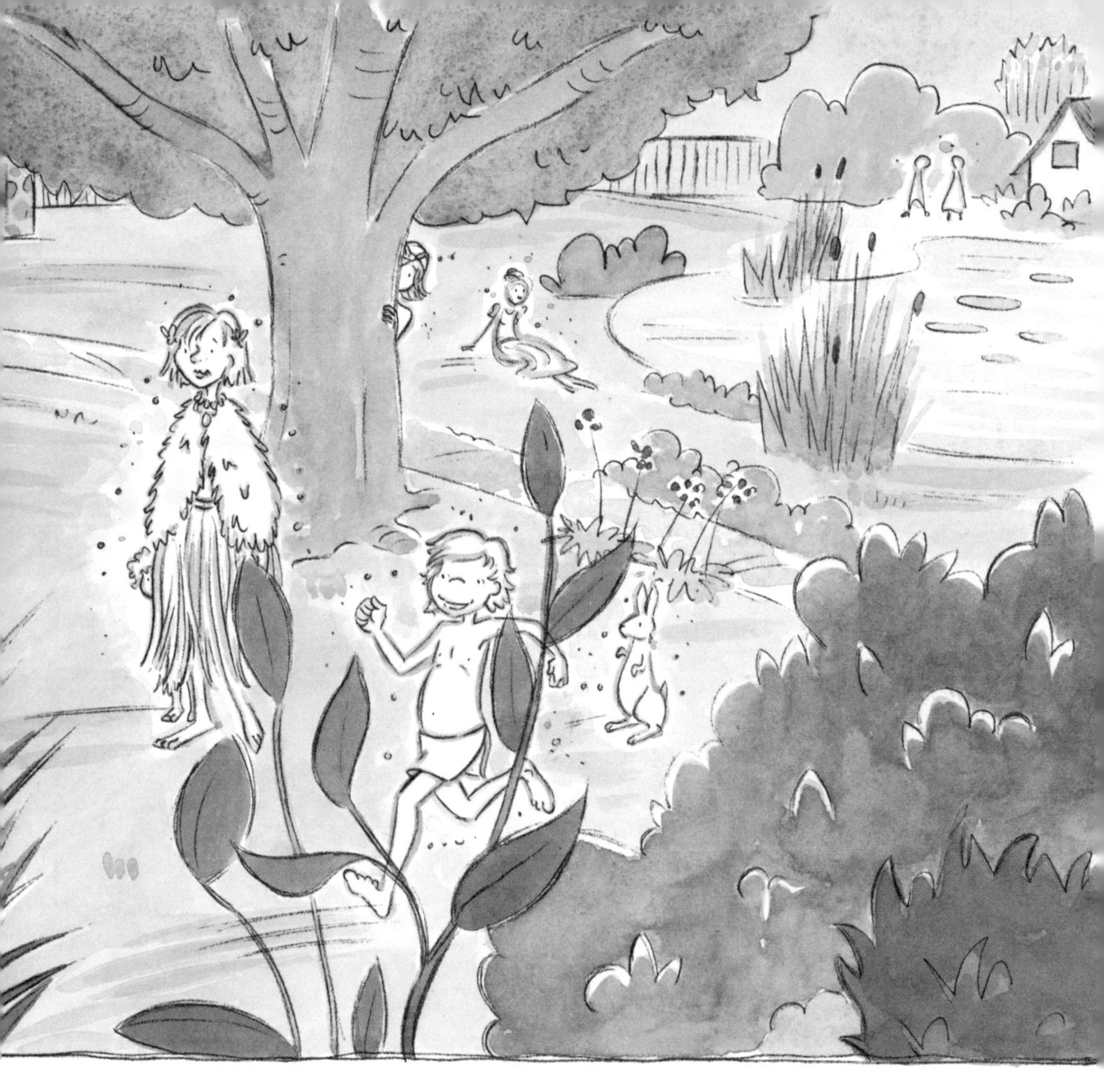

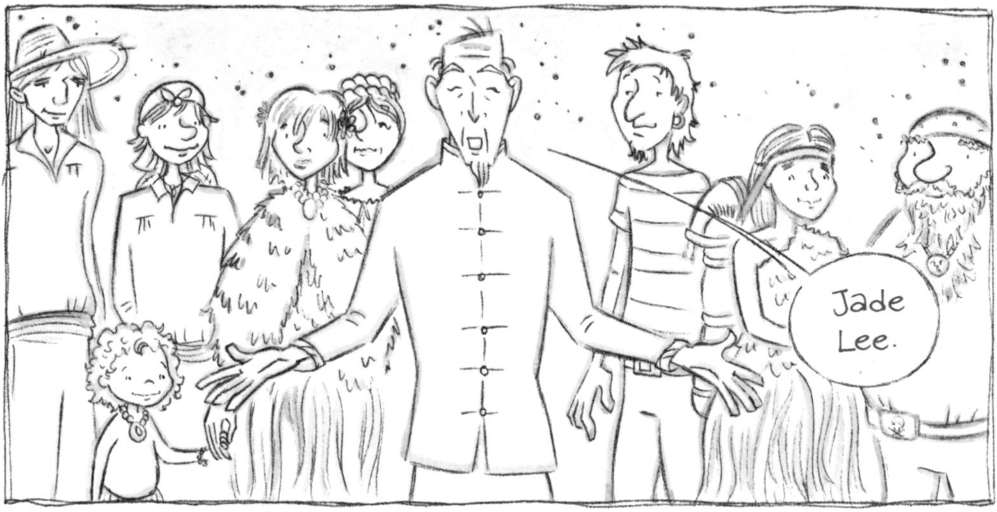
Jade Lee.

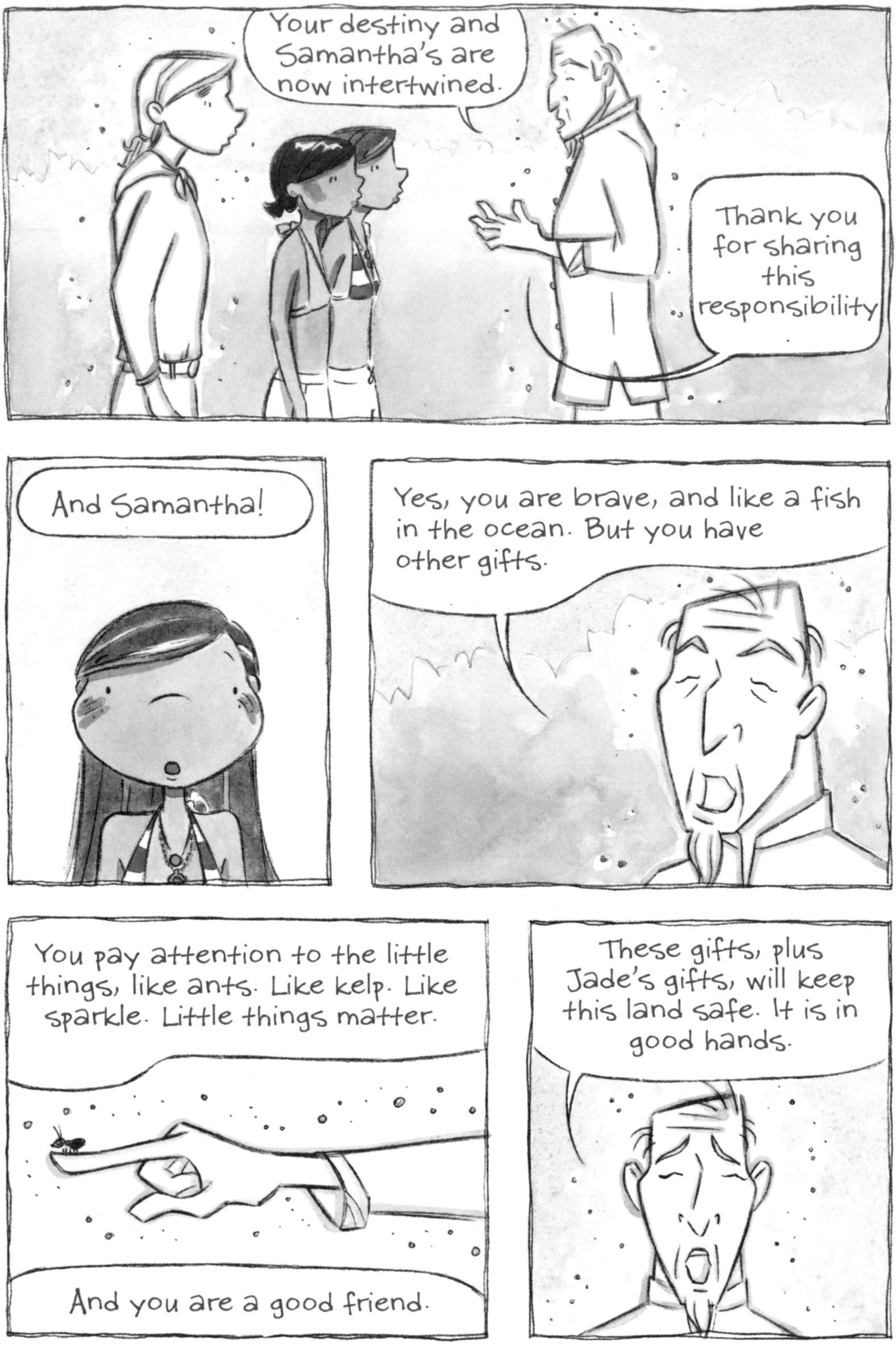
Your destiny and Samantha's are now intertwined.
Thank you for sharing this responsibility.
And Samantha!
Yes, you are brave, and like a fish in the ocean. But you have other gifts.
You pay attention to the little things, like ants. Like kelp. Like sparkle. Little things matter.
And you are a good friend.
These gifts, plus Jade's gifts, will keep this land safe. It is in good hands.

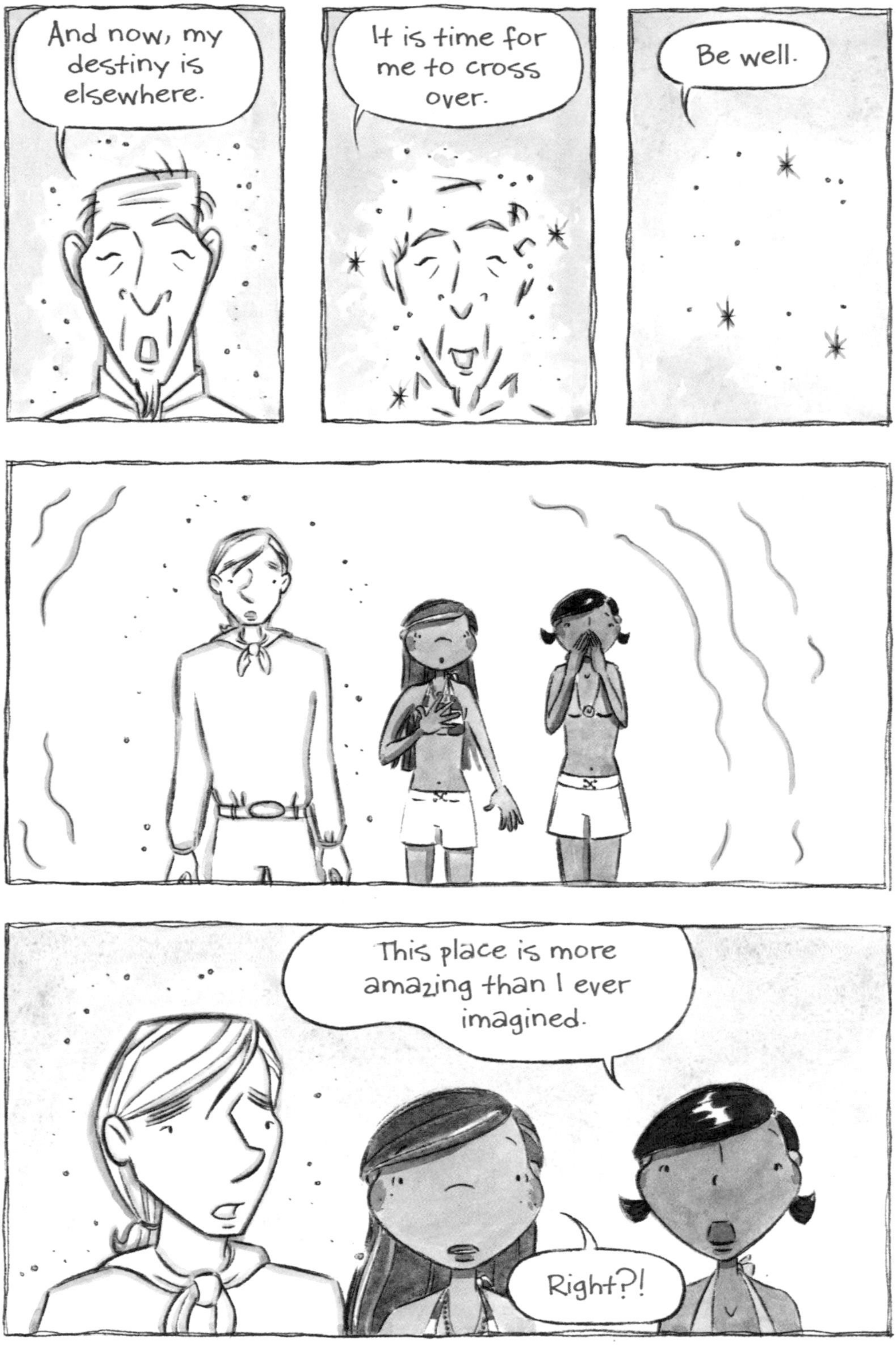
And now, my destiny is elsewhere.
It is time for me to cross over.
Be well.
This place is more amazing than I ever imagined.
Right?!

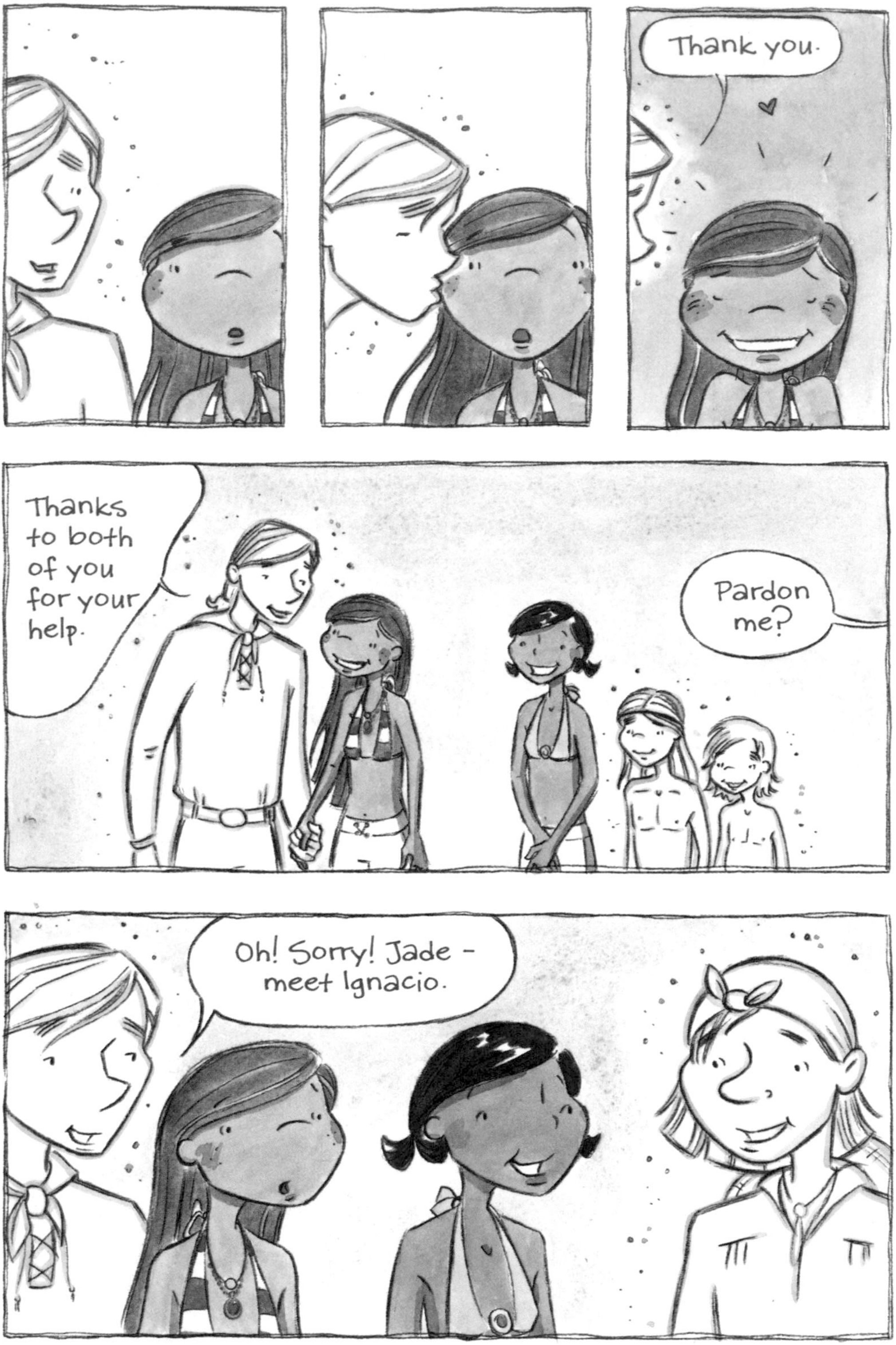
Thank you.
Thanks to both of you for your help.
Pardon me?
Oh! Sorry! Jade - meet Ignacio.

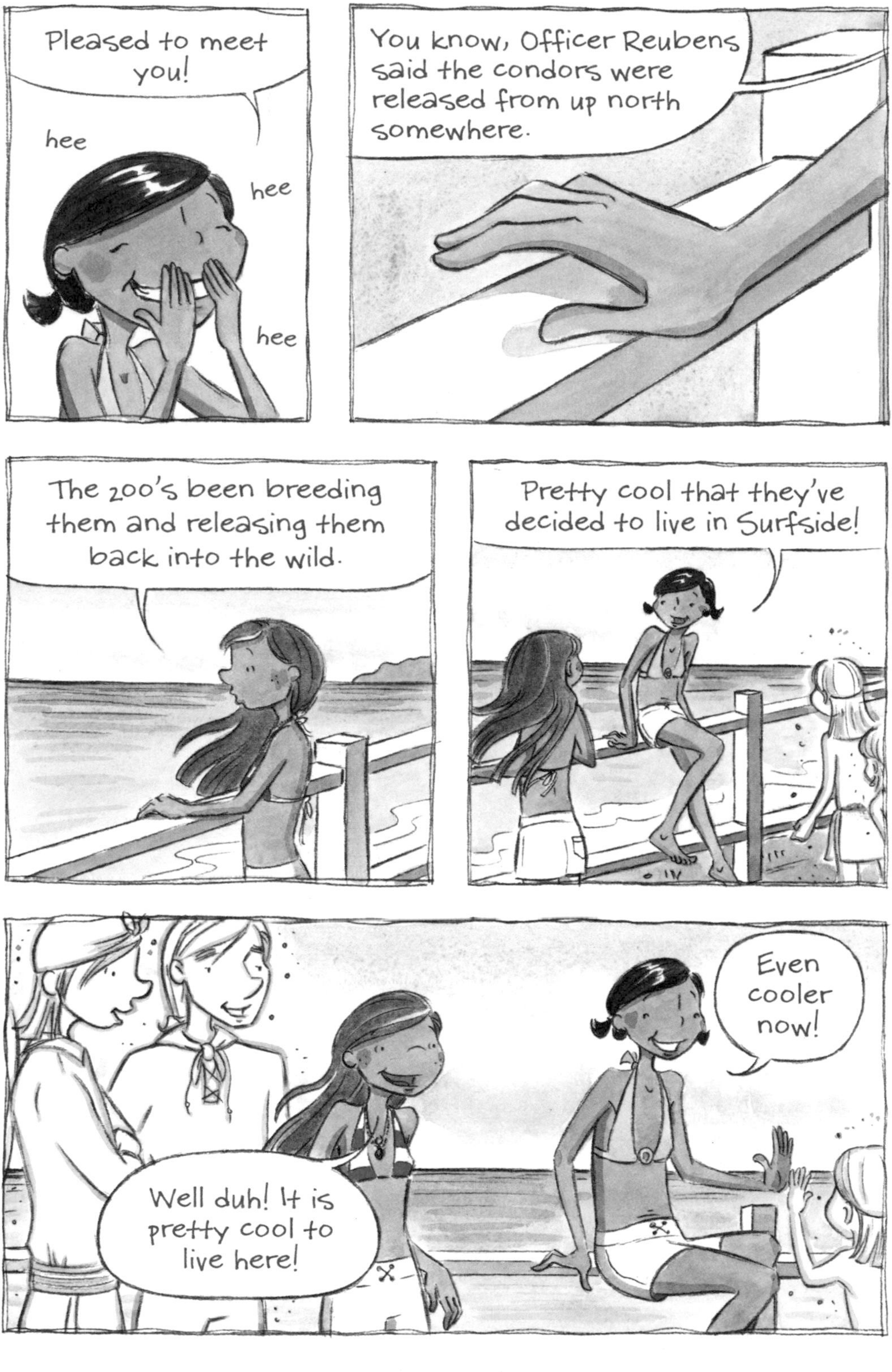
Pleased to meet you!
hee
hee
hee
You know, Officer Reubens said the condors were released from up north somewhere.
The zoo's been breeding them and releasing them back into the wild.
Pretty cool that they've decided to live in Surfside!
Even cooler now!
Well duh! It is pretty cool to live here!

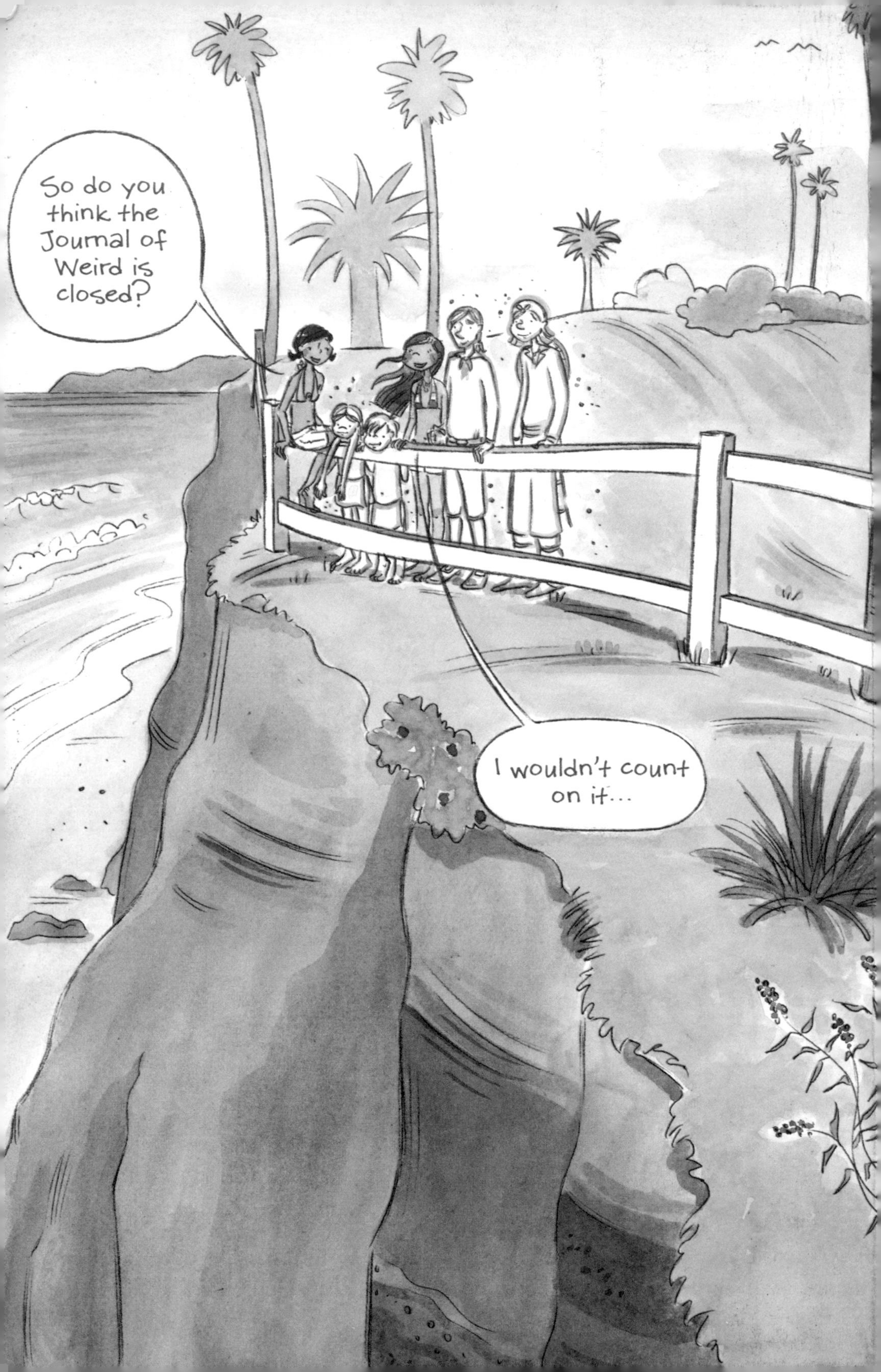
So do you think the Journal of Weird is closed?
I wouldn't count on it...